A Story in a Nutshell.

From Hon. George Bancroft to Friedrich Kapp, Esq.

Legation of the United States,
Berlin, December 10, 1868.

Rev. W. R. Alger, of Boston, proposed to Mr. Auerbach to take Roberts Brothers for his publishers. They, without Mr. Auerbach's consent or knowledge, published one of his works and filled the country with advertisements of their intention to publish the next which he should bring out. Messrs. Roberts Brothers then made Mr. Auerbach an offer, which he refused to accept without a modification. They, on their part, refuse to accede to his proposal. So that matter stands. Messrs. Roberts Brothers have received from Mr. Auerbach neither manuscript nor proofs of his new work, nor have they from him authority to advertise or to publish.

GEO. BANCROFT.

From Herr Berthold Auerbach to Messrs. Roberts Bros.

[Translation.]

Baden Baden, [Oct. 22, 1868.]

Messrs. Roberts Bros.:

Gentlemen—I have before me a copy of your letter to Messrs. Leypoldt & Holt, dated Boston, Oct. 3d. The statements you make therein are absolutely incomprehensible to me. Let me recapitulate the facts. You reprint the translation of my novel, "On the Heights," published by Tauchnitz, without my knowing a word of it. Mr. Alger, in sending me his own book, writes me a highly pleasing letter. In thanking him, I inquire whether he can find a publisher there who will pay me a satisfactory *honorarium* for my next book. I then receive a copy of your American edition of "On the Heights," and see that you already state in your announcement that you are going to publish my new novel, when up to that time no word of negotiation, much less of agreement, had passed between us.

A good while after, you make me a proposition. In my letter of July 15 I make my proposition in return, demanding a fixed *honorarium*, to which you object. I telegraphed you that only on condition of a fixed *honorarium* will I close a bargain with you, *else the new novel is otherwise disposed of.* You don't answer by telegraph but by letter, persisting on your previous propositions, though I had decidedly declined them. Herewith *the matter was completely finished between us*, and I really cannot comprehend whereon you base any lawful claim to the new book, "*Das Landhaus am Rhein.*" All attempts at coming to terms having failed, I legitimately made over my new novel to Messrs. Leypoldt & Holt of New York. This is the way matters stand. * * *

I have nothing more to add, and will be confident that you now will not interfere with the authorized publishers, Messrs. Leypoldt & Holt, of New York.

In this confidence I subscribe myself,

Most respectfully,

Berthold Auerbach.

Messrs. Roberts Bros. are now publishing an edition of the Novel.

Berthold Auerbach

THE VILLA

ON THE RHINE

BY

BERTHOLD AUERBACH

AUTHOR'S EDITION

With a Portrait of the Author, and a Biographical Sketch

BY

BAYARD TAYLOR

NEW YORK
LEYPOLDT & HOLT
1869

Stereotyped by LITTLE, RENNIE & Co.,
New York.

CONTENTS OF VOLUME I.

BOOK THIRD.

BOOK FOURTH.

BOOK FIFTH.

BOOK SIXTH.

BOOK SEVENTH.

BOOK EIGHTH.

BERTHOLD AUERBACH.

ALTHOUGH first introduced to the knowledge of most American readers by his story of "On the Heights," Berthold Auerbach has been for thirty years a familiar name in Germany. He is one of the small number of authors who have risen prominently above that dead level of elegant mediocrity which has been the affliction of German literature in our generation; and the place he has taken is there so well assured, and so generally conceded, that we shall have no difficulty in rendering it clear to those who now make his acquaintance for the first time.

Auerbach was born in poverty and obscurity, in the little village of Nordstetten, on the Suabian side of the Black Forest, on the 28th of February, 1812. His parents, being Jews, were inspired by the signs of the active and impressible intellect which he showed as a child, with the hope that he might become a light of the Synagogue, and they devoted him to the study of Hebrew theology. In Carlsruhe, where he studied, he also attended the Gymnasium, and gave a portion of his time to the classical branches. While completing his studies at the Universities of Tübingen, Munich, and Heidelberg, he gradually neglected Hebrew theology for philosophy, history, and literature, and it was not many years before the Hebrew element, so conspicuous in his early works, entirely disappeared from his contributions to literature.

His student-years were characterized by many privations and vicissitudes of fortune, the most important of which was his arrest in 1835, on account of his connection with a secret political society. He was confined for some months in the fortress of Hohenasperg, in which the unfortunate poet Schubarth had languished for ten years, half a century before. On being released, he determined to devote his life exclusively to literature. His first work, which appeared in the following year, was an essay entitled "Judaism and Recent Literature," which he designed to illustrate by a series of romances taken from the history of the Jewish race, under the collective title of "The Ghetto." Only two works of the projected series, however, were completed—"Spinoza," published in 1837, and "Poet and Merchant," which appeared two years later. Both these works attracted much attention in the literary world, and were the means of making the author's name known, although they did not become generally popular. His studies for the former led him to undertake the translation of Spinoza's works, which were published in five volumes, in Stuttgart, in the year 1841.

With these works terminated the first period of Auerbach's career as an author. The reputation which they achieved for him gave him admittance to the society of other authors and scholars, and his mind was thus insensibly led to broader and more important paths. From the literary circle of Würtemberg—Uhland, Schwab, Kerner, and others—he extended his acquaintance to that other and very different circle whose headquarters were then at Düsseldorf, and whose prominent members were Immermann, Grabbe, and the young Freiligrath. In the year 1842, while residing at Cologne, he received the news of the death of his father, to whom he was strongly attached. For a week or two afterward he wandered, alone, about the Drachenfels, and among the forests of the Seven Mountains, his mind entirely given up to memories of his boyish home, and the quaint peasant-life of those remote villages of the Black Forest. During this lonely ramble he conceived the idea of representing human nature as he had personally observed it in those humble associations, instead of seeking it in minds like that of Spinoza, or in the Ghettos of the Middle Ages. The first series of his *Dorfgeschichten* (Village Stories) appeared the following year.

The delight with which this work was hailed—its immediate and thorough popularity—determined, thenceforth, the field of his literary activity. German fiction, up to that time, had been treading (not very successfully, if we except the novels of Willibald Alexis) in the path of Scott. Only one author of real genius—Immermann—had, in his "Münchhausen," produced a story of Westphalian farmer-life, which, detached from its satirical envelopment, still remains one of the most admirable pictures of the characters and ways of the people, ever written in Germany. Auerbach can therefore scarcely be called the pioneer in this field, but he was certainly the first German author who devoted himself wholly to it. His "Village Stories" are models of simple, picturesque, pathetic narration. While he is as true to the features and fortunes of common life as Immermann, he is less coarsely realistic. A soft, idyllic atmosphere lies upon his pictures, and the rude and not wholly admirable peasant-life of the Black Forest is lifted into a region of poetry.

The "Village Stories" were not only read all over Germany, but they at once reappeared in English, Dutch, and Swedish translations.* A second series, which proved to be even more popular than the first, was published in 1849, and for a year or two thereafter, the revolutionary events in Germany seem to have interfered with his literary labors. He was a moderate—or, one might rather say, recalling the fantastic movements of that period—a *steady-headed* Democrat, and was thus not drawn into rash and fruitless undertakings, though he sympathized thoroughly with the principles at stake. He was in Vienna during the most eventful days of the Revolution, and related his experiences in a work entitled, "A Diary in Vienna, from Latour to Windischgrätz."

The success of the *Frau Professorin*—which, I believe, was one of the last stories of the second series—induced Auerbach to use his material for romances, giving them a more complete and artistic development than the brief stories would allow. He resided during this period in Dresden, but his summers were devoted to excursions among the villages of the Black Forest, and to newer and more careful studies of the people.

The first of these works, "*Barfüssle*" (Little Barefoot), appeared in 1856. It is not too much to say that it is one of the most exquisite idyls of humble life in any language. Its delicate humor and pathos almost defy translation, and are by no means reproduced in the English version which appeared soon afterward. This work, with its successors, "Joseph in the Snow," and "Edelweiss," were at once accepted as classics, and Auerbach found himself at the head of a school, with many and clever imitators springing up on all sides, yet none of them competent to endanger his supremacy.

As early as the year 1845 he had conceived the idea of an Almanac for the people, which, while attracting them by stories and illustrations, should also contain papers on politics, political economy, and science, adapted to their understanding. Such an almanac, under the title of *Der Gevattersmann* (the "Gaffer," or "Gossip"), he established, and continued for six or eight years. It was then relinquished for a completer form of annual publication, which still appears with the title of "Auerbach's Volkscalendar." Each number of the latter contains one or two of his stories drawn from the life of the people, and these have already accumulated to a number sufficient to form two or three volumes, of a character distinct from, yet equally original with, the "Village Stories."

"On the Heights" was Auerbach's first essay in that broader and more comprehensive field of fiction, which is to our day

* An excellent translation, made by Mr. Charles Goepp, was published five or six years ago, in Philadelphia, but—a fact difficult to understand—attracted no attention at the time.

what the drama was to former centuries. His success in Germany has not been inferior to that of his less ambitious works. A higher quality of genius is revealed in the fine, indirect irony which colors his pictures of life at a German court, and he has shown no little skill in interweaving this life with that of the lowest class of the people. No romance, since Freytag's *Soll und Haben* (Debit and Credit), has been more generally read in Germany.

Auerbach belongs, indisputably, not only to the class of self-made men, but to the class of authors who possess independent creative power. His continued success has never beguiled him to careless over-confidence in himself; his studies for each new work are as thoroughly and conscientiously made as if it were the first, and should determine his place in literature. His sense of the literary art has matured with his years, and a careful reader of his works can easily detect his progress toward an ideal of proportion, of balanced strength, such as only presents itself to genuine and unfaltering intellectual effort.

Personally, Auerbach is somewhat undersized, strong and stout of body, with a vigorous, compact head. His expansive brow, and large, lively, merry, gray eyes indicate both the thinker and the observer. A fresh, genial *bonhommie* characterizes his whole appearance. He is gay, witty, brilliant in conversation, an admirable *raconteur*, and with a natural gift of improvisation, which he has never cared to cultivate. His present residence is Berlin, where he moves independently through all ranks of society, from the Court-circle to the associations of working-men, and the commonest diversions of the people, in whom he still believes, and for whom he will always labor.

B. T.

THE VILLA ON THE RHINE.

BOOK FIRST.

CHAPTER I.

AN APPARITION WITH WINGS.

BE patient just a few minutes longer! There's a man making signs that he wants to go over with us," said the ferryman to the persons sitting in his boat—a man and two women.

The man was small, with gray hair and a bright ruddy face, and eyes which were good-natured, but absent-minded and weary. A rough moustache, which completely covered his upper lip, seemed to have found its way by mistake to such an innocent face as his. He was dressed in a brand new suit of that new-fashioned material which is sprinkled and spattered all over with white, as though its wearer had systematically rolled himself in a feather-bed. He wore, fastened to a belt, a wallet, elegantly embroidered with blue and red beads.

Opposite to him sat a tall, fine-looking woman, whose restless eyes and clear-cut features had evidently been charming once. She tossed her head impatiently at the delay, being evidently unused to waiting. She was dressed in pale yellow silk, and a white veil was wound around her gray hat, like the band of a turban. She turned her head quickly again, and then cast her eyes down and bored the side of the boat with the ferule of her large parasol, evidently intending not to concern herself about the stranger.

Beside the man sat, pleasantly smiling, a fair, slender girl, who wore a blue summer-dress, and held by its elastic bands a little brown hat adorned with a bird's wing. Her head was large, and her great forehead seemed yet more massive beneath the rich tresses of her luxuriant hair, two braids of which fell, to the right and left, over her shoulder and breast. The girl's face was as bright, unruffled, and clear as the beautiful day which bathed the landscape in light.

She put her hat on, and her mother adjusted it more becomingly.

She hastily exchanged her rough leather gauntlets for glossy ones which she took from her pocket, and as she drew them on she examined the new-comer.

A handsome, stalwart young man, with a full brown beard, a gray shawl on his shoulder, and wearing a broad-brimmed hat, came rapidly down the zigzag path to the shore. He stepped into the boat, and, removing his hat, displayed a noble white forehead, shaded by deep brown hair, and bowed, without speaking. His face was full of daring and resolution, and at the same time was one to awaken trust and confidence.

The girl looked down, while her mother tied and untied her bonnet again, throwing one lock of hair over her breast and the other over her shoulder, so as to make her look pretty and not at all formal. The man in the speckled suit pressed his white-headed cane to his lips.

The stranger seated himself at a distance from the others and gazed into the stream, while the boat moved swiftly forward.

The boat landed at the island on which stood the rambling convent, which now served as a school for girls, and the passengers stepped ashore.

"Oh, how beautiful! that must be where they study their lessons," cried the girl, pointing to a group of lofty trees, growing on the shore, so near each other that they seemed to spring from one root, and within which were placed low benches.

"Go on," said the woman, looking reprovingly at her daughter and giving her arm to her husband. The girl went forward and the stranger followed.

Nightingales, blackbirds, finches, and blackcaps sang in the bushes, as if saying, "Here is heavenly rest; no one disturbs us here." Dark fir-trees, casting broad shadows, grew on the shore, and long rows of brightly-colored larches stood motionless, and bees hummed amid the chestnut-trees.

They reached the convent, which was without any particular architectural beauty, but stood overlooking the gardens and meadows of the island, the stream, and the mountains.

The building was closed, and not a soul was to be seen. The old gentleman pulled the bell, and a portress, opening a little window, asked what they wished. They asked to be admitted, but she replied that it was impossible to-night.

"Take my card to the Mother Superior," said the old gentleman, "and tell her that I am here with my wife and daughter."

"Permit me to send my card in too," said the stranger, in such a beautiful voice that the three turned and looked at him. The stranger gave his card to the portress, adding, "Tell the Lady Superior that my mother sends her regards."

The portress closed the shutters, and the four stood before the door.

"I took you for a Frenchman," said the old gentleman, in a kindly tone, to the stranger.

"I am a German," he answered.

"You have some relative in the convent, and know the Superior?"

"No, I know no one here."

The stranger spoke so curtly that he did not give the slightest encouragement to continue the conversation, and the old gentleman seemed to be a man of position and character, not at all accustomed to make advances, but rather to be courted. He withdrew with the ladies to a beautiful bed of flowers, and seated himself with his charge on a bench near it. But the girl seemed restless, and wandered away through the grounds, plucking the hidden violets.

The young man stood rooted to the spot, and gazed at the stone steps which led to the convent door, as though he would read the fate of those who had gone in and out over them.

The old gentleman, as he sat on the bench, said to his wife: "That fine young man looks to me like a gambler who has lost his money at one of the watering-places near here; who knows but he wants to borrow money of the Lady Superior?"

The lady laughed at her husband, for this was the third person whom he had met during the journey and had taken for either a criminal or reprobate.

"May-be you are right," answered he; "but that's the trouble with those showy establishments, one supposes everybody he meets to be connected with them. It is with me just as it is with our child—"

"How is it with me?" asked the girl.

"Yes," continued her father; "how often have I been obliged to hear it said behind your back, 'What beautiful hair—where did she buy it?' No one believes in reality now-a-days."

The girl laughed brightly, and, putting a violet in her bosom, said, "I believe the stranger is a poet."

"Why?" asked her mother.

"Oh, a poet would look just like him."

The old gentleman laughed, and the mother said, "Child, you're inventing a poet for yourself! Come, the portress is beckoning to us."

The convent-door was opened, and the strangers entered. Behind the second door stood two nuns in long black robes, with ropes around their waists. The larger, an elderly lady, with a long drooping nose, said: "The Lady Superior regrets that she can see no one to-day; it is the eve of her patron saint, and she always remains alone till sunset then. Especially is it impossible to see any stranger, for the children"—so the pupils were called—"have prepared a festival with which the Superior is to be greeted after sunset. Consequently, everything is in disorder, as a theatre has been arranged in the dining-hall; the Superior has therefore given directions that the strangers should merely be shown through the convent."

Led by the two nuns, they proceeded through the great hall. The step of the nuns was loud and heavy, for they wore thick wooden soles, fastened to the feet by two bands drawn over the stockings. The smaller, delicate nun, whose fine face seemed oppressed and imprisoned in her close-fitting cap, kept herself timidly in the background, and always let the other one talk. Nevertheless, she occasionally spoke in French to the girl in the blue dress. Then the mother, highly delighted, would nod to the father: "Now, you see how wise it was to have the child learn something worth knowing. That was all my doing; I could hardly get you to consent to it."

The father could not keep from telling the German nun with the long nose, that his daughter Lina had only left the Convent of the Sacred Heart, at Aix-la-Chapelle, about six months before.

The stranger also spoke a few words, in French, to the delicate nun, but whenever he addressed her she drew back timidly; not exactly as if frightened, but smiling in a strange, nervous way.

The breakfast-hall, the school-room, the music-room, and the large dormitories were shown to the strangers, and everywhere were admirable neatness and order. In the sleeping-rooms everything was as quiet as if real human beings and restless children did not live there, but as if everything had been prepared for the inhabitants of story-land. Only in one little bed was there any uneasiness. Lina drew back the curtain, and a child looked around with great brown eyes. The young man also approached the bed.

"What ails the child?" asked Lina.

"Nothing but home-sickness."

"Only home-sickness," said the stranger to himself softly; and the lady asked:

"How do you cure home-sickness?"

"The Madam has an excellent remedy. A child who complains of being home-sick is declared ill, and must keep her bed. When she is allowed to get up, she feels relieved and at home."

"Go away! go away, all of you! Let Manna come! Let Manna come!" cried the child.

"Well, she'll come soon," said the nun, endeavoring to soothe the child, and explaining that no one but a certain American girl could quiet her.

"That must be our Manna," said Lina to her mother.

The twilight had come, and over the long corridor, through the golden rays of the setting sun, crept strange figures in long gray, blue, and red robes, and vanished in the cells.

The strangers entered the dining-hall, in the farther end of which a forest with a hermit's cave was represented, and there lay a young doe, bound with a red ribbon, which, looking at the strangers wonderingly with its bright eyes, arose and tugged at the ribbon, as if it wanted to run away. The French lady explained, that the children, aided by a sister who was very skilful in such matters, had prepared the decorations themselves. They had large choirs, and a pupil—an accomplished child—had composed the piece, which represented a scene in the life of the saint whose day it was.

The German nun, with the long nose, regretted that no stranger was allowed to see the spectacle.

A copy of a song to be sung in the piece, lay on a chair. The lady took it up, read it, and involuntarily handed it to the young man, who ran his eye over the verses.

"It is wonderful that a child should compose verses like that," said she.

The young man was obliged to say something, and so answered coolly: "Our German language—and especially our rhymes—are a piano so easily played, that any child can drum on it."

"Didn't I tell you he was a poet?" said the girl, glancing triumphantly at her parents.

As they were leaving this dining-hall, converted into a theatre, Lina told the French lady how sorry she was that she could not see her old friend Hermanna Sonnenkamp, for she had to go back with her parents that evening, having been invited to a reception to be given by the Countess Wolfsgarten next day at noon. She said this to the French lady, with such pride and emphasis, as showed that she thought that even here people knew what a reception at Count Wolfsgarten's meant.

The French lady noticed this and answered, "We do not know what each other's names were in thc outer world. Here, we only know our cloister names."

"May I know yours?"

"Why not? My name is Seraphia."

The girl seemed now to be more confidential with the French sister, since she could call her Seraphia, and it pleased her to think that she could tell at home in the village what a charming nun she had become acquainted with, who was certainly a princess.

They returned through the long corridors, and as they were going down stairs, a snow-white figure, with large wings on her shoulders, and a glittering diadem on her head, her hair streaming in disorder over her breast and shoulders, met them going up. Her face was pale, and her weird black eyes were brilliant beneath her heavy eyebrows.

"Manna!" cried out Lina, and "Manna" echoed from the vaulted ceiling.

The winged apparition seized Lina's hand, drew her up the stairs, away from the others, and said:

"Is it you, Lina? Ah, I have just left the poor little homesick child—the only living soul I have spoken to to-day."

"Oh, how wonderful you look! how glorious! You must have seemed a real angel to the child. Oh, how delighted everybody at home will be when I tell them."

"Don't say anything about it. Excuse me to your parents for passing them; but who—who is the young man with you?"

The stranger seemed to feel that he was spoken of, and looked up toward the wonderful apparition, shading his eyes with his hand, so as to see more clearly; but he could distinguish none of the features, and saw only the wondrous figure and the gleaming eyes.

"We don't know him either," answered Lina; "we met him in the boat for the first time. But," said she, laughing at her own cleverness, "you can easily find out who he is, for his mother sent her respects to the Lady Superior by him. Just ask. Isn't he handsome!"

"O Lina, what are you saying! May the holy Genevieve pray God to pardon you for what you have said to me; and me"—and she covered her face with her hands—"and me, that I have listened to it. Good-bye, Lina: remember me to the others."

As the winged apparition retreated along the corridor, she heard Lina call after her that she would tell the Countess Wolfsgarten to-morrow how she had seen her. The apparition vanished.

They left the convent, and at the door the old gentleman said to the young man:

"It's a very good thing for girls to be educated in an island convent, away from the world."

"Girls in convents, and boys in barracks! Yes, that's a fine world!" answered the young man brusquely.

Without answering a word, the old gentleman withdrew a few steps with the ladies; he evidently wanted no acquaintance with a stranger who entertained such opinions.

The stranger hastened to the boat to cross. The stream shone like gold, and the stranger, putting his hand into it, bathed his forehead and eyes.

He sprang lightly ashore, and turned to look back at the

island convent. He saw the man and his wife and daughter just stepping into the boat, and waved his hat to them; then he turned his steps toward the mountain beyond the ruined castle, from which the convent could be seen. There he sat for a long time, gazing at the convent on the island. He heard the children sing, and saw the long rows of windows lighted up; and, looking up at the stars, he said:

"O mother!"

What did he mean by that exclamation?

Could his mother have warned him that at some time he would meet an apparition?

The nightingale sang unceasingly in the bushes, and the youth listened to its song, and wished that it would stop, so that he might hear the convent children sing; for they almost seemed to have realized a dream of heaven, and to have become a choir of angels.

Alone, with beating heart, in the spring night and in a ruin!

"Is this thou?" the young man asked himself.

He descended the mountain, and as he approached the hotel, met the gentleman with the two ladies, going to the railway station. He felt like asking the girl who the singular apparition was, but did not. What good would that do? Better not know, and let the enchantment of it remain pure and complete.

He entered the hotel, sat down and read the bill of fare, without knowing what he was reading or what to order. He stared at the bill, till the waiter came and asked for it, to give it to another man.

He ordered "whatever was convenient."

"What wine will you have? We've a fine brand of *drachen-blut.*"

"Fetch *drachen-blut.*"

He ate and drank without knowing it—knowing only that he was mortal, and must eat and drink. Involuntarily he took up a newspaper lying on the table. What are convents, and what are ruined castles? What is an apparition of a girl with wings tied to her shoulders? Here is the world, the bustling, every-day, real world. Tired out with looking from mountain heights, you enter a hotel, and involuntarily snatch up a newspaper. Why? Perhaps because the mind and eye, wearied by the unmoved appearance of nature, are refreshed by your return to actual life and common events, where all is incessantly changing. It is necessary for you to hear ordinary words which all hear and which speak of the world in which you live, while you are dreaming, and are lost in deep speculation.

Yes, so it is! We can hardly imagine to ourselves to-day, how it was in other times when one could dream out his dream, undisturbed. At all hours, whether those of trouble, when even life seems a burden and the world to have grown indifferent, or in moments of exalted feeling, when we seem removed from and beyond all reality—at all times comes the newspaper and forces itself on our attention, demanding why we too should not be fellow-workers in the life of the world.

What now was America to the young man? And yet he eagerly read an account of the position of affairs in that country. The election of a new President of the Republic was arousing all the feelings of the new world, and the name of a man—Abraham Lincoln—universally held to be a model of uprightness and liberality, seemed to prevail, and with it a manifestation of the will of the people, that was to become historical. He read eagerly, and smiled when he thought how the French woman had told him that only an American girl could quiet the home-sick child, and how also the music of the festival had been of her composition. There was the child playing with a pious myth, while her native country was distracted by civil war. And again the young man's thoughts went back to the convent and the wondrous apparition.

As he was about to lay the paper aside, an advertisement caught his eye. He knitted his forehead, looked hastily around and read it again; then telling the waiter that he wished to retain the paper, betook himself to his room.

"A handsome young man," said the guests. "He is evidently a widower, who wishes to forget his sorrows by a trip on the Rhine; he wore crape on his hat."

CHAPTER II.

AGAINST THE STREAM.

NAME—Erich Dournay. Doctor of Philosophy, Ex-Army Captain. Place of departure—(name of a small University-town); Destination—"End of the journey."

In this way the young man registered himself at the hotel, early the next morning, and while doing so, noticed just above his name, "Justice Vogt, wife (*née* Landen) and daughter, from ——" (a little town of the upper Rhine was named).

That was the speckled gentleman of yesterday, with the two ladies.

Erich, as we shall hereafter call him, went with his luggage to the wharf where the steamboat lay. The morning was fresh and clear, exultant overflowing life was everywhere, only a streak of mist hung like a cloud half way up the mountains. With firm step, erect, and drinking in the morning air—Erich went along. He leaned over the baluster of the wharf and looked into the waves, whence a mist arose, and melted into air. Then he looked back at the island, where now the morning bell was ringing, arousing the children who yesterday seemed to themselves beings from story-land. How would that girl with long black hair and the shining wings open her lustrous eyes!

To banish this picture, Erich took the paper from his pocket and read the advertisement again.

The steamboat came up, breaking the waves against her breast.

Erich had not noticed that two nuns from the convent—and one of them the delicate, shy French woman—had been also awaiting the arrival of the boat. As soon as he was aboard, he noticed that they had embarked with him. He saluted them, but received no mark of recognition. The nuns seated themselves on the deck, and taking their breviaries began their devotions. Erich had at first intended to ask them who the girl with wings was, but now concluded not to do so. This whole affair should have no permanent effect on him,—he would concentrate all his strength on sterner things.

There were as yet but few passengers on the boat, and the early morning is always unsociable. The isolation of sleep seems yet to oppress the souls of men. Erich seated himself a short distance from the pilot, who kept whistling softly to himself, and in deep revery gazed at the ploughed-up water, and the landscape. He pressed his lips together and seemed determined to enjoy silently the storied beauty of the stream and landscape, and it annoyed him that men here and there would rob themselves of the freshness of morning and the repose of the scene by talking.

In the course of this story we shall often hear of this peculiar young man, and so we may as well know at the outset, that Erich was the son of parents universally respected, had received a careful education, and entered the military service, which, however, he had afterward left voluntarily, and devoted himself to study. He had been made a Doctor but a few days before, having worked very hard to take his degree, for only two months had elapsed since the death of his father.

On the evening of the day on which he received his degree, his mother advised him to take a few days' breathing-time. She passed her hand over his pale thin face and said:

"You will soon get your color back again. 'Living and working are duties,' that was your father's motto, and he lived by it till his dying day."

After Erich's return from this trip, they were to determine upon their future course of life. His mother felt this painfully, and could not avoid thinking that they would be obliged to leave the steady, easy-going life to which they had been accustomed, and lead a constantly precarious existence, for which their previous mode of living had not at all prepared them, and which she had never known or looked forward to; and with a sorrow which she could not overcome, but which she strove to conceal, she recalled an expression of Lessing, and seemed to see her son standing in the market-place asking for work. She hoped, however, that the reluctance which her son felt to receive any position, offered him through favor, would gradually disappear; at all events, he must take another vacation, and regain the freshness of youth. Had she seen him now, she would have been surprised to see how quickly he had been rejuvenated. Yes, a fire had come to his eyes, and a color to his cheeks, which had never been more bright and blooming.

It was only to give him an object, that she had sent a message by him to the Superior of the convent, and now he was returning home. A mere newspaper advertisement had given an unexpected direction and object to his journey.

"Wonderful!" thought Erich to himself as he put his hand on his breast-pocket where the paper was—"wonderful, how the mandates are given which drive the adventurous Odysseus to and fro." Yet he possessed youthful elasticity enough, not to forget the pleasure of his journey, in its object, and he enjoyed examining the machinery on the boat and the life on river and shore.

The two nuns left the boat at the second landing-place, and the delicate French woman nodded back to him as she stepped down the little flying stairs. When she was in the skiff, however, she folded her hands, and dropped her eyes, not even looking back when she had reached the shore.

From place to place the passengers changed. At one town came a troop of pilgrims, mostly women with white cloths on their heads; and at the place where they landed, a band of Turners in their bright gray uniform, came on board, and were soon singing on the deck while the pilgrims answered them from the shore. Bells rang in all the villages and cities which they passed. It was a bright, ringing, blooming spring day, and Erich felt all that intoxication with which the Rhineland life fills the soul—an expansion and elevation of all its powers, which can no more be explained than analysis can explain what it is that gives its life to the wine that grows here on the hills. It is the breath of the stream, the exhalation of the hill, the hidden virtue of the soil; it is the sunlight glowing alike in wine and men, which awakens winged happiness, from which none can escape, and which none can analyze.

Erich was frequently spoken to, but avoided any long conversation: he wished to be alone amid the crowd of men, environed only by the beautiful landscape. There are words which become an axis around which thought revolves. Erich heard one passenger say to another:

"I prefer to travel against the stream. You see everything more distinctly, and for a longer time; and it is a triumph of human ingenuity to be able to sail against the stream."

Against the stream! That was now the word which alone remained to Erich from all the thousands he had heard and thought. Against the stream! So lay the way which he must travel through life. He had left the beaten track, and boldly sought out a road of his own. It is well! thus would he learn to know the world, and, above all things, his own powers.

"Against the stream," said he, smiling to himself. "Let us see whither that will lead."

It was high noon when they reached the town known through all the world for its old gray towers.

A young man standing on the shore looked at him sharply, and then cried out:

"Dournay!"

"Herr Von Prancken!" answered Erich. They grasped each other's hands.

CHAPTER III.

YOUNG WINE.

THIS is the Rhine! One can hardly shake hands before he hears, "Let's take a drink!"

"It must be the river before your eyes that makes you long so for the fluid!"

So spake Erich to his companion, a slender, fair young man, about as old as he, who sat opposite to him, with his carefully-gloved hand resting on the head of a brown dog which lay on his lap. The dog surveyed Erich, whose full-toned voice probably moved it greatly.

"Now choose; here's the wine-list. What year and what growth? Shall we drink new wine, that's vigorous and hasn't gone to rest yet?"

"Yes, young wine, and from the hill there on which the sun-light rests so softly and where the cuckoo sings in the woods. We'll drink wine of the ground we stand on, and become blood relations of this lovely spot of earth."

Prancken addressed the waiter in a short, military tone: "A bottle of your best!"

The wine came; it flowed into the shining glasses like molten gold. The two men clinked glasses and drank. They sat amid the vine-leaves by the shore where the landscape opened before them, and the eye ranged over verdant islands in the river, over pretty houses, over hills, vineyards, and beautiful villas.

The boats by the shore were still again, for the waves made by the steamboat had subsided. On this side, and on that, far-off trains of cars rumbled along. The beams of the noonday sun flashed on the smooth stream, in which here and there white clouds were mirrored, and in the bushes nightingales sang.

"This is life," cried Erich, stretching out his arms. "After a day of loneliness amid the motley crowd of restless men, now to meet an old acquaintance so unexpectedly seems almost like home; and I must tell you that I take this meeting as a good omen."

Otto von Prancken nodded, well pleased. He did not know, but in the surprise of the meeting, he had greeted Erich more cordially than was consistent with his dignity. But now, when Erich called him "You," whereas they had been calling each other "Thou,"* he nodded complaisantly. Erich recognized his position, as became him. Prancken drew off his glove, and again stretched out his hand to Erich saying:

"You're travelling for pleasure?"

"No; I'm not now in position to do that, and it's no time. Perhaps you do not know that my father died two months ago?"

"Indeed! I shall always remain thankful to our good professor. The little that I learned in the military school—and it was little enough in all conscience—I have to thank him for entirely. Ah, what patience and unremitting zeal your good father had! Let us drink to his memory!"

The glasses rang.

"When I am dead," said Erich, and his voice trembled, "I hope some son of mine will remember me, with a companion, over their wine, as we now remember my father."

"Ah, to die!" said Prancken, seeking to turn the subject. "When I am dead, I shall like nothing better. It seems to me, to have been in extremely bad taste to place the graveyard over there in the vineyard."

Erich answered nothing, but only stared across the stream, and listened to the cuckoo singing in the churchyard.

"Are you an agriculturist?" he asked, rousing himself.

"For the time being, I have laid aside my lieutenant's coat for an indefinite period, and taken to high jackboots; but one is just as much a bore as the other."

As he said this, he took out his nail-cleaner, and zealously cleaned his nails; then, taking his pocket-brush, he arranged his already irreproachably parted, and somewhat thin hair. While doing this, he occasionally glanced at Erich. For

* The reader need hardly be reminded that with the Germans, "thou" is more familiar than "you."

a short time the two sat without speaking, closely examining each other. Two awkward men, who are helplessly in antagonism, immediately embarrass each other. Two clever men, who know their cleverness, are like two fencers, each of whom knows the other's skill, and hesitates to make stroke or pass.

Prancken bent over his glass, enjoyed the fragrance of the wine, and at last said, half smiling:

"You are probably converted from your communistic notions by this time."

"Communist? I would not have believed that you too, like so many others, would cover up so much that is disagreeable under that comfortable sneer—'Communism.' I wish I could be a communist; and, by that I mean that I wish communism were a practicable form of society, which it is not, and never can be. We must go to work in another way to free our existence from barbarism, when our fellow-men, equally entitled to the means of living with us, suffer for the commonest necessities of life. It makes me sad to think that I am sitting here composedly drinking the wine of the hill, on which even now poor oppressed men are toiling, who never taste a drop of it."

"It's Sunday to-day, and so nobody's working," answered Prancken, laughing.

The contrast between the young men can be seen in this first meeting. Erich also laughed at the unexpected quibble of his friend. He was wise enough to have no personal feeling in discussing a difference of opinion, so he returned at once to friendly ground, and the conversation flowed peaceably in reminiscences of boyhood and thoughts of the future.

Both the young men would easily be recognized as soldiers, from the stiff carriage of the neck, and the way in which they moved their arms when walking, but the stiffness in Erich's case was softened by a certain easy grace. Prancken was elegant; Erich, noble and refined. In every tone and movement of Prancken there was something that attracted attention, although he had that negligent insolence—or, if that is too strong a word, impertinence—which regards every one not belonging to "society" either as not existing or as a stranger, but when once he has obtained a foothold *there*, as being in the world too.

Erich's manners were as good, and more easy and dignified. His voice was a beautiful, strong baritone; while Prancken's was a tenor. Even in their manner of speaking, the difference between the young men was easily perceived. Erich spoke each word distinctly, and gave each letter its full sound.* Prancken, on the contrary, spoke far too lazily, as if vowels and conso-

* As is customary in German.

nants were too much for him, and as though obliged to avoid every strain on the organs of speech, and yet he liked to talk, and talked well, and to the point. His manner of speaking was rattling, like the short, quick gallop of the Prince's body-guard. There was something boisterous in his most ordinary expressions, as if he was always just coming from a society for the suppression of several bottles of sack, or going to one.

This conduct seemed new and strange to Erich, who had always been in the habit of thinking rather than speaking, and had lived shut up like a monk, engaged in earnest study.

"Herr Baron," said the waiter—approaching and bringing with him a bottle of the sparkling wine of the district—"your coachman wants to know if he shall put the horses out."

"No," rang out the answer, and Prancken continued to Erich, as he stirred the bottle about in the cooler, "I will not allow the brief pleasure of this meeting with you to be disturbed. Ah, you don't know how unspeakably tiresome all this greatly extolled poetry of being a landed proprietor is."

Filling their glasses from the uncorked bottle, he continued: "Compost—and compost again is the word. Olympus is a compost heap, and the god enthroned on it is called Jupiter Ammoniac."

Prancken laughed very loudly over this piece of wit; then he drank, and twirled the ends of his moustache complacently.

Erich returned to the beauty of this Rhine life, but here Prancken would not join him.

"If somebody would only come and rub the rouge off of those lying Loreleiers who talk about the beauty of Rhine life! The poets are always speaking of the dewy mornings, and to-day we had a fog on the hills, as though the angels in heaven had all thrown the milk from their coffee into the fire."

Erich could not help laughing, and said, as he sipped his wine:

"But the pleasure of the wine!"

"Yes, that's what all the people here drink, but not poetically—they make a business of it. There they sit, for hours together, always the same society, and they have the same half-dozen jokes in the garrison, or revive jokes that were worn out years ago, and then they go home drunk as lords, and roaring out a song—and that is what is called 'the gladness of the Rhine!' The only real pleasure in all this made-up lie about the Rhine is the Wreath Inn."

"What's that?"

"Well, some worthy gossip tailor or shoemaker has laid in a keg of particularly fine wine, which he neither can finish alone nor wants to. So he sticks up a green wreath at his house, and the old German sitting-room, with its comfortable old Dutch stove, decorated with green boughs, and the gray cat under the bench, is turned into a tavern. When they have finished in Schmied-street, they go to work in Hasen-street, Kirch-street, Salz-street and Kapuziner-street. The burghers lend each other a helping hand in drinking up their wine; and that's the only beautiful thing here."

"So let's enjoy the wine," said Erich. "See how the sun again glorifies the noble drink at which he smiles, and which he has ripened so carefully. I drink to thee, O Sun! past and present!"

With an eagerness unusual to him, he emptied his glass. "I always thought there was a poet in you," said Prancken. "How I envy you! I wish I had the ability to write a satirical poem, so peppered that all the world would burn its tongue with it."

Erich smiled, and answered that he, too, had once thought himself called to be a poet, but had discovered his mistake, and was now fully determined to lead a busy, active life.

"Yes," said he, drawing his newspaper from his pocket, "very probably you may be able to do me a life-long service."

"With pleasure, if it is not against—"

"Don't be disturbed; it has nothing to do with principles or politics. You might, perhaps, come to my aid as a matrimonial agent."

"You in love too? Handsome Erich Dournay, the Adonis of the garrison, needs some one to do his wooing?"

"Nothing of the sort! The business has only to do with the position of a private tutor. Here, look at the paper."

Prancken read: "I wish to secure a man of scientific culture and high breeding, to act as tutor for my son, fifteen years old, and fit him for a high station in life. Salary open to agreement. An annuity for life, after the conclusion of the engagement. Address and references to be left at Railway Station ——, on the Rhine."

"I know that advertisement; had something to do in getting it up; and I tell you, we were thinking of something extraordinary when we selected the expression 'high breeding.'"

"You probably meant a nobleman?"

"By all means. It's not necessary for me to apologize for what the disappointed beings in the daily papers call feudalism. Here the case is, that an instructor in a private house is to take particular care of a wilful pupil,—a position with an unquestionable title to be considered honorable."

"Certainly, that's all fair. But perhaps I've an unquestionable title too: I was made a Doctor only a few days ago."

Prancken nodded condescendingly, congratulating him, but quickly added:

"And have you quite forgotten that you left the service with the rank of a captain? I acknowledge that I would, in this case, lay great stress on being a soldier. But no, you're not fit to lead tigers. The boy is as stubborn and intractable as an American redskin, and understands how to find the scalp-lock, as he has proved with half-a-dozen pedagogues."

"Perhaps the undertaking would be so much the more pleasant on that account."

"And do you know that Massa Somnenkamp is worth several millions, and that the heir knows it?"

"That's no objection; it's only so much the more enticing."

"Good! I'll take you to the mysterious man myself. I have the pleasure of sharing his peculiar favor. But no—you'd better go with me to my brother-in-law's place. You must surely remember my sister Bella?"

"Well, I accept your hospitality. Only I beg you to let Herr Somnenkamp—and it seems to me that I have heard the name before, but never mind—to let Herr Somnenkamp know of my arrival, and allow me to go to him, afterward, alone."

Prancken cast a questioning look at Erich, who continued:

"I know how to value your good word, but you know that a stranger can never quite do himself justice in presence of a third party."

Prancken smiled at Erich's cleverness, and experienced a certain pride in having under his patronage a man so richly endowed. He drew out a pocketbook, and sat for a while with his silver pencil-case pressed against his lips; the doubt arose in his mind, whether he was doing wisely to recommend Erich for the position. Would it not be better to put him off, and recommend one who would be entirely his own creature? But as Erich would then make the application for himself, and, in all probability, receive the appointment, it would be better to establish a claim to his gratitude.

And yet, in the midst of these doubts, there arose an opposition to them. Prancken really felt a pleasure in being able to step forward here in the *rôle* of a benefactor, and for an instant was happy in the thought.

He wrote on a card, to Herr Somnenkamp, asking him to make no engagement, as a man of education, formerly an artillery officer, would apply in person for the situation. He cautiously avoided expressing himself in a more friendly manner in regard to Erich, as he was unwilling to take any decisive steps without his sister's advice.

The card was immediately sent away, and Prancken snapped the elastic band over his pocketbook, playing with it a few moments before putting it in his pocket.

CHAPTER IV.

DISSIMILAR COMRADES.

THE two young men drove in an open carriage through the street, and soon began to ascend the hill. The air was filled with dewy fragrance, and high above the vineyards in the leafy forest sang the nightingales. It was one endless chain of song.

They sat without speaking. Each knew that the other had overstepped the boundaries of his life, and it could not be foretold what would be the result.

When Erich removed his hat and fully displayed his fine face and the strength of character shown in it, it seemed to Prancken that he had never seen him before.

He shuddered as he thought how he was exposing himself to danger.

Anger and scorn, gentleness and smiles, appeared by turns on his face; he muttered unintelligibly, and occasionally broke out in a short, singular laugh.

"In fact I am surprised at you—utterly surprised," said he to himself. "I would not have believed it of you, my good Otto, that you could any longer be so magnanimous and self-forgetful—such an out-and-out friend! How often have you been told, and believed it too, that you were entirely through with such nonsense, and more knowing than you fully believed yourself to be! Shame on you, so to belie your own innocence and virtue! Here you sit, and are a friend, a most tender brother, a very high-priest of fate to another man who is a mere piece of philanthropy—nothing but philanthropy—pure philanthropy in a full beard. All his thoughts are most noble and devoted to the good of mankind, and yet a good streak of luck pleases noble philanthropy as much as anybody else."

Prancken laid his head back on the cushion and gazed smilingly at the sky. He would take good care that noble philanthropy, sitting here beside him in the carriage, should not interfere with his plans, and what he himself was unequal to, his sister Bella should do for him.

There was something violent in Prancken's ordinary demeanor. The uniform which he had worn from childhood, seemed to put a certain restraint on his actions, and had given him a character which drew him back from intercourse with the common run of men. He was perfectly at home when in the society of his comrades, or when on duty. He showed no peculiar ability, yet was a good officer, and knew how to command and exercise men and horses. Now, since he had doffed his uniform, and taken to citizen's dress, it seemed to him as though he would fall to pieces; so he carried himself bolt-upright and wished every movement to proclaim that he did not belong to the common herd of mortals. In the regiment he had always commanded others, but now he had entered the service of duty, where he had only himself to command. Cast upon his own resources, he found, to his chagrin, that he was nothing without companionship. The world seemed barren and stupid to him, and he had consequently assumed a bitter, ironical tone, that seemed to give him a certain superiority over this dreary round of life, without parades, play, or the ballet.

It was with a sort of envy that he looked upon Erich, who, without any external position, nay, even plunged in poverty, sat so quietly beside him enjoying the landscape as though it were a feast.

Erich was, in fact, in a better condition than Prancken. When he had entered military life, he remained under all circumstances a man centred in himself. He never had entered into familiar intercourse with his comrades; and now, since he had put on citizen's dress, his whole outward life had changed.

"I envy you," said Prancken, after looking at him for a long time without speaking.

"You envy me?"

"At first it grieved me to think that a man of your ability should be obliged to enter private service—and what a service! But it is probably very fortunate for a man to be obliged to do something for his living."

"That would be a hard task for the young millionare," answered Erich. "There are two things which arouse a man's strength—the idea and its realization."

"I beg pardon, I don't quite understand you."

"Let me explain."

"I am listening."

"He who calls his strength into action for the sake of an idea, almost becomes a genius, no matter how small and unnoticeable his sphere of duty may be. He who works for pay, in order to satisfy common needs or luxurious tastes, is a common worker, for common wants compel him. The hillside would not be planted with vines, the forest would not be cleared, the ship not steered, the plough not dragged, did not common necessity call to the work. Where both unite—and they are not incompatible—*there* is true manhood. A nobleman who enters the world, has the good fortune to be the heir of an idea—the idea of honor."

Prancken nodded, and yet was provoked. This man dared to pass judgment upon, and explain nobility. Nobility and faith should never be explained and proved; they are simply unimpeachable facts of history.

Both became silent again, asking themselves what would come of this unexpected association of their lives. They had been only slightly acquainted with each other in the service, but now something else might happen.

Shadows were already lying in the valley, but on the hills the sun yet lingered. They drove through the town. Happy crowds thronged the streets; girls were walking about arm in arm; the young men, singly or in groups, strolled along, exchanging pleasant greetings, nods and smiles. The old people sat before their houses. The fountain in the market-place gurgled from its fourfold jet, and farther up, along the road by the shore, there was merry singing.

"Oh, what a happy life we Germans lead!" cried Erich. "At evening laboring men enjoy the coolness of the shade in this treeless wine-land."

Again the men proceeded silently, and Prancken drew back hastily as, he knew not how—like a dream, like a far-off vision—he saw himself standing opposite to the man beside him, with a pistol in his hand—in a duel. Whence came the vision? He did not understand it, and yet—could it be a presentiment?

He turned eagerly to conversation. A peculiarity innate in his character, and which nature and education had developed, was a social virtue which may be called complacency with the world. And so, in order to banish the singular vision, as well as to bring his social virtue into play, he told where he had been. He had, at the recommendation of his brother-in-law, Count Clodwig von Wolfsgarten, been paying a visit to a very respectable landed proprietor of the vicinity, in order, provided it should be mutually agreeable, to become his pupil.

This landed proprietor, Weidman by name, who was sometimes called Marchminister (for in the year 1848 he had been minister for three days, as an ice-breaker to stem the incoming torrent of the revolution), was looked upon in all that neighborhood as an authority in agricultural as well as political affairs.

Prancken went on in his narration, and the more he did so, the more he enjoyed his own spicy way of talking, and the deeper he plunged into it. He began:

"I would like to know how he would please you. He has also—," and at the word "also" Prancken stopped and then proceeded quickly—"has also, like so many benefactors of the world, constantly at hand a large amount of good precepts, with which one might stock a convent of Capuchins."

They both laughed, and Prancken continued:

"Ah, the world only exists by means of superstition. All the fine poetry of being a landowner is nothing but money-seeking, which quickly takes the rouge from the 'evening-red' and the 'morning-red.' This Herr Weidman and his sons think of nothing but making money. He has six sons, five of whom I know; and they seem to be in impertinently good health, with pretentiously white, faultless teeth, and all wear long beards.

"All these hills which travellers admire so much are obliged to furnish wine for them, on their surface, and their bowels must give them slate and manganese, ore and chemicals. They have fine factories, and so they all work into each other's hands. I have heard that they draw forty different materials from beech-wood, and send the exhausted coal to Paris restaurants. Isn't that a beautiful enthusiasm for nature? And now for father Weidman. Don't you enjoy the singing of nightingales? Father Weidman has, during his reign, promulgated an edict of toleration, because nightingales eat insects, and are useful to agriculture in field and forest. Father Weidman inhabits a ruined castle, and yet if a minstrel should come to that castle to-day, he would not be listened to, unless he sang a stave from the noble ballad by means of which nitrogen and hydrogen unite magically to form Ammonia. My head is all in a whirl with superphosphate and potash. Do you suppose," asked Prancken directly, "that it is an object worth striving for, to increase the nourishment of mankind by a few sacks of potatoes?"

But before Erich could answer, Prancken added: "Ah! there is just nothing that one would really like to be! A soldier is about the only thing."

As they were ascending the steep hill, and could overlook the broad river with its islands, Prancken said, as he pointed up the stream to a bright white building standing on its bank, "See, there is the Villa Sonnenkamp, also called the Villa Eden. That large glass dome on which the setting sun is yet shining is the palm-house. Herr Sonnenkamp is an enthusiastic gardener; his green-houses and fruit-plantations excel those of the Prince."

Erich stood up in the carriage and looked back at the landscape, and at the house, where perhaps a new life had been prepared for him. When he sat down, Prancken offered him a cigar.

Erich thanked him, but had given up smoking. Prancken said, smiling:

"He who doesn't smoke is no man for Herr Sonnenkamp." He sharply accented the word "Herr."* "Next to his plants, his chief pride is possessing the greatest number of choice cigars, and he was peculiarly grateful to me, when I once told him he

* "Herr," in some connections, indicates more dignity than the English "Mister."

had a seraglio of cigars. I don't see how any one who refused his cigars could get along with him."

"I can smoke, but am not obliged to," said Erich, accepting the cigar.

"You seem to me to be not only a Doctor of Philosophy, but a veritable philosopher."

Still the travellers went on.

Erich looked down. A host of thoughts agitated his soul.

O wonderful world! Invisible powers hover in the air; a human soul wanders, and never dreams that another soul is pressing toward it, and that they both will have one destiny. It is the greatness of the human spirit, that there is a presentiment which calls up in the consciousness of the one, as though they two were to have one life, a man whose name he has never heard, whose face he has not seen, of whose existence he has no knowledge.

He who with an entire abnegation of self has devoted his life to the good of others, may at any hour free himself from his individuality, and become absorbed in thoughts of the universal good. Then does he speak the creating word, "Be soul of my soul," and the word which redeems from inborn sin, "I am my brother's keeper."

CHAPTER V.

THE OLD NOBLEMAN AND HIS BEAUTIFUL WIFE.

"TO Wolfsgarten," said the sign-post at the edge of the forest of tall trees which they were entering. Here we are, on the nobleman's territory. Every stranger who comes this way, and asks about that simple manor-house which he sees in the distance, with the old-fashioned gables, is told that there dwell two happy mortals, to whom nothing is wanting but to be blessed with children.

There are men who completely satisfy the soul. When two persons sit together and talk of one of them, each feels happy in the recognition and setting forth of the pure and beautiful in his life, and is grateful for any new light that the other can give him. But, singularly enough, one soon gets tired of the representation and explanation of the purely beautiful!

Then, again, there are men, who, when two are talking confidentially, furnish an inexhaustible source of remark, which, however, generally turns upon their disagreeable qualities, while the qualities which are attractive are kept in the background. When the conversation is ending, they feel obliged to add: "And yet, when I meet him as a friend, I'm not a hypocrite, for he has not only much that is deceitful about him, but much that is good too."

Clodwig was a character of the first sort: his wife, Bella, born Baroness von Prancken, was of the second.

Clodwig was a nobleman in the best sense of the word. He was not one of those affable men who win everybody at first sight, for he had a noble reserve and reticence. But the independent proprietor; the manufacturer as well as the day-laborer; the priest and the workingman; officers and merchants in the cities—everybody, regarded him with singular love and reverence, and looked upon him as an ornament to the landscape—a mighty tree on the hill-top, under whose shadow they could enjoy Nature's aspects, and which they prayed no storm might harm.

In every necessity, Clodwig von Wolfsgarten could be looked to for advice and aid, with the utmost confidence. He had always lived away from home till within the last five years, during which period he had married for the second time. Bella von Wolfsgarten was certainly more admired than loved. She was more affable than her husband, and, when seated in her little, low carriage drawn by a span of dappled ponies, she drove over the country and the town, everybody looked at her with wonder, for she held the reins while her husband sat beside her, and the servant sat on the back seat. Many old people who are always finding something singular in new fashions, maintained that her holding the reins was a sign that she was mistress elsewhere; but this was by no means the case. Toward her husband she was all humility and deference; so much so indeed as sometimes to make him uncomfortable by volubly rehearsing, even in his presence, his goodness, his uniform calmness, and his great wisdom.

Erich could only just remember the noise that Clodwig's marriage with Bella had made, for the event had happened just as he left the army. He had often seen Bella, but never Count Wolfsgarten, who had for many years adorned the office of Ambassador of his little country at the Papal court, where Erich's father had become acquainted with him.

Clodwig was known in the learned world through a little archæological work with very costly engravings; for, next to his passion for music, he pursued antiquarian science with all that seriousness and persistency which characterized his whole being. He was especially remarkable for not allowing any science or any art to go unnoticed.

Childless, and made a widower at Rome, he had returned to his native country, become a member of the National Assembly, and made himself illustrious in support of what is known as moderate progress; and here, during the session, he became intimate with old Herr von Prancken, who was also a member of the Assembly. There soon sprang up an interesting attachment to Bella von Prancken, who made an imposing appearance and was especially noted for her remarkable skill in playing the piano. Bella had—if such an unchivalrous expression is permissible—become a perennial flower. She had been, in her bloom, the handsomest woman at court, but now a new growth had sprung up in society, for which she had no affinity.

Bella had seen a good deal of the world. In company with two English women she had visited Italy, Greece, and Egypt, hiring a clever courier, who attended to everything for her. Now, having returned to court, she occupied herself in society with that resignation which becomes a superior nature when brought into contact with such commonplace things. She conversed much with Clodwig von Wolfsgarten, and he acted on the assumption that the frivolities of society hardly attracted her attention, for she had at the outset conducted herself as a ripe nature interested only in loftier things. She entered into Clodwig's favorite archæological occupations with great interest and attention. It will readily be understood that they met everywhere; and when either was not present, Bella or Clodwig was asked if the other was unwell or detained.

Bella had no porcelain figures or similar trifles on her table, but only choice imitations of antiques; and she wore a long amber chain, which had been found in the grave of a noble Roman lady. She had a large photograph-album, containing views of her travels, and was happy to go through them again with Clodwig, and receive information from him in regard to them; for him too she would sometimes play, though she had given up doing it in society.

The entire court once did something new. It continually carried between Bella and Clodwig the inspired things that one had said of the other, and even the highest authorities busied themselves in encouraging the pair, for it was perceived that both were backward in changing their relation. It was a success, however, and their betrothal was celebrated in the innermost circles of court society.

Evil tongues now declared—(they should surely be allowed to wag at last, which was no more than a fair compensation for being so exceedingly good hitherto)—that two interesting things had happened. Bella had stipulated that her betrothed should never mention his first wife, and old Prancken had asked the physician in ordinary how much longer Count Wolfsgarten would probably live. And he was said to have laughed very peculiarly when the doctor assured him that such old gentlemen, who live such measured, quiet, and passionless lives, reach an incalculable age.

Bella's conduct contradicted the calumny that she had hoped to be a rich young widow. A short time before their marriage, Clodwig had had an attack of vertigo, and Bella had managed so that from that day forth, wherever he went, and sometimes without his knowledge, he was attended by a servant. She tended the old gentleman with the greatest and most earnest care. He revived again, and now since they had returned to their estate, he had gained new vigor.

At the baths where they spent the summer, Clodwig and Bella were notable personages, and Bella was honored not only for her beauty, but for her immaculate constancy and the almost anxious care with which she guarded her old husband.

CHAPTER VI.

COLD MEAT.

THERE was yet daylight on the hill, as they approached the manor-house of Wolfsgarten. As they were ascending the last elevation, through the park, they saw a beautiful girl in a blue summer-dress, standing by the road amid the green trees.

The girl, who had caught sight of the carriage, turned around quickly. Two bright blue ribbons fastened behind, as the fashion was, played in the evening wind. The girl's appearance was buoyant, and at the same time delicate.

"Ah," cried Prancken, "we have hit the cold-meat society at my sister's to-day. That lovely child who turned away so quickly is the daughter of the justice of the peace, and comes fresh-baked from the pan of the Convent of the Sacred Heart at Aix-la-Chapelle. You will find her a genuine Rhine-girl: my sister has given her the appropriate name Musselina, there is something permanently summery about her. The girl has already announced us to the party."

Smoothing his hair with a pocket-brush, he continued:

"The family is very respectable, very honorable: the little one is somewhat too good an article to amuse one's self with, and so one keeps a cheaper quality to smoke in the open air."

Prancken suddenly perceived that he was speaking to Erich, and hastily added:

"That's what our comrade, Don Giovanno Nipper, who is always betting, would say. Do you know that that nonsensical fellow is now a cripple at Wiesbaden, and is dragged about in a hand-carriage?"

Prancken's whole existence seemed to expand; he sprang joyously from the carriage, stretched out his hand to Erich, and said:

"Welcome to Wolfsgarten!"

Several carriages were standing in the yard, and in the garden they met the ladies of the party. They were sitting on slight chairs, with fans and sunshades in their hands, around a circular bed of luxuriantly-growing forget-me-nots, in the midst of which arose blooming red rhododendrons.

"We are no disturbers of the peace. Keep your seats, ladies," cried Prancken pleasantly, as he approached.

Bella saluted her brother, and then Erich, whom she immediately recognized. He was introduced to the others—the justice's wife, Miss Lina—these were both happy to renew the acquaintance of yesterday. Then he was presented to the district-doctor's wife and her sister—the head-forester's wife and her mamma; then to the apothecary's wife, the burgomaster's, the school-director's; and then to the wives of two merchants and two manufacturers. The *élite* of the town seemed to be present in full force.

They said that the gentlemen had gone to a place near by, to take a look at the surrounding country.

Their conversation had probably not been very animated, and Erich's appearance awakened interest. The director's wife, a large, handsome woman, whom Bella called Frau Kleiderlied (lay-figure)—for, in fact, she was very skilful in dressing, and everything became her—took her lorgnette and examined the landscape, bringing Erich also into view; and the prospect seemed to be by no means unpleasing.

After the first questions as to how long it was since he had seen the Rhine, had been asked, and he had told how everything had seemed quite new again, and had almost intoxicated him with delight—Erich said how charming he found it to see the young ladies crowned with garlands of living flowers and green leaves; adding that it was undoubtedly natural affinity that gave woman the exclusive right of wearing garlands, while men, when they went on a pleasure excursion, were at most only allowed to wear on their round black hats a laurel-wreath, twined by some fair hand, which makes them appear extremely comical.

However trifling this remark may seem, the way in which Erich made it, at once aroused their good-will, and the whole circle smiled pleasantly, and felt at once that here was a man who could enter with gusto into customs with which he was not familiar.

Bella understood how to draw her guest out.

"Is it not true, Captain," she asked, "that the Greeks and Romans wore their decorations on their heads, while we moderns, who think so much of our hearts, wear ours on our breasts?"

Then she told about an antique laurel-wreath which she had seen at Rome, and asked Erich if they used to have class distinctions there; and without knowing it, Erich was led on to speak of the various crowns of triumph; and a great deal of mirth was occasioned by his relating how, when a general had succored a beleaguered city, he received a crown made simply of grass.

"And what did they call this crown?" asked Bella.

"Succoring crown."

This expression occasioned considerable merriment.

The girls, who were standing by in groups, and understood very well what they were about, called out to a pretty boy who was playing by a fountain farther down the hill, and sprang down with flying robes. But when they reached the spring, they did not trouble themselves much about the child, but told each other what an extremely interesting man the new-comer was.

"He's handsomer than the Architect," said the apothecary's daughter.

"And handsomer than Herr von Prancken too," added Hildegard, the school-director's daughter.

The justice's daughter, Lina, was in the enviable position of being able to say that she had met him yesterday at the convent on the island. Her father had conjectured that he must be of French extraction, for his family had, as his very name implied, been Huguenot immigrants.

The apothecary's daughter, whose brother was a lieutenant, and who prided herself greatly on account of it, promised soon to ask him for more definite information in regard to the Captain.

Lina, in her thoughtless way, proposed that they should make a wreath and put it on the stranger's head unawares.

The wreath was quickly prepared; but not one of the girls, not even Lina, was bold enough to carry out the odd proposition.

In the mean time, Erich sat among the women and told them earnestly how great he considered the happiness of those who lived surrounded by such beautiful natural scenery. "Even if one does not know it, his whole nature is expanded; and he feels the result of this when he is brought into contact with less eloquent landscapes." No one ventured to answer, until Bella said:

"When one praises the landscape in which we live, he seems almost to flatter us, as though he had said something in praise of our dress or house or something else that belongs to us."

They all assented, although it could not be told whether Bella had agreed or disagreed with what had been said.

Then she asked Erich about his mother, and mentioned quite incidentally, but nevertheless with some stress, that his mother's only brother, Baron von Burgholz, had died quite suddenly at

Madeira. So now the ladies understood that Erich was at least half noble.

Bella spoke so easily, that speaking seemed to be a matter of secondary consideration with her. Seeing and being seen were her principal objects. When she spoke she hardly changed a single feature; scarcely moved her lips even, and it was only when she smiled that her small and beautiful teeth could be seen.

Bella knew that when Erich spoke he regarded her closely, and she faced him with as much calmness as if she were standing before her mirror.

She now, in a very friendly manner, introduced Erich personally to the head-forester's charming wife, who was a skilful ballad-singer, asking him, at the same time, if he sang much now. He answered that he had been out of practice for years.

The evening was unusually sultry. An oppressive closeness lay on mountain and valley, for far off a storm was brewing. The ladies were in doubt as to whether it would be better to await the storm at Wolfsgarten or return home at once.

"If the gentlemen were only here to settle the point!" The chief-forester's wife confessed that she was afraid of a storm.

"There you sympathize with your sister," said Erich.

"Oh, I'm not at all afraid," said her sister.

"Pardon me! I do not mean you, but the noble songstress who lives in this shrubbery. Don't you notice that lady nightingale, who was singing so loudly a minute ago, has become silent?"

This remark set them all going again, and each one told how she was affected by a storm.

"I think," said Erich, "that not only our characters can be told from the effect which a storm has on us, but even the vegetative life of our brain—what is known as temperament and nervous disposition. We are so little in sympathy with the life of nature, that the sights and sounds of atmospheric phenomena awe us, as though what the ancients believed were true, and we suddenly heard a voice crying from the air, 'Lo! thou walkest and breathest in a world mysteriously moved!'"

"Ah, here come the gentlemen!" they cried out suddenly. Two beautiful setter-dogs sprang into the garden, aud immediately ran up to Prancken's dog, which seemed quite a stranger to them, and sniffed him, as if to learn what he had seen in his travels. After the dogs, came the gentlemen.

Although Count Clodwig was personally unknown to Erich, the latter immediately recognized him. That unruffled calmness, that settled affability in his smooth-shaven, elderly face, which, how-ever, bore no trace of decay or weakness, could only belong to Clodwig von Wolfsgarten. All the others had grouped themselves around him, and each showed toward him a certain deference, as though he were the prince of the realm.

Clodwig possessed two peculiarities seldom united in the same person: he was amiable, and, at the same time, imposing; and though he never evinced any aristocratic haughtiness, and was kind and affable to all, yet, from that very fact, it could be seen that he was recognized as their superior.

As Erich was introduced to him, his face suddenly lighted up, and pleasant recollections shone from every feature.

"Welcome as the son of my Roman friend! You have a right to come to me," said he, pressing his gold spectacles more closely to his eyes with the little finger of his left hand.

The manner in which Clodwig said this was so deliberate and feeling, that everybody received the impression that it had often been the subject of his thoughts; and in his tone there was something so eager, that the surprise seemed to be looked upon as the fulfilment of a long-expected gratification.

"You have your father's voice," said the Count. "I was much grieved to hear of his death. I had been intending to write to him for years, until it was too late."

Clodwig then introduced Erich to the other men, as though it increased his own dignity to do so.

"I introduce to you a new comrade," said he, smiling, as he turned to an old gentleman with a big red face and snow-white, closely-cut hair. This is our Major—Major Grassler."

The Major bowed, much gratified, and extended to Erich a hand which had lost its first finger; but the old man knew very well how to press a stranger's hand. He bowed again, but said nothing.

The other gentlemen were then introduced, among them the architect Erhardt, a handsome young man, wearing on his sunburnt face a fine moustache and imperial. As soon as he was presented he excused himself to the Count, saying that he had business at the quarry to attend to.

The school-director told Erich that Erhardt was a pupil to Professor Einsiedel.

The ladies called the Major away from the men, and gave him a scolding, and the justice's wife distinguished herself by rating him for having forsaken the women all day and keeping with the men—he who had always been so attentive to the ladies, and was their faithful guardian. So he had to beg their pardon.

The Major had hardly seated himself before the girls had put on his white head the wreath prepared for Erich. He bowed playfully, and wished that some one would bring a mirror, that he might see himself too. He shook his finger at Lina, and asked if she had learned such tricks at the convent.

The Major was evidently the target at which they discharged the arrows of their wit. There is hardly any company in which somebody is not either forced to act in that capacity, or to surrender himself with as good grace as possible. The Major made more sport for everybody who knew him than he himself was aware of, for everybody smiled good-naturedly whenever he was thought or spoken of.

A gust of wind blew over the broad top of the hill. The flags on the manor-house were lowered, and the cushioned chairs quickly brought under cover. A feeling of comfort came over them all as they sat cosily within the lighted saloon, while the storm raged without.

For some time nothing was spoken of but the storm. The Major gave an account of a little skirmish they had once had while it was thundering and lightning fearfully. He didn't tell it very well, but they understood what he meant—how horrible it was to murder each other while the heavens spoke.

The justice's wife told how a young man, who was just about to take a false oath, suddenly let his hand fall, as there came a clap of thunder, and cried out, "I did it!"

The head-forester said, laughing, that the storm was a very good thing, for it certainly tamed the game. The school-director gave a glowing account of how difficult it was to keep the children busy in the school-room during a storm, and how it was impossible to proceed with the lessons, and he absolutely did not know what to do.

All turned their eyes on Erich to see if he, too, had not something to say, but he only remarked:

"What seems to us, as we sit here, a furious tempest, is down there, on the Lower Rhine, or above in Alsace, only distant heat-lightning, which cools the unusual warmth of the day. There, they are comfortably sitting in gardens or on balconies, peacefully breathing in the pure air. I believe that in feeling there are geographical divisions and zones."

He said this calmly; he knew how to make the present forgotten. The forester's wife, who was sitting in an anteroom, in the darkness, pressing her eyes with her hands, now came into the saloon, tranquillized by Erich's words, which she must have caught.

Erich spoke much. In spite of manifold experience, he still believed that much was to be gained by conversation, that one's ideas become clearer by it, and that it is not simply a means of passing away the time. He therefore put his whole soul into the work, and gave it his best powers, not having the slightest suspicion that he might possibly be considered pert and vain while giving his animated discourses. His manner of speaking was not merely agreeable, for while addressing others he managed to look from their point of view, and they soon felt that he saw further than they; and Erich did this, not intending to offend, but simply with a desire to aid.

There is something impressive in being able to make another person's ideas clear and unimpeded—something which arouses in him a feeling of gratitude as though he had been liberated; but, nevertheless, most people under such circumstances retain a feeling of the imposingness of the process, as though they had been told, "I speak things which you, of yourselves, do not and cannot understand," and thus the utterances seem so much the more oracular.

The men, especially the justice and the school-director, shrugged their shoulders. The energy with which Erich unfolded the rich stores of his thought-life seemed strange to the men, and even wounded the feelings of some. They felt that this extraordinary bearing and unusual way of speaking, this arousing of the best feelings of the heart, attracted the women, and cast into the shade those who, like themselves, could only speak of such things occasionally, and even then without any real knowledge of what they were saying, or ability to say it well. The justice glanced at the kindling eyes of his daughter and those of the forester's wife, and whispered to the school-director:

"That's a dangerous man."

The conversation was now carried on in groups. Erich stood with Clodwig at the bay-window, and looked out into the night. Lightnings played over the opposite mountains, now showing a gleaming point on the horizon, and now rending the heavens as though behind them was another heaven. The thunder shook the ceiling, so that the lustres of the chandeliers rattled against each other.

"There are things and circumstances which bring back to us vividly what we have seen and thought long ago," began Clodwig. "I once stood with your father in the Campagna, as I now stand here with you. I do not know how it happened, but we were talking about that way of thinking which regards the things of this world from the standpoint of eternity, and your father said, and I think I can hear him now: 'Only when we look at human life as part of a great system, and regard it as an entirety, do we, as thinkers, find that rest which religion gives to its believers; for only then do we hold the world in the unity of God. He who looks at the zigzag path of the ant and its destruction when it is devoured by the ant-lion, does not comprehend its existence, for he has regarded only a single ant and its destruction; but when he looks upon the ant-hill as a whole'" . . . .

Clodwig stopped suddenly. They could hear in the distance the shrill whistle of the locomotive dragging its heavy train through the valley below.

"There was no shrill engine-whistle to disturb us then," said he, after a short pause.

"The whistle does not displease me," said Erich.

"Why?"

"Because it illustrates how man can steadily pursue his own objects, even amid the uproar of nature. What is the mission of men born in these times, if not to open the way through which he can make the forces of nature act freely, and is not this the whole object of his existence?"

Clodwig grasped Erich's hand. A long-continued, brilliant flash of ligntning shot over the landscape, illuminating Erich's earnest countenance and the calm face of the old man. Clodwig pressed the hand he held, as if to say: "Thou art welcome to me—thou art now mine."

It is often said that love touches two souls and makes them one. Is it not equally true of friendship?"

It was so now.

They were filled with no forebodings. They held each other as if they had found what was dearest, and knew that henceforward they should not be as strangers; they had forgotten that a few minutes before they had met for the first time.

They had embraced in the world of boundless thought, which knows no time; they could have stood long thus without speaking, after they had relinquished each other's hands. They were together, and *one* without word or contact.

With a voice filled with emotion, as though revealing a secret, that came reluctantly from his lips, but which he *must* tell, Clodwig said:

"In such storms as this, I have often thought back to the time when all this land, as far as the Odenwald, was a great inland sea, from which rose lonely mountains like islands, until the stream tore its way through the cliffs. And have you ever thought, young man, that chaos will come again?"

"Yes; but we can neither think ourselves back to the time when men did not exist, nor forward to the time when they will exist no longer. We can only fill, as best we may, our working hour, our three score years and ten."

The Major came and invited the two gentlemen to enter the saloon where the company was gathered. Again Clodwig touched Erich's hand lightly, and then said:

"Come!"

Like two lovers who had secretly embraced and kissed each other, Clodwig and Erich returned to the company.

No one knew why their faces were so bright.

CHAPTER VII.

A FLASH WHICH ILLUMINATED.

A PARTY that has been together during a storm, becomes particularly animated and homelike after the danger is passed.

The company had gathered in the music-hall, the dome of which, now that everything was lighted up, appeared almost solemn. Four platforms had been placed halfway up the room, and the grand piano stood in the middle. A circle had been arranged with an elevation at one side, on which Bella was enthroned with the majestic lady of the justice of the peace on her right and the forester's wife on her left.

The young ladies were walking arm in arm through the room, and Prancken was leading them playfully, carrying in his hand a rose which Lina had taken from her garland for him.

Bella asked the Major how Herr Sonnenkamp's remodelling of the castle was progressing. Nodding, as he always did several times before speaking, as if to confirm in advance what he was going to say, the Major explained that they thought there must be a fountain somewhere in the courtyard. Clodwig requested him to be very careful in preserving any relics of the Middle Ages or the Roman time, that they might find, and promised to come in person and oversee the excavation.

The forester said jokingly:

"Herr Sonnenkamp (everybody called him 'Herr,' but in such a way as to show that the title did not rightly belong to him)—Herr Sonnenkamp will now, in all probability, add the name of the restored castle to his own."

At the mention of Herr Sonnenkamp's name, it seemed as though a dam had given way, and from all sides the stream of conversation poured in.

"Herr Sonnenkamp has a great deal of sense," said the school-director; "but Molière said spitefully, that a rich man's sense is in his purse."

The apothecary added:

"Herr Sonnenkamp puts on the appearance of a hardened sinner, in hopes that he will not be believed; but he is believed."

Erich heard the names, Herr Sonnenkamp, Frau Ceres, Manna, Roland, Miss Perini—it was like the wrangling twitter of birds. It was not without a spiteful glance that the justice's wife said to Prancken:

"Men like Herr Major and Herr von Prancken may like to associate with such obscure foreigners; but women must be more reserved."

She gave them to understand that "old families ought to

wait a long time before they become familiar with such new-comers."

Bella spoke quite sarcastically of the long nails of Frau Ceres, but became silent as Clodwig said sharply:

"Among the Indians long nails take the place of long pedigrees, and are, probably, quite as good."

Everybody was astonished to hear Clodwig speak so slightingly of nobility. He seemed provoked at the abuse cast upon the Sonnenkamp family; for there was nothing mean in him, and everything little and hateful offended him like a disgusting odor. He turned to Erich and said:

"Herr Sonnenkamp of whom they are speaking is the owner of many millions. To acquire such wealth is strength: I would even say, that to acquire wealth is bravery; to take care of wealth when gained, is wisdom; and to spend it well, is both an art and a virtue."

He paused; but as no one spoke, he continued:

"I find that wealth has a certain title to honor. Wealth is an evidence of ability and industry; that is, wealth acquired by one's own exertions; and it seems to me that to be a man of such enormous wealth is a more difficult task than to be a prince. There accumulates in the man a strength which easily gives the character a certain arrogance. Such a man lives in an atmosphere of conscious power, and almost ceases to be a common personality; the whole world appears to him from the standpoint of prime-cost and price-current. Have you ever met such a man?"

Before Erich could answer, Prancken broke in, in a smiling tone:

"Captain Dournay wishes to become young Sonnenkamp's tutor."

All eyes were turned upon Erich. They looked at him as though he had been suddenly transformed and was dressed like a beggar. The men nodded to each other and shrugged their shoulders: a man who had entered private service, and such a service, immediately lost all dignity. The women looked at him compassionately.

Erich saw nothing of all this; he was looking at the floor. He could not think what Prancken meant by giving this unnecessary intelligence; he felt obliged to say something, but found nothing to say, and so remained quiet.

A painful silence followed Prancken's interruption. Clodwig placed his hand on his lips, which had become pale.

"Such a position," said he at last, "would do you honor, and be both honorable and fortunate for Herr Sonnenkamp."

Erich felt as though a broad hand had been laid on his shoulder, and as he looked around, he saw the smiling face of the Major, who, pointing several times at his heart with his left hand, broke in:

"The Count has said what I wished to say, but it is better that he has said it; and he has said it better and more finely than I could. Carry out your intention, comrade!"

Prancken now joined in, and remarked, in quite a friendly way, that it was he who had suggested and recommended Erich.

Lina had opened a window, and cried out joyfully, "The storm is over!"

A fresh, fragrant air entered the room, and relaxed the tension of their minds. Everybody breathed freely again. It was sprinkling yet, but already the nightingales were singing in the shrubbery. And now the head-forester's wife must sing. She struggled against it, but yielded when Bella, who was almost never heard, promised to accompany her.

She sang several songs, with such a fresh, youthful voice—so clearly and simply, that she rejoiced the hearts of all who heard her. Then Lina must sing. She protested that she couldn't sing to-day; but her mother looked crossly at her. Lina placed herself at the piano, sang a few notes, but absolutely couldn't sing any more. Quite ingenuously, as if nothing had happened, she said:

"There, I've proved that I can't sing to-day!"

Her mother bit her lips, and sniffed till her nostrils trembled, over the stubborn girl, who in the mean time acted as if nothing in the world had happened.

Then the forester's wife sang a song, and immediately Lina joined her, and said that she could sing in a duet, but not alone. In fact, she had a fresh soprano voice and sang purely, but with a nervous anxiety to please.

Without intending any liberty, but as if he were an old acquaintance, she called on Erich to sing. The whole party joined in her request; but Erich declined decidedly, and looked up in surprise when Prancken agreed with him, adding:

"The Captain is right in not producing all his various talents at one time."

It was said in the most obliging tone, and yet its malice was unmistakable.

"I thank you for coming to my aid in such a friendly manner," answered Erich, looking around.

The sky had cleared up, but the storm was yet rolling among the Taunus mountains. The company dispersed, greatly obliged for the glorious day and pleasant evening. Even the always-silent Frau Kleiderlieb spoke now, arrayed in her new-fashioned cloak, which she had arranged very skilfully. As they were about to break up, in came the district doctor. He had been making a professional visit in the neighboring village, and had been detained by the storm; he had hardly time to salute Count Clodwig and Bella, and then went away with the rest.

Bella drew a long breath as the "cold-meat" party disappeared.

There was a great deal of talking in the various carriages; but in one there was crying, for Lina was forced to listen to a long sermon about how she "had no manners, and was nothing but a stupid country simpleton. Instead of being pleasant and making the most of herself, she always acted as if she had been tending geese the hour before." Lina had been accustomed to these lectures for a long time; but now they seemed to go to her heart.

She had been so happy to-day, and this made the lecture doubly hard. She cried quietly to herself.

The Justice of the Peace, who did not appear to act in that capacity in his own household, did not interfere in the women's, quarrel. Lighting a fresh cigar at the stump of the old one, he said:

"This chatty Captain Dournay seems to me a dangerous man."

"I find him quite amiable," was the rejoinder.

"Woman's logic! As if amiability excluded instead of including dangerousness. But didn't you see the very transparent intrigue?"

"No."

"Well, put this together. We met him in the convent, where the daughter of this immeasurably rich Herr Sonnenkamp lives, and he acts as if he was acquainted with nobody and knew nothing. Now he wants to become young Sonnenkamp's tutor. My! how it lightens!"

There came a brilliant flash of lightning, which not only illuminated the landscape, but even distinctly showed the habitations of men.

Villa Eden especially was lighted up as distinctly in all the features of the building as if they were only a few steps from it.

"See now," continued the justice, "how that big building is illuminated, and yet nobody can see what is being concocted there. Wonderful world! Baron Prancken brings this Herr Dournay as a friend to his brother-in-law's and father-in-law's, and yet these two men are sworn enemies!"

The justice's wife was vexed with him. When he was alone with her at home, he was so clever and sharp-sighted, but in society he was always monosyllabic and dry, and let others shine.

"Who is his father-in-law?" asked his wife, in order to say something.

"Herr Sonnenkamp, of course! He's likely to be so, at least. The incalculable wealth of Herr Sonnenkamp is guano for

Baron Prancken, and he is very much in need of it, and won't inquire very closely where this guano comes from."

Lina drew her veil over her face and closed her eyes. The justice now determined yet more fully that neither he nor his wife should have anything to do with such affairs.

"The Captain-doctor is a dangerous man—dangerous in all respects!"

So he concluded, and spoke no more till they arrived at home.

CHAPTER VIII.

CONFESSIONS OF TWO SORTS.

OTTO von Prancken and his sister walked up and down in the garden. Otto was telling her that he had recommended Erich to Herr Sonnenkamp, but that he regretted it already.

Bella, who was always in bad humor after having entertained the common people at one of her "cold-meat" receptions, now vented her temper on her brother for having introduced to her, as an equal and a guest, a man who was even then, or was intending to become a servant; and that, too, at this Herr Sonnenkamp's house. She told Otto that he must be extremely fond of overcoming difficulties, if he would introduce such a captivating man as this Doctor—(she spoke the word "doctor" as though she considered it beneath the word "captain")—at that house. It was easily to be seen that the daughter of the house would fall in love with her brother's tutor.

"This Herr Dournay," she concluded, "is a very attractive person, not simply because he is unusually handsome, but because that simple frankness and honesty of his are very more charming. Whether genuine or not, they will have their effect, and especially on a girl of seventeen, who has been brought up in a convent."

Otto answered good-humoredly, that he had given his sister credit for less commonplace imagination; besides, Erich was a well-known woman-hater, who loved nothing feminine except the idea. He added, that he intended to call on Herr Sonnenkamp the next morning, before Erich could do so, and tell him that he had, much to his regret, been obliged to give the recommendation. Then he would ask him to refuse the candidate courteously, for Erich would be very likely to fill the young man's head with liberal ideas. One might even go further, and tell Herr Sonnenkamp that to admit Erich would be displeasing to the Court, which remark would settle the whole question. Prancken had very good reason to know that a recognition in Court circles was Herr Sonnenkamp's highest aspiration.

But Bella opposed this plan. She wished to stimulate her brother. To be directly opposed to such an antagonist as Erich, and to conquer him, would give her brother new energy. It would, besides, probably be well to have a man bound to themselves by gratitude, to represent the laity in opposition to Miss Perini, who was almost incomprehensibly religious. Yet more: there would undoubtedly be a secret and a continual war between Miss Perini and this most uncompromising Dournay; and so, in any event, the power of deciding and acting as umpires would rest in her and her brother's hands.

Bella forgot all her ill-will toward the "cold-meat" people as the whole web of intrigue rose before her, which would entertain her as well as lead to the accomplishment of her designs. She was Miss Perini's confidante, although she did not entirely trust her. Otto should remain Erich's friend, and thus they would have the whole house of Sonnenkamp in their hands, as it could not be doubted that Erich would soon obtain great influence.

Otto struggled against the *rôle* assigned him, but it was not changed.

When a cat is sitting patiently and quietly before a mouse-hole, it is difficult to get her away, for she knows the mouse will come out and she will nab it, which will be fine sport. Bella had an easy device for making her brother do as she wished; she had only to represent to him how irresistible he was, and that he must recover that self-reliance that had often done him such good service. Otto was satisfied with the position of affairs; not quite at rest, however, but he told himself that he would soon be so. And besides, this Dournay was poor and must require aid; on that very day he had borne the sudden allusion to his calling with good grace, and had conducted himself well.

While the brother and sister were walking in the garden, Erich was sitting with Count Clodwig in his study, which was lighted by a double lamp. They sat opposite to each other, in easy-chairs, by the long writing-table.

"I am sorry," began Clodwig, "that the Doctor came so late. He is rough, but genuine. I think you would like each other."

Erich was silent, and the Count continued: "I do not see why my brother-in-law mentioned your intended occupation so abruptly to the company. It will be much spoken about, and so the charm of your undertaking will be to a certain extent destroyed."

Erich answered earnestly, that it was well for us to let our actions be criticised.

Again Clodwig looked at him earnestly. He seemed surprised at the cool way in which this man had prepared himself for whatever might occur; and placing his hand on a little portfolio lying near him, as if he had registered something new, he continued:

"While I have been with you to-day, or rather *by* being with you, I have had a new and agreeable experience. Men generally consider private service a degradation, without considering that it does not make so much difference *whom* one serves, as in what spirit he serves. 'Ich dien' was the device of my mother's family."

The old gentleman paused. Erich could not tell whether he had concluded or was waiting for a reply. Clodwig, however, soon proceeded:

"It is considered very honorable for an army officer or a civil officer to take charge of a prince; is it any less honorable to teach thirty peasant-children? And now I wish to ask a favor of you."

"I have no dearer wish than to gratify you."

"Will you tell me, as succinctly as possible, how you became so—I mean how you became what you are?"

Most willingly; and I will do myself the honor of being entirely unreserved with you. I will speak to you as to myself."

Clodwig struck a bell that lay on the table, and a servant entered.

"Robert, where are the Doctor's apartments?"

"The brown room directly over the Count's sleeping-room."

"Give the Captain the upper bow-windowed chamber."

"Pardon me, Count, but Prince Leonhard's things are there."

"That's nothing. And now, Evis, I do not wish to be interrupted till I ring."

The servant left the room. Clodwig settled himself in his chair, and laid a red plush rug over his knee; then he continued:

"You must not suppose that I am asleep, if I shut my eyes."

There was something touchingly condescending, but far removed from all superciliousness, in the kindly tone in which Clodwig bade Erich to speak frankly. Erich began:

CHAPTER IX.

A SEEKER.

I AM twenty-eight years old, and when I look back over my life, I find that it has been a seeking. A special vocation leaves so many of our powers unused; and yet the pain of selection must end, and one finds at last that the whole man can live and work in any calling.

"I am the offspring of a perfect and happy marriage: you know what that means. From my third year I was educated in company with Prince Leonhard. There was always a natural antagonism between us, which I knew from the first would afterward result in open quarrel. Even at that early age, I saw that acting in accordance with motives which I did not feel, and which were totally at variance with the nature of familiar intercourse, though it had made me externally pliable, yet internally had made me restless and irritable. Perhaps there is nothing more at variance with the nature of childhood than incessant reverence and obedience.

"I entered the Cadet Institute, and there received marked favor because I had been the Prince's companion. I was now under the special instruction of my father, and remained at the school two years with your brother-in-law. I was not noted for my scholarship.

"One of the happiest days of my life was that on which I assumed my epaulets; and if the day on which I laid aside my uniform was not less happy, yet it was not free from a certain drawback. To this day I can't pass a battery without emotion.

"I'm telling my story forward and backward, and I must beg you to pardon the difficulty I have in collecting myself, for I have been through so much to-day. But I'll speak as closely to the point as I can.

"Soon after I was made a lieutenant, my parents moved to the University city, and I was left alone. For two years I enjoyed myself and was happy, like all around me. I remember the hour, a lovely autumn noon,—I see the tree, and hear the birds sing on its branches, at which I suddenly reined in my horse; and something in me asked: 'What dost thou in the world? Thou and thy companions are learning to murder thy fellow-men."

"Pardon me the question," said Clodwig quietly, "but did the military-school never strike you as being the place where men are trained for the business of your profession?"

Erich was somewhat abashed, but confessed that it had not. Then collecting himself, he continued:

"I tried to banish the thought, but it would not leave me. I was at war with my profession. I cannot express how useless to the world I seemed: all was stale, flat, and unprofitable. There were days on which I was ashamed of my uniform. To think that I, a strong, healthy man, should live such a vacant life and be so finely dressed, and that my horse should be eating the poor man's fodder!"

"That was a morbid exaggeration," said Clodwig.

"Certainly: I know that now, but in the first outburst of feeling it was different. At the breaking out of the Crimean war, I asked leave of absence, that I might learn real war. Prince Leonhard, who was my commander, unexpectedly asked me one day as we were exercising, which army I would like to join? 'You would certainly rather go with the fantastic Frenchmen than the solid English.' My tongue was paralyzed, and I saw it all. I was crushed, annihilated. From that day I hated my profession and longed to abandon it. Shall I recount all the petty irritations I suffered? I deserved them all, for my whole existence was a contradiction and a lie. Even my uniform was given me. I was not I, was not even a good soldier, for I was plunged in metaphysical thoughts, and wished to solve the riddle of existence. I am naturally sociable and communicative, and yet to lead the life of my comrades was impossible to me.

"For two years I endured it, and then asked for my discharge. I left with the rank of captain,—given me, I believe, out of respect for my parents. Now I was free! I've already told you how loth I was to leave that life.

"It was the pain of abandoning it that had made me weak, but now all that would change.

"I was free. Wonderful to ask the wide world: 'World, what shall I do for thee? What dost thou require? There lie around me a thousand activities . . . What shall I select?' I was ready for anything. I had a beautiful voice, and many believed that I might become an accomplished artist. I immediately received applications. But such occupations were distasteful. I longed to immolate myself for my fellow-men. Had I believed in the Church, I would have become a Brother of Charity."

Clodwig opened his eyes and looked at the earnest face of Erich. A short pause followed. Clodwig nodded to Erich, folded his arms over his breast, nodded again, and closed his eyes. Erich continued:

"When I first walked the streets, dressed in citizen's clothes, I seemed to be walking naked before all eyes, as often happens to us in a troubled dream. When one feels in such a lost condition he's very apt to become superstitious. The first person who met and seemed to recognize me, was my old captain, who had entered the civil service and become overseer of the male House of Correction. He had read of my resignation, and remembering an old taste of mine, asked if I intended to be a poet now; to which I answered, that I did not. He told me that he was in search of an assistant, and I instantly made up my mind to accept the situation, as I wished to devote my life to the instruction and elevation of my fellow-creatures. I immediately informed my parents of my new occupation, and my father answered that he fully understood my position, but clearly foresaw that my love of the beautiful would soon render such a course of life impossible for me; and he was right. I endeavored to subdue my love for the amenities of life, but did not succeed; or rather did not understand how to look from that liberal standpoint which regards all the appearances of life simply as phenomena of nature, and deals with them as such. In my uniform, the prisoners looked up to me with more respect than when I appeared in citizen's dress; and the knowledge of this haunted me. My life among the criminals, who were either hardened brutes or arrant hypocrites, was a peculiarly agonizing hell for me.

"I was extremely miserable, for I could not forget the world. I was impelled to follow every one into the inmost recesses of his mind, and was pursued by a restless desire to know what men thought and said of my actions. I seemed to see in their eyes that they held me for—excuse the expression, it's terse—an idealistic vagabond. That was a character which I neither was nor would be; and above all, my enemies and detractors should not have the satisfaction of knowing that my life was wasted in carelessness and vacillation.

"Ah, how I was troubled by this thought! for who has the time, desire, or impulse, to follow the life of one with whom he is no longer associated. Men bury the dead and then come back to their every-day life; and so, too, they bury the living. I don't trouble myself any more about it; it must be so.

"It became evident to me that I had not yet found my true vocation. I lived too much in myself; I classified everything around me and sought its reason and origin. I was as yet unwilling to see that the lives and vocations of men are not so logically constructed as I thought. I was too enthusiastic then; and above all, I was impelled by a steadfast longing for the beautiful.

"I thought of going to the New World; but what should I do there? Was I in all respects qualified—had I the ability to transform one little spot of the primeval forest into a fertile field? I had, to be sure, a special inducement to go to America. My father's only brother had gone there, and we didn't know whether he was alive or dead. He had been a jeweller, and in love with my mother's sister, but his offers of marriage having been refused by her, he had left Europe and gone to the New World. He had severed every tie which united him to home and family so thoroughly, that when a friend of my father had visited him in New York, and had begun to speak to him about us, my uncle had abruptly ordered him out of the house; he wished to hear no more of us, nor of Europe. I imagined that I would be able to change my uncle's feelings in this respect; and you know that when one is in desperate circumstances, he is ready to look for such means of escape as offer a prospect of adventure.

"My good father came to my assistance. I now saw clearly that what he had always considered my true vocation, and against which I had struggled only when dazzled by the thoughts of being a soldier, was the one for which I was fitted. The thirst for solitude awakened in me; I felt that I must seek some spot of earth where no sound could break the silence of my inner life—where I could bathe myself in solitude. This solitude, which is nevertheless locked up in every life, Philosophy alone afforded me. My father assisted me, explaining that my past life had not been lost, but had peculiarly fitted me for that which I proposed to lead. He came to me and brought a gift which had lain with me in my cradle; for the authorities of the University, at which my father had been an instructor before he undertook the education of the Prince, had given me soon after my birth a certificate of membership of the University, as it is the custom to give a new-born Prince a military office."

Clodwig laughed heartily, rubbed his eyes, and leaning forward, placed both hands on his knees, and then smiling kindly, begged Erich to proceed.

"I've not much more to tell. I was very early in life accustomed—or rather my father accustomed me to live only for what is universal, and to withdraw myself as much as possible from the merely personal. I entered earnestly on the study of the philosophy of the ancient world; and that impulse toward the beautiful which had made me love the vocation of the poet, now found satisfaction in the study of the classical world. 'Every one may boast of his own industry,' says the poet. I worked hard, and in my father's house I experienced the pleasures of childhood, and, as a young man, enjoyed intellectual growth. My father hoped that that success which had been denied to him would be granted to me, and gave me the heritage of those ideas which he could neither lay down in philosophy nor deliver from the professor's chair. If there was ever a happy home, where calmness reigned as in a temple, it was that of my parents.

"My younger brother died. In a few weeks, it will be a year since we buried him; and my father became sick at soul, for with all his stoical strength he was unable to bear this blow. It is now two months since he too died. I dismissed the sorrow occasioned by his death as well as I was able, and finished my studies. A few days ago I received my Doctor's degree. My mother and I have many plans, but nothing is settled. I took a trip to the Rhine, at my mother's advice, for I had overworked myself and needed recreation. I met your brother-in-law, and considered it my duty to accept the situation which he proposed to me. I am ready to enter private service. I understand what I shall teach, and believe myself fitted for the work. There was a time when I thought that I could only find peace in working for universal ends, but now I would be rejoiced to educate one single child of man; and to aid such a one as this, who by means of his great wealth will represent so much of life—to aid him in becoming a nobly-acting man, and one fully prepared for his great and arduous work.

"I have finished. I desire no one to think better of me than I deserve, but I wish to be considered what I believe myself to be. I am neither over modest nor conceited; I can afford to remain in profound ignorance of what others think of me, as I only represent myself to be such as I honestly believe I am. I intend to be a teacher. He who would lead a life of thought and cannot work as an artist, must be a teacher. The teacher is, so to speak, the workman of the soul, and like every workman, is skilful in proportion to his knowledge of an ability to use art. The best way in which man can serve man is by giving him a thought, and that which I give my scholar is thereby doubly mine. Pardon me for speaking like an instructor to you. I have placed, as well as I could, my whole existence in your hands: where there are things which you do not understand, I'll be glad to have you question me."

"Nothing further is necessary," said Clodwig, rising and laying beside him the rug which had covered his knees. "Yet one more question. Did you ever desire to marry, or has that wish never occurred to you?"

"No, I shall not marry. I have heard so many men say: 'Oh, Ideals! I had ideals too, but I am now living in the family, and for the family.' I will not sacrifice everything higher for the boon of a happy life. I know that I don't agree with the world. I have proposed for myself a difficult life-work, and can best accomplish it alone."

Clodwig stepped hastily toward Erich, and said:

"I again offer you my hand; as long as this hand belongs to a living man, it will not be withdrawn from you. I had something else to tell you, but cannot; and it is, moreover, no longer necessary, so I restrain myself. Enough! go calmly and steadily toward your goal, and where I can aid you, you have a right to ask my aid. Listen to me! You have a claim upon me in any emergency, in any condition in life. You cannot measure what you have given, and yet give me. Good-night, dear young friend."

The Count withdrew hastily, as if to escape giving vent to his emotion. Erich stood still for a while, looking at the empty chair, as if it had all been a dream.

The servant entered and conducted him respectfully to his chamber.

CHAPTER X.

THE GOOD GUEST.

WHEN one has laid out for himself his whole course of life, it seems to him so futile, so empty! What does it all amount to? How little and unsatisfactory he appears to himself!

But this was not the case with Erich. Below in the valley he heard the silver bell strike the hour of midnight in the tower where long ago a noble lady had placed it to lead travellers, lost in the lonely forest, back to the habitations of men. Erich listened to it, and almost seemed to see the confessional in the church, and believers humbling themselves there and coming forth to the world renewed and strengthened by a benediction. He had confessed to a man in whom dwelt the consecration of the pure spirit, and he felt, not impoverished, but rather, elevated and strengthened, and knew himself to be more reconciled to every tie which bound him to humanity.

He opened the window that he might breathe the refreshing air of night. A fine mist arose in the valley, and the village bells were striking the midnight hour, and lightly and modestly struck the clock of Wolfsgarten. Erich pondered the life and power of nature—how silently it steals up and down the tree, stirring in the branches and refreshing every bud! He heard a train of cars rumbling in the distance; the nightingales sang loudly and then suddenly became silent, as if overpowered by sleep.

Like troops of shadowy forms, all life, his own and that of others, thronged around him. Why had he lived till now without once crossing the threshold of the house which would perhaps have such an influence on his future life? He had redeemed his past life, and had a home of which yesterday he had not dreamed. Oh, how large, how rich is the world, in which dwell men impatiently longing to help us!

Erich felt all the fulness of the boundless life of nature and the human soul, and revelled in the Universal. His life was no longer his—it was taken from him—he was no longer an individual, but lived for and in all!

And now the moon arose over the opposite mountains and a shudder rustled through the forest trees. The nightingale sang again, and the moonlight came to him reflected from a distant dome—the dome of the Villa Eden.

It was only after a severe struggle that Erich yielded to weariness and closed the window. A black trunk bearing the arms of Prince Leonhard attracted his attention. Erich smiled;—had not Clodwig shown before the family and the servants that he honored his guest not less than the Prince who had been there a few days before?

Then he gazed at a bust of Medusa. The great face attracted him, it was so beautiful in its fierceness. On the head, with its wildly-streaming hair, were two outstretched wings. The large staring eyes were overhung by the thunderclouds of her knitted brows; on the distorted lips lay scornful, malignant words, and under the chin were coiled two snakes. The whole head repelled but fascinated him.

Opposite to the Medusa was the wonderful bust of Victory by

Rauch, the face recalling that of Queen Louise. The noble head, bound with a wreath of oak leaves, was bowed as if buried in deep thought. Wonderful that two such busts should face each other! But Erich had no time to ponder, for sleep was overpowering him, and when after a few hours he awoke, the day had hardly dawned.

There are hours and days when we feel a blissful confidence in all things, as though we had found the key that should open all hearts, and held the magic wand which reveals all hidden springs and brings us closer to every living being, as though we had found a comrade and a brother. The world is brightened, and the soul bathes in sensations of purest pleasure, and there seems to be nothing but existence, life, breathing, and loving.

Erich stood at the window and looked out over the stream toward the mountains, and saw castles, cities, and towns on the shore and heights. This is thy home; thou livest in a beautiful world!

He was soon in the open air, walking through the park and forest, not as if he himself walked, but as if borne on by an invisible power. To the early leaves of the forest trees, to grass and flower, drops of last night's storm were yet clinging. Not the softest wind was stirring, and yet the trees were shaking off the drops like rain; the sunlight dawned on bough and leaf, stirring them with occult power. Blackbirds sang in the bushes, drowning with their jubilant notes all songs but theirs.

Erich paused at an open spot, and stood beneath its leafy roof watching the flight of a hawk, which, sailing over mountain and river, alighted in the woods.

Why should he now think of Herr Sonnenkamp?

Was it the envy and fearfulness of little birds, slandering the large bird? and has he not a right to live according to his strength?

Then Erich thought of the boy, as if he would visit him in his dreams and say, "I come to thee."

He tried to find the glass dome, but could not, and turned toward the table-land where the house stood, to look again at the valleys, heights, and mountains.

He stood in a large field, and for the first time watched the planting of a vineyard. The laborers held in their hands intruments resembling large augers, which they sank in the spongy soil to prepare it for the slips of the vine, which they arranged in regular order. He spoke to the men, and they answered kindly, knowing from his voice that he greeted every stranger as a brother. He asked how long it would be before they could make the first wine; and when an old man explained it all to him, he felt that he had experienced a new delight.

This conversation brought him back from all his transcendental thoughts, from hovering in his endless speculation, and placed him again on the earth. He went away thankful, feeling that he must hereafter withdraw himself from the stream of his far-reaching thoughts, and plant his feet on the solid ground of a quiet, effective life.

He met laborers going to a quarry which, as they told him, belonged to the Count, who had leased it all, preferring not to manage his own estate. The overseer greeted him pleasantly, and showed him a cement factory near by, where he saw a stone for flooring, used in the time of the renaissance. The Count had advised the proprietor to copy it, and the imitation had found a ready sale.

Invigorated by the breath of nature and his communion with working life, Erich returned to the castle. A servant informed him that the Count was expecting him. Clodwig was already in full but quiet dress, and gave his hand to his guest, saying:

"I have yet many things to ask you, but only one now. Did your father die despairing of—or what shall I say? supported by a steady and well-grounded hope for the future progress of the world?"

With the full strength of his memory, yet more quickened by his morning impressions, Erich told the Count how his father, on the night before he died, had said that he considered his son fortunate in having been born into the new age, when the world is not wholly busied in abolishing violence and wrong.

"My son," said he, "my heart trembles with joy when I look into the centuries and see arising a beauty, a freedom, and a watchfulness over the rights of our fellow-beings, which we now see only in the germ. Look at this one thing, my son: the ancients desired that the state should educate the children, and now it does so in a manner of which Solon and Socrates never dreamed. You will live to see the time when men will hardly believe that there ever were slaves, serfs, bondmen, sects, and all the rubbish of a self-deceiving world."

Erich added how happy it made him to know that his father had passed away so peacefully, and that he, his son, might yet live to see the realization of his hopes drawing near. He spoke so ardently that the Count laid his hand on his shoulder and said:

"We will not go further into the subject this morning."

Nevertheless he expressed his joy that he was so hopeful for the future: it had always troubled him to think that he might have lost his confidence in the new age.

"We have finished our morning devotions, now let us take breakfast," said he, rising briskly. "Yet one more question: Did your father ever explain to you what preceded his sudden quarrel—you know what I mean—with the Court?"

"Certainly; my father explained it to me fully."

"And did he not request you to conceal it from others?"

'Certainly: from others, but not from you."

"Did he mention my name?"

"No; but he told me expressly to tell it to those whom I reverence with all my soul, and so I tell it to you."

"Speak a little more softly," said the Count, and Erich continued:

"In that last audience, which was kept secret, my father was to receive from the Prince a patent of nobility, in order to become eligible to a position at Court. He said to the Prince: 'Your Highness, you would destroy the happiness of my life-work—of the years during which I have devoted my best energies to the instruction of my Prince, if you could for a moment believe that I receive this for myself, or, especially, if you thought that I consider it of any meaning in the times in which we live.' 'I do not trifle with such things,' answered the Prince. 'Nor do I!' returned my father. Years after this occurred, as he told me of it, his lip quivered, and he said that that moment when he stood in silence facing his pupil was the bitterest of his life."

A momentary silence followed, and then Clodwig said:

"I understand, I understand; come."

They entered the saloon of the ground-floor, the doors of which stood open, and Bella soon joined them. She thought that Erich looked sharply at her, and turned abruptly to a sideboard to prepare the coffee.

"My wife," said Clodwig, "has sent an invitation to Miss Perini to-day, and I have taken the opportunity to inform Herr Sonnenkamp that you, dear Dournay, will call upon him this evening—or, yet better, early to-morrow."

"I must excuse my brother to you, for he went to the horse-market at Mannheim early this morning with a young man who is known here as the Wine-cavalier. Shall I give you coffee or tea?"

"Coffee, if you please."

"That's brave; that makes us good friends," said Bella, brightly. "It's abominably polite for men to answer this question so: 'It's indifferent to me.' If it's indifferent to you, dear polite soul, then choose something definite, and don't leave the choice to me."

This broke the ice, and they sat down at the table.

Bella knew that Erich was examining her, and she knew that she looked better in morning-dress than when dressed for society. Her movements were classically graceful. Her figure was slender and well built. Her soft, dark-brown hair, now half in disorder, was held back by a delicate lace cap tied under her chin, which gave her an improvised, careless air, as though she had glanced at herself in the mirror casually. Her complexion was as fresh as though she had just bathed it in milk; and in fact she did wash it in milk every morning and every night. She had a keen yet refined expression; all was nobly formed, but her upper lip was tightly drawn, and a sarcastic cavalier at Court had called it the lip of a poisoner. Bella's only trouble was that she had a man's voice.

She made good use of her playfulness and roguery during the conversation at the breakfast-table. She was surprised at Erich's appearance, when she came to examine it closely, for she had only seen him at twilight and when the candles were lighted, the day before. He was plainly one who must be seen by daylight. The happy emotions of his soul shone brightly on his face, and he looked at Bella as if he wished to say: "I have become almost the son of your husband; let us, too, love each other."

Bella was unusually pleasant: perhaps from the feeling that she had been practising a little deceit already to-day. A note written in Italian to Miss Perini, had contained the information, no less carefully worded than comprehensive, that the new-comer was to be examined closely.

When Clodwig told the servant that Erich would come that evening or the next day, she felt quieted and justified in the deception which she had practised, for Clodwig had never before detained a guest so obstinately; and no one else could boast of having so withdrawn him from his self-absorbed habits of life.

Clodwig and Bella had promised each other to live only for themselves, and they had hitherto faithfully kept that promise. "I am a weary soul," Clodwig had said to Bella, when he asked her for her hand, and Bella had answered that she would give the weary one rest. From that time Bella had severed every tie which bound her to the outer world, for she knew that friendly visits can only be for days or hours, and then only leave loneliness more lonely.

Bella was very amiable toward everybody, provided everybody would do her will and live as she wished him to. But she really loved no one—she had no need of others, and they must leave her at peace. She disliked the numerous connections which Clodwig had previously had with men and women, and Clodwig yielded to the wishes of his wife, who lived only for him, and narrowed the circle of his extensive correspondence and personal intercourse with others to the lowest possible limit. It was only with the society of their immediate neighborhood that they had any connection. We became acquainted yesterday with the society of the citizens, or as it was called up here, the "cold-meat" society; but twice a year the noble families scattered through the neighborhood were invited. Should this runaway Captain destroy all this?

In the triumph of the belief that she had banished him, Bella became yet more talkative. Erich could not help praising laughingly, that whimsical enthusiasm about the wine, that runs all through the Rhine-land, and attacks everybody who enters the circle of the inhabitants. At last he brought the conversation back to Sonnenkamp, remarking that the way in which his name was mentioned yesterday seemed puzzling to him.

Bella laughingly explained how enchanted she was to find that, instead of being the confirmed Philister she had thought him, Sonnenkamp was a conqueror, a mighty hero, and that in this stock-jobbing world there was nothing more noble to conquer than money.

An affinity seemed to exist between the adventurous nature of Sonnenkamp and that of Bella.

"I have often noticed," said Clodwig gravely, "that so long as a man is acquiring wealth, his success is looked upon with satisfaction by the world; but when he has reached his goal, then that same world, which before expressed itself as so well satisfied, deserts and criticises him. Do you understand horticulture?"

"No."

"Herr Sonnenkamp is a very notable gardener. Is it not remarkable that since we have subdued our passion for the French style of laying out our parks in imitation of nature, we should fly for refuge to fruit-raising, and there find protection in our common necessities. The English excel all the world in raising swine, producing some that almost look like four-footed flitches of bacon. The French, however, devote themselves to fruit, and draw fabulous profits from the cultivation of it. Yes," he concluded, smiling, "Herr Sonnenkamp is not only great at educating trees, but equally great at marring them. To-day I can speak more plainly to you; I have never liked Herr Sonnenkamp, and never will. With all his politeness and desire to please, a certain brutality is evidently inwrought in his whole nature."

"Yes," added Bella, "you would occupy a difficult position, especially as regards Roland."

"As regards Roland?" asked Erich.

"Yes; that is the name of the boy who would like to know much, but learn nothing."

The expression was so appropriate that Bella looked around, as if much pleased with herself. The parrot, perched in his cage on the veranda, cried out shrilly, as if to dispute her.

"See," said Bella, rising, "there's my tyrant; a pupil who tyrannizes over his mistress fearfully."

She took the parrot from his cage and placed it on her shoulder. It was enough to make one jealous to see the way in which she kissed and fondled it, and her motions were all beautiful, particularly the curving of her head and neck.

CHAPTER XI.

MEDUSA AND VICTORIA.

CLODWIG remained with his eyes cast down for a long time after Bella had left the room. He nodded to Erich as if to welcome him anew. Bella soon returned with the parrot on her hand, caressing it. She walked up and down the room for a long time, while Erich was relating how he had that morning left the immediate neighborhood of the Rhine, and gone farther inland, where he had conversed with several of the people.

Clodwig enlarged somewhat on his favorite theory, that traces of the early Roman colonists could still be seen in the physiognomy and character of the inhabitants. Bella seemed unwilling to be forced to listen to what she had so often heard, and said, with some appearance of temper:

"Whenever a person leaves the Rhine he has a feeling—at least it is so with me—as though some one, perhaps Father Rhine himself, were looking after him and calling: "Look back again!"

"We men have not always the desire to be looked at," answered Clodwig, as he called Erich's attention to a vase which the Justice of the Peace had brought with him the day before, and which was now standing on the sideboard of the breakfast-room. Erich was glad to examine it; and then the Count conducted him to an adjoining apartment, which was filled with all sorts of unearthed relics of ancient times. Erich, who had only just left the study of antiquity, seemed so well acquainted with these striking objects, that Bella could not help expressing her surprise.

"You are a good teacher; it must be a pleasure to be instructed by you."

Erich thanked her, and Bella amiably continued:

"There are many men who impart knowledge in order to appear brilliant, and others who do so against their will; but you, Doctor, do it in such a friendly way, that you seem like a benevolent person who is rejoiced to be able to bestow a gift which may benefit the receiver; and you do it, not only in such a way as to produce the impression that you understand the thing, but that the person to whom you are talking understands it too."

Clodwig looked up in surprise, for that was the same expression that he had used yesterday when recalling the fact, that it was only by means of the unselfish assistance which Professor Dournay had given him, that *his* little scientific work had seen the light.

After Bella had said this, she left the room, and the two men went together to Erich's chamber, where Erich showed him the thesis which he had written preparatory to obtaining his degree. It struck him now for the first time how singularly appropriate his subject had been, for he had chosen the apocryphal tract of Plato, "Concerning Wealth," and now he was about to undertake the instruction of a boy born in the midst of riches. The coincidence struck the Count as well as himself.

Clodwig desired Erich to translate the Latin into German for him, and found the essay replete with interest. The Count said, as he arose from his chair, that it must have made a peculiar impression on Erich, to see the Medusa placed directly opposite to the Victoria, but he confessed to a heresy which, although condemned by philosophy, was attractive to him personally. The Medusa appeared to him the representation of all-consuming passion, in which the transgressor is forced to see an image of himself, and it was well worthy of attention that the ancients had represented the chaos of the soul under the form of a woman, and that passion which overleaps all bounds appears yet more repulsive when brought in direct contrast with the female nature. On the other hand, Victoria von trast with the female nature. On the other hand, Rauch's Victory seemed to him the embodiment of the soul of modern culture, unruffled by the emotions.

"The face bears a wonderful resemblance—" He did not conclude the sentence, but stammered into another, and continued: "This is not that Goddess of Victory who haughtily wears her garland on her brow: it is the image of that Victory whose soul is torn by the feeling that she *must* conquer all who oppose her. Nay, more ; this Victoria is the goddess who has gained that most sublime of all victories—victory over herself."

After Clodwig had thus explained himself, he said:

"Now I will leave you : I have already—to-day and yesterday, conversed too much with you."

Erich remained in his room, and while he was writing to his mother, Clodwig sat with Bella, and said to her:

"This young man is an ideal nature, and ought not to remain confined for hours by his calling: he should be as free as a bird on its branch, singing, flying, without any settled object or any thought of time; but he should never be intruded upon. It is a pleasure to meet so deep a nature."

"Isn't he a little too conscious of his own importance?" asked Bella, with an evil light in her eyes.

"Oh no. He does not wish to shine: and yet he is pure light. When I am with him I seem to stand in the Spring sunlight of the soul. He is a man whose thoughts are pure, and I am as much at home with him as within the deepest recesses of my own nature."

As Bella did not speak, the Count continued:

"This peculiarity I find very agreeable in him; when one is speaking he never interrupts either by word or movement, but listens to the end. This, in a man of so much vivacity, and one whose mind is so well stored as his, is something more than mere politeness."

Bella was silent and worked industriously at her embroidery. At last she said, looking up pleasantly:

"Your pleasure is mine."

'And I would preserve that pleasure," answered Clodwig.

"He's a handsome man," Bella added.

"Now for the first time, when you recall it, do I remember how handsome he is. He does not parade his beauty, and I believe that that is the only true beauty which does not impress us while it is present, but the elements of which come back to us, new and beautiful, after the actual object has departed. Most handsome men seem to be continually looking in a glass seen only by themselves. Why should I relinquish this man to another, and that other, Herr Sonnenkamp? I am in a position to give him a home for years. Why should I not do so?"

"Why not?" said Bella, laying aside her embroidery. "I need not tell you that I have no pleasure that is not yours: don't forget this in your short happiness, your child-like trust in a new companion. I, too, feel the nobleness of his character, and that he both can and would give us exalted pleasure."

"Then why should we not keep him with us?"

"Because we wish to be alone! Clodwig, let us live alone! It is my wish that my brother should leave us soon. Any third party, even though nearest by ties of blood or spirit, will be an obstacle in our way, for when he is near I cannot live for you alone, nor you for me!"

While speaking, she had laid her hand on Clodwig's arm; now she took his hand and caressed it.

Clodwig went away, and Bella looked after him, shaking her head.

Bella appeared at the dinner-table beautifully dressed, with a single rose in her hair. The men seemed weary, but she was extremely animated. She told how happy she had always felt at the house of Erich's parents—a house in which no word not noble was uttered, for his mother lived an ideal life; she was a priestess on whose domestic altar an ideal flame was ever burning. Erich was happy, and he believed that his existence could know no higher pleasure.

At noon they went to look at the surrounding country. Bella was silent during the journey. They visited an ancient Roman camp, and Bella sat under a tree alone while the men examined the place.

When the lamps were lighted in the evening, Bella appeared like another being. She had dressed herself three times that day, and was now extremely lively.

Bella had not for an hour during her life been unsatisfied with herself. She easily excused herself for her actions, for she always said: "At the time when you did that, you were right in doing it." She wished now, above all things, not to appear to her husband's new favorite, as a quiet, unspeaking appendage to her husband. Erich should learn who she was. She was not only the wife of Clodwig, but also Bella von Prancken.

Clodwig had hardly expressed the wish that she would play, before she was ready. The hasty, nervous way in which she removed her bracelets, which Erich courteously took from her hand and laid on the marble table under the mirror; the manner in which she raised both hands like fluttering wings, and then brought them down upon the key-board like a swimmer in his element;—all this showed that she was determined to hold no secondary position. Never since she had been married had Bella played so before a third person; she had allowed Clodwig alone to know her wonderful skill at the piano, and now even he who knew every peculiarity of her playing, was surprised and charmed.

In a pause in the music, Erich appeared to have struck the right chord by saying that after such exquisite enjoyment found in intercourse with noble minds, and such glimpses of the large and untrammelled nature of the soul, there seems to be nothing left but the dying away of emotion in the limitless, shoreless ether of music. An empire of waking dreams, of boundless emotions arises within us which extends far beyond the word or the glance, which can nowhere be known in visible and audible nature, and has its foundation only in the deep and hidden recesses of the human soul.

"Mozart answered the question: What preceded in his mind the composition of his music? by saying: 'Nothing but music that *will* be expressed—the pure phantasy without defined feeling, without limited thought—nothing but a rhythmical tossing of the billows of music.' Let us again leave this world of sight and thought," continued Erich, "and through music enter that pure, that mysterious, yet all-surrounding kingdom of melody, which is chaos redeemed and working according to law."

Bella had seated herself in a large cushioned chair, and leaning back in it, appeared to be so absorbed in what he was saying, that Erich, who feared that he had outstepped the bounds of decorum by looking at her so intently, dropped his eyes.

To the surprise of both men, she abruptly arose and bade them good-night. She gave her hand to Clodwig, then to Erich, then again to Clodwig, and hastily left the room.

The Count remained but a few minutes longer with his guest, and then excused himself.

Erich went to his room like one intoxicated. How rich was the world! What a day that had been, from the morning in the dewy forest till now! Happiness is not the lie that men call it! Here are two mortals who are happy and at rest!

On the stairs he suddenly paused, and from the unconscious thought of Villa Eden, and the conscious thought of the blissful existence of Bella and the Count, arose the question: "Is not a life of beauty—the development of the soul by free intercourse with Nature, and satisfaction of the mind by means of the beautiful in science and art--possible only to wealth, to freedom from all care and want, and liberation from all labor and distracting needs?"

As he entered his room carrying the light, he stood horrified, as if he saw an apparition, before the Medusa, who looked at him with writhing lips and gnashing teeth.

What is this? How could that bust so suddenly acquire this resemblance? Did Clodwig know it? It is horrible!

Erich turned, and now, like devils' work, the Victoria looked like Bella, when she submissively and with quiet modesty bowed her head.

Had Clodwig any suspicion of this wonderful result of placing the busts opposite to each other, and had he not explained it all yesterday when speaking of his heresy?

Erich's pulse beat hard.

He extinguished the candle, and looked out into the dark night, trying to call up in memory the pleasures of the day.

CHAPTER XII.

MADAME ADVENTURESS.

EARLY in the morning Erich dressed himself in his captain's uniform, as Clodwig had particularly advised him on a former occasion. He had taken a horse, also at the instance of Clodwig; his trunks were to be sent after him.

Clodwig's troubled face became bright as he saw this handsome, stately man, who looked every inch a soldier, enter the drawing-room. While bidding him good-morning, Clodwig pointed to his arm and said:

"Take off the crape before you leave here."

Erich looked puzzled, and Clodwig said in explanation:

"Not being sentimental, you must confess that it is not exactly in good taste to enter a strange house for the first time with crape on your arm. You would seem to ask for a sympathy that you can lay no claim to. You'll have less trouble afterward if you tell yourself sharply at the very outset that you are entering service at the house of an immensely rich man who does not like to be excited. The more you keep your personal matters to yourself, the freer you will be."

Clodwig laughingly quoted a passage from Lucian's "Sale of Philosophical Souls," where the stoic who has been made a slave cries out: "They have sold me, but my soul is free!"

Erich good-humoredly removed the crape.

Bella had had herself excused for not appearing at breakfast; but had sent her farewell *au revoir* to Erich, and so the two men were alone. Clodwig handed Erich a letter for Herr Sonnenkamp, telling him expressly not to make an engagement until they had seen each other again. As he did so he muttered half-intelligibly:

"Perhaps I'll keep you all to myself."

Clodwig gave his young friend all sorts of good advice, like a mother who stuffs her son's pockets before he sets out on a journey.

"I am only slightly acquainted with the boy; in fact, all I know about him is that he is very handsome. Are you not of my opinion, that it is entirely wrong to give a young mind great principles on which to live before it has the fundamental materials of life or knows its currents?"

"Certainly," answered Erich. "It would be like building railroads in uncultivated or half-civilized countries before ordinary roads have been laid out to facilitate the exchange of agricultural or industrial products. The real cause of the sickness of men in modern times is that children are taught dogmatically the laws of the government of the world;—a luxurious fallacy, and unproductive because it neglects a prerequisite."

Clodwig nodded. "This was a man who might be allowed to go far out in the open sea: he always seemed to have a compass with him."

At last it was time to go. Clodwig said: "I will walk a little way with you."

Erich took his horse by the bridle, and as they went along side by side, Clodwig often looked at Erich with an affectionate troubled glance. He repeated that he considered it a high honor for the young American to be placed under the care of such an able man as he, and advised Erich to keep this steadily in his mind and avoid the slightest approach to obsequiousness in his intercourse with Herr Sonnenkamp. Herr Sonnenkamp allowed himself to be much talked about, either because he was too virtuous to care about it, or because there were facts in his life which he was glad to see covered up by this talk about trifles. It was, at all events, singular that he, though a German by birth, never had any relatives at his house. It was very evident from this that he, being of low extraction, was willing to help his relatives only on condition of their never coming to visit him. Major Krassler had once told him something to this effect.

"Now," said Clodwig, stopping, "do not say anything to Herr Sonnenkamp about your brief connection with the House of Correction. I do not wish to say anything too critical about him, but most people are apt to be shy of men engaged in that calling."

Erich thanked him. He saw this man's earnest desire to smooth his journey through life. They went a little farther together.

"Now," said Clodwig, "I will return; but let me give you one more warning."

"A warning?"

"Perhaps that is not the right word. I only wanted to tell you to be careful to put a high value on yourself in the world. He who in his life is seen to be occupied with something beyond common wants, common pleasures, and common honors, will appear an exalted being to men who cannot understand his predilections. The world cannot be just to such men; it must condemn them, because it sees its own pursuits condemned by them. If you remain true to yourself—and I believe you will—you will have a lifelong martyrdom to bear. Bear it in proud self-comprehension, and knowing that your new old friend understands and sympathizes with you."

The old man laid his hands on both of Erich's shoulders, kissed him, and turned hastily away. He did not once look back.

Erich mounted and rode away. When he reached the corner of the forest he turned and looked back. He saw Clodwig standing still.

Bella, who had been watching them from the balcony, which commanded a view of the whole road, now came to meet her husband. She was much moved when she looked in his face; she had never seen such emotion there. He seemed to have been weeping. Clodwig said hastily:

"You were right; it would be better for us to remain alone. Yet I love this modern age, it is so different from ours! No longer vacillating between those two poles, enthusiasm and despair, it has in it, if I may say so, a certain *intellectual* enthusiasm, and I believe it will accomplish more than we. I am glad that I am not too old to understand this youth. I admire and love the present age. The world knows to-day, as no other age has known, what it wishes and *will* have; this is true in all philosophy and all life."

Bella felt obliged to answer something, and said that it would be fortunate for young Sonnenkamp to have such a teacher.

"And it pains me to think that he shall enter that house."

"And yet you have just recommended him."

"Yes, that is what troubles me. Sooner or later, everything done in half truth, or with contradiction in the soul, revenges itself. I have brought myself nearer to Herr Sonnenkamp entirely against my wish. In that house I always feel as if I were in a family of horse-eaters. My God! It may be a prejudice of mine, and horse-flesh may be good to eat, but yet I'm troubled for the glorious young man."

Clodwig seemed unable to stop speaking of Erich, and as he recalled it all, he wondered how, in so short a time, he had come to know him so well, and pointing to an apple-tree in blossom, he cried out:

"Look at that blossoming tree; it is like this Dournay. He shakes himself, and covers us over and over with flowers, and yet remains so rich!"

Bella answered that it must be a difficult task for a man who was so highly thought and spoken of, to make his conduct always tally with such a high standard.

"When one is so fond of giving instruction," she asked quietly, "isn't he apt to be a little too self-appréciative, a little too vain?"

"Oh no! This young man does not wish to shine, but he is unwilling to lose a minute in frivolity. He lets his strength work, and it is quite natural that he should be pleased with the attention and sympathy of others. Unless he had this pleasure it would be impossible for him to love talking as he does. That is the faith which removes mountains of prejudice."

"Faith?" said Bella, smiling at her conceit before she uttered it; "it seems to me more like the permanent anointing of unbelief."

Clodwig explained with great earnestness that it was much rather a keen penetration into life. He spoke earnestly and long. Bella pretended to listen, but in reality hardly heard him: she smiled to herself as she thought of this old diplomat who was so inexplicably childlike—almost childish. She raised her head proudly as she dwelt upon her own steadfast virtue in so strenuously opposing her own husband, who wished to bring such a richly endowed man in contact with her.

In the mean time Erich was riding through the forest, filled with keen enjoyment of the good fortune that had come to him. He grasped his horse's bridle firmly. He was in that exalted state of mind when one feels assured that every undertaking will succeed, and all impediments be soon and easily removed. He wondered at his good fortune in meeting a man of such fine nature, and who was evidently so reticent with others, and in having so quickly and completely won him.

He had left his past life behind him: now a new one should begin.

He smiled as he thought: "So the heroes of antiquity must have felt who knew themselves to be under the protection of an Olympian god!"

He paused at a bend of the woods and took Clodwig's open letter from his pocket. He read:

"Neighborly greeting to Herr Sonnenkamp at Villa Eden. If I had had the good fortune to have a son, I would have regarded it as the fulfilment of my dearest wish to be able to give him this man as his instructor.

"CLODWIG, Count von Wolfsgarten.

"CASTLE WOLFSGARTEN, May 4th, 186–."

Erich put spurs to his horse, and rode merrily through the greenwood, while the birds sang in the trees.

As he rode through the village, he saw through the roses that clambered over the windows of the courthouse, a rosy-cheeked, brown-haired girl, who quickly drew back as he waved his hand to her from a distance. He wanted to look back and see if she was looking after him, but was afraid to.

It struck him now, for the first time in a long while, what a vain fellow he was. He had believed that the girl behind the flowers was looking for him; and there it was Lina watching for Prancken, and thinking it was his horse she heard!

Erich rode on through the valley along the bank of the river. He was so full of delight that now the old songs began to come back to his lips. He did not sing them aloud—only in his heart. All the fulness and infinite variety of thought, sight, and feeling stirred in his soul. As he saw the sun gleaming on the far-off dome of Villa Eden, it seemed suddenly like a flash of lightning.

"Why couldst thou not have such a free, beautiful life? Why must thou serve?"

And then the thought came to him: "What wouldst thou do in such a careless, selfish existence?"

This was the riddle—how to teach a rich boy? And—strange to say, such are the contradictions which coexist in the human mind—Erich, while he believed himself unable to solve this riddle, yet thought that he comprehended the way in which the ancients happened to embody the idea of the question and the enigma in the form of the Sphinx.

Again the question came to him: "How should a boy be educated who knows that such a villa and such wealth will be his own, and sees before him nothing to compel him to work?"

Erich's eyes had been cast down, but now he raised his head and smiled. Neither the teacher nor the pupil is simply a conception—an idea; ye are living, self-formed men. Such a question can have no general solution, and all riddles are like dreary out-door storms. Regarded from the confined air of a room they seem unbearable; but *there*, they are cool and refreshing.

In this spirit, he would accept the question as an escape from all his melancholy thoughts.

"Come riddle, I am here!" he cried out loudly, as his horse broke into a brisk trot.

In the midst of all his trouble, his face took on a pleasant smile. He wondered if he was not enchanted, and the whole overflowing life of youth came over him, as he spoke aloud to himself a letter which he would write to his mother that day:

"Dear Mother:—You must have yourself christened Lady Adventuress, for your son Doctor Adventurer, Captain, Valiant Warrior, has gone to Utopia in the midst of steam-cars and telegraphs, his belly filled with the sugar of praise, and the sweet almonds of protection, by a pair of spirits who guard the Sangraal. Your son is even now seated on a horse that looks as if colored with Isabel grapes, and has in his pocket the *Sesame* of a wise hermit, and the whole world is a little table covered with goodies, and everything says: 'Heart, what shall I help you to?'

"Dear mother! If you would like to have a 'lonely isle,' just say so, for I have any number of them to dispose of.

"There's a postscript too, dear mother! How would it be, dear mother, if this incalculable millionaire that I'm riding to should turn out to be Uncle Adam? That would just put a finishing touch to the fairy tale."

Erich stood suddenly still, as he thought that this fantastic idea might be the truth.

Then he rode briskly up the broad road, on each side of which nut-trees were dropping their blossoms on the ground.

His horse trotted along, his black mane fluttering. The rider took off his cap, and let the fresh stream of air cool his hot forehead.

BOOK SECOND.

CHAPTER I.

A MORNING IN EDEN.

THE ships sail up and down the stream, the railway trains roll hither and thither, and men of all climes and conditions enjoy the scenery. "Here or there," says many a one, "I might pass my life in peaceful enjoyment of nature, doing my chosen work alone or surrounded by those I love."

The shores of the Rhine are a beautiful place of rest, and yet they have motion enough. Before the threshold of the house lies the highway of business. Every hour, traffic changes the solitude into a scene of bustling activity.

Beautiful cities and villages lie along the shore with their castles and vineyards, and charming country-seats nestle among the hills—one unbroken chain of beauty.

In every city and in every house one may hear stories of the fortunes of inhabitants who have by determined exertion saved themselves from the flood, or at last, with the utmost effort reached the shore. Not a few, however, have been violently hurled on the beach.

He who comes hither from a foreign land, unknown and without credentials, can be sure of striking up a neighborly intercourse with the people, or if he chooses, of living alone. The steady stream of foreign business up and down need not interfere with the isolation of him who does not move with it.

"Who owns that beautiful villa, which when I first saw it in the distance looked like a white swan nestling amid the verdure of the shore?"

Passengers on the boats bound for some valley or mountain often ask this question, and receive the answer:

"The villa is called Eden, which is precisely the right name for it, for outsiders are not permitted to look into it; there are even spring-guns and man-traps all along the walls. The servants are only allowed to show the house and park to strangers when the proprietor is away; and they make a good deal of money in this way. The owner is a rich American. He built the house, laid out the park, and changed a swampy, useless meadow that ran down to the river into a fine orchard; and he raises better and larger fruit in it than was ever seen before in this section of the country. He restored that old ruined castle up there."

"What's his name?"

"Sonnenkamp. Almost all his servants are foreigners. He visits only very few of the neighbors and hardly ever receives a guest at his house. Nobody knows precisely who or what he is. He keeps fine horses, and yet he goes out riding or driving with his wife and a certain companion of hers, only to turn back at any spot in the open street that suits."

On this morning, as Erich was riding toward the Villa, the servants, dressed in their morning livery, had laid a large heavy carpet over the gravel-plot on the west side of the house. Near a pyramid of brilliant variegated flowers, the heavy odor of which filled the air, a round table, with a green damask cover, had been placed; and on the table had been set a cut crystal vase with artistically arranged shrubs and flowers, and plates laid for four.

At one side, near a bush of flowering heath and many-colored lilacs, a table had been placed, and a lighted tea-urn stood on it. A thin cloud of steam was seen rising from the urn. Two large, comfortable rocking-chairs were conveniently near.

A young man who had been standing near, without engaging in the table-preparations, but who was looking down the stream over the orchard and the fountain in which two white swans were swimming, and over the meadows and close-cut pasture-lands, now turned his head, and examining the arrangements said, "That'll do," and then withdrew with the servants.

The tea-urn steamed; the chairs and tables seemed to be watching for the company. A saucy finch perched himself on the back of one of the rocking-chairs, and whistled to his mate who was up in the tree. That was glorious, he only wished he could take such good care of his children.

The inquisitive and pert young father was soon frightened away. Some one was coming, and the bird started up incautiously and tried to fly directly over the tea-urn; but the steam seemed to scald him, and making a sudden turn he flew right over the head of the man who was approaching, almost grazing his hat.

The man was tall and broad-shouldered and dressed in a neat Summer suit. He wore a white neckcloth and a standing collar after the English fashion. He seemed to do all in his power to soften the effect of his Herculean frame, to make it small, but even the finest clothing, though it might help him in this, could not entirely accomplish it. He wore a broad-brimmed straw hat which shaded his face so completely that it could hardly be seen at a little distance. He limped a little with his right leg, but understood how to transform this limping into a carriage which gave to his mighty athletic frame a certain softness calculated to offset the intimidation it would naturally inspire. The young man who had pronounced favorably on the preparations of the table followed him, carrying a large portfolio. The man in the straw hat seated himself in a rocking-chair, and the young man stood before him. The occupant of the chair removed his hat, which the young man, Joseph the valet, quickly took. The man in the rocking-chair stroked his close-shaven, powerfully-moulded chin with a broad fleshy hand, on the thumb of which, in an outlandish fashion, he wore a frosted chain ring, the centre-piece of which was of iron. This was Herr Sonnenkamp. His face was of a bright reddish color, and his forehead, on which lay a streak of carefully-arranged gray hair, was broad. The unusual distance between his shaggy eyebrows made them look almost as if they had been violently torn apart. A person who had once seen this face would never forget it.

His deep-set bluish eyes showed determination and shrewdness, and his cheek-bones were high and prominent. His nose was large but by no means badly shaped, his mouth somewhat commanding, and defiantly curved. The whole face, although somewhat seamed by age, had not entirely lost traces of what had once been imperious energy of character. After having once seen him, no one would desire him for an enemy.

"Come, give it to me," said he, taking a bunch of little keys from his vest-pocket.

The valet handed him the portfolio with great deference. Sonnenkamp unlocked it, and Joseph gave him the letters it contained. Sonnenkamp quickly arranged them—those with foreign stamps in one heap, and the rest in another. Joseph now placed the hat and portfolio in the next rocking-chair, and rapidly cut the edge of each letter with a pair of scissors.

Herr Sonnenkamp hastily ran his eye over the opened ones and laid them aside. He only looked at the seals and address of a few of the inland letters, and directed Joseph to put them in the portfolio again, but he retained two of the foreign ones, and locked the rest in the portfolio himself.

The folding-doors leading to the terrace opened, and Herr Sonnenkamp arose and took his straw hat from the chair, as two ladies appeared. The first, who was slender, and had a pale, longish, and melancholy face, wore a fiery-red shawl and a morning-cap trimmed with deep-red ribbons; the other, whose face was angular and bloodless, whose hair was coal-black and closely confined, and who had piercing black eyes—one of those faces which have evidently never been young, but on which advancing age hardly has any effect—was dressed in black silk and wore a mother-of-pearl cross bound around her neck, shimmering and glittering on her breast.

Herr Sonnenkamp went as far as the steps to meet the ladies.

bowed benevolently to the one in black, gave his hand to the one who wore the red shawl, and asked in English how they were.

The lady, Frau Ceres Sonnenkamp, did not appear to consider it necessary to answer. She took her place at the breakfast-table, and a waiting-maid placed a napkin over her lap, while a waiter put an upholstered stool under her feet.

The lady in black—Signorina Boromæa Perini—went to the tea-table, and a servant held a tea-caddy for her, from which she took the necessary quantity with a spoon.

"Where's Roland?" asked Frau Ceres in a weary tone.

"He will be here presently," answered Sonnenkamp, giving a sign that he should be sent for.

Miss Perini brought the first cup of tea to Mrs. Sonnenkamp, for whom it seemed too hard a task to pour even the two drops of milk into it. Herr Sonnenkamp said, very submissively:

"Try to taste a little something, my dear."

Frau Ceres sipped a spoonful, then half a spoonful, and looked around as if exhausted. She seemed to consider it burdensome to feed herself.

"Where *is* Roland?" she asked again. "It's inexcusable in him to be so irregular. What is it, Miss Perini? Didn't you speak?"

"No, madam."

Herr Sonnenkamp said, in a very mild, conciliatory tone, that she ought to be patient a little. Roland had a tutor at last, it was to be hoped, who would be able to accustom him to regularity. Then he told them about the note that Otto von Prancken had sent him. At the mention of his name, Miss Perini let her biscuit fall into her tea, and fished it out again, while Herr Sonnenkamp went on to say that he would read no more applications till he had seen the man recommended by Herr von Prancken.

"Does he belong to the nobility?" asked Frau Ceres.

"I don't know," answered Sonnenkamp, but he knew very well—"he is a captain."

Frau Ceres understood nothing about the affair, but she wanted to know whether he belonged to the nobility or not.

Miss Perini understood what Frau Ceres meant to say; she looked smilingly at her, and speaking for her said:

"One very rarely meets such an accomplished cavalier as Baron von Prancken—at least, not in Germany. Why, he nearly excels Countess Bella in" . . . .

"I must beg of you," interrupted Herr Sonnenkamp, while his face took on an expression like that of a bull-dog who wants to be amiable—"I must beg that you won't praise anybody at the cost of the Countess. Herr von Prancken enchants the ladies, but for my part, the Countess Bella enraptures me."

Frau Ceres shrugged her shoulders expressively and held her gold spoon pressed to her lips.

"He boasts of being enchanted," she probably thought, "and yet his only object is to be able to speak a few complimentary words."

"I'd like to know where Roland is staying all this time," said she, rising on her footstool so that the table tipped, and everything on it rattled.

The servant came, and told them that Roland said he wouldn't come to breakfast, but intended to stay all day without eating, with Nora, who had had five puppies the night before.

"You tell him," said Sonnenkamp, while his face grew dark red to the roots of his thin hair, "that if he doesn't come instantly, I'll have all five of the pups drowned in the Rhine this minute!"

The servant vanished, and soon after a beautiful boy appeared, dressed in blue velvet. He was pale, and his beautifully cut lips were trembling. He had evidently been engaged in a hard struggle.

The child had grown up slender, and the features of his face were as exquisitely beautiful and pure as if chiselled. He took off his jockey-cap, and his dark-brown hair fell in large ringlets over his forehead.

"Come to me, Roland, and kiss me," cried his mother. "You look so pale! Is anything the matter with you?"

The boy kissed her, and said in a tone hovering between a falsetto and a man's voice:

"I am as well as my little dogs."

A fresh red color had come to his cheeks, and his lips were purple.

"I'll not punish you on the day when your new tutor is coming," said Sonnenkamp, following a hint from his wife.

"I? Another tutor? I won't have any!" answered the boy; "and if you give me one, I'll make it so hot for him that he'l soon be glad to go away again."

Sonnenkamp smiled. This stout defiance in his son seemed to please him.

As Roland, who had declared that he would not eat anything, now fell to work with great gusto, his mother followed his example, for her appetite returned when she saw how good everything seemed to taste to him, and Miss Perini could not help saying to Roland:

"See, Herr Roland! You ought to be more regular at your meals for your mother's sake, who never enjoys anything that you don't enjoy with her."

The boy cast a singular look at Miss Perini, but did not answer. There did not seem to be a good understanding between him and his mother's companion. But she continued in her friendly mood toward Roland, and promised to go with him and see his dogs after breakfast.

"Do you know why dogs are born blind?" asked Roland.

"Because God has so ordered it."

"But why has he ordered it?"

This seemed to be beyond her, and Herr Sonnenkamp came to her assistance by saying:

"A person who's always asking 'why?' will never get done, and Roland has got in the way of questioning because he's not willing to learn anything worth learning."

The boy looked at the ground; a certain hardness or stupidity, or perhaps both at the same time, appeared on his face.

Frau Ceres left the breakfast-table and, seating herself in a rocking-chair, set about examining her filbert-shaped, unconscionably long finger-nails.

Herr Sonnenkamp informed her of what a number of letters, in German, French, and English, he had received in answer to his advertisement. Most of the applicants had inclosed their photographs; and rightly, for personal appearance was of consequence.

Frau Ceres listened to him like a person who wants to go to sleep, and frequently closed her eyes. As Sonnenkamp added how much misery there was in the world waiting and watching for something to turn up by which money can be made, Frau Ceres suddenly looked at him out of the corner of her eye in wondering disability to conceive how one could live and at the same time be without means.

Miss Perini, the companion, was a good accommodation. As Frau Ceres evidently did not wish to participate in the conversation, she understood how to keep Herr Sonnenkamp talking by means of short answers and remarks, and occasionally glancing at him (she had the "convent-glance," looking *up* shyly yet graciously) while busied with her embroidery which she had taken out. In this way Frau Ceres could hear without particularly busying herself about what was going on.

Herr Sonnenkamp was always extremely polite to Miss Perini, who seemed to furnish him a means of practising politeness. He would probably have sent her away long ago, had she not become as inseparable from him as his "rheumatism-ring" which he wore on his left thumb.

Miss Perini always took care of Frau Ceres, who was never alone, but constantly kept with her a companion and guide; and when they went out riding Herr Sonnenkamp always seated Miss Perini on the front-seat with his wife, while he sat behind. He could never rid himself of her, and it was best to comport himself politely and attentively toward her. Besides, she had many excellent peculiarities, and the best of them was that she had not the slightest temper. She was always equable, never put herself forward but when asked, and always had an opinion which, as a general rule, was not disagreeable. Her feelings never appeared to be hurt; if no attention was paid to her, she knew how to conduct herself as though she had not noticed the neglect. If called upon to take part in the conversation she was charming and witty, always held her own, ready for others, and never talked about herself. She went to church every morning, Summer and Winter, and was always cheerful as if prepared at any moment to be called away. She knew where everything in the house was; and when travelling, was not of the slightest trouble. She was perpetually at her embroidery, and there was hardly a church within an hour's ride of the house which had not received from her an embroidered altar-cloth or some other decoration.

A singular coolness existed between her and Roland. She acted toward him as the young Herr, but further than this she had nothing to do with him, and had even, at the request of Herr Sonnenkamp, abandoned instructing him in the languages. She never overtespped the limits prescribed to her. She had been Manna's governess, had become Frau Ceres' companion, and that was she now, and nothing but that; and this latter fact really made her position appear more honorable.

The more Herr Sonnenkamp now said about the tutor recommended by Herr von Prancken, the more attentive she became. She uttered no definite opinion, and only when Herr Sonnenkamp asked her how *she* had felt when first introduced to the family in Nice, she said:

"I then had the happiness of being introduced to you by my noble friend Vormund, the Provost."

Roland was impatient and motioned to Miss Perini that he wanted her to go with him, but Herr Sonnenkamp requested her to remain with his wife. He thought that he ought to show some sympathy with his child's pleasure, and so accompanied him himself.

Nobody but Roland dared approach close to the bitch, and as Herr Sonnenkamp ventured to do so she snarled and showed her teeth. He was vexed, but controlled himself and went away.

Roland fetched his cross-bow and shot at the doves and sparrows in the courtyard.

Suddenly he stopped. A rider dashed up before the gate and skilfully drew up his horse.

CHAPTER II.

THE ARROW CAUGHT.

"SHOOT away, my boy! Don't be afraid—I'll catch the arrow!"

So cried the rider from his horse; but the boy did not shoot. He seemed astounded.

Erich had heard much about Roland's beauty, and yet now when he saw him for the first time, he was taken completely by surprise—the boy was so charming.

As he held his drawn bow in his hand, his whole being seemed also to be stretched to its utmost tension by terror and surprise. The rider feasted himself on the beautiful sight. The boy's head was uncovered, and his jockey-cap was on the head of a large dog which lay at his feet, raising his head as if asking his little master if it wouldn't be the right thing to spring up and drive the intruder away.

"Shoot ahead! Let her fly!" cried the rider in a haughty tone, as he sat before the gate. "Have you no courage, boy?"

The arrow whizzed from the string; the rider bent to one side and seized it with unerring hand.

"Either you shoot badly or would spare me," he cried.

"Perhaps you are Siegfried the bold."

"So?" answered Erich much pleased, "do you know anything about him yet? No, my boy," and he reached his hand to Roland and the boy grasped it, "Siegfried the bold didn't wear a uniform with a red cape. But now help me in with the horse."

"Isn't that one of Count Wolfgarten's saddle-horses?"

"Yes."

"Ivan!" cried the boy. A groom came and led the horse to the stable, while Erich and Roland followed. In a neighboring stall they heard a whimper and a helplessly awkward bark.

"You've some young St. Bernard dogs here somewhere," said Erich.

"Yes. Do you know them by the whimper?"

"I don't know the breed very well, but I saw one that looked like it in the courtyard out there. But these dogs can't be two days old, and are blind yet. I should think so, anyway, from the noise they make."

The boy looked at Erich as though he was an enchanter. He opened the stall, and told Erich not to come any nearer, as the bitch was dangerous, and was, besides, just now nursing all five of the puppies.

Yet Erich did go nearer, and the bitch looked at him without growling.

Again Roland wonderingly examined the stranger.

"*You* can certainly tell me why dogs are born blind," he began.

Erich smiled. A boy who asks is desirous and capable of improvement, and one must often instruct him by means of the things which move his inquisitiveness.

"Not only dogs," answered Erich, "but cats, eagles, and hawks come into the world blind. It may easily be that those animals which have especial need of sharp eyes to get their food and protect themselves, get their sight gradually, so as not to see the light of the world all at once, as they say. Although a man opens his eyes as soon as he's born, he can't see yet."

The boy started to hear the stranger talk in this manner; and, too, the tone of his voice had a wonderful effect on him, it seemed to seize upon him at once.

In the exalted state in which Erich had been for two days, and which, especially, he was now in, he seemed to himself to be living a fairy-tale—a dream, and one of those dreams in which one wonderingly says to himself: "Wake up, you are certainly dreaming!" He knew that he was experiencing all this in reality, and yet he felt as though he was only looking at it. He brought himself more under control, and said:

"You're the son of the house, aren't you? You're Roland?"

"Roland Franklin Sonnenkamp. And you?"

"Erich Dournay."

The boy was puzzled. He thought that he had somewhere heard that name during the last few days, but could not say certainly whether he had or not.

"You're an artillery captain?" said he, pointing to the uniform.

"I was. Do you know the uniform, my boy?"

"Yes; and Herr von Prancken doesn't call me 'my boy.'"

"Oh, I think we'll be good enough friends for that," said Erich, holding out his hand to the boy.

The child's hand was cold. All his blood had evidently returned to his heart. He was astonished, spell-bound, in spite of himself.

"If you would like to," he began, "you can have one of my puppies. I'm going to keep two for myself and raise one for my sister Manna. Baron von Prancken shall take the fourth, and the fifth you may have."

Erich's face beamed with pleasure as he looked at the boy. The love of giving must have a good basis in the character.

"Do you remember the custom of Homer's time," said he,

"of giving a guest a present to remind him always of his host?"

"I don't know anything about Homer."

"Didn't any of your teachers tell you about him?"

"All of 'em. They made a great fuss about him; but it was very tiresome."

Erich left the subject, and asked:

"Who helps you bring up the dogs?"

"Claus, the game-keeper. They sometimes call him the Krischer. He'll be pleased when I tell him that you knew how old the dogs were by their whine."

Erich nodded. A boy who takes such notice of a new event can be instructed. The only difficulty is to get control of him.

Erich then requested the boy to lead him to his father.

As they were about to leave the stables, a snow-white pony with a long mane turned its head and neighed.

"That's my Puck," said the boy. He was evidently very happy in showing the stranger his riches,—almost like a little child who shows its toys to one whom it trusts, to have him admire them. Erich could not help praising the noble beast, which looked at him askant with great, good-natured eyes.

Erich took the boy's hand, and they went together through the large plant-garden.

"Do you understand plants too?" asked Roland.

"No; I'm quite ignorant in regard to them."

"So am I," said the boy, glad to find that Erich had to confess ignorance of something; and that this ignorance was in regard to the same thing as Roland's, seemed to draw them both more closely together.

They crossed a spot of the garden where the ground was being cleansed and put to rights. A little old man with blear eyes, which were crafty too, was working there.

He took off his hat and bowed.

"Have you seen Father?" asked Roland.

"He's yonder," was the answer, as the man directed them to a hot-house.

The building was long, and made of pale-blue glass. The door stood open, and Erich saw a fountain in a basin of gray marble, in which lay pieces of rock covered with water-plants. A portion of the wintering trees were here, and in the front were a few weak ones bound carefully by their twigs and branches.

They heard some one speak.

"There he is, in the cool-house," said Roland.

Erich told the boy to go back, as he had to speak with his father alone. The boy stood still, as if rooted to the spot.

There was something not to be gainsayed in the way in which Erich had told him to go, and Roland could hardly think what had happened to him. When Erich had gone away, the boy stood for a while without stirring; then he turned, snapped his fingers and whistled.

Erich paused a minute to collect himself, and drew a deep breath. What if this boy were his blood-relation? What if he should now meet his uncle, whom they all supposed to be dead? With light and hesitating step he entered the cool-house.

CHAPTER III.

THE BANNER IS RAISED.

"WHO'S there? What do you want?" said a man rising from a bed of black earth. A sack of gray, coarse linen clothed the figure from head to foot: it resembled the dress that criminals or madmen wear.

"What do you want? Who are you? Whose house do you want to go to?" the man said again.

"I want Herr Sonnenkamp."

"What do you want of him."

"I want to recommend myself to him."

"I am he. Who are you?"

"My name is Erich Dournay. Herr von Prancken had the goodness yesterday to—"

"Oh! is it you?" said Sonnenkamp, drawing a long breath. He removed with trembling hands the sack in which he was dressed, and said smiling:

"You've surprised me in my working-dress."

He twisted the sack into a roll and threw it far away from him. Then he said:

"Wasn't there any servant near? Do you always wear your uniform?"

"Was it the uniform that frightened him?" passed rapidly through Erich's mind; and as he looked at the man he saw that it could not be his uncle.

"I am very sorry to have disturbed you," said Erich. He felt that the first impression which he had made was an unfavorable one. "I must ask you to pardon me," he stammered. "Count von Wolfsgarten, at whose house I was a guest, and from whom I bring a letter, has—"

"A letter from Count Wolfsgarten? Very satisfactory! I am glad to see you," said he, taking the letter. "We met each other under fearfully disagreeable circumstances; but then with us men it won't occasion any presentiment—I meant to say prejudice—embarrassment."

The tone of Herr Sonnenkamp's voice had entirely changed, having become affable, quiet, and almost obsequious.

He ran his eye rapidly over Clodwig's note, muttering:

"Much pleased—very satisfactory."

Glancing up from the page, he made a sort of bow, saying, as if sure of acquiescence:

"A nobleman—the nobleman, I should say, the Count Wolfsgarten. Are you as much of a favorite with Countess Bella?"

There was a dash of irony in the tone in which this was said.

Looking full at him, Erich answered firmly: "I am happy in enjoying the good-will of both equally."

"Fine, very fine," said Sonnenkamp. "But let's go into the open air. Are you a botanist too?"

Erich said that he was sorry that he had omitted any very near approach to that territory.

In the open air, Herr Sonnenkamp again measured the newcomer from head to foot. Erich noticed now for the first time that, forgetful of his military dress, he had absent-mindedly taken off his cap. And now as he saw how closely he was examined, he felt what it was to enter private service and give up one's whole personality to the authority of a single man.

There was something in Sonnenkamp's glance that made Erich feel as though he were standing in a slave-market, and as Sonnenkamp stretched out his hand and gave him a proprietary grasp, it seemed to him as though he would look at his chin, tear his lips apart and see if he still had all his teeth.

Erich shook his head as he thought of this singular notion, and straightened himself up proudly: he saw that he must be reserved with this man.

Sonnenkamp called a servant who was standing near, and ordered him to prepare a breakfast by the fountain.

"Did you come on horseback?" said he.

"Count Wolfsgarten was so kind as to lend me a horse."

"You've already spoken with my son?"

"Yes."

"I'm glad you came in uniform," said Sonnenkamp; but did not inquire how Erich had found the boy.

As if Erich had been only a gentlemanly, well-recommended visitor, Sonnenkamp now showed him his greatest pride. This was a complete collection of heaths, a sight that is rarely seen. He explained the fine varieties, and added:

"I have been at the place where most of these heaths come from. I was on the Table Mountain at the Cape of Good Hope."

"I am sorry," said Erich, "that my mother is not here, for it would give her great pleasure to look at these beauties."

"Does your mother understand botany?"

"Our professor of botany thought her knowledge on the subject quite wonderful; but she's very anxious to avoid any appearance of being a learned woman. It must be very difficult to keep these products of so many climates together."

"Certainly! and these heaths in particular require a uniform temperature and moisture. You must often have noticed that a heath with its tender blossoms, that are given to women for their flower-tables, withers away in a few days. These little plants cannot bear the dry air of a room."

Sonnenkamp suddenly stopped and smiled to himself. The stranger seemed to be making use of a commonplace trick, to appear agreeable by putting the rich man astride of his hobby, so that he should become communicative and think that he was shining. "I'm not to be caught with *such* bait," thought Sonnenkamp to himself.

"Will you have the goodness to take that pot from the stand and set it on the ground?" said Sonnenkamp, pointing to an arborescent heath.

The quick glance that Erich gave him, told Sonnenkamp that he was seen through; for he had wished to see if Erich knew how to serve—if he would humble himself.

Erich complied with his request with great good-will, but Sonnenkamp instantly determined, in spite of Clodwig's warm recommendation, not to take him into his household.

He had a double reason. The stranger had seen him completely frightened, which nobody else had done. He did not wish to retain him, and therefore he now persuaded himself that the stranger desired more consideration than would be agreeable to give him.

He would in the mean time accord him every honor of his house, as a man well recommended to him. It pleased him already, as he thought of it, to examine the man on all sides, to have him display his full powers in supposed certainty of the result, and then to reject him without giving any reason.

All this shot through Sonnenkamp's mind as he was turning back and locking the door of the green-house. The affair was locked up as closely in his mind as the door was locked.

"Do you speak English?" said Sonnenkamp, as he saw his wife sitting in her rocking-chair. She had discarded her red shawl, and sat in the chair arrayed in satin that shone like gold.

"Herr Captain, Doctor —— I beg your pardon—what is your name?" asked Sonnenkamp, introducing him.

"Dournay."

Frau Ceres nodded without noticing Erich, and as if she were not there; and then told her husband in a petulant tone that he had no eyes for her, for he hadn't yet said a single word about her new dress. Sonnenkamp stood without knowing exactly what to say at this sudden freak of his wife. Did she think it gave her an air of superiority to display her indifference before the stranger? No, she was hardly artful enough for that. He turned apologetically to Erich, and said that his wife was fond of gay colors.

Erich protested with the utmost sincerity that he entirely agreed with the lady; bright colors are natural in the open air, and people ought to surround themselves with brightness, as flowers do.

Frau Ceres smiled at this, and Erich proceeded in the same vein to say, that he considered it one of the disagreeable results of the manner in which people in society converse, that every expression of the truth, provided it is agreeable, is looked upon as politeness and flattery—words are robbed of their full meaning. The language of society is like a card of invitation to an evening party, which tells us to come at eight and means at half-past nine. If anybody should actually go at eight, he would only cause embarrassment.

Frau Ceres glanced rapidly from Erich to her husband, and as no one spoke, Erich continued in short, clear words to lay down the fact, that our dress should harmonize with the natural objects around us. He soon saw, however, that he was going too far in this strain, especially when he added how much the light floating dress of women resembled the plumage of birds.

Roland appeared at some distance, and his mother beckoned him to come to her. He pointed to the tower, and his mother looked up and smiled. His father looked up too, and saw the flag of the American Union fluttering on the tower.

"Who did that?" asked Sonnenkamp.

"I," answered Roland, smiling triumphantly.

"When?"

The boy's face quickly changed, and he looked stealthily at Erich. Sonnenkamp took his under-lip between his thumb and fore-finger, made a half-turn as if to go away, and nodded to himself.

Erich had noticed the boy's glance, and his heart started with pleasure. He asked the boy:

"You are very proud of being an American?"

"Yes."

Miss Perini approached, and while Erich was being introduced she took her mother-of-pearl cross in her left hand and held it fast, bowing at the same time very ceremoniously. Frau Ceres requested her to accompany her to the house. Sonnenkamp, Erich, and Roland were alone.

CHAPTER IV.

DEMAND AND SUPPLY.

GIVE me your hand, Roland," said Erich. The boy gave it, and looked at him earnestly and good-naturedly.

"My young friend," continued Erich, "I am grateful to you for raising the flag in honor of my coming, but now leave us alone; your father wants to talk with me."

Father and son looked in astonishment at this man who commanded in so unembarrassed and easy a way. The boy went away, Erich nodding pleasantly to him.

When the men were alone, silence succeeded for a little time. Herr Sonnenkamp offered Erich a large, dark brown cigar. He carried his cigars open, in his pocket. Erich accepted it, and as Herr Sonnenkamp offered him a light, he did not take the match from his hand, but quickly brought his cigar to the flame and said, as he took the first puffs:

"You'll easily agree with me that it's awkward politeness to ask a man to give you a lighted match, when you are almost sure to burn your fingers by doing so."

However trifling this remark was, it at once put them more at ease. Herr Sonnenkamp settled himself in his chair, filled his mouth with smoke, pursed his lips, and blew out rings that expanded until they melted into air.

"You have great influence over the boy already," said he at last.

"I believe that we like each other, and this makes me hope to remain here as his tutor. Only love can teach, as only love can work and fashion. An artist who does not love his calling—his work—can represent nothing truly. There are many who love every child they teach—I could only teach one whom I love."

"Fine—very fine—noble. But Roland needs coercion."

"Love does not exclude coercion, but rather includes it; for the lover not only wishes perfection in himself, but from the object of his love as well, and makes the highest demands."

Sonnenkamp, very well pleased, nodded kindly; but there was something sneering in his expression as he leaned forward and placed his arms on his knees, and looking at the ground said:

"Let us speak personally; there will be time enough to speak of such things hereafter. You are—?"

"I am a philologist by profession, but, by preference, have become a pedagogue."

"I know that—I know that," said Sonnenkamp, speaking to

the ground, "but I would like to hear something personal in regard to you."

He did not look up, and it was deeply painful to Erich to be obliged to relate the circumstances of his life again. He felt like a man who has come, filled with fiery wine, from the society of trusted comrades into the presence of a sober, watchful man. Yesterday he had laid his life fully and freely before Clodwig; to-day he was obliged to bring it to the market-place. So it is! The seller must always express himself more fully than the buyer. Power assumed quite a new appearance, coming under the guise of Wealth.

Erich looked at the broad back-head and neck of the man, who deigned him no glance; but his sensitiveness in regard to asking for work, quickly disappeared as he thought that he was not the asker, he was the giver. The pride of self-appreciation spoke in the tone of his words as he only said:

"I offer you spontaneous labor."

At these words Sonnenkamp quickly raised his head without changing his attitude, looked hastily at the speaker, and dropped his head again.

"I mean," said Erich, "that I offer you and your son the results of all the knowledge and experience which I have striven so hard to gain. I think next to nothing of pay as a compensation for my exertions; and I feel myself at liberty to do so, for whatever I do for you, I also do for myself, by striving to realize what I have worked and hoped for."

"I know what work without pay is," said Sonnenkamp, looking at the ground. Then he rose and said pleasantly:

"You haven't a learned man before you. I think we'll get at our object sooner if you treat me as a plain man, who wants, first of all, to get at some facts—"

"I had hoped," Erich interrupted him, "that my introduction by Count von Wolfsgarten—"

"I think very highly of Count von Wolfsgarten, higher than of almost anybody else," said Sonnenkamp; "but—"

"You're right," said Erich; "I will tell you." Whether it was the cigar or the painful position that made the perspiration break out on his forehead, at all events he laid down the cigar, and seemed astonished to find again that he was in his uniform. He began by explaining that he wore it to-day because Count von Wolfsgarten had advised him to.

Sonnenkamp now rose to his feet. He felt prepared and armed against this man, who, coming a stranger to his house, seemed to think that he could lord it over it, his wife, his boy, and even himself. He wanted to have the applicant talk himself tired.

"Proceed, Captain," said he, laying his right hand with

closed fingers on the table and drawing it back again, as if he had deposited a stake in a game.

Erich had fully recovered himself, and began quite humorously and in quite a different voice:

"Pardon me if the teacher can't forget his profession. In all poems, before the hero appears in his full development, the history of his parents must be told; and although I am no hero, and what I have to do requires no singular exhibition of power, allow me to draw a picture of my parents."

Erich briefly and concisely gave again the abstract of his life. Mindful of Clodwig's warning, he aroused no suspicion that he had believed himself called to instruct criminals. On the other hand, an incident occurred to him that he had previously quite forgotten. He said that he had once had the care of a gunpowder-mill.

"An agitating circumstance," said he, "deprived me of my overseership, for through some accident, unaccountable to this day, the powder-mill went up in the air, and four men were killed. And what did my superior say when he came? Not a word of pity for the unfortunates! He only said: "It's a pity about all that good powder!"

"What was that man's name?" asked Sonnenkamp.

Erich named one of the most distinguished names in the principality; and not a little to his surprise, Sonnenkamp said:

"A wonderful man—great and strong!"

After relating this incident, Erich proceeded quietly, and as he closed, said:

"I must beg you not to consider me a ne'er-do-well because I have changed my profession so often."

"On the contrary," Sonnenkamp interrupted, "I have lived long enough in the Old and New World to know that they are always the most capable men who give themselves up to their bent. He who changes his calling must either have a *true* one which is different from the one he has, or an external necessity for changing."

"Yet allow me one question. Do you believe it possible that a man who is not forced, or resigned, we will say, to accept such a—I don't mean menial, I mean dependent, I have almost forgotten my German, you know—I mean—would he of his own accord take such a position? wouldn't he feel always bound—obliged to serve, and unhappy?"

"Your frank objection honors me," answered Erich. "I know very well that the profession of a teacher necessitates a certain dependency from the time when it is taken up to the time when it is laid aside. Nothing could be more desirable to me than the assurance that you consider the matter as seriously as I could wish."

Again Sonnenkamp's face contracted. Erich did not appear to notice it, but continued with feeling:

"It is not mere force of circumstances which leads me to wish for the position of tutor in your house. I assure you that he who takes such a position out of necessity is not fit for it, although I do not mean to assert without qualification, that the inclination may not come from that motive, or as they say, a virtue may not be made of necessity. My knowledge is not great, but I have learned how one *must* learn, and therefore believe myself qualified to teach. I yield to none in honesty of purpose, and as far as I am capable of estimating myself, I can say that I would, even were I in the best of circumstances, joyfully take the vocation of a teacher, unremunerated."

"Very creditable! very creditable indeed! Go on!" Sonnenkamp broke in, and there was something in his tone that shocked Erich. He seemed to hear yet the echo of what he had said so impassionedly, which was now so suddenly cut short. Sonnenkamp said, with a certain triumph in his voice:

"Enthusiasm's a very good thing, but I prefer the man of business."

"I know that fully," answered Erich, "and I wonder at the matter-of-fact way of looking at things which men acquire in the New World." With great composure he proceeded:

"May I express a wish—a prerequisite, in regard to this matter?"

"And that is— ?"

Sonnenkamp again laid his hand on the table, as if he had deposited a stake.

"I wish that you could find it agreeable to regard me for a few days as a guest at your house."

Erich was silent. He had hoped that Sonnenkamp would consent, but he only bit in two a cigar he had just lighted, which did not seem to draw well, and threw it among the shrubbery. Again his face became red, and an evil smile played on his lips, for he thought: "Very good dodge! He only wants to stay here a few days and come his tricks over us, so that we won't let him go again. We'll see."

As he remained quiet, Erich said:

"It would be as desirable for you as for me to do so before we become any more closely connected, but I wish it principally on Roland's account."

Sonnenkamp smiled and sat watching two butterflies chase each other from flower to flower. He hardly heard Erich say that the boy was, on the one hand too old, and on the other not mature enough, to know how to select a tutor, and his voice ought not even to be listened to in the matter: he ought to become acquainted with him first as a guest at the house and then as his tutor, and he wished that Roland should never learn that he received money for teaching him—certainly not know the amount.

At the word " money," Sonnenkamp seemed to arouse from his watching the butterflies.

" How much do you ask?" he said, lighting a fresh cigar which he had long been holding in his hand.

Erich answered that not he, but Herr Sonnenkamp, ought to decide that. Sonnenkamp puffed his cigar till it glowed almost to a flame, and explained, with great unction, that he knew very well that no amount was a sufficient compensation for the pains-taking office of a teacher.

Then as he leaned back and threw one leg over the other, drawing the left one up and holding it tightly, he asked, evidently taking delight in showing the vastness of his mind :

" Will you not tell me, in a few words, the principle and method you would use in instructing my son?"

" I do not myself know the method."

" What! you don't know it yourself?"

" I must take my method from Roland, for it can only be determined by considering the nature of the pupil. Let me show you by an illustration drawn from your scenery. Look at the river. The pilots understand its bottom and know where there are sand-banks, and direct their course accordingly. It is equally necessary for me to know, above all things, the inmost nature of Roland."

Erich looked around, and continued:

" Or allow me another illustration, yet nearer. If you notice that your servants, in going to their quarters, choose to walk over a well-defined grass-plot, you will naturally go over this path yourself, if it is convenient, even though it may interfere with the manner in which your garden was laid out. This is the method which is determined by circumstances. There are such roads in a man."

Sonnenkamp smiled. In fact, he had laid out with the greatest pains, such a bed in the middle of the courtyard, had planted it with shrubs, and given strict orders that it must not be walked over; but had at last been obliged to make a path through it.

" Agreed as to the method," said Sonnenkamp. " But the principle?"

He smiled complacently as he thought what a nice distinction he had made; the man had convinced him that he might have a hard battle with him.

" I must enter somewhat further into that question," said Erich. " The great struggle which runs all through human history and human life, is most clearly seen in the education of one man by another. The two elementary forces are there opposed to each other as living persons. I may, for the sake of brevity, call them Individuality and Authority; or History and Nature."

"I understand—I understand," said Sonnenkamp, as Erich paused a minute, fearing that he was dealing too much with generalities. "Proceed," said Sonnenkamp.

"The instructor must represent Authority, and the pupil Personality, as it comes from the hand of Nature," continued Erich. "At the same time an arrangement—a treaty of peace, must always be kept up between the opposing powers, which must eventually become harmonious. To instruct a person simply as an individual, would remove him from life, and, for the sake of freedom, refuse him an existence in sympathy with mankind, or else would render such an existence hard for him. To make him subservient to law simply *as* law, robs him of an innate right. Man brings his law with him, but he also enters another law. It was the great mistake of Jean Jacques Rousseau and the French Revolution, to think (out of indignation against unreasonable tradition) that a man and a century could draw everything from themselves alone. An individual man has not everything in himself, nor does he receive everything from without. Consequently, I hold that there must be a uniting of both, which must constantly and unconsciously work together, conformably alike to nature and history; for man is a product of nature and a product of history. By means of the latter alone he is distinguished from the beast, and is the heir of the collected strength of all the ages that have preceded him."

Sonnenkamp nodded, very well satisfied. His expression seemed to say: "This man transplants into to-day the wisdom that he learned yesterday, very well." Erich continued:

"Man is only an heir, and to inherit is the most difficult of human arts."

"That's new to me. May I ask you to make it a little clearer?"

"Allow me to explain. The beast receives from its parents nothing but its personal strength and a capacity, which has been the same for ages. Man receives from his parents, in addition to this, an energy which has worked before—which he is not, but has and enters upon. Only man can inherit. And here let me say that it is hard to determine which contains the greater difficulty—to use properly that which one *is* as a man, or that, for instance, which your son enters upon as an inheritance. Most men exist only by means of that something which they possess. I do not, as you see, make too light of the latter, but—"

"Wealth is not a crime, and poverty is not a virtue," said

Sonnenkamp interrupting him. "I see how profoundly and well you seize upon the universal. I confess that it is new to me, and believe that you are right; although if you, having such opinions, should undertake to instruct a single child—"

"While engaged in teaching," said Erich, to reassure him, "I naturally would not always keep general principles in view: that would arrange itself. A man who loads a gun, aims and fires it, puts in operation the various physical laws which operate in such a case: he does not make them theoretically clear, but he must learn them in order to operate correctly."

Sonnenkamp was somewhat tired by this long conversation. He was not accustomed to hear such matters discussed, and felt that while he intended to impress the stranger with a sense of his importance, Erich had retaliated and made him appear ineffably small.

"Excuse me, Sir," said a groom, interrupting them just as Erich was preparing to proceed with his discourse. Sonnenkamp rose hastily, said it was the hour for his ride, waved his hand condescendingly to Erich, to signify that he would put off further remarks to a later period, and then went quickly away.

Roland came up the path and called out:

"Papa, mayn't I go riding with Herr Dournay?" Sonnenkamp nodded and disappeared. He mounted, and was soon seen on a spirited horse riding along the road which led to the shore. He looked strong as he sat on his horse; and behind him went the groom.

CHAPTER V.

A NEW PATRON AND A NEW TEACHER.

ROLAND had already ordered a horse to be saddled for Erich. They mounted, and rode at first slowly through a part of the town which reached as far as Villa Eden. Quite at the end stood a little house. It was surrounded with vines, and the window-shutters were closed. Erich asked to whom the house belonged and why it was shut up. Roland told him that it was his father's, and that the architect who built the Villa had lived here; and Herr Sonnenkamp also occasionally stopped at the cottage when he came from Switzerland and Italy, during the laying out of the park and garden.

"Now, sharp trot!" said Erich. "Take the bridle better in your left hand—so!"

They went gayly along, flank to flank, but suddenly Erich's horse shied and took to capering. Roland cried out, but Erich quieted him, and only saying, "I'll conquer him," discarded his stirrups and gave the horse such a run as made him smoke and very ready to obey.

He rode back to Roland, who was anxiously watching for him at the side of the road.

"What did you throw your stirrups away for?" he asked.

"Because I didn't want to hang in them if the horse should rear."

They now rode along quietly, side by side. Erich said:

"Which sort of riding do you like best—riding with an object or only going up the road to come back again?"

Roland looked at Erich as though perplexed.

"Didn't you understand my question?"

"Yes."

"And what do you think?"

"I'd rather ride with an object—for a visit."

"I thought so."

"Just think, I'm going to have another tutor!"

"So?"

"I don't want any."

"What do you want?"

"I want to go away from home—to a military school! Why should Manna go to a convent? They're all the time saying that mother couldn't eat if I should go away; but she'll have to eat when I'm an officer."

"Do you want to be an officer?"

"Yes. Why not?"

Erich was silent.

"Are you a nobleman?" asked the boy after a little while.

"No."

"Wouldn't you like to become one?"

"One cannot become one."

The boy played with the long mane of his horse, and looking around saw that the flag on the tower had been lowered. He called Erich's attention to the fact, and said proudly that "he'd hoist it again." The fine, plastically beautiful but pale features of the child, which often however wore a weary look, had taken spirit and color. There was an audacious expression in his face.

Without noticing his self-will, Erich said how beautiful it was that Roland took pride in being an American.

"You are the first person in Germany who has said I was right," cried the boy joyously. "Herr von Prancken and Miss Perini are all the time sneering at America: only you, dear—But pardon me, it's not right to be so familiar."

"Let it always be so—we will be good friends."

The boy stretched out his hand, and Erich grasped it affectionately.

"See! Our horses are good friends too!" continued the boy. "Have you many horses at your house?"

"I haven't any at all—I am poor."

"But wouldn't you like to be rich?"

"Certainly. Wealth is a great power."

The boy looked at him astonished. None of his tutors had ever told him *that*. They had all said that wealth was a vain and fleeting good, or else had set a flatterer's value on it.

After some time—the boy had evidently been thinking of Erich—he asked him:

"You are a Frenchman, to judge by your name?"

"No; I am a German, but my ancestors were French immigrants. How old were you when you came to Europe?"

"Four years."

"Do you remember America?"

"No; but Manna remembers a good deal about it. I only recall a humming sort of song by a nigger; but I can't put it together any more, and nobody can sing it to me."

They rode up the road leading to the mountain. The little man whom Erich had seen working in the garden was walking along the road and bowed to them very respectfully.

They stopped, and Erich asked Nicholas, or Grub-worm—as he was nicknamed from his constant digging, why he was going home so early?

He answered that he was only to pass the noon at home, and was then going into the forest to get the new earth which Herr Sonnenkamp had discovered. Over there in the forest there was a spring which contained iron, and Herr Sonnenkamp had ordered them to dig, and had found earth containing iron. In this he planted hortensias, and the flesh-colored plants became blue in it. Grubworm could not sufficiently sound Herr Sonnenkamp's praises—what a wonderful man he was, and how he knew everything and put everything to use, and how it was quite natural that such a man should become rich, for other people went stupidly up and down the world where there were so many millions lying everywhere, and did not know it.

As they rode on, Erich also expressed his admiration of a man who, in such a world which lay open to everybody, was always making discoveries like a Columbus. And the manner in which he recognized Sonnenkamp's greatness in this direction, from a single example, caused Roland to rise in his stirrups and look at him in astonishment. He had never heard his father praised so before.

"Is there no one in the neighborhood whom you would like to visit?" asked Erich.

"No—yet the Major, but he's up at the castle now. See! over there in the town Claus the huntsman—they call him the Krischer* sometimes—lives. He has our dogs; would you like

* Dialect for "Screamer."

to go with me and see him? I must tell him how Nora's young ones are getting along. He was at our house an hour before you came."

Erich was perfectly willing, and they rode up the rising ground on a short trot: then they turned to one side, halted at a little house and alighted.

Dogs of various breeds came up and jumped around Roland; and even Puck seemed to be pleased here and played with a brown terrier. An old man came out of the house and touched his cap in military fashion. He wore one of those short, light-gray cotton jackets that make the peasants of the Rhine look so free and comfortable, and was smoking a porcelain pipe, on which was painted in bright colors a picture of Napoleon apparently on a journey through the sky.

The way in which Roland introduced his new friend to the Krischer, showed that he knew how to treat his inferiors very imperiously.

"Take your hat off again!" said he to the Krischer. "Only just think! The Captain knew right away by their whine how old Nora's pups were and what breed they were of, without seeing them!"

"That can be done! According as a dog is of a wise or stupid breed he has a peculiar whine or bark. Stupid men cry and scream differently from wise ones."

He looked at Erich as a friend, and held his pipe in his hand a short time.

"You're right," said Erich; "and now that I notice you closely, I see that you've seen a great deal and thought much to yourself."

"Perhaps!" answered the old man.

He led them into the house, and when Erich asked who the saint was, whose picture hung on the wall, the Krischer answered, laughing:

"That's my only saint—Saint Rochus, from up above there; and I like him because he has a dog with him."

There were many bird-cages in the room, and the twittering and wrangling were so noisy that one could hardly hear himself speak. The old man took great delight in explaining to Erich how he understood accustoming birds who eat beetles and caterpillars to eating grain, and how he prepared maggots and meal-worms; but he scolded at Roland, who did not care for birds.

"No, I don't like any birds," the boy asserted.

"And I know why," said Erich.

"Do you? Why, then?"

"You don't like any free-flying animals which you cannot possess when they are at liberty; and you don't like to imprison them. You love dogs better; they are free, and yet they stay with us."

The Krischer nodded to Roland, as much as to say: "You didn't fall on your head *that* time."

"Yes, I like you better," cried Roland, who had two young setters in his lap, while their mother stood beside him rubbing her head against his side, and all the other dogs stood around him.

"And yet," said Erich, "jealousy and envy are the first things one notices in a dog. As soon as a man pats one of them, all the others want to be patted."

"There's one that doesn't trouble himself about it," laughed the Krischer.

A little brown dog was lying in the corner, occasionally blinking at them. Erich said that, judging from its appearance, he should call it a foxhound.

"He's right! He understands dogs!" said the Krischer turning to Roland. "He's right! I got Ranger there out of a fox-hole, and he's a treacherous and surly dog, and can't be trusted. You might give him what you liked, and he'd never be thankful or kindly."

The dog lying in the corner just opened its eyes once and then closed them again, as if it did not trouble itself at all about the conversation of the men.

Then Roland showed Erich his ferrets, taking them out of their cage, and they seemed to know him. He pointed out the yellow one as being quite a crafty, obstinate villain, and him he had named Buchanan. The name of the other he would not tell at first, but only called it "Knopf;" finally, however, he said that its name was "Dominie," for it deliberated so long before it went into the hole, and pursed its lips as if it wanted to give a long lecture.

They went into the garden and the Krischer showed Erich his bee-house. Turning to Roland, he said:

"Yes, Roland, your father's flowers help my bees too, but I wish the little things didn't have to fly so far as your garden. What difference does it make if I do pasture my cattle on a stranger's ground. It never was at such a pass before, that the rich could prevent the poor man's bees from sucking honey from the flowers."

An angry glance shot from his eyes as he said this: the whole resentment of the poor against the rich was in it.

The Krischer lamented that Sonnenkamp permitted so many nightingales to live there. They were good singers, it was true, but they ate the honey for the bees; that is, they ate the bees with the honey in them. The nightingale, of which men are so fond, is a notorious bee-murderer.

"Yes," answered Erich, "the nightingale doesn't know that the bees give honey, and shouldn't be blamed for considering bees monsters, for the destruction of which men ought to be thankful. But then she doesn't eat bees out of love for us, but love for herself."

The Krischer looked first at Erich and then at Roland, and shook his head, as if to say: "Yes, yes; but there's another way still of looking at it!"

Roland asked how much "Grip" had learned, and received the answer that he would fly at the man, but was too wild yet: his springing was not regular enough, but he had a beautiful grip. Roland wanted to see it tried, but the laborer whom the dog practised on was not at home. Roland said that the little gardener had come home, and he would do just as well. He went himself and fetched him.

When Roland had gone, the old man hastily seized Erich's hand and said:

"I'll help you! You shall get the boy—I'll make it handy for you!"

Erich looked at him in surprise, and the old man went on to explain to him that he knew very well why Erich had come, and that a man who knew how to do it could make a clever man of Roland. He added with a sly look, that Erich would be thankful to him if he helped him in getting the position.

Before Erich could answer, Roland had come back with the gardener, who allowed a pad to be bound about his neck and stationed himself by the garden-fence, holding fast to the palings with both hands. A large Newfoundland dog was let out of a kennel and jumped around awkwardly, but at a whistle from the Krischer placed himself behind him.

"Now!" called out the Krischer. "Seize him, Grip! Take hold of him!"

The dog went bounding through the garden at the man who stood at the gate, sprang at him and bit into the pad on his neck and tugged at him, till he fell; then he placed his right fore-paw on his breast and looked back at the Krischer.

"Bravo! Bravo! Do you see what a Satan he is?"

"You're right," cried Roland, "that's the right name for him. I'll call him so. Satan! Now the whole neighborhood shall be afraid of me!"

Erich was as much astonished at the tyrannical tone in which this was said, as at the quick way in which the boy had seen what use he could make of the dog.

He said to the Krischer that the name of a dog which had all its teeth ought not to be changed.

"Certainly," he answered. "You can't call him when his name is changed, for he doesn't know which is the right one."

"Besides," added Erich, "it is wrong to call a dog by such a name. There ought to be a C in it, and it ought to have only one syllable. A C is easily called out, and is sharp."

"You're a great scholar; I never met such a one before. You know everything!" said the delighted Krischer as he winked half stealthily.

Satan—for Roland insisted that the dog should be called so—would not leave the man, who was yet lying on the ground, although both Roland and the Krischer continued to call him. This was not in order; and it was only when the Krischer had shown him the whip that he released his prisoner.

Roland gave a piece of money to the gardener, who thanked him very submissively, and only wished that he could be thrown down three times a day by the dog, at that price. Erich looked on thoughtfully. "How shall a boy who is so rich that the world puts itself so readily at his disposal, learn to love—to work and toil for it?"

When the two left the cabin, the Krischer, surrounded by the crowd of dogs, conducted them a short distance. They led their horses by the bridle, and the Krischer paid exclusive attention to Erich, and brought out his whole stock of knowledge in regard to the training of dogs.

The Krischer considered himself immeasurably wise, and all scholars stupid. He seemed to wish to give Erich sly information, as he said: "The only time to begin with a dog, is just when it commences to walk decently, without stumbling over its own legs; and a principal thing is not to talk much with it, and use only loud, short words—simply, 'Come! Go! Here!' No long talks to let him know he's somebody. You must let him go whole days and not notice him, even if he wants to be friendly, for if you give yourself up too much to a dog, he becomes troublesome; and if a dog is afraid of *one* person, you'll be all right when you go hunting, particularly if you use him right at the start. If you've shot something that he can fetch, he'll like you and be true to you; but if you *miss*, he'll lose all his respect for you, and the game's up, for he'll never mind a word you say after that."

"Do you know Herr Knopf?" said the Krischer suddenly. Erich said that he did not.

"Yes, Herr Knopf has told me a hundred times," continued the Krischer, "that the schoolmasters ought to come to school to me. Dogs and men are just alike; only men are more respectable dogs, and show their teeth and bite only when their master lets them."

Erich looked at the man in astonishment. There was an inexplicable bitterness in his expressions; and yet he was the boy's friend. He turned away, and the Krischer smirked as he told him that animals receive a part of their knowledge from the men with whom they associate.

The Krischer seemed very happy; and as they were about to take leave of him after reaching the plain, the Krischer drew Roland aside and said:

"You bully boy! All your old fogies of dominies and school-masters weren't worth anything. *That's* the man for you! Your father ought to buy such a man for you—he'd make something out of you. But for all your money you can't get *him!*"

He said this apparently only to Roland, but Erich was intended to hear it, for he was to know that he was to have reason to thank the Krischer.

As they were mounting, the Krischer spoke again:

"Do you know that your father is buying the whole mountain? This cursed dividing up into districts! Your father's going to buy all Pfaffengasse. In a hundred years we won't have a hand's-breadth of all these wine-hills, for all our grubbing and digging! Must this be? Shall it be?" and he pointed to the broad Rhineland.

They returned to the villa on a brisk trot. Erich had decided.

Just as Erich was saying to himself, "Thou hast sworn to leave the boy no more," he saw a female figure disappearing around the corner of the garden which belonged to the vine-covered cottage.

Had he seen his mother, or only called her up in his imagination? With inconceivable rapidity, he thought that *here* his mother and his aunt should live; this house, with its little garden, its dwarf-trees, and its wide view of the beautiful landscapes, was prepared for them.

"Didn't you see the woman in the garden?" he asked Roland.

"Yes; it was Fraulein Milch."

"Who is Fraulein Milch?"

"The Major's housekeeper."

CHAPTER VI.

THE BREAD OF SERVITUDE AND THE BLESSING OF THE HUGUENOTS.

WHEN Erich and Roland had returned from their ride, they heard that Herr von Prancken had arrived. Erich's trunk had been immediately taken to his room. Joseph, the valet, introduced himself to Erich as the son of the janitor of the medical school at the University, and there seemed to be real gratitude in his account of how Erich's father had given him a

French grammar, in which he had learned his rudiments by heart, during the leisure moments of his profession as billiard-marker in the academical Casino. In this way he had laid the foundation of his present position, and expressed his joy at being able to thank the son of his benefactor.

Joseph aided Erich in the arrangement of his things; and while doing so, took the opportunity to give information in regard to the way in which the house was conducted—stating, among other things, that it was especially necessary for everybody to appear at the dinner-table in full-dress, which was looked at as a sort of solemnity of everyday occurrence, which took place during the summer in the pleasure-grounds, and in Spring in the Nizza, as a pleasant covered place on the terrace, where the sun shone, was called.

Erich took off his uniform; and as he was entering the arched passage, met Prancken walking up and down with Miss Perini. He approached Erich in a friendly manner, with an affable smile, which vanished almost as quickly as it appeared. In the consciousness of his rank and position in society, he could make use of an accomplished politeness, in which, however, the disposition of his mind could be easily detected. He merely bowed, joined Miss Perini again, and kept his walk and conversation uninterrupted.

Erich stood alone; and the suspicion that it would not do for him as a tutor to be sensitive, warred with his pride. It might, however, have been pure consideration in Prancken not to ask about his prospects for obtaining the situation.

Roland came up already dressed, and wondered when he saw Erich in citizen's dress.

"Is your sister's name Manna?" asked Erich.

"Yes: her full name is Hermanna, but we always call her Manna. Have you heard anything about her?"

Erich had not time to answer that Prancken and Miss Perini had frequently mentioned the name, for Herr Sonnenkamp appeared in a black suit, white neckcloth, and faultless yellow kid gloves. He bowed in all directions, very encouragingly—one might say appetizingly—as if to say, "I hope it will taste good to you." Herr Sonnenkamp was never more cheerful, more expansive, than during the quarter of an hour immediately preceding dinner.

They entered the dining-hall, a cool, four-cornered, vaulted chamber, lighted from above. The carved oak mouldings were extremely heavy. A large buffet, filled with beautiful old salvers and venetian glasses, showed a wealth of silver. It was consequently a sheer fable which was told in all the neighborhood—that Herr Sonnenkamp ate only from dishes of pure gold.

They were obliged to wait awhile in the dining-hall, but at last the folding-doors opened, two servants in the coffee-colored livery of the house stood like sentinels at the door-posts, and Frau Ceres entered the room between them like a princess. She paused as she crossed the door-sill, and bowed somewhat stiffly. Prancken went to meet her, and conducted her to the table.

A servant was ready for each guest, and held the chairs as they sat down. Miss Perini stood behind her chair, leaned her arms on the back of it, held her mother-of-pearl cross with both hands, prayed, made the sign of the cross, and seated herself.

Frau Ceres kept her yellow gloves on her hands all through the meal. She hardly touched any food, and acted as though she had appeared at the table only because her absence would destroy the dinner. She *always* waited till Herr Sonnenkamp said:

"Take a little something to eat, dear child, I beg."

In the way in which he asked her to eat there was a double tone, difficult to define. Sometimes it sounded like the summons, accompanied by the look with which an animal-tamer orders a tamed beast to eat the food lying before it; and again, it sounded like a father coaxing and flattering a stubborn child to eat for the sake of its own health. Frau Ceres ate only a little fowl, and some dainties.

Prancken comported himself like the guest of honor who has undertaken to show his host how pleasant and communicative he is. He gave a humorous description of the Mannheim horse-market, from which he had returned early that morning with his companion; he had bought a gray mare for the autumn races, and would be delighted to turn it over to Herr Sonnenkamp. He knew perfectly well how to please Frau Ceres, who had a particular antipathy against the family of the Wine-cavalier, which conducted itself very reservedly toward the Sonnenkamps. He recounted for her several ridiculous bragging speeches of the Wine-cavalier, whom he had only joined for the sake of company; and while doing so, gave some skilful imitations of the way in which different men speak and act, which not only made Frau Ceres relax her features, but even smile.

Then the conversation was carried on in Italian, which Prancken spoke tolerably well, but which Erich did not understand very well.

For the first time in his life, Erich was sitting at a table where he had to be as silent as the servants in waiting.

Frau Ceres considered it her duty not to leave the stranger entirely unnoticed, and so asked him in English if his parents were yet living.

In a tone which was evidently patronizing, Prancken set about describing Erich's father and mother. He did this in a pecu liarly friendly manner, and added with emphasis that Erich's mother was of noble blood.

"I should think, from your name, that you were French," said Miss Perini.

Erich repeated again that his ancestors had emigrated from France to Germany two hundred years before; he considered himself fully a German, and was glad to be descended from the Huguenots.

"What are Huguenots? Oh, yes! I know—they sing it!" said Frau Ceres, showing a childish pleasure in knowing so much.

Everybody at the table had hard work to keep from laughter.

"What are they called Huguenots for?" asked Roland; and Erich answered:

"Some think that the origin of the name is the fact that they were obliged to hold the religious meetings of their secret order at midnight, near Tours, where the ghost of King Hugo used to walk; but I accept the view of others, who hold that it is a German word, meaning Confederates (Eidgenosse), and that the French changed it to Huguenots."

Prancken nodded to Erich, as if to tell him how well he was beginning his work as a teacher.

"You seem to be proud of being descended from the Huguenots," said Sonnenkamp,

"'Proud' is hardly the right word," answered Erich. "You know, however, that the Puritans, expelled from Europe on account of their faith, were the source from which came that sturdy, virtuous, and brave stock of citizens of the New World. They came, as the Greeks in old times entered Sicily and Italy, bringing with them a complete civilization, and planting it in the New World."

The manner in which Erich spoke of this great fact of history suddenly gave a new direction to the conversation. It was all at once transported from the world of witticism and piquant personalities and placed in another region. Roland felt something of this, and looked proudly at Erich, happy in knowing that it was his thoughts which directed all.

Sonnenkamp recognized quite clearly the breath of a loftier nature, which moved only amid elevated thoughts; he could not refuse a certain respect for him, and asked:

"Why do you connect the Pilgrims to America with the Huguenots?"

"Allow me a short explanation," answered Erich. "Modern times have broken through the distinctions of mere nationality, and so, for example, the Jews, scattered among all peoples, have become important constituent elements of the traffic of the world. A proud and tyrannical king drove the Huguenots from France, and the Huguenots became Germans. The English Pilgrims planted their civilization in America, but the Huguenots, who fled to a people already civilized, were obliged to continue in the civilization of their new fatherland. You will certainly pardon me, Herr Sonnenkamp, if I take you as another example."

"Me? What do you mean?"

"You went to America as a German, and the German immigrants become constituent elements of their new home, and at the same time their children become Americans."

Roland's eye glistened, but whether it was that Prancken saw himself cast into the background by Erich, or that he sought to embarrass him, he said, with a curious mixture of humor and sympathy:

"It's very modest of you to put the Huguenots, who at least were most respectable creatures, on a parallel with the Jews."

"Although my ancestors were celebrated," answered Erich, "I consider it a matter of indifference that they engaged in ordinary business, and that my immediate ancestors were goldsmiths. But I readily admit their resemblance to the Jews. They all were driven into exile for their faith's sake, and their scattered society took upon itself two duties: first, in every nationality to keep the unity of humanity in view; second, to oppose with all their strength every fanaticism and every proscription. There is no religion which exclusively gives happiness, and no nationality which exclusively makes humanity beautiful."

Prancken and Miss Perini looked at each other in surprise. Frau Ceres had not the slightest idea of what it all meant, and Herr Sonnenkamp shook his head at the sermonizing manner of his guest, who had broken in somewhat violently upon their light table-talk with his broad ideas of history, but he could not escape the impression that he had before him a man who steadily occupied himself with genuine thought.

"You must give me a clearer explanation of these views sometime," said he, seeking to avoid further remarks.

Roland said:

"Louis the Fourteenth, who exiled your ancestors, was he the man who destroyed these castles on the Rhine?"

"Yes."

The conversation did not seem likely to be readily withdrawn from this subject, which made it somewhat dull, but a diversion was made by the appearance of a highly seasoned dish. Roland wanted to eat some of it, but his father refused to let him.

His mother, who noticed this, cried out in a shrill voice.

"Let him eat what he likes!"

Erich looked at him, and the boy laid aside the piece which he was just about to put in his mouth, and said:

"I would rather leave it."

Sonnenkamp directed the servant to help Erich to some more *Rauenthaler*. This seemed to be a sort of expression of his thanks for what Erich had done.

They did not again engage in light conversation. Prancken was dumb; and it was difficult to decide whether this was occasioned by his having nothing to say, or by a wish to give Erich to understand that his pedantry and pretension had disturbed the serenity of the meal.

They arose from the table, and Miss Perini again prayed silently. All stood still, and the servants removed the chairs from behind them, and then they went out on the verandah to take their coffee from tiny cups.

Frau Ceres gave a snow-white parrot a biscuit, and it cried out in English, "God bless you, massa!"

Then she sat down in an arm-chair, and Prancken took his place on a low stool close to her feet.

Miss Perini chose a place which was near enough to admit of her joining in the conversation if she should be wanted, and yet distant enough to allow Frau Ceres to talk with Prancken alone, if she wished to.

Sonnenkamp requested Erich to go into the garden with him, and Roland accompanied them without being invited.

A servant came and told them that Claus was with the new-born dogs, and would like to have Roland come and see him.

"You may go," said his father.

"I would rather stay with you," answered Roland.

There was a childlike affectionateness in his tone and bearing, as he insinuated his hand into Erich's.

"If your father says you may go, you should go," said Erich quietly.

Roland went reluctantly, stopping occasionally. But yet he went away.

CHAPTER VII.

AN EXAMINATION WHICH ENDED IN A LAUGH.

THE two men walked together for a while without speaking. Erich was dissatisfied with himself. He was yet too much absorbed in himself, and in the desire to conform everything to his own way of thinking, and to express it in the most specific terms. Actuated by this tendency, he gave himself up fully, freely, and in all *naïveté*, to the impulse of the moment, although he had in reserve a consciousness of the riches of his own intelligence. This not only aroused in his hearers a sense of their own deficiency, but impressed them with a feeling of the forwardness of the speaker. Erich always said this to himself the moment after speaking, and yet would immediately fall into the same error again, which made him doubly dissatisfied. Erich was aware, as if by magic, that all this was passing through Sonnenkamp's mind, although he did not know the full extent of Sonnenkamp's triumph over the enthusiast, for he smiled to himself over all this newly baked University-wisdom that Erich had served up. He knew that he was too old for all this stuff. There these men sit in a little University town, with no real men before them, and conjure up a phantasmagoria of humanity, and believe they have the burden of the world on their shoulders, and think it a piece of ingratitude that they are not called out by common mortals to rule the everyday world. Even this Captain-doctor who was walking beside him had only a little company of ideas to command.

Sonnenkamp whistled softly to himself—so softly that no one but himself heard his whistle. He even knew how to hold his lips, so that anybody could not tell by looking at him that he *was* whistling.

He seated himself, as they came to a little elevation, and asked Erich to take a chair too.

"You must have noticed," said he at last, "that Miss Perini is a strong Catholic. In fact, our whole house belongs to the Church. May I ask why you made such a point of your Huguenot descent?"

"Because I do not wish to disavow it, and want no one to be deceived in regard to me."

Sonnenkamp was silent again for some time. At last he said:

"I am master in this house, and tell you that your confession is no objection. But now"— and he bent forward and laying both hands on his knees, looked sharply at Erich, "but now—I came near falling from my horse to-day, a thing which seldom happens to me; for I was all the time thinking, while I was riding, of what you told me—now, briefly, for the principal question. How do you think a boy who already knows that he will not be obliged to work—that he will own a—or we will say several millions—how do you think such a boy can be educated?"

"I can give you a very definite answer in regard to that."

"So? I am listening."

"The answer is very simple. He cannot be educated at all!"

"What! not at all?"

"Yes, only the great unknown—only fate can educate him. All that we can do, is to prepare him—to accustom him to properly control and use the power he will have."

"Govern and use," muttered Sonnenkamp to himself. That sounds well, and I must say you remind me of an expression I have often made use of. Only a soldier, a man who has educated and enlarged his natural force, can do anything remarkable in our times. You can do nothing with books and lectures—you can't conquer the old world nor make a new one."

With a changed, almost a servile tone, Sonnenkamp continued:

"It may appear very strange that I, a man of small knowledge, who have had no time in the hurry of business-life to learn anything correctly, should undertake openly to examine you; but be assured, I ask only for the sake of information. I see already that I will probably learn more from you than Roland will. I ask, how would you—think of yourself as a father in my position—how would you educate your own son?"

"I believe," answered Erich, "that the imagination can represent everything in some fashion. But a relationship, which is a natural relationship, can, justly, only be experienced, not imagined. Let me answer from my stand-point as a stranger."

"Good."

"My father was a prince's instructor, and yet I believe his task was easier than mine."

"You don't place wealth above royalty?"

"Far from it. But in a prince the consciousness of duty is awakened very early; every instant, pride is aroused in him, but along with it the knowledge that he must comport himself as becomes a prince. The circumstance that surrounds him with unusual splendor, appears from the first as an office, a duty, and becomes the daily habit of his life. Virtue becomes, with him, a sort of virtuosoship.—Pardon me my scholarship," said Erich, smiling.

"No; go on—it's highly interesting to me."

Sonnenkamp leaned back and relished Erich's remarks like a sweet morsel. The man may go as far as he pleases with his fancies, so long as he doesn't call the chair on which he sits, the spot of ground on which he stands, his own; while Sonnenkamp, in the height of his pride, calls all around him his own, and can get yet more, as far as his eye can reach; yes, can, as the Krischer said, buy all the Rhineland, if he wishes to.

"Continue," said he, lighting a cigar.

"It may seem ridiculous," Erich proceeded, "but it is nevertheless true, that a prince receives a military rank in his cradle. As soon as reason awakes, he sees his father under the command of duty. I will not deny, that this duty is often performed very easily, if not totally neglected; but a certain appearance of duty must always be preserved. A rich man's son, on the contrary, does not see the duties which wealth enjoins, so plainly and imperiously brought before his eyes. He sees benevolence, concern for the public good, encouragement of art, hospitality; but all this is not duty—it is free personal inclination."

"Now you are coming to historical obligation. But I beg your pardon—You have a remarkable talent for teaching; and I am at all events grateful to Count Clodwig, and you too."

"An opportunity for a comparison occurs to me," began Erich anew.

"Go on," said Sonnenkamp encouragingly.

"There was a custom in the time of the Guilds which compelled German princes to learn a trade. Paying no attention to anything else, they learned to understand and value labor. A rich man's son should be obliged to do something similiar to this, without letting it—as happened in the other case—degenerate into a mere formality."

"Very profitable," said Sonnenkamp.

He had only intended to pump Erich—to have a certain enjoyment in letting a learned idealist express himself fully, but had no particular desire that Erich should do all this simply for his amusement, if he could draw instruction from it. He experienced a pleasure in making, for once in his life, a journey into the realm of the ideal. Everything looked very pleasant and orderly there; but only for an hour, for half a day. But he found that he had imperceptibly been drawn on to take a lively interest in the subject. He laid his hand on Erich's arm and said:

"You're really a good teacher."

Erich received this praise without replying, and continued:

"I prize wealth highly; it is a great power: it gives freedom and self-reliance."

"Yes," answered Sonnenkamp, "that's true. But do you know what one desires most, and cannot buy?"

Erich shook his head, and Sonnenkamp continued:

"Trust in God! See! the day before yesterday they buried a poor vine-dresser. I would give half my wealth if I could have bought from him his reliance on God, for the last years of my life. I could hardly believe the doctor, but it is true, the vine-dresser was a perfect hospital of diseases, and in the midst of all his suffering he steadily said: 'My Saviour has suffered more than I, and God will soon tell me why he has afflicted me so.' Now tell me, is not such a faith worth more than millions? And now I ask you, can you give it to my son without making him priest-ridden or a canting devotee?"

"I do not believe that I can give him *such* a faith; but there is a complete satisfaction of the soul to be derived from Reason."

"Is it *such?* and in what does it consist?"

"In my opinion it consists in working according to our strength, and in identifying ourselves with the interests of our fellow-men."

"If I'd had a teacher of your sort when I was a boy, I believe it would have been a happy thing for me," cried Sonnenkamp.

There was an altered tone in his words, and Erich answered:

"You could have said nothing which would have made me more happy and confident than that."

A hasty movement of the hand, as if he was throwing something away, showed that Sonnenkamp was displeased. This continued answering wearied him, he was not accustomed to it. This immediate settling of accounts, wounded his pride to a certain extent. Erich did not remain indebted to him, but seemed always to have something due to himself.

For a long time nothing was heard but the plashing of the fountain, the soft lapping of the Rhine, and the unwearied nightingale's songs amid the bushes.

"Were you ever a passionate gambler?" asked Sonnenkamp, half unconsciously.

"No."

"Were you ever passionately in love?—You look at me with astonishment, but I only ask because I would like to know how you became so mature a man."

"Perhaps a careful education and a philosophical persistence have given me what you are so kind as to call maturity."

"Good! you are more than a teacher."

"I shall be glad if that is the case, for I believe that he who would do anything great, must always do something more than his immediate vocation demands."

Again Sonnenkamp's features contracted, and again he made that motion as if throwing something away.

These ready and at the same time decided answers discom posed him.

They heard Prancken and Miss Perini wandering up and down in a by-path.

"You must be careful," said Sonnenkamp rising, "to be on good terms with Miss Perini. She is of some consequence, and not easily to be fathomed; and besides this, she has a great advantage over most men whom I know—a very precious advantage—she has no temper."

"Unfortunately, I cannot boast of having that advantage, and I beg your pardon beforehand if I ev—"

"It's unnecessary. But your friend Prancken understands very well how to get along with Miss Perini."

Erich considered it an obligation which he owed to truth, to tell Sonnenkamp that he had no right to call Prancken his friend. They had been acquainted at the military-school and the garrison, but their sentiments had never agreed, and that his own aims in life were very different from those of an "eldest son." He recognized Prancken's goodness in introducing him at Herr Sonnenkamp's house, but truth was more important than gratitude.

Sonnenkamp again whistled inaudibly. He was evidently astonished by this frankness, and thought that perhaps Erich was a skilful diplomat, and regarded it as the most important requi site of diplomacy to recognize no gratitude. "This man," he thought, "is either the most exalted of enthusiasts, or the basest of worldlings."

Erich felt that he had selected a bad time to make this announcement, but he could not have dreamed that this disclosure would obliterate the whole impression which his conduct had made on Sonnenkamp.

When they met Prancken and Miss Perini, Sonnenkamp saluted Prancken with the greatest cordiality, and linked his arm with his.

Erich walked with Miss Perini, who always had with her some fine little woman's work, and could, with her almost invisible instruments and thread, make a lace-garland with surprising rapidity. It was the first time that Erich had spoken to her, and he expressed great interest in her delicate work, which she called Ocki. It immediately seemed as though a written agreement had been signed by both: "We will avoid each other as much as possible; and when we are brought together in the same circle, we will each act as though the other did not exist."

In answer to the full voice of Erich, Miss Perini always replied somewhat hoarsely, and as she looked at Erich, evidently surprised at this tone, she said:

"I thank you for not asking me if I am not hoarse. You cannot think how tiresome it is to be all the time obliged to answer that I have spoken so from childhood."

The pleasant way in which this was said led Erich on, and he told how painful it was to a friend of his, who was born on the twenty-eighth of February, to be saluted by everybody who heard of it, with the remark: "It's fortunate for you that you were not born on the twenty-ninth of February, for then you would only have had a birthday every fourth year." He had accustomed himself to say, under fitting circumstances: "I was born on the twenty-eighth of February. It is fortunate for me that I was not born on the twenty-ninth, for then I would have only had a birthday every fourth year."

Miss Perini laughed heartily, and Erich himself was obliged to laugh.

"What are you laughing at?" said Sonnenkamp, approaching. Of all earthly pleasures, he loved laughing the best.

Miss Perini related the story of Erich's friend, and Sonnenkamp laughed too.

And so the day was yet more pleasant.

CHAPTER VIII.

THE EYES OPEN.

WHILE Erich was walking with Sonnenkamp in the garden, Roland and the Krischer sat looking at the little dogs, and the Krischer asked if "they had fastened the Captain yet?" Roland did not understand what he meant, and the Krischer laughed to himself, thinking that he might obtain a double advantage.

"What'll you give me if I work things so that the Captain stays with you as a comrade and teacher?" he asked. "Hu!" he interrupted himself suddenly, "you make a face like dogs when they open their eyes for the first time. Come, now, what'll you give?"

Roland could not answer. Everything was whirling and turning through his mind, and the little dogs were jumping about him.

Joseph now entered the stable. He lauded Erich's parents as saints, and ended by saying:

"You ought to be proud, Herr Roland. Erich's father taught the prince, and the son is going to teach you."

Roland was again unable to answer.

"Close the door, quick!" cried out the Krischer, suddenly. Joseph did so, and the Krischer lifted one of the puppies from the floor, forced his eyelids apart, and said:

"I saw that done once to a dog whose eyes had just opened. Now don't let any more light in, or you'll spoil 'em."

In his zeal for the dogs, the Krischer quite forgot his acute double plan. He entered the courtyard with Joseph and Roland; but the latter immediately left it. He saw his father and Erich sitting together, and scowled at Erich. "Why didn't he tell me right away who he was?"

But he quickly overcame this feeling, and would willingly have run up and thrown his arms around him, but restrained himself, and only approached when he heard them all laughing.

He pressed Erich's hand confidingly, and his look said: "I thank you—I know who you are."

Erich did not understand this look until Roland said:

"The others have had you long enough; now come with me."

He conducted Erich to his room, and then waited, expecting

that Erich would speak; but he only asked the boy to leave him alone. He was unspeakably weary. The thought lay upon his soul like a heavy burden, that he who gives himself up to labor—above all, he who takes upon himself the care of a true soul, which he is to instruct, hold, and lead—has no longer a life of his own, must not be weary, must not say, "Now leave me to myself:" he must be ever ready, ever expecting, ever living for another.

Roland was sorry when he saw the tired face of Erich, for the boy could not suspect that Erich was in the highest degree dissatisfied with himself. It was not that exhaustion which would naturally come after his long and continued conversation, which would easily lead to a certain barrenness in the soul; it was simply regret that he had allowed himself to enter upon such vast duties. And what was his object? To educate a single child.

But Erich's chief trouble was that he was obliged to acknowledge to himself that he was as yet unprepared: he ought himself to become more wise, before undertaking to instruct another. Absorbed in this misconception of his own position, he hardly heard the boy's various remarks about the singular beauty of the dogs, and how he kept questioning him, and looking anxiously in his face.

Then a servant came, and told them that the carriages were ready for their ride.

Erich was shocked. What sort of a life was this? To wander in the garden, to take a ride, to go on an excursion, to eat, then go out again and enjoy one's self—how could he preserve and sustain his inner life thus? How would it be possible, amid such surroundings, to educate a young soul rightly, and steadily develop it to the fulness of its powers?

Pride arose in Erich. Not for such a life had he worked so long, wearied himself with earnest and strenuous self-abnegation, for the sake of now filling out the leisure hours between riding and banqueting. This mode of life seemed impossible to him: he wished one of which he should be master, and to which he could give the color of his mind.

He went into the courtyard with Roland, and asked to be excused from accompanying the party in their ride, as he felt the need of a few hours' solitude.

Very various were the glances interchanged at this disclosure. Herr Sonnenkamp said hastily that he never attempted to compel his guests to do what they did not wish. Prancken and Miss Perini exchanged quick glances, in which seemed to lie a malicious joy, that Erich, through his self-will, which amounted to total absence of tact, should thus expose himself.

Roland said that he wished to remain at home with Erich, but Prancken said in a triumphant tone:

"Herr Dournay wishes to be alone, and if you remain with him, dear Roland, he cannot be alone."

He spoke the word "Herr" in a peculiarly snarling tone.

The second carriage was now taken away. Miss Perini, Prancken, and Roland got in, and Sonnenkamp seated himself on the box. To drive four-in-hand was a pleasure to him. Some people considered his four-in-hand turnout as sheer ostentation, but it was not—he took a particular delight in it.

Frau Ceres remained at home, as she had already exerted herself sufficiently to satisfy all social claims for that day.

Erich saw the party set out, and then went to his own chamber.

He sat there alone. No noise distracted him. He was so very tired,—for in accommodating himself to quite new circumstances, it had been a day of such exertion, and such unusual expenditure of strength, that it seemed impossible so much could be crowded into so short a time.

What had Erich not undergone on that day? His being with Clodwig, examining Roman antiquities, seemed to him an occurrence of years long past. In that day, he had been obliged to revolutionize and expand his whole existence. He had for the first time eaten the bread of servitude, and the feeling half of friendship, half of ingratitude: the enigmatical in Sonnenkamp, in Roland, in Miss Perini, and in Madam Ceres. When he thought back to home—to his mother, it seemed to lie far away, like a dream of long ago.

A longing for home came upon him, but he banished it. That must not be! The habits of his soldier-life aided him. This was his post—to look at all around him watchfully, and not become wearied!

"Not to become wearied!" he said aloud, and the consciousness of the strength of his youth came upon him. He felt that by the morrow he would be fully prepared for all that now seemed to him so full of mystery. And *one* feeling above all strengthened his soul, and set his heart free. He had remained faithful to the truth, and so would he always remain. Truth is the basis of that mother earth, on which the struggling spirit cannot be conquered and overthrown.

In the distance, at the railway-station, he heard the sound of a locomotive, which was now still. It rumbled, and blustered, and snorted like a horror of fable-land, and Erich thought: "This machine has to-day drawn its heavy train up and down; hundreds of human lives have committed themselves to it for a while; and now it has gone to rest, and can free itself from the pressure of its steam." He smiled to himself as he thought that he himself was almost such an engine, which had at last taken a moment to cool itself, to be ready on the morrow to be heated again.

Suddenly he was aroused from his dream—he had not known that he had been asleep.

A servant stood before him, and said that Frau Ceres wished to speak with him.

CHAPTER IX.

TWILIGHT MYSTERIES.

THE sun had set, but as Erich followed the servant, and looked from the corridors into the distance, a glowing exhalation lay upon the valley, and river, and mountain.

He was led through several apartments. In the last, which was lighted by a lamp of stained glass, he heard a voice say:

"Thank you. Be seated."

He saw Frau Ceres lying on a divan; a large armchair was before her. He seated himself.

"I remain at home out of compliment to you," began Frau Ceres. She had a feeble, anxious voice. Speaking was evidently difficult for her.

Erich did not know what to answer. Suddenly she raised herself and said:

"Do you know my daughter?"

"No."

"Were you not at the island-convent?"

"Yes; I had a message from my mother to the Lady Superior—nothing further."

"I believe you. I am not the cause of her becoming a nun—no, not I. Don't you believe me?" And laying herself back on the cushions, Frau Ceres continued:

"Don't stay with us, Captain—I warn you. I have learned nothing at all—he wouldn't let me; but don't you stay here, if you can get any other situation in the world. What did you want to come into this house for?"

"Because I believe—I did believe it an hour ago—that I could be a good teacher for your son."

And then Erich spoke out the whole despondency which he felt so deeply, now that he perceived that he was not competent to be the teacher of another man; and yet he dared to add, that no one else was fitted for such a position better than he, but perhaps another would more willingly undertake it. From the deepest recesses of his soul, he brought forth his newly-awakened longing for solitude, and lamented that men make for themselves an ideal of life and action, which is immediately shattered by reality. But this appeared to him an unsubdued selfishness, for which, not the world, but his own thinking, was to blame.

"I'm not learned—I don't understand you," answered Fiau Ceres. "But you speak beautifully—you have such good words, that I would like to listen always, even when I don't understand what you say. But you won't tell him that I sent for you?"

Him? Whom? Erich would have liked to ask. But she raised herself hastily and said:

"He can be horrid; he's a dangerous man—no one knows it—no one would think it. He's a dangerous man! Do you like me though?"

Erich shuddered. What could she mean?

"Oh, I don't know what I'm saying," continued Frau Ceres. "He's right—I'm only half-witted. What did I send for you for? Yes, now I know. Tell me about your mother. Is she indeed such a learned and distinguished lady? I was once a distinguished lady too—yes, I was too."

Erich shuddered again. Was this half sleepy, half wild creature really insane, and only restrained in society by the greatest circumspection.

That morning he had intended to write to his mother, and tell her into what a fairy-land he had come. The fairy-land was yet more wonderful than he had thought it.

With the greatest precision, as far as a son could, he described the character of his mother—how she was always happy because always thinking of the happiness of others. He told of the death of his father and his brother, and the greatness of soul with which she had borne all this.

Frau Ceres sobbed, and then said suddenly:

"I thank you—I thank you!"

She gave Erich her delicate white hand, and cried:

"I thank you! With all his money he has not been able to make me believe that I could cry again. Oh, how good it is! Stay with us—stay with Roland. He cannot cry. Don't tell him I wish I had a mother! Stay with us; I will never forget what you have done for me. I thank you! Now go, go, before he comes back. Go! Good-night!"

When Erich was again in his room, all that he had passed through seemed like a dream. The mysterious, secret life with which, at Wolfsgarten, he had seen the house of Sonnenkamp invested, returned to him with new force. Here were wonderful riddles.

Roland came to him fresh and joyful. The brief separation had given both a new and pleasant feeling at meeting again. They were as much rejoiced as if they had not seen each other for years.

Roland asked Erich to tell him about the Huguenots. They had evidently been talking about them during the ride,

Erich declined. It was not necessary, at least not at present, that Roland should learn the barbarity of men who had tortured each other for conscience' sake.

Roland told Erich that Herr von Prancken was going to the convent the next day, to see Manna.

Erich was in doubt as to what he should do. If he should tell the boy not to impart to him what he had heard, he would be likely to destroy the boy's wish to be confiding with him; and yet it was not right to allow him to speak of things which were evidently not intended for him to hear. He determined to ask Sonnenkamp to say nothing in Roland's presence which he did not wish him to know.

Again Erich was called to tea; but Frau Ceres did not appear.

Erich was anxious that evening; the feeling of full confidence had been taken from him. Should he tell Sonnenkamp that his wife had summoned him? But then he would be obliged to tell what she had said to him in broken sentences. It was nothing but a warning—a conversation so inarticulate that there was no connection in it.

Roland was always looking inquiringly at Erich. The boy felt that his friend was experiencing a trouble which he would gladly comfort, and so pity was added to Erich's love for him. There was evidently a sad domestic trouble into which the boy had not been brought, and it was fortunate for him that his young life was left to enjoy itself.

Erich kept thinking of his experience in the House of Correction. The most hardened criminals always appeared with the most brazen faces, and it was their greatest pride that they had been able so long to conceal from the world what they had done; while those who were not so obdurate, considered it a good thing for them to meet with immediate punishment, for the fear of discovery and the effort to conceal their crimes were worse than imprisonment.

Erich too had now a secret. Should he let the matter pass, at the risk of being betrayed by a servant, and himself appearing treacherous?

Just as he was about to go to bed, Roland came and asked him if he had nothing to tell him.

He said he had not, and the boy appeared grieved as he bade him good-night.

CHAPTER X.

YOUNG DAY AND DARK QUESTIONS.

THE morning dew glistened on grass, flower, and shrub, and the birds sang merrily, as Erich wandered through the park. Marks of regularity, industry, and care were everywhere.

On the shore, Erich heard the conversation of two women, who were unloading a boat loaded with garden-earth.

"God be praised," said one of them, "for sending this man to us. No one in this neighborhood, who is willing to work, need complain of hard times!"

"Yes," answered the other, "and yet the men are wicked enough to say I don't know what bad things about him."

"What are they, then?"

"They say he was a tailor!"

Erich could hardly keep from laughing aloud. But a third woman said, in a somewhat suppressed voice:

"Puh! a tailor! He was a pirate, and stole a ship full of gold from the Sultan in Africa."

"Suppose he was," said the other. "The man-eaters have gold enough left; and besides, they're heathen, and Herr Sonnenkamp does heaps of good with the money."

Erich was forced to smile at these singular stories and revelations; and yet he felt sorrowful, as he thought how great wealth always occasions bad reports.

He went along. As he looked from an elevation, and saw how beautifully in keeping with the park and garden the house and surroundings were, he was filled with delight. There were no trees near the principal building, except dark laurels, lindens, elms, and maples, which brought into full relief the bright architecture of the house, which was in the style of the Renaissance. Rows of laurels led to the dwelling, which seemed not to have been built into the scenery, but itself to have grown with it. The stone colonnades, the turf, the trees, the grading, all conducted to the house—all was in keeping. The verandahs seemed to be only supports of swinging plants. The whole was a masterpiece of rural architecture—a poem of nature, ruled by the laws of art; and at the same time, that which man had wrought appeared as fresh and bright as if it had just come from the workman's hands; and so well kept and satisfying, that it was evidently owned by a wealthy and luxurious man.

Erich did not long remain alone, for Joseph the valet soon joined him, and offered with a certain subdued humility to tell him, as a countryman of his, everything in regard to the house.

As Erich was silent, Joseph repeated that he had been billiard-marker at the University, as Heinrich XXXII, for all the billiard-markers had to take the name of Heinrich. Then he had become a waiter at the Bernhof at Berne, where Sonnenkamp, who had remained there nearly two summers, occupying the first floor—the best rooms in the world, Joseph said—had become acquainted with him, and had engaged his services. Joseph said, not without humor, that the servants in the house constituted a sort of menagerie, where specimens of the animals of all countries were gathered. It was like a poultry-yard where there are all sorts of fowls: and even the peacock was not lacking, which screamed so horribly and looked so fine; for Herr Sonnenkamp had travelled through all the world, gathering specimens. The coachman was an Englishman, the groom a Pole, the cook a Frenchman, the lady's-maid a thorough Bohemian, Miss Perini, an Italian-French woman from Nice. The master was very strict, and would not allow the gardeners to smoke in the garden. nor the grooms to whistle in the stable, for the horses were accustomed to their master's whistle, and must not be confused. Herr Sonnenkamp did not wish his servants to appear as such, or to wear anything that would indicate their position; and it was only a short time before, that he had so far yielded to the wishes of his wife, as to allow a few of them to assume livery. They were not allowed to talk much, and Herr Sonnenkamp had certain words which he addressed to them, and they had regular terms in which to answer; but they were all well kept.

In closing, Joseph said with some self-importance that he had already spread the fame of Erich's parents in the servants' hall, for "it was well to have them know where one comes from and so one will get more respect from them. In reality, Madame Perini ruled the house. She was unmarried; but the mistress always called her 'madame.'"

"The Krischer is right," added Joseph, "Miss Perini is a woman of seven-cat-power, and a marten might be thrown in."

Erich wished to stop these revelations, but Joseph begged him to let him talk it out, and excuse everything in an old college-acquaintance. He said that Prancken was to marry the daughter of the house.

"O, she's beautiful!—And yet not exactly beautiful, but a dear good girl! She used to be so strong and healthy! No horse was too wild, no storm on the Rhine too awful for her, and she hunted like a poacher. But now she's sad—always sad—dreadfully sad!"

Erich was glad to see the talkative young fellow take out his watch and say:

"The master will get up in a minute, and I must be with him. I tell you, he's always on time!"

Erich thought of all that he had heard of the daughter, and it seemed to him like fragmentary sounds, which, nevertheless, all belonged to the same melody. "Was not this the girl whom he had seen with the wings on, the day before yesterday, at the convent?" He paused involuntarily, and stared at a hedge, while a complete picture of life arose before him. Here was a child, sent to a convent, far from the world and intercourse with men, and then taken out and told: "You are Baroness von Prancken!" and she is happy with her handsome and agreeable husband; and all the glories of the world are hers through him. It is as if he had created the universe for her, and it may well be that she will not know what her husband is: yes, it will be well for her if she never knows.

He shook his head. What was the little convent-blossom to him?

Erich no longer saw the beauty of the garden. With hasty step—his eyes bent upon the ground—he wandered through the park, and as he emerged from the dense trees and came to the pond, Herr Sonnenkamp met him. He looked singular in his short, gray plush jacket trimmed with lace, but he was glad to find Erich already awake, and offered to conduct him through the grounds.

He called particular attention to a large spot of prairie-grass, which had really been brought from the prairies. He smiled as Erich attempted to draw a picture of how the buffaloes had thundered over it; and he made a motion with his arm, as he told Erich how he had caught many a one with a lasso.

Then he conducted Erich to a hill, beautifully girt with plane-trees; which, he said, was the centre of the place. He said that he took especial pride in these beautiful and flourishing trees, and added that, in this shadowless vine-land, one should be particularly thoughtful of shady places, for hot summer-days.

"See! I have increased the beauty of my grounds by working land that does not belong to me. Up there on that height there is a group of trees which I have procured and arranged, and I have laid out new roads, and made new plantings, in order to have a beautiful prospect. I did not build my house according to the views of others, but for myself to look at. That peasant-house up there is built after my plans, and I have naturally been obliged to contribute toward it. That shrubbery is to hide the glaring quarry. I built that delicate church-tower, yonder in the village. I got quite a notoriety for piety for that—almost had incense burned for me; but now I can confess to you, that the simple reason why I did it, was because I wanted a fine prospect. I must reconstruct the whole region, and that's tedious work; and there's where the selfishness of man can be seen. Look up there! A basket-maker is now building a house with a horrible red-tile roof. It offends my eye continually, and yet I can't get at the fellow. He wants to sell me the house at a high price; but what shall I do with it? He may just keep it, and accommodate himself to my arrangements."

There was something violent in the manner in which Sonnenkamp spoke, and Erich thought of what Bella had said—that he was a conqueror. Such a man is always inclined to tyrannize, and wishes to arrange the world according to his own personal taste or wish. The villages, churches, mountains, and forests were only points in his landscape which he wished to place at a favorite angle.

Herr Sonnenkamp led his guest through the park, and explained how he had given it a feeling of motion, by arranging hills and valleys; but had, however, only been obliged to set off some of his material, and bring it out so as to be effective. He called attention to the careful disposition of light and shade; and told how he had sometimes planted a group—a little clump of trees of the same sort which he had then permitted to combine with others, not abruptly and with violent contrasts, but gradually, as Nature herself works, into a group of various sorts of trees.

Sonnenkamp smiled very obligingly, as Erich, in indication that he understood him, answered that a park ought to appear like civilized nature; and the more one understands how to conceal man's hand, and man's intelligence, and let everything appear as a *naïveté*, so much the purer art appeared.

A little brook, which came down the mountain-side and flowed into the river, had been so skilfully changed, that it disappeared at intervals, and strangely appeared again, saying, by its murmur, "I am here."

They went on, and Erich hardly saw the beautiful and comfortable benches; and hardly heard Sonnenkamp say that he placed them not only in the open paths, but behind the bushes, so that here the solitude of the woods could be found ready-made.

Under a beautiful maple were a table and two seats, facing each other. Sonnenkamp explained that this was "the school," for Roland occasionally received his instruction here. Erich answered that he would never instruct in the open air. What one learns while walking is natural; but real and solid instruction, which requires the close application of the mind, requires the closed room, from which not even the voice can escape.

Sonnenkamp might now have taken the opportunity of telling Erich what his resolution was, in regard to what was of chief interest to him, but he was silent. Like an artist, rejoiced at the appreciation of an intelligent observer of a work of art, who lays before him hidden beauties, which he of himself would not have detected, so Sonnenkamp took delight in seeing Erich enjoy so understandingly and gratefully his manifold and novel arrangements of trees and shrubbery.

They stood for a long time, near a group where the dark cedar rose near the hardy pine, and the light morning wind played amid the foliage of tacamahac, and made the white leaves dance like the waves of a clear lake suspended in mid air.

A little pond with a fountain, and a bower of roses near it on a knoll, had been, as Sonnenkamp said, made to resemble a dream which Frau Ceres had had; and standing still, he said:

"That was the time when we were yet very happy in our retreat here, and everything was equable—healthy."

Erich stopped. Should he tell Herr Sonnenkamp of his singular adventure of the day before? Sonnenkamp stopped too, and said with a singular puffing sound, as if he were blowing a fire:

"My wife often has singular whims, but if one doesn't contradict her she forgets what she wanted."

He seemed to think suddenly that it was not necessary to say that, and with a haste unusual to him said:

"Now come with me, and I'll show you all my vanity. But one more question. You are a philosopher—is it not horrible to know, that we must die and leave all this, and it will blossom on, and he who planted it and struggled for the means of doing so, will not be there—will be moldering to dust?"

"I would not have believed that you would entertain such thoughts."

"You're right in answering me so. One should not ask, for no one knows an answer," said Sonnenkamp sharply and bitterly. "But the other thing. I wish that Roland should have the right understanding of this work, and extend it yet farther, for such a garden as this is not like a piece of sculpture; and it is still less like an artist's picture. It grows, and must be made anew. And why should it not be given to us to leave with confidence to our successors that which we toiled for and achieved, without any fear that strangers will some day call it all their own, and destroy it?"

"Notwithstanding you believe that I have no answer to your first question," answered Erich, "I must tell you, that I don't appreciate your second at all."

"Well, well, we'll talk further about it, or else not talk about it at all," said Sonnenkamp. "But now come, I'll show you all my vanity."

CHAPTER XI.

SONNENKAMP'S PRIDE.

EMERGING from the dense, shady park, the margin of which was planted with beautiful firs, they entered a wonderful combination of fruit-trees, which made the plane of several acres through which they were dispersed look like a scene of enchantment. The beds were enclosed with dwarf apple and pear trees as small as the taxus-bush. The bodies of the trees were supported hardly two feet from the earth, and the branches so laid out on wires, that often on each side limbs thirty feet long were bound fast. Everything was in blossom, and in such regular order that the arranging and constraining will of man was everywhere visible, and nature had been made a bold work of art, or had been dwarfed by over-refinement.

Beautifully arranged, sometimes in circles, sometimes in lines, the trees stood in all conceivable geometrical forms. Here was one with only four branches, which by regulated spaces indicated the four points of the compass. By the wall were trees with two limbs in the form of two-armed candlesticks: others had their limbs and twigs distorted so as to represent columns of basalt. Everything was regulated according to art, but yet all was thriving.

Erich listened attentively when Sonnenkamp informed him that the limbs must be pruned, in order to prevent the sap from forming wood in the stock and branches. All must be subservient to the fruit.

"Do you feel sympathy with these limbs?" asked Sonnenkamp.

"Not exactly that, but the natural form of the old and well-known fruit-trees—"

"Yes, yes," said Sonnenkamp, interrupting him; "men are ephemerals of prejudice. Does anybody find anything not beautiful, anything violent, in tapping the vine-stock three times every summer? Nobody! No one wants beauty in a vine, but beautiful fruit; and so, too, with a fruit-tree. As soon as men began to use their eyes, the way was pointed out. I am only a follower. The ornamental tree ought to be an ornamental tree, the fruit-tree a fruit-tree, and so throughout. This apple-tree must only have so many branches, and those in such a shape that it shall bear fruit as large as possible. I don't want wood from a fruit-tree, but fruit."

"But Nature—"

"Nature! Nature!" sneered Sonnenkamp. "Nine-tenths of what is called Nature is nothing but training and self-made grotesqueness. The spirit of Nature and the spirit of the people are two idols that you philosophers have made for yourselves. There is no Nature and there is no People; and even if there were both, neither of them would have a spirit."

Erich was surprised to hear Sonnenkamp speak so violently, as if to challenge contradiction; and he was yet more astonished when Sonnenkamp continued:

"The true man-teacher would be he who could teach men as I do trees—pay attention simply to the object, having nothing superfluous, and no loitering. That which is called Nature is a fable. There is no Nature; at least, only a very small one. With us men, all is custom, training, and tradition. There is no Nature!"

"That's new to me," Erich at last found words to say. "Gentlemen who follow tradition call us men of science atheists; but I have never yet seen or heard of a man who denies the existence of Nature. You are joking."

"Yes, I am joking," said Sonnenkamp bitterly; and Erich, who felt quite perplexed, said in a low tone:

"It might, perhaps, be said that those who derive the laws of our life from revelation deny Nature; or rather, that they do not deny, but reject her."

"I'm no scholar; and above all things, I'm no theologian," Sonnenkamp suddenly interrupted him. "All is Fate. Caterpillars injure the trees. There stands one entirely uninjured beside another that has been destroyed by them. Why? We don't know. All is Fate. Look here at these trees. I have cast a glance at the economy of what is called Nature. There must be a thousand germs produced, for one that is matured; and it is not otherwise in human life."

"I understand," said Erich. "Everything living has an aristocratic superiority over everything dead: the blossom which becomes fruit is rich, the other is poor. Do I understand you rightly?"

"Partly," answered Sonnenkamp wearily. "I wished to tell you, that I no longer seek for, because I no longer believe that I can find, the man who could so educate my son that he would go straight to that for which he is fitted by nature."

They walked again silently through the wondrously beautiful garden, in which the bees were humming, and Erich thought that perhaps these might be the bees of Jäger Claus.

Wonderful world, in which all things are so singularly adapted to each other!

The sky was so blue, the buds so fragrant! And yet Erich seemed to himself a prisoner full of fear. He stared at a tablet which rose over the orchard-wall, and read on it:

"Notice!—There are spring-guns and man-traps in this orchard."

He looked around at Sonnenkamp, who said, smiling:

"Your look asks me if that sign tells the truth. It does. People don't believe any more that one dares do that. Always keep in the path, near me."

Sonnenkamp seemed to feast on Erich's surprise and uneasiness. And yet he had lied, for there was not a spring-gun nor a man-trap in the whole garden.

Here by the wall there were stars, circles, and squares made of branches, and Sonnenkamp laid his hand on Erich's shoulder, as Erich remarked that only men possessed number and geometrical form. Geometrical form was evidently the basis of all appearances, which never occur as mere lines, but which man infers his knowledge of from lines. This was the mysterious feature of the doctrine of Pythagoras.

"I have long suspected," laughed Sonnenkamp, "that I was a Pythagorean. I thank you for calling me so. We ought to christen our new horticultural style the Pythagorean."

There was mockery in this expression; and yet Sonnenkamp was evidently gratified.

They had arrived at what was called "Nice," a colonnade in the Pompeian style, which went far into the second terrace of the garden.

"Now I will show you my house," said Sonnenkamp, as, pushing against a little door which opened into a subterranean passage, he conducted his guest to the dwelling.

CHAPTER XII.

A GLIMPSE OF HOUSE AND HEART.

THE servants and maids in the under-ground rooms started as Sonnenkamp and Erich entered. Sonnenkamp did not look at them, but said in English to Erich:

"The principal things which a retired man like me need care about, are the kitchen and the stable."

He showed him the kitchen. There were dozens of different fireplaces, for different purposes. Every sort of meat, every vegetable, every dish had special pots and pans;—fire sidewise, and fire open. The whole philosophy of preparing the sap and juices was here translated into cookery. Erich was pleased with it, as a work of art.

While they were in the under-ground rooms, Sonnenkamp showed Erich, laying particular stress on the fact, that every fireplace, every stove in the house, had its own chimney. He considered this of importance, for he had thus become independent of the direction of the wind. The architect had opposed it, and it had cost a great deal of thought and trouble to arrange the flues; but new advantages had resulted from it.

Then Sonnenkamp showed him the greatest part of the house, through which electric wires attached to the bells ran.

There were costly coverings on the stairs, rich candelabra everywhere, and broad beds in the sleeping-apartments.

All was arranged with splendor and taste; indeed, with massive splendor and discriminating taste. Gold, marble, and silk produced an artistic, and by no means ostentatious effect. Nothing was overloaded, or allowed to obstruct comfort. The pieces of furniture did not stand around like things seeking their places, but all was adjusted to the building, and was solid and home-like; and yet the whole house had an appearance of being uninhabited. It seemed as though the furniture was waiting for the people who would really use it, and live there, not merely go up and down and survey it.

The large, heavy silk curtains were in keeping with the upholstery. The large clocks in all the rooms were going, and little works of art were prettily arranged on mantelpiece and stand. But, on going further, one could easily see that this arrangement showed no particular turn of mind of the possessor. It was only that sort of taste which any upholsterer can produce; and, above all, there was no heirloom. Erich could not free himself from the feeling that the house was only inhabited by lodgers; and it seemed to him, all the time, as though Roland was walking behind him, and he was obliged to fancy himself in the position of the boy, who knew already that at some time all this would be his.

Here Sonnenkamp explained that he considered it ridiculous for men to have furniture which was mediæval, or in imitation of mediæval, and only of use for ornament, but not at all for comfort. When Erich remarked that Goethe was of the same opinion, Sonnenkamp answered:

"That's very pleasant. I think Goethe understood life."

Sonnenkamp said this in a very condescending tone, which plainly indicated his belief that anybody must feel delighted to have his merits recognized by Herr Sonnenkamp.

A recess with four sides had been added to the north side of the house, next to the great red-damask saloon, and in the middle of it stood a beautiful table of malachite, surrounded by seats. Four large windows—or rather panes of glass, as high as a man—gave an unimpeded view; and four representations of the hours of the day, worked in marble by Rietschel, were inserted in the wall at half the height of the windows. The ceiling was stuccoed, and a silver lamp seemed not to hang, but to be flying from it: the lamp was a flying cupid, carrying in his hand a torch, which, as Sonnenkamp explained, was lit like a gas-jet.

"It is only here," said he smiling, "that I have works of art; indeed (I lie neither to myself nor others), I have no appreciation of fine art. You, as the son of a professor of æsthetics, find this quite barbarous, don't you?"

"By no means; only honest, and I believe you have a right to it."

"Honesty is everybody's duty, not merely his right."

"Pardon me if I have expressed myself badly. I mean that the artist-world is jealous too. A man who has such a taste for landscape-gardening, may be satisfied with that, and can afford to do without expressing his spirit in other arts."

Sonnenkamp smiled. "This man knows how to get out of every scrape."

He led his guest into the music-hall. This was quite devoid of gold and velvet, and had simply stucco on the ceiling, and sea-green tapestry on the walls. In the niches, made by two little chimneys, stood swelling brown damask lounges and sofas. This saloon always seemed to be waiting for company to occupy it.

Sonnenkamp smiled, as Erich said that it pleased him to see the music-hall unornamented. Its whiteness gave one a feeling of sunniness, as though a sun hung on the walls; and as the eye was attracted to no particular object, one could listen more attentively. There was no competition between the senses.

Sonnenkamp was continually becoming livelier, and to Erich's question, Who in the family was musical? he answered:

"This room was arranged for my daughter."

"Singular," said Erich; "down in the garden the ruined chair is waiting for her, and here, the music-room."

Sonnenkamp, according to his habit, took his under-lip between his fore-finger and thumb, and seemed to be thinking of something, and deliberating whether he should act upon it.

"Since we are speaking of my daughter, I will show you where she lives," said he suddenly, opening a side-door.

They entered a little chamber. The venetian blinds were down, but Sonnenkamp quickly raised them. The view extended over trees and vineyards far away to the Upper Rhine. The room was without ornament, but all was exquisitely refined. A row of photographs, bound in a circle by a blue ribbon, hung on the wall, and in the centre was a large picture of the Pope. A white bed, with the curtains drawn back, showed a beautifully cut ivory crucifix on the wall, under which hung a colored picture in a frame,—a sort of diploma for Hermanna with the name Manna Sonnenkamp on it, as a sign that she had been received into the Society of Good Children.

A writing-table, a little book-stand, and delicate chairs, all showed that this was the dwelling of a girl who lived quietly in her own thoughts, and in pious reflections. There seemed to hover in the air of the chamber a soul-moving breath of prayer. One looked around involuntarily, as though expecting her to enter with that great child-glance; and then one cast down his eyes, feeling that he was in her sanctuary.

Erich looked at a large semicircular marble mantelpiece surrounded with living ivy; and in the recess stood flowers and leaves. There were no flower-pots to be seen, for they were skilfully concealed: all was a verdant, blooming mystery.

"Doesn't this strike you pleasantly?" said Sonnenkamp. "Yes, my daughter always keeps her mantelpiece covered with flowers during the summer; and I believe that Miss Perini keeps it so while she is gone, in remembrance of her."

Erich looked about him yet more closely. He thought he would be able to obtain an idea of the character of the girl who kept her mantel covered with flowers in the summer. Sonnenkamp laid his hand heavily on his shoulder and said:

"Have you candor enough? You did not come here for the sake of my son, but my daughter?"

"I don't understand you," answered Erich.

"Weren't you in the convent? Didn't you see my daughter?"

"Yes, what you say is true. But I did not dream of you, your daughter, or your son then."

"I believe you. But don't you think that perhaps, from being in my house, you might win my daughter's affection?"

"I thank you for this straight-forwardness, and will answer you with equal candor," said Erich. "I should consider it a misfortune to fall in love with your daughter."

"With my daughter! Why?"

"I should consider it a misfortune to love a girl of such great wealth, quite irrespective of her Romanistic views. I would never take so rich a woman for my wife, even though my heart should break. I beg you now—it will be utterly impossible for me as time goes on to avoid such a suspicion—I beg you now not to give me a position in your house. It is better to be your guest for this short time; and I thank you for your great kindness."

"Young man, stay! I believe and trust you. I thank you for having taught me again to trust and believe a man. You will stay! Give me your hand—you will stay! We will let it all rest. Besides, my daughter—and now I give you the best evidence of my faith in you—is as good as the bride of Baron von Prancken. Now come to my work-room."

They entered it. Here everything was arranged with ex

traordinary commodiousness. For every mood, for every season, for solitude and companionship, here were comfortable chairs and sofas with tables before them, so that the one apartment seemed to include several. The room was large, and yet had an air of retirement, and from the south side commanded a view of the landscape, where symmetrical beeches and plane-trees hid the vine-hills which often appeared bleak and bare, so that the glance fell upon the upper part of the forest-covered heights. In the midst, directly in front of the balcony, the ruined castle was to be seen, which, as Erich had heard, was owned by Herr Sonnenkamp, who was restoring it under the immediate supervision of the Major.

There was but one picture in the room—a life-size portrait of Roland, taken when he was seven years old. The boy was represented sitting on a fallen antique pillar, his hand resting on the head of a beautiful Newfoundland dog, and gazing off into the distance.

A large case, filled with armor of all sorts, also stood in the room.

While Erich was looking about him, Sonnenkamp shoved back two doors set in the wall, and led him into what he called his library. But there were no books to be seen, nothing but large boxes, vessels of clay and porcelain, and everything that a well-ordered apothecary-shop contains; and Sonnenkamp explained that these contained seeds from all quarters of the globe. From this seed-room a special flight of steps led to the garden; and the bannisters were quite overgrown with tendrils of the Chinese creeper, which clustered about them with their blue butterfly-leaves. Sonnenkamp led his guest back to his work-room, and here told how it had formerly been his wish to prepare Roland for the great employment which he had now relinquished. He spoke of business. Erich saw with astonishment the comprehensive views which Sonnenkamp took of the traffic of the world. For him there was no isolated activity, no separate production; one part of the world existed only by means of the others: the whole earth was to him a great market-place. He paid attention to iron, wool, tobacco, and corn at the same time in Sweden, Scotland, the East Indies, and Havana, and regarded each in its connections with the other.

Sonnenkamp seemed to wish to make Erich atone for having had so much to say to him before; and Erich was filled with surprise at the far-sightedness of this man, who preserved at the same time well-settled conclusions and perfect confidence in his own views, the surprising fulness of which appeared in every remark. He had seen the world with the penetrating eyes of Englishmen and Americans, who, notwithstanding they see so much, consume fewer spectacles than any other nations on the globe. He grasped the main points, letting minor ones go, and was unhampered by their reflex action. There was a remarkable realism in his manner of describing what he had seen in foreign lands, as well as that which he had transplanted hither.

Sonnenkamp was well aware of the impression he was making on Erich, and nodded, smiling, as Erich said how fine a thing it was, not only to possess, but to have and be.

"Think well," said Sonnenkamp, "over what you would, and what I ought to make of Roland. You have probably seen enough to know," added he with a triumphant glance, "that in case you undertake the instruction of my son, you will not alter me or my house."

This last expression nearly obliterated the impression that Sonnenkamp had made on Erich. All that he had said and done was for a purpose.

A servant came, and said that Herr von Prancken wished to take leave of Herr Sonnenkamp.

CHAPTER XIII.

SATAN'S TRAINING.

PRANCKEN'S horse stood saddled in the courtyard, and Prancken himself walked up and down, switching his riding-whip. With charming ease and vivacity he ran up to Sonnenkamp, and said that he must take leave of him. There existed a comical politeness between the two; and as Sonnenkamp said that Prancken was always doing something to surprise one, and never told his intention of going away till the minute of departure, Prancken answered, with hypocritical modesty, that he was convinced that by doing so he was in consonance with his friend Sonnenkamp, for there was nothing more repulsive, or more calculated to make life dull and insipid, than everlasting making believe, and denying, and cooking up. He *shot* the hares, and left the preparation of them to artists in cookery.

Prancken said this in his usual rattling tone, at the same time pulling the ends of his blonde moustache. He took a very cool leave of Erich, and said that he hoped to find him still there, after he should return from his short journey.

"If you shall have gone before I return, will you have the goodness to remember me to Madam—;" he paused, and then said, "to your mother."

He had taken off his glove to shake hands with Sonnenkamp; but now he drew it on again, and put out his hand to Erich.

This was evidently not an oversight. Erich was almost pleased by this coolness, for a part of his gratitude was taken away by it: the more Prancken acted as a stranger toward him, the more peaceable and independent their intercourse would be.

Prancken drew Sonnenkamp aside, and told him, that although he had cordially recommended the young scholar to him—speaking the phrase "young scholar" with marked coldness—yet he advised him not to decide before he was fully convinced, by personal observation, that he was fitted for the place.

"Herr Baron," returned Sonnenkamp, "I am a merchant,"—he paused to watch the effect of this—"and I also know the value of references; how one often cannot avoid giving them. I tell you, you are free from all responsibility; and as concerns my own observation . . . Herr Baron, I am a merchant;" again another watchful pause; "the young man is the seller, and a seller must explain, and let himself be known, more than the buyer; and it is just so here, where the seller is his own goods."

Prancken smiled, and called this most skilful diplomacy. He approached his horse, sprang lightly into the saddle, and galloped away. Sonnenkamp called after him, to tell him to see whether the magnolia was thriving in the convent court-yard. Nodding backward, to show that he had understood, he rode on.

"An amiable, charming cavalier! Always fresh and bold," said Sonnenkamp, and entered upon a prolix account of the steady, easy-going character of Prancken.

Erich was silent. In the circle into which he had come, there seemed to reign a continual desire to put people "to rights," and to criticise them. He knew Prancken, and he knew that rollicking way of his, which always makes one appear so very lively, even enthusiastic, if that word may be used in regard to a man who is forever pettishly sarcastic. But this rollicking manner has a lie at bottom, for it is impossible to be always so strained; it is brought about by an urgent desire to appear energetic, and in this continual effort the soul is, consciously or unconsciously, a liar.

Erich listened quietly to the long story, till Sonnenkamp asked him if he did not think that only a man who, from his childhood up, had been conscious of his own noble rank, could play freely in the game of life: then he answered, that no beauty in life was shut out from the common man.

Sonnenkamp nodded his appreciation. His horse had been brought. He mounted, and rode away.

Erich looked for Roland, and found him with his dogs. The boy wanted him to select one of the puppies immediately.

"And just think," he added; "one of the women just told

me that Grubworm has been hurt by Satan. Serves the silly man right. What does he want to undertake a thing for, when he doesn't know how?"

Erich was motionless. Was it possible that a young heart could be so hardened? He told Roland how cruel it was to look at a man as he looked at a puppy, and not to care about him after playing with him. His whole heart was full as he spoke. Roland dropped his eyes.

"Why don't you answer me?" asked Erich.

"I didn't know you'd be all the time lecturing me, like the others!"

Attracted by the boy's beauty and fearlessness, Erich had determined to become his companion, but now he was, for an instant, repelled from his resolution, only to be drawn again more closely to it. He wished to redeem and soften this soul, hard by nature, or hardened by education.

Roland came quietly up to Erich, and, after a while, asked him to take a ride with him. They rode together to the village; but Roland could not be induced to call on the gardener, and Erich found the little man lying on his bed, moaning and groaning. When he entered the Krischer's house, he did not find Roland, for he had gone up the hill with Satan.

The Krischer greeted Erich with less humility than he had formerly used. He pulled off his cap, indeed, but only to put it on again immediately, and approached him in the confidential manner of folk of the Upper-Rhine, where they always seem to be about to clink glasses and make themselves at home.

"Captain," said he, "is the business settled?"

"No."

"May I tell you something?"

"If it is good—why not?"

"That's as you look at it. That man down there," and he pointed to the Villa with his thumb, "is buying up the whole Rhineland. But look there at that foxhound—"

"Halt!" said Erich, interrupting him. He then said, decisively, that the Krischer had no right to speak so to him, and about others.

Erich was aware that he had not acted with sufficient reserve, or the Krischer would not have approached him so confidentially, and he now, in self-defence, spoke more sharply than he would otherwise have done.

The Krischer smoked his Napoleon-pipe more industriously, and then said:

"Yes, yes; you know how to catch the man down yonder by the gorge. I ain't smart enough for you. You want to do away with being obliged to me. Well, I don't want your thanks, and I don't want any wages for what I did."

He muttered to himself, that "you might just as well throw anything away, as offer it to the rich." Erich was forced to change his tactics, for the Krischer was the only person who could compete with him for influence over Roland. The Krischer received his friendliness with good grace, but remained silent.

When Roland came back, Erich said nothing in regard to his going up the hill, and nothing about the little gardener. Roland should ask him, but the boy said nothing about it, and the two rode silently home again.

Erich immediately found occasion to speak with Herr Sonnenkamp, and said that he must now enter into a definite relationship with Roland.

"Do you, too, find Roland a fine boy?"

"He has much bravery, determination, and—I know that a father can listen to this only with pain, but after your searching questions of yesterday, I am convinced that you have impartiality enough—"

"Certainly, certainly; speak openly."

"I find a certain hard-heartedness, and, what is surprising in so young a boy, a want of feeling for man, simply as such—for pure humanity," said Erich, and related how Roland had conducted himself in regard to the little gardener.

A peculiar smile played on Sonnenkamp's features as he asked:

"And you believe that you can bring such a spoiled disposition to perfection?"

"I beg your pardon, but I was not speaking of a spoiled disposition; I would much rather say that Roland is now in a state of mental transition, and therefore his disposition cannot be judged; consequently, he is much more in need of watchfulness and careful training."

"And what do you think of Roland's talents?"

"I do not consider them at all out of the ordinary: he has a naturally good mind, learns easily; but the retention of what he learns, is very questionable as yet; and I have already noticed that he follows well at first, but suddenly, in the middle of a thought, stands still, and is unwilling to go further. I am not yet clear in regard to this characteristic of his mind. If it cannot be bettered, I fear that Roland will not be happy, because he takes no steady pleasure in anything, and does not feel the delight and duty of perseverance. But perhaps all this is too finely spun."

"No, no; you're right. I have no very great reliance on my son's character; he is always fickle. Anything which he ought to do, is tiresome and painful to him, if the result of it is not immediately forthcoming."

"That's the way with children."

"But such children never become strong men. That's the reason why I wish that Roland liked plants. Then he would find that there is something that cannot be neglected or forgotten for a moment."

"I'm glad," answered Erich, "that you have brought me to the deepest point of the discussion. In the first place, a rich man and his son, just like a prince and his son, are always surrounded by friends who minister to their recreation. I am sorry that I have become the comrade of Roland in his pleasures, for now the earnest work which I have to do will seem repulsive."

"Then you don't think that pleasure and earnestness are compatible?"

"I hope they are; but earnestness should always be a principle."

Erich became silent, and Sonnenkamp asked:

"You had a second point?"

"Certainly. The other consideration is this: as I have already intimated, Roland must obtain one settled point—a steady, intimate connection with the things of the outer world. He who has no memories of youth, no firm attachment to the past, is shut out from the true source of deep and pure feeling. Ask yourself, and you will find, as your return to Germany proves, that what your soul eats and drinks—what might be called the mother's-milk of the soul—is a deep and earnest love for the memories of youth."

Sonnenkamp started at these words, and Erich continued:

"Homelessness is blighting your boy's soul."

"Homelessness?" asked Sonnenkamp, astonished.

A spasm passed over his face, his athletic frame seemed trying to wither, and yet he brought himself to a certain forced mildness, and asked:

"Did I understand you correctly? Homelessness?"

"I mean so. The child's inner life needs to be made at home. Travelling is perhaps not injurious, but at best is indifferent. A child gets no correct impression of the landscape while on a journey; he is pleased with the locomotive at the station, the windmill on the hill. One steady object in the soul makes the soul steady. If I said that a man must have a goal, let me add that he must also have a fixed point of departure; and that is home. You told me, and I see it myself, that Roland takes no real pleasure in anything. Doesn't that come from the fact that he is homeless, a child of hotels, having no place of rest, and worse still, nothing which he can steadily contemplate, no pictures in the midst of which he has lived, and to which his imagination ever turns? He has, as he told me, played in the Colosseum at Rome, the Louvre in Paris, Hyde Park in London, and by the Lake of Geneva; and now especially his living in Europe, and yet being proudly conscious of his American birth—permit me to ask you, does not all this make an unrest in the soul which prevents all natural growth?"

"I see," said Sonnenkamp, leaning his head back. "You are an incarnate, or perhaps I ought to say an in-souled German, who run through the whole world of reality and of thought, always stroking yourself with the greatest self-satisfaction, and saying: 'Oh, I'm so sympathetic; none of the rest of you are half as much so.' Pah! I tell you that if I give my child anything valuable, I believe it will be that he shall have no sentimentality about what is called 'sweet home.' The whistle of the engine drives away all that snivelling homesickness. We are in fact citizens of the world, and it is the great, unprecedented result of Americanism, that no national restriction or provincialism shall belittle the soul. The love of home is an old-fashioned disorder—a prejudice. Roland shall become a liberal man."

Erich was silent, but said after a little while:

"It's probably useless and tiresome to both of us to go into generalities. I only intended to say, that as little real pleasure is given by a journey which has no destination to reach—no object to accomplish, so little, and even less, can quietness and pleasure in existence be obtained by a life which progresses toward no activity and knowledge and enjoyment which it has planned out for itself. If Roland had a special talent—"

"You find that he has none?"

"I have discovered none, and yet it seems to me that if he had been born in different circumstances he might have made a good locksmith or groom. I hope you do not misunderstand what I say. I mean it only as an evidence of the similarity of men, and of the fact that it essentially depends on circumstances what a man shall become. Hundreds who are judges would, had the conditions been changed, have been scavengers, and hundreds of scavengers would have been judges. As I said, this is to me a sign of the universal capacity of humanity; only few have the genius which must necessarily result in one stated thing."

"I understand, I understand! And you think you can educate a child of whom you have so slight an opinion?"

"I have not a slight opinion of Roland—not of his mind, and not of his heart. He appears to me not incapable of feeling love; but love is to him only a pleasure yet, not a duty. He has the qualifications common to men not marked out for prominence, and this is sufficient to make him, by means of correct, scientific guidance, a good and honorable man, happy in himself and making others happy. I shall be very glad to find that I have made a mistake in my estimate of Roland's talents."

6

"I honor and appreciate your great earnestness," said Sonnenkamp; "But I'm in a hurry. Explain to Roland."

He seemed a little out of humor. He twisted his cigar from one corner of his mouth to the other, and turned to his papers as though Erich were not present.

Erich left Sonnenkamp's work-room, and went to look for Roland. He found the boy busied in chewing a half-raw piece of meat, and giving it to his newly-trained dog Satan: the Krischer had told him that this would make the dog his inseparable companion. Erich looked on for a while, and then asked Roland to send the dog away, as he had something to tell him.

"Can't the dog be by?"

Erich answered, "No." He saw that the companionship of the dog would have to be done away with. He looked at Roland a little sharply, and the boy said, "Come, Satan, wait out here by the door!" and then turning back, he said:

"Tell away!"

Erich took his hand, and said that he had come there to be his teacher. Roland rested his head on his slightly clenched hand, and looked at the speaker with great, burning, restless eyes."

"I knew that," he said at last.

"Who told you?"

"The Krischer and Joseph."

"And why didn't you speak to me about it?"

Roland made no answer, but merely looked at Erich, as if to say, "I know how to wait." Only once did he turn his eyes, when Erich told him that he himself wished to find out whether he would become his tutor before speaking about it.

Roland was still silent. The dog scratched at the door, and Roland looked toward it, but did not venture to open it. Erich did so. The dog sprang in and crouched to Roland; after which he went up to Erich and licked his hand. It seemed as though he was a mysterious messenger between the two—silent, yet saying much.

"He loves you *too!*" cried out Roland in childish delight.

The word *too* was the only one which at last betrayed Roland. Suddenly he sprang up and threw himself on Erich's breast, and Erich folded him in his arms. The dog barked as if he wished to speak.

"We'll be faithful friends," said Erich, releasing the child. "I had a brother of your age, and you shall be my young brother."

Roland held Erich's right hand in both of his, and did not speak.

"Now let us begin our life, fresh and brave."

"Yes," answered Roland, "we'll make Satan fetch sticks out of the water; he does it splendidly."

"No, little brother, we'll work. Let's see what you have learned."

Erich had noticed that Roland, whose knowledge of every thing else was quite scanty, was pretty well acquainted with geography. He tried him in it, and Roland was delighted to be able to give correct answers; but as soon as they entered on other sciences, Roland was all abroad; and above all things, he hated Latin with a personal hatred.

"We'll soon easily learn what's necessary," said Erich to comfort him, "and then we'll go riding, and shooting, and fishing, and rowing."

This prospect gave the boy a good deal of comfort; and now as the clock struck in the tower, he said suddenly:

"In one hour Herr von Prancken will be with Manna. I can learn to ride and fence and shoot as well as Herr von Prancken, can't I?"

"To be sure you can."

"I sent a letter to Manna, by Herr von Prancken."

"What language do you write in?"

"English, of course. Oh, now I think of it—everybody says such good things about your mother; why couldn't she come here and live in our little cottage with the vines all round it?"

The boy could not say anything more, for Erich lifted him up, drew him to his breast, and kissed him. The boy had expressed the thought which had occurred to him when he first saw the cottage. The boy loved to give, loved to put his benevolence into practice, and was already planning pleasure for him. All his hard-heartedness toward the gardener disappeared as a thing too slight to be noticed.

A servant came, and told them that it was dinner-time. Erich and Roland went hand-in-hand to the dining-room.

CHAPTER XIV.

A COMPETITOR.

THE table was as profusely spread as it had been the day before. Frau Ceres, who again appeared at dinner, did not show by word or look that she had had such a confidential interview with Erich. She often addressed him with some brief remark, but everything came back to the one important point, her being asked to "eat a little something." Erich was astonished at the patience with which Herr Sonnenkamp said this again and again.

After dinner, as they were taking their coffee, Sonnenkamp casually told Erich that a new applicant had appeared, who had been earnestly recommended by Roland's last tutor, Knopf the

Candidate.* He gave Erich to understand that he did not admit everybody to table at the outset, and told Joseph to lead the stranger in.

A slender, sunburnt man entered, and was introduced. Erich was called simply the Captain; the *doctor* was temporarily kept out of sight. The stranger, Professor Crutius, had been a companion of Candidate Knopf in his studies, had been much tossed up and down in the world, and of late had been for several years an instructor in the Military School at West Point, near New York. He said this very glibly, but somewhat bitterly.

Sonnenkamp seemed to have planned out for himself a pleasant after-dinner treat: if he could get the two scholars to tilt with each other, he could sit quietly by and smoke his cigar. He showed great skill in selecting points about which they might fight, but to his great surprise Erich suddenly lowered his weapons and expressed his pleasure at finding that he was forced to envy the stranger's great experience of life, and his large knowledge of the world; for he himself had always lived in the small circle of the Principality, and had only travelled through the world of books.

The stranger had with quick perception discovered that Miss Perini was the important personage of the house; and he found that he had had many experiences which were also hers. Crutius had accompanied an American family to Italy, and had thence gone to the New World. He pointed out, with great ease of manner and knowledge of his subject, the peculiarities of an American boy of the upper class, and how he should be treated. Without pointing directly to him, this remark was plainly intended for Roland, who was looking at the stranger with consternation.

Erich stood by Sonnenkamp, grasping the balusters of the verandah, and said that he knew that he himself was not so well qualified to take charge of the boy as the stranger was.

Sonnenkamp said nothing, but blew, one after another, smoke-rings from his mouth into the air.

"Magnanimity!" thought he to himself, "magnanimity—nothing but smoke and gas!"

The stranger conversed very industriously with Frau Ceres and Miss Perini. Roland went to his father and said as softly as determinedly:

"Send him away—I don't want him."

"Why?"

"Because I have Herr Erich, and because Herr Knopf sent that man."

---

* We have no exact parallel for the German word "Kandidat." It means one who has taken his degree and is a "candidate" for any position that may open.

"Go to your room," said Erich, "you have nothing to say here."

Roland looked at him with great eyes, but went.

Erich told Sonnenkamp that the boy was right—he could not hold any opinions in regard to Roland's bitterness toward his former teachers; but it was evident that he wished to be under a person who was entirely different from them.

Sonnenkamp was surprised at the affectionate sympathy which Erich had with the boy; especially when he went on to say what a pity it was that Roland should be transferred so from one person to another.

In the mean time, the stranger had been asking Miss Perini if Sonnenkamp had any relations—if he had always gone by that name—if he received many letters. He was evidently fumbling about in conversation to find what the people of the house thought about America; and when Sonnenkamp said, with great vehemence, that he wished America had a dictator to subdue the profligacy of the country, Crutius added that there were many people in the New World who thought and hoped, but did not dare to say, that America was likely to become a monarchy.

Sonnenkamp nodded to himself, and again whistled inaudibly.

"Where are you stopping?" he suddenly asked the stranger.

Crutius named a tavern in the village.

"Very good accommodations there!" said Sonnenkamp.

The stranger was disturbed, for he had evidently expected that his luggage would be sent for, and he be immediately received as a guest of the house. Sonnenkamp thanked him for his visit, and asked that he would give his address plainly, so that he might be written to. The stranger's hand trembled as he drew out his well-worn pocketbook and gave his card. He took his leave with profound politeness.

Sonnenkamp asked Erich to accompany his colleague part of the way, and handed him several gold pieces to give, as courteously as possible, to the stranger, who appeared to be in needy circumstances.

"Is this confidence or service?" Erich asked himself as he followed the stranger.

He overtook him at the wall of the park, and when he made himself known as a teacher, the professor's features changed and he cried out:

"Ah, a teacher too, and probably my competitor?"

Erich assented. Crutius had been delighted with the Captain's friendly encouragement, for he had taken him for a confidential friend of the house, and had been grateful for the praise which Erich had bestowed on him; and now to find that he was a teacher too! He gnashed his teeth with something like rage, as he thought how he had been deceived.

Erich offered the money to him with great delicacy, saying that he too was poor, and how impossible it was sometimes to refuse the offers of the rich.

"Ha!" laughed the stranger. "He knows me, he wants to give me a present, bind me and buy himself off!"

Erich said that he did not understand what Crutius meant.

"So?" said he laughing. "Innocence with the rank of Captain can be bought too! The whole earth is nothing but an old rag-shop. What's the difference? The den where the tiger eats his prey is very beautiful, very tasty. Masons and upholsterers can do a good deal! Excuse me, but I've been drinking wine this morning and am not accustomed to it. Good! give it to me! My most humble services to Villa Eden! Oh, a fine man! a fine man!"

Without giving another word of explanation, the stranger seized the gold eagerly, pulled his hat down over his eyes, and went hastily away.

Erich returned to Sonnenkamp in deep reflection. In a very affable way, Sonnenkamp requested him to be seated, and asked:

"He took the money?"

Erich nodded.

"And probably hardly said 'Thank you.'"

Erich said that the man himself had told him that he had been drinking wine that morning, and was not accustomed to it.

Sonnenkamp said, as he pointed to a large pile of letters, that all these were answers to his advertisement. He entered upon some very amusing remarks about how many things there were entirely dependent on chance. "One opens a honey-pot, and there he finds bees and wasps and gold-flies, not one of which he had seen a minute before." Then he continued:

"I can give you an addition to your knowledge of men."

"In regard to Herr Crutius?"

"No; in regard to your very much bepitied gardener. It's truly a pleasure to see what a glorious rascal he is. I knew, long ago, how sharp he was in stealing the black mould from the height up there, and now I find out that the story about the dog's hurting him is all humbug. I told Roland all about it, and am glad to see him come to know, so soon, the baseness and lies of men."

"You don't intend to keep the gardener in your service any longer?" asked Erich.

"Certainly! It amuses me to see the amount of rascality that the comical little fellow has. It's extremely pleasant to play with the rascality and cheating of men, and I wish I had half-a-dozen of this sort at hand, so as to teach Roland how this gentry is to be dealt with."

"Unfortunately, I would not be able to teach him that," said Erich.

"I should think not; you're here to do something else."

Erich left Sonnenkamp's room in deep thought.

A servant told him that Roland was waiting for him on the bank of the river. He went to him, and the boy wanted him to take a sail on the Rhine. Roland loosened the beautiful boat from its moorings and they sailed out on the water, now dark green; and above them, the verdant islands, covered with trees, seemed to be growing from the bosom of the stream. A fresh wind was ruffling the waves. Roland was delighted to display his skill in trimming the sails, and showed himself to be accustomed to the water. All his movements were so charming that Erich looked at him with admiration.

Erich was entirely unacquainted with boating, and gave Roland the triumph of being able to instruct him how to move the boat according to his wish or whim. There was a joyfulness in the boy's voice that Erich had never heard before.

And as they sped along with swelling sail, and the waves plashed against their boat, Roland told how Knopf, the Candidate, had made him thoroughly at home on the water; for as to rowing, sailing, steering, and bringing the boat around, all this Knopf understood better than the pilot, or even the pilot's wife, a great big woman, who had just now hailed them, as she was steering a large boat hitched to a tug, while her husband, not less mighty of frame than she, leaned against the mast.

Roland steered toward the tow, and fastened his boat to the woman's craft. She gossiped with him, but kept her eye on the business of steering. When he had gone far enough with her, Roland loosened his boat and went back with the tide.

He gave a somewhat humorous account of how the woman lorded it over her husband; but Erich brought the conversation back to Knopf, the Candidate. Roland would say nothing about him, or any other former tutor. They were evidently all indifferent to him, and he looked at them as at hotel-waiters who had attended to him the day before. They were all discharged servants. Who cares about discharged waiters? But from the way in which Roland let fall a few words it was evident that this Candidate must have loved his pupil very much.

The conversation now turned to the quarryman, and Roland appeared very indifferent to his rascality, for he was of the opinion that all poor people are rascals.

On this sail, Erich had obtained new and deeper knowledge of his pupil, and, in addition to his love for him, the pity which he had formerly felt was now increased. The boy had already learned to despise the world, and seemed to have nothing and no one to whom he could cling, or the thought of whom made him happy. He seemed to care for his sister only, as one congenial with him; and now, as they were approaching Villa Eden, Roland said:

"Manna is walking with Herr von Prancken now, just as I am walking with you. I believe that when Manna comes you'll like her too."

BOOK THIRD.

CHAPTER I.

A VOICE FROM BELOW.

A FRAGRANT strawberry beautifies the earth, is pleasant to look at, and good to eat. If one only had eyes and ears sharp enough to see and hear what is going on down there, at the root of the plant, he would perhaps find ammonia, not a very elegant and certainly a strongly-perfumed body, turning up its self-satisfied nose, and saying: "What would it all be without me?"

The potash, on the other hand, a shining, white, and odorous personage, has no need of saying anything, for its very look says: "All the learned men of the upper world praise me."

But the crabbed silicon rests with the greatest composure, and lets it be understood: "I am the original inhabitant, and what do all these parvenus amount to? They came yesterday, and will be gone to-morrow. I have outlived a great many already. They are all nothing but snobs."

The maggot feasts on the root, and thinks, winking with its cunning eye: "They like to serve others, but I—I just stuff myself!" The earth-worm comes wriggling along, putting on airs because it lays out the streets and canals where the rest can move. A mole, who has built his nest in the neighborhood, watches his opportunity, and when he sees the maggot complacently taking her nap, he goes to work and eats her up.

Such is the position of affairs down at the root, with its thousand-fold life and activity, and such was the state of things below, in the servants' hall at Villa Eden.

Herr Sonnenkamp had a wise law, although many considered it a hard one: all his servants were obliged to be unmarried. He gave them liberal wages, stinted them in nothing, but they had no title to family-life. No beggar was allowed to enter the well-fenced garden, for he would destroy its comfortableness. He received a gift from the porter, at the entrance, and the old cook was often heard to lament that "so many good scraps should be thrown away, when they might just as well have gone to hungry people."

It is noon. Here, in the servants' hall, they eat long before the master's table is spread above. Two grooms and a coachman, who have charge of the stables, eat alone, and in silence, for they have to relieve the watch at the stable.

The *Chef*, as the head cook is called, dressed all in white, is the great man here below. He is fat and pompous, has a beardless face, and a large, hooked nose. He plays the Lord here. His German is gibberish, but he rules the under-cooks and maids with a rod of iron.

The sentinels have finished eating. A long table is set for more than a dozen men, who straggle in one after another.

First appears—or rather, the preference is universally accorded to him—Bertram, the head-coachman, a gigantic fellow. He has a large, reddish beard, parted in two thick waves, and he wears a long, embroidered vest that comes over his hips, and over this is a jacket, striped with white and blue, which differs but slightly from that worn by the other denizens of the stable.

Bertram bows profoundly to the assembly, and seats himself at the head of the table, Joseph at his right, the head-gardener at his left. Next to him sits a little man, with a knotty face, and extremely restless eyes. This is Lutz, the courier. Now the others take their places, according to their rank, the stable-boys and garden-boys far down at the foot.

The head female cook, a personage held in high favor by Miss Perini, makes a point of having grace said before meat. Bertram, the giant coachman, a confirmed free-thinker, is always very busy in arranging his embroidered vest while the praying is going on, and pulls it proudly down over his hips. Joseph folds his hands, but his lips do not move. The rest pray silently.

The soup is hardly despatched and the wine sipped (for the servants receive their wine every day) before Bertram unfastens the gates of speech, and the conversation is occupied with one theme specially.

"I'm waiting to see if Lieutenant Dournay won't recognize me. I was in his battery."

"Yes?" said Joseph, very much pleased. "He certainly must have been a great favorite?"

Bertram did not think it necessary to answer this question immediately. He only said that he wouldn't have believed that Herr Dournay would have come to be a servant.

"A servant?"

"Yes; he's as much a servant as we are, only he becomes a tutor because he has a litttle book-learning."

Joseph smiled a melancholy smile, and took all pains to bring the company to a right opinion. First he sang of the renowned father of Erich, who had had at least twenty orders, and whose wife was of high nobility. He was delighted to throw hard scientific names at the heads of his companions—Anthropology, Zoology, Osteology, Archæology, and 'Petrofactology,' names which he had somehow picked up; and he told them that

Captain Dournay understood them all—he was a great university himself. But it did not become him, Joseph, to attempt to convince the present company that Erich was to be anything but a servant.

The head gardener said, in high-Prussian dialect:

"At all events he's a good-looking man, and sits his horse well, but he knows nothing at all about gardening."

Lutz, the courier, said that Erich spoke French and English very well, but as to Russian, Turkish, and Polish, of course learned men didn't understand them; for Lutz, who, as a journeyman tailor, had explored all lands, understood all tongues. He had formerly conducted Miss von Prancken (now Countess von Wolfsgarten) and two English women on their travels, and now served as courier to Herr Sonnenkamp, whenever he happened to be on a journey; but the rest of the time he was at leisure, unless carrying the letter-bag to and from the railway station, and playing the guitar and whistling while playing, can be called work. Besides this, however, he had a secret service.

At the table there seemed to be a tacit understanding that when Lutz said anything it was not to be contradicted at all. Only the second cook, a young lady with whom Lutz had a tender but not yet firmly established relationship, smiled at him.

A man with Sarmatian features, but whose manner of expression proclaimed him a Pole, boasted that it was Herr von Prancken again who had brought the man into the house. Bertram nudged Joseph, and then began to cover Herr von Prancken with extravagant praise. Joseph winked, as if to say, "That's the way! now you'll see again that the Pole is Herr von Prancken's spy."

And now they discussed the question whether Herr von Prancken would live here after he had married Manna, for it was settled that he would marry her.

A gardener, who stammered a little, said that "down in the village tavern it was all the talk that Herr Sonnenkamp had been a tailor." They all laughed; and the stuttering gardener, who, aside from his infirmity, was always the butt of the circle, was now drawn on to speak further, and badgered till he became blue in the face.

Bertram took both billows of his whiskers in his hands and cried out:

"If anybody talked so to me, I'd show him how his own teeth taste!"

"Oh, let the men talk!" said the head-gardener, and smiled in anticipation of his own wisdom. "When a man has good luck he must put up with backbiting."

One of the stable-boys told of a scuffle with one of the so-called Wine-count's servants, who had sneered at Herr Sonnenkamp's people because they were in the service of a man whom nobody nobody knew anything about—where he came from or who he was; and one had said that Mrs. Sonnenkamp had been a slave.

The secret and not very edifying history of many houses was here related, and at last the cook, a fat woman, cried out:

"Let's don't talk! My mother always said that whether a house is big or little, it always has a stone before the door."

The second gardener, a dried-up man with a long, pointed face, who was nicknamed Squirrel, and occasionally attended the prayer-meetings held by the pious of the vicinity, now commenced a long discourse on the evil practice of backbiting. He had originally been a gardener; and had then become a policeman in a northern capital. Sonnenkamp had there made his acquaintance, had brought him back to his first avocation, and now used him in many a case where particular circumspection was required.

An old kitchen-maid, who sat a little apart from the rest, holding her plate in her lap, cried out suddenly:

"You can say what you like, but this new-comer is going to marry the daughter. Mind what I say, and you just recollect it. He didn't come on the young master's account; he came on the young lady's. Once upon a time there was a prince and princess in a castle, and the prince dressed like a groom. Yes, yes; laugh as much as you like, but it's so!"

Joseph and Bertram looked thoughtfully at each other.

Now began general sport. Everybody wanted the old crone to tell his fortune. The courier sneered at them for being superstitious, but gave a forced laugh as Bertram cried out:

"Yes, yes; tailors are all great free-thinkers. They don't believe in hell!"

Everybody laughed loudly. A voice called from above:

"Bertram must hitch up the carriage, and Joseph come up here!"

The company broke up. The stable-boys went to the stable, where they smoked their pipes, and the gardeners proceeded to the park and hot-houses. Joseph told two servants to lay the cloth, and all was silent under-ground. Only the kettles boiled and bubbled, and the *Chef* regarded the progress of his work with an artist's eye.

An hour later, Lutz received the letters to take to the station, and said, casually, that the new tutor had a gang in the house, in the persons of Bertram, who had formerly belonged to his battery, and Joseph, who felt that through his University experience he had a claim on him.

It had never been said that Lutz was to be a spy among the servants, but it was well understood between his master and himself.

CHAPTER II.

A SUNDAY DINNER.

WHEN Erich was riding through the forest, amid its fragrance, brightness, and song, he determined to write a letter from fairy-land to his mother; but now it seemed as if years had passed since then. What had not Erich seen, thought, and experienced during the last few days? The letter had changed too.

On Sunday, the whole order of the house was transformed; breakfast, even, was not eaten as usual.

Herr Sonnenkamp met Erich in the garden, and asked if he would accompany them to church. Erich instantly answered, "No;" and added, in explanation, that to do so would be somewhat hypocritical: he might readily go to church as a sign of respect for the belief of others, but his action would be attributed to a different motive.

Sonnenkamp looked at him in surprise; and yet this straightforwardness had its effect, for he said:

"Good! One can easily know how to deal with you in such matters."

The expression was ambiguous, but Erich took it in its good meaning.

When all had gone to church, Erich sat alone, writing to his mother. He commenced his letter by saying that he seemed like Odysseus cast on an unknown island. To be sure, he had no companions to care for, but he was yet at the head of a good many ideas, and must take care that they were not changed into—

Just as he was about to write the next word, he stopped. This was not the right tone. He threw the paper away and commenced a new one. Concisely and simply he told of his meeting with Prancken, Clodwig, and Bella, and said: If the Homeric heroes were under the protection of the gods, he, in these latter days, was in different and better circumstances, for he was led by the spirit and honor of his parents. Speaking of Roland, he said that riches give a peculiar strength of imagination, and a sense of power; for Roland had, as well as he, thought of bringing his mother to the vine-covered cottage.

The bells in the village rang, and Erich wrote on rapidly, saying how highly he prized the vocation which gave him the privilege of leading in the right way a child to whom was intrusted the almost boundless power of wealth. And amid the chiming of the bells arose in his mind the history of the rich young man who came to Jesus. He could not recall, distinctly, what the young man had said, and the answer to it, and so he looked in Roland's library for a Bible. It seemed to him as if he could do nothing more until he had distinctly understood the whole circumstance.

He went below to the garden. There he met the gardener, whose sobriquet was Squirrel, and who joyfully said "Yes," when Erich asked if he had a Bible. Overflowing with pious expressions, the gardener fetched the book, and Erich returned to his chamber with it.

He wrote no further, but read for a long time. Then he sat gazing at the book, with his head resting on his hand, until Roland came from church, and laid down his prayer-book. Erich took the hand, as it was laying down the book; and the question rose in his mind, "Wilt thou be able to give this boy as firm a foundation, as an equivalent for this, if once—"

His thoughts were interrupted by Roland, who said:

"Did you go for a Bible?"

He told Erich, with childish pleasure, that the gardener had already spread the news of this throughout the house. Erich was obliged to stop and explain to the boy that he considered the Bible a book with which no other was to be compared, but by no means regarded it with the veneration paid to it by the orthodox.

"Do you know this?" Erich asked, as he showed Roland the passage referring to the rich young man.

Roland read it, and stared when Erich asked what he thought of it. He had evidently not understood the difficulty of the problem there laid down. Erich promised to tell him the meaning of it some other time: he must learn to wait. A seed lies at first powerless in the earth, until it is awakened by the force which is to mature it. Erich knew that such a seed had at that instant fallen into the boy's soul. He would wait patiently until it should sprout and appear.

He went with Roland to meet the Major, who always came to dine on Sundays. They walked for a while under the nut-trees in the street, and then ascended through the vineyard. At a large piece of land where only light vine-poles stood they saw the Major, whom we have already met at Wolfsgarten. He was in full uniform and wore all his orders.

As the chief families of the neighborhood were extremely reserved with the house of Sonnenkamp, the Major was the standard of gentility for the family; and Frau Ceres took especial delight in finding that a man with so many orders was so friendly with her. Evil tongues said, indeed, that the Major received a considerable addition to his not very enormous pension, as a consideration for entering Frau Ceres' service; but this was nothing but pure calumny, for the Major, or rather

Fraulein Milch, made a great point of refusing to receive aid from, or be dependent on, any one in the neighborhood.

The Major was very happy to see the two. "Have you got him already?" he asked Erich. "Be sure to keep a good hold on the bridle."

Pointing to the vine-hill, he said:

"A year from now, Herr Sonnenkamp says, we'll get the first wine from there. Did you ever drink Maiden wine?"

Erich said that he had not; and the Major was happy to explain that that was what the first growth was called.

The gait of the Major was a palpable rush, interrupted by an occasional bolt-upright strut. He halted at every two steps and looked around smiling. He smiled at everybody he met. Why should people be forced constantly to read in his face the disagreeable fact that he had lost his toes? He told Erich that he had frozen them in the Russian campaign, and had been obliged to have them amputated. He smiled very complacently as he went on to say:

"Yes, yes: our German proverb is right, in saying that everybody knows best where his own shoe pinches."

He nodded to Erich, as much as to say that the proverb was equally true in all conditions of life.

He then asked Roland if his mother was up yet; for every Sunday Frau Ceres went so far in her religious exertions as to rise at nine o'clock, and, what was not a less oblation, to accomplish her toilet in a single hour and go to church with the family. But she always compensated herself for her loss of sleep by going to bed again; and on her second rising she made her peculiar Sunday-toilet for the first time in the day.

As they came to the level street, the Architect, who was also going to dinner, met them. He joined Erich, and Roland walked with the Major. The men were all obliged to look at Roland's dogs before going to the saloon adjoining the balcony. Here they met Herr Sonnenkamp, with the Doctor and the priest.

Erich had hardly been presented, when Frau Ceres appeared in her robes of state. The Major gave her his arm. The servants opened the folding-doors, and the whole company went through several apartments before entering the dining-room.

The Major took his place at Frau Ceres' left, and the Priest at her right. Next to him Miss Perini seated herself: whereupon the Doctor, Sonnenkamp, the Architect, Roland, and Erich took their places.

The priest said grace in a loud voice.

The conversation was at first entirely incomprehensible to Erich, for it concerned persons and circumstances of which he knew nothing. The great wine-merchant, whose son, together with Prancken, had bought in the fine horses, was much spoken about. This gentleman had had a wine-auction in one of his cellars lying up the river, and had made enormous profits from it. It was said that he intended to relinquish the business entirely, in order to go to the Capital; for the shrewd old gentleman was very anxious to make himself known and liked at court.

"I give him credit for wanting to become a nobleman," cried out the Doctor.

Herr Sonnenkamp, who was just carrying a piece of exquisitely prepared fish to his mouth, suddenly breathed so heavily that all at the table became alarmed for him, his face was so red. He recovered in an instant, and explained that he had carelessly almost swallowed a bone.

The Major found it out of taste for the wine-merchant to have allowed himself to be made a candidate for the Chamber of Deputies, by the government especially, against such a man as Weidmann. Erich became attentive as he heard this man mentioned again. A respectful pause always took place when his name occurred in conversation: but the Doctor remarked that it was evident that the Wine-count only wished to satisfy his ambition for court favor by doing so; and as he had appeared in the papers as a supporter of the government, he would attain that object, although he knew he would be defeated in the election.

"Now, Herr Priest," he asked immediately, "which candidate will the clergy support?"

The Priest, a tall slender man with white hair and remarkably bright eyes, which looked out from beneath his heavy eyebrows sharply yet quietly, united dignity and cleverness in his deportment. He would willingly have remained silent, but now—moving his left hand and placing his thumb and forefinger together—he said that there could be no objection to the civil qualifications of Weidmann.

The Doctor was obliged to be satisfied with this evasive reply; but the Major, with much earnestness, extolled the noble character of Weidmann, who must win. The Major always spoke vehemently, and his face became purple to the roots of his white hair, not only when obliged to address his neighbor, but when the whole table listened.

"You speak like a brother Freemason," said the Doctor to him.

The Major looked grimly at him, and shook his head, to let him know that such matters should not be lightly spoken of; but yet he said nothing.

Herr Sonnenkamp explained, with great freedom, that although he was a tax-paying citizen of this country, he did not vote; he was accustomed to progressive ideas, and considered himself and family only as guests in Germany.

Erich and the Doctor glanced at each other, and then looked at Roland. What would become of a child who is told, "The state in which you live has no concern with you?"

The Doctor had begun early to make fun of the Major, and kept it up. The Doctor, who was known and liked as a jovial fellow, had been steadily since morning as good-natured as one who has just risen from a well-supplied table; and so his tone was singularly lively, and bore a strong contrast to the awkward bearing of the Major, who willingly let the pleasantry proceed. He seemed to hold it as a man's duty to serve his neighbor passively, and his face always appeared to say, "Children, be jolly—at my expense too, if you like."

In the mean time the Priest stood firmly by the down-trodden Major; but it was hard to say if he did not do so simply to keep the fun going, for the Major smiled yet more pleasantly at his assistance, directed as it was against the man who had assailed him. The Priest always spoke at first as if half inclined not to talk seriously, but when he found himself in the full current of his speech, he let his arrows fly in all directions, without for an instant losing his clerical demeanor, or failing for an instant to preserve his exquisitely courtly manners, or the graceful gestures of his delicate hands. Miss Perini's eyes always seemed to expand and feast on his clerical aspect, when she looked at him, and listened to him with her eyes. But she could not help being disagreeably impressed when he, in accordance with the manners of the snuff-taking clergy, took out his blue linen handkerchief, and, rolling it into a ball, waved it about. She breathed more freely when he put the blue cloth in his pocket again.

On the other hand, Miss Perini preserved an agreeable patience toward the constrained and awkward manners of the Doctor, who always dealt with her as a sort of member of the faculty; and, in fact, she was not without some medical knowledge. He had a peculiar respect for her, as she had never asked his advice in any little illness. She lived very abstemiously, and found but very little enjoyment in the great gatherings and sumptuous feasts given to the friends of the house. She had hardly any wants: she was a being who only existed to serve and please others. Doctor Richard, as a physician skilful and much sought after, did not need to stand on ceremony; he was moreover the amiable and recognized tyrant of the whole neighborhood, and particularly of the house of Sonnenkamp. He was talkative at table; and was able to be so, from the fact that the less he ate the more industriously he drank. He praised the wines, and knew them all from their earliest stage to their maturity. He asked for one which he particularly liked, and Sonnenkamp had it brought. The Doctor pronounced it "wild" yet.

At many a dish, Sonnenkamp looked doubtfully at the Doctor; but the Doctor would cry out, coming to his aid:

"Eat it! you needn't be afraid of it!"

"Drinking, I guess, would suit some people better than anything else in the world," laughed Sonnenkamp.

"It's a pity," cried the Doctor, "that you didn't know the precious youth who once uttered the great truth, that 'the greatest pity in this world is, that you can't drink what you eat.'"

Then turning to Erich, he said:

"Your friend Prancken doesn't speak very well of our Rhine districts; but this is only the result of the universal acclimating catarrh, which everybody must go through among us. I hope you will get rid of it more quickly than people generally do. Look at such a bottle of wine—all that poetry, that the drama, that art conjure up before us to give us emotions—all *that* is in this bottle. The drinker knows that he is not an ordinary beast of burden; he not only knows the beauty which is here corked up, but doesn't need to know it, for he feels it; he becomes, in fact, full of beauty."

"If there were only no adulteration," said the Architect.

"Yes, yes," cried the Doctor, loudly. "In old times, instances of drunkenness were very rare about here, and now they are quite common—all owing to the spirits they put in. Do you know anything about wine?" said he, turning again to Erich, and referring to him, as if, by common consent, he presided at the feast.

"Not yet."

"And yet you have probably made a good many drinking songs. You always say in them: 'Come, fill up your glasses, and drink, my boys, for jolly we've been, and jolly we'll be.' And when the gentlemen have drunk up their first bottle, they can't stand any longer on their poetical feet."

A glance at Roland seemed to bring the Doctor to his senses. It was not right to draw Erich into the sport so soon. He therefore turned the conversation, and gave Erich, whom with great urbanity he called "my worthy colleague," the opportunity of telling many entertaining stories of his University and soldier life. The Major nodded his satisfaction; he was left at peace by the interest which Erich's anecdotes awakened, and could now, without fearing any interruption, attack his food and drink. He loosened his uniform under his napkin, which he had tied by the corners around his neck. "It's a good thing that Fräulein Milch laid out a nice white vest, fit to be seen," thought he.

The Major had the best understanding with the servants, and had only to give the wink to Joseph, the favorite, and he knew what was wanted. So, while the wine was being changed, Joseph would always hastily fill the Major's glass with burgundy from a shining crystal flask into which it had been poured.

But now the Major stopped drinking too. The conversation had taken a happy turn while Erich spoke of the Geneva Convention for the care of those who had been wounded in the war. That was a point on which the Priest, the Doctor, and the soldier could unite their interests, and for a while a mutually satisfactory conversation reigned at the table.

The Major remarked, in a deep voice, that men who will not name themselves were at the bottom of this, as of all other humane movements. The Doctor told Erich—speaking in a low tone, as was his custom—how the Major attributed everything good that took place in the world to the Freemasons, and consequently that Erich, if he wished to remain in his good graces, should never say anything against Masonry.

The whole table listened with great attention as Erich said that we ought to be proud that such a movement, based on the love of humanity, had taken its rise in our century; and even the Priest nodded as Erich added that the Christian religion, in affirming itself up to its duties to the sick, had attained an elevation so pure and great that no former age and no other benevolence had ever reached it.

Roland was happy, as he saw with what interest they all regarded Erich—he was making them his friends.

They rose from the table quietly. Something like a blessing had been said over the food. The Priest prayed silently, and the Major came up to Erich and clasped his hand somewhat roughly, saying in a suppressed voice:

"You're ready for it: you must learn the signs yet."

Erich was so excited that he hardly heard what the old man said, although the Major had expressed his deepest feeling in acknowledging him as a brother Mason.

"See," cried the Doctor, overflowing with spirits, "our Major's hair has become whiter!"

And in fact it appeared so, for the Major's face was generally so red that it seemed impossible to deepen its shade at all; but now, by reason of the wine and the conversation, it appeared so much redder that his hair seemed whiter by contrast.

"The Major's hair has grown whiter," they all cried; and the smile that always played upon his lips grew to broad laughter.

CHAPTER III.

THE OUTER WORLD.

HARDLY had he risen from the table, when the Doctor was informed that several patients were waiting to see him; for it was known that he dined at the Villa on Sundays. He hastily took a cigar from Sonnenkamp, and told Erich that he would like to have him accompany him, as he had something to say to him. He said this in a matter-of-course way, as if certain of being obeyed.

As they came to the corner, the Doctor extended his hand to Erich, saying, heartily:

"I was a pupil of your grandfather, and knew your father at the University."

"I'm glad to hear it; but why didn't you tell me so at first?"

The Doctor looked at him a minute, from head to foot, then he laid both hands on his shoulders, and said, shaking his head, but in a hearty tone:

"I mistook you. I believed that the race of idealists had died out. You are Doctor of Philosophy, but not of shrewdness. Dear Doctor-Captain, what good would it do to let the people yonder know how we were connected? And then you want to live with Herr Sonnenkamp, too."

"Why not?"

"The man could not cry if he wanted to; and you—?"

"Well, and I?"

"Your tear-glands fill at every emotion. While you were speaking of your father there—of the great care of the sick—You have a talent for hypochondria."

Erich was disturbed. This way of being looked at was new to him; but before he could answer, the Doctor cried out to the group of peasants, who were waiting for him at the entrance of the porter's lodge:

"I'll come in a minute! . . . Wait here for me, I'll be back presently," said he to Erich, and went toward the group of men who all took off their hats and caps. He spoke to one and another of them, and wrote prescriptions on some slips of paper which he rested on the back of a broad-shouldered man, and gave them to some, while to others he only gave oral advice.

Erich stood and looked at the scene, while he thought that in fact he was without shrewdness; but a deep feeling of happiness came over him as he thought that his father and grandfather had here sent him a new friend. An uncomprehended, unmeasured inheritance seemed to be awaiting him everywhere, like a harvest ready for the sickle. He looked at the house and the great display of wealth, with a new feeling. He was not poor.

The Doctor returned, and said, pleasantly:

"Now I'm at liberty. Count Wolfsgarten spoke about you, but gave me a false impression. No matter! Everybody, standing in his own horizon, sees only his own rainbow. I only wanted to say that all that they're doing for you is hardly paying interest; for no one ever did more good to others than your grandfather and father. Now, let me take a good look at you. I saw you years ago, when you were coupled with the Prince."

The Doctor stepped away from him, and continued:

"The crossing is good. Father of Huguenot blood—mother genuine German, fair, delicate—correct mixture of nationalities. Come here, under the trees. Will you allow me a short and quick diagnosis?"

Erich smiled, for the whole way in which the Doctor reviewed and disposed of him was in the highest degree strange, and yet attractive, to him.

Knocking off the ashes of his cigar against a twig, the Doctor asked:

"Can you have daily intercourse with a person without esteeming or loving him at all?"

"I've never tried it, but I believe I cannot; but such work injures the soul."

"I expected that answer. For my part, I believe what Lessing said: 'It is better to associate with bad men than to live away from all men.' May I ask another question?"

Without waiting for an answer, he proceeded:

"Have you ever experienced ingratitude?"

"I don't think I have ever done anything to deserve gratitude. It's even a question whether we have a right to demand thankfulness, when all that we do for others is done for our own pleasure."

"Good, good—knew it! Only one more. Do you believe in total depravity; and if so, since when?"

"If by that word you mean the conscious wish to injure others, I do not believe in it; for I'm convinced that all crime is only a spreading of the boundaries of the natural impulse of self-preservation, but a spreading brought about by means of sophistry or passion. Perhaps belief in total depravity is only belief in passion."

The Doctor nodded several times, and said:

"Now one more question. Are you sensitive—touchy?"

"I might appeal to your friendly questioning as a proof that I'm not."

The Doctor threw away his cigar, which was not yet smoked out, and said:

"Pardon me, I made a mistake. My last question has yet

another to follow it. But now really to finish: Does it surprise you to find a well-dressed and well-spoken man or woman to be simply a ninny? And do you allow yourself to take such people for fools, and don't you think they have reasons for their conduct and understand other people's reasons too?"

In spite of Erich's good-nature, his patience was at last exhausted, and he said, not without some sign of irritation, that he had "gone through several singular examinations here already, but this last one was the most surprising."

"You'll probably understand it some day," said the Doctor in a low tone, while he took Erich's hand hastily, for he saw Miss Perini coming down the road, and went to join her.

The company met again at the fountain, chatted awhile, and then separated. The Priest and the Major asked Erich to visit them, and the Doctor asked Sonnenkamp if Erich and Roland might not accompany him on his round of visits. Sonnenkamp seemed disturbed to see Roland so brought into connection with Erich, but consented. Erich got into the carriage with the Doctor, and Roland took his seat by the coachman, who gave him the reins.

The day was fresh and full of fragrance. Bells rang and larks sang.

They went to a village lying inland. In a garden where lilacs were blooming they heard a beautiful quartette sung by men. In an enclosed place under the lindens young men and boys were engaged in athletic sports.

Erich could not keep from saying: "Oh beautiful, glorious Germany! This is life! This is our life! To build up the soul with song and the body with lusty motion, this makes a people strong and beautiful, and honor and freedom must become its own. Everything glorious belongs to us as fully as it did to the classical world!"

The Doctor laid his hand softly on Erich's knee, and looking at him earnestly said that if Erich should remain here he would like to make him more intimately acquainted with the real Rhine life; and he must not draw hasty conclusions if he should find much, both in-doors and out, that would be distasteful to him.

"And if you can (I believe that you alone are able to do it, and if you can't, I give it up entirely)—if you can give the boy in front of us pleasure not simply in that which he has, but also in that which he has not, in the great life of the people and of society, then you will have done a work which is worth the trouble of living. The chief point, however, is that during this time you must have courage to wish for nothing for yourself; otherwise you will not receive the blessing. Thus I understand the saying, 'Seek first the kingdom of God'—I mean, seek first the life of truth and love, and all the rest will come to you. Roland," said he, interrupting himself, "stop here."

The Doctor alighted from the carriage and entered a small but pretty house. Erich and Roland went into the gymnasium-grounds. They were at first looked at shyly, but when Erich showed a young fellow how to perform an exercise well that he was doing unskilfully, and when he took off hts coat and swung backward and forward on the bars, they all became more at ease. Roland tried a few exercises, but did not succeed, and Erich told him they would become easy by practice; but it was unfortunate that he must do them alone, for it was much more lively and beneficial when one has competition.

A servant came and called Erich and Roland to the house where the Doctor had alighted. Just as the physician was coming out of the house, the church-bell tolled. All the bystanders removed their hats; even the Doctor did so too, and said:

"A mortal is dead. The man has lived his years,—he was seventy-two years old; and yesterday, on his death-bed, he found comfort in the recollection of a little good deed. In the famine year 1817 he was wandering as a journeyman cooper over Lunenburg heath—he always called it Hamburg heath. At that time there were no roads, and at last, after wandering about for hours he found a miserable cabin, and children in it crying for bread. He had nothing but some dried eels in a tin box, and a little bread. He gave it all to the children, who ate it and were satisfied. 'Do you see,' said he to me only yesterday—'do you see, that always does me good, and I am glad that I was able to make the children happy, and they haven't forgotten either, that a stranger once gave them something to eat.' Is it not a beautiful thing that a man can refresh himself with the remembrance of one good deed? He has suffered much, and death is a deliverance for him. Yes, young man, this is the world. Out here all is blossoming, and men are singing, and exercising, and joking, and at the same time a man is dying. . . Pah!" said he, manning himself, "I didn't bring you to a funeral. Roland, drive through the whole town and stop at the last house." Then turning to Erich, he said:

"We're riding toward cheerful poverty, and you shall see something jolly. The man is a poor vine-dresser, has seven children, four sons and three daughters; and, in all their poverty, they are the jolliest mortals to be found on the face of the earth, and the jolliest of them all is the old man. His right name is Piper, but, because he sings with his children just as often as he can, and has taught them to sing pretty well, he is called the Seven-Piper."

They went toward the house. The daughters were sitting before the door, and the sons were at the gymnasium. The Seven-Piper appeared immediately, and said somebody ought to go for his sons. Then the Doctor asked him how he was.

"Ah, dear Doctor," rung out the answer, "it always happens that my youngest has the best voice." Then turning to Roland, he continued:

"Yes, young master, I make my children rich too. Each one of them receives his hundred or two hundred songs for his inheritance; and if they can't get through the world with that capital, they're good for nothing."

The sons came and struck up a merry song, so that the Doctor and Roland were overflowing with delight; and Erich, who quickly caught the melody, sang with them.

The old man nodded to him, and at the conclusion of the song said:

"You know how to sing too, Sir."

The Doctor always had a bottle in his carriage, and now he brought it out, and all were in high spirits, and the Seven-Piper explained particularly to Roland that the best thing in the world is to be healthy and make music for one's self.

The Doctor took his departure, and, as evening was coming on, Roland and Erich left the house with light hearts. The two eldest boys accompanied them to the shore, and, unfastening the boat, took them toward Villa Eden.

The river was wonderfully still and clear, and mirrored the red clouds of evening. Erich sat quiet and alone. He had a happy hour, having no thoughts, and yet having everything. Roland's oar kept time to those of the Seven-Piper's sons; then they let the boat float along noiselessly with the tide.

The stars were shining when they reached the Villa.

CHAPTER IV.

THE PARABLE OF THE RICH YOUNG MAN.

THE Architect came for Roland in the morning, and took him to the ruined castle, to make drawings under his direction. Herr Sonnenkamp reminded Erich of his promise to visit the Priest, and shortly after he had seen Miss Perini returning from Mass, Erich set out.

The parsonage lay behind a little garden, itself singularly quiet even in this quiet village. It almost seemed to Erich, as he stood at the entrance, that it would be impossible to make a loud noise in the house, it looked so peaceful; and had not the door-bell rang so loudly, and two Pomeranian dogs barked so testily, he would easily have believed it.

The housekeeper silenced the dogs, and asked Erich to go up stairs. He seemed to be expected.

Erich found the Priest in a sunny room devoid of ornament. He was sitting at a table, holding a book in his left hand, while his right lay on a globe which stood on a little pedestal before him.

"You find me busied with the world," said the Priest, as he held out his hand to Erich, and requested him to be seated on the sofa, over which hung a picture of St. Boromæus, which was much better in intention than execution.

There was an air of comfort and peace in the room;—an unassumingness and modesty, that asked nothing but to be shut up alone for days and hours in quiet thought. There were two canary-birds, who wished to express their joy at the stranger's visit; but when the ghostly father bade them be silent, they obeyed as if by magic, and looked inquiringly at Erich.

The Priest put out his delicate hand and drew the globe nearer to him, telling Erich that he had been tracing the course of a missionary on it.

"You are probably no friend of missions?" he asked immediately.

"I regard them," answered Erich, "as one of the first steps toward civilizing the world; and missionaries accomplish a great work by means of what they call the Holy Book, for they spread the knowledge of written language everywhere, and thus, to a certain extent, free the languages of nations from their inorganic condition, and make them organic."

The Priest closed the book that was lying open before him, folded his hands in a certain patronizing way, which was however the natural result of the habits of his profession; and then said, as he laid the tips of his fingers together, that he had heard very favorable reports of Erich, and from his own experience he had a prejudice in favor of men who had changed their vocation from conviction. It was true, that frivolousness and dissatisfaction were often the prime movers of such things, but where this was not the case, it was right to attribute them to some deep love of truth.

Erich thanked him, and added that the dignity of a calling did not lie in outward distinction, but in being broadly, universally human, which is possible in every vocation.

"Very just," answered the Priest, stretching out his hand as if in mild blessing. "Therefore the clerical profession is the highest for it seeks not gain, not pleasure, not fame, but only that which you, I know not why, call the universally human, whereas its correct name is simply the Divine."

A certain humility and reluctance to oppose any contradiction came over Erich, as he heard the Priest state his objection so mildly. After that word, it seemed as though a holy rest had taken possession of the room. No sound came from the outer world. It was as if all connection with it had been severed.

From the window they looked beyond the park and Villa, far away over the stream. The Priest noticed how delighted Erich was with the beauty of the prospect, and said:

"Yes, Herr Sonnenkemp has laid out all this for his own pleasure; but the beauty is also ours. It is only when I have to serve my flock, that I leave this house."

"And do you never feel lonesome in the country?"

"Oh no: I have myself, and my Lord and God has me. And as to the world—I had more of it in the great city. My parish, my church, my house—whatever else exists is not for me."

A recollection of his early years came back to Erich, and he told the Priest how, in the midst of the jovial life of the garrison, the thought had come over him that he was called to the clerical profession; but he could not take it without believing in revelation.

"Yes, yes; no one can give himself belief, but he can and must give himself humility, and the grace of faith will follow."

The Priest laid this down as if it were a mathematical axiom, and Erich answered quietly:

"Everybody obtains his stock of feeling and thought like his mother-tongue, from without. Might it not also be said that the soul acquires a language which has a tone of outer life, but which represents itself under the form of religion and habit?—which will not be uprooted, and if it is genuine cannot be, for, in the origin of it, root and ground are one."

"Have you studied the mystics?" asked the Priest.

"But slightly. I only meant to say that all real opposites must be able to unite in something unattainable and incomprehensible.

Again a holy silence took possession of the chamber, in which breathed two men, each seeking to serve his highest ideal in his own way.

"You are at the age," began the Priest, "at which young gentlemen begin to think of marrying; and, as is the fashion now, of marrying a girl with money—much money—very much money. You look so true-hearted, that, though I might do otherwise, I will ask you plainly: Is it true that you are courting Miss Sonnenkamp?"

"I?" said Erich, in astonishment—"I?"

"Yes, you!"

"I thank you," said Erich, in a clear voice, recovering from the shock he had received—"I thank you for asking me that now. You know I am not of your Church."

"And Miss Sonnenkamp *is* of our Church, and it would be hard—"

"I wasn't thinking of that," said Erich, interrupting him. "Wonderful; what tests I have to undergo! First an insolent Cavalier, then a Nobleman, then a Military-man, then a Doctor; and now I find myself in the clerical sieve."

"I don't understand."

"Ah, yes," began Erich; "and I tell you—I trust the nobleness of your mild and spiritual face; and so I confess that as I look at you, I admire the unbroken unity of your life, which the Catholic law of celibacy puts under the form of a dogma, and I allow myself to say that I arrive at the same result through reason instead of dogma. I tell you that he who wishes to live his ideal life, be he artist, scholar, or priest, can have no family. He must renounce such joys, and, living alone in himself, accomplish his mission in steady devotion to his ideal."

"*Divisus est! divisus est!*" cried out the Priest. "The holy apostle Paul says that he who is married is divided; and yet more divided, if he has the fate of children. The Priest has no fate."

A smile passed over his face, as he continued:

"Think of a minister married to a quarrelsome woman—there are peaceable women, mild and self-sacrificing; but there certainly are, also, quarrelsome ones—and now, shall the Priest rise in the pulpit, and speak the word of peace and love, when, an hour before, brawling and insult—"

He stopped abruptly, and musingly laid the forefinger of his left hand on his lips; for he recollected that he had strayed from his object. Had not Miss Perini informed him that Erich had been in the convent before he came here? He looked wonderingly at Erich. Was it his shrewdness, or genuine enthusiasm, that had so diverted him from directly investigating the affair? He hoped, probably, to arrive at his object another way; for, in an unembarrassed, but nevertheless watchful manner, he asked if Erich really thought that he would be able to educate such a boy as Roland, from such a standpoint as his?

As Erich said yes, the Priest asked again:

"And what would you give him first, and above all else?"

"To sum it up briefly," answered Erich, "I wish to make Roland pleased with the world. If he is so, he will give the world pleasure; I mean, he will wish to benefit it. If I teach him to despise the world, to think life a small thing, it will result in his abusing it, and the power that has been given him in it."

"I'm sorry," said the Priest, mildly, "that you are an unbeliever. You are on the road to salvation, but you wander.

Do you know what wealth is? I'll tell you. Wealth is a great temptation—perhaps the greatest of our age. Wealth is a force of nature, perhaps the wildest, most untamable and difficult to master. Wealth is a brute force, which nothing but Almighty God can rule. Wealth is below the brute, because no brute has more strength than is inherent to its own constitution. Man alone can be rich, can possess what he is not, and what can outlive his children and children's children. But here is the misfortune: he who takes so much from the world, lays up harm to his soul. I have tried to make this house and this boy acknowledge, at least before every meal, that what they enjoy so plenteously is only given to them. Do you believe that this boy of whom we are speaking, and this house, can be set right, except by the power of religion? A prayer before you sit down at meat is a recognition, an acknowledgment, that you have some one to thank for what you enjoy. That takes away the pride of vain-glory, and gives the humility which leads to giving others that which is given to one's self. Only where there is fear of the Lord—yes, fear—is there the blessed feeling of his almighty protection. On the table of this rich man, every day, there is a blooming garland of flowers—what of that? On the poorest table of the most needy peasant is a lovelier garland, brought by the word of prayer from the kingdom above; and a satisfaction of the soul comes with it, which makes the satisfaction of the body a blessing. That's only one thing. Up there on the Upper Rhine they call their furniture their movables; and so it is. In our times, riches are nothing but movables; and they are always moving away. Believe me," said he, laying his hand on Erich's shoulder, "believe me, government securities are to-day the curse of our world."

"Government securities? I don't understand you."

"Yes. It isn't so easy to understand. Whom can you lend millions to? Nobody but the government. If there were no government securities, there would be no one who could lend so much. There it is! Once, nobody could have so many millions, for he could not invest so much; but now, there are these securities, and the whole world is living on usury; and usury is canonically prohibited. Just look at it! in old times the rich man had a quantity of real estate; a great deal of field and forest. Then he was dependent on God's dear sun, and when all had reached its full time, and was ripe for the harvest, he gave a tithe to the Church. But now, wealth is laid away in fireproof and burglar-proof safes; not dependent on sun, wind, and weather, not to be seen by the world, and no tenth of the produce to be given, and only a little premium, in the shape of coupons, to be presented at the banker's. The harvest of the man who holds government securities consists in cutting coupons; these are the sheaves which he houses in his granary. If the Lord were to come to earth to-day, he would find no temples from which to drive the traders and money-changers, for they have built temples of their own. Yes; the citadel of Zion to which the rich men and princes flee for safety to-day is the Bank of England! Did you ever reflect on what will be the fate of humanity and governments, if this increasing of the national-debt goes on at this rate? Surely not! The whole earth will be one great hypothecation, pawned to whom? By him who lends long, but will some day demand his reckoning. A general conflagration will come, against which no safes are proof—a new deluge that shall swamp millions and millions of national-debt. I am no prophet of ill-omen, but I may say that I will probably live to see the failure of the Bank of England. Think of it! In the night comes the intelligence that all is lost! Then will thousands of weak men and women first see what nothings they are—when they find themselves suddenly robbed of all their glory, and thrown back upon the naked earth."

Erich smiled. The thought passed rapidly through his mind, that every man who lives in solitude, without intercourse with his equals, is very likely to become whimsical in his notions; and he said that, at all events, the world would be more burdened with debt than it would be worth if a purchaser could be found for it. But the true property of man was worth more than the earth, for his greatest possession was in ideal existence, in capabilities of work; and if all other wealth were blotted out, it would be the task of the new world to make use of its ideal and potential possessions. And he would add, that among the ancient Romans, also, and even in the time of the Republic, the wealth of individuals was as disproportionate as now. But the Priest hardly seemed to hear him, his feelings were so aroused. He went to his bookcase, took a large Bible from it, and, opening at a particular passage, handed the book to Erich.

"Read there the only way in which Roland can be educated. Read it aloud."

Erich took it and read:

"And when he was gone forth into the way, there came one running and kneeled to him, and asked him: 'Good Master, what shall I do, that I may inherit eternal life?' And Jesus said unto him: 'Why callest thou me good? There is none good but one, that is God. Thou knowest the commandments, Do not steal, Do not commit adultery, Do not bear false witness, Defraud not, Honor thy father and mother.' And he answered and said unto him: 'Master, all these things have I observed from my youth.' Then Jesus beholding him, loved him, and said unto him, 'One thing thou lackest: go thy way, sell whatsoever thou hast, and give to the poor, and thou shalt have treasure in Heaven; and come, take up the cross and follow me.' And he was sad at that saying, and went away grieved; for he had great possessions.

"And Jesus looked around about, and saith unto his disciples, 'How hardly shall they that have riches enter into the kingdom of God!' And the disciples were astonished at his words. But Jesus answereth again, and saith unto them, 'Children, how hard is it for them that trust in riches to enter into the kingdom of God! It is easier for a camel to go through the eye of a needle, than for a rich man to enter into the kingdom of God.'"

"And now stand up, and tell me," said the Priest, in a trembling voice, "tell me fairly, is not that the only thing?"

"Fairly, it is not! I love and honor him of whom the history speaks, probably more than many a churchman does; and in my heart I feel the peculiar force of the passage, which says: 'And Jesus, looking upon him, loved him.' I see the beautiful rich young man before the sublime Master. The youth glows, and is filled with honest zeal, for the Teacher wonderfully wins him as he looks in his face. Homer—"

"That's aside from the point—irrelevant," said the Priest, interrupting. "Come to the point."

"I must recognize the fact," answered Erich, "that according to my opinion, this doctrine sprang up in a time when all real power, the power of the State, wealth, and all earthly goods, were to be despised, and cast aside as things of no value, in comparison with the pure idea—in a time of oppression and foreign rule, that doctrine alone could preserve noble minds from falling. And it was well to teach this doctrine at a time and place which saw all that was valuable in the world passing away—which built on a new foundation, in which there was no ruler but pure thought. But if each one is continually giving away what he has, who is to receive it? And why, then, has not this tenet—that man must own nothing, become a positive command of the Church?"

"I am glad to see that you touch the right point," said the Priest. "Our Church has commands that are not binding on all, but only on those who wish to be perfect; as, for instance, the command to be celibate or poor. Only he who wishes to be perfect is obliged to keep them."

"I ask," interrupted Erich, "if the doctrines of Revelation, which are sufficient for all pure morality, are likewise sufficient for all the circumstances of the world? As humanity becomes more and more civilized, new relations come into existence; as from Nature, new natural forces, steam, electricity—"

"Man," answered the Priest, "is the same from eternity to eternity; it is only the citizen that changes. But I see now you are being led in the right direction. I do not demand (the

Lord himself did not do so) that everybody shall become perfect, and therefore the command to give away all his wealth, has no validity in regard to him who does not wish to become perfect; but I tell you, you will never be able to educate the boy unless you give him positive religion. The beast *may* do all that it can, for it has no conception of 'may;' but the man may not do all that he can. To do a thing for which one has strength, or, more accurately, inclination, is not yet the act of a human being; the *man* begins at that point where he tramples inclination under foot, and does that which God's law commands. If every one acted according to his inclination, no one could at any day know what would become of humanity. The law of God holds men together, and upright. Here lies the command of God: here lies the fall of man, which the gentlemen of natural science do not consider. The brute has strong impulses. Man can voluntarily arouse, increase, goad, and multiply his impulses. What shall limit them, except God's command? I'm not speaking of any Church. You have, I presume, devoted yourself principally to history."

"Not particularly."

"Well, you certainly know this: no people, no state can be free (at least history furnishes no such example)—no people, no state can be free without a positive Church. There must be something which is unassailable, and even the Americans of today are free because they submit themselves to religion."

"Or rather they make it optional," said Erich below his breath.

The Priest continued:

"You desire, as I think, to make this boy a free man. We too love free men and wish for them, but there can be no free man without positive religion, and certainly not without one which exacts steady, lawful obedience. The highest result of education is equanimity—understand me—equanimity. Can that philosophy of yours produce calmness of *soul*, and self-sacrifice too, seeing that our whole life is nothing but sacrifice? As I said, can you beget *that* as religion does? If so, you are at one with us. I, for my part, doubt that you can, and we're waiting for the proofs which you have yet to bring forward, although you've been daily occupied with them for thousands of years."

"Religion," answered Erich, "is a phase of civilization. But it is not the whole of civilization; and this is our point of disagreement with the clergy. But *we* are not to blame for the quarrel between religion and science."

"Science," said the Priest, "has nothing to do with the eternal life. Sewing-machines and telegraphs do not concern immortality. Revelation alone has disclosed the eternal life, and its contents will be the same though men in their finite existence make thousands and thousands of discoveries."

Erich, however, asked quietly:

"But how can the Church itself have possessions?"

"The Church does not own, she only administers," answered the Priest sharply.

"I fear we are becoming diffuse," said Erich. "Since we cannot expect that Herr Sonnenkamp and his son will give away all that they have, the question is how to find the correct way of educating the boy."

"Right!" said the Priest, rising and striding up and down the room. "Right! Now we are at the point. Listen to me faithfully. See, something new has entered the world, a position in the highest degree proper, and yet anomalous, and that is *haute finance*. You look at me in surprise."

"Not surprised, but simply questioning."

"Quite right. This *haute finance* stands between nobility and people; and I ask, what does it mean? Shall such a rich young commoner as Roland, thrown into the vortex without any limiting conditions, be lost?"

"Why should he be any more lost than the young nobles who wear the military or civil uniform? Do you think that religion saves *them?*"

"No; but something else, something positive—the historical institution of nobility saves them. Nobility, fortunately, makes those who inherit it pass their early years with the smallest disadvantages. The nobleman when youth is past throws himself back on his wealth and becomes a notable husband, fills his position with good grace, and even amid the mad life of the city is held within bounds by the consciousness of his place in society and at court. But what has the rich young citizen? He has no rank which he must regard, and has no social duties, at least imperative ones."

"You think then," asked Erich, "that it would be fortunate for Roland if his father should become a nobleman?"

"I don't know," answered the Priest. He was annoyed at having allowed himself to be surprised into disclosing the fact that Sonnenkamp had, a short time before, been discussing this question very earnestly with him. "I don't know," he answered; adding immediately: "If one could be ennobled by seventeen ancestors, it would probably be a good thing, but a parvenu nobility— But let us leave the subject. I meant to say that nobility has honor, an historical and constantly imperative obligation. Nobility has found a principle and must make it good. What great principle has wealth found? The most brutal of all, the purely animal. And do you know what this is called?"

"I don't know what you're driving at."

"The proposition which this desire of acquisition has for its highest expression is, 'Help yourself!' Every brute helps himself. Wealth holds that nondescript position attended by no duties, between the nobility and the people. I understand by the term 'people' not only common laborers, but also all men of science and art—yes, even the clergy. The people has work; the *haute finance* does not want honor, and cares for work only so far as to have others work for it, and reap the benefit of others' work. What then does it want? Money. What does it want money for? Pleasure. Who gives it this? The state. What does it do for the state? There's where it all lies. Do you know an answer?"

Erich's lips trembled, and he answered: "If the nobles feel themselves entitled and in duty bound to take—let us say briefly—the command of the army, for war, so ought the young men of wealth feel bound to become officers in the army of peace. An energy shall yet appear, self-raised to command, unsalaried and unselfish, which shall lead the common man on until he shall represent the entirety of the state, and be ready to offer himself a sacrifice for the universal good."

"Hold!" said the Priest, interrupting him. "That last is *ours*. You will never be able to organize that without religion. You will never be able to bring it to such perfection that men will be willing to leave their ease and luxury, and, from what you call a 'purely human motive,' enter the cabins of the poor, the helpless, the sick, the outcast, the dying, as we do."

As if the Priest had summoned to himself his high duty, the sacristan entered, and said that an old vine-dresser needed extreme unction. The Priest was soon ready, and Erich took his departure.

As he entered the street and breathed the clear air again, he felt refreshed. Had he not come from the atmosphere of incense? No! here was something more. Here was a mighty power which placed itself face to face with the enigma of existence. Erich wandered on, buried in reflection, and thought again how much easier life is to those who can propagate fixed dogmatic laws which do not come from themselves, but from others; but *he* was obliged to draw everything from himself—from his own consciousness.

And can that which comes from your consciousness, become the consciousness of another?

Erich stood still, and the thought, that while educating another he was educating himself too, made his cheeks flush. The boy should draw his knowledge from himself; for what is the culture that can be transferred? Nothing but giving the hand to one who moves himself, and leading him.

Erich was standing half-way up the mountain, in the road that led to the Major's house. He looked down at the villa which bore the proud name of Eden, and the history in the Bible came to his mind. In the garden of Eden stood two trees; the tree of life in the midst, and the tree of the knowledge of good and evil. Eden ceases for him who eats of the tree of knowledge. Is it not always so?

It seemed to be suddenly revealed to him that the possibilities of man are these—enjoyment, renunciation, and knowledge.

There is Sonnenkamp: what does he wish for himself and his son? Enjoyment. The world is a spread table, and one needs to learn only so much as will enable him to find the right ways and measures of pleasure. The world is a place of enjoyment, and we are to enjoy it. We have no calling on earth but to ride, eat, drink, and sleep, ride again, and—does the sun shine for *this?*

What does the Priest wish? Renunciation! This world has nothing to give. Her pleasures are deceitful shows, and only distract thee; therefore turn from them.

And what is thy wish? And what shall they whom thou wouldst have like thee, desire? Knowledge! For life is not divided between pleasure and renunciation. Knowledge includes both—is the union of both. Knowledge is the mother of duty and noble deeds.

In ancient times, heroes received from unattainable heights—from the hands of the gods—a buckler, which shielded them. Erich had received no buckler, and yet he felt equipped and prepared for all that might come. He was so happy in himself that he needed the aid of nothing and no one more: he was sustained by knowledge.

Then he walked onward. Calmly and at rest, he entered the Major's house, in the next village. Here, he knew, no examination was awaiting him.

CHAPTER V.

THE GOOD COMRADE.

THE Major lived in the charmingly convenient vineyard-house, near the castle, which belonged to a rich wine-merchant, or, more properly, a brother Mason; for Freemasonry was the central, and most holy point of the Major's life and thought, and whenever the enigmas of life were spoken of, his face always expressed: "These are no mysteries; all is clear to me. If you could only come to us! We see order in everything."

The side of the little house, where the wing occupied by the

Major was, looked toward the road, while the other was turned toward the river, and the mountains beyond it. The Major was firmly attached to his cottage, and his tiny garden shaded with foliage. He regarded the larger dwelling-house and garden with the eye of a warden, but did not live in them, nor did he once, during the many months in which they were empty, wish to occupy them.

Erich found him in his little garden, smoking a long pipe and reading the newspaper, with a cup of cold coffee before him. Opposite to him sat an extremely prim old lady, who wore a white cap and was darning stockings. She rose, as Erich entered, and hardly waited to be introduced, before she disappeared. The Major brought his hand to his cap in military style, and removing his pipe, said:

"Fräulein Milch, this is my comrade, Dr. Dournay, who used to be a captain in the Artillery."

Fräulein Milch bowed, took her basket of stockings, and went to the house.

"She's sensible and good, always contented and cheerful. You'll soon come to know her more intimately," said the Major, after she had withdrawn. "She's a great reader of human nature—there never was a greater. She sees men through and through. . . . . Sit down, comrade. You come just at the right time. I'll tell you how I live. I have hardly anything to do, but I rise early; it lengthens one's life to do so. And so I gain a victory every day over a lazy, effeminate fellow, and make him bathe in cold water, and then take a walk: often he doesn't want to, but he has to. Then, you see, I come home, and when I sit here of a morning, here's my white napkin on the table, here stand my coffee-pot and cream and rolls—I don't eat butter. I pour out the coffee, drink, dip my roll in the cup,—I like it so, I can't bite. Fräulein Milch keeps my teeth in order for me. With my second cup, I light my pipe, and smoke at the world and its history, which the newspaper gives me daily. My eyes are good yet; I read without spectacles, can hit the bull's-eye of a target, and hear everything distinctly. And my back is strong, and I walk as straight as a recruit. And you see too, comrade, I'm just the richest fellow in the world. And then I have my good soup every day—nobody in the world can make as good soup as she can—my piece of good roast-beef, my pint of wine, my coffee—she can make better coffee with four grains than other people can with a pound. And yet, a thousand times I've had to collar this fellow sitting here, and say to him: "Now, you're the most ungrateful fellow in the world: see how often you're vexed, and want this thing or that, which you haven't. Just think of how nice and delicate everything is—the good bread, the good chair, the good pipe, and so much good rest! You certainly are the luckiest man in the world, to have all this . . . . Yes, dear comrade! You—you are said to be a damned good scholar—pardon me, you are said to be deeply learned. Now, see! I haven't studied, haven't learned anything, have been a drummer. . . . I'll tell you again—yes, comrade—what was I going to say? Yes, that's it! You know a thousand times more than I, but yet there's one thing you can learn from me. Take life easier: *now's* the time; be happy now, and enjoy it, for this hour doesn't come back again. Don't be always thinking about to-morrow! Draw a deep breath, comrade. How's that for air? Is there any better, anywhere? And at the same time we've got good, decent clothes on! Ah, thank the Architect of all the worlds! Yes, comrade, if I'd had, at your age, some one to tell me what I tell you now—Heavens! but I'm an old chatter-box! I'm glad you came to see me! How are you? Is it true that you're going to drill our young man to stand fire? I think you're just the man to do it; you'll form him. No one but a soldier can do that. Only a soldier can school men. Strict drill 's the thing. I congratulate them: he'll get to be good, get to be good. Fräulein Milch always said he would, if he could only get into the right hands. The schoolmasters aren't any of them good for anything. Herr Knopf was real honest and good-hearted, but hadn't a good grip on the bridle. Thanks to the Architect of all the worlds! he's got the right man now! Thank you for coming to see me. If I can be of any service to you, remember that we're comrades. It's an excellent thing that you have been a soldier, and I've always wanted one. Fräulein Milch can bear me out in saying that I have said a thousand times, 'Only a soldier!' Now we'll make a soldier of Roland, an embryo soldier; he's got pluck enough, and only needs roll-call."

"I would like," answered Erich, "if I really take the position—"

"Really take it? There's no more doubt; that I say—Heavens! I'd bet something. But pardon me! I won't speak again. You were going to say something, comrade."

"I think we ought not to work with special reference to any calling. Above all things, Roland should be a cultivated, judicious, and good man; and what then seems to be his proper vocation—"

"Quite right! quite right! Well said. That's the way. The boy has given me a great deal of trouble. How foolish people are to wish for millions! And when they get them, they can't eat more than they want, and can't sleep more than eight hours. The chief thing is," said the Major, lowering his voice, and raising his hand, "the chief thing is, he must go back to Nature; that's all the world needs—it must return to Nature."

It was fortunate that Erich did not ask the Major what was the exact meaning of this mysterious sentence, for the Major would not have been able to explain it; but he was fond of the expression, and always made use of it, leaving his auditor to find out what it meant.

"To return to Nature—everything 's included in that," he repeated.

After a while he began again:

"Yes! What was it I wanted to ask? Tell me. You certainly had to suffer a great deal in your soldier-life, because you were a commoner and not a noble."

Erich said, "No!" and the Major stammered:

"To be sure! to be sure! You having been educated philosophically, suffered less. I asked for my discharge. I've already told you about that."

After a while, Erich told him that he had been at the Priest's house, and the Major said:

"He's an honorable man, but I don't leave anything for the parsons to do. I'm a Freemason, you know."

Erich bowed, and the Major continued:

"Whatever good there is in me, is owing to *that.* We'll speak further about it hereafter. I'll be your godfather. Oh, how delighted Herr Weidmann would be to become acquainted with you!"

Again the conversation turned on Weidmann, as though a beautiful piece of mountain scenery was being discussed. The Major continued:

"But now, as to the parsons. Just see here!" and he drew his chair a little nearer to Erich. "There's my drum, for instance; there's everything in it. You see, I was a drummer—yes, smile—now you see, the whole world says that this drum makes nothing but noise; and I tell you there is music in it as beautiful—I don't mean to offend anybody—as anything. Now just see! I tell you, and do you pay attention—I tell you that I don't contradict that you only hear a noise; and so, don't you dispute with me that I hear something else. See, again; I have often thought that men will make everything by machinery yet—machines are so clever: but they'll never be able to make drum or trumpet calls; for men's hands and mouths are needed for that. To be sure I've been a drummer—I'll tell you all about it presently. Now, see; I can tell by the tone what sort of a heart one has, when I hear him beat a drum: where you, brother, would hear nothing but noise and nonsense, I would hear music and sense. And so, for God's sake, don't let's have any quarrelling about religion; one's as much use or as little use as the other; they only sound the march; the chief thing is how one marches himself, how he drills himself, and what sort of a heart he has in his body."

Erich was quite refreshed by the singularity of the Major, in whom, notwithstanding his peculiarities, were deep earnestness and a moral independence all his own.

Placing his pipe beside him, the Major asked:

"Is there a man in the world whom you hate, and at the sight of whom your heart turns round in your body?"

Erich said, "No," and added, that his father had firmly impressed it on his mind that there was nothing so baneful to the soul as hate; and even for his own sake, a person should never allow such a feeling to take root in him.

"Here's my man! Here's my man!" cried out the Major. "Now we understand each other. He who's had such a father is my man."

Then he said that there was a man in the village whom he hated, and he was the Comptroller of Taxes, who wore the St. Helena medal, which the new Napoleon had given to his veterans for their valorous deeds in helping him to overthrow their fatherland.

"And just think!" cried the Major; "the man with the Helena medal has had himself painted, and the picture hangs, framed, in his office, and right under it, in a curious frame, hangs the diploma signed by the French Minister. I don't recognize the man, don't thank him for saluting me; won't sit at the same table with him. His idea of honor is very different from mine. And tell me, now, isn't there some way of punishing wicked men? I can only punish him by showing how I despise him. It comes hard; but oughtn't I to do it?"

The old man looked up in surprise, as Erich said that one ought to deal mildly with the man. Vanity was a very seductive force; and, besides, so many governments would be glad to see their officers decorated with Helena medals, that this man, who was in the state-service, was not at all to be criticised.

"That's true! that's true!" the old man cried out, nodding, as he usually did, a good many times. "You're the right teacher. I'm seventy years old—that is, seventy-three—and they may say what they like, I've never met a bad man—a really bad man. They do a great deal that's bad, in heat, foolishness, and pride; but, my God! they may thank their Heavenly Father that they're not what I might have become, many a time. I thank you—thank you. You've taken the adversary from my neck—yes, from my neck—where he's always been sitting, heavy and—Look! here comes the very man!"

The Comptroller was passing the garden; and the Major went nodding toward the fence, and even motioned with his hand, hoping, probably, that the man would be the first to speak. But as he did not do so, the Major suddenly cried out, in a voice that sounded as if a cannon had suddenly been touched off:

"Good-morning, Herr Comptroller!"

The man returned his salutation, and went by; but the old Major was quite happy, and patted himself on the heart, as though a stone or a burden had been lifted from it.

Fräulien Milch looked out of the window, and the Major asked her to come down, as he had something very good to tell her. She came down, looking neater than before. She wore a white spencer, which was fresh from the iron. The Major told her that the Comptroller was innocent, and had only received the Helena medal out of obedience to the government.

They went together to the house, and the Major showed his guest the chambers, in which reigned a spotless neatness. Then he looked at the barometer, and nodded to himself as he said:

"Fine yet."

Then he looked at the thermometer screwed beside the window, and wiped his forehead as if he had only just discovered how hot it was.

They heard the report of a gun in the distance, and the Major, calling Erich's attention to the direction from which the report came, said:

"They're practising at the fort. I find that rifled cannon make exactly the same noise as the smooth ones. Ah! comrade, you must teach me about the new art of war, for I don't understand it at all; but when I hear the firing down there below, I feel the soldier awake in me again."

He asked Fräulien Milch to bring a bottle of wine—the best. Fräulien Milch seemed to have been prepared for this, as she brought the bottle and glasses immediately, but made a sign to the Major, who understood her, and said:

"Don't worry, I know very well that I mustn't drink of a morning. Let me have your corkscrew, Captain, if you please. I consider you an honest man, and every honest man carries a corkscrew in his pocket."

Erich smiled, and gave him his knife, which had a corkscrew in it.

While opening the bottle, the Major said:

"An honest man can do another thing, too—whistle. Comrade, won't you be so good as to whistle a bit?"

Erich could not pucker his mouth for laughter. The bottle was open, and the two drank to better acquaintance. Then the Major said:

"Perhaps we're happier here than Herr Sonnenkamp in his big Villa. And, Captain, I tell you again, that an elephant is happy—and so's a fly. The only difference is that the elephant has the larger proboscis."

The major laughed till he shook, so pleased was he with his simile, and Erich laughed for company; and as often as they looked at each other, they burst out again.

"Now I understand the proverb," said Erich, "that says that a gnat may be considered as an elephant, and the fact is so. Organism is life, not size or measure."

"Right, right!" cried the Major. "Fräulein Milch, come here a minute."

Fräulein Milch, who had gone away, came back, and the Major continued:

"Captain, won't you just say over again what you said about organism? That's exactly the thing for Fräulein Milch, for she studies a good deal more than she tells about. Now, comrade, about organism again! I can't say it so well."

What was Erich to do? He explained the image again, and again they laughed.

Fräulein Milch recommended Erich to become acquainted with the village schoolmaster, who was a remarkably beautiful writer. The Major laughed and said:

"Yes, comrade, Fräulein Milch is the roll-list of the whole neighborhood. Ask her, if you want to find out about anybody; and for God's sake, don't take any of Countess Wolfsgarten's medicine, for Fräulein Milch understands all that much better than she—and nobody can set a leech as well as she can."

Erich saw the good old lady's embarrassment, and praise her beautiful flowers and plants which grew before the windo The Major assured him that it was probable that she undc stood gardening better even than Herr Sonnenkamp, and ı somebody would only write and say with how few expedients she preserved and grew them, *she* would receive the first priz at the Exhibition, and not the gentlemen who had big hothouses.

In order to change the subject, Fräulein Milch said to Erich that it was extremely unfortunate for Roland, the poor rich boy, that he had not the right kind of pleasures.

"Not the right kind of pleasures?" laughed the Major. "Just listen, will you!"

"Yes," nodded Fräulein Milch, and the ribbons and meshes of her cap nodded with her head as if to confirm her words. "He has just the pleasures and only the pleasures that cost money: but those are not the right ones; and anybody who goes sauntering through the world, without having anything to do in it, will seek pleasure in vain."

An agreeable glance from Erich's eyes rested on Fräulein

Milch, and at that instant there sprang up between Erich and her an undercurrent of confidence and thorough understanding.

Erich left the house, accompanied to the garden-gate by the Major and his housekeeper. As the gate was opened, a black-and-white setter sprang in on the Major.

"So!" said the Major, scolding and caressing the dog. "Ah, where's she been again, the naughty thing, the old vagabond—who knows where she's been? And here we've had a friend at the house, and, as old as you are, you won't learn manners and what's the proper thing to do? Shame on you—shame on you!"

The Major spoke thus to his dog Saadi, who was well known in all the neighborhood. He kept a bitch, because the dogs in the villages never fight with a bitch.

As the Major and Erich were leaving the garden, the Major said:

"Look at these two sentinels, these two ash-trees. I noticed that for several years the one that stands at your left always got its leaves ten or eleven days before the one at your right. Now one day there came along a sudden frost and nipped the leaves of the left-hand one, which suffered all through the Summer, and since that time has been shrewd enough to let the other one get its leaves first, and then puts out its own afterward. Oughtn't one to believe from this that trees have intelligence? Yes, dear comrade, everything is much better arranged in this world than we think. And you see, I am a retired officer on half-pay and have nothing to do; but I have so much to look at, that I often find the days too short. Now good-bye, and remember that you're always at home at our house."

As Erich shook hands with him, the Major said:

"I thank you. I've one more man to love, and that's the best thing yet: that nourishes and keeps me young and sound."

Erich had already gone a few steps, when the Major called after him to stop. He came up and said:

"Yes; in regard to Herr Sonnenkamp, there is yet—Don't mistake, comrade; low-minded men either make an idol of a fortunate man or they fall on him and tear him to pieces. Herr Sonnenkamp is a coarse-skinned man, but good at the core; but as to his past—who can praise his own past? What man can do that? I can't, at least, and I don't know anybody who can. I've not always lived as I may now wish I had. But enough; you're cleverer than I."

"I understand perfectly," answered Erich; "American life is a life without holiday—an endless working and searching for money, and nothing else. When men have led such a life for ten years, they've lost the power to do anything else; they persuade themselves that if they had enough—ah, he who strives for money never gets enough—they persuade themselves that then they would engage in nobler things. Ah, if it were only possible for them then! I assure you I admire Herr Sonnenkamp."

"Certainly, certainly," said the Major, agreeing with him, "he must have paddled around a good deal in the mud, as a gold-hunter, before getting so rich. Yes, yes; I'm satisfied. You're cleverer than I am. But now the important point occurs to me for the first time. Look at me and tell me, fair and square, were you at the convent with Miss Manna?"

"I was at the convent, and saw Miss Manna, but without knowing or speaking to her."

"And you didn't come here with the intention of building your nest in the house and marrying the daughter?"

Erich answered, laughing, that it was singular how this charge was coming against him from all directions.

"Comrade, see to it, that you drive the girl out of your mind, for she's as good as the bride of Baron Prancken. I'd rather let you have her, but the affair can't be altered."

At last Erich succeeded in breaking away, and, filled with happy thoughts, struck the road to the Villa. Good powers were co-operating to surround Roland with a circle of ideas and feelings from which he would never be able to escape.

He stood still before a nut-tree, and looked smilingly into its broad branches and foliage.

"Sonnenkamp is right," said he to himself; "the starting and flourishing of trees is under the influence of currents of air and the heights by which they are surrounded. There are nervous trees which perish in the wind, and others which strike their roots deeper as the blast tugs at them. Is not human life also such a plant? The persons by whom one is surrounded are his climate."

Erich was becoming more and more settled in the belief that he understood the conditions which would promote or hinder the growth of Roland.

"How rich the world is! Over there in yonder castle sits the Count, after a full and busy life, thinking his own thoughts; and by his side sits his young wife—here sits the old Major with his housekeeper. How Bella would turn up her nose to think of being compared with the housekeeper, and yet—"

Erich suddenly heard a carriage approaching, and the voices of a man and woman calling to him.

CHAPTER VI.

THE THIRD PARTY.

ON the day when Erich left Castle Wolfsgarten, a regular guest found his way thither; this was the son of the distinguished wine-dealer—the so-called Wine-count. He came once a week to play chess with the Count. He looked young and had a *blazé* air, and absolutely did not know what in the world to do. He did not like his father's business. He had money enough. He had studied a number of things, played, drew a little, and had various talents, but no leading one. Everything was a bore to him; the lees of life were stale and tasteless, but must be drunk with a good grace. Why should he deliver himself up to one definite profession for the sake of making money? It was by no means necessary. He was a director in several railway-companies; and for a while it had given him pleasure to rule and manage in this capacity and to be addressed and listened to reverentially by those below him. But this also became distasteful to him. Travelling afforded him no more pleasure, as he always carried an overload of ennui with him. He looked at the world with aversion, for it had nothing to do for him, and he nothing to do for it. He had developed only one single talent, and that was his talent for chess; and as Clodwig was also very fond of it, and was, moreover, a skilful player, he came to Wolfsgarten once a week, and played with Clodwig; this fact gave him peculiar importance, as well in his own eyes as in those of others.

He also had a secret but great reputation among the gentlemen of the neighborhood who could boast, as he could, of being rakes and appearing to the world as great gallants. He possessed a collection of indecent pictures of all sorts and subjects; and the man who could boast of having seen all of them, could also boast of being his very intimate friend. Certainly the Wine-cavalier was a very respectable man in the eyes of the world. No one had ever yet seen him drunk; and in the society of the citizens he played the part of the condescending bored gentleman, who is nevertheless so kind as to associate with these little people: one owes thus much to old acquaintance. Mothers always warned their daughters against the Wine-cavalier, as it is customary to warn children against the wolf that goes howling through the fields; but even the mothers were not very angry when he occasionally cast a languishing glance toward themselves, or whispered some tender nothings in their ears.

Lina was not so simple as her mother was always saying, for she said that the Wine-cavalier was the identical little enchanted fellow in the story who went in search of horrible things to learn how to shiver.

Every year the Wine-cavalier renewed himself in toilet, anecdote, and everything else needed by internal or external fashion, by a sojourn of several months in Paris. He did not speak, as his father did, of his friend the Ambassador So-and-So, the Minister So-and-So, or Prinee So-and-So, but he gave it to be understood that he lived on terms of the closest intimacy with the members of the Jockey-Club.

At other times the Wine-cavalier would find a certain little charm in paying impressively polite attentions to Bella, but to-day she looked at him as if he were not present, and as if she only heard at a distance what he said; and even the Count was so innattentive and absent-minded that he lost all the games with surprising quickness, and often looked with astonishment at his opponent, who sat in the same chair that had held Erich.

A new colleague for the Cavalier appeared; but even he was without effect to-day. He was a comely man, dressed with the greatest care, who had formerly been a celebrated basso, had married a rich widow in a neighboring commercial town, and had settled here in the midst of that beautiful region. Bella was generally glad to have him come, for he still sang pleasingly with what was left of his voice; but from the way in which he was received, he saw that he was not as welcome to-day as usual, and put Bella yet more out of humor by saying that he had only "happened in." Bella did not at all like to have people consider Wolfsgarten a place where casual calls could be made. When both the visitors had gone, Bella and Clodwig breathed freely again.

Clodwig entered the cabinet which contained his collection of unearthed relics, but here everything seemed changed. The urns for the ashes of the dead, the wine-urns, the tear-vases, swords, necklaces, and his multitude of *reliefs*, looked mournful even the clay cast of a warrior's face, only one half of which they had succeeded in excavating, looked grim to day. Everything looked as desolate as if the thousands of relics brought from the darkness of the earth to the light of day said in lamentable tones, "Why are we here? each of us misses something, each has lost a part of itself;" and if Clodwig could have put his own soul with all its emotions before himself like these remains, he—the full man—would have seen but fragments like these. Something was lost from him, since Erich had gone away.

With drawn lip and restless eye that seemed to be seeking something, he wandered for whole days through the house and park. Bella at last succeeded in drawing him into conversation, and he told her that he was now able to accomplish the ideal of his life, but that, singularly enough, he had not the courage to do so. He lamented, for the first time, the indecision and timidity of old age which he felt. He made a pause, hoping that Bella would ask him what he wished; but she was silent, and he told her, evasively, that one might allow himself many luxuries, and yet not possess that one of all others which was most desired. At last he said directly that he had made a mistake in letting Erich go: he had long wished for such a man, and would even say that in carrying out his own wishes he would be able to greatly benefit this young scholar with the Apollo mien.

Bella's lip trembled, and she said:

"The Captain"—she was thinking of the Captain in Goethe's "Elective Affinities," and as this thought passed through her mind, she went blundering on: "The Captain—I mean the Doctor, would certainly consider himself very fortunate. But, we may speak openly. I have the good fortune to bear a name above reproach, and we do not ask what people think."

"Speak everything you think," said Clodwig encouragingly; and Bella continued, after passing her handkerchief over her face:

"Don't you believe this young man—would sometimes—what shall I say?"

"Be in our way?" said Clodwig, coming to her assistance. Bella nodded, but Clodwig had already considered the subject in this aspect, and combated her idea by saying that it would be a certain oppression of the good, if they should be forced to relinquish a worthy object because the bad do their wicked deeds under a deceitful appearance of good.

Bella now urged her husband to send a message to Erich immediately, asking him not to bind himself. Clodwig pressed her hand, and entered his work-room with a step far more elastic than customary. He wrote for awhile, but soon returned to Bella, and said that he could not write, and it would be the simplest way to have the horses harnessed, and go to Villa Eden himself.

Clodwig usually avoided any immediate reference to Sonnenkamp and his house, so far as was possible, considering the close connection of his brother-in-law with them. To-day, however, nothing was said on the subject, and they were soon pleasantly on the road.

Bella would often draw her veil over her face and raise it again. She was ill at ease, for she was thinking of many things, and, as she noticed the rapid beating of her heart, she seized her husband's hand and cried:

"Ah, you're so good, so angel-pure! I would not have believed that I would be ever discovering new heights in you!"

Thus she spoke; and speaking so, silenced something that whispered stilly in the breast, which she would not recognize, even to herself—yes, which she denied to herself. It was an inexplicable whim, a play—not of passion, no; how could Bella find anything of passion in herself? It was the play of a demon! This young man must have some mysterious, some incomprehensible power of enchantment! Bella hated him, for he had withdrawn her husband from repose, and was now trying to accomplish the same result with her. He should repent it! She drew herself up proudly: she determined that by accompanying her husband she would overthrow his childish, transcendental plan; and if Erich would not notice her opposition voluntarily, she would call his attention to it, and make it the cause of his declining to comply with the Count's wishes.

As she thought of this, she became pleasant again; and Clodwig noticing the change, spoke of what apartments Erich was to have, and how the new household should be conducted. Bella should have a friend as well as he: he would invite Erich's mother to visit them. It was fortunate that Bella already knew and respected her. Clodwig said that the Dournays were noble too: their name had been originally Dournay de Saint Mort, and they had only relinquished their nobility when the Huguenots were expelled from France. In case Erich should make a marriage conformable with his position, he, Clodwig, would see that his title should be restored, and would probably be able to do yet more for him.

Bella asked, laughingly, if he did not want to adopt him as his son; and Clodwig said that he was not averse to doing so. Bella smiled bitterly, and yet seemed to be smiling gayly as she said that it would seem quite singular for her to have a son who was only a few years younger than herself.

Clodwig's antique relics fairly danced before his mind's eye, and cut strange capers. Bella, on the other hand, was very much out of humor. It was always a matter of wonder to her that her husband should be so earnest in regard to such matters. She had not deceived him when, in the Winter previous to their engagement, she had represented herself as a ripe woman, recognizing the deeper objects of life, and in sympathy with the art of classical antiquity, with science and the more lofty concerns of human interests; in truth, she had not deceived him, for she had never had any other idea than that such things were regarded by everybody, as they were by her, as practicable subjects of conversation, and mere tasty knick-knacks. As regards the history of past and present civilization, it seemed to her that there was a tacit agreement to consider it an elegant pastime.

She had learned to her horror that, in fact, great thoughts made up her husband's life: that he was troubled or pleased at all occurrences of world-wide interest, as if they were family matters; and that he was even religious. He did not speak as she did of God; but he could stand in wrapt adoration before the eternal divine order; and where there was an apparent contradiction, an enigma, he was aroused to a state of morbid, feverish excitement.

Bella did not acknowledge even to herself, that all this seemed to her shockingly like the conduct of a pedant, a preacher, or a professor; she had not known that she had married a pedantic professor, instead of a man who enjoys life. But, whether she recognized the fact or not, all this devotion to so-called higher interests, was wearisome to her. Everybody only played his own rôle in life—who would make earnest business of it? Let poor devils of scholars and philanthropists do so, but not a man of higher station. And then, again, she saw that Clodwig, by suddenly becoming associated with a stranger, might bring a disturbing element into an orderly life, which, although it was assuredly wearisome, was nevertheless passing quietly and honorably.

What was frequently said behind Bella's back—that she had married the Count in hopes of soon becoming a rich and charming widow—was black calumny. The old Chief-Equerry had been careful enough to obtain a good estate, and from the income of this large property yearly laid aside a considerable sum, which did not follow the entail. It was, as has been said, black calumny, to assert that Bella had gone to the altar in hopes of becoming a widow; but, to her horror—she concealed this horror in her breast, as often as she experienced it—she saw herself growing old before her time, beside a man who was old enough to be her father.

And who could tell how much money Clodwig would lavish on this Dournay, who never remained long in one profession, and who was, besides, out of favor at court. The worst, however, was that this young man, who knew so well how to obtain mastery, would draw her husband's attention entirely from her.

They would study together, make excavations, and in the mean time she—she who had so nobly, so faithfully, and with such entire abnegation of self, devoted herself to her duty to her old husband—would sit alone, forgotten.

Bella was deeply enraged at Erich, for he forced her to have evil thoughts, and suddenly she cried, looking at her husbaud:

"For God's sake! Your lips are pale! what ails you?"

Were her evil thoughts to be realized? But Clodwig answered:

"It's nothing. Do you see? There he is. What a wonderful form! I believe that as he stands there lost in dreams, and staring at the grass, his mind is filled with the loftiest inspirations."

The carriage rolled along. Erich heard his name called, and looked in surprise at them, as they greeted him. He was obliged to take a seat in the carriage, and a glance from Clodwig said to Bella: "Did you ever see a nobler man?"

Erich was asked if he had accepted the situation yet, and when he said he had not, Clodwig gave him his hand, and said: "Welcome to me!"

He could not speak further of this subject, for Herr Sonnenkamp trotted up to them on his black horse, and was extremely delighted to welcome such guests, but was surprised to see Erich so much at home with them. He rode close to the coach, and the guests were welcomed with great respect and satisfaction to Villa Eden.

They had hardly alighted, when another carriage entered the courtyard, and the Doctor alighted from it.

CHAPTER VII.

THE FIRST ROSE IN THE OPEN AIR.

A NEW importance was given to Erich by the arrival of Clodwig and Bella. Sonnenkamp called him "My dear friend" for the first time.

Herr Sonnenkamp offered his arm to Bella, who bowed, and accepted it: Clodwig should see what a sacrifice she was making. Her hand rested softly on Sonnenkamp's arm, and as she went forward, she stopped suddenly, filled with admiration at seeing an out-door rose-bush, bearing a rose in full bloom.

Herr Sonnenkamp hastened to pluck it, and offered it to her with a few delicate words. Bella thanked him earnestly, and pretended not to see his proffered arm any more. They immediately entered the green-houses. Joseph, who always appeared at the right time, as if called, was told by his master to announce the visit to Frau Ceres and Miss Perini. Joseph understood.

The Doctor had been called to attend Frau Ceres, but as soon as the lady heard who her guests were, she declared herself well again; but was cunning enough to tell the Doctor that it was simply his presence that had made her so. Doctor Richard understood.

In the mean time Clodwig had said to Erich:

"You will not stay here; you will go with us. I will not leave you."

He spoke these words shortly and hastily, as if he had had them prepared a long time, and yet as if the delivery of them was distasteful and annoying.

Roland was coming down the mountain, with his campstool and drawing-board, and Bella called to him while he was yet at a distance, and said pleasantly, "Welcome!"

"How handsome he is!" said she to the rest. "Who could fasten to the canvas such a picture as this beautiful boy? If one could change his campstool and portfolio into a spear and shield, one would have a picture from the Greek world."

Bella noticed the pleasure that shone in Erich's eyes, and said to him:

"Yes, Doctor; I once suggested to an artist at Court, that he should paint a scene in which I saw Roland. He had run across the street, and had thrown a gift into the hat of a beggar, who was sitting on a pile of stones; and as he ran back again, so slender and graceful, every muscle strained, and his face glowing with pleasure and benevolence, it was a wonderful sight—one never to be forgotten."

Clodwig looked down: Bella had evidently forgotten that it was not she, but he, who had seen Roland then, and had made the suggestion to an artist.

Roland was much surprised at the visit and the way in which he was welcomed, for Bella said to her husband:

"Clodwig, kiss him for me!"

Clodwig embraced the boy, who then looked at Erich with puzzled glances.

"If the Captain stays with us you must visit us often, Roland," said Bella.

Sonnenkamp could not think what this meant, but Roland immediately perceived that he was in danger of losing Erich, and looked at him as if seeking help. And now Erich knew what had been intended in regard to him, and understood, for the first time, what had been interrupted by Sonnenkamp's meeting the carriage.

They hardly looked at the green-houses, for Bella said that when everything was green and blooming out of doors, hot-house plants seemed to her imprisoned.

Miss Perini presently appeared, as the envoy of Frau Ceres, to inform the company that it was her intention not to be sick that day.

Bella and Miss Perini withdrew from the gentlemen; they had much to say to each other, and Erich was naturally the first subject they discussed. Bella could not avoid expressing to Miss Perini her admiration that she, Miss Perini, had instantly seen through this wonderful man, although Miss Perini had certainly not yet said anything about him. But this ingenious leader necessitated further conversation, which, nevertheless, was not by any means confidential, for Miss Perini said that German scholars awakened her admiration more and more every day, and would prefer to have Bella's opinion, as she was almost a scholar.

Bella refused to receive this equivocal compliment, and assumed a certain matronly air, as she acknowledged that she was not in harmony with the young people of the day—in fact, hardly understood them. Neither of the ladies appeared to express her opinion, and each seemed to impute to the other a secret inclination toward Erich.

"Do you know," said Bella, looking intently at the rose that Sonnenkamp had plucked for her—"do you know that this man with the double title has an insultingly contemptuous opinion of women?"

"No, I did not know it; but it may be a part of what Baron von Prancken calls that radical heresy, which he is so vain of, and likes to display."

"But what's your own opinion of Herr Dournay?"

"I've no opinion in regard to him."

"Why?"

"I'm not unprejudiced—he does not belong to our Church."

"But suppose he were a member of our Church; what would your opinion of him be then?"

"I cannot make such a supposition. That self-satisfied uprightness of his would be entirely impossible in a man who bowed before the Divine Law. His bearing has a certain air, as though he were a prince travelling incognito. As Baron von Prancken says, 'The man seems to go about the world in an invisible pulpit.'"

Both the ladies laughed.

Bella understood enough. She tried, very cautiously, to impress upon Miss Perini the necessity of making her influence tell against the acceptance of a man who prided himself on his unbelief. Miss Perini held her cross in her left hand and looked somewhat roguishly at Bella. Probably the Countess did not wish to have him here. Could she be devising some nice intrigue against her husband, and did she therefore wish to have Erich in her own house? She felt a certain malicious pleasure in pointing to the fact that, as Herr von Prancken had occasioned the whole trouble, it was his duty to relieve them of it. Bella informed her that there was also another reason why Erich was unsuitable for the position. And now Erich was for the third time called a dangerous man. Miss Perini had, it is true, said so with reference to two circumstances, one near, and the other remote; for Bella's remarkable agitation had not escaped Miss Perini's quietly shrewd eye. Hastily, and in order to conceal the fact that she had made this discovery, she said that such a man as Herr von Prancken certainly had no one to fear. She spoke of Prancken's journey with sympathetic interest, saying that it had probably been made on the impulse of the moment; that much must be pardoned to the passionate heart of youth, and that it often brought about the desired result in a better way than care and circumspection did. Miss Perini spoke only in inuendoes, and Bella answered in the same way, saying that she highly disapproved a certain tendency which Prancken had toward acting in opposition to the customs of society, but that she would have to let it pass, although not without anxiety.

The conversation again turned upon Erich, and Bella now spoke with the greatest magnanimity. She sympathized with his old mother, and expressed the belief that the self-conscious demeanor of the young man was simply timidity: he pretended to be proud, in order to conceal his dependent condition. A slight elevation of Miss Perini's eyebrows showed that she demurred a little to this; and Bella added quickly, that it is only pious persons who do not feel embarrassed by dependence, for their very nature places them above it—yes, makes them the equals of all.

Miss Perini smiled: she understood with what kind of tenderness Bella was dealing with her, and there was no need of that warm pressure of the hand to impress it upon her.

A servant came and informed them that Frau Ceres awaited Countess Bella in the saloon next the balcony. The Doctor had forbidden her to go into the open air, and consequently she could not venture to do so.

Miss Perini conducted Bella as far as the steps leading to the saloon, and there made a courtly obeisance. Bella took both her hands with apparent affection, and said that she wished she might have daily intercourse with such a friend as Miss Perini: she begged that she might soon have the honor of a visit from her.

When Bella had gone rustling up the steps, Miss Perini clawed with her little hands, like a cat who has waited and watched and at last caught something; her eyes, which were usually veiled, opened scornfully, and her little mouth said, half aloud:

"You're all duped!"

Frau Ceres lamented her constant suffering, and Bella comforted her by saying that she certainly had everything that heart could wish, and then—such lovely children. She did not know which was more delightful, the bewitching disposition of Roland, or the angelic nature of Manna.

It was seldom that Bella entered Sonnenkamp's house, but as often as she did, she experienced a passion pre-eminently feminine in its nature. True, she was surrounded at Wolfsgarten with an affluence which left nothing to be desired, but as soon as she entered the gate of Villa Eden, a demon came upon her, a demon whose name was Envy—envy of this woman living amid all the overflowing luxuries of life, not burdened with a decaying splendor, but born into a new one. And as often as she thought of Frau Ceres, her eyes became hot and dazzled, for she saw the glorious attire of Frau Ceres, which even the reigning Princess could hardly hope to equal.

She was now especially gracious and condescending to Frau Ceres, and her ability to be so made her happy. These persons could buy everything but a lofty name rendered illustrious by time, and even if Otto's design should be accomplished, this would but serve to cover their low estate with a new gloss, a gloss ever praying, "Don't touch me, or I'll rub off."

It was quite natural that Erich should be the subject of conversation here also; and Bella pressed the rose to her lips to hide her laughter, as Frau Ceres said:

"I would like to have the Captain for myself."

"For yourself?"

"Yes. But I believe I can't learn anything any more: I'm too old and too stupid. He'd never let me learn anything at all."

Bella would not hear of such modesty. Was not Frau Ceres young and beautiful? She might easily be taken for Roland's sister. Was she not clever and her presence dignified? Frau Ceres kept up a continuous smiling and nodding; apparently she believed that it was all true. Then Bella begged to be allowed to take leave; she could not think of longer disturbing the delicate organization of Frau Ceres.

At these words, Frau Ceres cast her eyes timidly around, not knowing whether this was compliment or the reverse. Bella kissed her forehead and withdrew.

Herr Sonnenkamp had left the Count and Erich: he had much to attend to in the house, and letters and despatches had arrived which required immediate answers. He sent for the Major, requesting him to come to dinner, and told the messenger that if he did not find the Major at home, he must look for him at the castle.

Clodwig went with Erich and Roland to their apartments, and, without knowing it, soon forgot Roland in the earnestness of their conversation. The boy sat quietly, looking first at the one and then at the other. He did not understand what they said, but probably felt how much pleasure it gave them; and when, at last, Clodwig withdrew to his own room, Roland took Erich's hand and said:

"I want to learn: I will study everything that you wish. I want to be like you and Clodwig."

Erich was deeply moved. What Clodwig wanted him to do, was the ideal of all that he could wish. But here was a living duty: he was no longer at liberty to decide.

CHAPTER VIII.

ICH DIEN.

FORTUNATELY, the Major appeared just as they were sitting down to dinner. He was extremely happy to meet Bella and Clodwig here. Every exhibition of friendly feeling was a cordial to him. It confirmed his belief that all men are boundlessly good, and furnished him, besides, with a means of confounding all scoffers and skeptics. He was as grateful to Clodwig and Bella as if they had done him a personal favor. He looked at the chairs as if to bid them be comfortable to their guests. He extended his hand to Erich as to a son. He had become entirely Erich's. And now he lamented, in the tone of a child who has been nibbling forbidden sweets, that he had let himself be led astray. He had wanted to see for himself, once and for all, whether the workmen at the castle were well fed: he had tasted their food, and found it so palatable that he had eaten his full before he knew it.

Erich comforted him by saying that he thought that he would certainly be able to find room for such dainty food as he would find here.

The Major nodded, and gave Joseph the brief command:

"Allasch!"

Joseph understood. He filled from a bottle surrounded by little glasses, which stood on a sideboard, and the Major drank the appetizing draught.

"That's a room-maker," he said to Erich, and his whole face laughed as Erich answered:

"Certainly; the spirit commands the common herd to give room."

Frau Ceres did not appear at table. The company had hardly sat down, before the Doctor was called away: he rose instantly. Sonnenkamp wished him to remain, but Clodwig said quietly that he would like to express the wish that the Doctor would go; for if one would place himself in the position of those who were waiting for the Physician, he would see how cruel it was to detain him here for mere pleasure, while they were suffering.

"He's a nobleman—a genuine nobleman!" said the Major to Erich; and Roland, who heard the words, looked around as if he had been grasped suddenly. Was his father, who had wished the Doctor to do otherwise, ignoble, then?

Erich felt what was passing in the boy's mind, and said to the Major, in a tone loud enough for the boy to understand:

"Herr Sonnenkamp spoke in view of the fact that the country-people often exaggerate the danger, and call the Doctor unnecessarily."

"That's true—I was wrong. Thank you, comrade."

Roland breathed freely, and smiled to Erich; he longed to throw his arms around him and kiss him.

Erich understood the smile.

The table seemed disordered, for the Doctor's withdrawal had made a gap; in order to hide which, the guests were forced to sit closer together, mentally as well as physically. The summons that had called the Doctor to the bed of some groaning patient surrounded by his friends, had disturbed the pleasant feelings with which they had sat down at table.

Erich, who knew very well that Clodwig and Bella had made this visit on his account, considered himself doubly bound to contribute his share toward making the company feel good-humored and at home. But while he was thinking in what direction to turn the conversation, the Major got ahead of him. He smiled pleasantly before he spoke, for he had something to tell, and now was just the time to tell it.

"Herr Sonnenkamp," said he, getting red in the face again to think that he had to speak before so many people—"Herr Sonnenkamp, the newspaper says that you'll receive a good many visits soon."

"I? The paper says so?"

"Yes. It doesn't say so directly, but that's the way I understand it. It says that it costs so much to live in America now, that there's an emigration from that country; a good many families are leaving the New World and coming to Europe, where they can live cheaper and better."

The Major repaid himself for filling the gap with something interesting as well as fitting, for, at one draught, he drank a glass of his favorite Burgundy, with the greatest gusto.

Sonnenkamp said, unconcernedly, that if that were the case, folks would be likely to form the same prejudice against Americans that they have against English travellers.

No one continued the conversation. Clodwig would have been listened to willingly; but he was embarrassed, and felt as though he had entered another man's house and had been received as a guest, while he was intending to rob his host. This made him dispirited and shy.

Erich put a different construction on his behavior, and gave the conversation a pleasant turn by referring to Goethe's poem, which extols America because it has no ruined castles; thus bringing in the favorite pursuits of Clodwig and Sonnenkamp, and drawing a parallel between antiquarian and horticultural tastes. Erich was very animated and communicative, and said things which he knew would arouse particular attention, and then would suddenly pause, in the midst of his exposition, to pursue some attractive accessory of the subject. Hitherto he had always innocently answered questions, and had only spoken to give information to others, or to explain something to them; but now he conversed with the intention—or at least the half intention—of being brilliant, and was greatly pleased with the effect of this or that expression. He was surprised at this himself, and yet spoke on. He banished the reproachful thoughts which accompanied this action, and only told himself that it was his duty to appear here in the character of an intellectual host. His eyes brightened, and he placed Clodwig and Sonnenkamp upon more agreeable relations with each other.

The ladies also did their part. But Bella had a way—and, since she had it, it must have been most excellent *savoir faire*—whenever she was not leading the conversation, no matter who was speaking, or what the conversation was about, of disturbing the little circle, by engaging her neighbor in a dialogue, and preventing him from escaping into the larger stream of discourse, even though he wished to do so. She was now engaged with Miss Perini, speaking volubly in Italian.

Erich was vain enough to notice her want of interest; it troubled him at first, but after a while he did not notice it.

Herr Sonnenkamp was very well pleased with this tutor, who not only let him shine in his own element, and placed him in the honorable position which rightly belonged to him, but who, by being present, was an ornament of his house, and brought to his table the *élite* of the land.

Clodwig again requested that he might be immediately informed of every relic of ancient Rome which should be found while the castle was being restored. Sonnenkamp promised this very readily, and with great vivacity expressed himself as highly amused by thinking what absurd reasons for rebuilding the castle were attributed to him. Some folks said that he wanted to see his name in Bädecker's "Hand-book of Travel," so that on the long summer-days, when people were sailing up and down the river, they might point out the castle to each other; and English tourists, bored to death as their manner is, might gape at it, and trace its name in the book with their fingers. In reality, his object was an æsthetic one. He knew quite well, that by restoring the castle he would have a fine termination for the view from his work-room; in addition to this, however, he would like to contribute something to the beauty of the German Fatherland.

Sonnenkamp always spoke the words "German Fatherland" with a peculiar twang: a bitter hatred might have been found in the tone, and yet it rather gave the impression of pity and compassion. Sonnenkamp knew that Clodwig was, above all things, a patriot, and therefore he loved to strike the chord that rang of Fatherland. Erich looked at Roland to see if he understood this piece of hypocrisy, for during the conversation on Sunday, Sonnenkamp had taken opportunity to speak coldly and contemptuously in regard to the election. But Roland's features were unmoved: and, on the one hand, Erich felt comfort in finding that the boy's innocent mind did not perceive the contradiction; but on the other hand, he saw a difficulty which would render his position as tutor more arduous; for it was one of his chief tasks to arouse and strengthen, in the mind of his pupil, the perception of the logical consistency and concatenation of all thought and action.

Sonnenkamp enlarged yet further on the singularities which were attributed to him; but the fact was that nobody had atrributed them to him, but rather it was he himself who, in conjunction with Prancken, had given out that he intended to assume the name of the castle—the family to which it originally belonged having long since died out. It was said that the arms of the Von Rankenbergs could no longer be distinctly traced, and yet it was intended to place them again over the gate of the restored castle.

Clodwig, who, with all his liberal ideas, took a certain pride in knowing the genealogies and arms of all royal and noble families, assured him that the arms of Rankenberg were perfectly well known;—that in the left field there was a "Moor's head," on a blue ground; in the right, a balance, as an emblem. The family had evidently distinguished itself in the Crusade, and probably had afterward risen to the higher offices of judicature in the kingdom.

Sonnenkamp smiled very pleasantly—almost grinned—and begged that the Count would send him a copy of the arms as soon as possible.

Erich's large store of information was again noticeable, and particular attention was aroused by his acquaintance with armorial devices. Considerable amusement was occasioned by parcelling out this or that motto to each of the assembled company—as the motto would sometimes be ridiculous from its inappropriateness, and sometimes an extremely shrewd expression of the person's character.

"What motto would you select?" said Sonnenkamp to Erich.

Erich answered only these two words:

"Ich dien."

CHAPTER IX.

DOUBLE ESCAPE.

ERICH and Bella happened to be walking together, and she, intending to accomplish a double design, said to him that she wondered at his close intimacy with Clodwig; for to live with him was not so easy as it seemed. She said this very guardedly, and it might have been nothing but praise. Erich answered:

"All the world, therefore, owes you gratitude, Countess; for the Count has received new youth from you."

Bella nodded. Erich had quietly and steadily taken the first step toward a better understanding, and had shown very delicately that he appreciated her sacrifice. She now spoke in an exalted strain of Clodwig, and said how happy she was in being able to do something toward preserving that pure man, and in having no selfish motive in doing so. It was so beautiful to immolate herself—to serve him silently, unrecognized and unnamed. She spoke in a half-childish way, in order to make Erich recur to his profession as a teacher.

Erich spoke readily and without embarrassment, so that Bella could not tell whether he had not understood her, or was only pretending that he had not. She hinted slightly at the peculiar difficulty of managing such a man as Clodwig, however unassuming and pliable he might appear. She begged Erich to aid her in making the evening of his life calm and blessed. There was a heartfelt earnestness in her tone that was not to be mistaken.

Erich told her plainly his doubts as to whether it was right to disturb such an unruffled existence by bringing into it a third party. He said that as yet he himself was unskilful, capricious, and passionate.

"You are so truthful that you have no need of being modest," answered Bella.

She looked piercingly at Erich, and dropped her fan. As Erich picked it up, she thanked him, giving him her hand.

Her bosom heaved as she told Erich adroitly, and yet with delicate emotion, how highly she prized the good fortune that had brought her into close intimacy with a noble man, and had given her a friend in whom there was no deceit.

Erich did not know whether this remark referred to himself or Clodwig.

"There he comes!" said Bella, suddenly. "Ah, see! he insists on not carrying a cane, and yet he needs one."

She went to meet her husband, who was approaching her

Clodwig sat down under a beautiful cedar, where light chairs had been placed. Erich and Bella stood before him, and he laid before them his whole plan. He spoke so earnestly of the beautiful and complete life they would live together, that Erich's cheeks glowed. With a trembling voice he uttered his thanks, and said how bound he felt to the spot where his heart had already decided him to stay.

Bella rested one hand on Clodwig's chair, and Erich went on to say how it rejoiced him to find that something so attractive was offered him; for this fact assured him he had made the right choice in that to which duty called him. A great and difficult task was set before him in the education of Roland, and it made him happy to think that another mode of life so enticing had been laid before him; for it renewed and strengthened his confidence that he had chosen his proper profession, and the presentation to him of this opportunity for change made him recognize the path of his choice as that of his deepest duty.

For a while Clodwig's eyes were cast down, and Bella, taking her hand from the chair, suddenly stood upright. But when Erich told of the pleasure he found in Roland, and the mysterious and deeply-felt attraction which drew him to the boy, even to his faults, Clodwig smiled quietly at the branches; for in the same way that Erich felt drawn by a romantic love toward Roland, Clodwig was drawn toward *him*. There was the same quality of feeling. Therefore, he would not let Erich go, and told him again that he could not educate Roland without assistance; for he would have to combat elements with which he had probably never contended.

"Ah! here comes the Doctor," said he, interrupting himself. "Will you call in a third party to decide?"

"I alone," said Erich, "can give the decision, however painful it may be. But I've not the slightest objection to hearing our friend's opinion."

It was given; but to the surprise of all, the Doctor disagreed with both. He wished that somebody would put Erich in a position to visit Italy and Greece.

Before Clodwig could answer, Erich said he was seeking employment in order to earn a living for himself and his mother.

Rising with difficulty, Clodwig said:

"Give me your arm, young friend."

He stood up and leaned upon Erich, while his arm rested heavily and trembled.

"I don't know," said he—"I hardly seem to myself a man who has gone through so much. I have had a better experience to-day. Is it age that makes it so hard for me to relinquish what I wish? Yet I have learned to do so. Yes, yes! one becomes childish—childish! A child cannot renounce."

He leaned yet more heavily on Erich, who was moved in his inmost soul to see so noble a man so shattered. He could say nothing, and Cloding continued:

"It seems to me as though I were not here—I know not where. Is it not stifling here?"

"No. Won't you sit down?"

Hastily withdrawing his hand from Erich's arm, Clodwig passed it over his face and said:

"Young friend, when I die, then—"

He had hardly spoken before he fell; but Erich caught him in his arms. Bella, who was walking behind them with the Doctor, gave a quick cry. The Doctor ran toward them, while Erich, bending down, took Clodwig in his arms like a child. All this was done in an instant.

Clodwig was carried into the great saloon, and laid on a sofa. Bella cried aloud, and the Doctor endeavored to soothe her. He had a medicine with him, by means of which he soon brought Clodwig to consciousness. As soon as Clodwig had spoken a few words, the Doctor begged Erich and Bella to leave the room.

When they had withdrawn, Bella threw herself on Erich's breast, and he trembled. He felt her breath, and shuddered as the beautiful woman leaned on him with such recklessness, such abandon, and cried:

"You are our helper, our friend in need! Oh, my friend, my friend!"

Sonnenkamp approached hastily, and Bella rising, said with wonderful composure:

"Herr Sonnenkamp, it is very fortunate that our common friend, Captain Dournay, is with us. He carried my husband with a giant's strength. Thank him with me."

Erich was amazed at her wonderful composure. The Doctor came out, and Sonnenkamp asked anxiously:

"What's the matter? what's the matter?"

He was reassured; for the Doctor said it was only a slight attack, which would have no bad result. Clodwig begged to see Erich.

Erich entered the chamber. Clodwig sat up, and, stretching out his hand to Erich, said with a wonderfully composed smile:

"I must finish my sentence. I intended to say: when I die, my young friend, I wish that you may be near me. But quiet yourself; it will be a long time before I die. Sit beside me. Where is my wife?"

Erich went to call her. She entered with the Doctor and Sonnenkamp.

The Doctor was not only ready to permit Bella and Clodwig to set out for Wolfsgarten immediately, but urged them to do so. Sonnenkamp decidedly opposed this. He wished that his noble guests would remain at his house, and said, with great munificence:

"Regard my house as entirely your own."

"Will you allow Herr Dournay to accompany us?" Clodwig asked.

Sonnenkamp hesitated, and answered adroitly:

"I have nothing to *allow* the Captain, but if you are determined to go, I would beg him to accompany you, with the promise that he will return to us."

"You go with us too!" said Bella to the Doctor, who readily consented.

And so the four went through the calm Spring night. There was little said, but once Clodwig took Erich's hand and said:

"You are very strong."

Erich and the Doctor passed the night at Wolfsgarten. Early in the morning the Doctor prepared to depart, but Erich was sleeping soundly. The Doctor awoke him and said:

"Doctor, stay here to-day, but no longer."

Erich looked at him with surprise.

"Didn't you understand me?" asked the Doctor.

"Yes."

"Good-bye, then."

Erich passed a whole day at Wolfsgarten again. Clodwig was as cheerful and clear-headed as usual; but Bella seemed shy, and almost timid toward Erich.

In the evening, Sonnenkamp drove up with Roland, and Erich returned with them to Villa Eden. Sonnenkamp was very pleasant, and all the blood rushed to Erich's face as he said:

"Countess Bella will be a handsome widow."

On the evening of the following day, the Doctor came to Villa Eden again; he had been at Wolfsgarten and brought good news. He took Erich aside and said:

"You told me in confidence that you neither have taken, nor expect, a decision from Herr Sonnenkamp personally. I grant that it would be done much better by letter. When you are away, you will be clear as to what it will be best to do, and so will he. I advise you to leave the house. Every hour that you spend here now is your destruction."

"My destruction?"

Erich shuddered.

The Doctor smiled and said:

"This forced exhibition of yourself for nearly a week is destroying you."

He paused, and then continued:

No man appears on parade for a week at a time, without

being injured by it. You're on conversational parade. You must go away, or become an actor or a priest, or maybe, both together. You repeat what you have learned by heart, and repeat it in view of, and with the consciousness of a certain effect. Therefore, go away! You've examined and been examined enough. Come with me, stay overnight at my house, and then in the morning go to your mother's, and wait there for something further to occur."

"But Roland?" Erich asked. "How can I leave the boy? His heart has turned to me, as mine to him."

"Good, very good! He'll have to wait—will have to long for you, and learn that the rich cannot have everything. He must ask for you, if it comes to that. All this will give you weight in the house, and a power with your pupil whose effects are incalculable. Now let me settle the affair for you. I am now what you will be day after to-morrow."

"Here's my hand. I will go with you," Erich answered.

Everybody in the house was surprised when it was announced that Erich was going away, and hardly had an hour passed before he was seated with the Doctor in his carriage.

Erich was glad that his parting from Roland had been hurried over. The boy could not understand what was going on: he could not speak, for emotion. When Erich was in the carriage Roland came to him, bringing one of his little dogs, and put it on his lap; but the Doctor gave it back, with the remark that the dog was too young yet to be taken away—it should be left with its mother; but he would see that Erich got it.

Roland gazed after them as they rode away. All that he had experienced during the few days that Erich had spent with him, passed through his mind. But Erich did not look back. In his father's house the boy seemed to himself an orphan and in a foreign land. He seized the puppy by the nape of its neck and was going to throw it away from him, but it whined so piteously that he suddenly drew it to his breast and said:

"Be quiet, it doesn't hurt you. I'm not a dog, and I don't cry; and don't you do it any more either. He didn't want either of us."

Roland took the dog back to its mother, who seemed very much delighted to see it again.

"I'll go to my mother too," said Roland; but he had to be announced first.

She allowed him to come to her room; and when he complained of Erich's abrupt departure, she said:

"That was right. I advised him to go."

"You? Why?"

"With your stupid 'why?' One can't be eternally answering your 'why?'"

Roland did not speak, and it almost pained him when his mother kissed him.

The boy wanted to go to his father, but he had ridden to the castle with the Major.

He stood, forsaken and alone, in the courtyard. At last he went to the stable, sat down by his dogs and looked at their funny antics. Then he went to his horse, and stood a long time leaning on its neck. Odd thoughts rushed through the boy's soul: "The horse, the dogs are mine. Only what one buys, what he possesses, is his own!"

Like a flash of lightning, hardly seen before it has vanished, the knowledge awoke in his soul, that there is no other possession between man and man than love. He was not used to moody thoughts, and now they gave him a headache. He had his horse saddled and rode in the direction that Erich and the Doctor had taken.

CHAPTER X.

THE PRACTICAL TURN.

ERICH sat beside the Doctor, quiet and thoughtful, and the Doctor did not disturb him by speaking. Erich seemed to himself driven hither and thither by wind and wave. A few days ago he had come here on a stranger's horse, and now he was going away in another stranger's carriage. He had entered the boundaries of the life-destiny of so many men; and the effects of this could never be destroyed in his life or in theirs. But he could not have dreamed that so much was lying before him.

"And you believe in instruction?" the Doctor asked at last.

"I don't understand you."

"I haven't the slightest faith in it. Men will be exactly what Nature made them to be. Under all circumstances they become what they are destined to become, as the saying is. As they lie in the cradle, so they lie in the coffin. Something of capability or knack has its effect; but when viewed in connection with the whole, such things are only of minor importance, for the real direction of all is in the hands of Nature."

Erich was unwilling to enter upon these discussions: he was tired of this continual talking.

The Doctor proceeded:

"I'm particularly unwilling to give you over to these people. It irritates me to think that these rich men should buy the fragrance and fruit of a knowledge beyond them; but it comforts me to think of the word of him who, standing at the centre of knowledge, said that no rich man shall enter the kingdom of heaven. The rich have taken in too much ballast; they have an over-refined life; they live far from the necessities of existence and avoid the natural force of the Seasons, for they fly from one climate to another, and have comfortable nests everywhere, like the swallows. It would be intolerable injustice in Fate if, besides all this, they should have those higher pleasures which are ours alone.

"There's no royal road in geometry, said Euclid," Erich began. "Knowledge and experience are obtained only through work, and I can sum up in one word what I intend to do with this boy. He must learn to draw from himself."

"You're right," answered the Doctor. "Yes; it is so! That in which we, who live according to the spirit, have the advantage of the rich, consists in this—we live for ourselves alone. The rich man does not know the etherial stillness of solitude. He always has so much, that he never has himself—himself alone. So I understand the expression in the Bible—What shall it profit a man, if he gain the whole world and lose his own soul? That is, if he never has himself alone, for himself in himself. He who has nowhere to lay his head, can carry his head erect and free. You see that I didn't study theology two years for nothing—till I learned that, although there's not much to be done by 'quacking' the body, there is more to be done by that than by quacking the soul."

The Doctor could hardly speak for laughing. At last he said:

"But the main question always is, how this endowment with all desirable material things is to give a corresponding catholicity of spirit? This will be your chief task—to awaken and develop catholicity in Roland. At first, he must learn only in the ordinary school-way. In regard to his knowledge of the world, he is yet a child; as to what he wants from the world, he is a man—one might say—a man who knows how to enjoy the good things of this life."

Erich had much to say in answer; but he smiled to himself as he thought—How easy it is to give instruction! The Doctor had spoken justly about his talking so much, and now he should see that he could keep silent. He did not speak, and the Doctor continued:

"I can, moreover, be of use to you, if you take the position. Unfortunately, you're not a Doctor; and, as I think, only a Doctor should be a teacher. Have you noticed that the boy has a stomach that doesn't digest well? A boy at his age ought to digest flintstones. I don't mean that only simple food should be given him. The rich and notable eat without hunger, and drink without thirst. The boy can have everything except *one*,—downright, genuine pleasure. Here, for instance, is a little thing, but yet it may be taken as an example:—new clothes give Roland no enjoyment. Strike this pleasure out of your childhood and youth. I must say that whenever I get a new suit it gives me pleasure, every time I put it on, for a week. What are you smiling at?" said he, interrupting himself.

"I was thinking of a theological friend of mine," answered Erich. "How astonished he would be to hear that the fall of man, which was immediately followed by a knowledge of nakedness, has become the basis of all woven, worked, and embroidered dress, in which we take so much delight."

The Doctor smiled too, but stuck to his theme, and proceeded:

"Victuals and clothes are the two most important things—the third in importance is sleep. It's the regulator of life. Air, food, and sleep are the three bases of vegetative life. I believe that I know something of you, Captain, already, but I understood you first when I saw you asleep. Our nineteenth century sleeps badly. The life brought about by our systems of education, work, and government, must be corrected, so that people can sleep better. I wish I knew enough to write a history of sleep, and show how different peoples and ages have slept. That would lay bare the deepest roots of the phenomena of civilization. But now, as to Roland—he's a singular mixture of temperaments, derived from his father and mother."

Tho Doctor spoke of Sonnenkamp's athletic frame, and how he was obliged, every minute, to struggle with his violent nature. His mildness, which everybody immediately looked upon as constrained and affected, seemed always to complement a certain unyielding strength in him. He was a restrained pugilist, and, indeed, had once boasted, in a careless moment, that he had a hand of iron. The ancient Germans, who crushed and mangled the mailed Romans with their naked arms, must have possessed such strength.

The Doctor burst out laughing, and was hardly able to tell how, when he first knew Sonnenkamp, he always used to be looking for the club which the man ought to have in his hand. When he was in a good humor he always seemed to be saying: "Don't be frightened—I won't hurt you!" Besides, the Doctor knew that Herr Sonnenkamp had a difficulty with his heart, and, consequently, was obliged to be very guarded against any violent emotion.

He particularly impressed on Erich the necessity of not being too accommodating with Herr Sonnenkamp if Sonnenkamp wished to have everything explained, for in doing so he would assuredly lose all hold on him.

"See," said he, "Priests, and we Doctors, give our Masses and recipes in Latin, for who would swallow our sulphuric acid if it stood on the paper in good German? Notice, too, that you will impress Herr Sonnenkamp only by means of a certain dignified reserve, for without it he will soon think that he has comprehended you."

The Doctor then described, with much humor, the sleepy life of Frau Ceres, whom the sharp-tongued but yet more envious Countess von Wolfsgarten had nicknamed Crocodilia, because she seemed to stretch herself on the shore in the sun. Herr Sonnenkamp had no object on which to bestow his great strength, and yet even as little work as he had would be an exertion for Frau Ceres. One ought not to think any the worse of her because she was dressed three times a day without even exerting herself enough to put a pin in her clothes—that she walked up and down in her room for whole hours, looking at herself in all directions, feeding her parrot, and patiently cultivating her nails. The poor body wanted always to live beautifully, and that could not be said of many wiser people. She had a peculiar weakness of the joints, but was not lacking in malice and ill temper.

Erich was on the point of telling the Doctor about his interview with Frau Ceres, but before he could open his lips the Doctor had begun to speak again.

"About a year ago, something happened which I would not have believed possible. I was called to Villa Eden to attend the daughter of the house, who was at the same time in a condition of tetanus and ecstasy which I did not understand. Miss Perini told me that the girl's hands had been clasped so tightly together that it took two servants to separate them, although the girl had not resisted; even when I came, the joints of her hands seemed cramped. I could not imagine how any external object exciting her mind, could have brought about such a physical effect. I only learned thus much: Herr Sonnenkamp had refused his wife something which she wanted very much. To be equal with him, she had told the daughter (who had previously looked up to her father as a sort of superior being) something which had excited the poor child up to that pitch. After she recovered, she remained melancholy until sent to the convent—where she is now, recovering her spirits."

Erich asked why Sonnenkamp was so much hated and slandered. The Doctor made light of his question, and said that the nobility, as a natural means of defence, sought out every spot in a man of such great wealth, and who spent money so lavishly that it seemed almost a personal affront to them. Herr von Prancken was friendly toward him, not only because he wished to marry the daughter, with her rich dowry, but because there was a natural affinity between them; for Herr Sonnenkamp was deeply interested in his own welfare, and Herr von Prancken cheated his neighbor as himself.

"And now, my friend," said the Doctor, in conclusion, "you see how you must comport yourself in this house."

"I've a favor to ask of you," said Erich, after a while. "Let me hear how you would speak to a friend concerning me, when I am absent. Will you do so?"

"Certainly; the question is not at all out of the way. You are an idealist. Ah, what a hard necessity men have with their ideal! You idealists, who are always thinking, working, and feeling for others, seem to me like tavern-keepers in the street, or near some beautiful prospect, who get everything ready, and pray to God, 'Let the weather clear up, and good guests come!' They can neither compel the weather nor the guests. Therefore this advice is simple enough: Don't be keepers of ideal-taverns. Let things taste good to you, and don't care for others. They can get their own portion, or they carry it in their knapsacks; and when this is not the case, they may go hungry and thirsty. I have found that there are two ways of being contented in life: to be neither dissatisfied with the world, nor with yourself. The young men of to-day have, as I understand them, a third way, and that is, to be dissatisfied both with the world and themselves."

"Unfortunately, that's my case."

"And for that very reason," continued the Doctor, taking off his large glove, and laying his hand on Erich's shoulder—"and for that very reason I wish that you had a different prospect before you. I don't know what; I look for it in vain."

A long row of wagons, containing beech-boughs stripped of their leaves, was coming up the road. The Doctor explained that various chemicals had been extracted from these branches, and that now they were going to a powder-mill. Erich answered that he understood, for he had been quite a time in control of a powder-mill, and had worked in it.

The Doctor became silent, and looking up, saw that he was recognized. A calash, drawn by two dappled horses, was coming toward them, and a handsome young man, who was driving, was nodding to them.

The Doctor stopped his carriage.

"Welcome!" he cried out to the young man.

They stretched out their hands to each other, and the Doctor said:

"How are Louise and the children?"

"All well."

"Were you at your mother's?"

"Yes."

"How are your parents?"

"Quite well."

The Doctor introduced the young man as Herr Weidmann, his son-in-law.

"Are you the son of Herr Weidmann, of whom I have heard so much?"

"Certainly."

"Where's your father?" asked the Doctor.

"Up there in town. They're settling about the arrangement of the powder-mill."

A thought suddenly flashed across the Doctor's mind. He turned quickly to Erich, but said nothing. The young man excused his haste, saying that he must be at the station on time, and they took short leave of each other. Young Weidmann said hastily to Erich, that he hoped to meet him again; and if he would come over, his father would be glad to see him.

The carriages went on, each in its own direction.

The Doctor told Erich that his son-in-law was a practical chemist, and muttered to himself:

"Trump called for—trump played!"

Erich did not understand him, and smiled as he thought of how Prancken had spoken about Weidmann's sons, with their impertinently white teeth.

The carriage went on. As they drew near the village, the steamboat from the Upper Rhine came up. The Doctor told the coachman to hurry, so that they could meet the boat at the wharf. They went along at a rapid gallop. The Doctor cried:

"Now I have it! Now I have it!"

He seized Erich's arm, not at all gently, but with violence, as though he was bringing his hand down on the table and making the glasses ring.

Fortunately, they reached the boat just as the gang-plank was being placed. The Doctor sprang quickly from the carriage, and told the coachman to tell his wife that he would not be at home till evening. Then he took Erich by the arm and went on the boat with him. Just as it was starting, Erich asked the Doctor if he was going to visit any patients. The Doctor nodded: he believed firmly that he had a patient with him on whom he would work a radical cure.

As soon as they were on the boat the Doctor was recognized, and a company who had prepared a "May-Bowl" offered him and his friend a glass. He filled it, but did not drink, explaining that he never drank doctored wine. The company was very lively, and a cripple who was on the boat was playing on the accordeon for them.

The Wine-cavalier was sitting on deck, at a little table, and opposite to him was a handsome woman with a great deal of false hair, but also a great deal of charming beauty of her own.

They were smoking little cigarettes, and chatting animatedly in French. The Wine-cavalier avoided meeting the Doctor's eye, and the Doctor nodded to himself, as if to say:

"Good!—a little shame left yet."

When they came in sight of the town of which young Weidmann had spoken, the Doctor said to Erich that he was purposely taking him to Weidmann. He was the man who knew how to help him; and Erich might, without any embarrassment, ask his advice. For a while Erich was troubled; but then it seemed to him to be another singularly good chance to undergo another examination, the value of which was beyond measurement.

He and the Doctor entered the skiff which took the passengers to the shore. The company on the boat bade them adieu, with their glasses in their hands, and the boat soon disappeared. Even the boatman knew the Doctor, and gave him a friendly greeting, saying:

"You'll find Herr Weidmann there, in the garden."

They landed at the quiet village. Erich was introduced to Herr Weidmann, who was a slender man, and, at the first glance, appeared somewhat dried up. His features were quiet and composed, but in his clear eye lay fiery energy. Wiedmann was sitting, with many others, at a table, on which were papers, bottles, and glasses.

He nodded pleasantly, and then turned again to his companions, with whom he had been conversing.

CHAPTER XI.

GET MONEY.

IT is not well for a man to hear much said about another, especially in praise, before he has seen him face to face. The great power which this man possessed seemed incomprehensible to Erich, and it appeared impossible that he should have any influence on his life. The Doctor was immediately called away; for the landlord's father was sick, and it was considered a piece of good luck that the Doctor had come. Erich walked up and down on the shore. He seemed to himself cast upon an unknown world, and surrounded by forces which he could not comprehend. How long it was since he had left Roland! How long since he had ridden past this village, which was then, for him, nothing but a name! And now there might arise a fate for him in this village, and its name would henceforth be unforgotten.

"Herr Captain," called out the boatman, "Herr Weidmann wants you to come into the garden."

Erich went back into the garden, and Herr Wiedmann met

him with a very different manner from his former one. He told him that he had been so busy that he had not had time to speak to him.

The Doctor soon came back.

The three seated themselves at a table in a corner of the garden, where the landscape opened before them; and it was not without humor that Weidmann spoke of the gusto with which the Doctor enjoyed administering his drastic medicines. He had skilfully selected a point where Erich agreed with him; and they two united in joking with the Doctor, yet did it in a way which showed their respect for him.

Erich learned that the Doctor had asked that the direction of the powder-mill should be given to him. Weidmann said that the difficulties were very great, that the state even threw all conceivable obstacles in his way; yet it was possible to find a market in the New World, and his nephew, Doctor Fritz, had sent over from America one of the men with whom he had dealt, and had recommended him highly. His nephew wished that an experienced artillerist could be found, who would go to America and set up a factory for the preparation of powder and slow-matches; for he would be certain to make a large fortune in a short time.

The Doctor looked at Erich, who, however, only smiled and shook his head.

Weidmann went on to say that an entirely new opening had just presented itself, for a stratum of manganese had been discovered, and a company was forming to work it; and a man who understood how, could easily co-operate in the undertaking.

He looked inquiringly at Erich, and then unhesitatingly made him an offer of considerable value—one, the profits from which would steadily increase.

Erich declined politely and gratefully, but he could have nothing to do with it, nor could he change his calling. The Doctor took him up sharply, and said that it was the beauty of our age, that men of scientific ability could enter a profitable business-life, and by means of their own property build up such a middle class of society, as no other period of history had known.

"That's our part, that's ours! we burghers can say. Isn't this your opinion too?"

"Certainly."

"Well, then, go ahead and do likewise."

And he added how gladly Weidmann's family would receive him into their circle.

Erich answered, smiling, that he must decline these deeply friendly propositions. He very highly esteemed the freedom which wealth gives, but he was not made for business-life.

"So?" said the Doctor, a little angrily. "Do you know what question is given to this age? It is, 'Will you work or be worked?' Why should you let yourself be worked by this Herr Sonnenkamp?"

"You surely would not wish that I should work others, and draw profit from their labor?"

"It's not well," said Weidmann, "to carry a personal question into such large generalities. I see, and was prepared to see, that the conflicting interests between the rich and the poor trouble you. But here is our Doctor, and he will agree with me:—social disorders are similar to bodily disorders. In the social pathology, we recognize this disease more clearly than any other one, but we know no remedy; and a disease must be long and thoroughly known before a remedy for it can be found: yet, in the mean time, we must be content to bear it, and perhaps it may do us good."

"Wouldn't you like to be rich?" asked the Doctor, who was still angry.

"It would be unwise to desire anything that I cannot obtain by my own strength."

Weidmann's eye rested quietly on Erich's face. Erich felt this, and although at that moment he believed that he could, with a wave of his hand, refuse all the riches of the world, yet the thought passed through his mind, what a great thing it would be if he, free from all care, could unite himself to the ideal of life, and he saw how he could gratify every wish of his mother and his aunt!

But no, his mother's first wish would be, that he should remain true to himself. And the more Clodwig there, or the Doctor here, tried to make him averse to his calling, so much the more clear did it seem to him, not only that he must remain within the sphere of his vocation, but also that he had contracted a moral obligation to Roland.

Weidmann remarked that he had received from New York a letter from his nephew, Doctor Fritz, who was about to send his little daughter to Germany to be educated. The conversation now turned on subjects and things with which Erich was unacquainted.

The ferryman approached, and said that the last steamboat was coming up the river.

Erich and the Doctor hastily took leave of Weidmann, who shook Erich's hand heartily, and begged him to make use of his aid in any circumstances where he might need it.

The Doctor and Erich entered the skiff which took them to the steamer. They hardly spoke a word during the trip.

As they approached the village, they saw men and women walking up and down, under the newly-planted lindens; for it is always a great occurrence when the boat arrives which lays overnight. The Doctor's wife was on the wharf, and she accompanied Erich and her husband home. She was very friendly toward Erich, with whom she had become acquainted at Wolfsgarten. Erich had forgotten her; for in fact he had hardly noticed the modest, quiet woman.

There were many people waiting for the Doctor at his house. Erich was taken to his room, and then to the library. He saw with great satisfaction that the man kept pace with all the discoveries of his science; and he hoped, by means of him, to fill up many gaps of his own knowledge.

The twilight had commenced. As Erich sat quietly in a large armchair, he heard the tramp of a horse before the house. He rose involuntarily and looked out. He believed that the rider who had just gone past was Roland; or had his imagination and his constant thoughts of the boy deceived him?

The Doctor's style of living was comfortable: everything showed him to be in good circumstances. Hardly had they risen from the supper-table before the Doctor was obliged to go to the neigboring village. Erich strolled with the Doctor's wife beside the river; and there was a double satisfaction in her words as she said, that she wished her husband always had such an intellectual and agreeable friend for his companion; for he often felt lonely here in the little village, and had to create everything for himself.

Erich was pleased, for he recognized in this, not only the friendly estimation in which he was held, but also the warm and intelligent appreciation of the woman who would gladly bring her husband a permanent good.

CHAPTER XII.

THE HAPPY VILLAGE.

HERE in the village was true neighborly life. People called to the friends who were at the windows and on the balconies, as well as to those who were walking about the streets. They joined each other, chatted and joked, and here and there the music of the piano and singing came through the open windows.

The Justice's wife and her daughter Lina joined Erich and his hostess. They were surprised that he was going away again—had thought that he intended to remain at Herr Sonnenkamp's house. And now Erich learned that in fact Roland had ridden through the village, and had passed the Doctor's house several times, making his horse gallop in a manner fearful to behold.

Lina was burning with desire to speak to Erich. She succeeded, for her mother and the Doctor's wife stopped to talk with the School-director and his wife, whom they met, and who told all about how the Forester's young wife was getting along, for she was lying in at their house. Lina took the opportunity and said abruptly:

"Do you know that your pupil Roland has a sister?"

"Certainly: I've heard so."

"You've heard so? You've seen her. She was the girl with the star on her forehead, and the wings, who met us at the convent."

"Indeed! Well?"

"Indeed! Well?" said Lina deridingly. "Oh, men are awful! I always thought that you—"

"That I—What about me?"

"Ah! my mother's right. I am too inexperienced, too awkward, and speak everything out too boldly. Now, I believed that you—"

"Go on. To be insincere is a sin, and doubly so in your case."

"Good!" said Lina, taking off her hat and shaking her ringlets over her shoulders—"Good! If you will say honestly that Manna made an impression on you, I'll tell you something else. But you must be honest and straightforward."

"My dear young lady, do you think I intended to say no? If you do, you cut off my road to honesty."

"Now I'll tell you—but pray, don't you know it? Manna asked me who you were; and that's a good deal for her. Ah, Captain, riches are a terrible thing. People go and court one because she has money. But no, I won't say that. Don't let Manna be a nun."

"Must I hinder that?"

"Did you see the nun's sandals? Horrible! Manna would wear things just like them, and she has such a beautiful foot!"

"But why shouldn't she be a nun if she wants to?"

"Oh," she said, complainingly, "don't you think I am a silly thing? Once upon a time a groom, or something of the sort, entered a castle. Well! And there I thought that the groom must be a tutor now; and here—."

She could not finish her dream, for her mother approached. It made her anxious to see her daughter walking with the stranger, and of course displaying her horrible *naïveté*.

"May one know what you are talking so earnestly about?" asked the Justice's wife.

Lina drew a deep breath, and put the elastic band of her hat in her mouth. Her mother had often forbidden her to do it;

but she did it now, nevertheless, as Erich said with the utmost coolness:

"Your daughter was reminding me that when we met at the island-convent I was not very attentive. Allow me to make my apologies now. To right myself in your eyes, takes from my soul a burden of reproach which I made for myself, and I beg of you to present my excuses to your husband. In travelling, one meets so many disagreeable people, who think themselves people of quality, that one becomes unsociable himself, and generally injures himself by it. Now, if I had not met you again, a false impression would have remained in my mind as well as yours. Ah! on such a lovely evening, by your beautiful river where everybody is so friendly and so happy, one feels as though he would like to do good to every one he meets, and say to him: 'Rejoice with me, fellow-fly, dancing in the sun for the little time which is called life.'"

Erich was very animated, and the Justice's wife was much pleased with him. The evening-walk was refreshing. Lina soon gave her mother her place near Erich, and went to talk with the Doctor's wife. They strolled about for a long time, and the Doctor's wife heard the rattle of her husband's carriage while yet it was so far off that the others could not distinguish it.

The Doctor came. He was cheerful again, for he said:

"I've been called to the confessional, and a singularly good admonisher of mine has died."

He explained that a man had lived in the next village, whose look had always stabbed him to the heart, for the man had sworn a false oath; he had sworn away from him a debt of a hundred guilders. Now, as time had passed on, he had been very thankful to this man, for he had done him good service, and had aroused his faith; for as often as he had met him he had believed in the baseness of man, which one is so ready to forget. The man had now confessed his crime on his death-bed and had restored the money to him. Now he stood there richer by one hundred guilders, but had paid for them by losing his faith. How could he laugh at the world any more, if he could not laugh at the baseness of men?

"What are you going to do with the hundred guilders?" asked Lina.

"What would you do with them?"

"I don't know."

"What would you do, Captain?" said the Doctor, turning suddenly to Erich. "What would you do if you could give away a million?"

"I?" said Erich, nonplused. He did not see why he had been asked so abruptly.

"Yes, you!"

"I've never thought of it; but I would immediately give large stipends to all the German universities. The rich man should think daily of how he can quicken the thoughts of the man of genius."

"Good!" answered the Doctor. "Every one thinks at once of his own circle. See! here is my little friend Lina. If she had a million to dispose of, she would spend it for muslin, and dress the entire female sex in blue muslin. Wouldn't you, Musselina?"

Lina was silent, and her mother said:

"Give a smart answer, Lina. Don't you know any?"

Lina seemed not to know any; but she and the Doctor liked each other well, nevertheless.

When they had separated, the Doctor said to Erich:

"You can see a new way of teaching here. The girl's mother tries as hard as she can to make her a sharp, worldly gossip; but fortunately the child has a simple, modest, unworldly nature; and when one talks with her alone, she's full of gushing life, and she justly deserves the name of Musselina."

The Doctor was particularly sociable with Erich, for he knew that earlier in the day he had tried to break into his life too rashly and violently. He was sorry that Erich had not become well acquainted with Weidmann; he had been too preoccupied to-day, or something else was the matter with him. He advised Erich not to take a false impression of Weidmann; and he laughed quite heartily as Erich said that he would not allow himself to judge of a Rhine landscape universally held to be beautiful, when he had only seen it through a rain or mist. It was evident that the Doctor had been thinking a great deal about Erich during his journey, and now he always addressed him, singularly enough, as Captain. This was soon explained, for he said, as he gave his hand to Erich, when they parted for the night:

"You're the first soldier that I've been able to live with, without a feeling of apprehension. Heretofore, when I've associated with officers, I've always experienced, I will not say fear, but a feeling as though I was near men who were armed, without being armed myself. You're always armed and prepared for an attack, though that's very well. I take my words back. Perhaps a soldier is a better teacher than even a doctor. Now, good-night!"

When Erich was alone, all that he had seen and felt during the day vanished, and the form of Roland rose before him. He placed himself in the soul of the boy who had ridden after him to see him once more. He tried to feel as the boy had felt, but could not fully do so, for Roland was filled with anger toward Erich, who had forsaken him—*him* who had so lovingly and faithfully given himself up. The boy had seemed to himself to be robbed, and so had ridden hither, and thought that Erich *must* meet him or must be waiting at the window to see him. The boy had gone back, crying with anger.

The world, of which he ought to possess so much, seemed to him inhospitable and strange; while it seemed to Erich, who owned nothing but his thoughts, as if suffused with a blessed dew. In the stillness of night, he thought of how kindly he had been received yonder by Clodwig, and here by the Doctor; and it seemed to him that hospitality was the most characteristic fruit of human progress. In old times men entertained gods and angels, and they entertain them yet; for in the free offering of what one has, to a stranger of whose existence, even, one was unaware till yesterday, the divine rises in the soul.

Yonder at Wolfsgarten, and here at the Doctor's house. . . . . There Erich had received fatherly affection founded on sympathy of thought: here with the Doctor, just as much affection based on dissimilarity, making their friendship as nourishing and homelike. There was Bella, always wishing to have something peculiar to herself; and here was the Doctor's wife, wishing nothing for herself, only longing that her husband might retain another friend who could talk with him of deeply-learned things, and thanking Erich in her heart for it. And now so many forms—was all this to be nothing but the fleeting experience of a journey?

CHAPTER XIII.

THOU ART ALONE AGAIN.

IN the morning," the Doctor used to say of himself, "I feel like a washed chimney-sweep." Summer and Winter he rose at five o'clock, studied for several consecutive hours, and let himself be called only in extreme cases of sickness. By means of this study, he not only kept pace with his science, but, as he bathed every morning in fresh water, his intellect was invigorated as well. Come what would, during the day, he had housed his piece of philosophic life. This was the reason—and we may be glad that we have got at the secret at last—this was the reason why he was always so animated, so earnest, and bold. He described these morning hours to an old friend as his "camel-hours," for then he drank himself full, and often, when in the desert, took a draught from his reservoir. However, life did not seem at all like a desert to him, for he possessed something that made everything bloom, and conquered whatever was barren; and that was his indestructible good-nature and equanimity, which he always attributed to his healthy stomach.

He sat thus studying now, and as he heard that Erich, who roomed immediately above him, was up, he sent a servant to invite him to come to breakfast. At this hour, the freshness of the man was yet undestroyed. His wife, who had some household matter to attend to, or pretended that she had, so that her husband would not be forced to speak of unlearned things on her account, had left the room, and was busied in the garden, where there were many seeds and scions from Sonnenkamp's garden. But the Doctor's conversation with Erich did not refer to scientific matters.

Portraits of the Doctor's parents and grand-parents hung in the breakfast-room, and the Doctor took from this circumstance the opportunity of speaking of his life. His grandfather and father had been shipmasters, and the Doctor had lived to see the golden-wedding of both, and hoped to live to have his own. When he had fully narrated his own battle with life, he asked Erich concerning his and his mother's circumstances.

Erich unreservedly explained the whole position. He said that his mother had noble and wealthy friends, on whom she relied; but he did not believe in their aid, and, to speak frankly, did not wish for it. The Doctor agreed with him that no one could materially aid them without giving offence, and displayed quite heretical views on the subject of benevolence, scolding at the giving of legacies and petty gifts which were only of value after the donor's death. He believed that it was much finer and better to make the life of a man or a family free from care, in order to enable them to be more useful. He related how he had often tried to persuade some rich man to do such a thing. This was impossible with Herr Sonnenkamp, for he would have nothing to do with a person into whose hat he had thrown alms.

The conversation then turned more particularly on Sonnenkamp. The Doctor undertook to make Erich promise, and even enjoined him to obey him in it, to settle all his outstanding affairs with Sonnenkamp.

"And don't trouble yourself any further with this man," said the Doctor, as he broke an egg. "See, all is but a change of material. We eat this egg with a good appetite, although the hen gets her food on a dunghill."

Erich was happy with this lively, practical man. He expressed the pleasure he felt in finding in this little village so many really admirable persons, making a rich and full social life. The Doctor disagreed with this, for he thought that the necessity of being cast on one another for company, and not having, as in a large city, the liberty of choosing one's own companions, made one sour, petty, and gossiping. In a large city one had no greater circle than it was possible to make for one's self; but the enforced union which existed here, prevented social life from being unrestrained and altogether agreeable.

"On the whole," he said in conclusion, "all that we get here from each other is the certainty of a full hand at whist."

It was time to think of departing. Erich left the house in a cheerful mood. The Doctor drove him as far as the railway-station, where he alighted and clasped Erich's hand warmly, repeating his wish that they could live together.

The train remained at the station longer than it usually did, for the train from the Lower Rhine, which had to be waited for, was behindhand. A troop of men, young and old, saluted the Doctor, and entered the car with Erich, to whom the Doctor explained that these were wine-tasters, who were going to a sale which was to be held that day at the vaults of the Wine-count. He called Erich's particular attention to a man whose face bore evidence of his calling, and said that this was the gauger, the finest judge of wine in the Gau. The Doctor laughed, as Erich said that he, too, had been trying the wine of the Gau.

"I've caught the spirit of the people."

"You have a singular way of translating everything for yourself," laughed the Doctor. "Count Wolfsgarten, Prancken, Bella, Sonnenkamp, the Krischer, the Seven-piper, Musselina, Weidmann, the Major, the Priest, Roland, and I—what a fine wine-list! Be careful that you don't reel when you get out of the cellar."

The Doctor suddenly turned and said:

"You might yet bring me to putting something into print. Although I am of the opinion that there must be consumers who produce nothing in return; and I believe that there is no 'graduate' in Germany, who has not, at some time, wished to write a book: and this probably helps study. But if you come again, get me to write my history of sleep."

The train, that had come from down the river, whistled, and the Doctor grasped Erich's hand again, and said with emotion:

"We are friends! Remember, that if one intends to cease being the friend of another, he is in duty bound to let him know it a week in advance. And now, good-bye."

The last word was cut short, for the locomotive whistled, and Erich was carried toward home.

He fixed his eyes on the floor; but suddenly heard some one in the car say:

"There goes young Sonnenkamp!"

He looked out and saw Roland again, who quickly disappeared behind a hill.

Erich heard nothing of the jovial conversation of the wine-tasters, which was often interrupted by loud laughter. He had much, both past and future, to think of, and was glad when the company quitted the car at the next station, and he was left alone. A disagreeable doubt would come to him, whether he had been right or not in not having severed all connection with Sonnenkamp immediately; but he manned himself again, and threw all regret aside.

Bodily we are carried along by the power of steam. And spiritually—how far are we masters of ourselves?

At several stations, school-boys entered the cars with their satchels on their backs. Erich learned, on questioning them, that their parents lived in the country-houses about and in distant villages, and that they went to school in the capital city every day, and returned home at evening. Erich thought much of what a different early life that was from his own. Early in the morning finding themselves placed in the midst of the noise of the railway, going to be instructed, and then back home again on the cars, these boys must soon learn, amid the unrest and bustle of the new age, to preserve their inner life, which will certainly be different from what ours was. He looked yet further into the future, where the fearful growth of large cities will disappear, and men leave them for places where they can have always before their eyes the green fields, the rippling of the stream, the blue of the sky, and where they may unite all the elements of civilization which the life of men in great cities affords. Love of the field again enters man's soul.

While Erich was taking leave of the Doctor, the Justice, with his wife and daughter, was enjoying his morning coffee. They were talking about the evening walk with Erich, and the lady was relating the honest way in which he had offered his excuses.

"That's very well, very well," said the Justice. "The man's polite and clever; but yet it's a good thing that he's gone. He's a dangerous man."

BOOK FOURTH.

CHAPTER I.

THE STRUGGLING HEART OF A CHILD.

THE sparrows on the alders and willows by the shore of the convent-island were twittering and chattering noisily to each other. They must have had a good deal to say about what they had seen that day; and who knows that a "to-day" is not a much greater length of time for them than for us. An experienced male-bird—it might, however, have been a female, for it already wore the undistinguishable dress of age—sat in the corner of a branch, leaning comfortably against the trunk. He told the others, with a knowing air, what a glorious time he had had over yonder at the inn by the shore, under the low, shady lindens. The waiters had neglected to remove the remains of an English breakfast, and he had found cakes there (but unfortunately the pieces were too big), eggs, and honey, and a lot of sugar—a feast without parallel. He contended that genuine enjoyment of life only begins when one enjoys the pleasures of eating and drinking exclusively, and knows nothing about anything else. This could certainly only result from travel and experience.

The others wouldn't listen to the swaggerer; and a fierce debate arose, whether, after all, lettuce-seed or young cabbage was not better than anything that men get up. A young rogue flew around a young "roguess," and informed her that behind the boatman's house there was a great big bag of linseed hanging by the window. The rogue assured her that her delicate bill was certainly fine enough to rip the seams; and he thought it was meanly spiteful in men to hang just the nicest tidbits in the open air, and then have them bagged up, so that they could not be got at.

A bird, flying up to the circle hastily, and out of breath, said that the scarecrow in the field was nothing but a stick with clothes hanging on it.

"Because the silly men think that it will scare birds, they believe we think so too:" he laughed, flapping his wings up and down, filled with astonishment and pity at the stupidity of man.

There was a nonsensical noise in the alders and willows; and nearly as nonsensical a one in the large meadow, where the convent-girls were teasing, laughing, chatting, and joking with each other.

At a distance from the noisy girls, amid the alders, where it was so pleasant to wander, walked a girl whose figure was slender, and whose whole appearance was lithe and graceful. Her eyes were lustrous—her hair deep black. At her side walked a woman dressed in the habit of her Order. Her form was dignified; and quiet and unobtrusive force of character spoke in her whole bearing. Her lips were naturally so firmly pressed together, that her mouth seemed only a small red line. Her forehead was bound with a white cloth. And her face—her grêat eyes, her delicate eyebrows, her thin nose, her compressed lips, and her sharp, yet not unhandsome chin—gave her an appearance of being grand and unimpassioned.

"Mother," began the girl, "you have read the letter from Fräulein Perini?"

The Nun—it was the Superior—only turned her face a little. She seemed to expect that the girl—it was Hermanna Sonnenkamp—would speak further. As Manna remained silent, the Superior said:

"Herr von Prancken, it appears, will soon visit us. He is a man of good family and position. He seems to be a worldling, but is not peculiarly so. He certainly has the impatience of the world, but I trust that he will intermit his wooing so long as you are here as our child—that is, as the child of the Lord."

She spoke very measuredly, and now stopped.

"Let us leave this place. The noise of the birds hardly lets us hear our own words."

They passed the churchyard that lay in the middle of the island, toward a little patch of woods, near a small, rocky place which the children called the "Switzerland" of the island. There they seated themselves, and the Superior continued:

"I am certain, my child, that you will avoid, in a becoming manner, any acknowledgment of love, or any expression that Herr von Prancken may use in allusion to his wooing."

"You know, Mother," answered Manna, whose voice was heart-stirring, and always seemed veiled with tears—"you know, Mother, that I have promised to take the veil."

"I know it—and yet, do not know it. For what you now say or mean is for us a word written in the sand, which the wind, or the pressure of a man's foot, may obliterate. You must first go back into the world, and conquer it, before you renounce it. Yes, my child, the whole world must appear to you like your dolls, of which you have told me—forgotten, idle, dead; a child's play, on which one can hardly comprehend how one has lavished so much attention, so much love."

There was silence for a time. Nothing was heard save the song of the nightingale in the shrubbery; while, over the river, crows flew and sang—men call it cawing—and fled to their homes among the crags.

"My child," began the Superior, after awhile, "to-day is the anniversary of my mother's death. I have prayed for her soul—in eternity, now—as then. When she was dying—what men call dying, but which is birth—my beloved forbade me to stand by her death-bed. It hardly cost me a struggle; for whether my parents be out in *that* world, or the other, is the same to us. See! the waves glow in the evening light; and out in the world men are standing—on mountain and shore—and talking, full of delight, of Nature—that new idol which they have made for themselves; for they are children of Nature. But let us be children of God, before whose eyes all nature appears empty, whether thus painted in color, or blossoming, or lying hid in snow."

"I believe I understand you," said Manna.

"Therefore do I tell you," continued the Mother, "it is great to conquer the world—to thrust it from you—to want it not an instant, and in its stead to receive eternal blessedness, even while wandering in life. Yes, my child"—she laid both hands on Manna's head, and continued—"I would give you strength—my strength. No; not mine, but that loaned to me by God. You must have struggled hard, and justly, with the world, before you enter forever, with us, into the anteroom of Heaven."

Manna had closed her eyes. And in her inmost soul the wish arose that the earth would open and swallow her, or that some mighty power would seize her, and carry her far beyond it all. As she opened her eyes, and saw the wondrous glory of the evening sky, the violet mist of the mountains, and the rosy stream, her eyelids trembled, and her hand moved deprecatingly, as if she would say, "Thou art nothing but a dull, a lifeless thing, on which we waste our love."

With a trembling voice Manna told how distracted and consumed her soul seemed. A few days before, she had sung and recited the message of the angel of Annunciation, and, deep within her soul, demons had rent her. She had prayed all day that she might be worthy to announce such a message; and in the twilight a man had appeared to her, and her eyes had rested on him with delight. It was the Tempter who had approached, and his form had followed her in dreams. She had risen at midnight, and cried, and prayed to God that he would not permit her to fall into sin and apostacy. She had prayed in vain. She spurned and hated the apparition; but it would not leave her. She asked, now, that a penance might be laid upon her. It might behoove her to fast three days.

The Superior comforted her tenderly, and said that she ought not to reproach herself so much, for these self-afflictions stimulated her imagination and emotions. When lilacs bloom and the nightingale sings, girls are easily haunted by dreams. Manna should not cry over this dream, but only banish and laugh at it; it could only be banished by derision.

Manna kissed the Superior's hands.

Night had come. The sparrows were voiceless, the noisy children brought back to the house, and only the nightingale sang on in the grove. Manna, holding the Superior's hand, returned to the convent. She went to the large dormitory, took holy-water and sprinkled herself. In her bed she prayed long and silently, and at last fell asleep with folded hands.

The river rippled by the valley, and by the Villa where Roland slept, his lip defiantly curled. It rippled past the village where Erich lay tossed in thought, in the Doctor's house; it rippled past the inn where Prancken leaned in the window and stared over at the convent.

The moon shimmered on the stream, and on the banks the nightingales sang. In the houses slept thousands of men, and forgot pain and joy till the morning awoke.

CHAPTER II.

A GREEN BOUGH.

ON the west side of the convent, amid lofty, broad-boughed and thickly planted chestnut, beeches, and lindens, and farther on, under firs with fresh shoots, stood some tables and benches fixed to the earth. In the mornings, girls dressed in blue sat here reading, writing, and busied with work. Sometimes there was a low humming, but not louder than that of the bees in the blossoming chestnuts. Sometimes, too, there was stirring or reseating, but not more than the fluttering of the birds above in the trees.

Manna sat under a large fir at a table, and not far from her, sat a child on a little stool, under a tall slender beech in whose bark many names were cut, and on which hung a picture of the Madonna. She looked up occasionally at Manna, who would nod to her, as if to say that *she* had to work, and the child too must be more industrious in studying. The child was called Cricket—because she had suffered so much from homesickness; and she had become the pet of the whole circle of convent-children. Manna had cured the child; at least it seemed so, for on the day after the performance of the sacred piece she had obtained permission from a lay-Sister, who had charge of the garden, to have a little garden given to Cricket as her peculiar property; and now she seemed to have become rooted among her flowers, even though they were not those of home, and she daily watched and tended them, but was inseparable from Manna.

Manna worked zealously. She had before her some faint-blue paper, on which she was painting the constellations with a fine brush, in gold color from little shells. Manna took particular pride in having the neatest writing-books; every leaf was edged with fine lines and with the greatest neatness, the writing being never too hasty nor too slow. Manna had, a few days before, received the highest honor which it was possible for a pupil to obtain—she had been unanimously appointed to the *ruban bleu*. The three classes of children, *Enfants Jesus*, *Anges*, *Enfants de Marie*, had elected her to this honor. There had hardly been any selection, it was so evident that no one but Manna could be chosen to the blue ribbon. This distinction made her, in some sort, a natural Superior.

As she drew, and occasionally glanced over the children who had been committed to her care, she had an open book beside her—Thomas à Kempis. In representing the constellations, which she did with that delicacy and clearness which, perhaps, is only possible in a convent, she murmured regular words from Thomas à Kempis, in order to take to her soul higher thoughts while engaged in this play-work.

The stroke of an oar sounded from the opposite shore, and the girls looked up. A handsome young man was standing in the boat, lifting his hat and waving it, as he saluted the island.

"Is he your brother?—your cousin?" the girls whispered to each other.

Nobody knew the stranger.

The boat touched the shore. The girls were full of curiosity, but could not leave their work, for everything had its regular time. Fortunately, a large, fair girl had used up her green worsted, and had to go to the convent for more. She nodded significantly to the girls that she would soon let them know who he was. But before the blonde returned, a sister had come and said that Manna Sonnenkamp was to come to the convent. Manna rose, and Cricket wanted to go with her, but Manna told her to stay where she was, and she sat down again on the stool near the Madonna. Manna tore a little twig from the tree under which she had been sitting, and laid it in her book, as a mark, and then followed the Sister.

Among the girls left behind, there was much questioning: "Who is he—a cousin? The Sonnenkamps have no relations at all in Europe. Maybe it's a cousin from America."

The children could get no satisfaction, and were in no mood to go on with their study. Manna had given one of them the sash which she wore on her right shoulder, to keep it for her; and the girl considered it her duty to keep a sharp eye on it.

Manna reached the convent. As she entered the reception-room where the Superior was, Otto von Prancken rose hastily and bowed.

"Herr von Prancken," said the Superior, "brings tidings to you from your parents and Miss Perini."

Prancken approached Manna and offered her his hand; but as Manna had her book in her right hand, she gave him her left hesitatingly. Prancken, he who was generally so ready, stammered—for Manna's manner had impressed him strongly—as he expressed his pleasure at finding her so well and grown, and said how pleased her parents would be soon, to see her so changed. The stammering, but yet deeply impressed manner of Prancken, did not diminish as he went on, for suddenly, in the midst of his involuntary emotion, he perceived that his evident feeling was not unnoticed by Manna, and not without a certain effect on her. He skilfully continued in the tone in which he had commenced, and congratulated himself on his art in being able so well to play the bashful, trembling, smitten swain. He knew perfectly how to delight her with news from home, and said how happy she must be to live on a blessed isle until she returned again to the continent, which, however, a charming circle of friends would make a welcome continent to her. It was not without self-satisfaction that Prancken looked about at this comparison, which seemed to him as delicate as new.

Manna did not speak for a long time; at last she said:

"Who is Captain Dournay, of whom Roland writes to me so enthusiastically?"

Prancken felt annoyed, but said with a smile:

"I was so fortunate as to find a poor young man, who could instruct our Roland—permit me to call him so, for I love him as a brother—for many reasons. I think it will not hurt Roland to be acquainted with this man."

"Roland wrote to me that he was your intimate friend."

"Herr Dournay has evidently told him so, and I would not contradict it, if Roland in that way would learn to respect a teacher. But, Miss Sonnenkamp, I would not say so to you; I am somewhat chary of the term 'friend,' and consequently would not—"

"But tell me something of this man who calls himself your friend."

"Allow me to make no more intimate disclosures. You yourself will agree with me in thinking that it is our duty to help an unfortunate, erring man, even though the past is not to be blotted out."

"But what has this Herr Dournay done?" asked the Superior. "I'm sorry for his mother, who was my companion in youth. She is, it is true, a Protestant; but is what the world calls good and noble."

Prancken seemed perplexed, but with a motion of the hand, by which he wished to indicate his consideration for others, and his goodness, and appeared to be mildly concealing something, he cast his eyes to the earth and said:

"Worthy Mother and dear young lady! Do not ask me to speak of such things in the convent; and I beg you to regard what I said as forgotten. When I look around me here, certain words which may be spoken in the outer world, seem as unfit for this pure air, as unholy, trivial pictures are to hang near the holy, glorified forms on these pure walls. Allow me to assure you, that I have reliable guarantees that this young man will not conduct himself unworthily."

Manna's aspect seemed to grow great and strong as she said:

"But I do not understand how a boy, my brother, should be given over to a man who—"

Prancken begged pardon for interrupting her, and conjured her by all that was great and holy, to forget that in his zeal for truth, he had said anything against a worthy comrade, he had done it unthinkingly, finding himself in the presence of purity and loveliness. He begged so earnestly and showed such a good heart, so full of the love of man, that Manna willingly gave him her hand now, and said:

"I believe you. Ah, how happy I am that you are so good!"

Prancken was happy, but resolved that Erich should not remain in the house. Every day it seemed more incomprehensible to him, that he should have hampered himself with such an antagonist. He was doubly angry at Erich, who had seduced him into being untruthful and unjust; and Prancken was too proud to relish this, especially as it would not have been necessary if he had been somewhat careful.

"May I ask you," said he, "to show me the lines? They will be of use to me—in seeing how Roland is already getting along with this man. Will you show me what your splendid brother has written about Herr Dournay?"

Manna blushed; but said that she did not now wish to speak more in regard to the Captain, and begged Prancken to use all his influence in expelling the man from the house. Prancken promised to do what he could; and he recovered all his self-control, as he begged Manna, in a cheerful tone, which was yet in keeping with the circumstances, that she would direct him to fight with dragons—like a knight of the good old times—and not give him such an easy task. And yet, while calling this task easy, he felt that it was no longer so.

The Superior arose. She thought that it was high time, and yet good time, to break up the interview. Prancken had aroused a new emotion; and that would suffice for the present. In fact, the Superior was not so exclusively devoted to the convent that she did not wish that Prancken would win Manna's love. Such a house and such a family, wedded to such wealth, might be especially useful to the convent and the Church.

"It was very kind in you to visit us," she said now. "I beg you to remember me to your sister, Countess Bella, and assure her that I include her in my prayers."

Prancken felt that he was dismissed. And yet he would willingly have said something definite, and received the word of assurance that his hope would be realized. His face burned as he suddenly said, so modestly and importunately that it was difficult to refuse his wish:

"Fräulein Manna! we erring men in the world love to hold a steady token in our hands."

"What do you want?" said the Superior, hastily and sharply.

"Holy Mother, I would ask," said Prancken, turning quickly and humbly toward the strong woman—"I would beg you to allow Fräulein Sonnenkamp to give me the book she has in her hand."

"Wonderful!" cried Manna. "Indeed, I will! I wanted to give it to you, to take to my brother. Ask him to read a chapter every day, beginning where the twig is, and then he and I will have the same thoughts in our souls each day."

"How happy this simultaneous elevation of the soul makes me! It would be impious to wish to define it."

The Superior did not know how to help herself; and Prancken continued:

"No; my honored young lady—pardon me, forgive my boldness—I would beg you to give me the holy book for my own edification, that I may keep step with my brothers and sisters."

"But my name is in the book," said Manna, blushing.

"So much the better," Prancken was about to say; but, fortunately, he restrained himself. He turned toward the Superior, laid his hands together, as if praying that she would grant his request. The Superior moved her head up and down, and at length said:

"My child, you may certainly grant Herr von Prancken this prayer. Now, farewell!"

Prancken received the book, and left the convent. As he took his seat in the boat, the ferryman said to him:

"I suppose you have a bride over there?"

Prancken did not answer. But he gave the ferryman a whole handful of money. His heart swelling with joy, Prancken walked up the shore and immediately sent a telegram to his sister.

CHAPTER III.

HERCULES IN A BARBER-SHOP.

THE telegraph-operator was greatly astonished, but dared not express his wonder, as the handsome, *distingué* young man, who looked so much like a man of the world, and appeared so quiet, and who yet showed such utter indifference for the dignity of a public officer—as this young man wrote a despatch couched in the following mysterious words:

"God be praised! A green bough from the blessed isle. New genealogical tree. Manna of heaven. Eternal possession. A consecrated one, new-born.

"OTTO VON PRANCKEN."

Prancken walked about in the tastefully arranged railway station, and looked out toward the mountains, and down toward the river and the island. The whole earth seemed to him created afresh; he seemed on a new world; a veil had been removed from all things, and all was beautiful and enchanting. In the shrubbery where no one could see him, he kneeled. Everything was unspeakably well with him as he kneeled here—he should never have arisen. He heard a noise near him, rose and carefully brushed his knees. It was a beggar who had disturbed him. Without being asked, Prancken gave him a considerable sum; and as the beggar departed, he called after him, and doubled the gift.

The air was full of spicy fragrance mingled with that resinous odor which opening buds exhale. Countless rosebuds hung on the balusters as if waiting, and from the steep wall of rock which had been blasted in building the railway, a cuckoo sang, and thousands of other birds answered. The whole world was filled with fragrance and song: all was untrammelled, free, blessed.

The people at the station thought that the young man who walked so restlessly up and down, now hurrying, now standing still, now looking out, and now fixing his eyes on the earth, must be expecting something important to come on the next train, but Prancken expected no one and nothing. What in the world could now come to him? All his desires were fulfilled. Only he did not understand why he should stay *here* and Manna *there*. Not a minute ought to pass without their being together—one, inseparable.

And now a finch flew from the tree under which he was standing, and sailed over the stream toward the island. "Ah, could I fly thither so, and look at her and greet her from the tree; and at evening fly to her window, and look in till she sleeps, and at morning when she wakes!"

All that stirs a young heart moved in Prancken, and he shuddered to himself as that demon of vanity and self-delusion which he had taken to himself, whispered to him: "Thou art a noble enthusiastic youth! In thee is all!"—He hated this demon now and found a means to banish it.

Amid some neighboring foliage he sat and read Thomas à Kempis. He read the admonition, "Learn to rule thyself, then canst thou rule the things of the world." Prancken had hitherto regarded life as a joke, not worth trying to make anything of. He had naturally that careless tone with which one commands a dog to jump over a stick, and now looked round amazed to think how it could have been so. Could this manner be maintained in connection with sacred things? In my father's house are many mansions, and it is well that children of the world should at some time learn that not to them alone is it given to play freely with the world.

Everything became in Prancken's eyes more wonderful, more enigmatical, and consequently more glorified. If the buds yonder by the hedge could speak when they burst, they would feel, as the light comes upon them, a sensation akin to that which now stirred in this young man's soul. Or if a man should find in the river below—a man who had lightly heard the story—the Nibelungen-treasure,—ancient, beautiful, glorious, wondrous, massive treasure—he would feel as Prancken now felt, when for the first time he discovered the Christian doctrine in this deep and searching little book. Everything in it is so wise: it shows you your strivings so mildly, and explains their origin, telling you how you may forsake your errors and lay hold on the truth!

Prancken sat long and pondered. Trains came and went. Boats sailed up and down the stream, but Prancken saw and heard all as in a dream; and it was only when the clock of the convent struck noon, that he awoke and returned to the inn.

Here he met a comrade who was on his wedding-tour with his young wife. Prancken was welcomed gladly—they were rejoiced to see him. They asked him to go sailing with them in the afternoon, and make a trip to the mountains; but he declined, he could not tell why. He looked at the young pair with burning eyes: so it would be—it would not be long before he would be travelling with Manna! He was wondrously happy at the thought that he would have her alone out in the great world! Why could he not withdraw her from the convent even now? He exhorted himself to learn patience.

The noon passed pleasantly, and Prancken congratulated himself on yet being able to make his jokes. His comrade ought not to tell about the military casino—it was not to be laughed at—and the big Kannenberg would not have bet ten bottles of sack that the pious frame of mind in which Prancken had been was anything more than a passing whim. Prancken produced his witty sayings like pieces which he had learned long ago, and it seemed to him a century since he had been on parade—yes, it must have been in a previous state of existence.

Prancken heard, accidentally, while sitting at the table, that on the next day there was to be a great pilgrimage from the next city. The young couple consulted as to whether they should not go and see the play at the place to which the pilgrims were going, and concluded not to decide till the evening.

When Prancken had accompanied his friends to the boat, he went to the station and bought a ticket to the city; he was glad that he would be able to attend vespers at the Cathedral. He went to the city, and smiled compassionately as the ready *valets de place* in the streets offered to conduct him to some place of amusement: he smiled compassionately as an attendant in the church asked if he should show "the gentleman" everything: Prancken knelt among the worshippers.

He left the church, strengthened anew and calmed. He wandered through the city, and stood for a long time near a barber-shop. No one would have thought, and Otto von Prancken least of all, that there was a special battle-field for him, not out in the wild conflict of arms, but before a large window filled with various perfumes, false hair for gentlemen and ladies, and dummies, whose glass eyes gazed out so staringly beneath their artistic brows and lashes. Over the door was a sign, saying, in gold letters, "Shaving and Hairdressing done here." Is it not ridiculous to think of this as a battle-field? Yet it is not ridiculous, but hard, bitter truth.

Prancken made the heroic resolution to go with the pilgrims, and yet he wished to do so without any exhibition of haughtiness, for he intended to pray and mortify himself with them. In order to excite no remark, and to indulge in the transformation of his moral being in solitude, he thought it would be well to have his moustache and whiskers removed beforehand; but his principal object in this was to make himself unrecognizable, for he feared that some one would meet him, whereby his frame of mind would be disturbed, and others would be led to the sin of making light of serious things. But before all, he was afraid of the newly-married couple, who would look at the pilgrimage as a play, and when they got home would give an account of it. How many persons would then be led to godlessness by laughing at it! And laugh they certainly would when they heard that Otto von Prancken was among the pilgrims. Therefore, for his own sake, as well as that of others, he must be unknown.

So, with this heroic resolution—and it was heroic, for who would willingly destroy so admirable an ornament, especially as it will not return at once when called?—he entered the fragrant shop, seated himself in a chair, and gazed in a mirror at his moustache and whiskers for the last time. A white mantle—truly a sacrificial mantle for the fated lamb—was laid upon him, and an extremely agreeable young man, who had no suspicion of his priestly office, asked:

"Shaved, or hair dressed, Sir?"

"Hair dressed!" answered Prancken, with the quickness of lightning, for this seemed a revelation to him. Curled, elegantly dressed, thus would he mingle with the pilgrims; that were more deep and subtle, and it would not be without its influence on holy things, for the pilgrims to see a stylish, unmistakably military man worshipping in their midst.

Beautifully curled, did Prancken proceed from the shop, and at every store that he passed, he stopped and gazed in the windows which shone like mirrors, and saw there, with deep satisfaction, his saved treasures—his moustache and whiskers.

He smiled at the world like a conqueror.

Prancken knew a hotel in the city which was much frequented by the nobility. Thither he turned his steps, hoping to meet some companion of equal rank, and persuade him to accompany him on the pilgrimage. He found no one, for as soon as he entered, he saw a celebrated actress, who was starring there, and whom he had formerly known: he affected not to recognize her, and went at once to his room.

The morning came. The bells rang for the departure of the pilgrims. Then did a mighty resolution seize upon Prancken. "Not too fast," he said to himself. "Make no great display; give the world no opportunity for misunderstanding you! One owes something to the world, and to the past; one must work progressively, and with due regard to the consistency of things in removing the old man and letting the new appear!"

As he sat at a window of the hotel and blew the smoke-clouds of his cigar into the air, he saw the pilgrims depart. Then he went to the station, took a ticket, and turned toward Wolfsgarten.

CHAPTER IV.

BITTER ALMONDS.

IN the land where the schoppen* reigns, the ladies gather to coffee; and the wine and coffee vie with each other, and adapt themselves to all seasons. In Spring and Summer it is delight-

* A wine-glass peculiar to Germany.

ful to drink on one of the low hills, amid the shadowy trees, with a beautiful landscape before one: in Winter, to drink in comfortable rooms, where sofa-cushions almost too much abound—cushions embroidered with parrots and swelling with worsted dogs.

The coffee-party offers something better yet, in that it circulates from house to house. And as the uses of the schoppen are not fixed facts, but are increased at pleasure, so is the coffee but a modest pretext for bowls of May-wine, and of fruit-cake, to follow. And she who would do something extraordinary, has carefully-preserved ice brought from the city by rail.

The Justice's wife began the circle of Spring coffee-parties. The little garden by the house was certainly very pleasant; and the alder bloomed there in all its exuberance. But people in the neighboring houses could look into it, and so it was better to transfer the festivities to the great room by the open balcony.

The worsted sofa-cushions, which had been covered with rustling chintz, were husked. The invitations had been sent, even one to the Countess Bella. She had sent word that she would come. But it was a steady custom of hers to send, an hour before coffee, a delicately-perfumed note, exquisitely written, to say that Countess Bella regretted that her painful neuralgia would prevent her from enjoying the long-expected pleasure —and render her unable to meet friends so highly respected as the Justice's wife and the company.

On this day, contrary to all expectation, the Countess came, and that, too, before any one else, which, to be sure, is not exactly the height of style. Lina was hastily sent by her mother to the parlor, to put another chair in it; for she had considered it certain that the Countess would not come.

"I expect my brother to-day—he has been travelling toward the Lower Rhine," said Bella. In fact, she intended to meet her brother in the village, so that she might learn something more definite in regard to Manna and the enigmatical telegram. She had also another design; and an opportunity for it soon presented itself.

The Justice's wife was sorry that Captain, or Doctor Dournay—

"Oh, what shall I call him?"

"Just call him Doctor."

That Doctor Dournay, then, had paid visits to the Priest, the Major, and the Doctor. Yes; the Major's housekeeper had told the Beadle a good deal about him. But, singular to relate (he seemed, otherwise, to be a man of good manners), he had forgotten the central point of the village, which assuredly was the courthouse. To be sure, on the evening when he slept at the Doctor's house, he had very modestly made his excuses.

And the Doctor's wife said that he would soon come back again, and receive a salary from Herr Sonnenkamp which would be double that of the Justice. Herr von Prancken had done a noble deed in obtaining this position for one who would, it was to be hoped—yes, who certainly would—show himself worthy of such recommendation.

Bella nodded, very well satisfied. She praised the lady who spoke thus, and so readily recognized the fact that one ought to help the unfortunate. She must, however, certainly see the danger of this. One could harm an unreliable man in no more effective way, than by helping him. Indeed, in this way, one only got enemies, who but awaited an opportunity of showing themselves in their true character.

The Justice's wife was enraptured at the way in which this lady, who was well known to hold herself very high, flattered her homely understanding. She believed—and she was happy in the thought—that as soon as one became personally familiar with the Countess von Wolfsgarten, one thought better of her, and understood everything about her, more clearly. They both smiled pleasantly; and found that each was more becomingly and tastefully dressed than either had thought—the palm, of course, being given to Bella. For it would be the extremity of folly to contend with her in anything.

In fact, Bella looked very animated to-day.

She told, incidentally—for no one must be allowed to misinterpret the fact—of the little attack which the Count had had at Villa Eden, where "Herr Dournay," who had excited the Count very much, conducted himself admirably.

The hostess now entered upon the praises of the Count, saying, too, how well he carried his age. Bella turned the conversation, and insinuated, very cautiously, that Erich had not visited at the Justice's house, on account of a certain shyness toward houses of Justice, and especially toward the servants of the reigning Prince. It was not without eagerness that the hostess asked for further information, and was told, under promise of greatest secrecy—but, of course, the Justice was to learn all about it—that certain political expressions, yes, even instructions, printed in a foreign paper—that is, one published just beyond the greenish-yellow boundary-post—had caused the honorable Lieutenant Dournay to ask for a discharge, rather than to receive a dismissal from the army.

"But why did they give him the rank of Captain?" asked the hostess.

"You're as shrewd as the Justice himself," answered Bella. She did not seem prepared for this question; and only said that it did not become her to hinder a poor young man in his endeavors to obtain bread. It had evidently been done—and here

Bella seized her friend's hand, and held it between both of hers, as a symbol of the great secret she was imparting—it had evidently been done for his mother's sake, who had been a favorite of the Prince's mother. And consequently it was natural that any noise about the affair should be avoided.

Bella smiled charmingly, and yet could hardly keep her smile from expressing a condescending pity as the Justice's wife said:

"Then, my husband was right again. As we were returning from your reception—ah, it was so lively and pleasant!—my husband said to me and my daughter: 'Children, I tell you this; Herr Dournay is a dangerous man!' Ah, men are much more clever, and understand each other better than we women do."

The Justice's wife seemed to be losing herself in universal speculations in regard to men: she loved to do so, and always maintained that a person who lived over a ground-floor full of court-records, received very mournful impressions of mankind. But Bella did not appear to be edified by these reflections, and asked casually:

"Has your husband, who saw through this Dr. Dournay so clearly, told Herr Sonnenkamp his impression?"

"It's clear," said the hostess, "that he ought to do so. Won't you tell him, Countess, that he ought to express his opinion to Herr Sonnenkamp? Unfortunately, he doesn't mind *me* at all, but he's always quite ready to obey *you* in everything."

"You must understand," said Bella, "that I can have nothing to do with the affair. My brother looks at him as a sort of comrade, although they were not in the same regiment; and besides, my husband has a morbid—I might say an enthusiastic—feeling in regard to the young man. You are quite right; your husband ought—"

Bella was getting on so securely that she felt certain that the Justice would be at Sonnenkamp's before evening, and this Herr Dournay be permitted to convert his self-assurance into money elsewhere; for Bella did not want Erich near her; he was disturbing—almost distressing to her. She held her closed fan clutched in one hand, and beat quick time on the other with it, and repeated to her soul what the Justice had said—"This Dournay is a dangerous man."

The Justice's wife was really a liberal-minded woman, and was the daughter of the Chief-Justice who had offered a determined resistance to the ministry in the days when Metternich ruled Germany. In addition to this, she had always been wealthy, and that is a great assistance to liberal views. She even felt the pride of a commoner, in not yielding in any point to the nobility; but in Bella she saw an amiable woman, he superior in intellect, and accordingly subordinated herself to her without perceiving that this subordination amounted to humility toward a Countess. Bella was shrewd enough to see this, and conducted herself toward the Justice's wife in that confidential manner which is used only between equals; but now she refrained from being extravagantly amiable, for that might lead her hostess to attribute her visit to another and a false motive.

Lina entered the room; she looked charmingly domestic in her blue frock and high white apron. Her mother sent her away immediately: the child ought not to be by, for perhaps the Countess had something important yet to say.

"Your child has developed wonderfully, and speaks French very well."

"Thank you," said the hostess. "I don't know how it is with other girls now-a-days, but Lina is very awkward yet, and has no piquancy, and is full of terrible *naïveté*. Just think, the child has been dreaming—it's incomprehensible to me how convents put such things in girls' heads—but she's been dreaming that this Captain Dournay only offered himself as Roland's tutor because he's secretly in love with Manna, whom he saw at the convent!"

Bella pretended to be very much struck by this, and wanted to hear again about the meeting with Erich, but the Justice's wife returned to the subject of the difficulty she experienced in making Lina a wide-awake girl. Bella might certainly have said to her: "You want to transform this simple, good child, who has no particular ability, no singular beauty, but is good-hearted and open. You are always worrying her with 'Come, be lively, be hoyden, be jolly, sing and dance around!' You are trying to make a dark-haired girl, with burning, brown eyes, out of your blue-eyed blonde." Bella might have said all this, but she was silent. She pressed her thin lips closely together, her nostrils trembled, and at that moment she despised all mankind. She was spared from expressing her feelings, for the ladies began to arrive. They were extremely glad to meet the Countess, and yet each one was angry that now she could not outshine *all* the others in finery and general effect.

Yes, such are the ladies when they meet for coffee!

There are things, institutions, and conditions which, having once got a bad name, always retain it; and the charming institution called a ladies' coffee-party, shares the same fate. At the first word spoken in regard to it, every reader and hearer is convinced that there is some hidden sneer or joke to be produced. For it has once been decided that coffee-parties are nothing but gossiping affairs, and masks for mutual admiration. And yet they are a fine thing; except when cards are played, and the ladies go so far as those court-ladies do who get up regular card-parties, and have a gilt-edged book, bound in beautiful black morocco, on the back of which is the inscription, "Hours of Devotion," but which contains nothing but blank leaves, where they score their points and make their reckoning. But that's only among the court-ladies. Here, in our comfortable little city, we have not reached such a pitch of civilization. Cards are not yet the book of salvation from all evil and weariness. Yet people here amuse themselves as much as possible. And why shouldn't they talk of people—and quite sharply, too, sometimes? What do others do—men, for instance—in higher regions, over their wine? Are they always discussing the Ideal? Here the news from the city is spoken of. And he who takes no interest in, or holds himself aloof from this, does nothing for the city—for his neighbor. And these ladies who tell each other this thing and that about what is known as the "gentry," and about the so-called "people," are the same women who have established, and kept up, benevolent associations. Let us, therefore, without any evil by-thoughts, be guests at the "ladies' coffee."

Here comes Mrs. White. Behind her back she is called Mrs. Coal; for her husband is a dealer in coal and wood. She has black curls—and a dark complexion, which always looks as if she had not washed her face completely clean. And as the good lady knows that she is called Mrs. Coal, she always dresses in what is known as "night-white," which certainly is not in keeping with her dark complexion and hair, in bright daylight, although she appears quite enticing by candlelight. Unfortunately, she has the unhappiness to squint, and yet, with such a sweet expression that one would think that her eyes forever held a languishing glance of love.

Yonder is the Cement-manufacturer's wife, large and stately, who never laughs, but is always unspeakably earnest, as if she carried around with her some vast secret; but she had no secret to disclose, except that she had nothing to say.

There sits the School-director's wife—beautiful, but a little too much inclined to *embonpoint*. She is known as Mrs. Clothes-horse, for she dresses well. She is always smiling; and one might almost believe that she would smile if she were to announce, or receive, the news of some one's death. She has very beautiful teeth.

Here is the Steamboat-agent's wife—lovely, and the mother of eleven children. The whole company is vexed with this brave, round, little woman, because she does not let her cup stand on the table, but holds it up in her left hand, and incessantly dips cakes in it; nods to, and agrees with, everybody, and seldom expresses her opinion, and even when she does, her mouth is so full that nobody understands a word she says.

Then there were two English women, who lived in the village. They were simply commoners, and were liked. They were not of any social eminence; but they appeared to be, for they were independent. They lived in their own house, needed no visits, and were like the island from which they came, which produces and possesses everything that man requires. Whenever they went to a company they were new-comers, and were always welcomed anew; while the amiable, helpless way in which they spoke German, and made outlandish grammatical constructions, challenged everybody's friendship—Bella's especially.

The chatting of the women was like the singing of birds in the woods. Each sings in its own way, polishes its little bill, and does not trouble itself about the others—hardly listens to them. Only two expressions were generally heard and repeated: for Mrs. White, called Coal, made the happy remark that even when Count Clodwig did not wear his orders, one seemed to see them; and the wife of the district judge would not be restrained from repeating this to Bella.

Another subject awakened general interest. They were discussing the question—not knowing what originated it—whether it was agreeable or not for men to smoke; and Mrs. Clothes-horse said that her good man often wished that he was a passionate smoker, so as to wean her from the love of it. Bella steadily smiled that agreeable smile which is so cold, but yet so enchanting.

The conversation barely touched on Sonnenkamp, but fastened on Erich. And why not? To be sure, there are thousands of people riding past the village during the summer, and a person might live close to the road that led to the ancient castle and other things worth seeing; but when would such a singular apparition as Erich come and remain at the village? Erich was a strange bird, who wished to establish its nest in the mysterious house of Sonnenkamp. He was not to be harmed, not a feather was to be ruffled. And yet, one would like to know where he came from, and say what one thought of him.

The hostess said that she had actually wanted to invite the Major to the lunch, for he knew most about the Captain-doctor.

Of course the ladies had tetting, embroidery, and needle-work with them, but this was only for appearance' sake—they did not wish to seem idle.

When they heard that Erich's mother was a lady of the best nobility, each said that she had thought so, for such a thing is not easily concealed. Upon this remark Bella lavished a gracious glance on the whole company.

The Justice now came in to spend a little quarter of an hour with the ladies, and Bella asked him to take a seat beside her. She expressed her hope that no disturbing element would ever be introduced into this innocent and happy circle, as the effect of such an occurrence could not be other than bad.

The Justice stroked his rough moustache, and looked at her with surprise in his good-humored eyes, for he could not suspect that this was to prepare him for what his wife was to say. He soon excused himself and left the room, and his wife now said that Lina had joined the singing-society of the village: they were practising for the great musical-festival which was to take place in the neighboring city, and Lina would evidently sing a solo.

Bella gave her opinion in a manner which was edifying and yet contemptuous. She hated musical-festivals, for she was convinced that nobody but herself understood music, and that that only was music which she herself produced. At such entertainments hundreds of ordinary young people of both sexes sing oratorios by Handel, Haydn, or Bach, and this vexed Bella;—and then these people are perfectly convinced that they understand music! If she had been able, she would have forbidden these festivals, under penalty of the law. For this reason Bella cordially hated oratorios, and only said: "I dislike them, and that ought to convince others that there's nothing in them."

She was full of graciousness and good-will. She had, as she said, nothing against the German masters of oratorio; but on the other hand, she did not like to think that the wives of the Justice and the School-director, the daughters of the pensioned Head-forester, as well as those of the tailor and shoemaker, should imagine they were working most artistically when, in fact, they had not a sound tone in their throats.

Lina now appeared with a new lustre, for everybody asked her to sing. The English women were very anxious to hear a German song; but Lina, who never gave herself airs, could not be persuaded to gratify them. Her mother's eyes rolled in wrath, but Bella laid her hand on the arm of the angry mother, and said that Lina was right, for to commence singing so suddenly would not be to her advantage. And now followed an unheard of event: Bella rose, went to the piano, performed a prelude, and then played a sonata by Beethoven, with the skill of a master. All were in ecstasies, and the house of the Justice was exalted beyond precedent, for no house but the Castle Wolfsgarten, and other noble mansions, could boast that Bella had ever touched the keys in it.

Bella received overwhelming praise, but deprecated it and said, half in earnest and half in sport, that everybody who wears long clothes wants to play the piano. Bella was like her brother in being able to be happy a whole day, whenever she succeeded in saying something sharp, and she was extremely delighted now, as she said:

"Every girl thinks that she must learn to knit a musical stocking."

She beat time, accenting the words "musical stocking," as if they were a musical measure. Every one laughed, but the English women seemed puzzled, and Bella was happy to be able to explain what she meant, and said:

"Yes, to knit a stocking of notes, and the principal thing with them is not to drop a stitch—a note. I really believe that the dear children regard the four parts of a sonata as the four parts of a stocking: the border is the introduction, the shank is the adagio, the heel is the caprizzio, and the tip of the toe the finale. Only a person who has a special talent should be allowed to learn music."

All the ladies agreed with her perfectly, and spoke of how much time is lost at the piano by girls who stop practising entirely when they are married.

The Justice had been called in, and if there is one heaven above the other, it opened before him as Bella praised Lina's singing, which she had heard, and asked that the girl might be allowed to spend a few weeks with her at Wolfsgarten, where, very probably, she might give her considerable instruction. The look which the Justice's wife gave him, spoke joy ineffable; and then how charming it was, that all the ladies had heard this request! The hostess seemed to herself wonderfully good-natured and condescending for being on such friendly terms with the Doctor's wife, Mrs. Coal, and the merchant's wife.

Bella now praised the excellent spice-cake which her hostess made, and wanted to know the recipe for it. She was told that what made it taste so good was a certain mysterious quantum of bitter almonds. The lady of the house promised to write out the recipe, but said that she was always forgetting it.

They had hardly tasted the May-wine, and discovered that nobody knew how to make it as well as the Justice, before it was announced that Herr von Prancken had arrived.

The Justice went down to meet him, his wife detained Bella, and Lina looked out of the window, and saw Prancken decline to come in for a moment. Bella took a very hasty leave, and went away.

After Bella's departure, it seemed to all the ladies as if the court had disappeared. They drew together more confidentially, and for the first time seemed really at home and comfortable.

The English women were the first to take leave, and the others soon followed, in order not to appear less fashionable than they; and soon the parents and their child were alone.

The Justice's wife took her husband into another room, and impressed on his mind that it was the duty of a justice of the peace to keep his district in good order.

The Justice discharged the duties of his office faithfully; and whoever spoke of him said, "He is the best man in the world." But he certainly was not too enthusiastic in his vocation, and always said: "What have I to do with other men's affairs? If I were rich, I would never in my life trouble myself with other people's grievances; but just live quietly, and enjoy myself." But now, since he had once been placed in office, he discharged his duties conscientiously. It was very much against his will that he was brought to interfere in Erich's affairs, and only yielded when his wife told him explicitly that it was Bella's wish that he should do so.

And now the husband and wife were in happy accord, when suddenly a great racket and crying was heard in the next room. Lina had let a whole waiter full of cups fall.

No greater evidence of her mother's happiness could possibly have been given, than what she said to Lina:

"Never mind, my dear child; the thing has happened, and there's no use in crying over spilt milk. Why! what's the matter? A minute ago you were so red, and now you're pale! I ought to thank God for sending us a little disappointment, for there ought to be a little of that in every pleasure!"

Lina was quiet, for she could not tell what she was thinking of when she let the waiter and cups fall out of her hand.

CHAPTER V.

THE SOUL OF THE WORLD.

WHY didn't you come in for a minute and see these worthy people?" Bella asked her brother as they sat in the carriage. Whenever she left a company where she had been particularly amiable, this frame of mind always lasted for a time, during which she smiled at the air, the cupboards, and the chairs. She felt in this humor now. She still felt the influence of her benevolent amiability: but her brother had come from a strange world; he had spoken to no one that day except —who would have thought it of him?—to his own soul, or, more properly, to Manna's.

"I'm going to leave the world," said he: "I want to forget it and have it forget me. I know it through and through—everything is narrow, empty, dry, a puppet-show. When you have been making these puppets dance awhile, you can put them away in the closet of forgetfulness again."

"You seem a little nervous," said Bella, laying her hand on her brother's shoulder.

"Nervous? That's another counter. Nervous? How often have I heard that word and used it myself! What does 'nervous' mean? Nothing. I have been broken down and built up anew. Ah, sister, a miracle has happened to me, and all miracles are plain to me. Ah, I don't know how I will ever come back to the world again!"

"Charming! I congratulate you; you are certainly in love."

"In love? God! don't say that! I am consecrated, sanctified. Ah, yet I am such a poor, frail worldling that I am afraid to acknowledge it to you, my only sister. I would never have believed that I was capable of such emotion—I know not what to call it—such rapture, such ecstasy thrilling through every nerve. Oh, sister, what a girl!"

"It's not true," said Bella, laying her head back on the cushion. It's a fable that we women are the riddle of the world; you men are much more so. Such romantic ideas to come over you, over Otto von Prancken, the exquisite connoisseur of the ballet! Good, charming! The strongest force is the force of illusion."

Prancken was silent: he heard Bella's words as if they came from a vanished world. When, where, had he thought and heard of the ballet? And yet as he heard that word, beautiful women, smiling roguishly, and charmingly dressed, danced before his memory.

His heart beat like a hammer against the book in his breast-pocket. He was on the point of telling his sister, that for the last few days he had hardly known himself, and that he had often been obliged to think of his name—of everything which he had desired and now longed for. He had gone as if drunk through the world, which had seemed to him like a phantasm! The rumbling trains of cars; the cities and castles mirrored in the river; all are but phantasms and will vanish. Only the soul exists—the soul alone.

Thus had Thomas à Kempis affected him, thus he had read the words on which Manna's deep-brown eyes had rested. All this now passed through his mind; he could not make his sister comprehend it—she could not conceive of it—he himself hardly did so. He determined to keep it all to himself, and, changing his tone with great self-command, he said smiling:

"Yes, Bella, the power of love has, in a certain degree, something consecrating, if such a word is allowable."

Bella said laughingly that he had made that remark in the tone of a Protestant candidate for the ministry, making a declaration of love to the pastor's daughter, dressed in rose-colored calico, and listening to it in the shrubbery of the parsonage-garden. She considered it a beautiful and honorable guaranty of the depth of his feeling, that he had not entered the Justice's house, and praised him for abandoning his intentions toward Lina.

Otto nodded as though a little ashamed, and took the opportunity of speaking about Manna; doing so with so much emotion and earnestness, that Bella was every moment more astonished. She let him tell his story quietly, but while he spoke she clasped her hands together, and whispered softly to herself: "Seven times nut-brown eyes, and three times gazelle-eyes, is glorious beyond measure."

They went through a little forest of firs fragrant with balsam, and it seemed to Prancken as if this odor exhaled from the book in his vest-pocket, and penetrated him and all things. With his eyes fixed as in reverie he said:

"Since the time of our great-uncle, no member of our family has entered the service of the Church. I will—"

"Surely not?"

"I will," continued Prancken, "devote my second son to the Church."

It seemed infinitely comical, and yet Prancken said it in deep earnest, as he leaned back comfortably in the carriage, sending out from his mouth dense clouds of cigar-smoke.

Bella, who usually had some quick objection or adroit approval ready for all occasions, was silent now, and Otto, who felt deeply the peril of entering on another subject, seemed to himself to be bewitched. He, the lofty, the supercilious, must, like a braggart who finds himself one of the company in a drinking bout, drink deeper and deeper, even though he does not relish doing so.

"I would like to give you some advice," said Bella, at last.

"I would like to listen to it."

"Otto, I believe that at this moment you feel what you say; I will even believe that the feeling will last: but, for Heaven's sake, don't let anybody notice it, for it will be looked upon as a hypocritical humility, assumed in order to win this rich and pious heiress. Also, for the sake of your dignity, for the sake of your position—not to speak of other reasons—leave off these extravagances. Otto, I'm not speaking my own opinions, but the views of the world—abandon these celestial raptures. Pardon me if that's not the right expression; but I don't know any other so applicable at present. In short, be just what you were before your journey; at least, be so before the world. Are you angry with me? Your face contracts so painfully!"

"Oh no; you're wise and good, and I'll take your advice."

As if a new stop had been pulled, Prancken asked immediately:

"How's everything at Villa Eden? Is the Allwise, the Soul-of-the-world, there yet?"

Bella smiled; her brother's old, sarcastic tone had returned, and Prancken was glad too that it had come back, and intended to retain it a long time, perhaps forever: it is a good weapon against a free-thinker.

"You must mean your friend," said Bella, not being able to keep from bantering her brother.

"My friend? He never was my friend, and I have never called him so. It was only out of pity that I let myself be humbugged. It's a peculiarity of our family that we can't bear to see an unfortunate person; and when I help such a man I'm very likely to get on more intimate terms with him than I ought to, or than it's natural and right that I should. If one wants to take a man out of the water he has to take him in his arms and to his heart, but that doesn't make him a bosom-friend."

Prancken said this in his old sarcastic, galloping tone, but the mode of expression had behind it a thought more of earnestness than was usual with him, as was natural after what he had experienced during the last few days.

Bella gave her brother a letter which Miss Perini had intrusted to her for him. Prancken opened it, and his face brightened as he read it. He put it in his breast-pocket, but it did not seem fit company for Thomas à Kempis; so he took it out and placed it in another pocket. Then he folded his arms over his breast and fell into a quiet, pleasing reverie.

"May I read Miss Perini's note too?" said Bella, stretching out her hand.

Otto took out the note, glanced hastily over it and gave it to his sister. It contained the information that Erich had gone away, but that he had had a secret interview with Frau Ceres, unknown to the other inmates of the house: the more important part would be told by word of mouth.

Otto said that he would like to know what this mystery meant.

"I know what it means," said Bella triumphantly. "Lina Justice—by the way, this Egmontian Clärchen* has no family name, and doesn't need any—Lina Justice has told everybody that Captain Soul-of-the-world was at the convent with her, and saw Manna, and, without saying a word about it, had himself introduced by you at her father's house the next day. You, as well as all the rest of us, have been deceived by this exceedingly exalted Soul-of-the-world.

---

* Clärchen, in Goethe's Egmont, has no surname.

Prancken drew a deep breath, and clenched his fist, and made a contemptuous motion with his hand. Bella went on to tell him, that, while at the coffee-party, she had taken care that this Soul-of-the-world (the term seemed to her to be very appropriate to Erich), should have to seek another home. The Justice would put an end to him. Bella learned, to her astonishment, that Otto did not like this proceeding. It was absolutely at variance with the higher life—he left it undecided whether he meant social or spiritual life—to make use of intrigue against a poor, deceitful wretch. He would much rather go to work openly, and explain it all to Herr Sonnenkamp immediately.

Bella was very serene, and not at all sensitive. She said that it was extremely ridiculous to make such a disturbance about the situation of a tutor: such a person, unless invested with an importance not his own, would always remain subordinate.

She admonished her brother that, in case he wished to profit by the affair, he had better not let the Justice be before him with it.

Otto determined to visit Herr Sonnenkamp the next day, and then and there cut through the meshes of Dournay's intrigue; but he let the next day pass, and the next, before he went to Villa Eden. If others' hands and others' tools should bring the affair to nought, it would be better yet. The Justice should have ample time to accomplish his purpose.

Otto read in Thomas à Kempis, and looked for a rule that would apply in such a case, but found none.

CHAPTER VI.

TACTICAL MANŒUVRES.

ON the third day after his return home, Prancken started for Villa Eden. He stopped at the Justice's house, for he wished to know what had already been done by him; but the Justice said, not less shrewdly than modestly, that he had considered it improper to make any move before Herr von Prancken, who had recommended his friend to the house, had told him to. He was ready to go immediately to Villa Eden with Herr von Prancken.

Prancken bowed his obligations; and so he was obliged after all to be personally engaged in the business. He did not decline the Justice's offer, for perhaps this pedantic little man would let himself be used as a sort of scout, and by means of him he would be able to tell how and where the enemy was posted.

In his new state of mind, Prancken did not relish entering upon intrigue, and told himself that he was not doing so; but manœuvring tactics are always permissible—nay, even commanded. One may and must injure the enemy where and how he can. Prancken drew himself bolt-upright and laid his plan properly; he would pretend to support Erich, so that he might give the Justice better and more energetic aid in accomplishing his design. He was again the jolly, self-reliant dragoon, ready to spring over any barrier.

The Justice asked him to see the ladies for a few minutes, as he had to prepare for the journey. He was not yet shaved. The good Justice lived the whole year in open violation of the law: every day his moustache was liable to be destroyed in conformity to the law; for, according to the rigid letter of the Prince's orders, no civil magistrate was allowed to wear a moustache. He always excused his moustache by saying that he wore it for the toothache; but the truth was that he wore it because his teeth were all gone.

Prancken went up stairs. The Justice's wife welcomed him, and could not sufficiently express how she had been enchanted by Bella, and the disappointment which the whole company had felt because he had not come in a moment.

"May one ask where you had been?" asked she.

"I was in the Lower Rhine, at the house of a dear friend."

"May I ask who he was?"

"Herr von Kempen."

The hostess congratulated Prancken on having such warm friends: if they were only always worthy! At this point the conversation might easily have turned upon Erich; but Prancken prevented this, and asked about Miss Lina. The mother said that her child was now learning to cook; for it was very necessary that a good wife should understand this part of her duties. It was, however, a great pity that cooks no longer understand how to teach their art. Prancken was loud in his praises of her wisdom in having her daughter learn this; and spoke of the worthlessness of servants, for which the revolutionists were certainly to blame, as they had demolished all fidelity and religion.

The lady found all this extremely true, and was on the point of speaking about Erich, when, fortunately, the Justice entered. He had donned his uniform, wore his sword by his side, and looked very ridiculous; but Prancken was highly pleased by this attention to the obvious requirements of the situation.

They set out together for the Villa.

Whenever Prancken left the Justice's house, he twirled his moustache with great pleasure and self-satisfaction. It was extremely honorable—outrageously brave many of his comrades would call it—in him to pay so little attention to the daughter. And the consciousness of his virtue (this was also a fine expression) made him very amiable and full of buoyancy; he was persuaded that not a second passed in which he was not giving something to the family, and such a present as was connected with no little sacrifice on his own part.

Lina looked after them from the window near the kitchen. She stood behind the flowers on the sill smelling a monthly-rose which had just opened, and a fragrance not less sweet filled her soul. When she could no longer see the carriage in which her father sat with the Baron, she hastened to the parlor, opened the piano, and sang love-songs clearly and ardently for all the world to hear. Her mother came to her with loosened hair, and could not conceive how she could be singing here while two kettles were boiling over in the kitchen.

"You're a stupid all your life long; and with the exception of the little language you learned there, the convent only made you stupider than ever!"

Lina went back to the kitchen and stood before the hearth, and dreamed that she was out in the world. She would have liked to hear what her father and Prancken were talking about.

But they were both talking very reservedly. Prancken praised the Justice for being so thoughtful of the purity of his district: the Justice lamented that he had accomplished nothing tangible, nothing but his own conscious satisfaction in the matter. He knew how to get Prancken to talk, and was told by him of many things of which Erich was, of course unwarrantedly, accused—even of something which looked very much like treason. But yet Prancken begged him to spare the poor young man, on whom even the Prince had had mercy, and thanked the Justice for counterbalancing an evil which he, being carried away by his good-nature, had brought about. The Justice did not exactly understand what he was to do, and felt uneasy when Villa Eden came in sight.

CHAPTER VII.

A NEW SUBSTITUTE.

ON the evening of their separation, Roland had fallen asleep with anger in his soul, and he awoke with longing. It seemed impossible that Erich could have forsaken him; and so firm was his belief that they were to live together, that he longed to go to Erich's room to beg his forgiveness for having had so bad a dream about him. And yet all, all was true. He entered the room. It was empty, and only Erich's Doctor's thesis lay on the table as a proof that it had not *all* been a dream.

Roland was not left alone long. He was called to his father's room and introduced to a man of elegant manners, who spoke only French and a little broken German. This agreeable young gentleman was called the Chevalier de Canne: he was from French Switzerland, and was warmly recommended by Sonnenkamp's banker at the capital. The banker himself did not know the ultimate authority by which this man had been sent to him, for Miss Perini was at the bottom of the whole affair.

Miss Perini was never seen to give a letter to the postman, for all that she wrote went through the Priest's hands; but her connections with the French clergy were of such a nature that, through means entirely unsuspected, a lay-pupil who could be relied on had been brought to apply to Sonnenkamp for the vacant position. The scorn with which Sonnenkamp would have received references from such a source as the French clergy was well known, and, consequently, Miss Perini had been obliged to act with great circumspection.

By means of his modest and quiet deportment, the Chevalier soon succeeded in captivating all the household, Sonnenkamp not excepted. His want of individuality was in strong contrast with Erich's nature. He never obtruded a strange or startling idea, he entered upon everything adroitly, and knew how, without a suspicion of flattery, to reiterate every person's words in such a way that what had been said would seem extremely fine and lucid to him who said it. He understood how to explain and interpret even the few words which Frau Ceres spoke, with a dexterity that would make one believe that he had known her for years. Such characteristics made him agreeable; and what made him doubly welcome to Herr Sonnenkamp was his extensive knowledge of botany.

He prayed with Miss Perini before eating, but so modestly, so delicately, that doing so only made him more pleasant to look at. Everybody except Roland was enchanted: the boy was always comparing the Chevalier with Erich, he could not say why; and now for the first time he asked his father to send him to some school—somewhere, he did not care where—and promised absolute obedience to the rules of the institution. His father, however, would not consent; but rather congratulated Roland on the fact that such an instructor as the Chevalier had been found for him.

Roland could not complain that it was one whit more difficult to learn under the Chevalier's instructions, and yet he could not banish Erich from his mind. He had already written two clandestine letters to Erich; and they were like the complaint of a maiden who is being forced into a loveless marriage, praying her lover to hasten to the rescue. He begged a thousand times that Erich—who knew nothing of the boy's rage against him—would pardon him for being for a moment unfaithful to him. He was steadfast in the hope that his father, who always spoke well of Erich, would ask him to return. So Roland wrote, but did not send the letters; and even carelessly left them lying open: the Chevalier saw them and gave Miss Perini an abstract of their contents.

Erich had an invincible advocate in Sonnenkamp's house; and that was Joseph. He kept asking Roland when Erich was coming back. He told the boy many things about Erich's parents, and even about his grandfather, and a brother he had who was about as old as Roland. A new longing for Erich was aroused in the boy's soul, for he thought that he would bring his brother with him, and then he himself would have a brother and companion.

In this way several days had passed. Roland was sitting on a camp-stool on one side of the road which commanded a beautiful view of the park, from the midst of which the tower of the principal building rose as if it had grown there. Roland was drawing, and the Chevalier, who was a master of the art, sat near him. Roland soon saw that hitherto too much of his work had been done by his master, and now he was very attentive and zealous. They were both drawing the same object, and compared their work from time to time.

The teacher had advised Roland to make a drawing of every view of the castle before it should be restored, and Roland had done so. Sometimes he believed that he had done it all himself; and then again the whole proceeding seemed to him like a farce, for his master had drawn the greater part for him.

Roland heard a carriage approaching: his heart gave a bound—surely Erich was coming. He hastened to the road and saw Prancken and the Justice. The Chevalier had followed Roland, who now stood motionless, looking at them. Prancken gave the boy his hand and asked him to introduce the Chevalier. Roland did so; and the Chevalier added in a tone of measured deference that he was Roland's tutor. Prancken nodded pleasantly, alighted and walked with Roland, gave his sister's love to him, and said that he wished to have a confidential talk with him soon, as he had something of importance to tell him.

Prancken praised the noble bearing of the stranger, and said that such a man was far better than a conceited German doctor.

"Erich might well be conceited, but he isn't," answered Roland boldly.

Prancken pulled his moustache; he must go to work more quietly: Erich might be let alone, now that he was gone.

Roland felt anxious, he knew not why, but he suspected that something was going on in regard to Erich.

At the Villa, Prancken left Roland with the Chevalier, to whom he nodded very graciously. He asked the Justice to see Herr Sonnenkamp alone first. The Justice looked at him with astonishment; but Prancken left him abruptly without waiting for a reply, and went to Miss Perini.

A very touching greeting passed between them—they gave each other both hands.

When Prancken asked about the Chevalier, Miss Perini pretended to know nothing about him. Prancken spoke of the good impression which the Chevalier had made on him, and acted as though he did not dream that Miss Perini had brought any secret influence to bear in the matter.

Then Prancken gave an account of his visit to Manna, and told partially—not completely—what a transformation he was undergoing. Miss Perini listened attentively, holding her mother-of-pearl cross in her left hand, and then told him about what she had only hinted at in her letter—Erich's secret interview with Frau Ceres. She also showed Prancken the letter which the Lady Superior had written in answer to her inquiries about the meeting between Erich and Manna, enclosing an abstract from Roland's letter to Manna, in which Erich was mentioned.

And now beamed forth all of Prancken's knightly soul, lifted to new heights by a flight of moral and religious sentiment. He stretched forth his hand as if to stay every breath that spoke of Manna, and said in clear and determined tones, that not by another syllable should Manna be drawn into such unseemly company. The whole tale was in reality nought but a phantasm engendered in the giddy brain of Lina, the Justice's daughter, by her convent-life. Not by the cloudlet of human breath should the glorious nature of Manna be obscured, for she was pure, and great, and exalted. Prancken felt that he was her knight, the chivalrous protector of innocence, and he was noble enough to exercise his knightly spirit toward Erich; for in this matter Erich was perfectly blameless: honor as well as dignity required that justice should be granted him.

Miss Perini regarded Prancken's noble ardor with amazement, as he continued:

"From this instant let us consider Lina's childish fancy as annihilated: neither you nor I, nor my sister, nor Sonnenkamp, who, as you say, fortunately knows nothing of the whole affair, will even cherish one thought of it in our souls."

Miss Perini, instead of being wounded by the magnanimity and penetration of Prancken, was delighted with it, and was discreet enough to make some little jest about the pettiness of women. She even said quite dexterously, that this was indeed knight-service; for the plain on which the tournament is fought in these latter days, is higher than in olden times.

Miss Perini was unwilling to be opposed to Prancken under any circumstances, for she knew what power she would lose if she were.

Quiet and well pleased with himself, Prancken left Miss Perini, in order to go to Herr Sonnenkamp. He could almost make apologies for Erich now, for Erich was no longer in his way. Calmly he laid his hand on the book in his breast-pocket —the man who spoke *there* might well be pleased with him.

CHAPTER VIII.

BALAAM.

PRANCKEN found the Justice and Sonnenkamp engaged in general conversation. The greeting between the master of the house and Prancken was very hearty, and Prancken seated himself astride a chair.

"I'll tell you, my esteemed friend," began Prancken—in public he always called Herr Sonnenkamp "my esteemed friend" —"I'll tell you about my trip by and by. For the present let me congratulate you that we've at last found for Roland a man who, to all appearance, is just what he should be."

Herr Sonnenkamp answered that he had hardly engaged the Chevalier yet—he was only in the house on trial. A certain something told him that this very learned Swiss was perhaps moulding Roland's disposition too much according to the ideas of the priests and churchmen. Erich was precisely the man whom he, for his part, would like to have.

Prancken looked around as if obliged to convince himself that the enemy was taking another position, and then said:

"We must by all means test the market-value of this man accurately."

Sonnenkamp looked at him sharply, as Prancken snarled forth the term "market-value." Did the Baron think that he must accommodate himself to him as to a merchant? He could not know that Prancken was proud of the phrase, and had saved it up very carefully, and Sonnenkamp answered:

"The market-value of this man is not small; and yet that Captain-doctor is an eccentric fellow. Eccentric men are very agreeable; but one can't rely on them."

With the vehemence of a person newly converted to the faith, Prancken now spoke of Erich's infidelity, and represented how necessary it was that Roland should be placed under the guidance of a man who was truly pious, and at the same time an accomplished man of the world. Sonnenkamp smiled, and said:

"You seem to advise that Roland should be made a parson."

"If it were his passion." Prancken played with his moustache; but as he saw the lowering glance of Sonnenkamp, he bit his lip, and hastily corrected himself. "If it were the natural bent of his mind, who would justify his being thwarted? It would probably be the fulfilment of his highest possibilities, to renounce the things of the world and gain everlasting treasures."

The perplexed Justice played with his sword-belt. These pious words of the cavalry officer seemed inexplicable to him, and yet they certainly were not said in jest. He avoided meeting the eyes, both of the speaker and the person addressed. But Sonnenkamp looked very serious. It was incomprehensible to him that the young man should tell him so openly that Manna's rich dowry was not enough for him, and that he wanted to get his hands on Roland's portion to boot.

In conscious superiority and triumph at being able to play with the men, Sonnenkamp told how Doctor Richard had depicted Erich so enthusiastically that one could hardly hurry fast enough with six horses to fetch the man back.

"Oh, the Doctor!" cried Prancken, moving his hand as though he had an invisible whip in it. "Oh, the Doctor! Quite natural! Atheists and communists hang together. Did the Doctor tell you that he had a private talk with Herr Dournay on Sunday?"

"No. Where did you learn that?"

"By accident. I heard—from—from a servant . . . They were pretending to have a medical discussion, and rubbed their hands and said that there was no need of having Herr Sonnenkamp know that there had long been a bond of union between them."

Sonnenkamp was very grateful for this intelligence, but was filled with suppressed anger. This confirmed his suspicion that Prancken had one of his servants in his pay. The Pole, to whom Prancken always spoke in such a peculiarly friendly way, was the man, and should be discharged from service.

Sonnenkamp whistled inaudibly, and only by looking at the corner of his mouth could it be known that he was whistling at all.

The Justice considered it his duty not to let the Doctor—the Court-physician—be assailed: solidarity demanded that he should not. After freeing the Doctor from every disgraceful imputation, "which certainly could not have been cast upon him in earnest"—during which proceeding Prancken had been twirling his moustache—the Justice made an unexpected turn by saying:

"Herr von Prancken recommended the young man, with the best intentions, but might I be allowed to express my opinion of the young man?"

Sonnenkamp answered that he had attached great importance to the opinion of the Justice. Now was the opportunity of bringing the tactical manœuvre into play! Prancken seated himself more securely in his saddle, encouraged the Justice to go right under fire and discharge his guns, and cried out:

"Tell it right off!—I'm ashamed that I didn't think of it myself. Connection with this Herr Dournay would be looked upon by the highest circles as an impropriety, and very probably as a piece of hostility toward them."

"Permit me," said the Justice, with something of the voice and manner one might use to call a prisoner to order in court—"permit me to remain strictly within the bounds of my position."

Prancken was exasperated with the Justice. This insignificant, almost decrepit little man, preserved a dignity which seemed quite incomprehensible. Prancken had expected that he would frighten Herr Sonnenkamp out of his wits, and especially impress upon him the hatred of the Prince toward Erich, and now what did he hear? An exceedingly mild, most carefully weighed, and even friendly view of the case. The Justice had called Erich "a dangerous man," only as a man—as a member of society; he said that he did not exactly know how to express himself correctly: he had meant it "only in a moral sense." He immediately retracted the word "moral," however, because Erich was known as a strictly moral man. And as he now touched upon the consideration that a connection with Erich would give rise to disfavor at Court, the face of the little man shone with a mild and genial loyalty.

"The princes of our house," he said, "are not revengeful, but exceedingly mild and peaceful; and our present ruling sovereign is especially so. Bless my soul! he has his peculiarities, but they're very innocent ones, and then his kindness is inexhaustible. And how then could he persecute the son of his teacher, the playmate of his own brother? I would rather assert that he will confer his favor on him who patronizes Herr Erich, since Herr Erich has made it impossible that he could patronize him."

Prancken was in despair. He looked at the Justice, as at a pointer who won't mind the whistle. He incessantly opened and closed his hand—the hand really itched for a whip; he winked at the Justice, all in vain. Prancken at last smiled bitterly. He looked in the little man's mouth, he thought that he must have teeth again—he spoke so fluently, so decidedly in fact. He had never spoken so before. "Oh, these officials," thought Prancken, while drawing up his top-boots—"Oh, these officials, there's no accounting for them!"

"I'm very much pleased," he finally exclaimed with a forced smile, "I'm most happy that our esteemed Justice banishes all fears. Oh, these office-holders know how to arrange their performances admirably."

The Justice caught the thrust, but it barely went through his uniform.

Sonnenkamp seemed tired of taunting them. With a triumphant expression, he went to his work-table, where several closed letters lay, tore off the envelope of one he had picked out, handed over the letter, and said: "Read, Herr Prancken, and you, too, Justice—read it aloud."

The Justice of the Peace read:

VILLA EDEN, May 186–.

"*Honored Herr Captain-Doctor Dournay:*

"You will not blame an old man of much experience if he, from his onesided practical point of view, begs you to consider whether it would not be doing wrong in devoting your mind, which is so richly gifted by nature and so well stocked with knowledge, to a single boy instead of a great community. Permit me to tell you that I look upon wisdom and knowledge as capital, and that you are investing your capital at much too low a rate of interest. I respect your liberality and your modesty, which are apparent in your offer, but being confident that you are deceiving yourself in thinking that you could be contented in so narrow a sphere, I must thankfully but decidedly decline your offer to undertake the education of my son.

"I wish that you might give me an opportunity, through placing you, by my exertions, in an independent position for a year, to prove to you that I am,

"With high esteem, yours,

"HEINRICH SONNENKAMP."

Thus read the Justice, and Sonnenkamp whistled softly to himself, beating time with his crossed foot: he evidently was very well pleased with the letter.

With a triumphant look, Sonnenkamp took back the letter, put it in an envelope, and addressed it to Erich. While writing the address, he said:

"I would like to take the man into my house in another way—he should do nothing but sit at the table and talk well. Why shouldn't that be had for money? If I were a prince, I would appoint conversation councillors. Aren't the chamberlains something of that kind?" he asked Herr von Prancken with a touch of irony.

Prancken was indignant. This man was sometimes so arrogant that not even the Court was sacred to him. Yet Prancken smiled graciously.

Lutz was called through the speaking-trumpet. The letter was put in the mail-bag, and Lutz went off.

Roland was waiting for Prancken, who now took him to a still place in the park, described his journey, and handed him a duplicate copy of Thomas à Kempis. He showed Roland the place where he should begin to read to-day; and keep on, but always secretly, whether he had a skeptical or orthodox tutor.

"Isn't Erich coming back any more?" asked Roland.

"Before I came, your father had written him a decided refusal, which is already posted."

The boy sat on the bench in the park with the open book in his hand.

CHAPTER IX.

THE SAD AND BRAVE HEART OF A CHILD.

FRAU CERES noticed at table that her son was very pale. She requested the Chevalier not to let him work so hard; and particularly, not to let him draw so long out of doors. The Chevalier found this in entire accordance with his views, and would have Roland turn his attention to drawing plaster-figures before taking him into the free open air again.

"The free open air," said Roland to himself, and wondered how that could be free into which one had to be taken.

Sonnenkamp was unusually pleasant at table, for to-day he had found new reasons for despising men, and had felt his own ability to play with them. He felt wonderfully relieved to know that this Herr Dournay, who caused him and others so much trouble, was at last out of the way. And yet he was obliged to confess to himself that probably he could not have selected a better tutor for his son.

After dinner Prancken had the Justice, who was in haste, taken to the village in one of Sonnenkamp's carriages, but he himself remained and engaged in a very confidential conversation with Sonnenkamp, who wondered at the art with which a young man who is courting an heiress works himself up into an enthusiast.

When Prancken had left, Sonnenkamp went into the greenhouse, where Roland soon joined him and said:

"Father, I want to ask you to do something."

"I'm glad, if you have a wish that I can gratify."

"Father, I'll promise you to learn the names of twenty plants by heart every day, if you'll give Herr Erich back to me."

"It was very kind in Herr Dournay to teach you to say that to me."

The boy looked at his father in surprise; his lips quivered, and looking timidly around as if to call the plants themselves to witness that he was speaking the truth, he said:

"Erich did not tell me to say anything of the kind, any more than the plants did: he did not teach it to me; and even if he had, he's the only person from whom I would have learned it."

"Not even from me?" cried Sonnenkamp.

The boy was silent, and the father repeated:

"Not even from me?"

His voice was full of passion, and his large hand was clenched.

"Not even from me?" he asked the third time.

The boy drew back, and cried in a heart-piercing tone:

"Father!"

Sonnenkamp's hand relaxed, and he said with forced calmness:

"I was not going to strike you, Roland. Come here: nearer—nearer yet."

The boy went to him, and the father laid his hand on his forehead. The boy's forehead was hot, the father's hand was cold.

"I love you more than you can understand," said the father. He bent down, but the boy stretched out both hands and cried in an agonized voice:

"I beg you, father! Oh, I beg you, father, don't kiss me now!"

Sonnenkamp turned and left the place. He expected that the boy would come after him and embrace him, but he did not.

Sonnenkamp stood in the hothouse by the palm-trees. He shuddered, for he was asking his heart: "Why hast thou not the child's love? Was that crazy agitator, that Dr. Fritz, right when he told thee in a public letter, 'Thou who hast destroyed the love of parent and child, how canst thou hope for thy children's love?'"

He could not comprehend why he should think of these words, spoken in a quarrel which he wished to forget, which had long since died out. Suddenly a loud call made the strong man shudder:

"God bless you, massa! God bless you, massa!" was cried out as if by a spirit.

He looked round and found his wife's parrot, which had been brought into the hothouse, in its cage. The gardener being called, said that Frau Ceres had ordered that the parrot should be placed here, as it was too cold in the house.

"God bless you, massa! God bless you, massa!" the parrot again called after Sonnenkamp, in English, as he was leaving the palm-house.

In the mean time Roland stood rooted to the spot where his

father had left him. The park, the house, everything swam before his eyes. Joseph came to him, and Roland was glad that there was *one* person who would sympathize with him in regard to Erich's rejection. He related what had taken place, and complained of his father.

"Don't tell me anything that I may not repeat to your father," said Joseph, interrupting him. He was a shrewd and faithful servant, never allowing himself to be used as confidant or tale-bearer; but zealously following, in this respect, the advice his father had given him when he left home.

Roland asked him if he did not intend soon to return to his native city; and Joseph answered in the negative, but gave a glowing account of how beautiful it had seemed to him when he had first gone home after taking his present position at the Villa. He described the road accurately, the persons he had met here and there, how his mother was peeling potatoes when he entered the house; and how his father had come in afterward, followed by all the neighbors, who believed that he certainly must wear golden clothes, being in such a rich man's service. Joseph laughed at their simplicity, but Roland did not even smile. He went back to the house, and felt as if everybody had cast him off. He entered Manna's room, thinking that perhaps that place would seem more like home to him; but the pictures on the wall and the flowers by the hearth looked at him, strange and questioning. He wanted to write to Manna and lay all his sorrows before her, but he could not.

Again he left the house, and went into the courtyard. He stood there a little while, looking around as if in a dream. The Chevalier came, and asked him if he did not want to work; but Roland looked at him as if he did not know him, and gave him no answer. He got his crossbow, but did not use it. The sparlings and doves flew hither and thither, the dogs came up and snuffed around him, but Roland hardly noticed them.

Followed by his big dog Satan, he went to the shore, and sat down under the dense, tall willows. He laid aside his hat, for his head was burning-hot. He tried to cool his forehead with the water, but it would not cool. He knew not how long he had been sitting there gazing at the water and lost in reverie, when he heard his name called. Involuntarily he put his hand on the muzzle of his dog, who was lying near him; and he himself hardly dared to breathe, lest his hiding-place should be discovered. The voice receded and was lost, and yet the boy sat perfectly still, softly bidding the dog to be quiet; and the dog seemed to understand him. Roland took from his pocket the letter which he had written to Erich, and read it. His eyes overflowed with longing and sorrow, and rising, he tossed the letter into the stream.

Night broke, and, silently as the hunter steals after his game Roland left his hiding-place, and followed the road leading fron the river—a narrow path through the wine-hills. He wanted t go to the Krischer, to the Major, to some one who would hel him. Suddenly he stopped.

"No, to no one—to no one," he breathed softly to himself, as if he would hardly trust the silent night. "To him! t him!"

He crouched so that no one among the vineyards might see him; and yet it was night. He did not rise to his full height till he struck a public road.

CHAPTER X.

MAKE A PLACE, OR FIND ONE.

AS one who has left a brilliantly lighted room, and, returning to the solitary lamp in his study, involuntarily rubs his eyes, which having became accustomed to a bright light, need it in order to see clearly, so Erich returned to his home.

The danger of wealth consists not merely in the fact that it can corrupt him who has it, but rather in the fact that it can work banefully on him who has it not. It is neither just nor philosophic, that the dejection and unrest which often exist in the soul of a poor man, should be named covetousness, jealousy, or envy. Properly it is none of these, but rather is that burdensome feeling which asks: "Why am I not as rich as he? Nay, I do not wish for that, but why am I not placed beyond the reach of care at least? The struggles of human life are hard enough, why then should be added this wrestling for the commonest necessities of life?"

The most disastrous of all the effects which the sight of wealth produces on the poor man, is that it instils into him a distaste for all work, disgust and consciousness of servitude; nay, more, it makes all exertion appear questionable. To what end is all this thinking and striving, this building up of lofty thoughts, so long as your fellow-man must be in want. The condition of the ant by the wayside is better, for he has no neighbor who swills while he goes hungry. How can toiling help us, so long as this fiend stalks in our midst? Can any philosophy, any religion, have valid claims to truth—that conquering force—if it cannot overthrow this monster?

Erich closed his eyes, and while the train rumbled forward, he dreamed this troubled dream of our age. The engine rushed on, and its motion played a strange accompaniment to the reveries of the silent traveller. His eyes were shut, and yet he noticed that the train was passing through a tunnel. Entrance nto the darkness of the earth interrupts all conversation; and o, too, does it break in upon every internal and unexpressed hought.

When the cars had emerged into the light, Erich's reflections ad changed. Over his face, which looked as if he were sleep-ng, a smile passed; for he thought of how suggestive an essay night be written by taking as a theme, the way in which the ncients admitted the fact as well as the idea of poverty into their hilosophy, religion, politics, and morals. The feelings in-pired by poverty were thereby transformed and elevated, for poverty was a subject of philosophical contemplation.

His thoughts went on, till he perceived that the natural aspect of poverty is the same as the historical. Man alone can be rich and poor. All social life is a chain of questioning glances from one individual to another, asking or saying: "Thou hast what I have not." Out in nature, no being regards another, no living creature troubles itself about its neighbor. Every bird of the forest has its own domain, and no other bird of the same kind builds its nest within the circle which another has marked out for itself, and consequently has not to struggle daily for insects and larvæ for its brood. Only animals who herd with those of the same nature, the same capacities and means of protection, live as one, but not united. It is only man who compares his own condition with that of others of the same species, who are endowed by nature with the same faculties as he, but to whom fate has given greater power.

The train moved monotonously forward, the locomotive whistled; and the thought arose in Erich's mind, that the greatest idea which has ever been revealed to humanity from the lips of any one man, is this: Rich and poor shall not exist, do not exist, when we turn our eyes upon eternity. The universal fatherhood of God annuls inequality and degradation.

The rattling of the wheels on the rails, as they went swiftly on, gave a new rhythm to the thoughts of Erich, who now opened his eyes, and said to himself, smiling: "Thus it is here, rich and poor alike are carried to their destination by one power—the power of steam; and so one great power impels the children of God to the destiny that awaits them."

At the various stations, the confusion arising from the entrance and exit of passengers was unnoticed by Erich: neither did it interrupt his thoughts. He smiled to all, and looked at them abstractedly, as in a dream, or as he would look at ants running hither and thither near an ant-hill, each with its little burden.

Erich did not wake from his reverie till he was asked for his ticket, when the train arrived at the University city. Then he arose as one arises from a heavy, dreamful sleep: he prepared himself to meet his mother. He alighted, but no one had been awaiting his arrival.

The surrounding hills, which used to seem so beautiful, so delightful to Erich, and amid which he and his father used to wander filled with great world-moving thoughts, now seemed small and mean; and even the stream looked thirsty. His eyes had become accustomed to larger and freer prospects, and he had unconsciously learned to compare all things with a higher standard than he had known in former days.

He saw the old figures by the railway-station, among them the half-idiotic hanger-on who is an institution among the students at every little University. He grinned at the Doctor and bid him welcome. He saw students sporting their many-colored caps, and fencing at the air with their canes or playing with their dogs. It all seemed like a forgotten dream; and yet—had it not once been his highest wish to live and teach here?

He walked through the town, but saw nothing which pleased his eye; everything looked narrow, angular, and insignificant. He entered his father's house, and the narrow wooden steps seemed so steep! He entered the sitting-room, but found no one there, for his mother and his aunt had gone out. He went to the library, and there saw most of the books which used to be so carefully kept on their shelves, where no one dared to disturb them, lying in confusion on the floor; and a tall, thin man raised his eyes in astonishment, and looked at him over his spectacles, which sat on the tip of his nose.

Erich introduced himself. The man took his spectacles in his hand, and gave his name, which Erich recognized as that of a well-known antiquarian from the capital. This man had come to buy the library.

"Then my mother's hopes have also failed," thought Erich. He called the antiquarian's attention to the valuable notes which his father had made on almost every page in the library.

The antiquarian shrugged his shoulders, and answered that these notes were worthless, and would rather detract from than enhance the value of the books. If his father had written a great work which had rendered his name celebrated, the notes would have been of consequence; but inasmuch as his whole life had produced nothing more than the *conception* of a great work, all that he had written in the books, even though it might be of the greatest value when considered in itself, would simply lessen the value of the books to the antiquarian.

Erich's eyes filled with tears, for after all that he had undergone, he did not need this last blow. Was it possible that all the work to which his father had devoted his whole life should be lost, or, what was yet harder to bear, be set aside as worse than useless! There was no page on which the eye of the dead had not rested, here was the home of his thoughts, feelings, and the rich stores of his knowledge: and now should all this be scattered abroad in the world, despised, or seized upon by some stranger and converted to his own use! Erich blamed himself for not having accepted immediately and decidedly the situation which Sonnenkamp had offered him: he should have done so, and then, when his work was accomplished, he would have had a considerable sum of money. He upbraided himself for having allowed the old chivalrous pride to get the mastery of him.

Erich looked sorrowfully at a large pile of manuscripts and matter for the press, which his father had been gathering and perfecting during his whole life.

Erich's father had intended to write a book which was to be called "The True Men of History," but had died before being able to accomplish his design. Many admirable sketches and even separate portions of the work were lying there completed; but hardly any of them could be put to use, as, for the most part, every conception had three different relations, and the leading idea had existed only in the brain of the dead Professor. All the sciences, and even the most recondite facts of history, had been brought to bear on the subject, but the leading and connecting idea had been buried in the grave with its originator; and there was no longer any possibility of shaping the work as he would have shaped it. Only *one* thing was often intimated—that the title should be "The True Men."

The first and larger volume was to collect those traits which, although dissipated during the lapse of ages, rehabilitate in man the image of God as it once appeared in true men. The second volume was to give an exact statement of the processes of the soul, which were to be as clearly defined as the processes of external nature; and then was to be shown the point at which Genius—that seeming miracle in the life of the soul—appears and forms the basis of new facts. Thus at least had Erich thought when he attempted to arrange the papers after his father's death; but the leading idea had again escaped his mind, and the collection made with such difficult and laborious endeavor seemed work thrown away. His father appeared to have shut up in his own breast the secret of what he had discovered and what he yet intended to discover,—like a seeker for hidden treasure, who is forced to carry away in silence the wealth that he has found.

Erich went back to the sitting-room; and the deep emotions of his heart, the whole enigma of his existence, the strange appearance of his home, all came with renewed force as he thought of the labor and trouble his father had undergone in vain. He looked about him over the room, and it seemed to him oppressively full of old furniture. He, who was accustomed to analyze his own mind so closely, did not suspect that the contrast between the luxury in the midst of which he had lately been living and the poverty which he now saw, had cast a dark veil over all his present surroundings. He collected himself in a moment, for he heard his mother and aunt coming back.

His mother gave him a warm welcome, but Erich was greatly moved when she told him that she would have considered it perfectly right if he had accepted the situation at Sonnenkamp's house, without waiting to consult her, for in their present situation this would have been a doubly good fortune.

Erich saw that his mother, who never before had been bent by misfortune, was now not only bent but broken; and as he looked at her sorrowful face, he felt, with pain, that she thought his self-sacrifice and deference to her had been superfluous.

Sorely at the expense of her pride, his mother had laid before the widowed Princess, at whose court she had once been a favorite, an account of her trouble. She had opened her whole heart to her, and had said that she thought the position of the Princess enviable, in being able to aid her who had never before asked a favor. She only wished an inconsiderable sum, in order to prevent the sacrifice of her husband's library, which was a family treasure and a matter of great consequence to her son. The tears stood in her eyes as she reviewed her letter.

And then the mother gave her son the answer of the Princess, which had been beautifully written by her secretary, in a few sympathizing and respectful words. A small amount of money had been enclosed, which was far from being sufficient, and which his mother had thought of returning—telling the Princess sarcastically that some underling had probably enclosed a less amount than had been directed. She did not, however, do this, for great people must not be affronted, and one must even thank them most submissively, so as not to lose their worthless favor.

Erich promised that within a week the library should be secured to them.

He went immediately to his own room and wrote a letter to Count Wolfsgarten. In a few straightforward words he told him what had happened on his arrival, in what condition he had found his father's house and his mother, and in conclusion echoed the words that Clodwig had once used to him: "I have such a strong friendship for you, that I can let you do me a favor."

Erich had written that his feelings toward Wolfsgarten would remain the same, even though his wishes should not be complied with. He felt that this was untrue, tore up the letter and wrote another, omitting the objectionable expression. It was no small thing for Erich to appear for the first time as a petitioner—almost (and he tormented himself with the word) as a beggar.

Erich now gave his mother a full account of his journey. She listened to him quietly; but when he spoke of Bella, she said: "Bella Prancken is an unaccountable woman."

Their old plans were discussed. Erich wished to establish a school, and his mother and aunt agreed with him. Both of them had connections with the best families of the land, and the only point on which all could not agree was whether it would be best for him to teach in a boys' school or one for girls. Erich was for the former, because he could co-operate better with his pupils if they were boys. His mother, however, thought that it would be best for him to pursue scientific studies for a few years longer, at the end of which time he would undoubtedly be able to produce some great work which would immediately make him famous: this would be far preferable to toiling on in some insignificant calling. In the mean time she and his aunt would earn enough in the capital, to let Erich live without anxiety.

They were all agreed that nothing was to be positively determined until Sonnenkamp's letter should come. Erich's mother said that it would fulfil the ideal of her life to occupy the little vine-covered cottage, and thought that she would be able to do great good to the boy, surrounded as he was by the dangers of wealth; and she would do so with redoubled willingness, for he was of the same age as her dead son.

Erich went to see his old friend and teacher, Professor Einsiedel. This man had been his favorite instructor. He was a high-priest of science—a man who lived steadily and exclusively in a world of thought and investigation, for the sole purpose of adding to the stores of human knowledge. He was frugal, living by law, unruffled by passion, eating and drinking with almost inconceivable abstinence, yet always smiling, always agreeable, always occupied with some new thought or discovery, always looking about on all sides in the wide kingdom of thought. Professor Einsiedel had been intimate with Erich's father, and always lamented that his friend, who always wanted to do the best and most perfect thing, had not done anything complete in itself. "We must always," was his maxim, "be content to have given some little thing as a contribution; and this will take its own place in the great totality. We produce a something which is up to the limit of our power, and to which we have nothing more to contribute. Only of God is it related in the history of creation that he could say of what he had made that it was good. Nothing but absolute spirit can make that which is produced correspond with that which was intended—the deed with the idea; but the immortal spirit always holds by the idea of that which it believed and intended itself to be able to do."

Whatever scientific problem Erich brought to Professor Einsiedel, immediately received a solution, and directions would be added as to the sources where it might be found. The Professor was always ready to give any one who asked it the benefit of his own laborious researches, and this he did with entire disregard of his own interests. It was a matter of indifference to him whether it appeared under his name or that of another, provided only that it appeared.

A picture by Rembrandt hung in the Professor's room—a little copperplate, which looked almost like a portrait of the Professor himself. The picture represented Faust in his nightcap, gazing at the magic circle illuminated by itself. Faust is an old, dried-up little man, who evidently needs the rejuvenating power of magic. Professor Einsiedel had no such magic draught; but every day he drank new youth from the writings of the classic world.

Erich visited him now to get aid and counsel; and as he entered, found the good old Professor (who lived quite alone, and was not near so much troubled by his solitude as by his want of means) in an unusual frame of mind. He considered it a pity that Erich did not intend to devote himself entirely to science; but, nevertheless, admitted that his nature was fitted for a practical, personal field of action. His face wore a peculiar smile as he said:

"You're a well-built man, and you must turn that fact into money, which is certainly a good thing. Yes, yes, that will help you."

In his restlessness and strong desire not to wait, but to accomplish something unaided by others, Erich went on the following day to the capital city; for he had heard from the antiquary that an elderly man who had hitherto conducted a school was about to withdraw from it, and was desirous of placing it in good hands.

He entered the city where for a whole year he had lived the life of a careless soldier, looked up to by the good citizens. Many of his comrades, dressed in the old uniform, went by him, and then turning, cried out, "Oh, is it you? Good-morning!" and then went their way. Erich walked through the streets of his native city, inquiring and studying his way as if he had been a stranger; but he hoped that soon, when he should become a permanent resident, he would feel at home once more.

The proprietor of the school received him well, and the terms were acceptable. The good position of his parents was of great service to him now; but he left the building without coming to a determination, for it would be necessary for him, in taking the school, to accept the old regulations and the old corps of teachers, and this fact made him hesitate.

As he was walking the streets again, he met an old friend of his father, who was now Minister of Education, and who called out to him as he was passing. This gentleman inquired about him and his mother, and offered him the position of custodian of the cabinet of antiquities, with the assurance that he had no doubt that in a short time he could become a director. Erich promised to consider the subject.

Just as he left the Minister, an elderly man, who had been waiting at the door of a house, approached and saluted him as if he were an old acquaintance. Erich was unable to recall his face, and the man told him gratefully that he had once been kind to him in the House of Correction. The man said that he was now pretty well off, and was the beadle's servant; and with an expression of face which was half cunning and half pious, he offered himself for any service in which Erich might require him. Erich thanked him, and did not reflect that many persons who passed by and recognized him, might think it strange to see him in such company. And now the man who had taken Erich's position in the army, and had become a veritable captain, returned from parade, and took Erich with him to the military casino; and Erich was in good spirits, and forgot all the troubles of life. In the casino there was much talking about how Otto von Prancken was going to marry a creole, who was worth a good many millions. Erich did not think it was necessary to say that Manna was not a creole, and that he himself knew something about the affair.

CHAPTER XI.

ROLAND! WHERE ARE YOU?

WHERE'S Roland?"

Sonnenkamp asks Joseph, Joseph asks Bertram, Bertram asks the head-gardener, the head-gardener asks the "Squirrel," the Squirrel asks the peasants, the peasants ask the children, the children ask the air. Miss Perini asks the Chevalier, the Chevalier asks the dogs—and Frau Ceres must not hear anything about all the whole affair.

Sonnenkamp rides hastily to the Major, the Major asks Fräulein Milch; but this time, the omniscient does not know. The Major rides to the castle, Roland's name is shouted into all the caverns and dark places, but there comes no answer.

Sonnenkamp sends the groom to the Krischer, the Krischer is out in the fields, and cannot be found.

Sonnenkamp rides to the railway station, taking Roland's pony "Puck" with him, and he often looks at the empty saddle. At the station he asks unconcernedly if Roland has not arrived yet, as though he was awaiting his return from a journey. Nothing has been seen of him. Sonnenkamp rides back to the Villa, and asks if he hasn't got back yet, and when he receives an answer in the negative, he rides away to the nearest railway station up the river. Here also he asks, but no less guardedly; but the boy has not been seen. The employees seem to spin round as if they were drunk.

Sonnenkamp returns to the Villa. The Major is there. Miss Perini has sent for him—perhaps he may be of service. She asserts that Roland has certainly gone to the convent to see Manna. The Major and Sonnenkamp rush to the telegraph-office, and send a despatch to the convent: everybody is full of impatience, for there is no immediate connection with the island, and it will be two hours before an answer will be received. Sonnenkamp will wait here, but sends the Major to the village, to ask the Doctor and everybody else for news—but quietly, so as not to make any excitement.

Sonnenkamp walks about the station, and lays his burning forehead against the cold stone pillars: all is silent and empty. He goes into the waiting-room, and finds that the seats there were never made to be rested on, which is horribly inhuman. In America things are different—or else there are no seats at all. He goes out again, and watches the workmen couple a freight-car to the train—how slowly they do it! He looks at a stone-cutter, who is using both a sharp and a blunt hammer—he examines as closely as if he wanted to learn the trade. These men all work so placidly. And so they might: they had not lost a son! He eyes the telegraph-wires, and wants to ask all the world, even those quarters of it where nobody knows either him or his son—"Where's my boy?"

Night is coming.

The train comes thundering toward him, and Sonnenkamp shrinks back, for it seemed to be rushing at him purposely. He collects himself, looks around, strains his eyes, but sees nothing of Roland. The passengers go to their homes, and again all is still.

Sonnenkamp went back to the telegraph-office, and sent another despatch to see if the first one had been received. The answer said, Yes. The tapping of the telegraphic instrument made him shudder, for he had often felt that same motion in the veins of his hand, at night when he tried to sleep. He wanted the operator to stay at the office all night, for who could tell whether some message might not come from somewhere, or he might wish to send one? But the operator refused, notwithstanding a large sum of money was offered him: he was not permitted to alter the arrangements of the office without authority from his superiors. He ordered the messenger to remain in the room while he was away: he slammed the door of the office and left. He was evidently afraid of Sonnenkamp.

Again Sonnenkamp was alone. He heard the stroke of an oar—somebody was coming up the river.

"Is that you, Major?" he called out into the starry night.

"Yes."

"Is he with you?"

"No."

The Major got out of the boat: there was no trace of Roland in the village. An answer cannot be received from the convent before early in the morning. And now they think that perhaps Roland has gone to Wolfsgarten. A message is sent thither, and they return to the Villa.

As Sonnenkamp gave his hand to the Major on entering the carriage, the Major said:

"Your hand is cold to-day."

It shot through Sonnenkamp's mind like an arrow, that with that hand he had that day offered to strike Roland. What if the boy had gone to his death in the waters of the Rhine, with that thought!

The ring on his thumb pressed into his flesh as if it were red-hot.

Joseph met them as they were returning to the Villa.

"Is he there?" cried the Major.

Sonnenkamp could not speak.

"No; but my lady has learned it."

In the village through which they were passing, men and women were standing round in groups chatting in the mild Spring night. They met the Priest, and Sonnenkamp asked him to accompany them to the Villa.

Arrived at the courtyard of the Villa, Sonnenkamp remained sitting in the carriage. He had forgotten where he was, and had to be spoken to before he would alight. When he touched the ground, he came to himself. Lights were being carried hither and thither in the house—they could be seen through the windows. And now they heard a shriek, and hastened up stairs. Frau Ceres was in her night-dress on the floor of the great saloon, half-kneeling by a chair, and pressing her face against the cushions. The Priest stood near her, and Miss Perini was shaking a powder into a glass. Sonnenkamp walked quickly to his wife, laid his hand on her shoulder and said:

"Ceres, be calm!"

The woman turned and looked at him with gleaming eyes. Then she sprang up, and grasping him by the breast, cried:

"Give me my son! Give me my son, you—"

Sonnenkamp covered her mouth with his broad hand. She tried to bite him; but he held her mouth fast, and she was still.

Sonnenkamp told the Priest and Miss Perini to leave his wife. Miss Perini wished to remain, but a motion of his hand bade her go, and she left the room with the Priest. Sonnenkamp took his wife in his arms as if she had been a child, carried her into her bedroom, and laid her on the bed. Her feet were cold: he covered them with a spread and wrapped them up so that she could not use them. After awhile, Frau Ceres seemed to be asleep. If she was only pretending, that was sufficient. He went to the room adjoining the balcony, where the Priest, the Major, and Miss Perini were sitting together. He told the Priest that he was very thankful for his kindness, but thought he had better go and take some rest. He told Miss Perini the same thing in a singularly courtly manner, and she could not do otherwise than obey; but he asked the Major to remain with him.

They sat together by the open door for an hour, looking at the heavens studded with stars, and listened to the lapping of the Rhine. Then Sonnenkamp bade the Major go to rest, for the morrow would bring peace, and all would be well then. He himself intended to sleep in the antechamber of his wife's bedroom. He went once more to her bed, shading the light with his hand: she was sleeping quietly, and her cheeks were flushed.

All was quiet at the Villa. Sonnenkamp was awakened from a sleep, for the messenger had returned from Wolfsgarten: Roland was not there.

"Is Herr Prancken coming?" asked Sonnenkamp. The servant did not know.

Sonnenkamp was tired and worn out, but he could not sleep. He stood on the balcony and listened to the singing of the birds, and the murmur of the stream. He saw the sun rise, he heard the bells ring—the whole world, so fresh and lovely, seemed to him a chaos. His daughter in the convent, his wife liable at any moment to make the most horrible disclosures, and his son lost—not a trace of him to be found! Perhaps his corpse is lying there under the waves! For an instant Sonnenkamp felt as if he must throw himself from the balcony and die: then he straightened himself up and lit a fresh cigar.

He went down into the park. The trees were shuddering in the early morning air, a rustling and whispering ran through the leaves as if the morning light had given them sound and motion. The birds were singing sweetly—they had a home, a family, they had not lost a child.

Sonnenkamp wandered here and there. This is his own

ground—-these trees are his, everything is blooming and breathing the freshness of morning. Did *he* yet breathe—he for whom all this lived—for whom it *should* live, for whom it had been planted and set in order?

"Why?—Why?" cried Sonnenkamp through the park, but no answer was returned from the outer world. Perhaps one came from within, for he pressed both hands against his breast.

He came to the orchard. There stood the trees to whose branches he had given the direction which *he* chose; they were in bloom, and now in the early light, their blossoms were falling like a light rustling rain, and covering the earth with a snow-white mantle.

And as the morning wore on, Sonnenkamp knew that Roland was there floating in the waves—they were so purple—the river was a river of blood. He groaned aloud, and stretched out his hands as if to grasp and strangle something. He seized a tree, and shook it till it had shed all its blossoms; he was covered over and over with flowers: and now he laughed outright in his bitterness, and said:

"Life shall not subdue me! Nothing! Not even you, Roland, not even you!"

At that moment he saw a white figure, with a singular covering on its head, steal through the garden and disappear behind the trees. What's that? He rubbed his eyes. Was it a phantom or reality?

He followed the apparition.

"Halt!" he cried. "There are mantraps and spring-guns there!"

A woman cried out piteously. Sonnenkamp approached, and Fräulein Milch stood before him.

"What do you want here? What's the matter?"

"I wanted the Major."

"He's asleep yet."

"I may tell it to you too," began Fräulein Milch, collecting herself. "It gives me no peace."

"Out with it—no introduction!"

Fräulein Milch drew herself proudly up, and said:

"If you're rude, I'll go back."

"Pardon me; what is it you wish?"

"I had a proposition to make to you."

Sonnenkamp controlled himself patiently, and nodded to her to proceed. She then said that it left her no peace—she did not know whether the Major had told him yet. Sonnenkamp impatiently broke off a twig covered with blossoms, and Fräulein Milch continued: She believed that Captain Dournay would certainly know where Roland was: a telegram ought to be sent to him.

Sonnenkamp thanked the old lady, and said, with great self-control, that he would wake the Major and send him down into the garden; but Miss Milch begged that he might be allowed to sleep quietly. She went back to her house, and Sonnenkamp walked back through the park.

The roses had opened during the night, and from a hundred stems and bushes they sent forth their fragrance to their owner, but it gave him no delight. Here is the park, here are the trees, and yonder is the house,—such things can be gained; but one thing is unattainable—a life—the life of a child, a child's heart, a union of soul with soul, inseparable, indestructible.

And back to his heart came that bitter word: "Thou hast slain the noblest emotions of thy fellow-men, the love of father and mother and child. Now thou art smitten!"

Why should that word, spoken by one who was struggling in the New World, haunt him so, to-day as well as yesterday?

Perhaps that man is in the boat which is now coming up the river.

He did not dream that at that very moment the child of that man was talking with *his* child.

CHAPTER XII.

HOW THE NIGHT WEARS.

IN the night, all the roses opened in the garden and in the boy's soul.

"To Erich!" said Roland, not aloud, but whispering to himself. The night was bright with stars. The crescent moon hung low, and Roland was so happy in its soft light that he often stretched out his arms as if to try a conscious power of flight. He walked swiftly, as if pursued; he heard steps behind him, and paused—it was the sound of his own footfalls.

Far off he saw a group of men standing still, and waiting for him. As he approached, they changed to black-painted palings, enclosing a vineyard. He slackened his pace, and wanted to sing, but was afraid that some one would hear him if he should. He paused at the top of a hill, and far below him in the river he heard the panting of a tow-boat, and saw the lights on the masts of the vessels as they were dragged along. How fast the lights moved! Roland counted them; there were seven.

"They're awake there too," said he to himself, and then for the first time it occurred to him that there are men who must earn their bread by waking and working through the night: some of them are down yonder in the tow-boat, working at the engine; the ferrymen, too, and the hands of the vessels that are being towed!

"Why should that be so? What forces the men?" The boy tossed his head in indignation. Yet what was it all to him? Ill at ease, he walked across the plateau, and ascended a hill behind it. He was filled with childish pleasure to see that his shadow accompanied him. He always kept in the middle of the road, for the ditches at the sides looked dark and awful, and he hurried past the shadows which the trees cast in the moonlight, and was glad when he emerged into the light. When he neared a village, he felt safe, for although all the inhabitants were asleep, he was yet among men. The boy had always been told that thieves and murderers wander about all the roads at night, and seek for victims. What had he with him to be robbed of? His watch and chain. He took them out to conceal them.

"Shame on you," he suddenly cried out, for he saw that he was afraid to the very bottom of his soul: and he *would* not be a coward. So he thought of other and greater dangers which he would like to encounter: he exulted in them, and cried aloud:

"Come on! here I am, and Satan too! Eh! Satan? Just let them come once!" he said, patting the dog. Satan bounded on by his side.

He passed through a village. Everybody was asleep. A dog barked, knowing by his scent that a strange dog was in the neighborhood. Roland bade Satan be quiet, and he obeyed. The boy knew the village, for he had been here one Sunday with the Doctor and Erich. Here was the house where the man had died; here, on the other side of the road, was the gymnasium where he and Erich had exercised; and at the end of the town he saw the house where the Seven-piper had lived: the whole orchestra was asleep. He stood still awhile, thinking whether it would not be well to rouse somebody in the house to accompany him; or, why not send a messenger to his father? He rejected both thoughts, and walked on.

The night was still; but occasionally he heard the distant barking of some dog aroused from sleep. A brook rippled beside him as he walked, and kept him company. How delightfully it prattled to him! But at last its path diverged from his, and all was still again. He passed through a ravine where the tall trees on either side cast such gloomy shadows that he could not see his path, yet he walked bravely forward, thinking how beautiful the spot must be in the broad light of day. He emerged from the ravine, and welcomed the high road again. Above the summit of a hill, a star shone large and bright! Slowly and steadily it mounted the heavens, and the boy wondered: "Does Manna see that star?"

As he approached another village, he saw a light in the window of the first house he passed, and heard people talking.

The housewife was crying and lamenting that in the morning their only cow was to be sold. He did not deliberate long, but placed some pieces of gold on the window-sill, and, rapping at the window cried out: "Here, folks! here's money for your cow. I've put it on the sill!"

He ran from the spot, hardly daring to breathe: for some unaccountable reason, he felt like a thief. He did not stop running till he fell into a ditch. He lay there and listened, thinking that the whole household might be pursuing him, and laughed as he thought how they would attribute his present to some spirit who wanders abroad at night to relieve the sorrows of mortals, and vanishes before a word of thanks can be uttered. When he found that he was not pursued, he proceeded on his way, and, blessed by the thought of what he had done, said to himself that some day when he had lots of money he would wander through the world unseen, and wherever he went all should be happy.

He had hardly struck the road again when he saw a frightful-looking man standing in a neighboring field, and holding in his hand a weapon pointed directly at him. The terrified boy stood still and demanded what the man wanted, but received no answer; the man did not even move. Roland set Satan at him, but the dog came back and shook his head. The boy approached the apparition, and laughed and trembled at the same time: the terrible phantom was only a scarecrow.

A wagon was coming after him, rumbling and creaking at a great rate. It screamed and clattered on its axles as the wheels jolted heavily over the stones. Roland thought that he could see that it was a two-wheeled wagon with only one horse. He stopped, in order to see more distinctly, and heard the tramp of two horses: when it came nearer, he saw that in fact there were two horses hitched tandem to a two-wheeled wagon. Roland stepped to one side, waited till it passed him, and heard the driver whistling and cracking his whip. Roland walked behind the cart, keeping at a little distance; for during the night a certain timidity had come upon him: and now he felt that he was near a man who was awake:—if anything should happen, he could call for assistance. He even thought how he would cry out, "Help! help!"

But no danger came near him, and as if sneering at himself, he said to his dog:

"It's too bad that somebody doesn't attack us! We won't have any chance to show our metal!"

But he felt a little afraid again when he could no longer hear the noise of the wagon, which had stopped at the toll-gate. His courage came back when he heard it rumble forward again. It stopped at the first house of the next village. The hostler, who appeared to have expected the driver, was not a little surprised when his lantern showed him a beautiful, bright-eyed boy, as well as the man for whom he had been waiting.

"Halloo! who's that?" cried the hostler; but his wonder and terror were so great that he could not shut his mouth again, for the big dog was sniffing at his legs, and showing his sharp teeth, and looking back at his master, waiting only for the order to "Seize him."

Roland ordered the dog to come back to him. The boy's voice appeared to have something in it which filled the driver and hostler with respect.

They asked him to drink a *schoppen* with them, and he consented; so they sat down at a table on which burned a single oil-lamp, and Roland drank to the wagoner.

The hostler was inquisitive, and said in a wheedling tone, as he pointed to Roland's delicate hand:

"That's a fine ring you've got on your finger. Lord! how the stone shines! Now that must be worth a good deal. Make me a present of it."

The host, who had heard what was said, came into the room looking like a ghost, for he was dressed only in his shirt and underclothes. He asked Roland who he was, where he was from, and whither he was going, but received only evasive answers.

The wagoner set out again. Roland accompanied him, and listened to him give an account of himself. The wagon carried new earthen jugs, which were to be taken to a neighboring mineral-spring, filled with the water, and then taken way off to Holland. Roland was astonished to learn how much work had to be done before those mineral-waters which he saw every morning on his father's table could be drunk.

The wagoner thought that Holland was at the world's end, and was greatly astonished when Roland told him that there were many countries, yes, even whole continents, more remote than Holland. The wagoner was amazed at Roland's vast learning, and inquired if he had ever travelled so far.

Roland stammered as he answered, and then the wagoner said that he himself was an honest fellow, that everything he wore had been earned by hard work, and that he would rather go hungry or be a beggar than possess wealth obtained by dishonest means. He advised Roland that if he had done anything wrong and feared punishment—if, for instance, he had stolen the ring—it would be best for him to go back and make restitution. Roland put him at ease on that score.

The road led through a beautiful little oak-forest. They heard the night-owl hoot, and the sound was like elfish laughter.

"Thank God you're with me!" said the wagoner. "Did you hear that laughing?"

"That wasn't laughing—it was a night-bird."

"Yes, a night-bird—the laughing ghost."

"The laughing ghost? What's that?"

"Yes, my mother once heard it in broad daylight when she was a little girl. Once on a time some youngsters went out in the woods to gather acorns. They put a white cloth on the ground to catch the acorns in, and then shake the trees, you know. Acorns are the best fodder for pigs. Well, one fine noon in the Fall, the children went into the woods; the boys climbed up the tree, and shook it till it creaked again. Then they heard a loud laugh in the thicket. 'What's that?' 'Oh,' says mother, 'that's a ghost.' 'Oh,' says one of the boys, quite bold, says he, 'if it's a ghost, I'd just like to see one once.' With that he goes into the thicket, and when he gets there, what should he see but a little man sitting on a stump, his head bigger than his body—all gray, and with a great big long gray beard. Then the youngster says: 'Was that you as laughed so?' 'To be sure,' says the little man, and gives another laugh just like the other one. 'You shook down the acorns, but one went under the cloth, deep in the moss; you won't find it, and out of that acorn a tree will grow, and when it's big enough, men will come and cut it down; and out of part of the boards they'll make a cradle, and out of the other, a door, and they'll put a child in that cradle, and when that child shall be able to open that door the first time, I'll be delivered Till that time I must wander about, because I was a poacher and lived by ill-gotten gains.' The little man gave another laugh, and disappeared into the stump. Since then he's been heard off and on, but nobody has ever seen him. Everybody knows where that oak-tree is, but nobody touches it."

Roland shuddered. He did not believe the story, but yet he listened, as the wagoner proceeded to explain yet more clearly how difficult it is to escape the consequences of living by unrighteous means.

As the day dawned, Roland gave his hand to the wagoner, and bade him farewell, for he wished to stop here and wait awhile before going on. The wagoner seated himself on the thills of the wagon, and prepared to take a comfortable nap: it was day now, and he could take a little sleep.

The boy seated himself on a pile of stones by the wayside, and gazed abstractedly before him, listening to the creaking and rattling of the wagon as it slowly disappeared in the distance. For the first time in his life, he followed, in thought, the life of another person. He saw, as in a dream, the wagoner arrive at the end of his journey, and lying in his shed on the hay which he would afterward give to his horses.

Never before had Roland been so completely alone, so cast

upon himself, with the consciousness that there was no one to guide him. It seemed to him as if he had never before seen the world and what is in it. He watched the path of a beetle which crept swiftly along the ground, and then clambered up the stem of a plant. Thoughts which he could not understand floated through the boy's mind. What boundless life there is in the world! In the hedges by the roadside where the wild roses had just opened, beetles and flies of all kinds sat motionless, while large bees flew humming from flower to flower. Here had beetle, butterfly, spider, and fly passed the night, and snails with their protecting shells dwelt in silence among the twigs.

He saw a field-mouse coming from its hole: at first it just put its head above the ground, listening, watching, and moving its whiskers; but after awhile it slipped out, and vanished in the grass, and dived into another hole. A bright-colored beetle ran hastily across the road, for it was afraid of the highway, and felt perfectly secure only when safely hidden in the cornfield.

A hare started up. Satan sprang after it, and Roland involuntarily brought up his hand as if his fowling-piece were in it.

Roland arose as if emerging from a stream of overwhelming impressions. The sun had risen; he could not support the splendor of its beams. Fixing his eyes on the road, he proceeded; but his step was hesitating, for something within him said:

"Go back to your father and mother!"

But suddenly he cried aloud:

"Erich!"

And "Erich!" was borne back to him by a thousand echoes: as if the mountains had commanded him, he journeyed on. He felt as if he did not walk, but as if he were lifted and carried forward by an invisible power. The sleepless night, the wine, all that he had experienced were like a confused dream, and he thought that surely he must find something never before known by man—something nameless, unimaginable, wonderful. He looked about to see if it would not appear: something *must* come, something that would say to him: "I have been watching for thee; hast thou come at last?" And now as he looked round, he found that his dog had left him. There was the wood close at hand, he must have run into it after another hare or wild rabbit. Roland whistled, and called, "Satan! Satan!" but with no result. Then he shouted the old name, "Grip!" The dog came running joyfully toward him: his tongue was hanging out of his mouth, and he was wet with the dew of the grain-field through which he had been running. Roland had some trouble to keep the dog from jumping on him, it was so well pleased to hear its old name, and looked up panting as if it perfectly understood the change.

"Yes, your name's Grip!" cried Roland.

The dog followed at his heels.

As the path now led through the forest, Roland left the roadside, and lay down under a fir-tree; above him the birds sang, and the cuckoo called. Grip sat beside him, and seemed quite disappointed at receiving no glance from his master. At length Roland turned his lips back and examined his teeth—how glorious they were! Then he said, for hunger had made him think of this:

"At the next town where there's a butcher, you shall have a sausage."

Grip licked his chops, sprang around as if he understood what was said, scared up the crows, who were already at work in the cornfield, and barked at the rising sun.

But soon the weary child fell asleep. Grip sat beside him, but knew his duty too well to lie down; he remained sitting, and would not sleep. He winked occasionally, as if it was hard to keep his tired eyes open; then he would shake his head, and keep faithful watch and ward over his sleeping master.

Suddenly Roland awoke. A child's voice had broken his slumbers.

CHAPTER XIII.

THE LILY OF THE VALLEY.

ROLAND rubbed his eyes; a child stood before him, a girl dressed in white and wearing a blue scarf. Her face was rosy, her eyes large and blue, and her long loosened hair fell in brown ripples over her shoulders. In each hand she held a bunch of wild-flowers.

Grip stood before the child and would not let her pass.

"Back, Grip!" cried Roland, rising, and the dog went behind his master.

"This is the German forest!" said the child with a foreign accent, and in a voice that might have belonged to the princess in the fairy-tale. "This is the German forest! I've only been gathering flowers. Are you the forest-prince?"

"No. Who are you?"

"I'm from America. My uncle brought me here this morning, and now I'm going to stay in Germany."

"Come, Lilian! Where are you staying so long?" cried a man's voice from the road.

Roland looked through the trees and saw an open carriage and a tall, stately gentleman with snow-white hair.

"I'll come pretty soon," answered the child, "I've got such lovely flowers!"

"Accept this from me," said Roland, plucking a full-blown lily from the stem.

She threw away all the flowers which she had in her hands, and took the one he offered; then, saying in English, "Good-bye!" turned and ran toward the carriage. The gentleman lifted her in, she pointed back into the forest, and then the carriage rolled forward, and Roland was again alone.

If one had been able to look down from the sky he would have seen a singular sight, for at the very instant when the child was speaking to Roland, Sonnenkamp was standing on the terrace buried in thought and shuddering in the morning air.

Roland pressed his hand to his forehead.

Had this really taken place, or had he dreamed it? The rumbling of the carriage, and the flowers lying on the ground told him that it was reality. But had the child really said that she came from America? "Why didn't I run after her? Why didn't I speak to the old gentleman? And now no one can tell me who the little girl is, or where they are taking her."

Roland stared at the flowers lying at his feet, but did not pick them up. Grip barked, as if to say: "Yes, and then folks say there aren't any miracles now-a-days." He sniffed at the flowers, and then followed the child's path and ran after the carriage, as if wishing to fulfil his master's desire and detain the old man and child, so that Roland might converse with them. Roland whistled and shouted, and so the dog returned and received a good scolding.

"You don't deserve a sausage, you didn't obey me."

Grip lay down at his master's feet quite humbly; he could not tell what good intentions he had had.

"Now we'll go," said Roland, and they started on again.

They heard a locomotive whistle in the distance, and walked in the direction of it. The two soon emerged from the forest and walked through the vineyards.

Roland saw some women walking up and down a by-road, carrying earth from a pile and placing it in a vineyard which had been recently laid out. By the hedge which bordered the field, kettles were standing over a large fire, and an old woman was stirring their contents with a dry branch. Roland stood still, and the crone called to him, asking if he would not like to share with them. He approached the group and found that they were boiling coffee. Presently the rest of the women, young and old, came up, and there was great laughing and talking; then they turned their baskets upside-down and seated themselves on these improvised chairs. They prepared a similiar seat for Roland, put some more fuel under the pots, and asked if he was not a prince. Roland said no. But the question flattered him; he was very condescending, and joked with the women.

An old vine-dresser who was overseeing the work, seemed to consider it worth while to speak to Roland, seeing that he was of the masculine gender, and advised him not to drink coffee, as that was a way in which stupid folks send money over to America and never get it back again.

Roland was struck at hearing America mentioned again, and the whole assembly listened with great attention when he said that it was not coffee that came from America, but sugar.

"All *our* sugar stayed in America, then," said the old woman, "for we haven't got a bit."

The first cup and the cream of the milk were given to Roland, together with a piece of black bread. He would willingly have paid something for what he ate, but he noticed now for the first time that he no longer had his porte-monnaie. He knew that he had it at the tavern: that sly-looking hostler must have stolen it. He suppressed his disappointment, and told the women that at some future time he would pay for what he had enjoyed by benefiting some one who was in want.

Again he sat out on his journey.

Thus had he at last experienced even this: Poor and helpless, he had enjoyed the goodness and generosity of poor people; this was the best thing that had befallen him.

The world is beautiful and men are good, even though hostlers are unable to withstand the temptation of a well-filled pocket-book. Feeling in this happy mood Roland walked on, and soon reached the railway-station.

He had carefully avoided entering the cars at one of the nearer stations, for he would in that case be easily recognized and found; he had therefore made a detour, so that he might take the train at a station further from home.

At the station, Roland was saluted with great familiarity by a man in tattered clothes, who had a boot on one foot and a slipper on the other.

"Good-morning, my dear Baron—good-morning, my dear Baron!" said the poor fellow, forcing himself on Roland's attention.

In such charming morning air, and after such a night, it was doubly disagreeable to enter an atmosphere of brandy fumes, such as was breathed by this half-drunk, half-crazy man, who became at last so disagreeably intimate, that one of the railway officials politely told him to leave the stranger in peace.

The poor man relieved Roland of his presence, but continued to make signs to him from a distance, very confidentially, and as if they had some mysterious secret with each other.

Roland learned that this man was connected with an illustrious, noble family. His relations being willing to aid him, gave him a yearly allowance, but this was entirely useless. He was at present boarding with one of the baggage-men, and the station was the only thing in which he took pleasure. He was treated with respect, for he was a baron, and very much to be pitied.

Roland was as much afraid of the man as if he had been a ghost. The agitation of the night, and all that he had experienced, was having its effect, and yet he could not help thinking how wonderful it was that this half-drunk, half-crazy man should be treated so respectfully because he was a baron.

Roland induced the *restaurateur* at the station to lend him enough money to pay his passage, and receive his ring in pawn for it. He purchased a ticket for the University city, and when at last he was comfortably seated in the car, he could not help saying to his neighbor :

"How pleasant it is to be carried forward now !"

His neighbor looked at him in surprise : how could he know how happy it made the weary boy to be carried forward toward Erich, without any exertion on his own part ?

"Where are you going, Baron ?" asked his neighbor.

Roland named his destination, but he was greatly surprised to hear the man call him "Baron." Had he indeed become one during the night ? At a branch-road where other guards entered the cars and his neighbor left, Roland caught the words :

"Pay good attention to the young baron inside."

He was very well pleased to hear this title applied to himself, and thought how fine a thing it must be to be a baron : everybody would call him by his title and pay him great respect. The thought soon passed from his mind, from which Erich was never absent. How happy he would be to see him ! His face glowed with impatience and longing.

Suddenly a fear fell upon him. Where had he left the dog ? He had forgotten and lost him. The train rumbled on through valleys, gorges, and tunnels, and Roland felt as though a year had passed since he had left home.

Not far from the University, where the road branched off again, some students entered the cars, and soon let their fellow-travellers see that they had been performing the heroic exploit of drinking a bowl of May-wine bought with their fathers' money ; and most certainly each one of their class can hold his own at a genuine drinking-bout ! They had also brought some of the May-wine into the cars with them, and, in their generosity or exuberant spirits, wanted Roland to drink with them; but he modestly though decidedly declined.

Twilight had come when they reached the University city.

Roland inquired for Doctor Dournay. One of the students, with a fine face, who had held himself aloof from the noisy young fellows, told Roland that he might go with him, as he lived near the Professor's widow. Roland accompanied him. And now a singular and anxious fear came upon him. What if Erich could not be found—if Erich would have nothing more to do with him? How much might have happened by this time!

His heart beat fast as he ascended the steep, dark, narrow wooden steps. A door opened on the landing, and in the door stood a woman and asked:

"Who do you want to see?"

"Captain Dournay."

"He's gone away."

CHAPTER XIV.

THE NEW SON.

ROLAND asked if he might wait there for awhile, and was conducted into the sitting-room. The servant-girl told him that Erich had gone to the capital city, but might possibly return that day. His mother had gone to the grave of her son, for to-day was the anniversary of his death.

The girl left the room to get a lamp, and Roland was alone in the chamber which was darkening in the twilight; he sat in the corner of a sofa, tired and filled with thought.

Strange that there should be so many dwellings in the world into which a man can enter and be a stranger in a strange house!

In the tower of the city, trumpets were sounding a choral as they had sounded it for many years past. Roland was lost in dreams; he no longer knew where he was, he only remembered that he had travelled through many lands and cities, and that everywhere men dwelt in houses and led their own lives, of which nothing was known outside.

Erich's mother entered and remained standing near the door. Roland rose and said:

"Good-evening, Mother."

Stretching out her hands, the lady cried:

"My God, Hermann—you?"

"I'm not Hermann, I'm Roland."

The lady tottered toward him: the aunt entered with a light

and now all was explained. Roland was so weary that he could hardly say that he had followed Erich, for he was never to leave him again. The lady kissed him, crying and sobbing.

A step was heard on the stair. Erich entered. Roland had not strength to stir, and Erich cried in astonishment:

"You here?"

Roland could hardly tell what he had done. He was perplexed and motionless to see Erich stand so coldly before him, not even offering his hand. When Roland had finished, Erich said firmly:

"If you were my son, I would punish you severely for this self-will and the anxiety you have inflicted on your friends by it."

"You may punish me—I won't stir. No one in the world may punish me as you may. You don't punish like—"

His emotion prevented him from telling with what he had been threatened, and perhaps a certain delicacy withheld him from complaining of his father. He had forgotten the other motive that drove him from home, and only felt his longing for Erich. Now he looked around, as if he saw his father's uplifted and threatening hand!

Erich's mother took him in her arms and said:

"Your willingness to be punished atones for all and blots it out."

"Stay here with my mother," said Erich firmly, "I will return soon."

He went hastily away and sent a telegram to Sonnenkamp asking whether he should send Roland home, or wait for some one to come for him.

On his return, Erich found that Roland had already fallen asleep on the sofa. He was utterly exhausted, and only with the greatest difficulty could be awakened and put to bed. Erich and his mother sat and talked for a long time about how wonderfully Fate was playing with them.

The mother told how she had returned from the churchyard oppressed by the sorrowful thought that she—his own mother—could no longer remember how Hermann had looked and acted. She could recall his face, which was represented in the photograph, surrounded by a wreath of immortelles, that hung in the window-niche, just above her sewing-machine: but how he moved, how he stepped out, how he threw back his head with its heavy brown hair, how he laughed and joked, the caressing tone of his voice, the gentle cooing laugh—all had vanished from her—her, his mother. Thinking of this, she had walked home, her eyes bent on the ground—sometimes suddenly stopping and struggling to recall his image. As she entered the house, a figure had started up before her—the exact image of Hermann, and with her dead boy's voice had said: "Good-evening, Mother!" She could not understand what kept her from fainting, and spoke of Roland with the same emotion that Erich had experienced when he first met him.

Then Erich spoke of the attractive and repellant circumstances connected with taking charge of the school, and also mentioned the offer which the minister had made him. He had now an opportunity of taking the position which his father had been unable to obtain; and which might perhaps have given him a longer life. His chief objection was, that he would receive the position simply because it was open and he had a patron, and through no personal merit of his own.

His mother endeavored to set his mind at ease in regard to both of these scruples, which were, in reality, but *one*, and that one superfluous, for he most certainly had a right to compensate himself for a wrong done to his father; or rather to collect an outstanding debt due to his father.

She quietly gave him to understand that this was one of the advantages of being connected with the nobility; in accepting this position, he would only be receiving what had long ago been earned by his ancestors, and would be able to transmit it to his descendants. She playfully added:

"Our professor of Political Economy always said that capital is accumulated labor; and in the same manner family-position is nothing but accumulated honor."

There were moments, which however were by no means frequent, when Erich's mother looked from her hereditary standpoint of tradition and custom, and saw in many of the feelings and sentiments of the commonalty a perversity, and even contumacy, which she deemed utterly inexcusable. Her husband had exhibited this objectionable state of mind very mildly, and only on rare occasions, but in Erich the feeling was more fully developed; he had that violent self-reliance which dislikes to be indebted to another for position or power. She never regretted that she had forsaken her rank in marrying her husband—she had been too happy to do this—but in Erich's fate she saw a disagreeable result of her own action. She never gave utterance to these thoughts, but nevertheless they influenced her words as she said:

"I can readily see that you are attracted to this American, for it's a grand thing to be a self-made man. Let us then accomplish both objects at once. You *can* effect this, for you have the boy so completely under your influence, that the American will feel necessitated to put him in your care, and at the same time you'll have an independent position in the service of the state."

Erich replied that his reason for objecting to the position did not lie merely in the fact that he would obtain it through patronage; but he hated the thought of being obliged to conduct through the art galleries parties of aristocrats to whom he was an utter stranger. He thought that he should decline the offer.

His mother suddenly remembered that there was a letter for him. She brought it; it was from Clodwig.

The noble man had placed at his service double the amount he had asked for.

Erich was delighted with the news, and his mother cordially nodded her approval as he said, that although the gift pleased him, he was far more rejoiced at meeting such striking confirmation of his belief in the natural goodness of men.

Erich and his mother sat together till after midnight, and then Erich advised her to go to bed, saying that he would wait till an answer came from Sonnenkamp.

He sat for a long time, buried in thought, but at last, sleep overcame him.

The ordinary course of individual human life as well as the life of nations seems to be, partially at least, under the control of the will; but at any moment an unlooked-for event may occur which suddenly shows that all this seeming freedom is in reality subordinate to immutable necessity; and thus had Roland's singular action seemed to make Erich's entrance into Sonnenkamp's house an inevitable necessity.

Erich went noiselessly to Roland's room; and so intently was the boy's soul fixed on Erich, that in his sleep he moved uneasily and muttered his name. Erich returned to the sitting-room, and then for the first time it occurred to him that there was no telegraph-station in the vicinity of Villa Eden, from which a despatch sent at night could reach Sonnenkamp. The father could not receive the news until morning. Then Erich went to bed.

In the house of the Professor's widow everything was belated next morning. Erich was the last to rise. As he entered the sitting-room, he found Roland with his mother. The boy was holding in his left hand a little wooden coffee-mill, the handle of which he was turning with his right. The mill was an heirloom handed down from the time of Erich's grandfather, who had been well known as a professor of anatomy at the University. The mother had been telling Roland this, and had also shown him various pieces of old furniture, some of which had come down to her from the times of the Huguenots.

"Oh, how nice it is here!" said Roland, as Erich entered. The atmosphere of antiquity which surrounded the family was not without its effect upon the boy, and now in the morning as they all ate together exchanging pleasant glances, Roland was happy in the simple old-fashioned house.

CHAPTER XV.

A SPECIAL-TRAIN.

I'VE gone through a great deal in my life—hope I may get through this! We'll be lucky if we come out with whole skins! This is what you might call tempting Providence. And you can't help yourself either!"

The Major found great difficulty in sputtering out these words, for he had fast hold of a tassel in a first-class car as it went rattling forward: he and Herr Sonnenkamp were rushing like the wind in a special-train. The Major looked sorrowfully at his dog Laadi which lay at his feet, but Sonnenkamp gloried in the foolhardy speed.

"In America, a special-train goes three times as fast as this," said he.

He appeared to take a mysterious delight in realizing and pointing out to the Major, that there is a courage very different from that displayed on the field of battle, which he possessed and the Major did not. He described how trains race in America. They stopped at a station to take in water, and Sonnenkamp left the Major, saying that he thought he'd take a ride on the engine, as he hadn't tried that sensation in some time.

There was only one car attached to the engine, and in that the Major sat alone with Laadi. He watched the trees, hills, and villages fly past as if torn up by a whirlwind, and thanked God that Fräulein Milch did not know that he had promised Herr Sonnenkamp to accompany him on such a breakneck journey in a special-train.

Why was the man in such haste? The Major could not understand it. Sometimes he was extremely parsimonious and retiring, did not wish to attract attention or be noticed; and then at other times he would almost throw money away, and do everything in his power to render himself conspicuous. The Major could not understand him. Evidently among all the things that he had been, he might have been a locomotive engineer!

"Yes, yes, Laadi," said the Major to his dog, "come here beside me. We never thought to live to see this, did we? Hope we may come well out of it. Yes, Laadi, she'd be sorry for you too, if we should be killed!"

The dog gave a low growl, as if bitterly enraged against this foolhardy Sonnenkamp.

Yet wilder became the chase: on they flew along the verge of hills which overhung the river, and the Major was in mortal terror every instant lest the engine should run off the track, and the car go crashing into the waters below. There came upon him such a settled fear, or rather, expectation of approaching death, that he braced his feet against the seat before him, and said in the silent depths of his heart:

"Come, Death! Thank God I've injured no mortal man, and have cared for Fräulein Milch so well, that she shall never know want."

Tears trickled from between his closed eyelids, and he made a remarkable face in order to dam the swelling flood: he did not wish to die, especially when his death was so uncalled for. He opened his eyes fiercely and clenched his fist; this special-train was all foolishness! To be sure, Roland ought to be secured, but so ought this madman!

The Major was very angry with Sonnenkamp, and still more so with himself for having consented to engage in this mad exploit. All his heroism had fled. He had not agreed to this, he had allowed himself to be overreached—he must look out better in future! Fräulein Milch was right; he was weak—he could not say No!

Every time that he looked out of the window he was seized with vertigo. He found a way of escaping this difficulty, by sitting on the other seat, through which manœuvre he saw what had been passed, but not what was to come. But this, far from bettering matters, only made them worse, since he now for the first time saw all the terribly sharp curves which the track made, and on which the car tipped up and almost turned over. And now indeed tears did fall from the Major's eyes. He thought of the Lodge of Sorrow which would be held for him when he should be dead, he heard the peal of the organ and the songs, and he said to himself:

"You praise me more than I deserve, but I've been a good brother. The Architect of all the worlds is my witness that I wanted to be so!"

The car rumbled forward at the same rate, and the Major tried to find comfort in the thought that there never had been an accident on this road. "But no," continued he to himself, "it's probably safer to travel on a road where there *has* been an accident; for where there has not been one, the people get so careless, and now I must be the first victim. Which would seem more dangerous to Fräulein Milch—a road on which there have been accidents or one which is yet to have them? I must remember to ask her that question. Don't forget, Laadi, we must ask her."

He had by this time entirely recovered his equanimity and was sufficiently at his ease to jest at his own anxiety, and think: "The millionaire out on the locomotive has a much more valuable life to risk, and wouldn't do this if there were any danger in it."

The dog must have scented peril in such swift travelling, for he kept trembling and looking anxiously in his master's face.

"You're a female, and you're afraid!" scolded the Major. "Take courage! You didn't use to be such a coward. Come! So—so!—put your head in my lap. There—there!" said he smiling, as the dog licked his hand.

In the very midst of the danger the Major drew pleasure from thinking how in a few days he would tell it all to Fräulein Milch, when they should be sitting together in the garden, in the peaceful shade. He stroked Laadi and ran over the whole danger in his mind, in anticipation of telling Fräulein Milch about it.

They reached the station where the track switched off and led to the University city. Here they were told that no special-train could be furnished them, as the only track was in use. They would have to wait an hour for the next regular train.

Sonnenkamp stormed and fretted at these stupid Europeans who hadn't the remotest idea of how to manage a railroad. He had ordered an open track by telegraph. All was of no avail. The Major stood at the station and thanked the Architect of all the worlds that everything was arranged with such nicety. He took a walk into the interior and saluted the grain-fields, which stood so quiet and flourishing, and would not be disturbed in their placidity by villainous locomotives. He was delighted to hear for the first time this year, the whistle of the quail, which has no home amid the wine-hills, and he gazed upward at the lark as it soared singing through the heavens.

A train had stopped at the station. The Major heard men singing beautifully, and learned that many of the villagers who had just taken their seats in the cars were emigrating to America. He saw mothers crying, fathers nodding; and while the engine stood still and roared, a troop of young fellows stood by the station singing songs of parting to their comrades. Their voices were filled with emotion, but they controlled their feelings as well as they could.

"Fräulein Milch will be pleased when I tell her of this," thought the Major, as, joining a group of those who were soon to be left behind by those they loved, he endeavored to comfort them: he also approached the emigrants and bade them remain good Germans in America.

An old man cried out through his tears: "What are you waiting for? Tell them to go ahead!"

The others were provoked, and gave vent to their feelings against such a hard-hearted speech, but the Major said:

"Don't misunderstand him: he feels so badly that he wants to have it over with."

The old man nodded to him, and the others looked at him in astonishment.

In the mean time the local train had arrived on which they were to go to the city.

"Major! Major!" cried the guards from all directions, and the Major with much difficulty succeeded in getting on the other side of the train.

Half laughing, half scolding, Sonnenkamp said to him: "One might almost forgive you, you're such a boy; you allow yourself to be attracted by every circumstance and drawn aside from your object like a child."

"Yes, yes," laughed the Major—he had completely recovered his jolly laugh—"Fräulein Milch often tells me so."

He told Sonnenkamp of the sorrowful parting of the emigiants from their friends, but Sonnenkamp appeared to pay no attention to it. Yes, even when the Major said that the Freemasons take a great deal of pains to frustrate the designs of those wretches who would cheat the emigrants, even then Herr Sonnenkamp said nothing. The Major sat quietly beside him.

They reached the University city, but no one was there waiting for them. Sonnenkamp was very indignant.

Breakfast was spread at the house of the Professor's widow. Roland was drinking his coffee from a cup on which Hermann's name was inscribed; and Erich was saying that in an hour he must be at the station, as Herr Sonnenkamp would probably arrive in the express-train, for no one could have foreseen that he was coming on the local train which did not connect with the train from the West. Just as Erich was saying this, a knock was heard at the door, and the Major entered followed by Sonnenkamp.

"Here's the young scamp!" cried the Major, "here's the deserter!"

This remark prevented the embarrassment which would have otherwise occurred. Roland sat motionless on his chair. Erich rose and went forward to meet Sonnenkamp, and then turned to the boy and bade him instantly beg his father's pardon for what he had done. Roland obeyed.

Erich's mother begged Herr Sonnenkamp not to punish the boy for his self-will. Sonnenkamp answered good-humoredly, that on the contrary, this bold exploit of Roland's was remarkably pleasing to him, it showed courage, determination, and self-reliance; he would rather reward than punish him for it. Roland looked at his father in surprise. He took his hand again and held it fast.

Erich begged his mother and aunt to take Roland with them to the study; but he remained with Sonnenkamp and the

Major. Sonnenkamp expressed his pleasure and gratitude to Erich, who must certainly be a magician, for he had enchanted his son in such a manner as to render it impossible for them ever to be separated.

"Indeed?" said Erich; "I'm obliged to express my own surprise."

"Your surprise?"

"Yes. Unfortunately I have no such powers; but yet I may say that I almost pity those who have."

Sonnenkamp cast a questioning look at Erich, who continued:

"You have accomplished a masterpiece of pedagogic. I see now that you told Roland that you had declined my services, in order to determine him to take the affair in his own hands: that would assuredly place him in my power as nothing else could."

Sonnenkamp looked at him in amazement. Was the man amusing himself at his expense? Did he wish to mock him, or to obtain yet further victory over him by means of this finely drawn shrewdness? Prancken was certainly right; under the mask of virtuous simplicity Erich was a sly trickster. Good; let it go at that.

Sonnenkamp whistled his old inaudible whistle; he would pretend that he didn't see through Erich. He acknowledged that he had been playing a subtle part with Roland, and smiled as the Major cried out:

"Fräulein Milch said—yes, she understands everything, and she said: 'Herr Erich is the man who sees completely through Herr Sonnenkamp's shrewdness.' Yes, yes, that *was* a regular special-train of cleverness."

Sonnenkamp smiled yet more modestly and gratefully, but his astonishment returned as Erich said:

"Unfortunately, life is such a self-willed thing, that it sometimes interrupts a line of conduct laid down with logical accuracy. I find that it will be necessary for me to decline your kind proposition."

Again Sonnenkamp whistled inaudibly.

Another stroke of diplomacy! He could not understand it. His enemy had lured him from his fortress: Sonnenkamp would engage him in the open field.

Erich said that it was in his power to accept the situation of provisional director of the Cabinet of Antiquities, and soon to become full director.

"Good!" thought the Major, as he nodded to himself—"good! give it to him! Make your own terms, like a prima donna whom every manager wants; you can have all you want, he must give it!"

But his expression suddenly changed as Erich continued:

"From your practical American standpoint, you would certainly excuse me if, as I am free to choose, I should use my refusal for the purpose of obtaining better terms, of some nature: but I tell you candidly, that I have no other reason for this refusal than the duty of gratitude toward my patrons."

Sonnenkamp perfectly agreed with this, and said:

"I'm very far from wishing to interfere with your prospects in any respect. I'm sorry to be forced to relinquish you, but I must."

"Yes," said the Major, interrupting, "you relinquish and he declines; but the boy—what's to become of him?"

Sonnenkamp and Erich looked silently at the Major, who had spoken the decisive word—"what's to become of Roland?"

Erich was the first to collect himself, and asked Sonnenkamp to put Roland in his charge for a year at the capital city; for he himself was obliged to confess that he would have no happiness or rest till he had exerted his best powers on the boy, to steady him in the right path of life. It would also be best for Roland to be educated in company with others, and he himself would see that he should have only good associates.

Sonnenkamp pressed his lip between his fingers, and then said:

"I can't think of it. I can hardly breathe when I don't know that that boy's near me. I must therefore beg you not to speak of it."

Then he asked the Major to leave him alone with the Captain. The Major readily complied, and seemed to think nothing of being so cavalierly disposed of.

When they were alone, Sonnenkamp said, as he rubbed his chin:

"I clearly see the difficulty of placing Roland in any one's charge but yours. I've already discharged the man who was at my house. But now, one question: Were you not a voluntary inmate of the House of Correction?"

"Why do you ask, when your question itself tells me that you know the answer?"

"And yet you think that you could be Roland's teacher?"

"Why not?"

"Don't you believe that the boy would be deeply shocked, or at least grieved, if he should accidentally hear that his instructor is a man who has also been the instructor of criminals?"

"Roland will not hear it accidentally, I myself will tell him; and he'll have sense enough to see that this does not degrade my personality, but rather—I say it with all modesty—elevates it. I voluntarily resigned an honorable calling in order to benefit my fallen fellow-creatures, and only regret my want of ability to do so. I'm convinced that every man, no matter what fault he has committed, can again become pure and upright. In that position, unfortunately, I was unable to advance the good work."

Sonnenkamp listened with closed eyes. He nodded; he felt that he ought to say something to show Erich how much he appreciated these lofty sentiments, but appeared unable to express his feelings. At last he said:

"I spoke of the subject merely to show you that I have left nothing unsaid. It's to be hoped that now we understand each other perfectly. May I ask you to call the Major and present me to the ladies?"

The Major came, and as soon as Erich and he were alone together, it was natural that the Major should give an account of all the horrors of the special-train;—the clatter had lost all rhythm—it had been one continuous crash and roar. He gave a wonderfully vivid description of how they had rushed like lightning past the stations, through the hills, and over the bridges—everything was told exactly.

Erich might have answered that he was thoroughly acquainted with the road, having gone over it only a few days before without saying a word, but buried in reflection; but the Major would not be interrupted. He asserted that no one else ever had travelled at such a rate, or ever would do so as long as Europe should be covered with rails, for Herr Sonnenkamp had built an American fire under the boiler.

Then he said:

"I've gotten to know Herr Sonnenkamp thoroughly since his boy's been gone. . . . . To be sure, I've no son of my own, and, therefore, can't fully sympathize with him; but such lamentings, such self-reproaches, such ravings, such curses! The wickedest corporal in the service is a pious man compared with him! What words he used! What Fräulein Milch says must be true—that in countries where good tobacco grows, and snakes and parrots, the hearts of men are a hotter soil, and things grow from them, and crawling and flying creatures abound, of which we can have no conception! I shan't say a single word about how Frau Ceres acted! But guess who was the first one to say where the young one was? Fräulein Milch! And what else do you suppose she said: 'If I were a young girl, I'd pursue Herr Erich over hill and dale!' But she said it in the most innocent way in the world; for she never loved any one but me, and we've known each other for nine-and-forty years, and that tells the story. But why should we speak of such things! There'll be plenty of time for that by and by. You're right; you're cleverer than I thought you. It was a good idea not to consent immediately. Now that he's come to your house, you can make what terms you please. When he was so tormented, he cried out: 'A million to him who gives me back my son!' You may have a million: it belongs to you, as I'll bear witness."

Erich explained, that although he felt almost irresistibly drawn toward the boy, he could not accept the offer without being guilty of the highest degree of ingratitude; for he would thus be obliged to decline the position so kindly tendered him, and in regard to which the Prince was certainly being consulted at that very hour. How could he stand before his patron and his Prince, who already had some cause of complaint against him, and say, "I thank you; but in the mean time I've made another engagement?"

The Major drummed as rapidly on the table with the first and second fingers of his right hand as if his fingers were drumsticks.

"Bad, very bad!" said he. "Yes, yes; Fate occasionally travels on a special-train! Yes, everything goes on a special-train now-days."

Erich added that there were difficulties connected with the acceptance of private service; and though he would probably be able to avoid any lasting loss of favor at Court, yet he feared that dependence on a rich individual would sometimes force him to think how much more independent he might be in the service of the state.

The Major continued to drum and say:

"Bad, very bad!"

He pronounced these words with such a singular inflection of voice, that it sounded like a crow gulping a grub in an open furrow.

CHAPTER XVI.

WE'VE GOT HIM.

WHILE Erich and the Major were sitting together, Sonnenkamp and the Professor's widow were in the library. Roland sat at the window, beside the aunt, looking at a large book containing outline-drawings of Greek sculpture.

The boy looked up, and cried:

"Only think, father, Erich has got to sell all this beautiful library, that once belonged to his father; and there's not a single leaf on which his father has not written, and now it must all go to strangers!"

"I would be glad, Madam," said Sonnenkamp, turning to the aunt, "if you would take a walk with my son; I wish to speak to Frau Dournay."

Roland and the aunt left the room.

Sonnenkamp asked if what the boy had said was true.

Frau Dournay answered that it would have been true, if the danger had not been obviated by Count Wolfsgarten, who had sent sufficient money to preserve the books.

As Sonnenkamp heard this name, and the amount which the Count had sent, a sudden change took place in his feelings. He said that he could allow no one but himself the right of aiding Erich in pecuniary affairs. And now that he had entered the sphere of beneficence, a new force seemed to bear sway in his breast; he congratulated himself on his ability to aid so noble a family, even though Erich was not to be connected with him.

The widow could not avoid acknowledging, in a trembling voice, that great strength of mind was needed to receive favors, and that her family was not accustomed to them. She then said in regard to her son:

"He's a child in disposition, without guile and incapable of intrigue, but at the same time strong, steady, faithful, and manly, clinging to all that is noble. I'm his mother, and perhaps ought not to say this, but I can only wish for your happiness. You may intrust to Erich the treasure of your life; and I tell you that he who loves Erich has a heaven in his heart, and he who does not love him has no heart."

Sonnenkamp rose and drew a long breath; he would willingly have said that he who could call such a woman his mother was a happy man, but he restrained himself. He stood before a flower-stand, which was so artistically and modestly arranged and so skilfully made to preserve the form of a pyramid, that it was a pleasure to look at it. He turned the conversation to botany. Erich had told him that his mother understood the science, and he was happy to find in her a co-worker in his profession, for he regarded botany as his profession.

He now dexterously and with real sympathy led the widow to speak of the past. He opened the subject by asking her if she would not like to visit the Rhine once more.

She answered that this would certainly give her pleasure, and particularly would she be glad to see again an old friend who was at present the Superior of the Island Convent, and director of the school.

"Are you so intimate with the Lady Superior?" said Sonnenkamp, and a feeling passed through him which he could not define; but he had evidently impressed this fact on his mind for future use. He smiled pleasantly as the widow laughingly said that life was a very strange thing; there sat one lady in her cage, and the other had built her nest in a little garden, and it was impossible for them to visit each other. The older one grows, the more enigmatical do the arrangements of the world appear.

She quietly closed her eyes, and added that this had been her lot only since the death of her husband; she used to tell him all her thoughts, and he would explain and harmonize all that seemed to her so confused and mysterious.

A feeling nearly akin to piety was awakened in Sonnenkamp's breast while she spoke.

Then she told him about her life at Court, and her eyes glistened as she spoke of the Princess Dowager.

"I had the good fortune and the honor," said she, "to visit and inspect the various benevolent institutions of which her Highness is patron—not only with her, but oftener in her name and by her authority. It was a far more important, but often a sorrowful and yet blessed duty to visit or make inquiries in regard to those unfortunates who addressed to the Princess heart-rending appeals for aid. The greater part of her letters was given to me to notice and answer. This was a difficult but, also, as I said, a blessed and elevating office."

As the lady spoke thus, and laid her delicate hand upon her heart as if to still the welling emotions caused by this remembrance, her whole face was lighted up and glorified by ineffable goodness.

Sonnenkamp rose abruptly, as if violently moved, and said with emotion:

"Might I offer you, noble lady, a recompense for what you have lost, by asking you to live near us, if you feel so disposed. I am no prince, but probably am not therefore less a recipient of letters which call for my benevolence. Our good Major helps me in many a situation where inquiry is needed. But, honored Madam, you could give me yet more aid, for even if one cannot be of practical service in every case, it is always a source of comfort to the poor to receive at least a friendly answer, and your very look carries with it the blessing of a mother."

It was an hour in which Sonnenkamp experienced a happiness of which he had not thought himself capable, and his firm determination was: "It must be; at this point I can begin a life for which I have long wished, and which will redeem the past."

Sonnenkamp had preconceived a very different opinion of Frau Dournay and her sister-in-law, from that which he now entertained. In Erich's mother, he saw a dignified, refined, and noble woman; she was pale, and this paleness was heightened by her black cap and mourning-dress.

But the aunt seemed to him yet more beautiful.

Sonnenkamp made a singular grasping motion in the air, as if seizing both the women, for in spirit he had transported them to his own beautiful apartments, where he saw them doing the honors of his home, adorning and adorned by the house; and he thought how, on reception evenings, whist-parties would spring into existence almost of their own accord.

Sonnenkamp could hardly keep from asking the ladies at once if they played whist, and his face was flushed by the consciousness of thinking of such a thing and his endeavor to master himself.

During the conversation Roland had left the room, holding the aunt's hand; he now returned with Erich and the Major, bringing a letter which bore the ministerial seal.

Roland said:

"Please, let me read it, Aunt."

They were all astonished at the boy's appearance, as, raising the letter, he explained:

"Aunt told me that here is the decree which places in your charge the beautiful antique statues of bronze and marble. Erich, I'm neither bronze nor marble, and when you go there among the figures, you'll freeze, and I shall freeze too, always, if you leave me. Erich, don't go—for your sake as well as mine. Stay with me; I'll stay with you. I beg you, Erich, don't leave me. I'm not clay and marble—don't forsake me. Oh, don't leave me, Erich, don't leave me!"

All shuddered at the sight, and as the boy ended, the Major said:

"He's no longer a child! The boy spoke as if a holy spirit had descended upon him!"

Erich went to Roland, lifted him in his strong arms, and held him close, and said:

"Roland, as I hold you and you hold me, so cling to me with all the strength of your life! We'll fulfil our destiny together; here's my hand upon it."

The letter had been forgotten. The mother begged to be allowed to open it, and had hardly glanced at it, when she cried out joyfully:

"Thank God, Erich, you needn't be ungrateful!"

The letter expressed regret that the situation had already been given to a young man of noble family, who had rendered himself invaluable by diplomatic services.

Sonnenkamp requested that the letter might be given to him, as he might probably find use for it as a document against those enemies of Erich who pretended that he was in disgrace at Court. Then he wanted the mother and aunt to set out immediately with him for Villa Eden; but Erich decidedly objected to this. He, for his part, had promised to come, but his mother and aunt would not be ready before Autumn: he wished to be alone in the house with Roland for a time.

No one was happier at the turn affairs had taken than the Major. He was obliged to depart to-day, but when the ladies should become his neighbors, Fräulein Milch and he would do all in their power to render them comfortable. The Major could never avoid an opportunity of speaking of Fräulein Milch. Then he asked to be excused for an hour, as he had friends here in the city whom he wished to visit, and with whom he was not yet personally acquainted.

When the Major had gone, Sonnenkamp said with a benevolent and patronizing air, that the Major had certainly gone to visit his brother Freemasons. Erich also asked to be excused. He merely wanted to bid a friend good-bye.

He went to Professor Einsiedel.

The Professor was always ready for a friendly visit, but he was also always vexed when his visitor forgot at what hour he lectured, and if any one came within half an hour of this time, he was apt to be very angry. His wrath expressed itself in the following words:

"But, my dear friend, how can you forget, when you certainly know that at two o'clock I lecture, and can talk with nobody. No, I must beg you to be very, very, very careful to remember when I lecture."

Then he would clasp his friend's hands with great warmth.

As Erich said that it would be of no use for him to remember this hereafter, Einsiedel asked him at what time the train departed—he would probably meet him at the station; he would not promise to do so, for if he promised, it would disturb him in his lecture. Erich left the house.

The Professor accompanied him to the door of the room, took off his little black cap, and excused himself for not seeing him down the stairs. Then he returned to his room, muttering to himself, "I beg you to be very, very—I lecture at two o'clock." Erich knew that the Professor would meet him.

The towns-people were greatly excited when they saw the six persons going together to the station. Sonnenkamp escorted Frau Dournay, the Major, the aunt; and Erich held Roland by the hand. They were obliged to wait for the arrival of the train. Suddenly, Professor Einsiedel appeared. This was a great feat, for the lean little man had interrupted his day's arrangements.

Erich introduced the Major and Sonnenkamp to him. Sonnenkamp did not know what to say, and even the Major, in spite of his love for all mankind, could find no point of contact with this delicate, fragile apparition whom Erich presented as his master and teacher. But Roland, on the contrary, grasped the soft, childlike hand of the little man, and said:

"Do you know how you seem to me? You're my grandfather, for Herr Erich is to be my teacher, and you're his teacher; so you're my grand-teacher, and if you'd like to have a dog I'll send you one."

The Professor quoted in Greek a few words from Plato, expressing delight in a beautiful spirited youth, and then patted the boy's shoulder, thanked him for presenting him with a dog, and said that he did not like to take leave amid noise and bustle, and would therefore say farewell before the train arrived. He now appeared to regard the rest as already gone, and, taking Erich aside, said in a voice filled with emotion:

"You're now well enough provided for, and must get married, for the Apostle Paul says: 'He who careth for the things of the world should marry.'"

Then he asked him to write him a further account of Clodwig's investigations, and gave him his hand. Roland also shook hands with the Professor.

Erich gazed after the little man, who, as he walked away, seemed to him like a wandering temple of the spirit of science; and the good man rubbed his tiny hand on his coat, for Roland had grasped it a little hard.

The train arrived. The parting was brief. Roland kissed his mother and aunt again and again, and Sonnenkamp kissed the mother's hand.

As they were parting, the mother said softly to Erich:

"Thou art leaving me; I am at peace, for I know that thou wilt not forsake thyself, and thus thou wilt ever be near me. Go then; keep thyself in thyself, and me in thee, and I will be at rest and thou also."

When they were seated in the car, the Major bent toward Erich and whispered softly in his ear:

"I've learned something about your father."

"What?"

"It's good news for you and me too. Your father, who has gone to his eternal home, was a member of our order. You have now the right to ask, and I the duty to give you support. My only request is, that you will never thank me: we must not thank each other."

At the next station the Major took Erich aside, and asked him if he had made any agreement in regard to salary, and indemnity in case he should be dismissed, as well as a pension after the conclusion of his duties. Erich treated this matter very lightly, and the Major gave him to understand that he could make his own terms. He advised Erich to strike *now*, while the iron was hot; but as Erich did not seem to agree with him, he desisted and, laughing to himself, muttered:

"And then Fräulein Milch is always saying that I'm not a practical man; but here's a man who's studied ever so much, and who could turn and twist seven times before I could get on my feet, and yet he's less practical than I am !"

The Major was almost jubilant as he thought how unpractical Erich was; *that* would be something worth telling Fräulein Milch.

During the journey, the diamond-ring was released from pawn, and Erich said to Roland:

"Give the ring to your father; I prefer that you should not wear a ring hereafter."

Roland obeyed, and the Major murmured to himself:

"He's got him! He's got him by curb and snaffle."

It was evening when they passed the vine-clad cottage. Roland's face beamed with pleasure as he nodded to Erich and pointed to the house; but he did not speak. They entered the grounds of Villa Eden; a flood of air redolent of roses blew upon them as they rode toward the house, for all the roses in Sonnenkamp's garden had bloomed.

"We've got it!" said the Architect to the Major, as the latter alighted.

"You've got what?"

"We've found the fountain at the castle."

"We've got something too," cried the Major, pointing to Erich.

From that day on, the Major would often commence his stories with the words:

"About the time I went with Herr Sonnenkamp in a special-train."

BOOK FIFTH.

CHAPTER I.

HIGH UP.

IN the garden, during this Spring night, the roses had opened; and in the youth's soul, blossoms for which there is no name.

Roland welcomed this Erich whom he had conquered, with unbounded bliss. Swiftly and lightly he ran through the house to his mother; but she was so affected that he was not allowed to see her. He forgot what a stranger Miss Perini was to him, and informed her with joyful eagerness, that Erich was in the house, and would stay; she should please tell his mother so.

"And you do not inquire for the Chevalier at all?"

"No, he's gone—I know it: he wasn't with me, even while he was here. Ah! forgive me, I hardly know what I'm saying. Why doesn't the whole world dance with joy?"

But Roland's joy received its first rebuff, when Miss Perini said that it was still impossible to tell what irremediable injury his mother might retain from the pain which Roland's flight had caused her.

The boy stood silent, but he was convinced that now everything would come right; the whole world must be well and bright.

In the yard he met Joseph, and informed him joyously, that now he knew Joseph's native city too. He nodded to all the servants, he smiled at the horses, the trees, the dogs; all should know and rejoice at the tidings: "Erich is here." The servants looked at him with astonishment; and Bertram, the coachman, pulled his long beard with both hands and said:

"The young master has got a man's voice in these last two days."

Joseph added with a smile:

"Why yes, one day at the University has made another man of him, and what a man too!"

Roland had indeed changed entirely. He returned home as from a voyage across the ocean, almost as from another world. He could not yet believe it, everything seemed changed, brighter: he had been alone with himself, and he had gained himself.

Erich had decided nothing about salary, and Sonnenkamp said smilingly to the Major:

"There's always a hidden smartness in these exalted idealists. This man acts like one asked to dinner: he lets the master or mistress of the house help him to a good dish; and is sure to get more of it than if he helped himself."

Erich had made only one demand, that he and Roland should occupy together the remote suite of rooms in the tower, which commanded a beautiful prospect.

This was granted, and Erich felt himself wonderfully free, in these large, handsome rooms, with the view of the river and the landscape.

How compressed life is, in the little low room of the University town! but how widely can the spirit expand, away beyond these narrow limits! And these carpets, this well-ordered furniture, how soon one gets accustomed to it all, and it is forgotten and unnoticed, just like the prospect of the wide country beyond! Still, Erich felt so well here, so contented, so exalted; as though—he could not help laughing, when the comparison passed through his mind—as though he lived on horseback. It is pleasant enough to ply your staff over hill and valley, but to be on a horse, and dash away and be one with an outside power, which may be doubled, tripled, and which raises you above your ordinary level—that fills you with a rare joy.

Roland came to Erich, and the latter expressed his pleasure to the boy about the beauty and tranquillity which would mark their life here; but Roland begged:

"Give me something to do; something real hard: pray think of something."

Erich understood very well the emotion under which the boy was laboring, and placing him by his side, he took his hand, and explained to him with great calmness, that life but very seldom offers us the chance of any one deed to which we could devote the whole force of our will, but that they should work together steadily and calmly, and thus continually make each other better and wiser. The boy was satisfied; he looked long at Erich, as though he must take him into his soul through his eyes, so that he should be his own. Then he softly touched Erich's shoulder, as if to get new assurance that he was really with him.

Now they settled themselves comfortably, and Roland was happy in doing all sorts of little offices for Erich. Erich had entered into the new relation so suddenly, and, in spite of all reflection, so hastily and rashly, that he had scarcely regained his self-possession. Moreover, much had been left to be discussed with his mother, as to what he should take along, what leave with her; but everything was postponed for future arrangement by letter.

When some degree of order had been attained, Erich consented to go up to the platform of the tower with Roland. Here they sat for a long time in silence, and looked all about them. Erich could not refrain from telling the boy how fresh and fair life appeared to him. In old times they built castles on these heights, for war and strife, and plunder of the men who might pass by: but we, we work with the forces of Nature, we try to acquire wealth; and then we build our dwelling on a height or in a lovely valley, and desire nothing but to enjoy the eternal beauty, which robs no one of anything. The great stream becomes a thoroughfare, along which extend the villas of industrious and liberal people. Coming generations will have to acknowledge that in our day men commenced to worship Nature as never before in the history of mankind; ours was a new religion, even if it have no form, nor should ever acquire one.

"Speak on, speak on forever!" said Roland, nestling against Erich. He could not say that he only desired to listen to his voice: he closed his eyes and repeated again, "Speak on."

Erich understood the appeal, and he related how, when standing on the Rigi for the first time, watching the setting sun, he tried to imagine some act, some arrangement, something which could serve as the expression of the Nature-worship of all the persons there assembled. But he had learned that this was not possible, nor even necessary; that Nature and the love of Nature gave to each one his own happiness and peace independent of association with men. Then speaking enthusiastically of the good fortune of being able to take in the world and the whole beauty thereof, from a tower built by one's self to one's own house, he explained how wealth, both in its acquisition and in its possession, could form a great moral power. Wealth, he declared, is but a result of liberty, of the unrestrained exercise of strength, and it must lead back to liberty.

Roland was happy. He did not yet comprehend all this, but he felt that, for the first time, wealth was represented to him neither as something objectionable, nor yet as a source of pride.

Till now, all his teachers had sought to instil into his mind either the one view or the other.

Joseph came up to the tower, and asked whether Erich and Roland wished to dine alone in their rooms. Both said, "Yes."

The two sat together happy, and Roland exclaimed repeatedly:

"We, too, are living on an island; and when I shall live in the castle you must be with me too. Do you know what else I wish for?"

"Ah! you have still another wish?"

"Yes; Manna ought to be with us. Don't you believe that she's thinking of us now too?"

"Most certainly not of me."

"Oh yes; I've written to her about you, and this evening I shall write to her again and tell her everything."

Erich was embarrassed for a moment, and he was at a loss what to do. Should he prevent the boy from writing to his sister about him? There was no reason for it, and he would not disturb Roland's ingenuousness.

CHAPTER II.

THE VOICE OF A SPIRIT IN THE NIGHT.

ROLAND sat in his room writing, and occasionally he spoke aloud the words that he wrote. Erich sat by, and stared into the lamp. But of what avail was all meditation now? He stood long before the books he had unpacked: there were but few of them. During the last quarter of an hour, before entering the carriage, he had gone again into his father's study, and put away his father's papers; and as he glanced over the library he took out a book, it was the first volume of Sparks's fine edition of Benjamin Franklin's works. This volume contained the autobiography and its continuation. Some extra leaves had been fastened into it, and bore his father's handwriting.

And now, during the first night of his new vocation, he read these words written by his father. They were as follows:

"So! Here is a true man, the genius of sound sense and firm will. The air always contains electricity; but the electricity does not always collect and form the lightning which clears the atmosphere. This is genius. Genius is nothing but the collected electricity of the atmosphere of the mind."

"Cast away on an island, with nothing but this book, a man would not be alone, but in the midst of the world."

"By profession, neither philosopher, poet, statesman, artisan, nor a student, and still all of these at once; a mother's darling—the darling of Mother Nature and Nurse Experience; a lost child, who, without scientific guidance, finds all the healing herbs in the wild forest by himself."

"If I had to educate a youth, not for any definite calling, but only for true manhood and good citizenship, I should lay my hands on his head, and say: My son, grow to be like Benjamin

Franklin, no, not like him, but develop *yourself*, as Benjamin Franklin developed *himself*."

Erich rested his chin on his hand, and peered into the dark night. How is this? do miracles occur in our life? He looked to the right and to the left, as though he expected to hear his father's voice, not in the written page, but speaking: "My son, grow to be like Benjamin Franklin!" Erich forced himself to continue, and he read:

"It is well, if we form ourselves after the first people of the ncient world: that was the time of elementary creative being. The figures in the Bible and Homer are not the creations of one single highly gifted mind; they are the creations of the primeval united spirit of a whole people, extending far beyond the span of one man's life. Understand me well. I declare that I know no other man in modern history, after whose life and thought a man of our days should be modelled, but Benjamin Franklin.

"Why not after Washington—a man so great and pure?

"Washington was both statesman and soldier, but he did not construct his universe within himself, he did not develop it out of his thought. His influence lay in governing and guiding others, Franklin's only in governing and guiding himself. When the time shall come, and it will come, when men will speak of war, as we to-day speak of cannibalism, when honest, industrious, faithful work shall constitute the history of mankind, then Franklin will reign."

"I should not like to fall into the sermonizing tone, yet that relic of priestcraft always revives in us when we approach the eternal sanctities. But our strain should be entirely different from theirs who profess to speak in the name of a spirit which is not their own.

"To Moses, Christ, Mohammed, God appeared in the solitude of the wilderness, to Spinoza in the solitude of his study, to Franklin in the solitude of the ocean." (This last sentence had been crossed out, and then restored.) "Franklin is the man of sober intellect, who knows nothing of sentimentalism."

"The world would not be remarkable for beauty, if all mankind were like Franklin; his being was entirely devoid of romantic flavor," ("to be expressed differently," was the remark set in the margin opposite this last sentence,) "but the world would know uprightness, truthfulness, industry, and charity. Now they speak of love, and revel in their fine feelings, but you cannot speak of love, until you have verified these other four." (This last phrase was underscored in red ink.)

"Franklin has something of Socrates in him, with a spice of

humor which is remarkably happy. Franklin gives us many a hearty laugh."

"Franklin's whole being is good prose, sensible, tangible, clear."

"It is not our function in this world to educate geniuses. Every genius educates himself, and can have no other instructor. For this world, we must educate thorough, effective citizens. Whatever else you make, whether shoe-nails or marble statues, is not my affair but yours."

"We shall never judge the world fairly till we believe in its purity, that its motives are the highest: otherwise the inmost soul of mankind will never be revealed to us. There is no safer armor against temptation, than the belief in the good which others do, and which we ourselves ought to do; and this faith plays within us a march with which we can keep step, freely and cheerfully, through the battle of life."

"The most honorable and distinctive feature in Franklin's life is just this:—That he was the first self-made man." (The words "self-made man" were written in English.) "He was self-taught, he discovered for himself the treasures of knowledge and the forces of nature, he is the representative of those who, transplanted from Europe to America, expand and flourish anew, after the danger of withering and perishing is safely passed."

"Were we to intend, like the ancients, to form a mythical figure representative of that other world which is called America, which took its material, I mean its historical ideas from Europe, and yet created a life independent and individual—were we to wish a human form to represent this conception—there stands Benjamin Franklin. He was full of knowledge, though he had no teacher; full of religion, though he had no church, and full of love of men, though no eye was keener than his to detect the evil in them. He knew how to control the lightning, not only in the clouds, but in the stormy passions of the human soul. He had mastered that wisdom which shields us from inner discord and fits us for self-control."

"The reason why I would take him for a guide and an example in the training of a man is this: he represents simple, sound, common-sense, firm and sure, not the intellect which dazzles by its brilliancy, but that homely intellect which builds up the happiness of the people, which is calmly scientific and moral, and which improves always."

"Luther was the conqueror of the middle ages; Franklin is the first modern, self-made man. The man of our day is no longer a martyr: Luther was none, Franklin much less. No more martyrdom."

"Franklin introduced no new principles into the world, but he developed fully whatever an honest man can find within himself. There was about Franklin, neither for himself nor for others, anything strange, exciting, intoxicating, mysterious, brightly luminous, dazzling; he was as the water of life, the water which is essential to all creation." A note in the margin read: "Here deep waters lie hidden; they must be bored for and collected in wells. The man of the past eighteenth century had no conception of popular life, and could not have it, it was all simply a striving and fermenting of independent thought, onward to the climax at the close of the century—to the revolution."

"Whoever wants to create, stands in opposition to that which is, or at least, stands independent of it."

"Franklin is the son of this century; he acknowledges only the powers innate in men, not those conventionally inherited. (This must be developed.")

In pale ink, apparently of later date, were the words: "It is not a mere chance that this first free man—free not only in thought, for many philosophers have been thus free—but also free in action, was a printer. In a world of books there is no room for 'heroism;' (for I believe that the conditions which produce 'heroism' are past); but in them lies the manhood of the later time."

"While we work through books, there can never again be a great personal redeemer." Here between two brackets were two interrogation and two exclamation points, and across the last remark, the words, "To be expressed more accurately," were written in pencil.

Then in conclusion, in Roman letters and in blue ink: "Abstract rules form no being, no man, and produce no work of art. Living man, and every organic work of art contain all laws, as language contains all grammar; and this is good and beautiful."

"Whoever knows the true men who lived before him, in such a way that they revive in him, enters into their ranks; he enters the hallowed ground of existence, which has been consecrated by the predecessors who have trodden it."

And again, much later, with a trembling hand, running across the whole, was written:

"Whoever takes an active part in the political and social organization of his day, either through holding an office or making laws, and whoever stands in the midst of the science of his day, must, in the process of reconstruction which comes after him, become antiquated; consequently he is no prototype for the future. Such is he only who conceives the eternal laws of the human mind, which are the same from the beginning to all eternity, who analyzes them and masters them; therefore Franklin is not a pattern, but rather a method."

And last came these words, which were doubly underscored:

"My last proposition is—Organic Life, Abstract Laws. You can make brandy of grain, but you can never make grain of brandy. Whoever understands this, knows all that I would say."

This was what Erich read, and now he leaned back and tried to enter into his father's spirit and into the thoughts which he often but half expressed. He felt as if on a mountain height, wandering through a mist, and yet he saw the path and the goal clearly before him.

He placed his hand on the written leaves, and a happy smile passed over his face; then he rose and almost laughed aloud, as the words which the Architect exclaimed at his arrival, occurred to him—"We've got him now!"

"Yes," he exclaimed, "I've got it now. I have the fount which shall yield its pure, life-giving waters to Roland and to me."

He could not sleep; he opened the window and looked long out into the night. The air was full of the odor of roses, the sky full of the brightness of stars; here and there a nightingale sang, and then was still; and in the distance, where a portion of the Rhine had been dyked off near the bank, the frogs croaked in noisy confusion.

Now Erich heard a man's voice on the balcony below. It was Prancken, who said:

"We're making too much ado about nothing. The best way would be, to put such a tutor in livery."

"You're very merry to-night," replied Sonnenkamp.

"Quite the reverse; very serious. The sacred order of things, without which neither society nor the state can exist, has a firm support in the preservation of rank. Let every one show his station. Servitude—"

Erich closed the window softly; it was beneath him to listen. Without, the nightingale sang in the bushes, the frogs croaked in the marsh.

"Every one sings his own song," thought Erich, as he thought of his father's message, and of the young Baron's remark.

CHAPTER III.

OLD FRIENDS WITH NEW FACES.

THE first thing in the morning Roland wanted to go out riding, but Erich, whose principle it was, that the only way of consecrating a day was to take something good into the soul, made Roland read to him the opening chapters of the life of Benjamin Franklin. This was the consecration of their new activity, and when they were called to breakfast, they both felt a new life within themselves. They could boast of an edification equal to Miss Perini's who came from mass with Herr von Prancken.

Erich had not been mistaken, Prancken was here. He saluted Erich with a certain respectful elegance, but he likewise fulfilled the demands of truthfulness, by openly acknowledging, as a man who has nothing to conceal, that he had at times believed that it would be better if Erich should not take this position. He added with much firmness and with a tone of satisfaction, that there are mysterious processes of the soul, which we must accept humbly; and Roland's spontaneous action was a sign of destiny, which imposed on Erich, as well as on all of them, the duty of submission.

Erich gazed at Prancken with astonishment. He had been mistaken in this man; Prancken could assign reasons for his actions—a thing of which he had never supposed him capable.

Breakfast went off merrily, for the Major furnished topics for conversation, even more by his absence than by his presence. He had of course related to Prancken the terrors of that ride on the special-train, and Prancken repeated the tale in a manner which caused much amusement to his listeners; he imitated the Major's peculiarities of speech with his heavy pronunciation, and Fräulein Milch he never mentioned otherwise than as Miss Milch with the black eyes and the white cap.

After breakfast, Erich requested Herr Sonnenkamp to excuse him and Roland in future from appearing at this general meal, so that they might be left to themselves till dinner.

Sonnenkamp looked at him in surprise, and Erich explained that he demanded this on the first day, in order to prevent the establishment of any custom. It was very necessary to keep Roland attentive, and his mind free from distraction; and this could only be attained by having at least half the day and the freshness of the morning. Sonnenkamp agreed with a shrug of the shoulders.

At breakfast, it had been casually mentioned, that Bella and Clodwig were expected to dinner the same day.

Erich comprehended at once, that the principal difficulty of his position lay in his preventing diversions from becoming interruptions. He drew a boundary line, invisible, yet impassible, between himself and all the other inmates of the house; but especially against Sonnenkamp. This was particularly difficult, as Erich was not reticent, and always willing to discuss a thing. But where was this boundary line? There was something about him which told every one not to ask him for more than he communicated of his own accord. He worked with Roland, and informed himself carefully where the boy had thorough knowledge, where it was imperfect, and where entirely wanting.

A carriage rolled into the courtyard.

Roland glanced up at Erich. But the latter seemed not to have heard the sound of the wheels.

"Your friends have come," said Roland. He did not like to say that he himself was eager to greet Clodwig and Bella, and hear their praise under the guise of blame for his having done the bold deed.

But Erich insisted that they had no friends just now except duty; nothing and nobody ought to exist for them till they had done their work.

Roland clenched his hands under the table, to force himself to patience.

Suddenly, in the midst of a mathematical problem, he said:

"I beg pardon, but they've chained up Grip—I can tell it by his bark. It's wrong, it spoils him."

"Never mind Grip or any thing else; everything must wait," persisted Erich.

Roland threw himself back like a horse which feels the bridle and the thighs of his rider. But soon Erich went down to the yard with him. Roland had heard aright—Grip was chained. He released him, and the boy and the dog both seemed freed from chains as they frolicked together.

Bella was with Frau Ceres.

A servant informed Erich that Clodwig was expecting him. Clodwig advanced toward him with much heartiness, greeted him as "neighbor," and expressed much pleasure at the energy which the boy had displayed. "If we still lived the life of the ancients," he added, "this deed would have given the boy a new name."

There was noble-mindedness as well as good-breeding in Clodwig's manner of speaking of Roland.

When they were assembled for dinner, Erich heard Bella joking with Roland; the boy's face beamed with joy, for Bella was telling him of Roland the hero.

Bella's reception of Erich was very friendly, but reserved; she called him "neighbor" repeatedly, and was very much at her ease. Perhaps she now looked back upon it as a foolish whim and piece of timidity, that she had done her part in trying to keep Erich away from the neighborhood. Had this man indeed made an extraordinary impression on her? It seemed to her a dream, a mistake.

Erich had looked forward to this first meeting with some dread, now he blamed himself for his vanity.

"Shall you have your father's library brought here?" asked Clodwig.

Erich answered affirmatively, and Bella looked at him fixedly. Now he knew why Bella treated him with so much ease and freedom—he had received money from her husband; this had at once changed his relation to them.

At table he also saw Frau Ceres for the first time, and when he approached her, she said in a very low voice, "I thank you;" nothing more. The words were very significant.

At table the company was in good spirits. They said the trip would do Frau Ceres much good—the journey to the baths. It would be a good experiment. They discussed one day and another, as feasible for beginning the trip.

Erich did not know what all this signified. Roland saw his questioning look, and whispered to him:

"We're all going together to get Manna to go with us to the baths. Then we'll have a good jolly time!"

Again it struck Erich that the principal objection to so luxurious but aimless a life was, that the whole family, and the boy perhaps most of all, lived either on the remembrance of some diversion, or in the hope of one. He thought he would wait quietly till his views were asked, and then make his decision tell.

After dinner, it seemed as if it were by chance, Bella walked with Erich. She told him, first, how happy Clodwig was that Erich was going to remain in the neighborhood after all; then suddenly standing still, she said with a searching glance:

"You will meet Miss Sonnenkamp again within a few days."

"I?"

"Yes; aren't you going with us?"

"No one has decided anything about it as yet."

Bella smiled.

"But you will surely like to meet Miss Manna again?"

"I didn't know it was she, when I met her."

Bella smiled again and said:

"I've seen enough of the world to have no prejudices. The daughter of the house, and my brother Otto—But you know what I mean."

"No, Madam, you give me credit for too much knowledge."

"I ought to feel offended to see you reserved toward me,

while you have such friendly intercourse with all the dependants of the house. The Major's servant is said to boast of your being her favorite, and you pretend not to know of the secret engagement?"

"Not till the present moment. I congratulate you, and feel myself honored that you, Madam, initiate me with so much confidence into your family affairs."

"Do you know," said Bella suddenly, "do you know that I expect much enjoyment from you?"

"From me? what can I do?"

"Oh! I don't mean that: let's speak openly. I've thought much about you; you're of an impulsive nature, but are still a riddle for me, and I hope I'm one for you too."

"I've not yet permitted myself—"

"I permit that you permit yourself. Well then, Captain or Doctor or Herr Dournay, or neighbor, which is perhaps best of all, let's enter into an agreement. I shall try to comprehend the contradictions and peculiarities of your being, and watch you as much as possible; but I shall allow you to do the same in regard to me. Don't you find the prospect attractive?"

"Attractive and dangerous."

Bella drew herself up to her full height, and Erich continued:

"Dangerous for me, for you know what friend Hamlet says: 'Use every man after his desert, and who should 'scape whipping?'"

"I'm glad to find that you're not polite, but then you should not be modest either."

"I mean that it might be dangerous for me, not for you, Madam."

"I'm too proud either to owe politeness or squander it. I'm glad to see that you're too proud also. And now tell me how you saw Manna, and how she impressed you."

Erich described the chance meeting, and how he had not known the name of her he had met until he heard it from the Justice's daughter.

"Take care, take care, Lina," said Bella, and her fingers moved very fast, as if she were playing the piano in the air. It was an agreeable discovery to behold this play of feeling, for Lina had a decided inclination for Otto. But the *naïve* innocent knew also that Otto turned to Manna; so it was not a bad speculation to procure Manna such a handsome suitor.

While Bella was walking with Erich, Prancken had very affectionately taken hold of Roland's hand and gone with him to inspect the stables and the young dogs: then he led him to the less-frequented part of the park, which extended along the road. The conversation seemed to turn spontaneously on

Erich, and Roland did not tire of relating how all-wise and all-good he was. In a severe manner, Prancken blamed Roland for applying such words to a man; and he impressed on him, strongly, that although he could learn from this worldly man much that was of use in the world, there was a supreme interest, with which he must not trust him, and in which he must in no wise obey him.

And now he spoke of Manna. There was an expression of reverence in his words as well as in his tone. He drew the book, which he always carried on his heart, from his pocket, and showed Roland precisely what Manna would read to-day; and though by his flight Roland had missed several days' readings, he could nevertheless now catch up with her at his leisure. But above all, Herr Dournay must know nothing of it, for Roland must let no unbeliever come in between himself and his God.

Prancken sat down with Roland under a nut-tree by the roadside, and read him some impressive passages. The boy regarded him with astonishment. The Wine-cavalier rode past; he greeted Prancken boisterously: the latter answered with a motion of the hand, but immediately resumed reading.

It seemed a release to Roland when he saw Bella and Erich approaching, laughing and talking merrily. He called to them, and soon he walked with Erich, leaving Bella next to her brother, who twisted his moustache and admired his fine boots for a long time. When Roland and Erich had left them, Prancken drew himself up and commenced to reprove Bella severely for trifling and jesting with a young man.

Bella stood still: she seemed undecided whether to laugh at her brother, or to retort upon him sharply; she decided for the former, and ridiculed the new convert.

"Ah!" she exclaimed; "it seems you're somewhat afraid that this Herr Dournay might find favor with the sainted Manna, and think me capable of the same weakness. Well, you've hit it. The man has about him something fascinating for us women, whether we live under the restraint of the marriage tie or of the convent."

Prancken did not enter into her mood; he repeated, that all trifling, all jesting, are borderers upon sin itself, and that by jesting, especially, the border lines are imperceptibly changed. He grew so earnest that he drew the book from his breast-pocket and read Bella an appropriate passage.

Bella opened her eyes wide, to see Otto with such a pious book; but she explained to him that there was such a thing as proven virtue, that she was simply playing with the young man, who had a self-confidence which was perfectly exasperating. Besides, Otto might be well satisfied if the semblance of a connection between Erich and herself should arise; why, she would even make this sacrifice for him, her virtue was safe from all misinterpretation; she would assume appearances, in order to free Otto from a dangerous rival.

But now, seriously, she concluded: "Must good people deny themselves all bright enlivening intercourse, because wicked people hide all improper things under its guise? That would be a strange order of things, that would be a subjection of the good to the bad."

Bella did not know, or did not care to know, that in saying this she was decking herself with one of her husband's maxims.

Prancken looked at her in amazement. Was he indeed misguided by his new zeal, or was all this only disguise, woven of arrant hypocrisy? He was embarrassed; he did not know what to say in reply to her frolicking, laughing tone, and her smooth and ready evasions.

CHAPTER IV.

A DISAPPOINTMENT.

IT was a difficult task for Erich to keep the attention of his pupil centred on his studies, for he thought of nothing but the journey.

The day of the trip to the convent had come; and it was bright and sunny.

Erich begged to be allowed to remain at home. Sonnenkamp agreed at once, with the kind remark that it would be pleasant for Erich too to have a few quiet days to himself. Erich was very much pleased with this considerateness, and returned it, in expressing his desire not to place himself between Roland and his family.

Prancken drove up with his sister; and Bella told Erich that Clodwig invited him to keep him company during these few days. Erich remarked only now, that he had not been invited at all to join the excursionists; but he at once dismissed the whole train of sensitive feelings which are apt to arise from such occurrences. Roland alone begged, earnestly, that Erich should accompany them, and he said frankly:

"Manna will be very angry if you don't come with us: she will want to see you too."

Sonnenkamp smiled strangely at this argument, and Prancken turned away to hide the expression of his face.

Roland took a passionate leave of Erich; he was for the first time to be parted from Erich for hours, even for a whole night; but he promised to tell Manna much about him. Something strange must have been passing in the boy, for at the very last he said to Erich:

"You and the house, you stay safe at home."

Erich pressed his hand warmly.

They went to the steamboat in three carriages; Prancken rode with Frau Ceres, Sonnenkamp with Miss Perini and Bella, and in the third carriage were Roland and the servants.

They rode some distance up the river to meet the boat; and when it shot quickly past the Villa—where Erich stood on the beautiful, shaded hill which commands a view down the river to where the mountains overlap each other, as if the river must be stopped and formed into a lake—Roland waved his hat from the boat. Erich answered in like manner from shore, and said aloud:

"Farewell, my young soul!"

Whoever understands the fact that Erich could not wave his salutation even to a distance where he could not be heard, without pronouncing a distinct word—some loving message, whoever understands this, knows the profoundest depths of Erich's soul.

The boat rushed past; the water near the shore was stirred for a little while, rocking the beautiful rowboat from side to side: then everything was still.

The steamboat glided down-stream and the company on board was in excellent humor. Prancken was most assiduous in his attentions to Frau Ceres, who sat on deck covered with fine shawls.

Roland had received permission to take Grip along, and every one on board admired the beautiful boy; some even expressed their admiration aloud.

The Wine-count and his son, the Wine-cavalier, travelled part of the way with them. The old gentleman, a tall elegant-looking man, wore his red ribbon in his button-hole. The young gentleman was extremely glad to meet Prancken, and especially happy to pay his respects to Bella. Toward Sonnenkamp and his family the two old residents were rather reserved; to-day, to be sure, they seemed inclined to change this reserve into an advance, but Sonnenkamp's manner was rather repellant: he did not want them to approach him now, when they found him in noble company, and he was visibly relieved when the Wine-count and his son stepped ashore at the second landing, where there was a famous water-cure establishment. On the wharf stood the Court-chamberlain, with his sick son, expecting them. Bella was favored with an especially respectful bow from his excellency, and she told Herr Sonnenkamp, as they glided on, that it was as good as settled that the rich wine-merchant's daughter would marry the sickly young nobleman.

It was a bright day, there was scarcely a breath of air stirring on the swiftly-gliding boat. Roland occasionally heard people whisper to some new-comer: "That's the rich American, he's worth ten millions."

There was a private table set on deck for the Sonnenkamp party, which was now being decorated with flowers, and glistening wine-coolers under Joseph's superintendence: Sonnenkamp's servants, in their coffee-colored livery, waited on the party.

At table Roland asked:

"Father, is it true that you're worth ten millions?"

"No one has ever counted my money," Sonnenkamp replied with a smile. "At all events, you'll always have enough to order a dinner like to-day's."

The youth did not seem satisfied with this answer, and Sonnenkamp added: "My son, all wealth is only relative."

"Remember those words, all wealth is only relative," repeated Prancken; "it is a great thought." Sonnenkamp smiled, he was pleased to hear any one endorse one of his sayings so emphatically.

"Ah! travelling is delightful—so jolly! If only Erich were with us!" cried Roland.

No one answered. The boy seemed very talkative to-day, for when the champagne sparkled in the glasses and Bella drank to Manna's health, Roland said to Prancken:

"You ought to marry Manna!"

The women looked curiously at the two men. Roland had expressed what was the wish of all.

He became more and more exclusively the subject of their jokes and conversation, and they made him more loquacious, more excited; he uttered the wildest nonsense, and at last he yielded to Prancken's teasing, and mimicked the candidate Knopf. He pushed back his hair, took snuff from his left hand, which he held as a snuff-box, and tapped this snuff-box repeatedly; suddenly his voice and face were completely changed, he went through the fourth conjugation in a stiff, gawky manner; explained the Pythagorean theorem, and recited a lot more of the most incoherent stuff.

"Can you imitate Herr Dournay too?" asked Prancken.

Roland was struck dumb; his face grew rigid, as though he had seen a monster. He was suddenly sobered, and he regarded Prancken with a look as if he would crush him.

"I shall never mimic candidate Knopf again, never again—I swear it!—from this day!"

The boy, who had been much excited with the wine and with talking, became suddenly quiet and disappeared, so that the servants had to look for him. They found him on the lower deck, beside his dog: great tears were in his eyes. He agreed to go back to his party; but he was reticent, and remained so.

The boat glided on and on. The vine-clad hills shone in the bright noonday sun, and soon some one said:

"Only two landings more, then comes the convent."

Roland went back to his dog and said:

"Grip, now we'll see Manna! Cheer up!"

The sun was still high in the heavens, when they went ashore under the hanging willows, and entered the refreshingly cool park which surrounds the convent. The servants had remained in the large hotel on the opposite shore.

There was no one on the shore to welcome the party, although they had sent word that they were coming.

"Manna not here?" asked Sonnenkamp, as he jumped ashore; and the ferocity which he knew how to hide at other times, appeared in his countenance.

Frau Ceres quietly turned her head toward him, and he was subdued and gentle.

"I do hope the dear child is not ill," he added in a voice which would have well suited a penitent hermit.

They went to the convent. It was locked, the church alone was open, and here a nun, with her face hidden, lay in prayer, while without lay the bright sparkling sunshine. The new-comers, who had reached the threshold, turned away in silence: they rang the bell at the convent; the portress opened.

Herr Sonnenkamp asked whether Fräulein Hermanna Sonnenkamp was well. The portress said she was; and added that if they were the parents, the Superior invited them to come into the parlor. Sonnenkamp requested Bella, Prancken, and Miss Perini to remain in the garden. He desired Roland to remain with them, but the boy said:

"No, I'm going with you."

His mother took him by the hand, and speaking now for the first time, said:

"Yes, you stay with me."

Grip remained with those outside. The parents and Roland went in to the lady Superior, who received them with much cordiality and dignity.

She requested a Sister who was with her to leave her, and then invited the visitors to be seated. It was cool and pleasant in the large room; pictures of saints, painted on golden backgrounds, hung on the walls.

"What about our daughter?" asked Sonnenkamp at last, drawing a deep breath.

"Your child, whom we may also call our child, for we love her no less than you, is perfectly well. She is generally gentle and patient, but occasionally she has an incomprehensible obstinacy, even stubbornness."

A quick glance from Sonnenkamp's eyes flashed to his wife, but she only looked at him, and slightly curled her upper lip.

The Superior did not notice this, for while she spoke she

generally closed her eyes, or looked down into her lap; therefore she continued calmly:

"Our dear Manna consents to see her parents, only on condition that they will first promise that she may remain with us in the convent during the coming winter: she declares that she does not yet feel herself strong enough to enter into the world."

"And you allowed her to make this condition?" asked Sonnenkamp, and passed his left hand through his white neckcloth, to loosen it.

"It is not for us to allow her anything. You are her parents, you have unconditional power over your child."

"Of course," burst out Sonnenkamp, "of course, if such thoughts are instilled into her— But, I beg your pardon, I interrupted you."

"Not at all, I have finished. It is for you to decide whether you grant this condition in advance; you have full parental authority. I will call a Sister to conduct you to Manna's cell. It is not locked. I have but given you the child's message; now act according to your own judgment."

"Yes, I shall do that, and she shall not remain here another hour!"

"If her mother were allowed to give her opinion—," began Frau Ceres.

Sonnenkamp looked at her, as though a dumb object had suddenly commenced to speak; but Frau Ceres was not talking to him, but to the Superior.

"I, as her mother, declare that we shall not force her to anything—I accept the condition."

Sonnenkamp got up quickly. He took hold of the chair convulsively: he seemed to be passing through a violent inward struggle; but suddenly, he said in an exceedingly affable tone:

"Roland, go now to Herr von Prancken."

Roland had to leave the convent. His heart trembled. Up there is his sister—what will happen to her? Why will they not let him go to her, embrace her, kiss her, and loosen her black locks as of old? He went into the open air, but he did not go to Prancken: he went into the open church, and there he sank on his knees, and prayed with deep devotion. He could not say what he was praying for, but he prayed for peace, for beauty; and suddenly, on looking up, he started.

Before him hung a large picture of St. Anthony of Padua; and—marvellous! the picture resembled Erich—the same noble, beautiful face as Erich's.

The boy looked at it long and earnestly: at last his head sank upon his hands, and—oh blessed childhood!—he slept.

CHAPTER V.

LOVE—STILL AND SECRET.

THE parents entered Manna's cell. Manna advanced calmly toward them, and said:

"Welcome! May Heaven bless you!"

She gave her father her hand: it shook as she touched the ring on his thumb. Then she threw herself on her mother's breast and kissed her.

"Forgive me," she cried, "forgive me! Do not think me heartless, but I must—no, I will. I thank you, for granting my request."

"Of course we will not force you," said the mother; and Sonnenkamp, who had not yet given his consent, was obliged to yield.

Manna's countenance brightened suddenly; she was very glad to see her parents looking so well, and told them that she prayed for them daily, and that Heaven granted her prayers. Manna had a voice in which one heard suppressed tears: this voice seemed to induce Sonnenkamp to lay his hand on his heart, and his attitude and expression were those of a man registering a silent vow.

When Manna inquired after Roland, he said with the air of one who talks to a sick person who has but just recovered, that Roland was in the park, and he hoped that she would go down with them to see the ladies and Herr von Prancken.

When her father pronounced this name, a slight shudder passed over Manna; but she said, with ready self-control:

"I want to see no one but you and Roland."

A servant Sister was sent after Roland. In the mean time, Manna declared that she should, in accordance with the law, return into the world for one year, and afterward—she hesitated a moment, before she continued—if she were still firm in her present resolve, she should take the veil.

"And will you never tell me why and how this thought grew within you?" asked Sonnenkamp, in eager supplication.

"Indeed I will, father, when all is over!"

"I can't understand it! I can't understand it!" cried Sonnenkamp aloud.

Manna hushed her father's loud voice, with a motion of her hand, telling him that in the convent they did not speak so loudly.

Roland, for whom a long search had been made, started up and staggered back when, suddenly awakened by a black figure, he found himself in the church.

He was taken to Manna. He threw his arms around his sister with passionate tenderness, and cried:

"You good, naughty girl you!"

His excitement prevented him from saying more.

"Come, don't be so impetuous," the girl said soothingly. "Dear, what a big boy you've grown to be!"

"And you so tall. And you look something like him too: but Erich is still handsomer than you. Yes, you may laugh! Isn't it so, Mother? isn't it so, Father? Ah! how glad he'll be when you come home, and how much you'll like him too!"

Talking incoherently, now of St. Anthony, and now of Erich, Roland told what an excellent man his teacher and friend was; and when Manna declared that she should not come home before Spring, Roland concluded:

"You can very easily picture Herr Erich to yourself. If you go into the church, only look at St. Anthony; that's just his face, just so good. But he can be strict too, he was an officer in the artillery."

Her father again assuring her, and her mother joining in the assurance, that she should be free to return to the convent, they both begged her to accompany them a few days on their journey to the baths.

Manna replied that she must not interrupt her studies and the habits of her convent life.

The wondrous, heart-reaching tone of her voice had something overpowering in it; and while she told them how she hoped to grow firm and clear in all things, and to face life bravely, the tears came into her mother's eyes. But her father stared at her in wonder; yet he scarcely saw his child, he scarcely knew where he was. He heard a voice which he had heard once before, many, many years ago; and as he stood there, he no longer noticed the girl, or anything around him; he saw nothing but a neglected grave in the churchyard of a Polish village. He passed his broad hand over his whole face, and like one just waking up, he looked around and heard his child repeating:

"I shall face life bravely."

He had heard everything that had passed here, but his thoughts and his eyes had been far away: it was a twofold existence, hardly comprehensible.

Now he repeated his request that Manna would come into the park to welcome her friends—she ought not to offend them; but Manna insisted that it was impossible.

Manna had requested a servant Sister to go for Cricket. The child came, and looked wonderingly at the strangers. Manna told the child that they were her parents and her brother.

The child scarcely looked at the parents, but clung to Roland when Manna said:

"See, this is my brother, of whom I have told you."

"I like you," said the child, "I like you."

And she was as much at home with Roland as if she had always played with him.

"Will you be my brother too?" asked the child.

Manna said how happy it made her feel that she could be so much to the child.

Sonnenkamp grumbled to himself:

"Yes, yes, that's the way. I know what you are—a child fostering a strange child. But enough!"

He rose quickly.

The parents and Roland left the cell. Manna remained alone with Cricket.

On the stairs, Sonnenkamp said to his wife:

"You have brought this on me! The child turns from me; you have estranged her from my heart, you have told her—;"

A strange laugh, a laugh that seemed as if it came from a different person, burst forth from Frau Ceres. Roland looked at her fixedly; here was something which he could not understand.

The parents and the boy joined their friends in the park, and Sonnenkamp explained, with much composure, that to prevent all interruption of her studies, and the disturbing influence of the outer world, he had permitted his daughter to remain in the convent till next Easter. Prancken cast a curious glance on Sonnenkamp; then he quickly expressed his admiration of the great ease with which Herr Sonnenkamp managed everything.

Bella and Miss Perini had taken a walk through the island. They were not to be found for a long while; at last they came from the room of the lady Superior.

Evening had set in, and when they got into the boat, Roland called up to the convent:

"Good-night, Manna!"

Manna had heard the cry; she had stolen down into the park, she had looked after the departing friends, and then she had quietly entered the church.

When they reached the opposite shore, they heard the chorus of clear girl-voices ringing from the convent above.

"That may sound well to him who has no child among them," said Sonnenkamp to himself.

In the large hotel, there was a stir and a bustle, as if some prince with his suite had arrived, for sometimes Sonnenkamp liked to make a show of his wealth. The large garden was brilliantly illuminated, the Sonnenkamp party was most assiduously waited upon, and whatever guests arrived that evening were scarcely noticed.

When all was quiet, a small boat crossed to the convent. In it sat Prancken. He stood on the island, and listened to the sounds of the harp from an open window. It was Manna, he knew it. Gradually lights became visible in different cells, windows were opened, girlish heads appeared, and looked out into the night; then the windows were closed, the lights were put out, and the tones of the harp were still. Prancken saw the open church; he entered, knelt down, and prayed in silence. Suddenly he heard a low footstep, he heard some one kneel before the altar; he started, nevertheless he did not rise, he could recognize nothing by the dim light of the solitary, eternal lamp. The figure rose, and went toward the open door. The moon threw a broad stream of light into the middle aisle; and now, as she stood in the doorway, Prancken advanced toward the figure, and said:

"Fräulein Manna, a friend. Do not be alarmed--a man who owes his highest bliss to you, stands before you. I did not come to shake your sacred resolution, I wish only to tell you what I have become through you. No, I cannot express it, but this you must know: if you take the veil, I also shall renounce the world, and as long as we remain on this earth, we will, separated from each other, live only for Heaven. Farewell, a thousand times farewell, thou pure, thou lovely one! Farewell!"

The young man and the maiden regarded each other as if both were transported from earth. Manna could utter no word, she only dipped her hand into the font, and sprinkled Prancken's face three times.

With hasty steps, Prancken went away toward the shore. Manna stood still, and passed her hand over her brow. Was all this a mere dream of her imagination?

Then she heard the stroke of the oars in the river, and once more a voice cried:

"Thou pure, thou lovely one!"

Then all was quiet.

A chain rattled on the other side, the boat was fastened to the shore; no sound was heard; only the waves of the river, whose sound is not noticed through the day, tossed and splashed and murmured audibly in the silent night. Manna thought she must hear the coursing of her blood, which now rushed to her heart—her heart so full, so heavy, and still so happy.

CHAPTER VI.

A DAY FREE FROM WORDS.

ERICH stood on the shore, looking after the boat from which, far off, Roland was still waving his handkerchief to him. Seeing a person so faithfully attached to you fly past on a boat, is like loving a bird in the air, which soars aloft, free and unattainable. And still it is different: Love binds men together with invisible ties; and this beckoning from a distance is a sign of community of thought, of a mutual grasping and holding, in spite of all separation of space.

When the boat had disappeared, and only a lingering smoke-cloud melted softly away on the mountains, Erich yet stood on the hill; and like the clouds floating in the air, Roland's parting words floated through his mind: "You and the house, you stay safe at home!"

What a heaving, working, seething, there is in a young soul, before it bursts forth like a flower into the full expression of itself! The reserved and the concealed has no less beauty and tenderness within itself, but it does not appear before us, does not charm us with its bloom and fragrance. Thus thought Erich, as he stood looking at an acacia, which was loaded with blossoms, but showed not a single green leaf.

Erich was now quite alone in the Villa. He inhaled the silence, the peace, the perfect calm in full deep breathings, as if, after standing long days and nights on the roaring locomotive, he had suddenly come into the quiet forest; nay more, as if he lay deep down at the bottom of the river, and above him rippled softly the cool waves. He did not read, he did not write, he only indulged in an infinite repose. He would not respond to Clodwig's invitation before the following day. Erich was certainly free from all egotism, but the liberty of living a whole day with closed lips and alone, charmed him as if he were now for the first time, after the long imprisonment of servitude, given back to himself and to freedom again. Once more he remembered that Clodwig was expecting him, but he said almost aloud:

"I cannot!—I dare not!"

For one single day he wanted to live for himself, to hear no strange word, to speak to no one, to be alone, mute, solitary, independent. For a moment he thought of writing to his mother, but rejected even that. Nobody should have anything of him, he wanted all of himself. He felt his constant thinking for others, his toiling for them, his love for them, like a pain, like a sickness, and from the depths of his soul he longed for solitude. Only for one single day he wanted to be an egotist, to live in perfect quiet; no book, no human tie, no purpose should rob him of a particle of his solitariness. Eden was the name of this Villa; he would be for one day the first man—alone in Eden. He contemplated a tree, and nodded to it. As immovable, as self-contained as this tree, he would live for one single day. He lay in the park under a large beech, in lazy reverie. There is an easy, blissful rippling of being and feeling, without decided thought or will, of which the incessantly thinking and working man is most deeply conscious. Thus Erich lay, happy with himself, merely gazing and breathing, alone, so that a gardener's step on the grating sand roused him as from a dream. The gardener commenced raking the path: it scratched strangely. Erich would have liked to ask him to stop, but he refrained, and smiling, said to himself:

"You are yourself a path-raker like him."

He looked into the branches of the tree, and as the soft wind moved them to and fro, so he let his thoughts move hither and thither; with no desire, except to live without aim.

Everything was peace.

How often, from its first budding, is a leaf moved to and fro by the wind, the long summer through, till it falls! and then—what then?

A smile passed over his face.

We are no longer alone, for here is another man, and he too is conscious that he is a thing to be forgotten. And the thought carried him still further on. Yes, solitude means rest on mother Earth; it is the legend of Antaeus, who was permeated with new strength out of the eternal strength of mother Earth, every time he touched her. Our thinking continually raises us from the ground, and renders us powerless. And still further, ever further, his thought and fancy strayed. This is one of the burdens of wealth, its curse, that it can neither enter Heaven nor descend into the primitive power of earthly being; for the rich man possesses all things save one, and that is separation from the world, seclusion in himself.—"Ballast, ballast, too much ballast!"

The doctor's words occurred to him; and the word *ballast* was repeated constantly in his brain, as the finch on the tree above him repeated again and again the same tones.

With all his dreaming and thinking, sleep overcame him; and when he awoke, he felt fresh and endued with new life. It was the first time, in a long while, that he had come to himself again. He smiled to himself, for now it was all clear to him; he was like one enlightened. Adam slept in Paradise, and when he awoke, he saw his wife before him; a world was his own, and also another being who was to be one with him.

It was a day and an hour in which all that has past away, and all that exists, and all that humanity has ever dreamed of and conquered by labor, stands before the eye, newly illuminated, and shining by its own light. All riddles seem solved, all is peace, eternity, and unison. So must he feel who realizes the waking from death, and eternal life opening before him.

But for the present, he must nerve himself afresh, to encounter the struggle of existence.

Erich wandered about in the park, through the house, and greeted everything with eyes that seemed new and fresh; he had forgotten everything—put it far away from him; and now he saw it as a new, recuperated man. It is well for us that the world stands firm, and is ever ready when, forgetting ourselves, we return to it.

A whole day passed, during which Erich neither read nor wrote a single word.

The next morning Erich had his horse saddled: he mounted, and rode on his way to see Clodwig.

But he had scarcely ridden a quarter of an hour, when a boy called to him and handed him a paper. He read, nodded. and turned cheerfully toward the village.

CHAPTER VII.

OUR FRIEND KNOPF.

ON a bright summer day the people sail merrily up and down the river; everything sparkles and glistens in the sunshine and is full of joy. Who stops to think then how much misery, how much labor, care, and sorrow are in the houses yonder? Look up there to the village on the hill, which looks so fair when seen from the river, and even now sends us the sound of its bells; there a poor village-schoolmaster wends his way from the church to the school-house, with sad, sorrowful mien. But to-day his countenance brightens, for before the school-house stands a faithful friend, and holds out his hand to him.

"What! you here, Herr Knopf?" cries the schoolmaster.

"The free republic of the United States has made this a free day for me. You see an independent man before you. Ah! dear Fassbender, I seem born to be a teacher of girls. I tell you, before the deluge of their first ball, the girls are the loveliest flowers on our planet."

Knopf related to his colleague how fortunate he was in having a lively, uncommonly apt American lady as a pupil: his by no means handsome face gained an entirely fresh expression as he spoke.

Knopf's face was indeed ugly; everything was so knotted there. The nose, the mouth, the forehead, yes, even the eyebrows, which projected rather far over the pale blue eyes (especially when, as now, he had removed his spectacles), everything seemed as if kneaded of dough. But now as he spoke of his pupil, a light passed over his features.

He explained that he had come to give Roland's present tutor some hints about the character of his pupil, and the manner in which he was to be governed in future. He had started on his journey early in the morning before sunrise. It had been a refreshing walk; but now he felt that he ought not to go to the Villa, so he intended asking the new tutor to come here, and he begged for a boy to take a note to Captain Dournay. Gradually the children came up and greeted Herr Knopf, whom they recognized as an old acquaintance. A curly-headed boy was very happy to carry the message to Villa Eden, instead of being obliged to sit in school. Knopf knew a pretty spot beyond the village on the summit of the hill, under a wide-spreading linden-tree: to this place he walked leisurely, and lying down under the tree he gazed upon the landscape with delighted eyes.

"I love to lie the flowers among,
And hear the distant flute and song,"

he said almost aloud to himself. And as in our steam-roaring times the flute is heard no more, Knopf screwed up his cane, which was a perfectly constructed flute, and played the tune to which Konradin Kreutzer has set Uhland's song.

The thought that others would hear this at a distance, pleased him more, almost, than his own enjoyment of it.

He allowed no vessel to pass up or down the river, without waving his white handkerchief to it. Even if they were strangers, what did it matter? He has given them a sign that he is happy up here; may they be happy on their journey down there! This is what the signal is meant to tell them.

Yes, Knopf deserves that we should know him better. The son of a poor schoolmaster, Knopf had struggled through the University with much difficulty, and had passed his examination; and then his great misfortune befell him. In his trial-year he was hooted by the boys the very first day; and the more he begged for silence, the more insolently did they deride him. The director came to his assistance; but scarcely had he left the schoolroom, when the noise and the hooting began anew. Knopf was allowed to pass his trial-year in a distant town, but an invisible power seemed to have noised his misfortune abroad, for soon after he commenced his regular instruction he was hooted there too. Then he withdrew altogether from the field of public education.

In the capital, Knopf was much liked as a teacher of girls; he was so fabulously ugly that mothers could allow him to instruct their half-grown daughters, quite confidentially, without the fear of their falling in love with him. He was also conscientious and careful, but he had no success. He was very popular in every household, but no parent cared to have him as an inmate for any length of time: he was a teacher in case of need. No other man had as many deceased pupils as he, for many were given to him for instruction only after they had fallen sick

Knopf had also been much at watering-places. If the parents could not take their children to the baths themselves, especially to the all-curing salt-springs, they were put in Knopf's charge, and he was teacher and nurse at once. For a short time he was even teacher in an institute for idiots, and his conscience reproached him then, and sometimes does even to this day, for not having remained there; but he insisted that he was too much accustomed to the sight of beauty. Indeed, he wanted to investigate how the Greeks and Romans conducted their philanthropic institutions. He found that their children were neglected in a far less degree, both morally and physically. Then Knopf formed a project which he revolved in his mind for a long time: he meant to found an institution for the care of sick children, at some salt-spring; for Iodine is now the panacea of all scrofulous and cultivated, that is to say, all wealthy people. He hoped St. Iodine would send him a helpmeet in recognition of his devotion.

In the mean time he was and remained an assistant teacher, especially for girls.

Greek and Roman mythology was his specialty; and it is very important for girls of the upper classes to be perfect in this study. But his favorite subject was the explanation of the poets, especially of the romantic school. Of course he was a poet himself, but only modestly and in private. There are, in the capital, but few albums, commenced early and then neglected, which do not contain a neatly written sonnet, or still more frequently a triolet, from Emil Knopf for his dear pupil. He was also sufficiently musical to superintend the girls' practising. He was especially firm in keeping time—even unmerciful. He could also draw enough to assist in this branch, especially in drawing flowers. He was as skilled as he was popular in the arrangement of games for the bridal eve, when one of his pupils got married. He not only understood how to let the allegorical girl-flowers say, "I am the rose—I am the violet;" but he could also insert an occasional joke, even of a personal nature. While the bride's beautifully dressed friends acted and formed charming groups on the stage, he sat in the prompter's box, and whispered the words to them. And how happy he was at the feast, and how approvingly he nodded when this or that speaker delivered, either by heart or from the written page, the toasts which he had composed!

Emil Knopf was one of the handiest of men. He was proud of never having advertised in the newspapers: he had always been recommended from mouth to mouth, and for the most part, by beautiful mouths; one mother praised him to another, and the fathers smiled and said: "Yes, Herr Knopf is a most conscientious teacher." When he was in a house where smoking was not sanctioned, he chewed roasted coffee-beans, and got along very well on them. Knopf was very fond of taking snuff, but he did it very quietly, and only when he was alone: he carried a colored pocket-handkerchief and a white one, to prevent his patrons from noticing that he took snuff. Only one single, very queer habit he could not give up—he was constantly hitching up his trowsers on both legs, as if he feared that they would fall off.

But this is surely no sufficient reason for his being apparently destined to be forever only a needy assistant, forever only a pedagogic nurse for a few weeks at a time. Knopf is kept until trouble and sickness or any thing else is past in the house; then he is dismissed again with very polite, very cordial words, —but still he is always dismissed. For fourteen semesters (Knopf always reckoned by semesters, and we must do like him) Knopf had lived in the capital, and during this time he always intended laying in a large stock of a peculiar kind of cigars which suited him; but he never did it. For fourteen semesters, from one week to the next, he always smoked sample-cigars: he asked continually how much they were by the thousand, but he never got a thousand.

Knopf was by nature one of the most awkward of men, but he trained himself and became a most able swimmer and gymnast; so that for awhile he became a teacher of gymnastics. Two positions which he had filled in the country, where it was so difficult to get a piano-tuner, had induced him to learn even this accomplishment; but this he only practised in the house in which he lived at the time. Some people averred that he could even knit and do fine sewing, but this was decidedly a calumny. The darning of stockings he really did understand to perfection, but no one had ever yet seen him at it. He always did it secretly by himself.

To Herr Sonnenkamp, Knopf had of course come as a candidate in need, and as an instructor in need; but here a longer stay seemed promised him, and a future free from care. Knopf had an enthusiastic love for Roland, and although the boy really learned nothing under him, Knopf often said to the schoolmaster Fassbender, to whom he had become attached:

"The gods did not *learn* either—they *had* everything. Who can say who was Apollo's music-teacher, under what butler Ganymede learned to wait? Beautiful natures have everything in themselves, and need not learn anything. We are, after all, but cripples, with all our studying; we allow ourselves to be imprisoned by the tyranny of the four faculties, but life is no square."

Such, then, is "our friend Knopf," and "our friend Knopf" he was called in the first houses of the land.

Knopf had just stopped his flute-playing; now he sat there, his tablets on his knee, and looked first at the landscapes, then hastily wrote a few words, then took his pencil between his teeth again, and seemed to be chewing a phrase.

To a great distance he could look along the road which leads from the village past the Villa to the neighboring hamlet. Presently Knopf saw a horseman approaching. He quickly transformed the flute again into a walking-stick, concealed his memorandum-book, and hastened through the vineyards down to the road.

"Yes, one who sits a horse like that is the proper teacher for him," said Knopf. He took off his hat while still at a distance: the horseman nodded to him.

CHAPTER VIII.

A WALK IN THE OPEN AIR.

THE horseman came nearer, and now he was beside Knopf. The latter looked wonderingly at the splendid man, he could not utter a word; but Erich said:

"Have I the honor of seeing my colleague, Herr Knopf?"

"I am he."

Erich quickly jumped from the saddle, and held out his hand to Knopf.

"I thank you," said he. And with every word that he spoke, at the sound of his voice, Knopf's countenance brightened more and more, and all over his face still more elevations and depressions appeared. Erich continued:

"It was my intention to call to see you soon; but I did not want to do so until I had formed an independent opinion and thoroughly proved it."

"Very proper," replied Knopf; "the judgment of another may give rise to a prejudice."

With still increasing admiration, Knopf looked at Erich and said—it sounded like a declaration of love: "I am really glad that you are a handsome man. Smile, if you will, and shake your head. It gives you great influence in that family, and upon Roland especially. It was a wise practice, that of the Spartans—to be sure, it was cruel, very cruel, but there was deep wisdom in it too—their practice of putting misshapen children to death. Really, all men ought to be handsome."

Erich laid his hand on Knopf's shoulder. He could not utter a single word; admiration and inclination to laughter struggled within him: admiration was victorious. A man of Knopf's appearance must have celebrated many a conquest over himself, before he could reach the philosophy of such expressions. Erich walked with Knopf toward the village, and said that Knopf could just as well have called upon him at the Villa; and if he wished to avoid the family, he would have found him quite alone, because they had gone with Herr von Prancken to the convent to get Manna.

"Ah! poor girl!" lamented Knopf. "I may say that I have had more than fifty pupils, fine girls all of them, and not half, no, not a third of them have married as I should have wished. Ah! my dear colleague, I've never in my life told one family how another lives; and you may take my word for it, it has been a difficult job too. The old ladies, as a rule, want to know what happens here and there, but I never tell a thing. It's a matter of principle, you see. Whoever talks to me of other people, will talk to other people of me; that's what my mother used to say. I've remembered it, and I've got along the better for it."

Erich was delighted with the honest fellow, and soon banished all thoughts about Prancken having gone to get the rich bride from the convent. What was the girl to him?

He left his horse at the village tavern, and Knopf led him to the linden on the hill-top, and there developed for him his conception of Roland.

"I'm like a child," he began. "I must always acquaint you first with my latest discoveries, and my most recent pains. You are not in haste, I hope. I confess openly that nothing in our age vexes me so much as the everlasting hurry that everybody is in."

Erich told him that he had the whole day at his disposal, and bade Knopf go on.

"So this is my latest pain; it dates from this morning, when I came over the mountain, up there past the forest chapel. The fresh dew lay on everything, the birds sang merrily, alike unmindful of the morning chimes of the chapel above and the ringing of the bell in the depot below. What does self-contained Nature care for these things, in the time of young spring-love? But, dear me, this isn't at all what I mean to tell you," he interrupted himself, placing his hand on the memorandum-book, which no doubt contained a poem on this subject.

"It was only this. As I walked along the forest path, I heard children's voices, clear and merry; and another soft and pacifying one seemed to control them. And up the mountain came a lovely girl—I beg your pardon, but how lovely she was I found out afterward, for I had given myself a treat, and taken off my spectacles in the green woods. Now I put them on again, and the first thing that struck me was two beautiful round white hands. The girl saw me—and—who knows what she had just been thinking of?—but she seemed to be frightened, and took the elder brother, a boy of thirteen, by the hand: two younger ones walked beside her. I passed them and wished them good-morning. The girl thanked me in a low voice, but the boys said a hearty 'Good-morning!' We passed each other.

"I looked after them a long while. I returned to the chapel. The silence, the whole aspect of things up there, where no people dwell, but all is prepared for their worship, the vessels, the pictures, the candlesticks, and the priest so reverend—it does not seem to me possible that a man who bends as he did, kneels down and raises his hands aloft as he did, can do it all in mere mockery. If he could, the lowest criminal in a house of correction would be an angel in comparison with him. The sermon itself was, of course, no better than a hospital broth. But would you believe it, I had hoped to see the girl again there; but I was ashamed of having come to the chapel with that intention, and stole softly away. Then all personal interest fell from me, and the great misery came over me."

"What do you mean?"

"The misery of our freedom oppressed me. Here's a young girl but just from school, walking with three younger brothers in the early morning through the mountain forest, and they are going to the forest chapel, whose bells are calling to them to come. But consider these four human beings to have no object for their morning walk, no such good, fixed object—what would pilgrimage be in that case! A walk in the open air, nothing more! The open air, what does that mean? It is nothing, it is nowhere. But to enter a temple where the organ sounds and holy hymns are sung, must have a refreshing influence on these young souls, and they must take home with them a greater and entirely different satisfaction from that given by a mere morning walk in the open air. And up there, divine service is performed whether the people come or not; there is nothing designed for the peculiar character of a community or for any one degree of culture of any one man. Like eternal nature itself, it always goes on unconcerned whether it is received or not: whoever comes may take part—no one asks where he came from, and no one needs to know. Could I believe, I should be a Catholic or an orthodox Jew. But what is our life? A walk into the open air—into the unbounded, but also into the uncertain! You can conceive that this must make me sad, for I cannot force myself into anything else, to anything positive. And this is as impossible to all my fellow-creatures as to myself: still, we must try to arrive at something, our life must not be a simple walk into the open air, but through the open air to some sure, safe, homelike, peace-giving goal. Oh! if I could only express it, only conceive it, and the millions of languishing souls with me! And then you see," concluded Knopf—"then I thought of you and Roland. You understand me fully, do you not?"

"Not quite."

"Of course, I haven't kept close enough to the point. Well, then, to speak in plain words, the thought that occurred to me was and is: 'Whither can you lead Roland?' Into the open air? But what will he do there? what does he find? what has he? what binds him, what attracts him? There's the rub, there lies the difficult problem. The faith—the moral castle to which we must guide the rich youth, has neither walls nor roof, it has no pictures, it has no hymns, it has no consecrating formula. There, that's it. Is it plain to you now?"

"Yes, yes, I understand you now," said Erich, taking the other's hand; "you've touched the thoughts at the bottom of my soul; but I trust that we may succeed in giving a man a hold within himself, without the support of any datum from without. Both of us here, have we not this hold?"

"I think so; or, I venture to say, I know so. I thank you, you make me happy," cried Knopf enthusiastically. "Oh, the world! To think of our sitting down gazing ahead, waiting for some sign to appear, some all-penetrating or re-creative word! But it will not come from without, it can only come from within. And in Roland there is the germ of a thorough man, a sterling original nature, in spite of all the slime with which they have covered it; he unites an obstinate daring with a surprising tenderness. He has many good impulses, but youth cannot analyze its feelings; if it could, it would no longer be youth. Roland has all the needful elements, but we grown people do not understand a child's heart. Let us ask ourselves, whether in our childhood we were understood, even by the wisest and nearest? You'll accomplish it, you have a call to do it."

"I?"

"Yes, you! A great inscrutable plan guides and governs all existence. A wondrous law reigns over the world, call it Providence or call it Fate, which ordains that a man like you, at a distance, must pass through various callings and be prepared, and now stand here so beautiful and noble. Ah! do not shake your head, let me say it. It inspires a feeling of devotion to reflect that a recondite power, which we must call God, brings you here to develop a man, by and to the beautiful—an Apollo-like man, who has no business on earth but to be beautiful and to feel the Beautiful. I did not guide Roland rightly. I sowed my seed, before I knew that the ground was loosened. To-day, when I watched a man harrowing in the vineyards, I thought, 'This is Copernicus.'"

"Copernicus?" asked Erich with astonishment.

"Do not misunderstand me; the first man who took a sharp stick, a horn, a bone, or a piece of stone, and dug up the earth for the purpose of putting in seed, moved the world; he became the sire of modern culture, as truly as Copernicus who at last discovered that the whole planet moves."

"What would you propose now to make of Roland?" asked Erich, returning to the subject of conversation.

"What to make of him? A man whose existence is beauty. Is it not a mistaken idea to educate a man to good by the sight of all sorts of misery and crime? That makes one low-spirited, sentimental, weak. The Greeks had a different method—that of strength, gayety, self-confidence,—*that* makes men strong. Our virtue is no longer manliness, but womanish lint-scraping. Ah!" continued Knopf, "the beautiful man—the real man—is the *unexamined* man, a species no more to be found in Europe. We are all born to be examined. The Greeks were great, inasmuch as they had no examining-boards. Plato never graduated. And that's what constitutes the greatness of America too—wherein she resuscitates ancient Greece. There too they have no real examinations—"

"That's not as nearly true now as it once was," interposed Erich.

"Yes," resumed Knopf once more, "Roland is the unexamined man: let him learn nothing, for the mere purpose of being examined upon it. Why must a modern man 'be something?' '*Civis romanus sum*,' that's enough for the generality of men."

Again Erich led him back to the matter in question, by asking:

"Do you know of a calling for Roland?"

"Calling? calling? The best that we learn is not put down in curriculums, nor paid for in ready-money. This division of callings, of which we are so proud, is at best only a mechanical tyranny, a virtue made of necessity. Vulgar natures pay with what they accomplish—noble ones, with what they are. That's a fact. Take a handsome and harmonious man who lets himself develop according to the law of his own being—why, he ornaments humanity and helps it. I attempted to preserve in Roland the *naïveté* of wealth. People are not made to be drilled into Brothers of Charity. It's not everybody's function to serve. Developing yourself is a beautiful calling. I honor that precept in Cicero, which says: 'Whoever does nothing, is a free man.' A free man is an idler."

Erich contested this, and Knopf was not a little surprised to find Erich's recollection of the passage in Cicero very exact, and to hear him prove that Cicero advanced simply the proposition, "No one is free who cannot sometimes be idle—*non aliquando, nihil agit*." He went on to say that there could be a beautiful state of being without accomplishing anything, without action, but that the German poet's expression to the contrary was a mistake. But he tried to turn the conversation away from these general contemplations altogether. Of what use was all this pondering and discussing, concerning the vocation of mankind, on the part of two men, on the mountain-side? It seemed to strike Knopf too that he had strayed too far, and he said:

"You ought to take Roland away from home."

"That would indeed be the wisest course; but you know that it's impossible."

"Of course! of course! I also frequently considered the possibility of forcing on Roland the impression that he was poor; but if, logically speaking, there's such a thing as the comparative of a negation, then this is even more impossible. I have read Jean Jacques Rousseau's Emil, and found in it much that is good. I've also studied the treatise on Wealth, ascribed to Plato. Aristophanes too has a profound perception of the relation between wealth and poverty. When you call to see me at Mattenheim, I shall be ready to submit it all to you."

Erich made a slight effort to discover the reason why Knopf had left the house; but Knopf did not tell him, he only indicated that Roland had been led off by the French valet, Armand, and Armand had then been dismissed from the house. With unusual haste, he went on to say that he had felt some hesitation about going to see Erich; but Herr Weidmann had read his wish in his eyes, and persuaded him to do it.

Erich promised to come over to Mattenheim soon, and Knopf seemed very much pleased when Erich told him of Roland's industry and devotion, and how the Life of Franklin not only enabled him to give Roland a personal ideal, but also gave him occasion to let Roland recognize and supply the defects of his own life and knowledge, by studying the process of Franklin's development.

"Shall I tell you," cried Knopf, springing up, "what can confer even more happiness than Archimedes' great word, 'I have found it!' There lies even greater happiness in 'Thou hast found it!' Yes! You've found it," cried Knopf, giving his trowsers an extra hitch. He would have liked to embrace Erich, but did not dare.

And on Erich's telling him that he had reached this simple method through some of his father's memoranda, Knopf cried out into space:

"Blessed be thy father! and blessed be thou, Eternal Spirit! Oh world, how fair and great thou art! Now we know where we are going when we walk in the open air—the free air; we are going to a free man—Benjamin Franklin. Here are two men on a mountain-top on the Rhine, who hail thee to all eternity!

But pardon me," he said, "I'm not often thus, you may take my word for it. But, Captain, if ever you want me to do something great for you, something hard, remind me of this hour; you shall see what I can do."

Erich ingeniously slid past this topic, by begging Knopf to tell him something about his pupil.

"Yes," began Knopf, "there's an example. The parents have sent the child to Germany, because they feared that her soul might not remain free in yonder land of freedom, for Doctor Fritz and his wife are liberal in their religion, and are generally looked upon as noble characters. They sent the child to an American school, and after the lapse of six months she commenced trying to convert her parents to the Church, and always pronounced her intention of becoming a Presbyterian. She wept and prayed, and said she could find no peace, because her parents were unbelievers. Isn't this a remarkable experience? So the parents sent the child to Germany—of course to the best family that could be found."

Knopf took the letter from his pocket; it was from Doctor Fritz, who, as a representative of German honor and philanthropy in the New World, was busily working at the removal of that blemish which still rests on mankind in the existence of slavery. Doctor Fritz gave the teacher a very accurate characterization of his daughter, which gave evidence of the father's entire impartiality. He explained, in like manner, how the child was to be guided. The letter also enclosed a photograph of Doctor Fritz, a vigorous-looking man, with fair curly hair and full beard; something childlike, and yet something that spoke of great aspirations, shone through the strong, manly features.

Very mysteriously, Knopf then confided to Erich that, though her lot had been cast in the New World, the child had lived entirely within the magic circle of Grimm's fairy-tales; and—it was wonderful, and he could not make out whether it was imagination or reality, but something had happened to the child on her journey which sounded like a fairy-tale.

"The child's name is Lilian," continued Knopf; "and, as you know, the Mayflower is called lily-of-the-valley in English; and the child received a mayflower from an apparition in the woods which did not know her name. This has started a wonderful fairy-tale in her little golden head, for the child insists that she has seen the wood-prince."

"You're a poet at the bottom," said Erich.

Involuntarily Knopf's hand felt for his breast-pocket, where his tablets were concealed, as if Erich had taken them out.

"I allow myself to hammer out a stanza occasionally, but you needn't fear, I've never yet tormented another's ear with my poetry."

Erich grew very fond of this man, apparently so prosy, and still so deeply enthusiastic; and when the bells again rang in the village, Erich said:

"Now come, and make me acquainted with the village schoolmaster."

CHAPTER IX.

SAINT ANTHONY.

THE village schoolmaster was an awkward, formal apparition; he behaved very humbly when the Captain called on him. Soon the three sat together in the tavern, and he related the history of his life.

He was sixty-four years old, but still appeared very active. The complaint unfortunately universal among village-teachers, had in this instance special justification. With a blending of pride and bitterness, he said that he had a son twenty-one years old, who was now in young Herr Weidmann's cement-factory, getting double the salary that he—the father, had, after thirty-two years of service. He had four sons, but not one of them should be a schoolmaster. A second son was a merchant, and the eldest was a master-builder in America. "Yes," said he aloud, "we schoolmasters will never be any better off till there's a general strike."

"Would you continue to teach," asked Erich, "if you had a good enough income without?"

"No."

"Then if you had had the income, you would never have become a teacher?"

"I believe not."

"That's the worst of it," cried Knopf, "that wealth always says, and with truth too, 'I must not relieve want, for it is want which produces and forms the great and the beautiful—want makes our aspirations and our virtues.' Do you see, Captain colleague, that Herr Sonnenkamp is an important man of much worldly wisdom, and he says: 'I must take no notice of the lives round about me. Neither shall Roland, else he will be cheated out of his life; he can't drive out in his carriages without thinking of the misery and hardship everywhere.' See, that's where we again come upon our riddle. How can one be an ideally disposed man, and at the same time rich? We teachers are the guardians of ideality. Look at the villages round about: each one has a visible steeple and an invisible steeple, and this invisible steeple is the ideality of the village-teacher, who sits there with his children. I honor you for having become a schoolmaster."

Erich looked around as if aggrieved; in his inmost soul a

certain vanity was hurt at his being called a schoolmaster, but he got over it quickly, and was glad of it.

He succeeded in inducing the village-teacher to continue his history. He was a good mathematician; he had entered the revenue service and become an officer of the custom-house, had lost his position when the German Zollverein was established, had roved about nearly starved for two years, and finally had taken to school-teaching. But he had married well—that is, richly; so that he had been able to give his sons a better education.

The evening had come on.

Erich promised the schoolmaster to employ him in the instruction of Roland.

Knopf accompanied Erich a good part of the way; then he begged him to mount his horse.

Knopf stood still a long while, looking after Erich till he disappeared behind a bend of the mountain, and Knopf's thick lips murmured low words after him.

On his way home, it seemed strange to Erich that he thought less about Roland than about Manna—for Manna would be home to-night.

Foolish old stories floated through his brain—of a poor tutor falling in love with the rich daughter of the house, and being sent away by the hard-hearted father. And then he stands before the illuminated house; he hears music; above, the fair one celebrates her marriage with a high-born fop. Then a pistol-shot—no, some other situation on a more solid basis would be, after all, rather more sensible.

Erich had sufficient good sense to ward off any such notions toward the daughter of the house; he would remain distant, reserved, and respectful.

When he entered the Villa the carriages had arrived; and Erich was immediately given to understand that Herr Sonnenkamp had been displeased with him for not having had the complaisance to remain at home, or to remember the hour fixed for the return.

After all that he had been discussing with Knopf, the sensation of servitude seemed something strange to him: or was this reception only meant as a lesson in regard to his behavior toward Manna?

Erich took the reprimand, for such it was, without replying.

He went to Roland, who embraced him ardently, crying:

"Oh! it's sweet to be with you! All others are—"

"Don't speak of others," interrupted Erich.

But he could not prevent Roland from telling of the universal ill-humor caused by Manna's not returning with them.

Erich breathed more freely.

Roland related, rather incoherently, that, on the way back, Bella had gone ashore at the water-cure establishment, because she had received a telegram from Clodwig, who expected her there. But he finished:

"What does all this concern us! You're at the convent too, and I've told Manna so: you look just like St. Anthony in the convent church, Yes, you may laugh! If he were to laugh, he'd have to laugh just as you do; he looks at one exactly as you are looking at me now. Manna told me the legend. The saint was praying earnestly to Heaven, and then the infant Christ lay down on his arm in the solitude, and he's looking at him so devoutly, so fondly!"

A thrill passed through Erich: upon his hands too is a pure child-life. Is he worthy of holding it, and of letting the child's pure gaze rest upon him?

The two sat for a long while without speaking, then Roland cried:

"We'll leave each other no more, never again! To-day, as I was sitting on deck, it seemed to me—I was not asleep, I was perfectly wide awake—it seemed to me as if you came and took me on your arm, and held me there."

Roland's face glowed, all his pulses throbbed feverishly, and it cost Erich much trouble to reduce his overexcited mind down to its usual tone. But the dogs succeeded easily in accomplishing what was so difficult for him. Roland was again the same light-hearted child when he saw the puppies, which had grown wonderfully during these few days.

Prancken also joined Erich with great familiarity, and told him how he admired his power of arousing younger intelligences; for Roland had displayed an activity of mind and an adaptive tenderness of feeling which one could not have expected in him.

Frank reader, you may say what you will! Yesterday—yes, even one short hour ago—you thought meanly of a man's judgment, you recognized plainly the pettiness of his being. Suddenly he shows how he understands you, he praises you, he exalts you, and as suddenly, without your acknowledging it to yourself, your opinion of the man formerly looked upon as one-sided and narrow-minded, changes—especially if you be still wrestling with yourself, still educating yourself, if you despair frequently of yourself.

And so it happened with Erich.

Prancken seemed to him possessed of good judgment, amiable indeed; and Erich even went far enough to say that it would please him very much if the friends of the family would assist and encourage him in his difficult vocation of instructor.

Prancken was satisfied: Erich obviously recognized his position; he proved it in not taking part in the trip, and in thus refraining from intrusion upon the family; and though a certain pride had part in it, insomuch as he might not wish to travel and be confounded with the "companion" and servants, at all events Erich seemed not quite devoid of tact.

Prancken knew how to give to this patronizing protection the air of a sort of friendly familiarity.

CHAPTER X.

THE ALLUREMENTS OF THE WORLD.

ERICH and Roland lived together in "the castle"—as the apartments in the tower were called—as if they had entered a remote dwelling-place and were entirely alone. No noise came to them from the outer world—nothing but the song of birds and the chiming of the village bells.

Regular work was their rule; until noon they knew nothing of what was taking place in the house, and Roland lived almost absorbed in thoughts of Benjamin Franklin.

Roland was continually finding something new and attractive in Franklin's character; and when this American youth, who had never in his life felt want, saw before him a life full of renunciation, his ideas underwent a surprising change. He lived and moved in the life of Franklin. He spoke of him at table as if he had just come into existence; and as if he was the unseen companion of all his thoughts and actions. Roland immediately wished to follow Franklin's example, and keep a diary by which to criticise his own conduct, but Erich dissuaded him; for he knew that the boy was too unstable to carry out his project for any length of time. Such strict self-judgment is only fitted for one who lives alone or strives to find the right path without assistance; but Roland was continually with Erich. They imitated Franklin's physical experiments, pondered his little stories; and almost at every occurrence, Roland would exclaim:

"What would Franklin say of this?"

Erich had been in doubt as to whether it would be best to tell Roland that he had conversed with Herr Knopf; but he considerately waited for a more fitting opportunity, as he did not wish to disturb the serenity of a life that was every day becoming more and more firmly settled.

Prancken came almost every day for a short time, and at table spoke much of the Prince of the Church: he never called the Bishop anything but the Prince of the Church. A second court-life seemed to have opened before his vision, and this court had some holy prerogative, some power of arranging its own conduct, without the need of a chamberlain. Herr Sonnenkamp was continually, and with great interest, asking questions in regard to all the arrangements of the Episcopal court; but Frau Ceres showed not the slightest curiosity; for she had understood that it gave no balls, and that, as a general thing, there were no ladies to be seen there—excepting, perhaps, some of the most noble and distinguished nuns. But Frau Ceres had a great aversion to nuns, principally because they have such large feet, and wear such awkward shoes, and cotton gloves. Frau Ceres hated cotton gloves, and whenever she thought of them, a nervous shudder ran through her.

The days were quiet. The fragrant southern trees grew green with those that were growing in their native soil. But the silent days were numbered, for the family began to make preparations for a journey. Lutz was the director; and already great trunks had been made ready and sent forward.

It was a rainy morning. Erich and Roland were sitting together reading the Life of Franklin. Erich found that the boy was inattentive, and often looked toward the door.

At last there was a knock, and Sonnenkamp, who had never before disturbed their morning work, entered. He expressed his pleasure at seeing the course of instruction so well begun, and hoped that the journey would occasion only a short interruption of it; for, on their arrival at Vichy, it could proceed again.

Erich asked, in surprise, what was meant by speaking of Vichy, and heard that the whole family, together with the servants, male and female, as well as Roland and himself, were to go to the springs at Vichy, and thence to the sea-shore at Biarritz.

Erich endeavored to compose himself, and succeeded sooner than he had hoped; he then said that he did not know what Roland thought of it, but, for his part, he had decided that he could not go to the springs.

"You cannot go with us? Why not?"

"It pains me to be forced to discuss the question in presence of Roland, but I think that he is old enough to understand the affair. I think—I am perfectly convinced, that earnest study cannot at present be taken up at a fashionable watering-place, and then continued at Biarritz. I cannot commence my instruction after my pupil has been at the spring, early in the morning, listening to pot-pourri music. Under such circumstances, no one can think quietly or clearly. As I said, I consider Roland old enough to decide for himself. I will, if you wish, remain here at the Villa until you return."

Sonnenkamp looked at Erich in amazement; and Roland, imploringly. Sonnenkamp did not seem to give himself credit for sufficient self-command to oppose the tutor in a becoming manner; therefore he said, quietly, that they would speak of the subject again in the evening. He excused himself, half sarcastically, for not having told Erich of his summer arrangements when he visited him in the University city.

Again Erich sat alone with Roland, who fixed his eyes on the ground and did not speak. Erich did not disturb him for awhile; but said, at last, that now the first decision was to be made—now he was to be put to proof.

"Do you understand why I am unable and unwilling to pursue this work-life of ours at a place of pleasure?" he asked at last.

"I do not," Roland answered, obstinately.

"Shall I explain?"

"It's not necessary," the boy answered, sulkily.

Erich did not reply, and the silence gave the boy an opportunity of thinking of his conduct; but a struggle was taking place in his breast; something within him revolted against anything resembling servility. He gave no intimation of this, but said:

"Haven't I been sufficiently industrious and obedient?"

"As was your duty."

"Don't I deserve a little pleasure now?"

"No. One cannot be paid for doing his duty—certainly not paid by pleasure."

The boy did not answer, but sat angrily turning the leaves of Franklin's biography, which he had been reading. Erich, without speaking, took the book from him and laid it aside. Laying his hand on the cover, he said:

"What do you think Franklin would say to you now?"

"I can't tell."

"You can, but you won't."

"No, I cannot," said the boy. He stamped with childish rage, and his voice was choked with tears.

"I have a better opinion of you than you have yourself," said Erich, taking Roland's chin in his hands. "Look at me—don't look at the floor—don't be pettish."

Roland's face was unmoved. Tears stood in his eyes, but did not fall. Erich continued:

"Is there any good thing in the world that I would not like you to have?"

"Well, but—"

"But what? Go on."

"Oh, I don't know. And yet—yet—you might go with us just to please me. I couldn't enjoy myself if you were not with us—I there, and you here all alone!"

"And would you like to go without me?"

"I won't—you must go with me!" and the boy sprang up and threw his arms around Erich's neck.

"I tell you most decidedly that I shall not go."

Roland loosened his hands. Erich took them, and said:

"I might do as you did, and say: 'Do it for my sake, and stay with me!' but I will not. Come, look up pleasantly, and think what a fine time we might have here, all alone. Your parents go to the baths, and we stay here till they come back, studying regularly, and much more comfortable than we would be on the promenade amid the music—happier than at the sea-shore. Think, Roland, I have never seen France and the ocean; I renounce it for the sake of duty; and do you know where my duty is?"

"Oh, Duty could travel along with us!" said the boy, smiling through his tears. Erich was obliged to laugh too, and said after awhile:

"*This* duty cannot travel with us. Your attention has been sufficiently distracted all your life. Come, be my dear comrade, my good boy. Trust to me, even though you do not entirely see the use of what I want you to do."

"Yes, I trust you, but you can't think how beautiful it is; and I want to show it all to you."

Roland seemed seized and whirled about by a tempest of incongruous feelings. Should he who had subdued Erich and forced him to be his daily companion—who had compelled his father to give Erich to him—should he now leave his friend? But, on the other hand, *there* were pleasures enticing him, music and the delights of travel, ladies, and those jolly girls who would play with him! The boy rose and knew not what to do. Suddenly he cried out: "Erich! your mother!" for she had said to him at parting: "Be worthy of Erich's eternal companionship." The thought of this awoke in his soul, but on the other hand, there were the coaches, and the gay equestrians, and he himself riding in their midst. How was it possible that that aged, melancholy lady in mourning, who stood that day by the wayside, could hold him back? It was like a waking fever-dream.

"Erich! your mother!" he cried again; and then said, as he embraced his friend:

"Erich, I will stay with you! But now you must help me, or I shall be taken away without you."

"You should not be disobedient to your parents, but now you have a duty to me as well as to them; you must not leave me, as I will not leave you."

It was only after a hard struggle, that the parents could be brought to consent to leave Erich and Roland at the Villa. Frau Ceres was the first to yield, but Sonnenkamp continued his opposition, and Roland was in continual perplexity. The wish again arose in his mind that his father would remain inflexible and Erich be prevailed upon to accompany them.

Erich took Sonnenkamp aside and told him that, in his opinion, it would be ruinous to withdraw Roland from the path which he had voluntarily selected: the boy had hitherto been hindered from being steady in his pursuits by sheer idle distractions. He said further, that although it would give him great pain to do so, yet he would feel obliged to leave the house if Roland should go to the baths. He had not told this to Roland, for Roland should never think of the possibility of their separation. He then asked Sonnenkamp to use a little strategy, which, in such a case, would be by no means inexcusable. He requested him to tell Roland that he had been testing his stability, and was glad that he had stood the trial—he had hoped that Roland would make the proposal to remain at home with Erich, and then he would have agreed to it.

Sonnenkamp was vexed, but nevertheless acceded to this proposition, and Roland found himself rejected on the one hand and bound by his promise on the other.

On the next day, the parents set out for the baths. Erich and Roland accompanied them to the station, and just as the approach of the train was signalled, Sonnenkamp took his son aside and said to him:

"My boy, if you find it too hard, jump into the cars and leave the Doctor alone. Believe me, he won't run away; I've a golden whistle that charms everybody. Pluck up courage, my son!"

"Father, is this another proof of my steadiness?"

"You're a brave boy," replied Sonnenkamp, surprised and touched.

The train arrived. A great number of black trunks, studded with yellow nails, was put aboard, while Joseph and Lutz showed their surpassing abilities as marshals of the journey. Trunks, chests, boxes, bottles, and bundles were placed in the first-class carriage, in which sat Sonnenkamp, Frau Ceres, and Miss Perini. Roland was kissed once more, and his father whispered something in his ear. The train rolled away, and Erich and Roland were left standing alone on the steps.

They went silently to the Villa. Roland looked pale, every drop of blood had receded from his face. They entered the grounds; how quiet and deserted it all seemed!

When they had alighted from the carriage, Roland took Erich's hand, and said:

"We two are alone in the world now."

What was to be done at such a time?

A storm-wind rushed through the park, shaking the trees and making the blossoms dance and whirl in the air: the river cast high waves on the shore. A storm was brewing.

Erich hastily had the carriage made ready again, and entered it with Roland, who asked:

"Where are we going?"

Erich assured him that he would show him something wonderful. They rode along the road where the wind shook the nut-trees till they roared. Overhead lightning flashed and thunder rolled.

"Where are we going?" Roland asked again.

"We're going to school with Franklin. I can show you now how lightning is made prisoner." They rode swiftly back to the station.

The telegraph operator saluted Erich very cordially, and Erich showed his pupil how the electric current was collected in a delicate little glass box, where a blue spark jumped about and disappeared in the conductor which was connected with the wires. At every flash a report could be heard in the feeder, and at the same instant a little blue spark appeared and vanished.

Erich was delighted at being able to show this to his pupil, and the operator was very ready to give all the information needed. He told how sometimes, while standing near the conductor during a storm, one would be seized by a nameless fear; how unintelligible words would come over the wires; and how he had once been struck by the lightning. He showed the manner in which the electricity was led to the ground, and said that sometimes the feeders would be cut in two as if by a delicate file.

All light had been excluded, and only the blue sparks could be seen, at which Roland looked with childish curiosity. Here was a good opportunity to explain the *modus operandi* of the telegraph, and Roland said:

"Even if Franklin did not foresee this, he was the first to chain the lightning. Do you suppose that he knew what would be the result?"

Erich tried to make Roland understand that all action, all investigation and thought, are but a vast unity, a continuous, self-promulgating revelation; and there, in that dark room, while the blue sparks appeared and vanished, and where the three sat, scarcely speaking above their breath, a feeling of devotion entered the boy's soul and elevated it far above the petty affairs of common life. The separation from his parents, the pleasure which had seemed so enticing to him had vanished, as if he had ascended to a star far above the earth.

The storm had ceased, but the rain was yet falling, and as the windows were opened, Roland said, as he looked out in the night and pressed Erich's hand:

"Might not one think that the soul moves in the human body as the electric spark moves in the wires?"

Erich did not answer. He saw that the enigma of life was presenting itself to the boy's mind; he must ponder it for himself.

Erich could not and dared not help him yet. But this subtle question gave assurance that the boy could be brought into the higher life; he had subdued the desire for distracting amusement, and had given himself to something that could not be rendered subservient to his will.

The operator gave a description of the singular way in which Sonnenkamp had looked and acted at the office on the night of Roland's disappearance. He told Erich in a low voice that he had been afraid of the man, and in spite of the large sum promised him if he would remain and watch all night, he had pretended that it was inconsistent with his duties, whereas the real reason was that he would not be alone with Sonnenkamp for all the money in the world.

Erich noticed that Roland had heard the latter part of this discourse, despite the low tone in which it had been spoken; so he said laughingly, that a man who is always manipulating the nervous system of the earth is very apt to become nervous himself.

The operator agreed with this, and knew of a very curious incident bearing on the point.

As Erich entered the waiting-room with Roland, he noticed how quick the boy was to remark any ridiculous peculiarities in men. He had paid so much attention to the singularities of the operator, that he was now able to give very skilful imitations of them. Without expressing any decided objection to this, Erich sought to impress on his mind the fact that men whose professions place them on the territory which separates manual from scientific labor, as apothecaries, leechers, lithographers, photographers and telegraphers, easily acquire a sort of double nature, in which the artisan and scientific man are both represented. Telegraphing engenders a certain sensitiveness and nervous quickness, for it forces one to be always on the *qui vive*, and places his mind in a perpetual state of tension.

Erich tried to explain all this to his pupil, for he wished to instil into his mind that sense of justice which is the basis of all perception of psychological truths, but he soon recurred to the wonderful things they had just seen, in order to impress them firmly upon the boy's mind; and he succeeded.

The stars were shining brightly again as they rode toward home. They had been contemplating the mysterious primitive force of the world.

Erich could not help fancying that he had awakened in the soul of his pupil emotions like those which, of old, the people of the desert must have felt on the evening of the day in which the Godhead revealed itself to them amid the thunders and lightnings of Sinai;—that he felt as those thousands must have felt—as though the earth had been created anew.

Erich hardly knew what he said as they rode homeward thus amid the cool air, in the starry night; but they both—the boy as well as the man—were filled with holy thoughts, and when they reached home neither wished to speak, and they silently bade each other good-night. Is the light in the soul of man a mysterious electric spark which cannot be detained for an instant, but flashes out in a resolution or an action and then vanishes? When all is calm and no storm vexes the sky, we send at will our messages over the wires; but when the great, eternal, and unconquerable powers speak, the word of man ceases, and the sparks flash of their own accord along the wires. Chaos speaks the Incomprehensible.

There will come a time when thou wilt no longer be lord of thy pupil's inner life—when the all-moving powers let loose shall rule within his soul and accomplish that for which they were destined. What then?

Nothing is sure for all time. Now thou must be content to accomplish the duty of thy day, silently and strong.

CHAPTER XI.

THE VINE BUDS AND BEARS.

ALL is quiet amid the vine-hills; there are no longer men between the green rows called "Zeilen," for the vines which have hitherto been allowed to grow free are now bound up, so that the blossoms may not be destroyed by the wind. The buds have not yet appeared, but a soft, sweet fragrance fills the air. Now the stock needs the quiet sunshine of day and the soft breath of night. The blossom must become fruit; but the fire and seasoning and all the strength shall not come till the autumn months. When the blossom has developed, then storm and wind may come—the fruit is strong and sure of its future worthy end.

Erich and Roland wandered hand-in-hand through the country; their way did not lead to men. How quiet it was in the village! how deserted the scattered country-houses seemed!

Bella, Clodwig, and Prancken had gone to Gastein, the Major to Teplitz, the Justice with his wife and daughter, to Kissingen. No one but the Doctor had remained at his post; and he was alone, for his wife had gone to visit her daughter and other relatives.

Even before Erich had heard of the proposed trip to the baths, or had known that he would be left alone with Roland, he had determined to avoid everything likely to distract his pupil, and every temptation to enter upon other pursuits; he wished to ally himself exclusively and implicitly to Roland.

They were now inseparable companions from morning till night.

Only he who lives day after day with Nature, knows all the fitful changes of Her light and shade; and only he who lives alone with one man, knows and understands how suddenly everything within him is lighted up, and how his character is newly illumined and more clearly defined. Erich noticed that Roland occasionally thought of the pleasure and distraction of the baths, and was obliged to conquer himself in order to remain within his settled round of duties. Something within him yet revolted and resisted; but Erich knew that this was only the intractability of the unbroken horse, who will yet be proud of the bit and bridle against which he now rebels.

Innumerable elements are busied with a growth; they move, form, and pour in upon it: man chooses and directs that which moulds itself, but he cannot control the action of the powers which he has used.

Erich employed three different elements with his pupil. They read steadily at the Life of Franklin, for it was desirable that Roland should view a whole man from every point. Roland was yet too young to comprehend the political life into which Franklin gradually entered; but it would be well for him to learn to aspire toward that higher field of action; and Erich well knew that no one can comprehend the power which the half-understood has over a young mind. The White House at Washington became, in Roland's imagination, like the Acropolis at Athens, or the Capitol at Rome, and the boy often expressed a wish to make a pilgrimage to it.

It was difficult for the boy to fix his attention upon the founding of the American republic, and the establishment of its constitution; but he was obliged to persevere. Erich selected for particular remark, Bancroft's History of America.

Then they read Plutarch's Life of Crassus, and afterward Longfellow's Song of Hiawatha. The impression made by this poem was so great, as almost to obliterate his previous reading, for in it the New World has enshrined its heroic and romantic age of Indian life, in such a manner as to make one imagine that the poem was not written by a single man, but the whole poetic spirit of the people. The planting of the maize is a mythological picture, not excelled in vigor and life by the mythologists of antiquity. Hiawatha invents the sail, makes the stream navigable, and annihilates sickness; but Roland was most impressed by Hiawatha's fast, and the feverish, world-forgetting life of self-devotion that is shown in it.

"No one but a man could do that!" cried Roland.

"Do what?" inquired Erich.

"No one but a man could fast—voluntarily renounce food."

From this dreamland of the past, which must necessarily yield to the world of reality as civilization progresses, they returned to the history of the founding of the great American republic. Franklin, who again made his appearance, seemed to Roland the central point of the record, even surpassing Jefferson, who not only first clearly enunciated the doctrine of the eternal and inalienable rights of man, but also made them the basis on which to build up the life of a government. Roland and Erich studied together, and saw how this "Robinsonade" on a large scale—as Friedrich Kapp calls it—was made the basis of a civilized government; but that miserable weakness and timidity which dared not at once aboilsh slavery, presented a difficult subject for contemplation.

"Do you think that negroes are men like us?" asked Roland.

"Undoubtedly; they speak and think as we do."

"I heard once that they can't learn mathematics," said Roland, interrupting him.

"That's new to me, and is evidently a mistake."

Erich would enter no further into the subject. He did not wish to cast blame on Sonnenkamp, who had once owned a large plantation worked by slaves; it was sufficient that the boy had begun to question.

Nothing better could have happened to Erich and Roland, than that they should learn something together. The Architect, a man skilled in his profession, and fortunate in having been permitted to work out such a beautiful undertaking while yet so young, was communicative and instructive. The castle, like so many others in the Rhine country, had been destroyed by the barbarous acts of the soldiers of Louis XIV., just one hundred years before the French Revolution. One of the old principal towers still had remains of Roman masonry—gutter-walls—as the Architect called them.

"What is a gutter-wall?" asked Roland.

The Architect explained that it consisted of pieces of quarry-stone arranged in layers, which were built with a space between them into which stones were thrown irregularly, and mortar afterward poured on these stones to cement them. Only one-third of the tower was of this nature, two-thirds being solid masonry.

Since that time, the whole neighborhood had used the castle as a quarry; and the corners especially had suffered, for they were of the best stone. It was entirely overgrown by shrubbery, the barracks had entirely disappeared, and the castle itself, which had formerly been a Roman stronghold, had been rebuilt in the style of the tenth century. Only very little which was characteristic could be gathered from a drawing in the archives; but from individual stones and angles much could yet be concluded in regard to the form of the building, and the Architect showed them how he was now building it, and he was particularly pleased at having discovered the fountain, out of which had been taken, as he said, "a lot of stuff and rubbish."

It was very interesting to Roland to see a man so completely wrapped up in his profession, and master of it; he followed with delight the process of restoring the building, and both he and Erich regarded it as a pleasant reward after the completion of their day's study, to be instructed by the Architect, and even to be allowed occasionally to render him assistance. It was a favorite dream of Roland that one day he might live here alone in the castle which he had helped to build.

It was by no means accidental that Erich and Roland came to the castle every Saturday evening when the masons and other laborers received their wages. On that day the workmen left their work an hour earlier than usual. The barber came from the village and shaved the masons, who then washed themselves at the fountain: the baker's wife came too with bread to sell. The workmen would gradually assemble under the shelter of a little cottage which had been built for temporary use; and Roland would sometimes stand in the room among the overseers and catch such words as these:

"Your wages are so and so much."

He saw the toil-hardened hands receive their money. Sometimes he would stand outside of the cottage among the workmen, or a little apart from them, and watch their actions and words,—especially those of the mortar-boys, who were about as old as he, and to whom he would always speak kindly when they saluted him. Most of them had under their arms loaves of bread wrapped in cloths. They walked to the villages where they lived; and sometimes singing could be heard in the distance.

Erich knew that in allowing Roland to become acquainted with this sort of life, he was acting in opposition to Sonnenkamp's wishes, for he had once heard him say: "A man who intends to build a castle should not know all the wagoners and stone-breakers in the quarry."

And yet Erich considered it his duty to let Roland have unimpeded intercourse with this hitherto unknown life. He noticed the expression of Roland's large eyes, as they sat together on a projection of the castle amid the fragrance of thyme, and looked out over hill and valley, and heard the bells ring for the coming Sabbath. He was happy, for he knew that eyes that had looked so pitifully on toil-stained hands, and followed so earnestly the path of the weary laborers as they returned to their homes, would never look coldly on the sorrows of others. Thus were the seeds of moral and intellectual life sown in the youth's soul, and Erich carefully fostered their growth.

One evening they were sitting together near the castle. The sun had gone down, and only the glory of departed sunset lingered on the hills; the castle with its blue slate-roofs seemed hovering in a dream amid the mists of coming night, and Roland said:

"I wonder how it seems in America—there are no such castles there."

Erich repeated to Roland the following verses of Goethe:

America, du hast es besser Als unser Continent, das alte; Hast keine verfallene Schlösser, Und keine Basalte. Dich stört nicht im Innern Zu lebendiger Zeit Unnützes Erinnern Und vergeblicher Streit. Benutzt die Gegenwart mit Glück! Und wenn nun Eure Kinder dichten, Bewahre sie ein gut Geschick Vor Ritter-, Raüber-, und Gespenstergeschichten!	America, thou art more fortunate than our continent—the old. Thou hast no ruined castles and pillars. In thy living age, no useless memories and vain struggles weigh upon thee. Use the present wisely, and when thy children shall sing of thee, may good destiny preserve them from legends of knights, robbers, and ghosts.

Roland learned this by heart, and wished to know more of Goethe.

In their quiet walks Erich often repeated the poetry of Goethe, in which not a mere human soul, but Nature herself seems to find expression.

The lofty spirit of Goethe was now united to the calm and considerate judgment of Franklin, to Hiawatha and Crassus.

Roland was greatly influenced by the elemental power of the master-spirits in whose sphere he lived. When he and Erich were in the right mood, and fitting occasion was offered, Erich could—thanks to his retentive memory—furnish Roland with extracts from the classical poets of antiquity as well as those of his own Fatherland. This revealed to Roland the twofold basis of all life, and made him long for that which is genuine and abiding.

One day Erich and Roland sat by the border of a field, and saw a hare, which would nibble, and then run and nibble again, and Roland said:

"Timid little hare! and why shouldn't he be timid, when he has no means of attack or defence, and can do nothing but run away?"

Erich nodded, and the boy continued:

"Why is the dog the enemy of the hare?"

"What do you mean?"

"I mean that it's very easy to see why dogs and foxes are enemies, for they can both bite; but the dog hates the hare and runs after it, and the poor little thing can do nothing but jump and run. I don't understand that."

With all his learning, Erich often found himself in a predicament from which there was no escape but conjecture, so he said:

"I think that in its wild state the dog finds its chief food in destroying harmless and unprotected animals, as the fox does too. The dog is nothing but a tame cousin of the fox, and cultivation has changed his nature only so far that he kills hares but does not eat them. Animals that live on plants live in the open air; beasts of prey live in dens."

The boy did not speak for some time; then he said suddenly:

"Wonderful!"

"What is wonderful?"

"You'll laugh at me, but I've just been thinking"—and a pleasant smile passed over his face, dimpling cheek and chin—"yes, it is so. Wild animals have no regular meal-time, they eat all day long; but we men have accustomed dogs to eat only at stated times."

"Certainly," replied Erich. "When civilization begins, men learn to divide their life into regular intervals of time."

Then Erich, without long or perplexing details, told his pupil what it is to measure time, and to bring the universe, even the whole starry heavens, into rhythm with the life of man.

It will hardly be believed, but it is nevertheless true, that from the time of this conversation, which, beginning with the small and readily comprehensible reached toward the limits of the universe, Erich and Roland determined on having stated hours for study; the boy would have no more unregulated time. What had formerly seemed tyranny to him was now law which he himself had made.

But a few weeks had passed before Roland relinquished his dearest comrades for the sake of Erich. It was quite natural that they should be accompanied by the dogs in their wanderings over field and hill and to the castle. Erich was always ready to agree to every request of his pupil, but there was always a troublesome companion from whom it was difficult to become separated, for Roland never went out without taking one of his dogs with him, and it was impossible to fix the boy's attention, for his eyes were continually wandering involuntarily to his dog. The dog would always be looking at his master, wanting notice, and the boy's thoughts would be jumping about like his dog. It was with some difficulty that Erich succeeded in persuading him to leave the animals at home. He did not directly order him to do as he wished, but often said, when asked certain questions, that it was impossible to answer them while one had to be thinking about what the dog was doing, and watching him jump. When Erich had repeated this process several times, Roland left the dogs at home, and knew from the way in which his questions were answered, how Erich was rewarding him for his self-denial. Erich led his pupil into all the domains of science, but was careful not to give him too much at once. He would often promise to explain to him at a future time, and encourage him to follow his own thoughts.

In the vineyard grow the clustering grapes in which are collected and transformed all the elements wafted in the air or lying quietly in the ground; but more important than all, is the undulating current that bears to the fruit an imponderable strength, a mysterious fragrance. Day and night the fruit is growing; sunshine and cooling dew, rain and storm, and even hail come upon it, and yet the plant steadily develops to its maturity.

Who can say that all which Erich fostered in Roland grew and bloomed at one particular day or hour? And yet unintermitting persistence is the mysterious and yet obvious force which fashions life.

Every morning and evening, Roland and Erich were present when the lawns were irrigated, and the trees and flowers were watered, and the aid which they thus gave to another growth than theirs—for they would sometimes assist the gardeners—gave them a feeling of satisfaction; they seemed to be doing acts of benevolence in thus furthering the growth of shrub and flower, and aiding the day and night in their task of refreshing the earth.

Roland once said, timidly, "Will you tell me why thorns grow on the stems of roses?"

"Why?" replied Erich. "Certainly not that men may prick themselves. Bees and butterflies do not get hurt by the thorns of the rose, nor by the prickles of the thistle; they draw honey and pollen from the calyx of the plant. Nature has not directed her powers with reference to the muscular system of men, nor generally in such a way as to injure men. Everything exists for itself, and for us only so far as we know how to use and enjoy it. But, Roland," said he, thinking that the boy did not quite understand this, "your question was badly put. 'Why?' 'For what purpose?' These are questions for us, not for rosebushes."

The park and garden were in bloom. All was made ready, and in waiting for its master's return. And in Roland, too, had a garden been planted and fostered. What thought will one day be the master of this garden? and will these fruits and flowers refresh their owner's fellow-beings?

The nightingales had become silent in the park, the sensuous odor of the blossoms had fled; everywhere was silent growth.

And although the days were passed in intellectual activity, in the quiet nights, Roland and Erich wandered together among the hills, and looked at the moonlit landscape, where, on one side, the mountains cast their shadows, and the sharply-defined moonlight slept among the vineyards and shimmered in the stream, and the stars glittered overhead. An atmosphere of silent rapture lay upon the landscape, and the wanderers breathed it silently, hardly caring to speak. These were hours of deepest blessedness, during which the soul wished for nothing but to breathe, see, dream with open eyes, and be conscious of the fulness of the nature within, and of the power silently yet mightily streaming upon the soul from without.

The vine draws from the earth, draws from the air, and at such hours there ripens in the soul both that which it draws by its own ineffable powers from itself, and that which streams in from Nature which environs it.

CHAPTER XII.

PLEASURES AND PAINS OF THE CHASE.

ERICH was very careful not to change Roland's naturally bold and determined disposition into one that would be sentimental and brooding. During the intervals of study, he gave the boy regular bodily exercise in fencing, vaulting, riding, swimming, and rowing. It was fortunate for Erich that no other teacher was needed, for, by instructing his pupil in such exercises he obtained new power over him, and was always with him.

With Fassbender's aid he also taught Roland surveying in the open air. Fassbender was very skilful at this, but had a certain cringing manner of dealing with Roland that was very irritating to Erich. Once when he said that he would tell his friend Knopf how industrious and clever Roland had become, the boy shook his head, and was much displeased. It was evident that he did not wish to hear anything more about Knopf; perhaps, too, he remembered something which he did not wish Erich to know.

Erich prepared a shooting-place for Roland. He did not wish to withdraw him from his customary life in the open air, or from his habits of wandering about; but he steadily maintained that outdoor exercise should only be taken *after* mental exertion, never *before*.

One of the principal difficulties which he met, was in attempting to moderate Roland's love of hunting. Erich did not desire to entirely suppress it, but to bring it within proper bounds. As it was now Summer, the only game was wild rabbits; and the Krischer came to invite Roland to hunt with him. His former teachers had always allowed the boy to go alone with the Krischer; but now Erich accompanied him, and had a new pleasure as they walked through the vine-hills.

Erich was more than usually attentive when he heard the Krischer say that Manna, even when she was a little child, hardly a grown girl, had been not only a bold rider, but had always hunted in company with her father, and was untamable in her wildness. Rose and Thistle had once been her dogs; and even now when anybody said "Manna," the dogs would prick up their ears and look around as if they thought that she was coming.

Erich would willingly have asked how it happened that a young girl who had enjoyed hunting so much, and had been so bold and courageous, should now be living like a penitent in the convent. How incompatible the two pictures seemed!—this one, a girl with a gun and followed by dogs, *that*, a winged apparition. But he was careful not to ask Roland, and acted toward the Krischer as if he had known it all before.

Herr Sonnenkamp had given Roland his two favorite dogs, Rose and Thistle. They were small, but strongly built, with broad breasts and strong spines, and seemed to understand how highly Roland valued them. The smaller of the two, a female, had red chops, and a head that bore the scars of many battles, and kept licking Roland's hands as he told how brave she was, but dropped her head as he remarked that she was not as obedient as her male friend, Thistle. Thistle blinked bashfully at Roland with his bright eyes, as the boy told Erich that he could not govern this dog except by using English words, but that *then* he was very tractable. If he said: "Zurück!" Thistle would look at him as if deaf; but as soon as he cried out, "Go back!" the dog would follow close at his heels.

As they were passing an oak whose branches were within reach, Roland took a twig, and shaking it over the dog, said in English, "Hang!" Thistle sprang into the air, seized the twig with his sharp teeth, and clung to it till Roland told him to let go of it. Rose performed the same trick, and even excelled herself, for she whirled round two or three times as she hung in the air, and then, with a skilful tug, broke the switch and brought it to Roland.

The boy and the dogs were very happy with each other; and the dogs knew where they were going.

When they reached the Krischer's house, the two ferrets were placed in a basket; and when they arrived at the edge of the forest, Roland took the little yellow, snake-like animals out, put muzzles on them and caressed them. They entered the thicket and found fresh burrows. Nets were placed at the opening, the ferrets sent into the hole, and Roland was delighted to see how skilfully Erich fastened the nets with wooden pegs which he made of twigs. Almost as soon as the ferrets entered, a whirring sound was heard, and the rabbits came out into the nets, where the dogs worried them to death.

The ferrets were sent in again, and the huntsmen placed themselves before the opening and shot. Roland missed--Erich hit.

Erich would not say anything in regard to the cruelty of netting the animals, and letting the dogs bite at their eyes and tear them till the poor things gave their last gasp; for he himself was sportsman enough to disregard this. The Krischer lightened this cruelty, by continually scolding at the devilish rabbits that nibble and destroy the young vines, and the best of the crops. He gave a very comical imitation of a peasant rushing about with a stick after a rabbit, and shrieking: "I've got ye at last, ye damned beast."

Rose was sent into the next hole, and soon a bark like that of a fox was heard underground. Erich himself was excited, and they all stood still, watching. Then Thistle was placed in the hole; and he barked too, but no fox appeared. Rose came out presently with her muzzle covered with blood, looked at the sportsmen, and ran back again. They heard a whimpering and barking; and at last the dogs came out covered with blood, but still no fox appeared. They waited a long time, but it would not come out.

"They've choked him," said the Krischer triumphantly. "We won't fight him any more."

Roland was filled with tenderest sympathy for the dogs, but the Krischer comforted him by saying that the wounds would soon heal. Roland told the Krischer that he did not understand how the dogs could bite the fox to death, when the fox had such sharp teeth. The Krischer shrugged his shoulders, but Erich said:

"Foxes bite sharp, but don't hold on long."

Roland looked at Erich in surprise. This was a man who could teach him everything!

All Erich's learning had probably not impressed the boy so much as this one remark.

The ferrets were again sent into a fresh burrow, but only one came out: the other had disappeared. They waited a long time, and then left the Krischer to watch for it, but the second ferret was nowhere to be found. Roland was inconsolable for the loss of the animal, which was so clever and which he had tamed so well. The boy walked silently beside Erich as he told him that now the animal's liberty would be of no use to it, for, being muzzled, it would die of hunger. Suddenly Roland opened the basket, took out the remaining ferret, placed it on the ground, and then deliberately shot it. He left the dead animal lying in the forest, and without saying a word walked with Erich toward home. He looked long and sorrowfully at his gun; Erich knew that it would be long before its report would be heard again.

But from this time forward, Roland was sullen and silent, a certain dulness and unwillingness to be ruled took possession of him; he was not precisely disobedient, but seemed to take no interest in his pursuits, and often looked coldly at Erich.

Erich did not know what to do, and for several days was deeply troubled. He felt that he was no longer new to Roland, and that the restlessness natural to the wealthy, who soon tire of that which presents no novelty, added to the fact that Roland had passed most of his life in travelling, was engendering ennui and almost disgust. It was Erich's task to instruct him in such a way that each new day would be greeted with pleasure, even though it brought nothing new, and was simply a repetition of yesterday.

One day the Krischer came, and taking Erich aside, said to him:

"I've found the ferret that ran away that day."

"Where is it?"

"Out in the woods starved to death because of its muzzle, and half-eaten up by ants."

"We will not tell Roland about it."

"Certainly not. Do you know what the ferret's name was?"

"No."

"Its name was Knopf. He only called it Dominie when you were around. It often angered me, for although Herr Knopf is superstitious, awfully superstitious, he's the best man in the world. He's spoiled Roland with his old fogy ghost-stories. Roland told me as a secret, that when he was on the journey that brought you back by main force, he saw a ghost early in the morning. It came to him in the woods, and was a princess out of the story—as stupid superstitious people call it . . . A pretty girl with her hair all in ringlets, who spoke English . . . I wonder now, do ghosts speak English? Herr Knopf put that in his head. I don't want to say anything against Herr Knopf; he's a good man, and teaches poor children for nothing, and does a great deal of good—but belief in ghosts and such stuff, won't do. Haven't you noticed how bad Roland looks? I believe that it's all owing to his faith in ghosts. Drive it all out of his head if you can."

Erich did not believe that this was the cause of Roland's long-continued ill-humor; but it troubled him to think that Roland had preferred the Krischer to him as a confidant in this matter

But he would not intrude himself on the boy, or disturb him; he would wait patiently till the cloud passed away.

CHAPTER XIII.

NEW WINE, NEW MUSIC, AND NEW GLORY.

THE Doctor had called now and then, but only for a brief quarter of an hour at a time. He praised Erich for having taken such good care of Roland, and for having devoted himself so exclusively to him; he didn't mean, either, to interrupt in the least, the genial flow of their daily intercourse by any intrusion of himself.

But as he was now at hand, Erich held fast to him and expressed his anxiety about Roland, who was looking so pale that Erich feared he was getting ill.

"So, so!" cried the Doctor. "Has it come already? I'm glad that it has broken out so soon and so unmistakably."

"What now? What's the matter?"

"It's all right—all as it should be, my dear young friend. Simply a cold; I generally call it the May-cold. But be careful! Roland was born a hunter, and I feared you were trying to make a collector of pebbles or beetles out of him. I understand you, you would bring him to take a deeper hold upon life; but there lies the danger too—he may take it too seriously, while the best thing for our life is, that we take it easily."

Erich agreed with him; he asserted that he was far from seeking to make a model youth of Roland—one who is evidently just what he ought to be. The Doctor went on:

"What's the matter with our stripling now is, as I said, the May-cold. In every new situation, notwithstanding all the happiness in life—a change of calling, marriage, in which one's former independence is given up after a few weeks which are the blossoming-time—a chilly spell comes on, just as out there in nature in the May season. It's said that it comes from the Alps, from the melting of the glaciers; perhaps it is the melting of glaciers in the soul. At any rate, it's the last battle of Winter with Summer—a battle of the spirit of loneliness with the social spirit. Don't be concerned about it. Let these chill saint-days pass over the youth, and all will be well again. Give way to him freely at this time; it's the feeling of compulsion that's aroused in him. But I'll leave him a medicine. He must be made to think that he's not quite well; that will help him and you too, for then you can indulge him with freedom: a sick person may be permitted to be wilful, and one may give in to him without fear."

The Doctor now came more frequently. He proposed to Erich, in response to Weidmann's invitation, to take Roland on a visit of some length to Mattenheim; the varied aspect of a social life, bristling with industrial activity in all directions, would freshen up both teacher and pupil. Erich answered that he did not feel at liberty to leave for so many days the house that had been intrusted to his care. The Doctor agreed with him; he bethought him, too, that it would be better for Roland first to learn to feel more at home on the Rhine.

After this, Erich and Roland frequently accompanied the Doctor on his rounds, and both of them were thus brought into more intimate contact with the social life of the Rhineland. The Doctor declared that it was not without a good object that he thus led them into the home-circles of the country, into its inner life; he held it to be a right and proper aim of life to seek to make the best possible wine. Roland might and ought to do that. To offer to the world a good article of wine was the same as giving it a beautiful work of art. And if a strong attachment for the Rhineland were implanted in Roland, noble results would flow from it, especially if he were brought at the same time into association with the house of Weidmann.

The Doctor was an excellent guide; he knew every house, and knew its occupants thoroughly, and he weighed the character of each in nicely-poised scales—he brought out the shadows as well as the lights. From house to house animating pictures were presented, and from cellar to cellar refreshing draughts. They learned to drink as the vagrants—on the march.

"Much is said," observed the Doctor, "about the decline of the race; it seems to be a long sickness, but at any rate not a very dangerous one. The people fight their way and drink their way along; and so it has ever been and ever will be. If the sun is very hot, one must drink; if the weather is disagreeable and damp, one must refresh himself with a good drink."

They turned aside to a house where the statue of the Virgin Mary, with a lantern in her hand, was displayed.

"Up there," said the Doctor, "it is an actual fact that pure wine is made; the occupant of this house supplies the churches and the heads of the church with sacramental wine. The father of the man is a very famous embroiderer of church vestments; his brother is a respectable painter of sacred subjects. If the common people do turn their religion to their private gain, it is nevertheless a sacred thing with them. The main point is, we must not asperse the honesty of the believers; they should therefore give us unbelievers the credit of honesty as well."

Farther on they came to another house, and the Doctor said:

"There dwelt a lusty rogue, who has, in fact, left a ghost in the house. He was a wily old owl—a mason by trade. Now, it's known that he made himself a little chest at the cabinet-maker's, and fitted a key to it at the locksmith's, and that while he was laying up the walls of his cellar, when he was alone, he hid it in the wall and stoned it in. It's thought that great sums of money are concealed in it; and yet, perhaps he was rogue enough to put an empty box into the wall, so as to cheat posterity. The people don't know whether to tear down the house in search of the box or not: an empty box may be found, and then the house is torn down."

The Doctor always gave his observations about men and things such a turn as would make them useful to Roland.

The Doctor saluted a crafty-looking old man, who sat before his house, very familiarly. The man asked the Doctor whether he would not have another drop of the "black cat;" and the Doctor followed him with Erich and Roland to the cellar, where they drank a fiery wine from a cask upon which, in fact, the black cat was couched. Of course it was only an imitation, with glowing glass eyes. The old man was very jovial, and striking glasses with Roland, he said:

"Yes, yes! We're all mere bunglers, compared with your father."

He praised Sonnenkamp's hardness and cunning with evident relish, and Erich looked anxiously toward Roland, who meanwhile seemed but little affected by the old man's words. As they went away, the Doctor said:

"There's your true peasant, for your true peasant is always altogether too much of a self-seeker; he's always thinking only of his own advantage—the rest of the world may go to ruin. Such a man was the old countryman yonder. When his neighbors, who were working along in a small way, were hard-pressed, he lent them money; and when a bad year came, suddenly foreclosed upon them without pity, so that the hillside vineyards which they had cultivated were brought to public sale, and now he's in possession of the largest stock of vines in the neighborhood. Ah, he's a cunning old wretch!"

This story made a much different impression upon Erich than upon Roland, for the latter took the roguery of the man to be a matter of course. Erich called the Doctor aside to question him, for he did not understand how he could be so friendly with the old man; he asked, too, whether the man was respected in the neighborhood. The answer was given with emphasis, for wealth gives respectability in the country.

They entered the house of the gauger, who was truly "hail fellow well met" with the whole country round. He led them through his cellar, and made them drink many a drop of wine. The gauger was fond of telling good stories, which were not quite fit for the ears of a youth, but the Doctor knew how to lead him off readily from his bent. The gauger always had near at hand a loaf of white bread, which he called his sponge. "With straw," said he, "our vines are made fast, and with this bread, which is grown upon the straw, I tame down the effect of wine. Water wastes one away, as the nun said when she washed her veil, and then ate a whole loaf of bread. It was reckoned that the gauger, in the course of his life thus far, had drank seventy large casks of wine, but he asserted that this was laying it too mildly on him. "I've drunk," he said, "far more."

It was a jovial, lusty life with which Erich and Roland were brought into contact; and when they returned to their close work, the consciousness was still in the background of their souls, that they were living in a joyous land, in which existence flowed along lightly.

It was mid-summer; then came the cold, wintry, blustering days, when one begins to doubt of the permanence of all things, and yet the Summer is not at an end; it must get warm again. The nightingale became mute—she had not ceased altogether to sing—she still often warbled a few tones, as from memory; the thin notes of the linnet or the deep short calls of the blackbird were more often heard. The trees showed that the Summer had reached its height, and that it was now receding; the woods had attained their growth for the year, and now too the gush of song was hushed in them, only the indefatigable blackcap chirped, and the magpie chattered.

Erich and Roland often rowed out upon the Rhine, singing as they went; and Erich was pleased when Roland said: "Yes, it is time. Man can sing at all seasons of the year, if he's in the humor for it."

Erich nodded; he felt that a sense of art and of the superior freedom of man was springing up in Roland: he said, they would now leave home for a few days on some little trip. He proposed to Roland two plans: they would stray off either to Herr Weidmann's, of whom so much had been said, or to the great musical festival which was to be held at the garrison-town. Gayly decked boats bearing the singers were stemming the current, and were saluted at every turn of the river with discharges of artillery. Roland begged to go to the festival, and he asked to travel a part of the way afoot; for he wanted—and this time by Erich's side—again to see the road which he had wandered over in the night.

They went on their way in good spirits, and Roland was very full of talk, and related to Erich all that happened to him. They came to the woods; Roland told him that he had here fallen asleep, and had a wonderful dream. He blushed as he said this, and Erich did not ask him what the dream was. Roland was silent and went toward the woods.

"There it is! There it is!" he cried abruptly. "There is my porte-monnaie! God be praised, it was not stolen from me. Come, let's go to the village where the hostler is whom I suspected. I'll give him all the money."

They went to the village: the hostler was no longer there; he had been drafted into the military service.

Roland was very sorry, and wrote down the name of the man in his note-book.

They went on through the country, which still overflowed with the lusty life of summer: they came to the railroad and were carried on their way to the garrison-town. There everything was dressed up in gay bunting. From all directions, by boats and by the cars, the singers came—men and women—singing loudly, and heartily welcomed, and Erich, pleased with the sight, said to his pupil:

"Look! This is all ours. Neither Greeks nor Romans had such festivals as this, nor any other nation but us Germans."

The throng of people spent the night in town, and in the morning they all assembled—hundreds of singers, men and women, and a great mass of listeners—in the gayly-decked festal hall, where on work-days the fruit-market was held. Then there ran a vague murmur among the crowd, the singers shook their heads and gave signs of anxiety; and among the listeners there was a wavy motion and a kind of seething process.

A man of noble voice and of tried skill was suddenly taken sick.

"Look there!" said Roland; "there sit some nuns; and these are the pupils, all dressed as they are in Manna's convent. Oh, I wish Manna were here!"

Erich said to Roland:

"Stay here, I'll see if I can give any help. I depend upon it that you will not leave this spot."

He went up among the singers on the platform: he placed himself beside the Conductor, and spoke earnestly with him. The man kept passing to and fro before them while they were talking together. Suddenly all eyes were turned toward Erich, and a buzzing and a murmuring went through the assembly. Ferdinand the Conductor raised his baton; his glance, which inspired and governed everything like a charm, was bright and pleasant. Silence ensued, and in a winning voice he said:

"Our baritone is unfortunately taken ill; this gentleman here —he is unwilling to have his name given—offers very obligingly to undertake the solos of our sick friend. You will join with us in gratitude and grant him your kind indulgence, as he has not rehearsed with us."

General applause was the response.

The choral singing began, and created deep excitement in the soul of Roland. Then Erich stood up—all hearts beat. But at the first tone he sent forth, every singer and every listener looked to his neighbor and nodded. It was a voice so full, so deep, so penetrating, that every one listened with suspended breath. And when he had ended, such a storm of applause broke forth that the hall seemed about to fall in.

Erich sat down, the chorus and the other solos followed; but he rose again and sang a second and a third time, and his voice grew stronger, and seemed to penetrate all hearts with increasing power.

But among the thousands who heard him, and felt the echoes of that manly voice in their souls, how was it with Roland as he listened?

The choruses swelled up like towering waves of the sea, and as Erich sang, it was as if he stood upon a high ship and guided and governed all; and this voice seemed to Roland so lovingly near him, and yet so high above him! The youth experienced that delicious, dreamy pleasure which music brings, steeping the listener deep in his own life, and bearing him along amid dreams, until sunk in delicious melancholy he loses all consciousness of self.

Roland wept. Erich's voice bore him up into the invisible world; and then the chorus began anew, and it was as if he was born circling up and up to a heavenly existence.

Roland wanted to tell his neighbor who the man was, for he heard it asked and guessed on all sides; but he said softly to himself:

"Nobody knows him here but me."

Then he turned his eyes again over the cluster of maidens dressed in blue, and now one of them nods to him. Yes, it's she! It's Manna!

He begged those sitting next to him to let him pass through: he wanted to go to his sister, he wanted to tell her who he was who had brought so much happiness to the hearts of all. But he was pointed back to his seat with vehemence; those near him scolded about the bold boy, who was so unruly and wanted to make a disturbance.

Roland kept quiet; he let the pauses slip by, in which he might easily have made his way to Manna.

The oratorio was finished, but the song of jubilee, in which the whole throng participated, and which was to conclude the entertainment, had not yet been given. There was a general cry, that the stranger should give his name.

"His name! His name!" was tossed and shrieked from a thousand lips.

The Conductor bowing pleasantly to Erich, who was hesitating, rose again by his desk, and all cried out:

"Silence!"

Erich rose, and said with a subdued voice:

"My heartfelt thanks. It was in the service of God, in the service of the sacred art that I appeared here, and as I do not wish that the emotion which this work excites in you should be invaded by the sound of a stranger's name, I am reluctant to give you mine."

"Name! Name!" was again the cry from the whole assembly.

"I am called Doctor Dournay."

"A flourish! a flourish of trumpets!" they cried on all sides to the orchestra, and the orchestra sounded a triple flourish, and the entire throng cried out:

"Hurrah for Doctor Dournay!"

Erich was almost torn to pieces; his shoulders were bruised and sore with the hearty slaps they had received. He saw pressing around him those who now recognized him, and those who wanted to know him.

The crowd broke up.

Erich looked around for Roland, but did not find him. He went out upon the courtyard before the music-hall and walked around it: he re-entered the hall; all was noise and confusion, for they were preparing the tables for the feast. He stayed there some time, for he felt sure that Roland had lost himself in the crowd, and would now return thither.

At last Roland came: his cheeks glowed.

"It was she!" he said. "I went with her and her companions to the boat; they are gone already. Oh, Erich, what a grand thing it is that she was present and heard you sing! And she said that you ought not to be so irreligious, when you sing so piously. She told me not to tell you, but she's a little cheat, and really wanted me to tell you. And oh, Erich, Lina the Justice's daughter was among the singers too; and there was the Architect too: they went away arm-in-arm; they knew you at once, but they did not betray you. Oh, Erich, how you did sing! it seemed to me as if you could fly too; I was all the time thinking to myself—now you will spread your wings and fly away."

The youth was in a fever of excitement.

One of the managers of the festival came to them and invited Erich and his brother—as he took Roland to be—to remain to the banquet, and to take a seat beside the conductor of the performance.

Others who knew him came from this side and that; and many strangers wished to become acquainted with him.

A photographer, one of the solo singers, begged Erich, before he went to the table, to let him photograph him;

for all the singers—a hundred or more—would want to have his picture.

Erich thanked them all for their friendly advances, and with the next boat was on his way to the Villa.

Roland had gone to the cabin and was soon fast asleep. Erich sat alone upon the deck, and began to be troubled in mind because he had brought himself out so publicly. But he said to himself: "There are moments when our powers are not our own, and when we cannot determine for ourselves what we shall do. I have done what I was obliged to do."

When they arrived at the station, Roland had to be awakened. He had to be almost carried into the ferry-boat; his wits were so turned about, that he did not seem to catch any recollection of what had passed.

When they had at last landed, Roland said:

"Erich, your name is now known to thousands and thousands of men; you have become very famous."

Roland, who had never taken to singing before, now sang all along the way a melody from the piece they had heard.

At the Villa, letters from Erich's mother at the University city, and others from Sonnenkamp at Vichy, awaited them. Erich's mother wrote that he must not mind it if he should hear the reproach that he had lightly and foolishly sold his genius; people were only vexed, and partly with reason, because he had gone away so—without leave-taking.

Erich laughed; he knew right well that at the black-table, as it is called, of the club-house, where year in and year out the shiny oil-cloth is spread upon the dirty table-cover, people spent their witty phrases on him. It seemed to him incomprehensible that he could ever have thought it possible to spend his little day of life or enjoy the serenity of its evening-hour there.

Sonnenkamp's letter left a quite different impression upon him, for Sonnenkamp authorized Erich, in case he thought it advisable, to set out alone with Roland and come to him at Biarritz.

"It is also gratifying to his father, that you have been received with so much honor; the nuns who accompanied Manna said, of course, it was not judicious in you to come out so publicly."

Erich looked about him with a troubled air. The sense of dependence and servitude came upon him. He had devoted his whole personality to the service of Sonnenkamp, and he must in every act or omission place before himself the question, whether that course will suit his master.

All the rest of the day was strewn with ashes, and instead of the high feelings with which he had before been animated, he now felt a vague sense of depression in his soul.

CHAPTER XIV.

OUR FELLOW-MEN.

AGAIN the days passed on quietly between work and recreation. One day the Krischer came and begged that Roland would make good his promise and show him, for once, the whole Villa from top to bottom.

"What do you wish that for?" asked Erich.

"I would like to see just once what all the rich have, and what they do with so much money."

It was a cunning glance which the Krischer threw out of the corners of his eyes. Erich gave permission. He was about to send a servant with them, but he went himself: he was a little suspicious of the Krischer; he did not like to leave him alone with Roland. He did not know why, but he feared that the manner the Krischer kept constantly bringing forward the distinction between wealth and poverty might confuse Roland's ideas.

They wandered on from floor to floor, and the Krischer, who hardly dared to set down his foot, was always saying, half to himself:

"Yes, yes, all this a man can have for money! What can't a man have for money!"

In the great music-room the Krischer climbed upon the stage and called down to Erich and Roland:

"Captain, will you let me ask a question?"

"Certainly, if I can answer it."

"Tell me truly, and on your honor, what would you do, if you—you are, in fact, a liberal-minded man and a friend of the people—what would you do if you were the owner of this house, and so many millions besides?"

The voice of the Krischer was a sonorous one, and reverberated in the great hall.

"What would you do?" asked the Krischer again. "Don't you know an answer?"

"It's not necessary that I should give you an answer?"

"Well, well; it's all clear enough."

He came down from the stage, and said:

"My business is, as you know, to keep watch over the fields; and so I must keep on the go all night, and it's as if an evil spirit had taken hold of me—I can't get rid of it. I keep thinking and thinking to myself, what would you do, now, if you had so many millions? It makes me almost wild—I can't get rid of it; and, as it seems, you don't know any answer either."

"What would you do?" asked Erich. "Don't you know anything about it?"

"If I had a great deal of money," answered the Krischer, with a cunning laugh, "I'd first beat the district judge to a jelly, if it cost a thousand florins—it's worth it."

"But then—?"

"And then—then I don't know what I'd do."

Erich looked toward Roland. Dismayed, with lustreless eyes and compressed lips, Roland gazed up to him. The *naïveté* of wealth, as Knopf had termed it, seemed disturbed—prematurely stirred up. The mischief could not now be undone, and yet Roland was not ripe enough to make a clear way out.

Erich said to Roland in English, that it was all clear to him, but that it wasn't possible to give a just answer to an uncultivated mind.

"Is his question then a senseless one?" replied Roland in the same language.

Erich was mute, for he dared not, for his own peace and quiet, confuse and taint the frank, pure mind of his pupil.

"He, he!" laughed the half-wit, scornfully; "now I'm clear of it—you have it now. Standing or walking, you will hear the question I've put, in all the halls—all the rooms. Very well! If you ever get an answer, let me into it too."

He put on his hat and went away. For all the rest of that day it was impossible to keep Roland's attention fixed upon any thing. Roland sat in his room alone. Late in the night, when Erich had already been asleep, he heard him in the library-room; he had gone to fetch something.

Erich let him take his way: then he went to the library and found that Roland had taken away the Bible. He probably was reading the parable of the rich young man; the seed which had hitherto lain dormant was springing up.

Erich had thus far worked along, quietly preparing the way, and a power from without had entered—a power that obeys no rule or measure in its approaches—and had awakened that which ought as yet to have slumbered. But there it was. What is all our teaching—our well-laid plans? It is just as out in nature; the buds grow quietly in themselves, and a wild, stormy night comes and breaks them open at once. The wild, stormy night had come upon Roland. Erich could not shield him now.

Early in the morning Roland came to Erich, and said:

"I have a favor to ask."

"Ask it, if I can grant it."

"You can. Let's forget all about our books to-day, and come with me to the mountain."

"Now?"

"Yes! I have set my heart on it. I will myself know all about it. Give me only this one day?"

"What then?"

"I will work as the mason's apprentices do up there in the mountain, and I will eat nothing except what they eat and drink, and will trudge up and down with burdens like them."

Erich went with Roland to the mountain, but on the way he said:

"Roland, your purpose is a good one—I'm glad to see you so earnest in it; but think it over again. You're not undertaking an equal task with those up there; you're undertaking a much harder one, you're not used to it; a day like this will be ten times more fatiguing to you than to them, for you will set about the work under different circumstances. What is a daily habit with them, is new to you and a double burden; and besides, you are not equal to them, for you bring muscles which have been nursed and pampered for a long time; you come from a bed which they know nothing about, you have tenderly-cared-for hands, the strength you bring is altogether unequal to the task. You will not learn in any such way, how those poor people feel who have nothing but their own native strength of limb to sustain their lives with."

Roland stood still and asked—it was an echo from what he had read in the night, for he asked it with trembling voice:

"What shall I do, then, that I may share in the common life of my fellow-men?"

Erich was struck with the tone and manner of these words. He could not tell Roland how happy he felt; for he was at that instant sure in heart, that a soul which has willed what these words of Roland's implied, which has borne and cherished the purpose in itself, can never more go astray, can never lose its hold upon the common heart of men—its sense of a like duty and destiny. He forced himself meanwhile to speak his mind and said:

"My dear Roland"—it was the first time that he had called him dear Roland—"the world is a great system of work, the same task is not laid upon every one; but upon every one is laid the duty to feel as the brother of his fellow-men, and to consecrate himself as the keeper of himself and his brother. What we can do is only to be ready, to hold ourselves ready and to make ourselves ready, as often as the call of our brother-man comes to us, to stand by his side with a helping hand. The task which you will have some day, is not like that of the man yonder who is carrying stones and mortar; your task is a harder one, but also a more blessed one. Come. A time has come when you can see much and learn much."

CHAPTER XV.

OVER THE WORLD AND OVER LIFE.

IT is told in the Bible, how the youthful Isaac went by the side of his father, the patriarch Abraham, to the mountain where the sacrifice was to be made. The boy walked on in silence, thinking to himself, till finally he asked:

"But where is the victim?"

He did not know that it was he himself.

Thus Roland walked by the side of Erich, thinking quietly to himself. He had been willing to sacrifice himself: the sacrifice was refused. What shall now be done?

They sat down on the brow of the hill, where they could look down upon the country lying below. The odor of the thyme was breathed about them. Erich took his pupil's hand in his own, and began:

"It must now come. I could wish that it might come upon you later; you ought to have been, for a long time yet, free from this question, to have approached it from a different direction. But, now, do you know what wealth is?"

"Yes; when one has more than he needs."

"How do men get this 'more than needful,' this superfluity?"

"Through inheritance and labor!"

"Can a beast become rich?"

"I think not."

"Certainly not. Every brute, has and is only what it had and was at the beginning of its existence. But let us go further. Are the men of to-day further advanced than those of old?"

"I think so."

"And will men continue to advance?"

"I hope so."

"By what means?"

"Through knowledge."

"Is knowledge—culture, possible where a man is compelled to work from morning to night in order to satisfy his mere bodily wants?"

"Hardly."

"How then is it possible for a man to labor for his own improvement and that of his kind?"

"By having his time free."

"And can he have this freedom otherwise than by having an accumulation of working-power—that is to say, of riches?"

"It seems not."

"Hold fast, then, to this. Wealth is an accumulation of reserved force, of power which no further labor is required to obtain."

"Wait a little," said Roland. He looked down thoughtfully; at last he said:

"I have it. I understand it now. Go on, please."

Erich continued: "What ought the man to do, who has come into possession of so much power that he is not obliged to work for more."

"I don't know."

"I'll tell you. It is by having more than common necessity requires, that man attains to the adornment and elevation of life, to art and to science. Wealth alone renders the progress of the human race possible. That man should first become rich, is the condition of his higher destiny; not till then does he live through others or for others. Without this accumulation of unexpended power, without riches, there can be none of the higher ideas of life, no adornment of it, no science, no art. Wealth therefore affords both for one's self and one's fellows, the possibility and the assurance of the nurture and increase of the higher fruits of existence. The rich man is not rich through himself; whatever of knowledge, of improved mechanism, of inventive skill, of enterprise, has been brought to bear in order to enable him to possess more than necessity requires—all this progress he owes to others who labored before him. The rich man therefore is, in fact, not rich through his own exertion, nor, indeed, for his own benefit; he is only a manager of the accumulated results of labor, and he must use them so as to make them contribute to the elevation of man. Look yonder, over the outspread fields and the hillsides covered with vineyards! Whose are they? Here and there lie landmarks upon the earth, and the walls of division run as traced by the law, separating mine from thine; no one dares overstep the boundaries of another and enter upon his domain. Yet these scattered stones are to the mind's eye the stones of a temple, the great temple of law and order, which protects mankind. The dividing walls that run through the entire sphere of life are not as evident to the sense, but they are laid no less firmly. You dare not break into that which belongs to another—into the products of his labor and his native vital force. Look! Down there the seaman steers his ship, there the vinedresser rakes the ground so that the roots of his vines may drink up the rains; the bird flies above the stream in quest of food, men pull the oar or dig the soil, and animals fly above the earth or creep along its surface. Then comes the man, a tempting spirit, and speaks: 'Let others work for thee; maintain thyself by their sweat, their bones are thine; look not upon them, regard them not, instead of their toil do thou take gold; gold does not weep, gold hungers not; it only shines

When thou hast me thou canst sing, dance, walk upon men's heads, over their crackling arms. Be bold. The world is a field of spoil, each one takes what he can seize.' So speaks the tempter. But the spirit of true life says: 'Thou art only that which thou art in thyself; whatever of earthly possession has been assigned to thee is indeed thine, but thou art not one with it; in the morning it may no longer be thine. To-day, however, it is still thine, and thou mayst work with it and produce a thousand-fold, so that it may go well with thee and thine, and those about thee. Art thou one to whom genius has not been given? Let not that dispirit thee, be of good heart and seek culture; this it is in thy power to attain, and with it comes all that is truly worth the desire, fame and greatness are fine things, but not every one can achieve them; but every one can be a contented man, active in doing good. Wealth is an instrument placed in the hands of many a one, but it only occasionally happens that the holder knows how to use it. You cannot annul the evils of the world, hunger, sickness, and all its toils, but you may not throw away the power which does lie in your hands; it is your high duty to achieve with it the good and the beautiful. Be glad then of your wealth, for it gives you the power to create happiness and beauty. First of all, create joy and beauty in your own soul, the power to deprive yourself, the spirit of work, and hold yourself ready to stand firm in yourself when external supports are removed from you. Whoever places his being's centre on something outside of himself, upon which he rests for support, will fall to the ground whenever the support gives way. Stand firm in yourself, keep the centre of gravity within you, learn to know and govern yourself, and to know and govern the world around you. Now is the time of preparation; you have as yet no duties toward others. Your duty is now, first of all, to yourself. Keep your powers well in hand, do not waste your own being, and if you possess yourself, you are rich to eternity. If you do not possess yourself you are eternally poor; and if millions were yours, and if in addition to them you owned yourself, you would indeed be the lord of your wealth."

They sat in silence for a long time. It is impossible to divine in what direction a thought once seized may lead, what latent germs in the soul it may bring to development.

"I would like to know," began Roland, "how it came about that America was discovered."

Erich explained to the youth what a revolution in thought the great discoveries of the sixteenth century had made. Then in a small German city arose a man, who proclaimed and proved that the earth upon which we live is not a fixed point, that it turns continually upon its axis and revolves around the sun. The entire system of thought, which had prevailed among men for thousands of years was changed at once. We wander about on this ball which we name the earth, we hew and build, we journey by land and sea upon a ball which keeps continually turning. How must this thought have first fallen upon the heart of man! a shudder must have run through it; the canopy of heaven was removed, there was no longer a heaven, and that old representation of a king of the world sitting up there: heaven itself, and all that was included in that name, became naught else than the innumerable ranks of stars, which move according to their own laws and meet and pass in the great void.

Another man came and said: There is no man upon earth, who, sitting on his throne, comprehends within himself the infinite mind, and is competent to teach and determine what men shall believe and for what they shall hope. The schism in the Church broke out and tore the system of the world, as it then existed in men's minds, to tatters.

And still another man embarked with his few comrades, and sailed to the west and discovered a New World. In our human dwelling-place, there was suddenly opened an immeasurably vast space, in which men lived to whom as yet no report of all that we had accomplished had come; and plants, and animals, and measureless forests and streams were there, and we knew nothing of them.

Copernicus, Luther, and Columbus—what these three in common and at the same period unfolded to the vision, must have produced a revolution in the minds of men, with which nothing in our time can be compared. Let us suppose that to-day some one was able to remove from the world all the rights of private property, so that no man could any longer claim anything as his own—the revolution in the thoughts of men would be no greater than it then was.

Roland looked with wonder upon the man, who had thus placed him upon a height, where all life and being rolled forth before his eyes new and transformed.

Erich checked himself, lest he should disturb or cover up the evidently deep impression which this revelation had made upon his pupil. He questioned within himself, however, whether he had not set before the boy ideas and views which he was not able to comprehend. But he comforted himself with reflecting on the custom of the Church; there the youthful soul is brought into contact with truths for which he feels no craving and which he cannot as yet fully seize; the hope is cherished that later in life they will recur to him. Ought we not, are we not obliged to do the same?

Their quiet meditations, as they gazed out into the illimitable space, were interrupted by the superintendent's coming to them and announcing that a Roman tomb had been found, containing an urn, a chain, and a skeleton. Erich went with Roland, upon whom this exhumation of a man who had long ago disappeared from the earth made a profound impression.

What is the world? What is life? A later age finds the skeleton of a man; it is a matter of indifference to it; it only asks—are there any remains of the ancient world with it, any traces of some old form of industry? Such is Life!

How attentively Roland listened, while Erich expressed his satisfaction over this discovery, which would so gratify Count Clodwig. Roland now gave his thoughts to this subject, and all his broodings seemed forgotten. Erich was pleased to observe this double power of youth; one moment it is deeply immersed in some new exciting thought, but when another thought comes, the first is covered up and forgotten. Such is the buoyant and happy nature of the youthful mind.

Roland also wanted to make a collection, and Erich encouraged him in it. He could here point out a kind of property which represented the pure idea of property: such accidental discoveries do not belong to him who calls them his; they belong to the world, which derives from them a knowledge of the past; no one dares claim them for himself alone. That is the pure unmixed idea of property, freed from all material weight, and thus we must look at all the wealth of the world.

After this incident, a calmer tone of thought seemed to settle upon them. But, as they were on their way home, Roland asked again:

"Now tell me, Erich, what would you do, if all this wealth were your own. Do you know the answer yet?"

"Not with certainty. I think that I would spend much in experiments—in attempts to help and strengthen suffering men. I have hitherto pondered much on the subject. I, first of all, asked myself, what is a million, or many millions—what are they worth?"

Erich checked himself, and Roland asked:

"Have you found it out yet? What are they worth?"

"I have made it clear to myself in this way: To know what such sums include, I have first asked myself how much bread could a man get with a million; and by means of this somewhat childish-sounding question I hit, as I think, upon the right road."

"And it is—?"

"I sought to calculate how many families a million represented; that is, how many families could live upon a million. That, I think, is the road; I haven't reached its end yet, of course. But, I repeat it, we must first of all cultivate in ourselves the firm resolution, in every situation of life, to do what is right. What the hour and the circumstance may demand of us no one can determine in advance."

"Keep always by me, and help me!" said Roland. Erich seized his hand and pressed it.

They returned in silence to the Villa.

CHAPTER XVI.

AT A GOOD NEIGHBOR'S.

AN accident often occurs which seems a summons. While at the castle they had been speaking of Clodwig, and when they got back to the Villa, they found that he had sent word that he and his wife had returned from the springs, and would visit Roland and Erich on the following day.

The sun had browned Clodwig's face during the summer trip, and Bella looked rejuvenated; and as she walked about the house and park with her train sweeping the ground, she bore no little resemblance to a peacock. As soon as they arrived, Roland showed what he had found at the castle; and his face lighted up as Clodwig told him that he ought to make it the basis of a collection, which would probably give him more pleasure in his future life than almost anything else. Roland nodded to Erich. And Clodwig said that during his journey he had made several valuable acquisitions which would soon arrive. At the baths he had had daily intercourse with a celebrated antiquary, who had once been Erich's teacher.

Erich regretted that he had so greatly neglected Clodwig's friendship, and had not been to see him before he went away; but it was again evident that Clodwig's nature was not easily ruffled, for he did not show the slightest trace of sensitiveness on the subject. In this respect, good-nature and self-confidence aided him; he readily pardoned any neglect, and like a man accustomed to be wronged, hardly gave a thought to an injury or slight.

"You are elevated beyond the necessity of making excuses to me," said he to Erich, taking his hand and holding it as if Erich had been his son. "You have cured me of an egotism of which I would not have believed myself capable. Yes, my young friend, you must live your own life, and let me enjoy the pleasure of being your neighbor: good neighbors were not a political fiction among the ancient Romans."

They pledged good neighborly feeling; and as the old gentleman drank, he looked with beaming eyes at Erich.

As the husband and wife prompted each other's memory, it was pleasant for Erich to hear that during their travels they had intentionally made a detour in order to spend a night a the University city, and visit his mother and pass a day with her. At last Clodwig allowed his wife to speak without interruption, for she spoke earnestly and with deep feeling of the life of the noble lady.

How homelike seemed the picture she drew of the corner where the piano stood, and where the beautiful and estimable lady sat working at her flower-stand. By the window before her hung the pictures of the dead husband and son, over which a lock of her grandmother's blonde hair was framed and covered with glass; and at the right and left of this hung pictures in pastil of her grand-parents. She was not melancholy, but on the contrary was good-humored, and ready at any remark to enter into conversation.

Bella told of walks through the lovely valley, of their excursion to the mountain chapel, and Erich could almost hear his mother's voice; he saw her sitting near this beautiful lady, and nodding approval to Clodwig. Erich passed an hour of deep and homelike pleasure, listening to what was said of his mother.

But Roland was not less interested, and broke out with the question:

"And didn't she say anything about me?"

"She hardly spoke of her son as much as of you," answered Bella.

She turned again to Erich, and seemed never to tire of saying how deeply she had been interested by the sight of a lady who lived happily in a world of her own, not longing for a wider sphere, but having her world in herself; regretting nothing, and yet denied so much.

Clodwig smiled, for Bella was repeating the very words which he had used, but she added of her own accord:

"I think that it is only since becoming acquainted with your mother that I understand you, Herr Captain. We agreed to correspond, but she would not let me bind myself to keep it up."

Erich was continually growing more and more at home with Clodwig and Bella; and it seemed as if the spirit of his mother was present, blessing their friendship.

"But we must not forget the aunt," said Clodwig, adding that he had renewed an old acquaintanceship with her: he well remembered the dazzling beauty of Fräulein Dournay, and what an excitement was caused when she, a commoner, was introduced at Court, and received in the best society. It was said that she and Prince Hubert, who died when quite young, had been deeply in love with each other, and that after his death Fräulein Dournay had steadily declined all offers of marriage; but of this Clodwig did not speak.

After dinner, as they were strolling in the garden, Bella said to Erich:

"Your youth was beautiful and richly endowed, but one thing you lack."

"And that is—?"

"A sister."

"I would fain believe that you were my sister," replied Erich softly.

Bella's eyes were fixed on the ground for awhile, and then she called Roland.

They went to the castle, and Clodwig, in the interest of his young friend Roland, desired the Architect to be very careful of any relic of antiquity that might be found.

They sat down on a ressault of the castle, where the Major had caused comfortable seats to be placed.

Clodwig walked with Roland, and Bella sat beside Erich. She was in her idyllic mood. She had been at Paris and brought back the latest style; but she said to Erich: "How silly it is in us to dress so extravagantly."

Then, without any very apparent reason, she added how much she was misunderstood. People believed that she was extravagant, but nothing would give her so much pleasure as to live in some well-warmed and comfortable room in some fisherman's cottage by the Rhine.

"And who's to tend the fire to keep this room warm?"

Bella was shocked.

"You're right; we must not be idyllic."

Then there was a long pause.

"You have become acquainted with my mother," began Erich; "had you known my father you would have liked him too."

"I did know him. But I thank you; I know that you wish me to share everything that is yours."

She said this with deep feeling; her eyes shone, and she looked at Erich in such a way that he dropped his eyes. Pursing her lips, she added:

"It must seem strange to you—yes, it certainly *has* seemed so—to be regarded thus by me. Now, then, I see that I must accomplish a wish of Clodwig's, since I think that I can do so. Clodwig wishes me to make a drawing of you. I will try to, but I want our young friend Roland in the picture. Herr Roland, come here," she cried as she saw Roland approaching.

Then, with a blush on her cheek, she said that she had intended to give Clodwig a birthday surprise by giving him the drawing; but she saw now that this was impossible, and therefore must speak openly.

"Pray, Roland, seat yourself in the Captain's lap. So—that's right. Put your right hand on his shoulder—a little further forward. So--now turn your head a little to the left. Say something, Captain; you must seem to be telling Roland something."

"I don't know what to say," said Erich, smiling.

"That's sufficient, I see the movement of your lips. It will be pretty hard, but I hope to fix it. When will you give me a sitting?"

Clodwig was pleased, and said that he was not very fond of surprises; an expected and hoped for pleasure was much more agreeable and satisfying. He wished Erich and Roland to visit them at Wolfsgarten, and remain there till the family returned, but Erich declined not less pleasantly than decidedly: he did not wish to disturb the course of life upon which they had entered. Clodwig instantly agreed with him, and promised that he and Bella would come to the Villa again before long, when the drawing would be commenced and finished. Bella wanted a photograph of Roland and Erich, taken in the pose which she had chosen; but Clodwig opposed this, for a drawing made with the aid of a photograph always gives a feeling of stiffness and unnaturalness. He was opposed to photographs of human figures, as they only give the architectural elevations of what they mean to represent, and do even this untruthfully.

Roland then expressed his opinion; he thought that Grip ought to be included in the picture. Clodwig agreed with him, for this would help fill out the foreground.

Bella was vexed: after being surrounded with such pleasant society, it was too bad that she should again be shut up in a solitude which was only enlivened by specimens of the antique, among which she probably included some that had not been dug out of the earth. A visit from Erich and Roland would be welcome to her, as a means of passing away the time—she wished for nothing more. But this proud and learned Captain was so reserved, and always had some principle or other to apply to the most trifling affairs; and her husband—displaying his worst infirmity, the weakness of old age—immediately agreed with whatever the Captain said, and never had any opinion which was not that of the young man.

Her face suddenly fell; she seemed to lose all spirit, but noticing this, she soon collected herself. She became extremely pleasant, and as Erich kissed her hand at parting, he felt it pressed against his lips; but probably this was his own imagination or the effect of his own awkwardness. While he was thinking of the occurrence, Roland said:

"I don't know why, but I felt uncomfortable when the Countess was looking at me. Did you? And then she looked at you so strangely!"

"Oh, that's the way in which artists look at people," replied Erich; but he was by no means at ease.

Who knows but this answer expressed the whole truth?

CHAPTER XVII.

THE FASHIONING OF A MAN.

THE Major did not send word in advance that he was coming, but came. He looked quite fresh with his short, snow-white hair, and his ruddy face, browned by the sun, and said that as often as he took the warm baths he thought that he experienced the same sensations that he did when he was bathed for the first time after he was born. He seemed literally a new-born child, and always felt as though an invisible nurse were bending over him smiling, and bespattering him with water.

He laughed to the trees, the walls, the roofs, and finally to the faces of his friends.

He was greatly pleased to find that Erich had taken his pupil from the line, and was drilling him in private. To be sure this was more difficult, but he would learn more in one day than in whole weeks under the old system.

He begged Erich to send a couple of words to Fräulein Milch, excusing himself for not having visited her during her loneliness, and asked him to come and see him soon, for he would then meet the old head-master.

We must bear in mind that the Major lived in one of the little houses belonging to the Villa estate, which was finely situated on a little elevation, over which he had a sort of jurisdiction. The Major was very careful to preserve the independence of his life, but always felt under obligations to the head-master, who, although celebrated by the Major for his kindness, was yet more lauded by him for his conversational powers. It was the Major's constant desire to bring to him every good thing which he found; and what did he now possess better than Erich, whose praises he was ever chanting to such an extent that he, who found it so hard to talk except on this topic, poured forth floods of eloquence which always wound up in his characteristic way?

On the first evening when he was at leisure, Erich visited the Major, and soon obtained Fräulein Milch's forgiveness. The Major laughed so heartily that he got into such a fit of coughing that Fräulein Milch had to slap him on the back; and all this was owing to the unprecedented fact that the Major had made a joke—he had said that Erich had been lying in and had been delivered of a fine boy, and consequently had been obliged to stay in the house for the first six weeks.

Fräulein Milch said that Erich had become quite famous at the concert, and the Major said:

"That's good! We always have celebrated singers at our concerts. Can you sing 'In diesen heiligen Hallen?'"

Erich regretted that the glorious aria was too low for his voice.

"Sing something else; sing for Fräulein Milch."

Erich had some difficulty in refusing this friendly request; but Fräulein Milch came to his aid, and the exhibition of his artistic talent was deferred to another evening, on which it was agreed that he would sing.

The conduct of the so-called head-master was as disagreeable as that of Fräulein Milch was kind and confiding, for it was to some extent offensively patronizing; he seemed so accustomed to flattery, that no one but a man as humble and grateful as the Major could live happily, or even contentedly with him.

The Major took all pains to make the two men friends, but did not succeed. The head-master conducted himself with calm superiority toward Erich, whom he addressed by no other title than "young man;" he imparted instruction to him, and gave him advice, as if Erich's true instructor had at last been found in the person of the head-master. Erich had need of all his self-control to keep from showing the man the impropriety of his conduct, for the head-master was audacious enough to talk about the inexperience of the "young man"—who had, most assuredly, come to him to hear the oracle speak. The whole tenor of his conversation was oracular to a degree, and the movement of his left hand was that of a husbandman scattering seeds broadcast upon the earth.

Erich's sense of humor was keen enough to allow him to look at this insolence as a curious natural phenomenon; he submitted patiently while the man anointed him with the unction of superior wisdom, and when he departed the head-master said to the Major:

"The young man has ideas."

To be sure, he had never heard any of Erich's "ideas," but as he concluded that they were the same as his own, he gave him his meed of praise; and this was a great deal for the head-master to do, for no one but himself ever had "ideas," and the whole world ought to come to him alone for instruction.

As Erich was again entering the Major's house, a messenger came from the Villa with the intelligence that on the next day Clodwig, Bella, and Prancken would visit there. Roland had gone into the yard with Fräulein Milch, where he stood admiring the young ducks.

The Major asked Erich if he was on good terms with Prancken, and Erich could only say that Prancken's conduct toward him was very friendly and considerate.

The Major, who from a drummer had become an officer, had

a strong and lasting grudge against the haughtiness of those of his comrades who belonged to the nobility: nevertheless he advised Erich to be very friendly in his conduct toward Prancken, who, notwithstanding he was well-mannered, was noble, and had brought about Erich's entrance into Sonnenkamp's house, and was also the means by which he had obtained such a distinguished friend as Clodwig.

As Erich and Roland were walking home, Erich said:

"Now, Roland, we will show that we intend to let nothing interrupt our work; come what will, we will continue our studies unintermittingly, and will place only our leisure hours at the disposal of strangers. See, Roland, this is one of the difficulties of life. One often injures himself by pliability to the world, and by endeavoring not to seem cold and ungrateful. We, on the other hand, will remain steadfast to ourselves. Each man must live for himself first, and then for the world. He who cannot exist for himself is owned by the world, not by himself."

The consciousness of fulfilling his duty made Erich strong, and at peace with himself, warding off every disturbing influence.

CHAPTER XVIII.

UNDER-CURRENTS.

THE guests came. Prancken rode beside the carriage in which sat Clodwig and Bella; and a large frame covered with paper, and a beautifully inlaid box containing crayons, was on the seat before them.

Erich and Roland received them, and Erich begged that they would make themselves at home; everything had been prepared by the servants, and he himself would be at their disposal in an hour, when he would be through with his instruction.

The visitors looked at each other in amazement.

Prancken was singularly changed; deep seriousness was expressed by his face, but now he shrugged his shoulders, and burst out in a short, harsh laugh.

Bella considered Erich's conduct very unmannerly and pedantic; Clodwig thought that it illustrated a fine and manly character; but Prancken found in this regard for duty nothing but ostentation; the young man—he said this almost as the head-master said it—the young man wanted to make a display of his strict attention to duty.

Nevertheless they entered, and flowers, and the evident attention paid to the preparation of the rooms, showed that Erich had cared for the comfort of the guests.

The hour was soon over, and Erich came to them with that

freshness and good-humor which nothing but the consciousness of duty fulfilled can give.

He had selected for the temporary studio a room facing the north, and, after a little intermission, the sitting commenced.

Clodwig remained with his wife; Roland, whose presence would not be needed at first, went to the stables with Prancken, who comported himself in the house as the natural substitute for Sonnenkamp, or as his son. He had the horses brought out, examined the garden, and praised the servants.

"I never saw you look so serious and melancholy as you look now," said Clodwig to Erich; and in fact his face was clouded with care, for he suspected that Prancken was speaking of him to Roland.

Of what value is instruction, or endeavors to direct a pupil's mind, when one cannot be sure at what instant a foreign and incongruous element may be brought to bear upon it? Comfort must be found in reflecting that no one individual can educate another—it requires the whole world. Erich had no suspicion of Prancken's real intention with Roland.

Prancken asked Roland if he read every day in the book which Manna had sent him.

Roland said he did not; and then gave an account, by no means very clear, of Benjamin Franklin, Hiawatha, Crassus: of their observation of the storm at the telegraph-station, and of Bancroft's History of the United States.

Prancken nodded, and asked Roland if he frequently wrote to Manna. Roland said that he did. Prancken then said that he was breaking a snow-white Hungarian horse for Manna, and added:

"You can write that to her or not—just as you choose."

He knew very well that there was no likelihood of Roland's forgetting a communication when the propriety of making it was left to his own judgment, especially in this instance, where a snow-white horse with pale-red nostrils was to be spoken of. Prancken promised that Roland himself should ride the white horse sometimes.

"Has it a name yet?" asked Roland.

Prancken smiled, for he noticed that his confiding in the boy had produced a great effect. Then he replied:

"Certainly, it has a name—Armida."

Roland was summoned, being needed for the sketch; and when the first outlines of this were completed, Bella paused from her work.

In a tone which was half confidential and half imperative, Prancken asked Erich for a private interview, and entered on a discussion of the way in which Roland should be educated, in a manner that was not only very, but exceedingly friendly.

Erich now for the first time heard Prancken seriously express his deep feeling for the Church. He was surprised. Was all this assumed, so that Prancken might more easily and securely win the heiress *religieuse ?*

But why should Prancken clothe himself with spirituality here, where no one would see him, or on his travels, or at the baths? It was much more probable that this natural-born worldling had experienced the new birth: on such natures as his, the strength, sternness, and controlling influence of the Church have a powerful restraining effect.

"I regard it as my duty—and *you* will recognize the strength of that motive," said Prancken abruptly, as he laid his hand on his heart—"to tell you something in confidence."

"If I can be of service, I feel myself honored by your confidence; but if I can do nothing, a confidence will only be unnecessary trouble to me."

Prancken was astonished at this reserve, and very nearly became angry, but controlled himself and continued in a lower tone:

"You know that Herr Sonnenkamp—"

"Pardon me for interrupting you. Does Herr Sonnenkamp know that you are communicating with me in confidence?"

"But, Sir!" said Prancken, flashing up—"But no, I honor discretion in a man situated as you are."

He paused for an instant: it occurred to him to give a confidence other than that which he intended, and warn Erich against becoming too intimate with Bella; but would not that be placing his sister in a dilemma? He returned to his first idea, and said shortly:

"I think I may tell you that I am the son of— Miss Sonnenkamp is as good as my wife."

"If Miss Sonnenkamp is at all like her brother, you are to be heartily congratulated. I thank you for your confidence, which is so unusual, and hitherto unmerited. May I ask why you honor me with it?"

Prancken was every minute becoming inwardly more discomposed, and outwardly more composed: he moved his right hand nervously, as if longing to use his whip, but he smiled very obligingly and said:

"I have not been deceived in you"—he paused and then added: "I fully understand your reserve."

Nevertheless he did not directly answer the question as to the reason of this confidence; indeed he hardly had opportunity to do so, for Roland called to Erich that he was wanted to continue the sitting.

"One might believe that ten years had passed between the time when you went away and now, you look so much older," said Bella to Erich.

Erich could not tell what was passing in his mind. The way in which Prancken had acted toward him, and he, on his side, had comported himself toward Prancken, made him uneasy. He sat quietly, but seemed to himself dragged hither and thither by contending emotions. He felt that at the bottom there was a lie in his conduct, and that they both understood their natural antagonism; they should have been either enemies or indifferent to each other, and yet there was something which attracted them, and made them persuade themselves that the case was different.

All misery has its basis in a lie. If one always had the courage to act truthfully, and in spite of internal antagonism would not allow himself to be drawn into lasting entanglements and engagements, ever laying to his soul the flattering unction of the pretext, "it will all come out right—the business is not so difficult after all"—the world would be far different, much misery would be unknown. But in a thousand circumstances the danger is veiled, hidden, or clothed in deceptive colors, as it is in that expression of the Bible, where the serpent silences the repugnance, the conscious antagonism, by saying: "Eat; ye shall not surely die, but become wise!"

The great penalty exacted by a connection based on a lie, is that it demands continued untruthfulness—often unconscious or veiled by self-deception, and finally makes the lie a virtue, changes the whole gist of the question, dissolves the antagonism felt before the man was contaminated, and says: "Thou must be faithful; ye have been friends so long, thou hast received so much from him, or hast done him such service, that it would be a dissolution of thy life, would leave it incomplete, if ye should now separate; no, now is the very time to hold together."

And so the lie grows and poisons life. All sorrow and misery, treachery and deceit, come from this—the victim has been faithless to himself. The devil of lies yet goes up and down the earth seeking whom he may devour.

Of course it is true that there is no devil: you can't see him in such a shape as to catch him and put him in the ranks like a soldier, but close to the divine ideal, which is, in its last results, nothing else than truth; close to *that* dwells the lie, and well it knows how to imitate the form and language of its neighbor.

All this was torturing Erich's soul as he was sitting for his picture. If any one could have fixed the attitude of his soul on the canvas, it would have been a distortion beyond parallel.

Bella declared that she would not draw Erich so, and broke up the sitting.

They went to dinner, and had a pleasant meal, for the Doctor came and ate with them.

In the evening they sailed on the Rhine, and Roland said

that Erich was a fine singer, but Erich could not be persuaded to display his powers. They joked him considerably about his distinguished success at the concert; and Prancken joined in the pleasantry, but was bitterly sarcastic.

When night had come, and fire-flies were hovering in the fragrant air of the garden, Erich walked at Bella's side, while Clodwig sat in the house near the balcony, turning the leaves of an album filled with large new photographic views of Rome, and often lifting his eyes and looking far away, filled with memories of the past.

Roland walked with Prancken and talked of Manna; Prancken knew very well how to give the boy the impression which he wished him to convey to Manna in his letters. They occasionally passed Bella and Erich, and Prancken was surprised to see that Bella was leaning on Erich's arm.

Witty words and inuendoes flew through the air like the fire-flies, but their brilliancy lasted longer than that produced by the insects, as the two walked along.

Bella and Erich conversed in a low tone, and often paused when Prancken and Roland passed them.

Bella was again speaking of her good husband—she called him her good husband—and of how consonant his nature was with Erich's, and how Erich seemed, so to speak, to *affectionate* him.

"You create words!" answered Erich, as Bella repeated her new-found word with delight, as if it had been a newly invented coiffure which was becoming to her alone.

Erich was pedantic enough to return to the real theme of the conversation, and said, warmly, how blessed it was to possess beauty and peace, not merely as ideals, but to meet them in real life, to stretch the hand to them and look into their quiet, beaming eyes.

"You're a good man, and, I think, truly honest," said Bella, taking off her glove, and striking him softly on the hand with it.

"It's no advantage to be honest. I wish I could be dishonest. I do not mean positively dishonest, but more reserved."

It was beautiful and encouraging to see how thoroughly Bella appreciated the happiness of an open nature; she said with deep emotion that if she had only known how to pretend the least little bit of love, she might long ago have achieved a brilliant destiny. Erich did not know what to reply; and this was one of those pauses which Prancken noticed, as he passed by with Roland. Bella went on to say how blessed it was to do something for the conservation of a human being; the one—and she nodded to Erich—does this for another in the morning of life, the other for one in the evening of his existence, and the sacrifice, silent and unrecognized, is rewarded only by the consciousness of duty fulfilled.

At a turn of the road it very naturally happened that Erich left Bella and walked with Roland, and Prancken proceeded with his sister. Roland was jealous of Bella—he was jealous of everybody to whom Erich gave a word or look. He wished to have him, he alone. And as Roland said this with childish pettishness, Erich shuddered. He had not only let his soul be led away from Roland, but had probably entered upon another error. It is yet time to turn. He went to talk with Clodwig, and was almost glad to find that he had already gone to bed.

CHAPTER XIX.

SEEN IN ANOTHER LIGHT.

WHEN Bella examined the picture next day she was uneasy and dissatisfied. All that she had so carefully done seemed false and distorted. She was vexed, and wished to begin anew, but Clodwig soothed her, and so kindly and delicately called her attention to the good points of the work that Bella recovered her good-humor. Nevertheless she said, with a certain bitterness, that it was her fate that everything she undertook turned out differently from what she intended. Clodwig told her that this was necessarily the case with every attempt to realize the ideal. On this she became cross, and said peevishly: "I am not what I am." The cause of her ill-humor was unfathomable. It was not simply that disgust and anger which artists feel at their want of skill.

Nothwithstanding Erich's firm resolve, the course which he had laid out for himself and Roland was broken in upon. Bella knew that she could accomplish anything she undertook. Her motto was: "Men must only *think* that they settle what is to be done."

Roland soon brought the conversation to his one absorbing topic, the Life of Franklin; and as Bella expressed a wish to learn something about it, Clodwig offered to read from it. Bella listened to a summary of the preceding chapters, and then Clodwig read, commencing where Erich and Roland had left off. Roland and Erich listened with interest. Bella kept up a lively commentary on the book; for she had a great knack of quickly seeing the gist of everything. Nevertheless, Erich started as she said that she detected "a certain stupid pedantry in the man, and knew that he must have been very mean and stingy." Erich felt a shudder run through Roland, who was sitting in his lap.

In our age, it is impossible for a young man, situated as Roland was, and having undergone what he had experienced, to live fully in accordance with his ideal. Perhaps it would be beneficial to Roland to see his ideal assailed, nay, even distorted, provided it be justly and opportunely done.

Erich said, as impressively and forcibly as he could, that the problems of life present far greater difficulty to one who is an unbeliever than to those who have the Church to say to them, "Follow me." We modern men must recognize the lofty and pure in exalted natures, even though somewhat of the narrowness of the age or natural disposition of the individual still clings to it.

Bella worked very rapidly, and kept nodding to herself, as he was saying this. When he had concluded, she looked him full in the face, and said:

"You are the best teacher I have ever seen."

She turned; her eyes glistened and her cheeks glowed.

"That depends upon who is my pupil," said Erich pleasantly.

"Now I would like," blushing more and more as she proceeded, "I would like to have you place your hand on Roland's head. Do it, please;—that is just what I wish. Pray do as I ask you."

He complied, but said that he did not like the position; he would have Roland learn to carry his head free.

Bella shook her head and worked on, not touching the figure of Erich, but confining herself to Roland. Suddenly she said:

"Now I have it! That's it! You look like Murillo's St. Anthony."

"I discovered that too," cried Roland, "and Manna scolded me for saying so, at the concert!"

Bella's opinion was also confirmed by Clodwig, who said:

"That is my favorite picture, and as you spoke I seemed to see it. The whole form of St. Anthony as he kneels; his staff beside him; the landscape merely intimated; a tree in the background; and the shrubbery; angels playing on the ground and hovering in the air; an angel turning the leaves of the Saint's book—another holding an earthly lily to the angel in the heavens, and the flower itself forming a connecting-link between heaven and earth—all is like a heaven on earth."

Erich was embarrassed as Roland related how strangely he had felt in the convent where he fell asleep in the church, and on suddenly waking found the black-robed nun standing beside him, and saw the picture above him.

Erich made a request which produced peculiar feelings in each who heard it; he asked Clodwig not to read further, giving his reason for doing so by saying:

"I see clearly that thoughts can neither be firmly held nor pursued, as we would wish to pursue them at this moment, when we are forced to preserve a physical condition which is opposed to, or at least unconnected with our thoughts; there is a mysterious connection between our reflections and our physical state.

This remark set each thinking in his own way. To Erich himself was represented his position as a teacher. Roland thought of the castle-walls, and wondered how the builders felt as they stood on the scaffolding, or as they chiselled the stones. Recollections of the past must have been summoned up in Clodwig, for he shook his head sorrowfully and pressed his lips together; but Bella was more affected by these words than were the others, for her pencils dropped from her right hand, and the bit of bread which she had in her left, and which she had occasionally used to rub out a line, fell to the floor. Erich hastily handed them to her; she took them without speaking and seemed lost in reverie, for his words had shown her the picture of her wedded life.

It was long before a word was spoken.

The presence of Clodwig and his wife at Villa Eden occasioned much remark in the neighborhood, and seemed to give the tutor a new importance. But Prancken regarded it with far different eyes and, in his capacity as future son-in-law of its master, invited to the Villa the Justice with his wife and daughter, who had just returned from the baths.

They came, and Prancken was particularly attentive to Lina; they two strolled through the garden and Lina gave him a description of cloister-life which was entirely new to him. Lina had a very happy way of drawing the comical traits of the Superior and her companions. She had gone to the convent for no other earthly purpose than to obtain a good knowledge of foreign languages. Lina's persistently light and cheerful disposition brought solace to the melancholy heart of Prancken, and something of the old Prancken said within him: "Why should the present be desolate and drear? Shall Bella weave her charms around the Captain, and thou not enjoy thy day with Lina? Why not revel amid trifling pastures—perhaps enjoy the blessed sense of a reawakened emotion? Thou canst at any moment be master of thy passions."

The old Prancken—the Prancken of palmy days—took his moustache—preserved from the fell swoop of the barber's knife—in both hands, and twisted it on high.

It is right; one may pause awhile and enjoy a little by-play with Lina, the Justice's daughter. It will be a very easy matter to lay all this aside,—transfer it to the time before that visit to the convent, and for the rest—Manna would have a good deal to overlook in his past life, and might add this to it.

But Lina treated all his homage very lightly, and was just as confiding with Erich as with Prancken, always calling him her brother-singer.

There was pleasant jest and laughter in the park and Villa, and Prancken even asked his brother-in-law to go sailing with him and Lina, while Bella worked at the picture. He wanted Roland to go with them too, saying to himself in a devil-me-care mood, that they ought to be alone together once at least; but Roland would not leave Erich, and even openly avoided intercourse with Prancken.

Lina sat in the boat and sang merrily. She was in good-humor, and sang love-songs as she had never sung them before; and Prancken, looking at her, was forced to drop his eyes. When they returned to the Villa, Clodwig told his wife that Lina's singing was as beautiful and simple as a wild-flower.

Bella asked the Justice and his wife to let Lina go to Wolfsgarten with her: the Justice objected, but his wife overruled him, and Lina was overflowing with happiness, as she set out with Clodwig and Bella.

Prancken rode beside them.

After the excitement of the last few days, Erich and Roland felt the loneliness of the Villa. Erich was out of humor, weary, and listless. It was burdensome to him to devote his life to another from the time when he woke in the morning till he went to bed at night: it wearied him beyond measure to be endlessly following Roland's mind in its uncouth, and often capricious flight, and to recall or give it direction. He wished for the society of Clodwig, and even more—he hardly acknowledged this to himself—did he long to be with Bella. There was something fresh—something that aroused and excited him; a spirit of gracefulness had filled these rooms, and now all was so empty! After a few days he yielded to Roland and agreed to make the promised visit to Wolfsgarten.

Erich was unwilling to leave the house, the care of which had been intrusted to him, and Prancken assumed the responsibility; but there was gall in his words as he said to Erich:

"You went to the concert and left the house alone with the servants. But, as I said, I take the responsibility."

CHAPTER XX.

TRESPASSING ON ANOTHER'S DOMAIN.

IN the valley on the bank of the river, where the waters glide past so swiftly, and yet without agitation, it is beautiful to stand and to watch how they glisten by day—how they mirror every changing tint of the sky, and carry the swift vessels up and down; and, when evening has come, to listen to the quiet murmuring of the waters, through which shimmers the light of the moon. How beautiful, too, to stand on a mountain-height, and gaze down into the world, over forests and vineyards, villages and cities, and the far-stretching river.

There was a new life stirring at Wolfsgarten, where all were animated and refreshed. The picture of Erich and Roland was brought nearer to completion; while, at the same time, Erich arranged Clodwig's collections, and introduced his pupil to the knowledge of antiquity. They sung and laughed, they went out riding and driving in the surrounding woods, and many a pregnant conversation was carried on.

In her rambles with Erich, through the park and the groves, Bella often took with her a parrot, which sat on her shoulder, and was very cross to Erich, and scolded him.

Bella often allowed the parrot to fly away, saying to him: "But be sure to come back in the evening, Koko!" and Koko flew up on a tree, flew into the woods, and away from the woods, and still he was sure to return in the evening. At such times Bella called him her liberated slave.

But now Koko had not returned for two days. Clodwig did all in his power to capture the parrot again; he did not notice how calmly his wife bore her loss.

It came about seeminlgy by chance, that Bella always went about with Erich, while Roland and Lina romped through the woods, and Lina was happy at being allowed to carry on like a wild-boy. At times, too, when Bella and Erich strayed through the park and the groves, Roland would sit in the potter's workshop, where the clay which was dug out of the neighboring mountain was moulded. He watched the whole process of manufacture, and he often saw how much care and trouble one single pot required. Two youths of his own age trod the clay with naked feet to render it pliable. The journeymen made architectural ornaments, floor-tiles, and earthen vessels. At a wheel sat a fine-looking, powerfully built young man; he moved the wheel with bare feet, fashioned the clay with great care into a pot, shaped the rim and the spout, lifted the completed article almost tenderly from the wheel to a board, and placed it in a row with the others. His heavy hands never made a pressure which he had not intended; and he never took more clay than was necessary for the one pot.

Roland watched all this in deep thought. Would money bring any relief to all these people?

No. You could render their life more comfortable, but they must work.

The young man who shaped the pots was dumb; he looked at Roland good-naturedly, and continued his work. The master praised the dumb man, and Roland feeling a desire to do something for him, gave him a fine pocket-knife, which contained a variety of instruments, and the dumb man was delighted with the present.

Roland told Erich of all that he had seen and thought, informing him that old women and young children brought the laborers in the factory their dinners from a great distance, and asked him whether something couldn't be done to change this.

Erich listened to it all, looking at the youth with a strange expression. How glad he had been at other times, when Roland had not passed by with indifference the existence of his fellow-beings, but sought to comprehend their life. Now Erich's life seemed to be all wrapt up in something else.

A piece of news which a finely lithographed paper brought to Wolfsgarten, furnished much matter for conversation.

The Wine-count's daughter was betrothed to the son of the Court-chamberlain. It was considered strange that the young man, whose speedy death was quite certain, should nevertheless enter into an engagement; but that the girl, a young, luxurious creature, should have made up her mind to it, seemed stranger still. Lina, who was very well versed in the gossip of the neighborhood, related that the Wine-count's daughter had declared that she would be well satisfied to be the widow of a baron.

There was an appearance of deep depression, an indication of something which did not find full utterance in Bella's manner of speaking of the engagement, especially to Erich, as if he must know what it was that she concealed.

The newspaper brought the tidings, that the prince's brother had returned from America, that he had seen a great deal there, and had brought the prince a beautiful negro, a freed slave.

While they were still sitting together, discussing the impression which the contemplation of the American republic must make on a German prince, Roland came running in from the woods crying:

"I've got him!"

He had hold of the parrot by his claws.

"Why here you are, my freed slave!" cried Bella. The parrot tore himself away from Roland, and flew to his mistress's shoulder, scolding Erich vociferously.

Clodwig could not easily be disturbed when a discussion was once begun, and now while he continued to explain his views about the world in general, Bella took part with much vivacity. But occasionally it appeared to Erich, that Bella's talkativeness did not go beyond a certain superficiality; then again he rejected this view as pedantic.

Book-life, he said to himself, had rendered him unimpressible by a light, graceful, and charming manner, and harsh in his judgment upon it; his vocation as instructor led him to look for and develop a web of thoughts and emotions, where there was nothing more than a simple utterance of nature. He now gave himself up entirely to the delight of a more intimate intercourse with a nature so finely planned and so richly gifted. He believed that butterfly inconstancy was a justified peculiarity of female nature, which he only was apt to handle too roughly.

Hitherto he had known only the almost manlike conscientiousness and industry of his mother and aunt: here was a nature which seemed to desire nothing beyond the graceful sipping of froth. Why expect her to be otherwise?

Erich and Bella were walking together in the park, Roland and Lina sat with Clodwig, and Bella complained to Erich that she often had religious doubts which she could not overcome, and still existence would be a cruel problem without a belief in another compensating life. Without wishing to shake this opinion, Erich sought to impart to her that comfort which can be attained through pure reason. There was a strange contradiction in both of them; they had the sensation of ever speaking of something surpassing all life, and still at the bottom of life itself, and in a manner and direction which they would not acknowledge to themselves.

Suddenly Bertram came riding up on a foaming horse, and cried out at a distance:

"Herr Captain, you must come home at once!"

"What has happened?" demanded Erich.

Clodwig came up with Roland and Lina; Prancken also appeared at a window and asked:

"What has happened?"

"Thieves, robbers!" cried Bertram. "A burglary has been committed—Herr Sonnenkamp's room."

Erich and Prancken were soon in the carriage on their way to the Villa; Prancken was very much put out, for he had taken the responsibility.

For a long time the three did not speak a word. Roland first broke the silence, asking:

"Erich, what do you suppose Franklin would have said and thought of such a robbery?"

In an angry tone, Prancken interposed:

"I should think that a son's first question ought to be: What will my father say to it?"

Roland and Erich were silent.

Again they rode on for awhile in silence. Erich was racked by tormenting reflections; he appeared to himself as a double thief. Yonder the rooms of the Villa had been broken into; and what had he done? He had forgotten a soul confided to him, and still more, accepted by him through friendship and kindness; he had sought, by words, and thoughts, and looks, under the guise of intellectual intercourse and high aspirations, to attract to himself the most precious thing confided to him—the wife of his friend. He pressed his hand to his heart; it beat as though it must burst. Those men who have stolen coined gold are punished by the law, and thou—who shall punish thee? He sat deeply perplexed; and when he saw that Roland's glance rested upon him, he cast down his eyes.

With trembling voice he said at last, collecting himself, that he must take the entire responsibility on himself; he was sensible of Prancken's kindness, but he felt that no one could become his substitute—he would bear all the consequences of his neglect of duty alone. He blamed himself so unmercifully, that Roland as well as Prancken regarded him with astonishment.

CHAPTER XXI.

LEARN TO UNDERSTAND WICKEDNESS.

VILLA EDEN had hitherto been surrounded by a mysterious charm. Vexation, envy, and fear had spread the opinion that all was not as it should be with its inhabitants; not with Herr Sonnenkamp, who showed himself much abroad, and not with Frau Ceres, who showed herself rarely at all. The notices on the walls, threatening trespassers with spring-guns and man-traps, had produced in the minds of the people a dread almost as of something supernatural; they said Herr Sonnenkamp had impregnated the points of the traps with a poison against which there was no cure. The servants of the house had something of their master's reserve; they rarely had any intercourse with others, and the people barely exchanged salutations with them. But now, through the robbery, it appeared as though the mysterious dragon, which lurked around the Villa, one scarcely knew how or where, was nothing more than a scarecrow. It seemed as if the decoration of the beautiful white house was suddenly removed, as if the glistening window-panes were obscured; all locks seemed to have burst, and soon the rumor that the servants of the house had committed the theft spread and took root. The people on the roads, and in the villages through which they passed, looked up at Erich, Roland, and Prancken, as they drove rapidly by, and nodded to them. But few of them raised their caps, and these looked confused, for all really wanted to say: "It's all up now with your secrecy, now the justices are coming to find out what your goings-on are up there, among you."

The two men and Roland arrived at the Villa: here they found everybody cast down and uneasy.

The steward at once asserted that the burglary could have

been committed only by people belonging to the house. Everything had been well locked, no dog had barked; consequently the thieves must have known the house well, and been intimate with the dogs.

The magistrates and officers had already come.

Sonnenkamp's room had been broken into; precious things, whose value could not be estimated—among them a dagger with jewels on the hilt—had been taken away. The thieves had also tried the fire-proof safe, but in vain. From the dining-room, large gold and silver vessels, which had been standing on the buffet, had disappeared; and Roland's gold watch, which, at his departure for Wolfsgarten, he had left on the table before his bed, was gone too. Roland's pillow had been taken; it was found on the wall, where pieces of broken glass had been set up to prevent any one from climbing over, but now it had proved a soft support, preventing all injury.

Footprints of two kinds were discovered in the park and behind the greenhouse. Where the garden mould was prepared the thieves must have stumbled, for the impression of a human body was plainly visible on a great heap of earth. Here one of the thieves had fallen. Here, too, lay a pair of old boots belonging to Grubworm. They were compared with the footprints in the garden; they fitted exactly. This gave an indication, but a very unreliable one. Just then Grubworm came up the path, to go about his usual work; he heard with astonishment what had happened. He was allowed to work on undisturbed.

The examining justice and his assistant, the mayor of the village, and a few noted men, were assembled in the balcony-room; they made and rejected many guesses. Roland stood aside, staring at the pillow which had been taken from his bed and served the thieves in crossing the wall.

With a pale face he heard them consult together, trying to liscover something about one man and another.

Grubworm came up to the assembled men, and said that he also had been robbed of a pair of boots. The examining judge replied at once:

"To be sure, the robbery has been committed in your boots."

Grubworm stared stupidly, as if he did not understand what this meant.

The examining judge had him arrested at once. He lamented that suspicion always fell on the innocent, and Roland begged to have the poor old man released.

"I'll strangle the first one that touches me!" cried Grubworm. He appeared a changed man.

The judge beckoned to two men, and instantly Grubworm's hands were tied behind his back.

Erich led Roland away. Why should he become acquainted with the dark side of human existence?

Fortunately the Major came up at this moment. Erich gave Roland into his charge, and the Major said:

"My boy, here's a lesson for you: you can be robbed of everything except what you've got in your brain; and as long as your heart's in the right place they can't rob you of that either. Remember that."

The examining judge sent for all the servants, and examined them in regard to everybody who had lately been at the Villa. They mentioned many persons; but the steward said:

"The Captain took the Krischer all over the house, and when the Krischer went away, he said to me: 'You're taking care of the rich man's money and things, and it would be much better if you wrenched the doors off their hinges, and scattered everything behind them to the winds.'"

Erich could not deny that the Krischer had examined everything closely, and talked confusedly about rich and poor, but he thought he could vouch for the Krischer's honesty.

The judge said nothing, but sent two officers to the Krischer's house, to institute a search there.

The Krischer smiled, and shrugged his shoulders, when he saw them depart on this errand.

They found nothing. But in a kennel a dog was chained, and barked incessantly.

"Loosen the dog from the chain!" said one of the officers to the Krischer, who, mumbling inaudibly, had followed them all over the premises and about the yard.

"Why?"

"Because I want you to. And if you don't do it right off, now, I'll shoot the dog."

The Krischer unchained the dog. The kennel was searched, and here in the straw were Roland's watch and the jewelled dagger. The Krischer protested his innocence, but he was at once arrested and fettered. On the way from his house to the Villa he continually held up his chains, as if he would call on the fields, the vineyards, and the sky above: "Look at me, see in what state I am forced to walk about!"

A list of the stolen things was made out, so far as they could be named. Roland was called, and he had to put his name under a legal instrument, for the first time. Erich stood by, and said to the Major:

"It's impossible to foretell how deep an impression this may have on the youth."

"It won't hurt him," replied the Major. "He has a sound heart; and Fräulein Milch always says, 'A young heart and a young stomach digest quickly.'"

But Fräulein Milch wasn't right this time; for when the Krischer was led away in chains Roland burst out into bitter lamentation.

A further trace was found. The groom, who had been a spy of Prancken, and in his pay, had been dismissed by Sonnenkamp, but within the last few days he had been seen in the vicinity, and recognized, although he had rendered himself almost unrecognizable.

Telegrams were at once sent in all directions to arrest the supposed thief. A telegram was also directed to Sonnenkamp.

The Priest came, and expressed regret tempered with noble mercy; but begged of Erich not to take the matter too much to heart, as he, fresh from the pursuit of science, was not sufficiently acquainted with the depravity of men, and might, therefore, allow himself to be too much overcome by it. Erich was very humble; the Priest could have no suspicion of the reason. Erich had once said that whoever devotes himself to Truth must renounce all else; now he tormented himself with the reproach that he stood opposite a man who realized this doctrine in his way, while he, Erich, had become faithless to himself by yielding to the seductions of a spirited play. And when the Priest now told him, repeatedly, how we must at every step be prepared for the wickedness of men, Erich, who scarcely knew what to reply, said that he realized it all perfectly; that he had voluntarily passed some time in the penitentiary, there to guide guilty men back to their better self.

When the priest praised this action of Erich's, neither he nor Erich noticed what an impression this disclosure had made on Roland. He was in the hands of a man who had sought to convert convicts—who had lived in the penitentiary!

A deep dread and estrangement took root in the youth's soul. The purpose for which Erich had gone there was entirely lost sight of. Roland felt himself degraded. He sat for a long time mute, and absorbed in himself, his face covered by his hands.

The Priest at last went up to him, exhorting him not to allow his soul to be desolated by this occurrence, but rather to learn from it, to put no trust in earthly goods; not in that which we possess, and, above all, not in the so-called faith of mankind; for this faith, he said, was deceptive, and every day gave us occasion to question it. Faith in God, in that exalted Being, eternal and unchangeable, which had never proved false, was the only thing which would remain ever firm.

When Erich and Roland were alone, Roland still remained mute and brooding. At last he asked:

"Does my father know what you have been?"

"Yes."

"And why didn't you tell me of it?"

"Why? I had no reason for concealing it from you, and none for telling it."

The youth again hid his face in his hands; and now that Erich had something to defend, wherein he was pure, and while at the same time there was something in his soul about which no one but himself reproached him, he explained to Roland how he had thought it his duty to devote himself to these most unfortunate of men. Erich spoke so impressively, that the youth suddenly removed his hands from his face, and held one out toward him, exclaiming fervently:

"Forgive me! you are better than all other men!"

These words cut Erich to the quick.

Justice and her myrmidons had left the Villa; Prancken, too, had ridden away. Roland continually looked about timidly, as if he had seen a spectre, or a demon. Criminal men had gone up the stairs; at these doors they had tested their tools: a desecration had come over the house, and over all property. He had not lost his pleasure merely in the things that had been taken, but in those it had been impossible to take away—in what the evil-doers had had to leave behind them.

Roland begged of Erich not to leave him for a moment—he felt so uneasy. Night had come. Roland did not want to go to bed; it seemed to him that he could no more find repose where thievish hands had robbed him of his pillow. He begged Erich to stay with him, and the latter promised to do so.

When Roland was in bed, Erich said to him:

"I still owe you an answer. You asked what Franklin might have said concerning this theft. I think I know. He would have had no pity on the thieves, and would have committed them to the rigor of the law; but he would have maintained that we must not allow the wickedness of individuals to rob us of our faith in the general goodness of mankind; for him to whom thieves could do this injury, they would have robbed of more than hands can lay hold of."

Roland nodded. And when he had gone to sleep, Erich still stood at his bedside, looking contemplatively at the youth, who must so early become acquainted with all this evil. Of what use is all pondering—of what avail all deliberate guidance? An invisible, unconquerable power, the great connection of all life, does far more toward educating a man, and in quite a different way too, than any one individual can do. Erich stood a long while at the window, and looked out over the river and the vine-clad hills. We all toil with our best strength, but the result of our toil lies not under our control, it lies in the power of that invisible, all-controlling force, whose essential nature we cannot fathom, but only name—God!

Erich was deeply shaken. The incident could not exert as deep an influence upon the youth as upon him, for he saw himself torn away from the abyss by a force which was more powerful than all his reflection. He looked into space, and within himself he formed a strong resolution.

He was called away. The examining Judge had sent over a telegram from Sonnenkamp—it was as follows:

"'Give up trip to sea-shore; coming back; shall discover thieves, no matter what their position."

BOOK SIXTH.

CHAPTER I.

THE MASTER IS BACK AGAIN.

AS a monarch returns to his palace, where a mutiny has lately broken out, Herr Sonnenkamp returned to his Villa. Every step that he took in the house, every glance to a servant, said: "I have come back again, and with me order and power."

Erich did not shift his guilt to Prancken's shoulders; he confessed that he had been guilty of an act of negligence, and Sonnenkamp seemed to find pleasure in humiliating Erich deeply. Sonnenkamp liked to govern others. He was humane enough to desire voluntary obedience, but when he saw that this was not yielded, he did not rest till he had crushed the other; and when he had crushed and overthrown him, then he took pleasure in raising him again, for then he was sure of his own power. This self-reliant Captain-doctor had assumed a bearing which was unbecoming his station; now he was humbled, and had to be grateful for all kindness and indulgence. Sonnenkamp had no idea how willingly, and for what reason Erich humbled himself; he only recognized in this ready submission a victory of his own power; while Erich acknowledged to himself that, enslaved by Bella's charming witchery, he had lost the strict watchfulness which was his duty.

Sonnenkamp soon discovered that the theft was not of much consequence. With a certain maliciousness, he said:

"The scoundrels have stolen the dagger with the jewels. The point is poisoned; whoever scratches himself with it is lost."

Erich could scarcely state that the dagger was already in the hands of justice, for he was filled with horror. Why did this man keep a poisoned dagger?

Prancken and the Major soon arrived, and Prancken was honest enough to take the responsibility on himself: but he could not refrain from saying that before the event Erich had left the house to go to the musical festival, and had acquired a surprising renown there.

Sonnenkamp smiled and said:

"You kept Roland from joining us on the journey to the baths, to guard him against all diversion—did you carry out your purpose?"

Erich could not reply, for the Priest came in, and Sonnenkamp, who had never yet made a donation to the Church, declared at once that the gold and silver vessels which had been stolen from the sideboard should now belong to the Church. In apparent anger, he added:

"I don't want them in the house any more. Your Reverence will consecrate them anew."

Erich, who stood by, said in a low voice to the Major, how glad he was of this, and what a good impression this would make on Roland, whom the thieves had robbed of the greater part of his peace of mind. But Sonnenkamp heard him, and said:

"Most worthy Captain, I don't care much about fine feelings, and confess, openly, that I am glad that Roland begins early to know the lower classes, of whose genial disposition we hear so much; and understands that there is nothing there but a secret conspiracy against the whole wealthy class, which only awaits favorable opportunity to break out—or rather, to break in."

Sonnenkamp was extremely bright and animated, he only found it unpleasant that there was so much talk about the affair in the neighborhood, and that so much valuable time would be lost in going to court. Frau Ceres did not say a word about the robbery—it seemed almost as if she knew nothing of it: she only expressed herself pleased at Roland's having grown so much in the mean time. To Erich she said that she had met at the baths a relative of his mother's, who had spoken of her in the most exalted terms, and that the lady was as high-born as she was charming.

On the first evening after the return of Sonnenkamp and his family, a carriage drove up, in which were Bella and Clodwig. Erich was very glad to see his friend; but he was rather shy of Bella. She said to him in a low voice, behind her fan:

"We have come, to protect you against this wild man; he must see that you belong to us. And now leave everything and come with us."

A tremor ran through Erich; a mute bow expressed his thanks.

Bella observed how timorously Clodwig stood near Sonnenkamp: the polished, dainty little man always felt a new uneasiness, a certain timidity, whenever he came in contact with Sonnenkamp's herculean figure. Bella playfully relieved his embarrassment, saying:

"Herr Sonnenkamp, you have seen much of life; have you ever heard of thieves who confess openly that they have stolen or intend to steal?"

Sonnenkamp looked at her in amazement

Bella exclaimed, laughing:

"Look at us, we are thieves in broad daylight."

Then turning to Clodwig, she continued:

"Now you go on, dear Clodwig."

With much hesitation, Clodwig said that he desired to engage Erich's services. Sonnenkamp cast a sharp glance at Bella: he had raised the forefinger of his left hand. He meant to tell Bella, with a pleasant warning: "I understand you"—but he laid his finger on his mouth and said:

"I am glad that our Herr Erich"—he emphasized the word "our" strangely—"that our Herr Erich stands so high in your favor."

Erich was curiously struck by the peculiar stress on the word "our;" he seemed to have become property. And he received a new surprise, when Sonnenkamp held out his hand to him, saying:

"You will remain with us, will you not?"

Erich nodded.

Bella now related at great length the particulars of the visit she had paid Erich's mother in the University town. She evidently wanted to impress on Herr Sonnenkamp that a man of Erich's rank and station was not to be put down because of an act of carelessness.

Sonnenkamp whistled inaudibly; a plan seemed to be maturing within him.

Bella again succeeded in being alone with Erich for a short while, and she told him how pleased she felt that she had at last succeeded in the management of an intrigue. She had known that Herr Sonnenkamp would not dismiss Erich, but she had known also, that he would try to humiliate him because of his negligence; therefore she had induced Clodwig to come here. Erich was all gratitude.

"Did you observe," she asked in a low voice, "how this Herr Sonnenkamp raised his finger, how his glance fell on me? This man believes that our friendship is something more than friendship. The impure do not believe in purity. I hope you will not misunderstand me, if I sometimes neglect you intentionally in the presence of this spying rogue."

She extended her hand to Erich and held his clasped for a long time: he trembled. Neither imagined that two eyes had peered out of the bushes and that a sharp ear had heard all. As they passed on, Sonnenkamp, who had held his breath, again breathed freely.

CHAPTER II.

WHAT CANNOT BE STOLEN.

THE next morning news arrived that the groom, whom Sonnenkamp had dismissed shortly before leaving home because he suspected him of being Prancken's spy, had been arrested in the capital, in the act of offering a large silver-bowl to a secondhand dealer.

It was Roland who brought this information to Erich, and it seemed, indeed, that all their retirement and study were likely to be interrupted at all hours by reminiscences of this occurrence. Of what use was study, in the midst of this perturbation of mind? What would take root now? Erich thought of going out hunting with Roland more frequently: he must have some diversion, and acquire new energy and a brighter view of things by means of other pursuits. But he turned in exactly the opposite direction: not diversion but deeper application was to aid Roland. How happy it made him to hear Roland say:

"Let us forget everything else; let us go on with our work quietly."

The youth had acquired a desire for study, which made him disinclined to all diversion, and let him find his greatest enjoyment in his books.

Roland soon perceived that a new animation had come over Erich, but he could not divine whence it came; it was the animation of a rescued man—one who was rescuing himself. When Erich thought of the days at Wolfsgarten, of their playing and trifling with everything that fills the heart of man, he appeared to himself like a thief. He had thoughtlessly squandered all his intellectual property, which he had acquired by assiduous labor; he had permitted himself a flirtation, disguised under the exchange of great thoughts, with Bella, the wife of his friend: a flirtation—he went further, he called it a love affair outright. He looked on himself as a church-robber; and small, infinitely small in comparison, was what these poor people had done. Erich was deeply crushed in his own estimation. How gladly would he have gone on a pilgrimage with Roland to some temple where he could purify himself, and strengthen Roland anew! Whither should he turn?

It is much easier for a man, hunted down by others and heavily laden in his own consciousness, to enter the high-towering visible temples of the earth than the invisible ones of knowledge. Still, Erich succeeded. And what for himself he could only have conquered by hard labor, or perhaps not at all, he accomplished now as a matter of duty toward another; he plunged into knowledge, and everything appeared clearer and more transparent. As a practised swimmer, rejoicing in the rush of the towering waves, dives, and makes his way back again to the light, and parts the waters with robust arms, so Erich plunged into science; and it made his heart beat high with joy to see the great waves come roaring on: then all petty dread and hesitation, and all battling with himself ceased.

Roland, too, experienced a deep revulsion of feeling. He often went about like one in a dream; the earth beneath him which he now knew to be in perpetual oscillation, rocked before his eyes; the heavens no longer existed; the world of faith was demolished; a new world was discovered. And mingling with all these ideas, came whizzing a feeling as if all private property were abolished, and all men were equally poor and equally rich. Erich noticed the great commotion in his pupil's soul. One day Roland asked timidly:

"Tell me, Erich, will there ever be a time when there will be no private property in the world, and no thieves?"

Erich was startled when he observed that a strange thought abode in the soul of the youth. He explained that he had only made the statement in the way of an illustration; the conception could never be realized: he had only wished to indicate comparatively, how great a change might be brought about in the feelings of men and their mode of being. And again indefinable fermentation appeared in the soul of the youth, who now begged Erich to go with him to the Krischer's house, in order to see how the wife and the children fared. He said that he had met the Krischer's son, who was a cooper in the Wine-count's employ; that he had offered to shake hands with him, telling him that a son should not be blamed even if his father did do wrong, but that in this case his father had surely not done the deed. But the cooper had refused to take his hand; he had stared at him, taken his hammer from his leather apron, played with it, and finally gone on.

Erich went with Roland to the Krischer's house; the birds in the cages sang; and high above all, the blackbird sang over and over again his "Life let us cherish." The dogs frisked about merrily. The wife looked grief-worn and wretched; she broke out in lamentation, and told her visitors that as soon as her husband was arrested, she had wished to let all the birds fly away, but that her son, the cooper, insisted upon having everything unchanged until his father returned, for he would surely be set free very soon. The Seven-piper had, in the mean while, taken upon himself a portion of the Krischer's duties, and the cooper, who had to work hard enough by day, had undertaken the night-service. Everything was to be carried on as before, so that her husband might enter upon his duties at once.

Erich offered the woman money ; but she declined, saying that she would take nothing, because her son, the cooper, had forbidden her accepting anything from the house of Sonnenkamp.

As they were driving to the Villa, Roland asked: "If the Krischer is innocent after all, and I really believe that he is innocent, who will recompense him for all the torments and the disgrace which he must bear?"

Erich did not know what to answer; all he could say was, that in this matter it was again evident that the best part and possession of life cannot be replaced by money.

CHAPTER III.

A NEW ALLIANCE AND A SUMMER FESTIVAL.

SCARCE two weeks were past when the continuity of the instruction was interrupted. Frau Ceres, who was silent as a rule, and took no interest in what went on about her, now mentioned frequently that she had promised the wife of the Privy-councillor, whom she had met at the baths, to take Roland to her very soon.

A trip to the capital was resolved upon. Erich was not invited to join the party. They drove in two carriages ; Frau Ceres, Miss Perini, and Roland sat in one, Sonnenkamp and Prancken in the other.

Prancken expressed his delight at Sonnenkamp's generosity to the Church: he had taken measures on his part to secure the co-operation of the higher clergy, whose influence at Court was very great in the execution of the plan. Prancken's conscience smote him somewhat for deriving court influence from his spiritual regeneration, and from his acquaintance with the Bishop; yet there was sufficient worldly vanity left in him to make him willing to have the spiritual illumination in which he secretly gloried, pass for sagacity in the opinion of the world, and especially of Sonnenkamp. He was very glad at the ease with which the acquaintance with the wife of the Privy-councillor had been brought about: it was possible to influence the lady through favors, with which the husband must be approached very carefully, if at all.

They drove past the handsome Villa, all of whose shutters were closed, and Prancken hinted that Herr Sonnenkamp must buy the Villa, so as to sell it again to the Privy-councillor's wife for a trifling sum; she having for a long time entertained a desire for a place of the kind. Sonnenkamp was ready to do so, provided the goal could be reached in this way. Prancken added that this was one of the levers, but of course not all.

The two gentlemen were all alone by themselves, but neither named the goal definitely, until at length Sonnenkamp said that the wife of the Privy-councillor had informed him that the Wine-count was to be ennobled. He wished that this elevation might be granted him first; he thought he had a greater claim, although he proposed to marry his daughter, not to a nobleman doomed to a speedy death, but to one in the fullest enjoyment of health and life.

Prancken smiled his appreciation of the flattery, but he replied that the precedent of the Wine-count—it was a precedent, by no means a precedence—was rather advantageous than otherwise; for then Sonnenkamp's elevation to the nobility would not be so singular.

"Your case is more difficult than the Wine-count's," he added: "the Bishop stopped at the Wine-count's house on his last journey through the diocese. The Church-party goes for the Wine-count, and it is as influential as it is modest; while you, I would say *we*, have no party at all. So much the better, the victory will be ours alone."

They arrived at the capital.

The Privy-councillor's lady was in good spirit, and said to Prancken, to whom she constantly addressed her conversation—as if he were the chief person, the president of the company—how very glad she was to see a watering-place acquaintance ripen into friendship.

Prancken suggested gracefully that they might possibly become neighbors. The Villa was described in glowing terms, and cautiously, yet not without making it tell. The statement was made that Sonnenkamp had bought it, and was ready to dispose of it on moderate terms, if in that way he could induce noble friends to settle down as his neighbors.

The Privy-councillor's lady was delighted: she knew the house well; it had formerly belonged to a friend of hers, and she had visited there at intervals. She called those happy who can establish themselves upon such an estate, and have noble men for their neighbors. She related that she had told her husband that it was a shame that a man like Sonnenkamp had not yet received an order.

After this introduction, Prancken developed his plan; and her ladyship added, that society must be highly pleased to have a gentleman of Herr Sonnenkamp's character and influence raised to a higher rank. Sonnenkamp acted very modestly, even bashfully; a girl who receives a proposal, which she has expected, could not look down to the floor more demurely—he even blushed.

They moved their chairs closer together, as if they could at length venture to indicate that confidential relations existed between them. The Privy-councillor's wife requested her visitors not to speak to her husband of the matter, she would put it properly before him; still, it would be well if others co-operated. It might be best to have Count Wolfsgarten broach the matter at Court; then it would be easy to play into his hands.

Prancken spoke of the very strong friendship which Clodwig entertained for Herr Sonnenkamp; but he thought that the matter ought to be pushed very gently and delicately, and that could only be done by a person of her ladyship's well-known tact.

Sonnenkamp said again that he would not ask to be raised to the nobility—the honor must be offered to him; his friends must bring that about. He enjoyed the delicacy with which her ladyship handled the matter, and he handled it in like manner. The expression of his face clearly said, "Well! this is a new way at last."

He moved his hand through the air as if he were stroking the fur of a remarkably smooth cat.

"Do any vineyards go with the Villa?" asked the Privy-councillor's lady, suddenly.

"If I remember rightly, three acres, and most favorably situated," replied Prancken.

He winked at Sonnenkamp, to make him understand that he must buy this land.

Sonnenkamp suddenly lost his modesty and bashfulness; the question was becoming a money-question: now he was master. He wanted to tell the lady that he would only consent to bargain piece for piece—she was not to receive the Villa, with the vineyards, until he had received his patent of nobility; but he was afraid to say so in Prancken's presence. And, again, it did not seem necessary to disclose his plan of action at this early stage. When the time comes he will be man enough not to allow himself to be taken by surprise. A smile of victory played about his features.

The Privy-councillor entered. He greeted Sonnenkamp with courteous politeness, and thanked the company for the attentions which they had shown his wife at Vichy.

They went to the drawing-room, where Roland had been talking to a son of the Privy-conncillor, who was a cadet; and soon Roland, whose beauty made every eye brighten, was the centre of the group. His lordship expressed his approval of the choice of a well-informed, though somewhat eccentric man, like Erich; and when Roland, being questioned, declared that he wanted to become an officer, the Councillor advised his parents to send him to the military academy as soon as possible.

In a low voice, Prancken said to the Privy-councillor that he agreed entirely with Herr Sonnenkamp, in his wish of not having the boy enter until the family were ennobled. The delay would spare him many unpleasant experiences; indeed, it would be awkward if the young man were suddenly to become noble while at school; he would be subjected to much teasing from his comrades.

The Privy-councillor spoke of the restoration of the ruined castle, and of Sonnenkamp's celebrated gardens, and stated that they had been mentioned favorably at Court.

Sonnenkamp begged to be allowed to send some of his fruits to the palace, especially some fine bananas, which had turned out beyond his expectation. Prancken extolled the great skill by which Herr Sonnenkamp was enabled to have grapes on his table every month in the year.

The Privy-councillor replied that he did not doubt that Herr Sonnenkamp's kindness would be appreciated, but that he could not act in the matter; the Court-chamberlain, a cousin of Herr von Prancken, would certainly accept the offer.

Prancken immediately took Herr Sonnenkamp to the Hofmarschal's house. Roland rode out with the cadet Frau Ceres remained with the Privy-councillor's wife, who appeared much embarrassed when Frau Ceres urged her to accept the coral necklace which she herself wore, and of which her ladyship had expressed great admiration.

Her ladyship had to comply, but she besought Frau Ceres to look upon her acceptance of it as a token of intimate friendship, of which no one need know. She affirmed again and again, that she worked for her friends without any selfish consideration. Of course she felt convinced that Frau Ceres was leagued with the others in the design of winning her over by presents, and she hinted at it very cautiously.

Frau Ceres looked at her with a face full of astonishment: again she appeared terribly stupid in her own eyes; the lady spoke of matters which she could not comprehend.

It had not been the intention of the Sonnenkamp party to remain in town overnight; but when the Privy-councillor's lady proposed a drive to a summer-resort, Prancken insisted on their staying all night; for it was of the greatest importance to have Frau Ceres and the Privy-councillor's lady, Sonnenkamp, Prancken, and the Privy-councillor drive in open carriages through the town to the resort where the best and most select society was to be met. The best society should acknowledge Sonnenkamp's connection with him and the Privy-councillor as a fact.

On this drive, the wife of the Privy-councillor had an idea which was as kind as it was clever. She was pleased with both qualities, but more with her good-nature: she gained a supporter, and she helped a poor woman. With charity and condescension she spoke of Erich's mother, who had romantically sacrificed her position to a so-called ideal love. The Privy-councillor's lady and Prancken had come to so perfect an understanding, that she did nothing without his approval; a slight nod showed her that she might venture still further, so she asked Herr Sonnenkamp to do something for Erich's mother, if possible to take her into his house. Aunt Claudine, too, she spoke of in terms of the highest praise.

Her ladyship saw clearly that the intimacy between her family and Herr Sonnenkamp's would be confirmed more easily, if Erich's mother and aunt lived at his house, for she would then cultivate them, rather than this man; indeed it would be her duty to visit the noble ladies, to alleviate the unpleasantness of their dependent position; and all this it would be very easy to do if she lived in the Villa, to which several acres of vineyards were attached.

So the various motives were intermingled, and the mixture was good and refreshing.

Sonnenkamp smiled very benignly; but in his own heart, he thought: "This noble set hang together more firmly than a gang of thieves; and now they are a gang of thieves. All the broken-down nobility mean to have me set them up again."

He agreed politely with her ladyship; but he thought, "You haven't got the Villa yet, and Frau Dournay may sit and work at her sewing-machine a little longer."

They drove past the country-seat of the Prince, who had lately returned from America. Everything was well kept; and in the small pavilion, in the wood by the roadside, a table was set, and servants stood by. A military band was playing in a public garden, and colored lanterns were hung upon the trees. The officers of the Guards had gotten up a summer-night's festival, and scarcely had the one band played a piece when another began on the other side. In the centre of the garden, under a large tent, a table was spread for the officers; near by, around smaller tables, sat the dignitaries of the capital, with their wives and daughters in bright summer-dresses.

There was quite a stir when the two carriages, drawn by Sonnenkamp's fine horses, drove up. Prancken made all the necessary arrangements very quickly, and the company sat down at one of the best tables. Many eye-glasses were directed at them. Prancken went to his comrades, shaking hands with one and another, but he returned soon to Sonnenkamp and the party.

Her ladyship leaned on Sonnenkamp's arm, and was wonderfully affable. Prancken escorted Frau Ceres. Roland had gone with the cadet to the shooting-gallery; he hit the bull's-eye every time.

Herr Sonnenkamp was presented to the General, who, upon Sonnenkamp's invitation, promised to call upon him soon.

Prancken was happy to be able to say, that he brought a recruit, and pointed to Roland.

It grew dark—the colored lanterns were lit. Then the guns were fired, the trumpets sounded a flourish, and cheers rent the air; the Prince had driven over from his country-seat to attend the supper of the Guards. Both bands struck up the national hymn, and all were supremely happy; but the happiest man of all was Sonnenkamp, for he was presented to the Prince, who, to be sure, addressed only a few unmeaning words to him. However, the world had witnessed the introduction, and seen the Prince talking and bowing to him.

Highly pleased with the day, the party drove back to the capital. The colored lamps still shone, and the music still floated through the air.

The following item appeared in the morning paper: "Last night the cuirassiers of the Guard celebrated their anniversary at Mount Rudolph. His Highness Prince Leonhard honored the festival by his presence. Among the guests we noticed Herr Sonnenkamp of Villa Eden and his family."

CHAPTER IV.

THE PLACE IS FILLED.

WHILE the Sonnenkamp family were in the capital, Erich rode over to Wolfsgarten. He had conquered every treacherous, dishonorable thought, or rather he had never allowed any to spring up. Now he only kept thinking that it was his duty to improve the friendship which was certainly honorable on Bella's part, in order to make her more fully appreciate her husband's truly exalted merits, which were indeed worthy of all respect and devotion. This is what he intended to do. Bright, and full of spirit, he rode along.

He found Clodwig alone. Bella had gone out riding, with stranger visiting them. Clodwig was very happy to be quit alone with Erich; on his former visits he had so often left him to the boy, and accompanied Bella. Clodwig now told Erich that the son of an old friend who had lived in Naples as Russian ambassador, had come to him to pursue the serious studies of Farming in Germany, under his guidance.

The great fact that the Emperor of Russia had abolished serfdom, produced a still greater one, both morally and economically: landowners must now increase their own power, as well as that of the soil. Instead of mere landowners, they must be landtillers. Clodwig told Erich that this young prince, like all of his class, had drifted about in the whirlpool of Paris life; but there was a good germ in him, and a force of will, which allowed his friends to hope for the best. "The Russians," he continued, "have a sort of passion for self-sacrifice, and a devotion to the lower classes; and this passion often takes such powerful hold of worldlings that it appears like the reform of those regenerated sinners who, coming away from wild orgies, become suddenly conscious of their moral duty."

"Now observe," said he, as if instructing Erich. "There is no aristocracy as eager for culture as the Russian; but, unfortunately, the men are only zealous in the pursuit of ideas for a year or two, then they are apt to become careless. They have a great talent for imitation, but it remains to be tested how long this will last, and whether they will ever produce anything new. Perhaps the abolition of serfdom is the great moral turning-point of their history."

Erich pointed out that it was a glorious sign of a new free spirit, that this great act was not the work of the Church, which ought to have considered it its business, but of pure humanity, which bears no religious impress.

"This way of looking upon it is new to me," replied Clodwig, adding his thanks.

The two men were still engaged in far-reaching dissertations about the power of the intellect. Clodwig was just explaining how his soul was often pained at the thought that after all brute force still had more influence on the mind than men cared to acknowledge, when Bella entered.

Her face glowed as Erich advanced to meet her. And the young gentleman, who was of aristocratic appearance, but had a somewhat weary air, greeted Erich very courteously; he was charmed to hear Erich speak French fluently, as he expressed himself but imperfectly in German. He added that one could not help perceiving at once that Erich was of French descent; there was something in his pronunciation which only the French organ can produce.

After having separated for a short time they all met again at luncheon, in the summer-house.

Clodwig must have urged the Russian to attach himself to Erich; for the young man soon said to him:

"I shall be very glad if you will let me learn something under your instruction."

He said this with a certain childish submissiveness, and so cordially, that Erich offered him his hand saying:

"I am sure I shall be able to learn something from you."

"Excepting whist, which I play pretty well, as I am generally told, I don't believe that anything can be learned of me," laughed the Russian.

And as a man who turns for information about the products of the country to the producers themselves, he said:

"I am told philosophy is no longer the fashion in Germany. Can you tell me the reason?"

Clodwig nodded. The theme was well chosen, and the question modestly put.

Erich confessed himself unable to give precise information on the point; but suggested that perhaps philosophy was less prominent as a science, but that it had become the method of all the sciences.

"Are you also of the opinion," asked the Prince, "that Kant's 'Categorical Imperative' and the French revolution produced the same results?"

Bella leaned back her head, and gazed at the blue sky. The men are now going to discuss subjects which, out of deference to the lady, they ought to postpone to some other time, but she will be patient and listen.

Erich explained that Kant's maxim, "Act so that you may wish your rule of conduct to be all men's rule of conduct," established the same ideal which the revolution had established in decreeing equality before the law; all privileges were to be done away with.

"But does not this equality destroy all greatness, all genius?" asked the Russian.

Now Bella thought the time had come to sit silent no longer, and with ready wit she added:

"I would ask more: Do not superior beings create new laws in the intellectual, the moral, the political, as well as the æsthetic world?"

Clodwig smiled at Bella's leading out her whole stud at once, but Erich replied very seriously:

"This is the misery for which Jesuitism in the Church and frivolity in the world are equally accountable. We are willing to accord to certain characters, and certain characters demand for themselves, rights and exceptional positions, the general maintenance of which would destroy human society. Superior endowments impose additional duties, but do not confer extraordinary rights. Before God and eternal Morality we are all equal; Christianity expressed this truth exhaustively, in saying that we are all children of God. Children are equal before their father. But now the Church has created indulgences, the state primogenitures, and a sophistical system of ethics, illegitimate privileges. No one iron man will come to establish the new kingdom of equality: the kingdom has come; the iron rail is its pathway, steam its horse."

"You talk very well; I am glad to have made your acquaintance," said the Prince to Erich. "I shall be delighted to have you call on me often; or will you allow me to look in upon you?"

Erich, who had become excited as the conversation proceeded, declined the honor; remarking, that he must devote his time and strength to his pupil. He was angry with himself for giving up, at every demand, the full contents of his being; he had no social small-talk; he thought he understood the meaning of the young man's praise, "You talk very well." Yes, this is the way with the aristocracy! New dishes, piquant sauces, new music, charming caprizzios! Is not he a fool who allows them to peer into the sanctuaries of his being?

Erich was startled when he caught Bella's eye; it had a strange, fixed look, for she thought: "Have I deserved that he should thus teach me—that no one can claim a special law for his own conduct?" She was highly indignant, yet only smiled painfully; but she soon recovered her composure, and managed to have the two young men go through an intellectual tilt in her presence.

But the Prince was Erich's superior in the statement of facts and in the knowledge of the world. Erich yielded gladly on many points.

When they were walking in the garden, the Prince, who had in a very cordial way put his arm in Erich's, asked him whether he knew Herr Weidmann, into whose house Count Clodwig wished to send him.

Erich said that he had only seen him for a few moments, but that the gentleman was generally much liked.

"If you had a friend like yourself," said the Prince, pressing Erich's arm—"if you knew of a man who would like to be my companion, my teacher, I could procure him a life-appointment, or—you will excuse the question—perhaps you would yourself—"

Erich expressed his gratitude, but promised to think of a proper person.

Bella joined them, and Erich walked beside the two, swayed by conflicting emotions. He had pondered so much, to find a way back from that border-line of friendship on which so many dangers lurk; now his reflection had become unnecessary—his place was occupied by another. Although he would hardly acknowledge it to himself, his vanity was wounded; a man of the world had come, whose insignificance was only hidden beneath elegant externals; yet he became at once a greater favorite than Erich, with his clumsiness and his perpetual freight-train of historic learning. He was vexed at Bella's intimacy with the Russian, and a strange confusion of feeling arose in his heart. Ought he to rejoice because she was simply a coquette, who flirted now with one man and then with another? or did Bella act thus, simply to render her confidential manner toward him less striking?

He was in a peevish, discontented mood. At one time he felt glad because he had received this lesson, and could now return home unburdened and unfettered; and then again he was vexed because he could not readily comprehend and assume the easy manners of society.

The Doctor came, and the conversation took a different tone. He cast a penetrating glance at Bella, Erich, and the Russian; he seemed to understand the situation. There was always a secret feud between Bella and the Doctor.

CHAPTER V.

A SEVERE JUDGMENT.

THE Doctor asked Erich to fasten his horse behind the carriage, and ride with him as far as the Villa.

When they were seated in the carriage, the Doctor puckered his lips, and for some time indulged in an inaudible whistle: then he said:

"Countess Bella is a handsome woman and a clever one: she loves her parrot and evidently might let it fly free in the woods, for it would come back again and sit on her shoulder."

"Allow me to make a remark," said Erich, interrupting him: "I find that people here in the country, who have a very small circle of acquaintances, like to speak of third parties, and certainly—I am not speaking of you, but have often noticed it in others—not in the kindest manner. Doesn't that seem to you like narrowness, or whatever you choose to call it?"

The Doctor must have seen that Erich did not wish to enter on the subject, but yet he replied:

"The most prolific subject of contemplation is the *genus homo*, the most inexhaustible theme in this genus is the variety *mulier*. Nevertheless, I am not speaking of Bella, but of myself —I have discovered a totally new variety in this lady."

"Why certainly, Doctor, the Countess seems entirely normal."

"Have you known her long?"

"But slightly," said Erich, unwilling to commit himself. "But *I* know her. She made a *mariage de convenance*, like many another woman, and I don't blame her very much for that. My opinion differs from that of most men on this subject. In fact, the Countess is less proud of her talents than of her morals. I know that before they were married she told the Count that she was too insignificant for him—was not worthy of him. Intellectually that was just, although the modest humility of it was slightly exaggerated. She has ability, but no soul; she offers nicknacks, but would let one starve for want of good, solid meat. But morally speaking, this confession was the exact truth—morality is with her nothing but convenience."

"I must ask—," said Erich interrupting him.

"And I must ask," cried the Doctor, "that you will allow me to finish my sentence. I mean the morality of the great world, which considers it necessary to be honorable in appearance merely, and is only troubled about a lapse from virtue when it is seen. Everything pure and beautiful is a stern and holy law to the Count; his nature is essentially hostile to all that is impure and unlovely; he would not touch it even though no mortal eye should see him."

The Doctor paused. Erich's heart swelled. Did the man hold the purity of Clodwig before his eyes to show him how base would be even the slightest impulse to deceive or injure such a being?

The Doctor proceeded:

"There can be no higher honor than to be Clodwig's friend. I do not love aristocrats—yes, I may say I hate them—but in this Count Clodwig there is a loftiness of character which, perhaps, is never seen but when fostered from generation to generation; whereas we commoners have to achieve it by individual endeavor, and when we get it, it smells of fresh varnish, liable to rub off at any minute. Even the air by which Clodwig is surrounded seems to be warmed steadily and gently by him; there is no hot flame—always a soothing, pleasant warmth. You see," said he, interrupting himself for the sake of making a joke—"you see that I too have learned from you the art of drawing similes. His only passion is quietness, and this fact makes his giving up so much of his ease for your sake, only so much the more noteworthy. I do not agree with the wicked world, which says that Countess Bella is a dragon. Every week, or at least every month, she must have an honest reputation, or better yet, a dishonest one, to worry like a cat; and like a well-trained dog, she prefers to snap at the eyes of some poor little hare. Having done so, she's satisfied and extremely polite, and harms no one. At the same time she's not particularly bad and cruel. She speaks well of one so long as he's in trouble; when one is subdued, she likes to be clement to him: as soon as one is sick she's kind to him, but as long as he's well he has nothing but harshness to expect from her. Her hair is luxuriant and beautiful, but this doesn't please her so much as it does to be able to say: 'This or that woman has so many pounds of false hair.' She's happy when she can say that this or that lady is scrofulous, for none but the Pranckens are perfectly sound. When she has once asserted anything, she never retracts; she would sooner believe that her husband, Prancken, and the whole world were illogical, than that she was wrong;

Bella von Prancken could never have been wrong. She has never worn an unbecoming dress, and never said a word that might not be graven in stone; and that she calls 'character—strength!' Never to confess an error! It's enough to drive all the logic of the world to the devil. You know the egg-dance, in which a person is blindfolded and dances under somewhat difficult circumstances. Well, Bella can execute the conversational egg-dance with the greatest ease. Did you ever receive one of her delicate notes? So to speak, she knows how to dance on the paper with exquisite grace and dexterity."

Erich passed his hand across his forehead, and hardly knew where he was. The Doctor threw away his half-smoked cigar, and continued:

"The wicked world wishes—and unfortunately its desire could not be fulfilled without cutting the glorious Clodwig to the heart—that some time or other this dragon would meet its unsaintly George. He would have to be a man who strongly craves what is called 'success with the ladies;' but not one to whom the terms 'love,' 'magnanimity,' and 'higher aspirations' are serious words, and yet one who does not use those terms as a cloak for other designs."

Erich knew not what to say: he clenched his hands without speaking, for he felt that he was trembling. The Doctor pulled a string, the break came against the wheel and they drove down the hill. The carriage screamed and grated; below them could be seen a little brook rippling among the rocks. When they reached the valley they proceeded quietly again, and the Doctor continued:

"When I say the wicked world, I'm not using a figure of speech merely, but I must show you what the new variety is with which I have become acquainted in Bella. It is this. There have been and are a good many ladies who really, or in their own imagination, it matters little which, are or think themselves very unfortunate, because they have such insignificant husbands; they themselves are great, unappreciated, etherial souls, but their husbands love horses, dogs, and nothing else. Now, the new variety represented by Bella is this—she is unfortunate because her husband is so distinguished. Had she married one of those military puppets, whose only object in life is to fill a court-uniform, she could regard herself as a lovely victim decorated with flowers for the sacrificial altar: she might patiently renounce the world and bewail herself; yes, perhaps gradually develop into a more exalted being, capable of the loftiest feelings. But, wedded to such a man, she becomes daily more disagreeable and narrow-minded. He offends her, for he makes her see her own deficiencies, expressing his dislike of her frivolity by simply raising his eyebrows. And at bottom—I don't think she confesses it even to herself—she hates her husband, for he looks at her trifling with most serious eyes; he forces her to recognize her absurdities and sillinesses, but he pays a sufficient penalty for doing so. I have come to understand the fable about harpies. Our modern harpies befoul every noble thought and make it nauseating and distasteful, and consequently Clodwig is obliged to fight and struggle for his simple daily-bread of the spirit. And yet she's not altogether devoid of nobleness; she likes to help the sick, only she's somewhat tyrannical in administering her doses. But do you know what's the most dangerous thing about Bella?"

"No, I don't; and I can't conceive what climax you're coming to now."

"A very simple one. In the Church they call it the devil, but at present he appears in the form of a very pliable, noble and self-sacrificing demon, who comes and says: 'Lo, you are this woman's friend, she has trust in you and is gentle, use therefore these means to lead her in the right path; you must teach her to value her husband justly, and reverence him as he deserves.' Now this sophistical demon, however refined he may seem, is the clumsiest of all, for nobody ever learns to appreciate another—certainly no wife to appreciate her husband—by receiving information on the topic from third parties. Life and love are kept in existence by vital force, which can only come from the man himself; and where this does not exist, *there* nothing will avail, though one spake with the tongue of angels. Have you seen the Medusa? The ancients considered it Theseus's most glorious exploit that he vanquished Medusa. She is deadly beauty. In the old time, she turned men to stone, *now* she effeminates them. I have a singular hatred of this woman; and do you know why? Every time I go to Wolfsgarten, she makes a hypocrite of me. I ought not to be so polite to her; and my love for Clodwig is no excuse for my being so. No mortal ever made me so bad as this Bella does; I'm a hypocrite in her presence, and feel so savage that I'm lost in amazement at myself. She's a quack-doctor. If I prescribe a medicine, she knew beforehand just what it would be. Medically speaking, I've had some experience, but Lord! I don't touch her in this respect. She has picked up some domestic remedies and professional terms, so that some people might think that she has investigated the science, but the very essence of her nature is disrespect and impertinent interference in everything, for she thinks that everything is a swindle; and she has no self-respect, for she knows that she's a swindle too. One essential feature of her soul is that she's ungrateful. No matter what is done, she's ungrateful. If you want to see her exact opposite, look at the Major, who is thankful for everything, even the air he breathes. The Major—the old child—is sixty years old, and does not yet believe in the badness of men! If the very devil should come to the Major, the Major would find some good in him. There's no reason for this Bella's existence. When a man is bad, there is always something left of him that may be of use to the world; but when a woman is bad, she's all bad, and only bad. Do you know who just suits Frau Bella?"

"I don't know anything by this time," cried Erich in despair, and feeling as though he must jump out of the carriage.

"The only man who suits her—who can tame and master this whole menagerie, as Bella calls it, is Herr Sonnenkamp; and, at the bottom, they have a deep sympathy with each other."

Erich was glad to find something to laugh at, but the Doctor went on:

"My young friend, I'm a heretic. I believe that women are an inferior race. Men can never be as bad and hypocritical as women. They're not responsible for that last fault, though, for from their childhood up they're continually told: 'Only *act* so; the world cares for nothing but appearances.' But the main point is that they've no *reason;* they never try to find out what a thing *really* is. Everything is painted, embroidered, and sewed for them, as a milliner makes a bonnet or mantilla. And then, too, they're like the lower animals in this respect: they have not the slightest idea of what humanity means; a piece of slander is a sweet morsel for their bloodthirsty throats. Through all animate nature, the female is always the more cruel."

Erich sat still, and listened patiently to this tirade, and as they had now reached the place at which they were to separate, the Doctor returned, for a time, to his inaudible whistle, and then said, with a very red face:

"At least, I've made myself easy in regard to a matter that has long been troubling me. I thank you for listening so patiently. My young friend," and he laid his hand kindly on Erich's shoulder, "I'm enraged at the poets too, for they've dressed up a sham *lady* for us, because they're afraid of the *woman.* If I have said too much about Bella, as is very possible, I beg you, nevertheless, to retain what of it is true and unexaggerated, and what I will maintain under all circumstances."

Erich did not mount, but took his horse by the bridle, and walked silently and thoughtfully toward home. It pained him to hear Bella spoken of in this way, and himself to utter no word in her defence. With reverent thankfulness he looked at the cloudless sky; he would keep himself uncontaminated by the sin of self-deception. His soul turned to Roland, and he thought: "Now I hope to educate a mortal; for no frivolous trifling with thoughts and feelings shall ever again overcome me. Yes! I was vain; I rejoiced to seem brilliant, and be praised by a beautiful woman and to feel the touch of her warm glove upon my hand. I was not then the man to say, 'I will educate a mortal to purity;' now I hope the man is here!"

With a heart at peace, he went on, and soon reached the Villa.

There a telegram informed him that the family would pass that night in the Capital-city.

Erich was alone.

CHAPTER VI.

RECEIPT FOR THE FIRST PAYMENT.

FRAU Ceres said on the next morning that she was not glad to go back to the Villa. The fête at Mount Rudolphe had made a great impression on her, and she wished to have one like it on the day of her arrival. She urged the Privy-councillor's wife to come home with her, and remain for a time at the Villa. Her request was declined, but the lady promised that she would soon pay her a visit.

Frau Ceres was not at all in good-humor, and so, to cheer her up, Sonnenkamp let Prancken sit with her in the carriage, and took Roland himself. When he was alone with his son, he asked him questions of every sort, and did not hesitate to inquire how often and how much Erich had been with Countess Bella, and if they had often taken walks by themselves.

Roland was perplexed.

On their way, they overtook the saddle-horses which had been sent on before them; they were completely covered with blankets, and only their eyes and feet could be seen. Sonnenkamp paused for an instant, and the horses looked out from their coverings wonderingly at their master. He gave the groom a sharp reprimand: he had noticed, while yet a long distance from the horses, that the groom, instead of walking patiently beside the beasts, was mounted on one of them. He threatened the man with instant dismissal on a repetition of the offence. They drove on, and Roland said:

"Our horses are better clothed than their drivers."

Sonnenkamp said nothing, but looked askance at his son, and seemed perplexed.

Suddenly Roland called out to the coachman to stop. He saw the wagoner who carried the clay jugs to the mineral-spring, and with whom he travelled on the night when he went to find Erich. He got out of the carriage, gave the man his hand, and told him to say to the hostler when he should see him, that he was innocent. Roland entered the carriage again, the wagoner stared after him, and his father questioned him in regard to this singular meeting.

Roland told him all—even the story of the laughing-ghost; but it did not make Sonnenkamp laugh, and when the boy said that he liked to associate with poor people who have to work hard for their daily bread, Sonnenkamp whistled inaudibly to himself. The more Roland spoke, the more his father was surprised at the quickness of his intelligence; but that conversation at the castle, occasioned by the Krischer's question, was told very confusedly and with many unintentional distortions.

Sonnenkamp had an inward struggle in regard to what he should do. It would not do to dismiss Erich immediately, on account of Roland, who would be likely to hold these preposterous ideas even more obstinately should Erich be sent away. Equally disagreeable would it be to bring about a rupture with Erich, on account of the Privy-councillor's wife, who had laid great stress on obtaining the assistance of Erich's mother. But above all, regard must be had to Clodwig, with whom not Prancken but Erich had been able to bring about anything approaching to intimacy; and Clodwig was the stoutest lever which Sonnenkamp could use in the execution of his design.

Sonnenkamp felt a double cause for jealousy; churchmen had drawn one child away from him, and now a layman was depriving him of the other. He did not so much oppose Erich's ideas, as he endeavored to instil into Roland the fact that there was no need of being so subservient to a man who was paid to teach him; it was not necessary for him to be so completely absorbed by his studies;—that was for people who had to achieve a position in life, but not for a young man who only needed to learn enough to enable him to take his place in the world. He warned his son not to let his life be spoiled by whimsical notions; and it was not difficult to renew the fascination which Roland had felt for the brilliant soldier-life of the capital.

Shortly after the first words of greeting had been spoken, Sonnenkamp asked Erich where he had been on the preceding day. He asked this in the manner of a master who has the right to dispose of his servant's time, and can ask him to give an account of himself.

Erich gave an account of his visit at Wolfsgarten, and dwelt particularly on the description of the young Russian prince.

Sonnenkamp smiled; it was pleasant for him to find this haughty virtue so skilful in concealing its own derelictions.

Roland now began to be inclined arbitrarily to break through the strict rules which Erich had established, and which he himself had re-enacted. He was listless in his studies, and it was evident that his father's advice was already having its effect. Erich often saw from the boy's actions that he was regarded almost as a jailer. Hitherto Roland had viewed the world as if his eyes were Erich's; he had enjoyed all that he had experienced, as if commissioned to enjoy it for Erich: but now all this was past; the boy seemed always to be hearing the far-off trumpet-call, and seeing the careless, light-hearted officers sitting together and enjoying themselves.

Erich noticed the change in his pupil, and was deeply grieved. He determined to devote all his powers to Roland. But Roland received this renewed attention with the utmost coolness; and now, when forced to impart instruction to one who was reluctant to learn, Erich felt a return of his dissatisfaction. Again the difficulty of his profession rose before him; and thoughts of his past life filled his mind. In the garrison city, after leaving the service, he had lived for himself alone. Afterward, in his father's house, he was allowed to do as he pleased, for his mother treated him as she had treated his father, having learned from experience that a scholar ought never to be disturbed by others, for he has to carry enough in his head without being troubled by more. He was never disturbed, and could pursue every thought that entered his mind. But now, at table or during their walks, he was obliged to answer the questions which Sonnenkamp and his son were so ready to ask; and these were neither few nor easy. He had long been used to a life of independence and self-culture; but now he seemed to be losing his individuality in such a life as this. He was only the ghost of his former self: nothing new or enjoyable any longer sprang into being within him, and it was only with difficulty that he could arouse his former thoughts and feelings. Erich bewailed his own desolation. Hitherto he had hardly confessed to himself how much life he had drawn from Bella. But that could no longer be. What remained to him?

He saw with horror that he had allowed unhallowed hands to profane the sanctuary of his being, and rousing from his lethargy, he saw that the coldness of Sonnenkamp and his pupil was a righteous punishment for his crime. He redoubled his zeal, but in vain.

An unexpected and insignificant event caused the quarrel to break out. Sonnenkamp paid Erich the first instalment of his wages in Roland's presence, at the same time looking triumphantly at his son. Erich trembled; but quickly controlled himself. He took the money in his hand, and made a step toward the window where Roland was standing; and Sonnenkamp almost thought that he was going to throw it out, but Erich said, with forced calmness:

"Here, Roland, take my wages, and carry the gold to my room. Wait there till I come."

Roland took the money, and looked with perplexity at his father and Erich.

"Do me this small service, and take the gold to my room," Erich repeated. "Now go!"

Roland went. He carried the money in his hand as if it had been a heavy fetter. He went to Erich's room, and laid the money on the table. He wanted to go away; but thought that he must stay and watch the gold. He might lock the door—but then he remembered that Erich had told him to wait till he should come. So he remained where he was, and could not comprehend what was the trouble. What had happened?

Prancken came to bid him good-bye. He congratulated Roland on the fact that he would soon be rid of Erich. And then it flashed through Roland's mind what had happened, and what would happen. Prancken spoke slightingly of Erich, as a man whom he had recommended only from pity; and then bade Roland a pleasant adieu. When he had gone, Roland felt that he could never love Prancken again. He felt this to be a loss, and stood silently by the table looking at the gold spread out before him. Then, like a child, he counted it to see how much Erich had received. But how long did it take him to earn this? He could make nothing of it, and turned indignantly away, and looked out at the window. The gold lay behind him, on the table. And it seemed to him as if some one were with him, softly whispering in his ear, "Forget me not!"

In the mean time Erich stood in the room with Sonnenkamp, who looked at him in amazement and said:

"You are wilfully destroying the attachment!"

Erich replied that he might, perhaps, have chosen another time for taking this measure; but the way in which he had been paid forced him to take it now.

"Have I hurt your feelings?"

"I am not particularly sensitive, and I value money as much as it should be valued, and am proud of my honest earnings. I love your son perhaps more than—But there is no measure for love; it can be measured by nothing other than itself."

"Thank you!"

"Pardon me; I wish to finish my sentence. Because I love your son, I would rather that a stain should rest on me than on you."

"On me?"

"Yes, I might have paid you back well for giving me my money in such a manner before my pupil. I might have told you that free labor—I am not speaking of love—I mean, simply, that unremunerated labor, with which man serves man, can never be paid for. I suppressed it, because I wish your son to love and honor you more than any one else—even me."

Sonnenkamp clenched his fists, and looked at Erich with staring eyes; but soon turned his face to the ground. He was obliged to control himself with a powerful effort, or Erich would have seen that he was trembling. At last he opened his lips and said:

"I do not know what you meant to insinuate by certain words you used, and I don't want to know! But I am a man to put a bullet through the brain of any man who tries—"

"I do not understand your excitement," said Erich, calmly rising to his full height, and looking composedly at Sonnenkamp.

"Who are you? Who am I?" asked Sonnenkamp, his face fearfully distorted.

"I am the teacher of your son, and I know the responsibility of my position. I am in your service; this is your house, and you can send me from it this very hour."

"I don't want to—I don't want to! Did I say that? I only want to explain matters to you, and you must do the same to me. Didn't you tell Roland that there will come a time, or that it is now one, in which there will be no private property?"

Erich said that such a thought had never entered his mind as to say that to his pupil. He was sorry that he had chosen this by way of illustration, and regretted that Roland had misconceived his meaning."

"Let us be seated," said Sonnenkamp—his knees were shaking. "Let us talk quietly, as reasonable men—as friends, if I may say so."

He whistled softly to himself, and then said, in a voice entirely changed:

"I must say that, aside from the question of its truth or error, your way of thinking seems to me dangerous to my son. You seem to me, in short, to be a philanthropist, and I have a great respect for philanthropists. You are one of those men who thank every street-sweeper for his trouble, and, as far as possible, put their gratitude in a material form. You see that I believe your philanthropy is genuine, and not that it is only a dodge to make yourself popular; but this philanthropy—I speak my mind plainly—is absolutely worthless to my son. My son will have a princely income some day. Now, if a rich man were to go through life, continually looking for people in necessitous circumstances, or poorly paid, he would be condemned to greater misery than if he were a beggar. The worst thing that could happen to my son would be to be filled with sentimentality, or that snivelling soft-heartedness. I am not, and do not wish my son to be, one of those men who have a perpetual longing for the inexpressible, and, as I believe, the unattainable. I wish him to look for a life of pleasure which he can obtain. Believe me, such ideas are only a sort of smuggling traffic in illegitimate sentiments; one persuades himself that lower men have the same feelings as himself."

"I thank you for thus setting me right; and am glad you have given me opportunity of telling you in what way I wish to make Roland good-hearted, but not weak-hearted. He should recognize it as a great privilege of his life to rely on himself for all that is most beautiful and exalted—he shall become the noble steward of the great power which will one day be his."

Erich explained his meaning yet more fully, and Sonnenkamp stretched his hand toward him, and said:

"You are—you are a noble man; you have yet something to teach me. I now trust you unconditionally. I trust you, and believe that you will not withdraw my child's heart from me; that you will not make him a sentimentalist—a universal benefactor of his race."

Sonnenkamp said this somewhat impetuously, for it vexed him to think that the man whom he had intended to humble had humbled him; and that he seemed like a beggar, asking a stranger not to take his child away.

"Why, pray," he soon began again—"I only ask because you have reasons for everything"—in spite of all his apparent humility there was a sneer in this—"why did you deprive Roland of his liberal allowance of money as soon as I went away?"

"I cannot produce valid reasons for all my conduct, but I have a very good reason for this part of it. Roland squanders money—throws it away. He does so through ignorance and generosity; but I regard the management of money as a part of management of self."

And then Erich first told Sonnenkamp what an impression the theft had made on Roland. Sonnenkamp cried triumphantly:

"I'm glad he has learned so soon what a crowd of impostors there is in the world, for it will make him cautious when he comes to be his own master. Yes, my dear philosopher, write down in your books: 'The chief superiority of man over beasts consists in his ability to lie, and play the hypocrite;' and the sooner and more thoroughly my son learns *that*, the more I'll be pleased. I wish that Roland had already gone through the second school."

"The second school?"

"Yes. The first is, 'Do good to men, and then see that they are scoundrels;' the second is, 'Play hazard, and think you'll win.' Debts of gratitude and gaming debts nobody likes to pay."

Sonnenkamp assumed a sort of fatherly tone, as he warned him against the badness of human nature, praising at the same time his idealistic benevolence. His one great maxim was, "Man is a wolf to man."

When Erich went to Roland, the boy came toward him holding out both hands, and said:

"I thank you for neutralizing what my father did; I want no more money! I beg you to pardon my father for paying you like a servant."

Erich endeavored to explain to Roland what had happened, without shocking and perplexing the boy's simple and unaffected nature. The son *must* love and honor his father.

"Put the gold away," said Roland, imploringly. Erich placed it in a box; he saw why the sight of money troubled the boy.

Roland then said to him: "Give me something."

"I have nothing to give," replied Erich. "But from this very hour you shall know that something more valuable than all the gold in the world. We will both hold by the proverb: 'A friend who can forsake a friend, was never a friend.'"

Roland kissed the hand that had received the money. Erich was opposed to all sentimentality, but here he felt as if the first fragrance was breathing from an opening flower, and that flower was a young man's heart.

"We will go to the Major," said Roland. It was evident that he wished to be with a man who knew nothing of all this trouble, and who lived peacefully within his own heart.

They went to the Major's house, but did not find him at home. They wandered about till night, and neither spoke a word.

Sonnenkamp, too, wandered through the park in the midst of the silent night, cursing that hard fate that had given him a secret that must forever be concealed; for one word, spoken to-day by Erich, had roused within him a bitter struggle. That word was "unremunerated labor." When his thoughts recurred to what he had done, he could not conceive why he had intentionally wounded Erich's feelings, wishing at the same time to have Erich's mother at the Villa. The thought flashed through his mind: "How infinitely kind this act will make me appear in the eyes of men!" Would that he himself could believe that it was kind! But he knew his own design. Very well! If the world believes in the noble and tender, why—let it! The woman of fashion knows that her cheeks are painted, but what does she care, so long as the world does not know it? She is happy, and can pretend that she is young!

Sonnenkamp had expressed the wish that Prancken would effect the purchase of the neighboring villa, which would then be handed over to the Privy-councillor's wife. Prancken had just as pleasantly declined, for assuredly it was Sonnenkamp's wish to have a good neighborhood. Sonnenkamp did not know whether to hope or fear that Prancken had been shrewd enough to secure the villa long ago, so as to make a little speculation on his own account. But was he to be duped? And yet it was a fine thing to know that his future son-in-law was shrewd enough to secure such an advantage.

During the next few days Sonnenkamp paid but little attention to the house and garden, and as little to Roland and Erich. He made inquiries about the villa, offered to buy the vineyards attached to it, and became fully convinced that Prancken had taken no steps in regard to the matter. This was, to a certain extent, satisfactory, but nevertheless somewhat humiliating; for it forced him to see that he did not yet fully understand the ways of the nobility. Prancken was a man who scorned to have anything to do with the common affairs of business.

The Wine-count was the chief person with whom Sonnenkamp had to compete for the ownership of the villa. It was said that he wished to obtain it for his son-in-law, the son of the Court-chamberlain. Sonnenkamp instantly bought the place.

CHAPTER VII.

INDIGESTIBLE FOOD FOR A GUEST.

IF the Krischer could have heard, as he lay in prison, that Sonnenkamp had bought another villa, he would have said again, in a tone of the deepest conviction:

"Well, he'll buy the whole Rhineland yet."

The investigation dragged along, and the Judge was so friendly as to have the testimony of Erich and Roland taken again at the Villa; and this troublesome and protracted business occasioned greater interruption in the boy's studies than was thought.

Neither were hospitalities wanting, for Roland said to Erich, one day:

"There's to be a great *fête* at Wolfsgarten; Father and Mother are quite delighted, and you and I are invited."

Sonnenkamp was well satisfied that Prancken had brought this about, Erich's assistance being utterly forgotten. It had been settled with Prancken that Clodwig, the most powerful member of the commission having charge of such matters, must be gained to further the all-important object in hand, and, indeed, to be very earnest in taking the initiative.

Sonnenkamp stood before his arsenal; he stood before his great fireproof safe, which was sunk in the wall. Here were powerful and effective forces—here alone could he work in person. For awhile he was despondent; but then he drew himself up proudly: these weapons had never failed him before—why should they now?

On the day of the invitation, Sonnenkamp had had a severe struggle with Frau Ceres. She wanted to take all her jewelry to this midday feast; and even Miss Perini could not dissuade her, although she repeated it as a rule firmly settled in society that diamonds must not be worn by daylight. Frau Ceres wept like a child; she would stay at home, if they would not let her wear them.

Sonnenkamp begged her not to wear them and offend the Countess, who never wore one-twentieth part of the jewelry worn by Frau Ceres. She should dress plainly; and was promised, as a recompense, that she should wear it all at the next *fête* given at the Villa.

But Frau Ceres persisted in refusing to go, if she could not wear her jewelry.

"Good!" said Sonnenkamp; "I'll send a messenger to Wolfsgarten to say that we'll come without you."

He summoned a groom to the chamber, and told him to saddle instantly and go to Wolfsgarten; then he left the room. Frau Ceres looked after him with an expression of intense anger; she was the poor child who had to stay at home all alone when the rest went to the feast. After awhile she ran through the house to Sonnenkamp's room, and said that she would go as they wished her to.

Sonnenkamp regretted that he had already sent the messenger. Frau Ceres burst into tears, and begged him to send another to say that she *would* come.

Sonnenkamp told her that this was impossible; but at last he gave in. He himself went to the stables, and had nothing more to do than tell the groom to "unsaddle again!" He had not sent him, for he knew beforehand that Frau Ceres, that spoiled child, would come and beg him to let her go. So they set out for Wolfsgarten.

Bella was extremely delighted to meet the Privy-councillor's wife as a guest; she was very gracious, and looked more beautiful than ever. She was friendly to everybody, but particularly so to Erich. She thought that she had made a bad impression on him during his last visit to Wolfsgarten, and wished to obliterate it by making a good one now.

Erich received her attentions gratefully, but it did not escape the shrewd lady that his conduct was extremely cold toward her.

Sonnenkamp, who had a sharp eye, held his breath like a sportsman about to bring down his game. "So," said he to himself, "she plays her cards well." The virtuous air of this house had been very depressing to him, but now he moved about with a certain sense of being at home.

It was a little court that had sprung up here; freer manners were allowable, for it was in the country, but at the same time all was no less well-modulated than in the capital. A crowd of eventful lives had assembled here, which perhaps appeared only the more striking in the midst of country life. It was a presentation of isolated existences, withdrawing themselves from seclusion. Pensioned military men, and others who had resigned their commissions, furnished the largest quota; orders modestly showed themselves as red, yellow, and blue ribbons in buttonholes; the hair of old gentlemen was carefully dressed and their beards newly dyed; and the ladies showed that their yearly sojourn of a few weeks in Paris had not been entirely in vain.

The conversation was conducted in French, to please a few French ladies.

A celebrated musician, who was resting from his musical tours at the house of a colleague who had married one of his pupils—an heiress, and settled in the neighborhood—had been invited.

With the exception of Erich, Herr Sonnenkamp and the musician were the only commoners in the assembly. Genius had elevated the artist, and millions the rich man, into this unaccustomed atmosphere. The Wine-cavalier might be regarded as having already been ennobled, for it was known that in a few days his family would receive its patent of nobility. The young couple had been invited; but on the day of the feast a note arrived, regretting with extreme politeness that, as the prospective bridegroom was slightly unwell, the bride could not come. None of the Wine-count's family appeared except the Cavalier, who again expressed his regret at the trifling indisposition of his future brother-in-law.

And then there was a renowned portrait-painter; he had been for some time at the Wine-count's country-seat, making a life-size picture of the future bride and bridegroom. He was quite in fashion, and succeeded best with pearls, laces, and gray satins; only they all had a suspicion of very dark blue. Nevertheless, he was a great favorite at Court, and it did not admit of question that he alone could paint the aristocratic bride.

Naturally, the Russian Prince was the bright, particular star.

Sonnenkamp received the place of honor beside the Countess, and the Prince sat on the other side of her. Clodwig had Frau Ceres next to him; and the Major was near, as help in case of need.

Clodwig amused himself very agreeably with Frau Ceres, who ate a great deal to-day without being encouraged to do so by Sonnenkamp.

Sonnenkamp had burnished the weapons of gallantry with

which he had never failed; but to-day they seemed to have no effect, for Bella only half-listened to him, and was always trying to catch Erich's conversation with the Russian.

Suddenly all general conversation ceased, for the Prince asked Herr Sonnenkamp:

"Do the Americans call their slaves 'souls'?"

"I don't understand."

"In Russia we used to call our serfs 'souls'; we say a man has so many hundreds or thousands of souls; do they say so in America?"

"No."

"It certainly admits of question," said Clodwig, "whether or not the negroes are really human souls. Humboldt says that savages believe apes could once speak, but intentionally left it off for fear they would be forced to work."

All the company laughed, and Clodwig continued:

"Whenever we find even the most trifling object made by the Greeks or Romans, we find it beautiful, but, so far as I know, the negroes have not produced a single new and beautiful form."

"It is said that they have never invented even a new mouse-trap," said the Prince.

"True enough," replied Clodwig.

"It is questionable whether negroes are capable of receiving or transmitting civilization, for they have not inherited the beautiful human form, as it passed from Egypt, Greece, and Rome to us; therefore they cannot advance art—and art alone represents the nobility of mankind; neither can they create beauty in their own likeness, for though it is written that God created man in his likeness, it is equally true that man creates his gods in *his* likeness, which cannot be done to very good advantage by negroes. They may, perhaps, be able to create something which shall influence their own future, but not that of others—properly, they are not included within the general insurmountable barriers of humanity."

Sonnenkamp looked up in surprise. A man of such undoubted humanitarianism speaking thus!

"That's true," said he. "People are not sentimental in America. To be sure, our clear head and solid views are considered heretical by sentimental schoolmasters, and placed under the ban for being vastly inhuman; but there are Priests of what is termed 'humanity,' who know how to turn inquisitors as well as other people."

Sonnenkamp spoke in a tone of concentrated ridicule and with contempt which plainly showed how impertinent the remarks of the Prince seemed to him, although they had been made in all politeness. Clodwig felt himself obliged to come to his assistance, and began in a low voice, which became gradually more excited as he went on:

"He who regards historical events calmly, and from a philosophical standpoint, sees how the Idea gradually develops itself. It works patiently and silently, but irresistibly, and this noiseless working continues till an unlooked-for event occurs, which to all appearance has nothing in common with the idea; and then are seen its accomplishment and development. The idea but prepares the stage—the event is final and dramatic."

Bella spoke very softly to the Prince, who sat at her right. But Clodwig knew that she was making excuses for his somewhat tedious and always logical remarks. His face contracted almost imperceptibly; he compressed his lips slightly, and continued:

"I am convinced that the emancipation of the serfs would not have taken place when and as it did, had it not been for Sebastopol. And who can tell when and how it would have occurred? Now, as formerly, Saul goes forth to seek an ass, and finds a kingdom—a kingdom ruled by the Idea. The Crimean war was undertaken in order to humble Russia, and ended by making Russia establish within itself a free peasant-class, and regenerate its own life. These are great deeds of history, which we have not accomplished."

"This is new to me, surprisingly new," said the Prince; and Clodwig proceeded:

"The Russian ambassador told me that during the Crimean war a report was circulated—no one knew whence it came, but it was on all lips. It was this: 'Every one who fights at Sebastopol, or enters the army voluntarily to free the Emperor from the allies, shall, at the conclusion of the war, receive free land, and be an independent peasant.' This idea was universally held. Where did it come from? The idea of the emancipation of the serfs, which had long been discussed in books and the higher classes of society, and took form in the consciousness of the people, and became a recognized fact, which needed only the imperial decree."

Clodwig ceased for a minute, as if tired; but then aroused himself again and proceeded:

"That is a beautiful expression: 'Swords shall be beaten into ploughshares.'"

The whole company exchanged perplexed glances. They could not see the drift of Clodwig's words: only Erich looked at him with a beaming face. He was startled by a hand laid on his shoulder, and turning, saw Roland, who said:

"You once told me the same things."

"Sit down and be quiet," said Erich.

Roland went to his place and waited till he caught Erich's eye; then he drank to him.

Bella looked about as if seeking help—there was no conversation at the table; she looked at Erich and nodded, as if asking him to turn the conversation from these hateful subjects.

The servants were just then pouring Johannisberger into delicate glasses, and Erich, holding his glass before him, said:

"Herr Count, the ancients never had wine such as this in those stone vases which we have just dug from the earth."

Bella nodded encouragement to him; and when he stopped speaking, said:

"Is anything definitely known in regard to the way in which the ancients cultivated the vine?"

"But very little," replied Clodwig. "But it is very evident that they had no idea of seasoning—of that fire of the wine, for they never fermented it."

"I by no means wish to lay claim to great learning," said Sonnenkamp, "but it is very evident that without pruning, one can have no thoroughly ripened and strong bunches of grapes; and no developed and matured wine, without putting it in casks."

"In casks? Why in casks?" asked the Russian. "Do the fibres of the wood make the wine better?"

"I think not," replied Sonnenkamp; "but casks let the air in, and let the wine ripen in cellars—let it mature and complete its cultivation. Wine is stifled in stone jars, or, at most, remains in the same condition in which it was when poured into them."

Bella added skilfully:

"I am glad to know that; now I see again that cultivation makes even natural productions more pleasant."

Sonnenkamp was in his element; he made brilliant and ineresting observations, and appeared at his best, and the converation became general.

Everybody was comfortable and good-natured; everything disagreeable seemed forgotten; and when the company rose from the table all eyes were bright and all cheeks glowing.

CHAPTER VIII.

HELP YOURSELF.

THE gentlemen sat by themselves in the garden, drinking coffee. The ladies had withdrawn.

The Prince, who wished to appear affable to Sonnenkamp, spoke of his intention of going to America; and Clodwig encouraged him to do so. He regretted that he had not done so in his youth, and said:

"I believe that he who has not been in America does not understand what man is when he gives his powers full play. In that country, life develops entirely new energies in the soul. While struggling for the possessions of the world, each must, in some sort, become a Robinson Crusoe, and must discover new resources in himself. I might even say that America has something which makes it resemble Greece. Greece saw men bodily naked. America sees them spiritually naked, which certainly is not a very fine sight, but may result in producing a regenerated humanity."

The Musician, who was thinking about making a professional tour in America, said:

"I don't see how people live in a country where there is no wine grown, and no larks sing in the air."

"Allow me to ask a question, Count," said Erich, joining in the conversation. "It is strange that no new names are produced in America: their names of rivers, mountains, cities, and men are taken either from the aborigines or from the Old World. And I would like to ask, in addition, has the New World yet been able to produce a new ethical law?"

"Certainly," said Sonnenkamp. "The best of all laws."

"The best? What is that?"

"The two significant words, 'Help yourself.'"

Clodwig shook his head, and said:

"'Help yourself' is, properly speaking, not a human, but a brutish principle; for every animal helps itself, with all its powers. It's a dogma which was just and in place only as opposed to a false and over-refined moral philosophy, or the social philosophy of a State which absorbs the individual. 'Help yourself' is a good motto for an emigrant; but as soon as he gets among those who are settled in a country he must regard the rights of others, and his duties toward them. In the western part of America 'Help yourself' is out of place, for there neighbors help each other a great deal. At the outside, 'Help yourself' is only of value to individuals, but not to society at large. The serfs could not help themselves; and the slaves will not be able to do so. Moral solidarity says, 'Help your neighbor as your neighbor helps you; and if you help yourself you help another.'"

They had now fully entered upon the theme which had appeared at table, and been so fortunately dropped. No one appeared to wish to take it up again; and Clodwig continued:

"It seems as if every people must be admitted into history by one idea. I believe that America has been called to a great destiny: it is to drive slavery from the earth. But this is, as I said, the realization of an idea which had long been working. I would ask, Has America a new moral principle?"

"Perhaps the sewing-machine is a new moral principle," said Prancken, pertly, at which they all laughed.

"And yet there is a moral principle in 'Help yourself,'" said Erich. "In Europe, men have some distinction, either having inherited it or received it by the favor of their rulers. The American does not wish to succeed through the help of others, but wishes to become only what he can become by his own exertion. And in opposition to that belief which would have one shipped like a bundle to his heavenly destination by a spiritual expressman—in opposition to that, I say, the American proverb, 'Help yourself,' is valuable. Nobody will send you by express. And we Germans have a similar proverb—'Everybody must carry his own hide to market.'"

"May I ask a question?" said Roland.

They were all surprised, but, most of all, Erich and Sonnenkamp.

"What is it?" said Erich, encouragingly.

"When I heard the Count speak in regard to inheriting civilization, I wanted to ask, How do we know that we are civilized?"

The boy was embarrassed, and Erich encouraged him:

"Explain your meaning more clearly."

"Perhaps the Turks, or Chinese, consider us barbarians."

"You want," said Erich, helping him, "an unmistakable sign by which to know whether a people, an age, or a religion, is advancing in civilization?"

"Yes; that's what I mean."

"Good! I'll show you. In what does a man of culture differ from an ignorant man?"

"In having good thoughts and clear views."

"Good! Where does he get them?"

"From himself."

"And how does he learn to define and give them shape?"

"By comparing them."

"With what?"

"With the thoughts of great men."

"And does he recognize their validity by finding that they agree or disagree with those of others?"

"By finding that they agree with them."

"And where do the others live?"

"Around him."

"Have not other men lived before him, also?"

"Certainly."

"And can we also compare our thoughts and views with those of men who are dead, or learn directly from men of the past?"

"Certainly; for we have their writings."

"Good! Now, if a man or a people has a doctrine or a culture which is in no way related to those of the past, what would you call this?"

"Not an inheritance."

"I did not expect that answer, but I will accept it. Good! Then, if a man or a people cannot inherit a civilization, is he at unity with humanity, or isolated?"

"Isolated."

"And there we have it. We know that we stand at the middle point, or rather are progressing in civilization, because we take from the Persians, Jews, Egyptians, Greeks, and Romans the results of their civilizations and enlarge them. Turks and Chinese who do not, or cannot do so, are isolated and die away in themselves. It is no undue pride in us Germans to consider ourselves in the vanguard of civilization, for there is no people that accepts and develops the work of humanity more than the German, or let us say the Germanic race, for that includes your native country as well as ours."

"Bravo! bravo!" cried Clodwig, and they all rose. Clodwig went up to Sonnenkamp and said:

"Never was a recommendation better grounded than that which I gave the Captain; and, Herr Sonnenkamp, I have learned something—you are right. 'Help yourself' is a new and great principle—not moral, however, but educational. See, our friend teaches your son in the highest sense; his is the modern Socratic method."

Erich and Roland had now become the central point of the company; the Prince went to Erich and said, as he shook him by the hand:

"You are truly a teacher."

A messenger came from the ladies asking the gentlemen to come to the saloon, and when they arrived there they had a very pleasant time. The jolly Austrian officer, who had elevated to the ranks of the nobility the daughter of a merchant in the neighboring city, sang comic songs. Prancken, who had learned a good many tricks from a conjurer, was prevailed on to amuse the company with them; and the musician played on Clodwig's old violin.

Sonnenkamp seized the opportunity of speaking to Clodwig as they sat together in a retired corner of the room. He began by speaking of the affectionate interest which Clodwig took in Roland, and here Clodwig readily chimed in with him. Then he proceeded with extreme caution, and there was a certain piteous, old-fashioned tone in the way in which he said that he had nothing more to wish for himself in life, and that it was his only wish to place Roland in a secure and honorable position. Clodwig did not doubt that with such an instructor as Erich for his friend he had already acquired habits and views of life, and would acquire yet more which would render him secure in himself and admit him to the society of the noble.

Sonnenkamp fastened on the expression, "society of the noble." He had not studied the natural history of bribery in vain, and Clodwig was to be corrupted by being taken into the committee of establishment and receiving ideal dividends; but Clodwig pretended that he did not know what Sonnenkamp was driving at. Sonnenkamp consequently became confused and, instead of asking Clodwig's aid, asked his advice, and Clodwig objected very earnestly, even using such hard words as to tell him that it was very wrong to try to become a member of a decaying institution, in which he could never be at home. Sonnenkamp was obliged to express his great gratitude for this disagreeable counsel. Clodwig seized a favorable opportunity of mingling with the other guests, and Sonnenkamp was brilliant no more.

They returned home while it was yet day, and the hosts accompanied them part of the way.

Sonnenkamp had Roland sit with his mother and Miss Perini; he did not wish to bear the brunt of his wife's affliction occasioned by her looking at Bella's beautiful pearl necklace, so he took Erich and the Major in his own carriage.

"There's a German society for you! Our host is an old professor!" said Sonnenkamp. No one answered him.

He then said to Erich in English that he admired his tact in being so cautious about displaying his friendship for the Count and his lovely wife, before Roland, who was yet so young. Then he said, as he laid his hand on Erich's shoulder:

"Young man, I might envy you; I know, of course, that you will deny it all, but I congratulate you. The old gentleman is right. Help yourself is not a moral principle."

Erich could do nothing but resolutely decline this praise; at the same time he felt severely punished for a fault, carelessly and almost innocently committed, and it was a source of great comfort to him that he could say:

"I may accept it; I have proved the proverb, 'Help yourself.'"

Sonnenkamp too was thinking of the proverb, and it made him angry, for he was at that very time engaged in a struggle for something in which self-help was not all-powerful; he had to seek aid from others. He wished to obtain an honored and distinguished position, and found the endeavor more difficult than that which obtains possession of money and goods; honor comes only from the participation and aid of others, and now the first and most influential of all men, and one who ought to work with him, was reserved and disinclined to aid him. It seemed impossible to win Clodwig.

CHAPTER IX.

THE BOUQUET.

ROLAND'S distraction of mind daily increased; it interfered much with his routine of study. But Frau Ceres was perfectly happy, for now had come her opportunity to show off all her finery; and Miss Perini, too, was in her element, for she had a chance to open the boxes that kept arriving from Paris. There were only two such gowns on earth; one of them was the Empress's, the other belonged to Frau Ceres.

The old-established and much-respected family of the Wine-count had hitherto held themselves decidedly aloof from all intimacy with the house of Sonnenkamp; but now, after the fête at Wolfsgarten, an invitation was extended to the Sonnenkamps to attend the wedding of the daughter of the house with the son of the Chamberlain.

Erich had much trouble in restraining his pupil from constantly talking about the great fête, for Roland was full of reports concerning the fireworks which were to be set off upon the Rhine and the wooded hilltops, and every morning he repeated—"If the weather only keeps fine!—It will be a great shame if it doesn't!" He often went out with Prancken, and, after several hours' absence, returned much excited; he was evidently concealing something from Erich, who, for his part, refrained from all inquiry.

On the day of the fête, the General, with whom they had become acquainted at the capital, also arrived.

It was still bright midday when they set out in three carriages for the house of the Wine-count. In one of the carriages Frau Ceres was seated with the General; she was so puffed and voluminous in her dress that the General sat in a flood of drapery. In the second open carriage sat Sonnenkamp with Miss Perini and Prancken, who appeared to-day in full uniform, and with his two decorations on his breast; he wished to accompany the Sonnenkamps as one of the family. Sonnenkamp did not speak of it, but it was easy to see by his look how thankful he was to the young man, who not only had brought him the General as his guest, but also was introducing him into society. In the third carriage sat Roland and Erich. Roland thought it very wrong that Erich had not also put on his uniform. A long row of carriages was drawn up before the Wine-count's villa, which stood by the roadside with broad, stately front, and well-laid-out and shady gardens on either hand. The General offered his arm to Frau Ceres. They were shown to the garden by servants in rich livery. Along the paths rose walls of shrubbery and fragrant flowers, beautifully arranged. As they descended the garden steps, the Wine-count met them, and bade the General surrender to him the arm of Frau Ceres. Various groups wandered here and there in the garden, or seated themselves in its beautiful bowers. The spouse of the Wine-count, a large, well-preserved woman, had not heard to no purpose that she resembled Maria Theresa; she had for this occasion arrayed herself throughout in the costume of the Empress, and wore a beautiful diadem of brilliants.

Sonnenkamp was presented to the bridal pair. The bridegroom looked very tired, but the bride, with a wreath of roses on her head, appeared full of life; it was only regretted that Manna was not also present at the fête.

The bride's father, the Chamberlain, was glad to meet Herr Sonnenkamp here again, and to make the acquaintance of his wife and his handsome son, of whom he had heard so much. It was honor enough for the whole evening, when the Chamberlain said publicly, in a voice intentionally raised, that only yesterday there had been very honorable mention of Herr Sonnenkamp at the Prince's table. Frau Ceres kept her place beside the Chamberlain, and still held her white mantle drawn over her magnificent robe.

The Wine-count, decorated with many orders, was everywhere. He was a man of impressive manners, being in constant intercourse with the entire aristocracy of Europe. In the time of Napoleon, when he was as yet only an energetic travelling-agent for the elder house, he was employed on various missions by the astute Metternich, all of which he discharged with great skill. There was scarcely a French field-marshal whom he did not know; he had even twice had interviews with Napoleon himself. The Wine-count had three sons and three daughters. The eldest daughter was already married to an officer of noble rank. Of the three sons, one had gone to America, and had squandered a great deal of his father's money; a second was a member of the orchestra of a theatre in a capital city of Middle Germany, and it was said he had written to his father that he, for his part, would not accept the noble rank. The third, or, to speak properly, the eldest son, was engaged in the wine-business, and had taken to the new honors with great enthusiasm, and made himself very happy over them.

The Wine-count conducted himself on this occasion with great suavity, and in the whole manner of the spare yet active old man, with his snow-white hair, there was an unwonted elasticity; he went from one to another of his guests and had an apt, friendly word for each; he received everywhere the good wishes of the company, all the more fervently expressed because on that day the Prince had ennobled him. He thanked them very modestly; and he could truly say that he could have attained this honor ten years ago, but that at that time a certain patriotic enthusiasm raged among the people, with which even a certain Wine-dealer became infected. His constant answer was that the high favor of his Prince made him supremely happy.

Sonnenkamp laughed quietly to himself: he saw how they would soon be paying like homage to him, and he prepared himself to accept it with becoming modesty.

Frau Ceres sat very uneasily beside the Chamberlain, who, when he found that he could not get a word out of her, allowed her to sit in silence.

But at last her turn came too, for the wife of the Privy-councillor entered: the Chamberlain resigned his place to her, and she was extremely rejoiced to meet her friend here.

Her luck rose still higher; for soon after, Frau Bella entered, who, even in this circle where there were so many of her equals, seemed to hold a certain pre-eminence.

She was very gracious to Frau Ceres, and bade her take her arm and go with her to the garden saloon, for there the rich array of bridal gifts was to be seen.

From those whom they met on their way back, they heard universal exclamations of admiration, and saw looks of envy.

Frau Ceres bore her long train very awkwardly, while Bella held hers gracefully in both hands, and walked along as if she floated through light waving clouds.

Sonnenkamp was greeted by the Russian Prince very familiarly; he offered him his hand. Sonnenkamp was much elated, but all was suddenly strewn with ashes, for the Prince said:

"Oh, I forgot! you must give me a more particular account concerning the treatment of the slaves; I fear that I shall find no more of them when I make up my mind to set out on my American travels."

He soon turned away, for the General was presented to him.

Sonnenkamp felt new and out of place in this circle: his spirits however were heightened and restored when he saw Bella and Frau Ceres so confidential together.

"You haven't paid your respects to the Countess yet?" said he to Erich.

"Ah, I was thinking of something quite different," answered Erich. "I would like to know how our new Baron here will say to his servants: 'John, Peter, Michael, from this day you must call me, My Gracious Lord or Herr Baron!' He must certainly find it a ridiculous position."

"Perhaps 'Doctor' is a grander title," answered Sonnenkamp sharply—"a title one is born with, possibly."

He found Erich's critical manner somewhat disturbing, and would willingly have seen him out of the company.

He was, however, suddenly restored to an amiable mood, for Bella came near him and said:

"Do you know, Herr Sonnenkamp, why we are here, and what all these festivities mean? It's simply a baptismal feast; and isn't it a fine joke which our gracious Prince has perpetrated here? The Wine-dealer has vexed himself so long about a title, and as he has now even brought his daughter as a sacrificial lamb, the Prince could not escape giving it to him at last. And isn't it magnificent, the name which he gave him, Herr Von Endlich?"*

She described, in a very entertaining way, how fine it would be, if so old a baptismal candidate should suddenly cry out—"I don't want that name, give me another."

Turning to Erich, she sketched in turn almost every member of the company, with a few characteristic but rather spitefully drawn lines. She was most scornful in her manner over a group of young girls, who looked all the time as if they felt the weight of their friseurs; for the hair-dressers of the neighboring watering-places, and the castle, had from early in the morning been hurrying from house to house to truss up the heads of the young girls in a fashionable manner. Bella created much merriment by her skilful imitation of the young ladies, as they whispered hurriedly to one another:

"Do tell me, is my chignon on still?"

She was particularly witty over a great tall Englishman, who was accompanied by a fat wife and three lean daughters, with long-drawn locks, but showily dressed. In Winter, he lived in town; in Summer, at his country-seat. He spent his time in fishing; his daughters spent theirs in drawing. He passed for very rich, and his wealth had a queer source. Years ago, a brother of his wife had been transported to Botany Bay. Being an experienced merchant, he was successful in establishing there a large export-business, and thence arose the great wealth of the family.

Bella was full of charming witticisms, and Erich felt that in his opinion of her he had been doing her an injustice. He had listened to the Doctor's sharp, judicial sentence—his nice dissection of her, and he felt it his duty to fight resolutely against the impression he had received. He kept looking at her meanwhile, as if he had a favor to beg; and Bella was much pleased, and displayed a liveliness and freshness of manner which added to her power of fascination. She singled Erich out in a marked manner from the whole company.

Count Clodwig now joined the circle; he could not refrain from saying that he was always astonished to see how many

---

* At last.

strange characters collected here on the banks of the Rhine. The Major stood near by, and looked to Herr Sonnenkamp with a glance that seemed to mean: "Don't, I beg you, go the same way; stay with us? I'd forego taking home the most delicious bonbons with me to Fräulein Milch, if I could take word, that it isn't true what is reported about Herr Sonnenkamp." For Fräulein Milch had learned at once the closely-kept secret.

Erich condoled with the Major for looking so unusually dull to-day, and it fell to him to know the cause of his low spirits, for the Major said:

"It's just as if a Christian should become a Turk! Yes, laugh if you will, Fräulein Milch is right. Gold, beautiful gold, stores of gold, won with so much toil, will now be thrown away upon the nobility, and we plain citizens must stand aside and be thought nothing more of."

Erich quietly pressed the hand of the Major, and the latter said:

"But where's Roland?"

Yes, where is Roland? Soon after their arrival, Roland had disappeared, and was now nowhere to be seen.

The evening gradually drew on, and from amid the close shrubbery a bugle was sounded in tones of wonderful beauty. For awhile all those who were dispersed in groups through the garden stood quiet, but then it seemed as if the music made them all the more talkative.

Erich looked for Roland, but no one could give him any news of him.

The music in the garden died away; the night came on apace. On the balcony of the house appeared a trumpeter, clad in the costume of the middle ages, and blew forth signal-notes that vibrated in the air; the company gathered in the house; they climbed the stairs to the great drawing-room, and the rooms that opened into it.

Only a few chairs were placed here—two fauteuils in front, wreathed with flowers, on which the bridal pair were to sit; behind these a row for the oldest and most distinguished of the company.

Frau Ceres held a place beside Bella; Miss Perini very adroitly pressed up against her, and tugged at her mantle. Frau Ceres understood it, and all eyes, which had been turned upon the bridal pair, were now turned upon her. Such a *parure*, representing a wreath composed of wheat-ears, every kernel of which was a large diamond—such a robe, so bespattered with pearls and diamonds, never were seen before; a whisper rustled through the company, and was long in composing itself.

Frau Ceres stood by her chair as if bound by a spell, till Bella bade her be seated. Bella looked smilingly upon the gorgeous array of Frau Ceres:—"So indeed! The American ladies can put on finery like that; but I know a neck and shoulders they can't put on!"

It was now seen that the wall before them was only a curtain; it was drawn up. Vine-dressers of both sexes appeared, and in song and speech proclaimed the glory of the house, and at last presented the myrtle-wreath.

The curtain fell; every one was in ecstasies. They were about to leave their chairs, but a voice behind the curtain cried out:

"Keep seated!"

The curtain soon rose again; but a fine gauze remained, and behind it, among shepherds and vine-dressers was seen an Apollo, and the Apollo was Roland. The curtain had to be drawn up a second and a third time, for all were in raptures over the tableau, especially over Roland's personation of the god.

Bella nodded approvingly to Erich, who stood by her side, but he remained as if transfixed, for he asked himself: "How will this affect Roland, and how could Roland conceal it from me?" It did not last long, for Roland made his appearance among the company in his usual dress; he was admired and praised on all sides, and was almost carried about on their shoulders.

Frau Ceres was congratulated even still more on having such a son—one who was so genuine a representation of the god; they again regretted that her daughter was not at the fête also. Frau Ceres took everything in a very pleasant way and always said: "Thank you kindly, you're very good." Miss Perini had taught her that.

New rooms were thrown open; the tables were spread; they sat down.

Roland sought out Erich.

"But you've nothing to say to me about it?" he asked.

Erich was silent.

"It cost me much trouble," Roland went on, "to conceal everything from you; and it was a great effort to give attention to my studies at this time, but I wanted to surprise you."

Erich, on reflection, thought it best to attach no importance to the affair, if no injurious effects followed; he only reminded Roland to be temperate with the wine; and Roland was made so happy, that he resigned the place which had been prepared for him at the bride's table, and sat down next to Erich, to show him how temperate he would be.

Prancken, who, with the portrait-painter, had arranged the *tableaux vivants*, was strangely excited this evening, for it kept buzzing through his head that he might have married the beautiful daughter of the Wine-count. Here, it is true, a freshly lacquered nobility shone to view, but it was all transparent enough; there will now be a charming widow, or an amiable, unhappy wife. He nevertheless banished the thought, and said to himself that he loved Manna.

As the former comrade of the bridegroom, and as the friend of the house, Prancken pronounced the toast to the bridal couple. He spoke well, and, as was best, in a humorous vein. Hilarity and good feeling prevailed everywhere.

The boom of a cannon announced the time for the fireworks. They flocked to the veranda and the garden.

CHAPTER X.

FIREWORKS AND—NIGHT.

WITHOUT Erich's observing it, Bella had suddenly placed herself by his side.

"You're uncommonly serious," she said to him.

"I'm not used to the tumult of fêtes."

"It seems to me all the time as if you had something on your mind to say to me."

Erich was silent, and Bella continued:

"Is it so with you, too, that, when you see your nearest friends in a large company, you meet them as strangers, and as if struggling against a torrent, in which you are borne away?"

"Ah! bravo!" was suddenly shouted forth.

A sheaf of rockets had been set off, and at the same moment the music burst forth, and from the opposite hill a trumpet was sounded in response. Far along the shore, they saw the men from the towns and hamlets gazing up, their faces touched by the light.

"Ah," cried Bella, as it again became dark, "we are still all slaves! One should live thus—that were a life indeed!—as a rocket in the air; then let Night and Death come—they are welcome!"

Erich trembled; he knew not how it happened that he held Bella's hand in his own.

At that moment bright fires again streamed up over the river and on the mountain side; it was as if all the people, who were gazing out over the water, must have seen Erich's hand in Bella's. Erich drew back. At that moment the Prince came, and Bella took his arm. Erich stood alone; he saw Bella, on the arm of the Prince, wandering up and down the road before the house; he wondered whether he had not said to Bella, "I love you." It seemed to him as if he had spoken aloud; yet it could not be. Fire-wheels, the name of the bridal pair, balls of light, were set off; and last of all, a large golden wine-flask shot up from a boat on the Rhine, burst in the air, and scattered globes of fire about like a shower of suns. Music rang forth, and along the shore jubilant cries arose, as if all the waves had suddenly found voice.

Erich's head whirled round; he no longer knew where he was, who he was. He suddenly felt an arm laid in his own. It was Clodwig. Erich would willingly have knelt down to him, but he felt unworthy to say a word to him, and he inwardly vowed to himself: "I'd rather put a ball through my heart, than that it should beat again with such an emotion!"

Clodwig spoke of Roland, and said he did not approve at all of their bringing him out into the world. Erich answered in a distracted manner. Clodwig thought that Erich must know the plan, but Erich thought he referred to the military service; and he was so wandering, and trembled so, that Clodwig recommended his young friend not to overtax himself so much, nor to vex himself unnecessarily.

Erich avoided bidding Bella good-night.

It was late when they returned to the Villa; they were driven home, as they came, in their carriages. But this time the Privy-councillor and his wife went with them; they were to spend the night at Villa Eden.

The wife of the Councillor rode with Sonnenkamp and Prancken. Their talk was naturally about the brilliant fête, and that the old and famous firm would now become extinct—the Wine-count would sell off his whole stock of wines. The Councillor's wife said that Bella had confided to her her intention to invite Erich's mother and aunt to be her guests. Prancken acted as if he knew it already; he was, in fact, much surprised. And here, as they were alone and had no one to fear, the Councillor's wife said with emphasis, that no one could more easily and naturally prompt the bestowal of the new honor upon Sonnenkamp than the Professor's widow. It was not actually commanded that Herr Sonnenkamp should invite the mother and aunt to Villa Eden, but the duty of hospitality was enjoined upon him.

Sonnenkamp laughed to himself; for he had a more comprehensive plan, in which he could make use of these ladies. The General had frequently given it out that Erich's mother was the trusted friend of his sister, the Mother-Superior at the Island convent. It was, in musical phrase, a double stop, which was now to be drawn.

Erich rode again with Roland, in the third carriage; they sat for a long time in silence, and the carriage drove on slowly. A voice was suddenly heard by the roadside:

"Good-evening, Master!"

Erich ordered the driver to halt. It was the Cooper, the son of the Krischer, who had come that way; he brought Erich, from Mattenheim, the salutations of Knopf, the Master of Arts; he said that he had gone there to summon Knopf as a witness in his father's trial to-morrow.

Roland rubbed his eyes open, and looked about him here and there, as if he were in a new world. He bade the Cooper to take a seat in the carriage; the Cooper thanked him, and told what a strange sight it was to him, as he came over the heights from Mattenheim, when suddenly, out there on the Rhine, the wonderful fires shot up to heaven; and that he stood on the spot where the echo of the cannon was thundered back. He held out his hand to Erich; he did not offer it to Roland.

And as they went on their way, Roland said:

"The Krischer too heard in his prison the sound of the cannon, and perhaps saw the fireworks. Poor fellow! he has not even a dog with him to talk to. How often I pitied him because he had to wander, day and night, through the fields! And now he longs to be trudging away again. And while he mopes in prison everything is growing outside; and the thieves, the foxes, and the hares know that nobody knows their tricks so well as the Krischer, and I believe, for all, he is innocent. Why are there any poor and unfortunate men? Why isn't all the world happy?"

For the first time, Erich found himself obliged to advise Roland not to tell his father that he had had these thoughts about the Krischer, and poor and unhappy people.

Erich was reassured and content. Roland's appearance as an Apollo, and the admiration it had called forth, had not spoiled him.

CHAPTER XI.

A CRAMPED HEART.

WHAT are we, if we place ourselves before the judgment seat, with our inmost thoughts laid bare?"

This was what Erich had written in his answer to an elegant note which Bella had sent him. She had requested him to send the robe in which she had drawn him; she wanted to introduce a few more details of its peculiar cut in the completion of her picture. The manner in which she subscribed herself frightened Erich, for there stood her name, Bella, but in the place of her family name an interrogation-mark, between brackets; through this a stroke of the pen had been drawn, as if she repented having made it, but it was still easily traced.

She threw the robe on the lay-figure in her atelier. A strange mood had come upon her; she stood with her hand resting on the shoulder of the lay-figure.

"What are we, if we place ourselves, with our inmost thoughts laid bare, before the judgment-seat?" Such were Erich's words, and now 'twas as if the lay-figure spoke them.

Bella shuddered; she trembled as if in the presence of death, and at that moment, as she stood there with her eyes fixed upon the floor, her hand upon the coat of this strange man, it was as if she must sink to the ground. In that instant of time her whole life lay before her.

The days of childhood—there was no fixed image of them. Her teachers praised her for her quick understanding. A French *bonne* was engaged; a severe English woman was given a place in the house. Bella learned languages readily, and good manners seemed native to her. While yet a child, her witty fancies were admired, and she heard them often repeated: that flattered her vanity, and blighted the simplicity of her childhood.

The men and women who came to the house, or whom she met here and there, praised her beauty, by their glances as well as their words. The day came for confirmation, but the sacred ceremony seemed to her simply as a sign of her release from the nursery, of short dresses to be put off and long ones to be worn, and when she went to the altar, the thought that reigned over all others, was: "I am the most beautiful." The evening before, the Bishop had dined with her parents; to her, therefore, he was not now an extraordinary personage as to the others; he had spoken familiarly to her, and in the church she seemed to herself the central point of all.

Her father consented, and during the very next winter, when she was but fourteen years old, Bella was brought out in society. Her dêbut was a brilliant one, and she was much courted; every one was captivated with the bloom of youth that rested upon her and heightened her charms. But very early a certain coldness began to appear; she was called, in jest, the Maid of the Sea, and there was in her eye, if one may say so, a cold fire. Even the reigning prince sought her out. She carefully preserved, as a sacred treasure, the tablet of her first Court-ball, and the withered bouquet lay with it.

From that time on followed an uninterrupted chain of conquests. Bella, ever ready with apt repartees, was the life of every circle. While she was still a child, they praised her to her face for her beauty; now that she was grown, they enlarged openly, or if behind her back, in such ways that she was sure to hear of it, upon her extraordinary mind. They encouraged her to make sharp remarks and criticisms, and they passed her witty sayings from one to another. Her reputation for wit, her fresh, spirited playing on the piano, and above all, her skill in design, made her the wonder of society, and she was set up as a pattern for imitation to many a young girl who followed her in their introduction to the social world.

Not yet sixteen years old, she had already given refusals to many suitors for her hand, and she heard with a smile of the betrothal of this one and that one, for she could say to herself, "I might have had him, if I had wished to." Her mother would have married her early, but her father was unwilling to give away his child so young; he kept hoping that a prince of the collateral line would lead her to his home.

On her seventeenth birthday, which was honored at break of day with a burst of martial music, and on which tokens of homage flowed in on all sides, one might have noted a change in the look of Bella's full eyes; for as she awaked beneath the tones of the music, a thought rose in her mind that never lost its hold, and this thought ran: "I do not believe in love; all that they say and sing of the might of love is idle tradition!" The teachings of her mother had conduced not a little to this condition of mind, for her mother had eradicated early in life all her power of loving, by continually representing to her daughter that the great thing was to win a brilliant lot in life. And in fact Bella had never loved any one; she only could not bear that any one toward whom she felt an inclination, should not throw himself at her feet. And very strange, in contrast, sounded the suggestions of a cousin of her mother, who often whispered to Bella, half in mere bitterness of heart, half in earnest: "That only is genuine love which is bestowed upon a man of humble birth. If you fell in love with the drawing-teacher, in whose atelier you are working, your music-teacher, or your teacher of languages, that would be real love." But to show an affection to a teacher, seemed to Bella the same as if one should choose to love and wed a liveried servant, or even a being of another species, as a horse.

On that seventeenth birthday, that cold, glassy, Medusa gaze which looks away off, through and beyond men, as if they were only shadows, was for the first time observable in her; but no one thought about it, and on that day it was as if something had hardened in her which would never after be waked to life.

After her year of mourning upon the death of her mother, Bella, though not yet twenty years old, withdrew coldly from society—its edge was worn off. She only allowed herself at times to take part in it as a disagreeable duty. She read, drew, studied music, conversed with artists, savants, and statesmen; but a certain rigidity settled in her bearing and her expression, whenever she was not flinging her witticisms about her. These were all the more telling in effect, because Bella had a deep, somewhat masculine voice, which her appearance would not lead you to expect.

It made a great sensation when it was learned that Bella had overcome her parents' opposition to her younger sister's marrying first. Bella stood by her sister's side before the altar, and through the bridal-veil of her sister she saw the dark, brown eye of the Adjutant-General, recently become a widower, fixed upon her. She curled her lip. "You will waste your courting on me," she said to herself, and gloried in her pride. To shatter, to ruin, to torment the hearts of men, to beguile them on and then cast them off—that was her pleasure. She once said to her father: "I would be willing to marry, if I could still do what I chose; but to go before the altar and, for weal or woe, say the yes! I was frightened when I heard my sister say that. I thought I should cry out, No! no! no! And I can't be sure that even before the altar I should not involuntarily say 'No!'"

She devoted herself to the companionship of a sick Princess, who was bid to spend a year at Madeira. The Princess died at Madeira. Bella went home; and she smiled when she was told that the Adjutant-General had married already. She had no reason to complain that the homage of men grew less frequent and fervent; but she was vexed for all that.

She again went abroad; this time with two English women, whom she accompanied through Italy and Greece. Lutz, Sonnenkamp's young courier, was at that time hers. She wiled away a whole winter in Constantinople; and the wicked tongues of the capital said that she was seeking a man of position, no matter what else he was; she would marry a gray-bearded Pasha. Bella returned; and then appeared in society in plain velvet robes.

Then followed Clodwig's courtship, and within four weeks, to the great surprise of the whole town, their betrothal and marriage. Bella retired with her husband to Wolfsgarten; she was not at all changed by marriage: that completeness which marriage gives to the nature of women was denied her. And what was there yet lacking? She was mature in mind, and as supremely happy as it was possible for her to be; for she had discovered in Clodwig what she had in vain, not so much sought for, as hoped to find—true nobility of soul.

She felt, for the first time, humble and modest; her life now flowed on peacefully, and in a well-defined channel. Clodwig was attentive, communicative, and as full of homage as on the first day of their marriage; there reigned in his soul a calmness and constancy, such as is attributed only to the gods: in every interview he was very respectful and gentle. His real warmth of nature, which found vent in his close, compact sentences, was only fully revealed when topics affecting the general welfare were under consideration. Bella recognized in his excitement at such times the evidence of a full, comprehensive soul, which, though created for a larger sphere of action, had been forced to develop itself in a narrow, contracted age, and under the mean conditions of a petty State.

Clodwig often lamented that, having for his whole life trusted confidently in the realization of his lofty views, he found, when it was too late, that one must work stubbornly on, regardless of results. But as soon as he came in contact with men and especially when he entered the Court-circle, he became mild and forgiving. Clodwig was always full of admiration of his wife; and if he sometimes found fault with her in a gentle way, and exposed the frequent superficiality and one-sidedness of her views, she may for a moment have felt a little rebellious; but when she regarded his refined, serene bearing, every defiant impulse vanished. She was happy in proving to herself, and in exhibiting to the world, how much she cherished a man of so much worth and importance. She knew that watchful eyes were upon her, though the world could not understand her conduct.

But now in this peaceful circle a man had suddenly entered, who exercised so sure and irresistible a power over her and her husband, and the entire house, that she was at first ill-affected toward him, and so expressed herself to Clodwig. She tried zealously to prevent his coming to the neighborhood; but as Clodwig, with a generous enthusiasm, extolled all the more the excellent character of the man, and even against her will invited him to the house, she yielded to the pleasure which this refreshing intercourse gave her.

Thus, then, Bella stood before the picture that *would not* be finished; she ground her teeth in angry self-contemplation. She had become at last settled in her relations to the world, and now once more a childish and senseless emotion like this has come upon her—for childish and senseless she called it—and yet she was unable to free herself from it. Was it because it hurt her self-esteem; or was it because it was the first time that she had extended her hand and not had it taken?

Her large eyes flashed; whoever had looked into them then would have seen the Medusa-look.

She suddenly left her atelier; she went to her dressing-room. She there placed herself before the large mirror, unbound her abundant hair and looked fixedly into the glass; and upon her pressed lips lay the question: "Are you then so old already?" She parted her lips like one who is sick with a fever, or is faint and would drink. Her eyes sparkled with joy, for she said to herself: You are beautiful, you are strong enough to look at yourself as you would at a stranger. But what avails this childish, this senseless emotion?

She took in either hand the long masses of her hair and brought them together under her chin; she was terror-stricken;

for now for the first time she saw that she was like the bust of the Medusa up there in the guest-chamber.

"Yes! Then I will be a Medusa! He shall be subdued, changed to stone, destroyed! He shall kneel before me, and I will spurn him with my foot!"

She raised her foot, but suddenly pressed both hands to her face, and tears burst from her eyes.

"Pardon, pardon my pride, my fierceness!" a voice within her seemed to cry. Contrition and wild passion, pride and humility contended within her; and it was as if that in her which, on the dawn of her seventeenth birthday, had hardened to stone, was suddenly unbound, had burst open like a flower-cup which has long been closed. A longing awoke in her—a longing for a home, as in the heart of the wicked child that has been forsaken by its parents in the woods; she longed for a place where she could remain hidden and protected—for a home. Where is it? Where?

She longed for a soul into which she could disburden all her own soul.

"Pardon! Pardon me!" her heart cried within her again and again. At first this appeal was made to Clodwig; it was now to Erich.

"Pardon! Pardon my pride! But you cannot know how proud I was. And I offer thee more than a thousand others, more than the whole world can dream of or understand!"

She shuddered at being alone; she rang for her maid, and bade her prepare her toilet.

"Tell me! How old am I? Do you know?" she asked abruptly.

The dressing-maid was startled by the question; she was not ready with an answer, and Bella added:

"I never was young."

"Oh, my good lady, you are still young, and have never looked better than now."

"Do you think so?" said Bella, and she raised her head haughtily, for the thought arose in her: Why should you not be young again? You are! You are what you are made to be, and let the world too be what it must.

"What is all this? What are all these vases? Volcanic ashes! All ashes! What is all this antiquarian pottery? What means this raking together of unearthed fragments of antiquity—this constant thinking and talking about humanity and progress? It is all a foreign, dead thing—a conversation over a death-bed, nothing but distraction of mind—self-forgetfulness, no life, no hope, no future in it, never out into the day, always back into the night—the night of the past, the night of humanity in the abstract, in the idea. But I am not the past, I am not this idea of humanity! I belong to the present! I will belong to the present! Ah me! where am I?"

She went to the garden. She saw two butterflies that flew from flower to flower, and then up in the air, circling about one another, joining and separating in their flight.

"That is life!" she cried to herself. "That is life! they do not haunt the ruins of the past."

Then a swallow came whizzing down, snapped up a butterfly and flew away.

"What has become of thy life now, poor butterfly?"

Down over the Rhine, clouds of vapor rolled up from the steamboats and vanished in thin air; and Bella thought:

"Who would be thus absorbed, dissipated, lost? What do we, then, here! We warm with our blood this dead earth, that it may not be without life. Every breath of our life is but a puff of vapor, mingling with a thousand others; and that we call life, and it is blown away like the thousands—"

The gardener's children, just come from school, crossed her path: they saluted their lady.

Bella stared at them.

"Why are these children here? What means this senseless renewing of mankind?"

As if seeking to hide from herself, she fixed her gaze upon a bush in blossom. She left the park. She watched a dove, as it cooed about its mate in the courtyard. The demure mate picked quietly at its food and scarcely listened to the amorous cooing, and then flew to the ridge of the roof and trimmed its feathers. The male bird followed after it; but it again gave its head a shake and flew away.

She turned her gaze to the ground again, and saw a boy bringing oxen under the yoke. He first laid a pad upon the head of the animal, and upon that the wooden yoke.

"That is the world! that is the way of the world!" she said to herself. "A pad between the yoke and the head, a pad of ready-made thoughts, of conventional sentiments!"

The boy stood astonished, for the lady stared at him so, and now put the question to him:

"Doesn't it give them pain too?"

He did not understand the question; she had to repeat it, and received the answer:

"The ox is used to it, he don't know anything better. Since our gracious lord has done away with the double-yoke, each ox has now its own yoke; they are harder to manage of course, but they draw better than in the double-yoke."

Bella gave a start.

"Double yoke—single yoke," kept sounding in her ear, and suddenly it seemed to her as if it were night, and she a spectre wandering about. This house, this garden, this world, is all a mere realm of shadows that vanish away.

It became disagreeably sultry and close: Bella thought she would suffocate. Then a fresh breeze blew over the heights; a storm unexpectedly rose, and hardly had Bella reached the house, when it broke loose with thunder and lightning and driving rain.

Bella stood by the window and looked out into the distance, and then rested her eye again upon a lofty ash-tree, whose branches were tossed about in the wind, and whose stem bent to and fro. The tree leaned toward the house, as if it would there seek help. Bella thought to herself: "Year after year this tree has sent out its roots here, and keeps growing; no storm can root it up or snap off its branches. Does it know that this one will pass over it, and only give it a new store of life? I too am such a tree, and I shall stand fast. Let the storm come, with its lightning and thunder and its dripping rain, it shall not loose my hold upon the firm earth, or shatter me."

"Erich," she suddenly said aloud. At that moment Clodwig entered and said:

"My dear wife, I have been seeking you."

Bella, when she heard the words "my dear wife," let them sink into her soul. Clodwig showed her a letter which he had written to Erich's mother and aunt; in which, according to Bella's wish, he had invited them to a visit of several weeks at Wolfsgarten.

"Do not send the letter," she exclaimed, abruptly. "Let us be quiet and alone again; I don't wish to be unsettled by the Dournay family."

Clodwig was sure that the noble lady would not introduce a disquieting element, but rather a beautiful social one; and that they would thus, in a pleasant, informal way, have Erich often with them.

The storm had passed over. Bella opened the window; a refreshing breeze blew in. She held the letter in her hand: the storm, with its lightning, rain, and thunder, had that day rushed through her soul, and here was the renewed and purer life. She assented to the wishes of her husband; she said to herself that the society of the noble lady would restore her to her true self. For a moment it passed through her mind that she would confess everything to Erich's mother, hold nothing from her; but then the thought came that that would not be necessary. It was easy to add that Erich would come to Wolfsgarten, and their intercourse would return to a peaceful train.

CHAPTER XII.

REVELATIONS OF JUSTICE AND WEALTH.

WHEN the inmates of Villa Eden arose on the morning after the fête, and prepared to attend the trial of the men accused of the robbery, their heads were in a whirl; for they had not yet recovered from the excitement occasioned by the snapping and cracking of the fireworks, and the sound of the horns.

But Prancken remained at the Villa, having undertaken to conduct the guests through the newly acquired country-house and grounds. Sonnenkamp, Roland, and Erich, the Castellan, the Coachman, Bertram the Head-gardener, with two of his assistants, and Squirrel, set out for the Court-city to attend the trial. As they passed the house of the Wine-count, now known to the world as the Baron von Endlich, they saw the sticks and shells of rockets, and other remains of last night's display, but the house was closed. The family were yet luxuriating in the first sweet sleep of nobility.

Erich spoke of the beautiful and pious conduct of the Priest in regard to the prisoners. For the good man acted in accordance with the great doctrine which teaches us to devote ourselves to the faltering and the fallen; and said that whether they be innocent or guilty, religion bids us give aid and solace to both. The Doctor, however, had taken the affair very coolly, and said that in all probability it would be a very good thing for the Krischer to live awhile under shelter. With this exception, little was said, and they reached the city in good time.

Sonnenkamp went to the telegraph-office, as he had some dispatches to send, one of which was to Erich's mother, at the University city.

Roland and Erich strolled, for awhile, along the banks of the Rhine, which flowed before the city. All was fresh and filled with exultant life; but the two friends did not speak. They returned to the city, passing the Corn-exchange; and as Roland looked at the crowd and bustle his face brightened up, and he said:

"Doesn't it seem to you, too, as if ten years had passed since then? It was so different then from what it is to-day! Don't you believe, too, that there were as many rascals among the singers as there are there in prison—and perhaps greater rascals too?"

Erich was deeply pained to see how early in life Roland was made to feel its bitterness and contention. They went together to the Court-house.

The President and judges sat on a little dais—at their right the jury, at their left the advocates and prisoners. The tribune was filled with spectators; for there was great curiosity to hear this mysterious Herr Sonnenkamp speak openly, and—who knows what other exciting things might be experienced?

Grubworm, the Groom, and the Krischer sat in the prisoners' dock, Grubworm snuffing furiously, the Groom looking round with brazen face, and the Krischer holding his hands before his eyes.

Grubworm was in good condition, and seemed benefited by his imprisonment. He stared about the hall with an almost happy look, apparently enjoying the flattering fact that so many people should bother themselves about him. The Groom, who had been very careful to curl his hair and trim his beard, looked disdainfully at the assembly.

The Krischer appeared deeply humiliated, and turned his back on his fellow-prisoners; and once, when Grubworm tried to whisper something in his ear, moved indignantly away from him. He looked up at the spectators. There he saw his wife, two of his sons, and his daughters, but the Cooper was not with them. His children seemed grown since he had seen them last, and were dressed in their Sunday-clothes to witness the shame—no, surely to see the honor of their father firmly established.

The Krischer stirred uneasily on his bench, and moved his lips as if saying something to his wife, but no audible word escaped from them. He was saying to her: "Don't worry; we'll go home together again in a couple of hours."

Sonnenkamp, Erich, and Roland sat on the witnesses' seat.

Roland was between his father and Erich, and clung to his friend as if frightened. Knopf sat beside Erich and nodded to Roland.

"In court, one man's testimony is as valuable as another's," said Roland softly to Erich, who knew what was passing in the boy's mind. Had he not already subdued his pride, it might have offended Roland to see that the Castellan's testimony was of equal worth with his father's.

The accusation was read. Closer examination had brought to light the fact that a receptacle within the safe, which was sunk in the wall but disconnected from it, had been opened with a key and afterward locked: a considerable sum of money had been taken from this place, which was afterward found nearly untouched in the possession of the Groom.

At his own request, Sonnenkamp was examined first, and identified the stolen goods as his property.

Roland straightened himself up as he heard his father speak so benevolently and mildly, for Sonnenkamp said that he was sorry that anybody should come to grief in this way, but justice must be done.

Sonnenkamp was allowed to leave the stand. He had hardly made his bow, intending to leave the court-room, when the Groom's counsel requested the President to ask Herr Sonnenkamp what amount of money had been deposited in the closet sunk in the wall; for if he did not know this, it would be impossible for him to say with certainty what amount of valuable papers and coin had been extracted.

The entire assembly was breathless; for now the measureless wealth of Sonnenkamp was to be disclosed. For a time there was utter silence, and then Sonnenkamp asked if the law could compel him to answer such a question, or whether it was optional with him to answer or not. The President was obliged to say that it was very necessary that the amount stolen should be known, in order to regulate justly the amount of punishment.

Again there was a pause. Sonnenkamp unbuttoned his coat; then he unbuttoned his vest and took out a little book, approached the dais, offered it to the President, and said:

"Here is a full statement of the valuable papers payable to bearer, needing only my signature, and also a statement of the amount in cash."

Sonnenkamp paused half-way up the steps of the dais, on which sat the President and judges, for the counsel for the accused cried out:

"We have an incontestable right—entirely incontestable—to know the contents of that paper; there is no document that the President may read, and we may not."

"Very well," said Sonnenkamp, turning; "I'll read it. Twelve million dollars in papers, payable to bearer, three million only payable to my order, and only two hundred thousand in cash. Is that satisfactory?"

The spectators began to applaud, and the President said that on a repetition of the noise he would order the galleries to be cleared.

Sonnenkamp stepped down again: he had intended to leave the court, but changing his mind, sat down with the other witnesses. Roland dropped his eyes and took Erich's hand, which he held fast. There was great whispering and moving in the galleries, the President again ordered silence, and Sonnenkamp left the room.

The Head-gardener was then examined, but his testimony was hardly heard. The audience did not become perfectly still and attentive till Erich was called.

He gave the whole story, and said that the Krischer was accustomed to speak bitterly about the difference between the rich and poor, but added that he considered the man incapable of any base crime.

There was great whispering among the spectators as Erich

said that the Krischer had once asked him: "What would you do if you were worth millions?" And so the question was put before everybody.

Knopf was called, and the first thing he did was to produce a writing from old Herr Weidmann, stating that the Krischer had been his (Weidmann's) servant for several years, and that the writer considered him an upright man, incapable of deceit, let alone a crime. Knopf then added, on his own account, that the Krischer was always bothering his head about what could not be helped.

Roland was then called, and stepped boldly up before the court. The Krischer nodded to him.

Roland was a minor, and therefore could not be sworn, but he produced a good impression by saying that his word was as good as his oath.

He recognized the stolen articles as his. He believed that his father's rooms had been locked, but would not swear to it, for he had not been near them for several days before the robbery. And then, without being asked, stated his conviction that the Krischer had no part in the crime.

At these words the Krischer rose to his feet, and the officer behind him had to lay his hand on his shoulder to make him sit down again.

The Krischer had now only to answer for receiving stolen goods. The other two could gain nothing any longer by denying, and sought only to cast the blame of the burglary on each other.

Erich was again called to testify to the fact that, a few days before the crime, the Krischer had been shown through the whole house. As Erich sat down, Roland rose and said:

"Herr President, may I speak again?"

"Certainly," answered the President, encouraging him; "speak as much as you wish."

Roland stepped forward erect and boldly, and his voice was almost as powerful as a man's as he cried:

"I here raise my hand to testify that my poor brother here is as innocent as he is poor. It is true that he often used to lament that one man starves while another feasts; but, before God and man, I assert that he has often told me that the hand must wither that gets property unjustly. Could a man who would say that break into another's house at night and steal? I beg, I entreat you, to say that this man is as innocent as any of you—as I myself!"

He paused and stood rooted to the spot, and for a time a breathless silence reigned throughout the court-room.

"Have you anything else to say?" inquired the President.

Roland appeared to be waking from a dream, and said:

"No—nothing more, thank you."

He turned to Erich, who took his hand and held it fast; it was cold as ice, and Erich tried to warm it in his own. Knopf fumbled for the other hand of his former pupil, but could not grasp it, for he had to take off his spectacles and wipe them—they were wet with tears.

It did not take long to finish the proceedings. The Head-master was on the jury, who now retired, and entered again almost immediately. The Head-master had been chosen foreman, and, laying his hand on his heart, announced the verdict, which was, that Grubworm and the Groom were guilty, and the Krischer not guilty.

When the crowd had withdrawn from the court-room, Erich pressed through the group of children around the Krischer. The wife and the Cooper were also there, and grasped the Krischer's hand.

The Krischer broke away from them all, saying that he must see Weidmann's son, who had been one of the jurors. The man was just approaching, and the Krischer told him, with great emotion, to tell his father that now all was atoned for, for the world knew what Herr Weidmann thought of him.

Young Weidmann went up to Erich, and congratulated him on having educated his pupil so well, and others did the same. Erich requested young Weidmann to remember him to his father, and tell him that he would soon make the promised visit to Mattenheim.

Knopf stood in the midst of the group, begging the men not to praise the boy, for that would spoil him; and, from sheer desire to keep the others away, did not offer the boy his hand.

And then Sonnenkamp appeared. All respectfully took off their hats. What manner of man is this, who has such incalculable wealth and yet wears a coat and stands on his own feet just like the rest of us! . . . Sonnenkamp filled them with awe. How *can* the man be so rich? Some sat in the seat of the scornful, and maintained that Sonnenkamp had exaggerated his wealth, and others, who could see further through a millstone than even these, held that the man was richer than he pretended; but these latter received but little attention. Sonnenkamp saluted the crowd on all sides, and then approached the Krischer and congratulated him. Then he called Roland aside, and, for the first time, the boy stood before his father and knew how rich he was; he dropped his eyes and thought that he must look up to him as to a mountain. But Sonnenkamp laid his hand kindly on his son's shoulder, and told him to return home with Erich, for he himself was obliged to remain in the city and wait for a telegram.

Roland requested and urged the Krischer and his family to ride with them in the carriages.

The Krischer refused; but the boy begged so earnestly, that at last he yielded and got into the carriage with his wife: the children could walk.

Roland conducted the liberated man in triumph through the city and villages. The woman was very much ashamed of travelling in this manner, but the Krischer looked boldly around, and often said:

"It has all grown finely without me, and will grow just as well when I am over the ocean."

He told Erich of his intention to take his family and go to America.

CHAPTER XIII.

THE MAJOR VANQUISHES.

THE same sun that shone on Wolfsgarten, where Bella sat engaged in fierce struggle with herself—the same sun that shimmered through the green curtains of the court-house upon the bench where sat the accused, fell through the closed jalousies into the quiet room, in the old University city, where sat Erich's mother. She sat quietly working in the piano-nook near the window filled with flowers, and thought of her son, wondering why he should be called to tread so peculiar a path in life. She raised her eyes sorrowfully to the picture of her husband, who would have said to her: "My child, we both, and you more than I, have trod a peculiar path; and this destiny will continue from generation to generation. But let us be at peace; the spirit of our son is steadfast and sure: he may be cast down by fate, but cannot be utterly subdued."

So the mother quieted herself, and Erich's letters brought peace. He had promised faithfully to let her know of all that should occur; but afterward had begged her to forgive him if his letters were irregular and hasty, for he must, for awhile, forget himself and all that was his, in the hope, now almost a certainty, of winning yet another soul. At first, he had spoken much of Bella and Clodwig; of how he felt fully at home with his friends, and was learning to believe in the happiness of perfect rest; but after awhile he said nothing of Bella, except occasionally to send her compliments. Erich's mother had not noticed it, but his aunt Claudine, who seldom talked, but always said something to the point when asked her opinion, remarked, when asked what impression Bella and Clodwig had made on her, that she had noticed, while Bella was at the house, a certain restlessness in her actions; and that she had looked at an old picture of Erich in a manner which showed that she took an unusual interest in it. Frau Dournay was obliged to say that she had noticed something similar in Bella's actions when she asked so earnestly in regard to Erich's early life. Nevertheless she told her sister-in-law that Bella was not merely a dilettante, but an artist, and looked at the picture, which was very well painted (she had once been offered a considerable sum for her collection), with the eye of an artist.

The rooms where the two ladies lived were very quiet; they themselves lived almost as noiselessly as the flowers which thrived so well under their care. The postman brought a letter, the handwriting of which was Clodwig's; and in every word he himself could, to a certain extent, be seen. The characters were neat and delicate, never made in haste, but never with too much care; the lines were symmetrical and sufficiently far apart, although no space was lost. The first casual glance at the letter put the ladies at ease, and the contents and mode of expression were just as clear and calm as the handwriting. He said that Frau Dournay would place him under obligations to her by accepting the invitation to pass a few weeks with them. He spoke of the pleasant intercourse he had once had with her husband, and which he had renewed with Erich,—thus bringing back to him reminiscences of his early life, for which he had never dared to hope. In conclusion, he appealed to their personal acquaintance, and there was a written smile in his words as he added that never in the course of a long life had he experienced a heartfelt pleasure which had not been reciprocated; he therefore begged her not to put him to the blush now in his old age. He closed by saying that he begged to be permitted by the mother of his friend Erich to subscribe himself, "Your friend Clodwig." There was no overstrained courtliness in the letter, but yet all was delicate and refined.

Under this were a few words from Bella, written hastily and in large characters, requesting the mother and aunt to honor her with a visit. She said that she only wrote a few words, being convinced that she would soon be permitted to have more intimate intercourse with the venerated mother and lovely aunt. In a postscript, she added a request that they would bring Erich's music with them.

The Doctor had enclosed a letter appealing to them as a pupil of the old Professor. He good-humoredly offered his assistance in case they should need medical aid, and added his belief that his mother's presence would be a sure preventive or cure of any sickness his young friend Erich might have.

This expression set Erich's mother thinking; and she had determined to accept the invitation, when another knock was heard at the door, and Sonnenkamp's dispatch arrived.

She had hardly read this when another rap was heard, and the Major entered.

The lady started, for she did not recognize him: she saw only the ruddy face with its short, snow-white hair, and the badge of his order on his breast. She thought at first that the intruder was an officer of justice, whose arrival boded some ill—she knew not what—to Erich. The Major was not very skilful in relieving her anxiety, for he said instantly:

"Frau Professorin, I come with authority—yes, yes, but I shall not drive you from Paradise, but shut you up in the Garden of Eden."

The Major had been thinking this up during his journey, and had said it to himself certainly a hundred times, and now it came out so bunglingly that the widow could not rise for trembling.

Then the Major cried:

"Keep your seat; nobody puts himself out on my account—everybody knows that. I never distrust anybody, and like to have people keep their seats when I come,—don't you? Then you're *sure* that you're not making trouble."

"Do you come from my son?"

"Yes, from him too. See now; I'm no saint, but then I'm no great sinner either, but I can boast of *one* thing, and that is, that never in my life have I envied anybody but you. I envied you when you said 'my son'—then I did envy you. And why can't I say so too? Oh, if I only had such a son!"

And then at last Peace entered that house.

The Major delivered a letter from Sonnenkamp, and one from the Privy-councillor's wife; he desired that they would read them immediately, for that would obviate the necessity of his saying anything.

The widow read; and the Major, chuckling and nodding with internal delight, looked at her as she read.

The lady again welcomed him, and called her sister-in-law, who came.

The jalousies toward the street were opened, and a full stream of light entered and shone on happy faces.

"What shall we do?" asked Aunt Claudine.

"We need think no longer, but accept the kind invitation."

"Whose?"

"Why Herr Sonnenkamp's."

"Right!" said the Major, smiling. "Will you allow me to light a cigar? Did our brother, your husband, who has gone to eternal rest, smoke?"

"Certainly."

Aunt Claudine's delicate fingers held the light for him.

"Good! good!" cried the Major. "You have given me fire, and I promise to go through fire for you."

After this gallant burst of eloquence, the Major was happy, and puffed away with delight.

Of course much was to be done before they could set out. The Major promised that Joseph should come and pack up everything, not a thread should be left. He himself left the house, promising to return in a few hours, after having seen his brother Masons.

Midday saw the Major and the two ladies seated in a first-class car, *en route* toward the Rhine, and the Major was as proud and happy as if he had conquered the enemy and taken all his munitions of war.

CHAPTER XIV.

POTATOES, AND SOMETHING BETTER YET.

ERICH and Roland rode with the Krischer and his wife. When the Krischer reached his own territory, he stopped the carriage, and got out.

"No, I won't ride here," said he. "And now look at my hands; my hands have been chained. What shall they do now! Take vengeance? On whom? And even if I knew whom, what then?"

He took some earth, and throwing it into the air, cried out:

"I swear by you to leave the country. The New World must give me, too, my own land. I've taken care of others' soil long enough in the Old World!"

Erich and Roland alighted, and accompanied the Krischer to his house. Suddenly they heard some one calling to them from the vineyard, and the Seven-piper approached, bringing the halberd which the Krischer had always regarded as the symbol of his office as guardian of the fields. He handed it to the Krischer, and said:

"Take it back now, I have guarded it faithfully for you."

He accompanied them to the house. All the dogs in the yard began to bark, and all the birds in the room jumped about and twittered as their master entered. But the blackbirds outsang all the others, for they whistled, "Life let us cherish," but stopped at the second line. The Krischer looked at everything as one just awakened from sleep; but finally things became more natural to him, and the whole family sat down at table, where they ate the first new potatoes, which a neighbor had cooked for them. Roland had never tasted such food, and all laughed as he said:

"Claus, potatoes come from the country where I was born, and to which you are going. They were born in America, and are immigrants here, just as we are."

There seemed to be a hearty good-feeling between these good people and Roland, and the boy wished to give the Krischer the watch which had been stolen and recovered. He wished him to keep it as a remembrancer; but the Krischer would not take it, although Erich and the Seven-piper urged him to.

"Take it, father," said the Cooper, and then at last the Krischer consented.

The Seven-piper led the conversation. He poo-pooh-ed the Krischer for always bothering his head with stupid notions, and never letting up on them. It wasn't necessary to be rich. To be sure, a man was always hollow, but he couldn't eat and drink more than his fill; and a rich man couldn't sleep better than well; and it didn't matter in what sort of a bed one slept, provided he had a good sleep; and it was all humbug to ride in a coach; 'twas a good deal better to ride on shank's mare, with a good walking-stick.

They also talked about Grubworm, and the Seven-piper said:

"When any one goes to find his grave, he'll have to take a ladder."

"Why?" asked Roland.

"'Cause they'll hang him."

But the Krischer didn't want to talk of wicked men.

The Seven-piper was, and always continued to be, the personification of jolly poverty. He had sent one of the children to his house; and just as a flask of wine arrived from Fräulein Milch, singing commenced at the Krischer's. The entire orchestra arrived, and the Seven-piper and Erich joined with them.

At last Erich urged the necessity of returning home; and just as they were leaving the side-road and striking the highway, a carriage approached, in which sat the Major, gesticulating, and crying with mighty voice:

"Battalion, halt!"

They halted, and the Major came up with Erich's mother and aunt.

"That's the only thing I was wishing for," cried Roland. "Herr Major, the Krischer is released, he's innocent!"

The mother embraced Roland, and then her son. They had all alighted, and Erich walked toward the Villa with his mother, who was leading Roland, with her hand on his arm. The Major politely offered his arm to the aunt; but she declined it, excusing herself by saying that it was a whim of hers, never to be led.

"It is certainly better—Fräulein Milch thinks so too. You will become acquainted with her; you will be good friends, depend on it. She knows everything--everything. It's incomprehensible where she learned it all! She knew that Count Clodwig had invited you. But we understand strategy—we got ahead of him. It's the lucky man who takes the bride home—that is, they say so."

Music was heard in the distance, and the Major explained that they were still rejoicing over the marriage at Herr von End lich's house.

"Oh, mother, if ever again I should be dispirited and sad, I will recall this hour, and be happy again"

The mother's heart was full: she could not speak.

The guests were warmly welcomed at the Villa. The Privy councillor's wife embraced and kissed the Professor's wife. Frau Ceres sent her excuses. As night approached, Sonnenkamp appeared.

The moon shone brightly, as Erich and Roland conducted the ladies to the vine-clad cottage; and here upon the balcony the mother again clasped her son's hand, and said:

"If your father could see you, he would be pleased with you. You have still your good and pure look. Yes, everything is well now; you have still your pure look."

BOOK SEVENTH.

CHAPTER I.

MOTHER IS HERE.

"MY mother is here!"

Erich felt as if surrounded by a flood of lifegiving dew. He heard the voice of a child waking from its dream; it was he himself who had given utterance to these words. He closed his eyes again and dreamed himself back to the days of his childhood; all that had perturbed his spirit since that time—all that had oppressed and torn his soul, had vanished and sunk into nothingness.

"My mother is here!"

And thus, too, duty called.

Erich stood by Roland's bed. It was never necessary for him to rouse the boy with words; one full glance upon his sleeping face was sufficient; and now, as he opened his eyes, his first words were:

"Your mother is here!"

And thus the words that Erich had heard in his dream were now spoken by another. He laid his hand on the boy's forehead, and looked at him with delight, and yet with sadness. Why was it that this child, poor in the midst of his wealth, was unblessed by a mother's love?

The day was now doubly welcome, for Erich and Roland went first to the mother.

As they walked by the shore, Roland cried out to the stream:

"Father Rhine! Erich's mother is here!"

Erich smiled—the boy's cheek was glowing.

They went to the mother as to a temple, and came from her as from a temple; for every word, every motion, every glance of this calm and pure woman seemed a blessing; and she showed them the sacredness of order and steadfast adherence to duty, by saying that she would consider it only a perfect proof of their love and constancy if they worked as steadily now as heretofore. We must do our duty in every circumstance of life, be it sorrowful or joyful.

Erich and Roland were soon at work again; to-day they read the return of Ulysses to Ithaca. Erich was not very attentive, for every thought and emotion was merged in feeling that he was again near his mother. He endeavored to overcome his distraction, for he wished to confine himself to, and think only of his present duty, but before he was aware he again detected himself thinking of his mother, as he looked at Roland. Ah, why could not he, too, know the blessedness of such a feeling? The best source from which man can draw happiness and life is a mother's love. Man's love must be gained, conquered, and earned—struggled to through opposing difficulties. A mother's love alone is forever ungained and unearned.

And now his thoughts turned to Bella. Erich hoped that he had freed himself from all treason to himself, to the world, and to all that is pure; and with a power which was stronger than ever before, for it was attained through hard struggles, he returned to his duties, and transferred himself and his pupil into the life of another so completely, that all around them was forgotten.

It seemed almost like a new pleasure to recall at noon the presence of the mother. They were all in the garden together, except Frau Ceres, who excused herself through Miss Perini. Sonnenkamp smiled, for he knew that his wife had never thought of sending her excuses, and that Miss Perini had taken upon herself the responsibility of making them; and she was perfectly warranted in doing so, inasmuch as Frau Ceres was naturally obstinate enough to be unwilling to meet any society obtruded on her, and her chief strength always lay in refusal. Miss Perini evidently took pains to make herself as agreeable as possible to the Professor's widow, and expressed an almost childish delight when that lady taught her a new piece of fancy sewing.

But the Privy-councillor's wife was eminently useful in putting everybody at ease. The way in which she modestly subordinated herself to the Professor's widow influenced all the others; and, together with the respectful deference which she paid to her, at once and peremptorily secured for that lady a position which doubtless she would otherwise have acquired, but only after the lapse of some time; and this result was aided by her repeating that, in her day, Frau Dournay had been the most honored lady at Court, and was even yet referred to as a model of high breeding. At first, Frau Dournay was somewhat humiliated by hearing herself so highly praised; but nevertheless she was grateful to her friend, who was evidently striving to transform her poverty and dependence into sources of respect and admiration.

Even Miss Perini was subdued by the widow's character, for Frau Dournay had such quiet dignity, such a serene and mild countenance, in which dwelt such youthful enjoyment of life, and there was such a kindly light beaming from her whole nature, that everything ignoble and impure seemed totally unknown to her. At the same time the youthfulness of her feelings was evident; and she was full of enthusiasm, which, nurtured by the idealistic life of her husband, again sprang into full bloom in the companionship of her son. She said the simplest things with a sweetness and grace which gave them a meaning, and with a freshness that made them seem new.

While they were together at noon, a letter came from Bella. She welcomed Frau Dournay, and requested a visit from her on the following day.

Frau Dournay wished to send an answer by the same messenger, but he had—no one knew why—immediately been dismissed. But Sonnenkamp had arranged that; and when Frau Dournay had given her letter to a messenger belonging to the house, it instantly found its way to Sonnenkamp's cabinet, where it was skilfully opened and the contents found to be satisfactory, for it contained a polite but decided refusal of the invitation. Sonnenkamp smiled, for the lady said that she had been received kindly as the guest of the house, and only asked that the visits paid to it would also be granted to her.

Again Sonnenkamp smiled: his expectation was being fulfilled; and through the Professor's widow he would yet conquer a position among the neighboring families, and be received into their society as an equal.

CHAPTER II.

SHE WHO HAS NEVER LEARNED ANYTHING WISHES TO LEARN.

WHEN Sonnenkamp came from his cabinet, he went to his wife's chamber. In the ante-room, a waiting-maid told him that her lady wished to speak with no one. He did not heed her, but went on. He found Frau Ceres lying on the sofa; the windows were curtained, so that the large room seemed to be in twilight. Frau Ceres looked at him with her great dark eyes, and gave him her small delicate hands with the long nails, but did not speak. He kissed the hand and seated himself beside her.

For some time he was silent, but at last began to explain to his wife, that he was accomplishing his plan by means of the guest who was now in the house; for by her hand the doors leading to the halls of the Prince's palace would be opened.

At the word palace, Frau Ceres roused herself a little. She did not speak; but her restless glance showed that interest was awakened within her; for beyond the ocean and amid all their wanderings, Sonnenkamp had told her that it was his highest aim that she should enter Court-circles. And Frau Ceres had thought of life at Court as of a glorious fairy-tale, representing some blissful sphere beyond the earth where were eternal brightness and glory, and the abode of the gods. She had already learned that the representation was exaggerated, but everywhere she heard of that happiness, and saw how all were struggling for admission at Court, and she was angry at her husband for not having obtained what had been so long and so often promised. She was in Europe, had retired into solitude, which, men say, is so lovely, and was always expecting to be summoned to Court.

Why was it so long in coming? Why were people so distant? Even Bella, the only person who showed her any attention, seemed to regard her as a parrot—a foreign bird whose plumage was to be looked at and admired, but with whom one must have no more to do, than occasionally to give it a lump of sugar or to say "Pretty poll." Even the recollection of how she had outshone all the other ladies at Herr von Endlich's fête was not more than half satisfying.

Notwithstanding all her apparent idleness and ennui, Frau Ceres was always busied with one thought, and that one thought had been planted in her mind by her husband; it had become stronger than he wished—it controlled her whole being.

He now told her, with much address, that the house would gain new lustre and be led more surely to its goal by the Professor's widow, to whom even the wife of the Privy-councillor deferred, because she had been the favorite and most powerful lady at Court—nay, had been the friend of the widowed Princess herself.

Sonnenkamp was so skilful in displaying his shrewdness, that at last his wife brought herself to say:

"You're very shrewd. I'll talk with the tutor's mother."

He then undertook to instruct her how she should comport herself; but, like a spoiled child—almost like a wild beast—she cried out, as she gesticulated and stamped:

"I'll have no instructions! Don't say another word! Bring the woman to me!"

Sonnenkamp, anxious and troubled, went to Erich's mother; he would willingly have given her advice as to her conduct, but feared to, and said:

"My dear little wife is somewhat spoiled, and very nervous."

Frau Dournay went to Frau Ceres, who remained lying on the sofa. She was shrewd enough to know that the less accessible one shows one's self, the more deference is likely to be shown.

Frau Dournay bowed gracefully, and Frau Ceres instantly forgot everything, and before the other could speak, cried out:

"You must teach me to do that! I want to bow so! People bow so at Court, don't they?"

Frau Dournay did not know what answer to make. Was this something more than nervousness—insanity? Yet she found strength to say:

"I can easily imagine you, belonging to a republic, find our manners somewhat strange; but I find that it is better to simply give the hand at a first meeting."

She extended her hand, and Frau Ceres did the same, and was sufficiently forgetful to rise.

"You are sick—I will disturb you no longer," said Frau Dournay.

Frau Ceres thought it would be better to pretend sickness, and said:

"Oh, yes—I'm always sick; but pray stay with me."

And as the mother spoke to her, the earnest tones of her voice made such an impression on Frau Ceres that she closed her eyes, and when she again opened them, large tears stood on her long lashes.

Frau Dournay regretted that she had agitated her, but Frau Ceres shook her head and said:

"No, no: I thank you. It is years since I have been able to cry. These tears lay here—here," and she beat her breast. "Thank you!"

Frau Dournay wished to withdraw, but Frau Ceres rose hastily and approached the wondering lady, who could not help shrinking as if grasped by a mad woman, for Frau Ceres threw herself on her knees before her, and cried as she covered her hand with kisses:

"Ah, protect me! Be my mother. I have never said Mother to any one—I never knew a mother!"

Frau Dournay raised her and said:

"My child, I can be your mother—I can and will. I am glad to have so beautiful a calling here, and accept it with my whole heart. But now, I beg you be calm!"

She led Frau Ceres back to the sofa—a curious complication of soft cushions in which the delicate lady always lay wrapped up as if buried—laid her tenderly down, and covered her with a large shawl.

Frau Ceres held the mother's hand close, and sobbed like a child.

Frau Dournay now spoke of their happiness in having two such sons; but spoke less of Erich than of Roland. And as she related how Roland, appearing to her in the gloaming, had seemed so like her only dead son, Frau Ceres turned and kissed her hand. And the lady went on to say that she, too, was a woman of many peculiarities, with whom it was not easy to live: she had too much accustomed herself to solitude, and feared that she was not young and cheerful enough to be the companion of a lady who could lay every claim to a life of brilliancy and pleasure.

Frau Ceres asked Frau Dournay to draw the curtain a little;

and then as she saw the stranger more clearly, she smiled; but her face with its delicate, half-opened mouth, soon took again its old expression of dulness, and she took up her fan and fanned herself. At length she said:

"Ah, yes, to learn! You can't think how stupid I am; and yet I want to be clever, and should have liked to learn so much, but he wouldn't let me, and was always saying, 'You are loveliest and dearest as you are.' Yes, perhaps so to him, but not to myself. If Miss Perini were not so good, I don't know what I should do. Do you play whist? Do you love Nature? I'm a foolish thing, ain't I?"

Frau Ceres probably expected that Frau Dournay would contradict this assertion: she did not, but on the other hand, said:

"If there is anything which you can learn from me, it is entirely at your disposal. I have known women like you, and might tell you why you are always unwell."

"Why? Do you know? You?"

"Yes, but it is not a very flattering reason."

"Oh, tell me what it is."

"My dear child! you are always unwell because you are always idle. When one has nothing to do, he always finds employment in thinking of his health."

"Ah, you're wise," cried Frau Ceres, "but I'm weak."

In fact there was something weak and defenceless about her. She regarded herself, and Sonnenkamp regarded her, as a fragile toy. And she was utterly lazy, the smallest thing was a burden to her. She could not decide which was the most trying, to hear or to see; but thought that on the whole the latter was the more burdensome, for when one reads, one must hold a book and pay a certain degree of attention to its contents: the consequence was that she always had Miss Perini read to her whenever she could exert herself sufficiently to listen, and then—what an advantage it was to be able to fall asleep when she felt like it!

A somewhat similar occurrence took place now; for while Frau Dournay was speaking, Frau Ceres dropped her hand, and it needed only a glance to see that she had fallen asleep; and her companion sat in that rich and beautiful apartment as in fairy-land. She held her breath, and did not know what to do. What is all this? Here all is mystery. She did not dare to stir, for fear of waking the sleeper; but Frau Ceres turned and said:

"Go now—go now; I'll come pretty soon."

Frau Dournay went.

Sonnenkamp was waiting for her, and said anxiously:

"How does she act toward you?"

"Like a good child," answered the mother. "But I have a

request to make. I think I can cure the over-excitement or sluggishness of your wife, but I beg you never to ask me what we talk about. If I gain your wife's perfect confidence, I must be able to say conscientiously, 'She speaks with me alone; what she confides never passes my lips.' Will you promise to indulge us women?"

"Yes," replied Sonnenkamp.

It was difficult for him to do so, but there was no help for it.

CHAPTER III.

A CULTIVATED NEIGHBORHOOD.

ON the following day Prancken called, and, summoning up all his fine airs as a man of the world, he made his salutations to the widow. The latter at once caused him to understand that she regarded him as the friend of the family. This she did so unobtrusively, and with such charming tact, that Prancken was highly delighted.

When she thanked him for having obtained for Erich his present position, he denied all claim to her thanks; it was only a slight acknowledgment of his own debt, for he owed all that he had of knowledge and culture to the late Professor.

There was a tone in these words that won the widow's whole heart. She knew quite well how much to ascribe to the excess of politeness, but she was convinced that the kernel was truth; whoever came within reach of the voice and eye of her husband, if not wholly indifferent and careless, must have received an enduring impulse toward a nobler life.

Prancken spoke of his brother-in-law and his sister, and told how much Erich was loved at Wolfsgarten. Then giving a skilful turn to his speeches, he had the art to say that he promised himself that the presence of Frau Dournay would prove a calming and quieting influence upon his sister, who had recently become much perturbed in mind. He touched upon this point very cautiously, and only intimated how difficult a task it was to live with so old a man, though one, it was true, of so noble a nature; and how an emotion which has been apparently subdued, often unexpectedly seizes the mind anew.

Frau Dournay understood this better than Prancken imagined, and she was much pleased to meet in him a young man who, in the quiet of a country life, was addicted to the study of the intricate machinery of the human mind.

Prancken could not restrain himself from giving some account of his religious conversion; he did this as a token of his trust and confidence in her. And then suddenly, as in a vision, he saw this lady by the side of Manna, and the latter opening her whole soul to her. She therefore would assure Manna that he acknowledged his change of heart before the world. It even came to him just then, that the Mother-Superior had spoken very highly of this lady in the presence of Manna.

A smile touched his lips, as he thought to himself, "This lady can be used to a good purpose in dissuading Manna from her childish project of taking the veil, although it is certainly unfortunate that this lady does not belong to the same Church with her."

He then, at Sonnenkamp's request, invited Frau Dournay to go with him to the villa, which the wife of—he corrected himself quickly, and said—the Privy-councillor wanted to buy. She would surely consent, so as to help Herr Sonnenkamp obtain such agreeable neighbors. The objection of Frau Dournay, that she was hardly sufficiently rested as yet, was waved aside with many flattering speeches.

The carriage drove up.

The wife of the Privy-councillor and Sonnenkamp entered; the Widow must go with them to inspect the villa which was offered for sale. On the way thither, they were all very pleasant in their manners; but somehow the thought crossed her mind that she was in the midst of intriguants, and that in her innocence they wanted to make use of her for some purpose—she knew not what. She experienced a positively uneasy feeling, which was rendered still more defined when, upon their entering the villa, Sonnenkamp said the villa belonged to him; and he was glad that, in parting with it, he could make so pleasant a lady his neighbor.

What does this mean? Are they going to surprise her? Does Sonnenkamp mean to place the villa in her hands?

She soon was conscious of her error; for the wife of the Privy-councillor immediately went on to portion out the rooms to herself, to her husband, to her children. She had two sons in the service; one of her daughters was already married, and a room was set apart for the grandchild; and when she began to select favorite spots in the garden, Sonnenkamp promised to have new grounds laid out. She was surprised how much could be made out of this piece of land.

Sonnenkamp was very complaisant; he had indeed desired to give the villa as an equivalent for the coveted elevation of rank—for the small sum which the Councillor paid was only for appearance' sake—but he had been obliged to submit to Prancken, who asserted that this was not practicable; that it was more prudent simply to place one's self in neighborly relations with a man of so much power, that thus all the rest would follow very naturally.

The wife of the Privy-councillor took the Widow aside to a

seat in the garden. She knew in her heart, she said, that Frau Dournay would surely be glad to use her great influence in procuring for the Sonnenkamp family the deserved honor. She did not, for the present, go further than this; but it was her decided plan not to appear herself, or have her husband appear as the chief lever in this undertaking, but to use the Professor's widow as such. If it miscarried, they would remain concealed, and only the scholarly widow would be committed; and she was considered eccentric anyhow.

Amid high-sounding speeches, overflowing with pure and generous sentiments, an intrigue was concealed which could not be easily penetrated.

When Sonnenkamp was alone with Prancken and the Councillor's wife, he smiled as one who, by way of sport, allowed himself for once to be overreached. He listened with a very friendly air as Prancken showed him that the Privy-councillor would have to acquire and occupy the villa at once, for if it was transacted later, soon before or soon after the wished-for event, there would be occasion for malicious talk.

Sonnenkamp smiled, and recommended his young friend to a diplomatic career—he was decidedly adapted to it. Prancken did not deny that in the future, instead of confining himself to a country life, he would undertake such a position; naturally, however, only in concert with his relations and his paternal friend, as he called Sonnenkamp.

Prancken mentioned a notary well versed in the most ductile legal forms. In the evening, the notary was at hand.

The purchase was concluded. The Privy-councillor became the neighbor of Herr Sonnenkamp.

As Sonnenkamp was out walking with Prancken, enjoying the mild air of the night, the latter was for the first time shocked by the language of his future father-in-law, who said:

"My dear young friend, you have undoubtedly had som dealings with the usurers in your day. I know this compassion ate brotherhood well—they hang together like a secret priest hood. But I was going to say that the most interesting insight into what is called the human soul, is offered by the history of bribery. I am familiar with the most diverse nations and the most diverse races, and I have tried it everywhere, and it has never failed me."

Prancken looked strangely at the man. He had much confidence in him, but when he spoke in that matter-of-course way about the corruption of all nations, he began to feel a degree of repulsion, and to find it an unpleasant thought that he was to be the son of this man.

Sonnenkamp continued, with good-humor:

"You, also, are probably affected with the old prejudice that bribery is a wicked thing, as, a short time ago, usury was considered. It is, in fact, only a regular department of business, and it is a piece of folly in the government to exact from men an oath that they will not permit their acts to be changed or determined by the reception of money. It may, so far as I am concerned, be imposed upon the judges, though even there it is ordinarily only a form; for, if it comes to the pinch, a rich man can get clear, provided the business is not carried on too clumsily. It's remarkable that, among other nations, Roman or Sclavonic men always take the gold offered them, and even, under one or another cover, offer themselves to the highest bidder; but with the prudish Germanic race the women act as the intermediaries in these operations. And very naturally! Among no people in the world do we see so many cows put in harness for agricultural uses, and so they harness up the cows in this business too. Therefore, the women have to be courted with the utmost gallantry. And I must say that I prefer to deal with women—they keep their word; for nothing occurs more frequently than that a bribe is given and the person bribed does not keep his word, unless the bribe is at least doubled. My father—"

Prancken was startled. For the first time in his life, Sonnenkamp had mentioned his father; but the speaker continued calmly:

"My father was a virtuoso in the art of bribery, and in Poland he never bribed but by giving a hundred or a thousand gulden note, which he always tore into two pieces; one of them he kept, the other he gave to the contracting party, and he did not deliver the reserved half until what he wanted was brought about. You don't think it is necessary to tear a note with the Councillor's wife, do you?"

Prancken felt offended to hear a lady of rank so characterized and set down. He gave Sonnenkamp the most positive assurances of good faith, and the latter explained:

"I find everything in order. That which is designated in the language of our forefathers as bribery, is a necessary result of advanced culture. As soon as a people develop to a more complicated system of relations, bribery appears, can't but appear, sometimes openly, sometimes clandestinely; and nothing is more varied in its forms than bribery—I know that."

Prancken having stopped in astonishment, Sonnenkamp taking his arm under his, continued:

"My young friend, if I buy an agent or a voice to be under my dictation as member of Parliament or Congress, or if I buy an agent or a voice in order to become ennobled—it's all the same. We in America do it, only more openly. Why shouldn't this Privy-councillor and his wife make the most of their position. Their position, you know, is their whole possession. It pleases me so—it's all right. Must a genteel cloak be thrown over it in Germany? Well, let it be so. If, as I hope, you enter the diplomatic career, I shall have many other little lessons to give you."

Prancken professed himself ready to profit by his instructions, but he nevertheless felt in himself an inexpressible fear of this man,—a fear that alternated with contempt. He made up his mind, if he should ever win Manna, to keep himself as far as possible from him.

But Sonnenkamp was so happy in finding a new confirmation of his knowledge of human nature, that he sought to share it with his own son.

In the morning, when they had risen from breakfast, to which the wife of the Privy-councillor had been invited, he took Roland with him into the park and said to him:

"Look at these high-born people!—All a mere cheat! This Privy-councillor and his family, I raise them from beggars to people of means. Do not let them see that you know it, but you should know it. They are all mere rabble, the high as well as the low—they all have their price for what they call their soul. Everything in the world may be had with money."

It pleased him to unfold these views at large; he had no suspicion what a profound disturbance, what repulsion he was producing in the soul of the youth.

Roland sat mute, and Sonnenkamp questioned in himself whether he had done well; but he soon quieted his doubts. Religion, virtue—it's all nothing but illusion! Some people—this Herr Dournay is one of them—believe in their illusions; others know that they are illusions, and merely play off before themselves and the world. It is better, he finally quieted himself by saying, as it is,—everything illusion.

CHAPTER IV.

A NEW ATMOSPHERE.

FRAU DOURNAY had been but a few days at the Villa, when she comprehended her son's complaint, of how difficult it was for him and Roland to preserve a settled mood or pursue any fixed line of thought; he had constantly to contend against a roving habit of mind. In such a family, with its extensive possessions and its numerous engagements in this quarter and that, that persistency of mind which is so necessary to the mastering of any branch of knowledge was broken up; it was difficult therefore under such circumstances not to lose one's self-control. It was now their intention, without sketching out a formal routine, without at least announcing any, to preserve an independent attitude; for it is only when a man is self-collected that he is able, when it is required, to be anything to any one.

Erich and Roland went every morning to Frau Dournay to receive, so to speak, the day's blessing, and soon a devoted circle formed about her. Whoever approached her assumed a loftier attitude than his wonted one, toned his speech to a moderate and well-ordered key. She was a lady of substantial culture, who made no claim to genius either in her own estimation of herself or in the estimation of others. She was not brilliant but logical, and what she examined and decided upon, seemed necessarily true. She made as little show of her knowledge as of her dress, which, as was to be expected, was neatly ordered.

Neatness, in the highest and purest sense of the word, best characterizes the impression made by her appearance and character. She was clear and pure in everything; in all that she thought, and all that she felt. She had lived at Court for thirteen years, and knew the actual world; but an air of ideality still clung to her. She knew what vice was, and believed in virtue. She was quick in thought, but self-restrained; ready at repartee, but considerately yielding.

If the Widow were compared externally and superficially with Bella, the elder lady stood at a disadvantage, but on closer consideration, Frau Dournay was within her range more satisfying, while Bella was more fascinating.

Bella was always making a demand on you, not simply your attention to her appearance, her sensibility; she liked to originate themes for discussion, to start the most difficult questions; she always wanted to take the initiative, to lead off. To whatever was said on any subject, she returned a very fluent and ready answer; and she knew how to set off what she had heard to the best advantage; all which was very charming on first acquaintance, but with longer intercouse it showed itself to be a merely superficial trick of speech.

The Widow, on the other hand, made no demands; she received willingly and thankfully whatever was brought her; and to everything that was submitted, she gave quiet and deliberate thought.

Externally, the ladies could scarcely be compared, for Frau Dournay did not present at all what you would call a distinguished appearance. She was somewhat full in person, and had that fresh, neat look which is seen represented in the pictures of the comfortable, well-to-do Holland women. Her chief power lay in her constant self-control; she could listen quietly to everything said; and if she had anything to say in reply, she could hear patiently, and wait till the right moment.

When questions which she really did not wish to answer were

put directly to her, she was skilful in turning them off, as if she missed hearing them; and if she was then urged to give a decided reply, she answered no nearer the mark than she actually wished. She never permitted herself to be forced beyond a certain border-line.

She was thus the centre of the circle. The fundamental trait, however, which was manifest in her whole life, lay in this: She was true; she never spoke a word merely for show; she never even smiled where there was nothing to smile at; she gave to each expression its natural tone, and to everything that she heard, the attention that was due it. This truthfulness was not opposed to her habit of reserve. She never said anything that was contrary to the truth; but it was not always necessary to declare what she knew and thought. That is not subterfuge; it is much rather a simple dictate of prudence, and prudence is a virtue which is the stay and support of all that is good. Nature herself is prudent—and veiled.

The Widow was perfectly happy in having her botanical tastes gratified and enriched in Sonnenkamp's beautiful collection of plants, and in the practical information which he was able to impart concerning them.

Erich's mother and aunt lived in beautiful harmony, and were nevertheless very different in character. As they devoted themselves to different realms of knowledge, and drew thence their inspiration, so it was in actual life. They were passionately devoted to the two most beautiful studies in the world. The Widow was a botanist; Aunt Claudine was an astronomist, but she sought most studiously to avoid all show of learning; she spent many a quiet evening hour in the tower, making her observations, generally with a small telescope—without any one's noticing it.

Every day the Widow spent many happy hours in the forcing-houses, and among the plants of the garden; and when Sonnenkamp one day showed her his orchards, she did not, like others, express her admiration and astonishment, but showed rather an extensive, detailed knowledge of the new art of French gardening, and remarked how peculiar it was, that the restless French, when they withdraw from the turmoil of life, pursue the cultivation of fruit with such tender and persistent care. She glanced into Sonnenkamp's face, as she added, that the cultivation of fruit, as practised by him, called for the talent of a general, for it was evident that he must decide justly which fruit can attain the largest growth, and to cherish this he must sacrifice the others, plucking them off in their unripe state.

Sonnenkamp thanked her very courteously, but laughed to himself, as he penetrated, as he thought, her fine, courtly manners. This lady had evidently, before she came, hastily posted herself in botany, in order to make herself agreeable to him. He accepted this homage with apparent ingenuousness, but he promised himself not to be caught by such arts.

He wished to return politeness for politeness, and spared no pains in placing everything at the service of the two ladies, in the most hospitable manner.

Toward Frau Ceres, Frau Dournay held a well-defined relation; she only permitted her attention to be claimed by her for brief periods, and, contrary to all her previous habits, Frau Ceres visited other apartments than her own. She asked Frau Dournay whether she might not, occasionally, be admitted to see her; which was sometimes granted, sometimes not.

But soon Frau Ceres also came under the consecrating influence of her mind, for Frau Dournay was always inspired with the right thought for every nature: she was like a priestess whose duty it is to keep alive the fire upon the altar. If Frau Ceres wanted to know, again and again, how such and such a thing was done at court, the Widow succeeded in awakening unexpectedly in her some degree of thought and of wider interest.

The Aunt, on the other hand, while she was extremely reserved in her manner, introduced an enlivening element into the house which was not anticipated. The grand-piano, which had for a long time stood mute in the music-room, now sounded with clear, sonorous tones; and even Roland, who had abandoned all exercises in music, was seized with a desire to renew them, and became the pupil of Aunt Claudine. The house, which Erich had once spoken of as dry, because no music was heard in it, was now refreshed as with drink. There was a pleasant life there with the new guests; and Sonnenkamp's countenance showed an expression of satisfaction such as had never before been observed in it, when on one occasion Frau Ceres, sitting beside him in the music-room, said:

"I can no more realize what sort of life it was here, before these noble ladies came among us."

After Aunt Claudine had been playing beautifully one day, and a favorite piece of Erich's had been twice repeated, Frau Ceres said to his mother:

"I envy you, who understand and enjoy all this so profoundly."

She was evidently anxious to make sure of the effect of this studied speech, by repeating it, but Frau Dournay involuntarily tore off the little piece of finery which had been put on, for she said:

"Each one has his own pleasures, either of nature or of art, provided he is true to himself. We do not need to understand a thing thoroughly to derive pleasure from it. I take delight in viewing these mountains, without knowing how high they are and what kind of rock forms them, and whatever else the learned know about them. You can enjoy music in the same way. Seek, first of all, truth for its own sake, and for nothing beyond it, and everything else will follow."

No one suspected, not even Frau Ceres herself, that she left the music-room that day another being; for no one can know what particular word has wrought upon an impoverished, but inquiring, longing nature. Frau Ceres did not know it, but she felt it. One can, without having learned or acquired anything, but by simply relying upon that which he brings from nature alone, participate in the higher pleasures of life and knowledge.

The quiet, busy life of the house was suddenly broken into; a carriage drove up over the grating sand of the courtyard. Bella and her husband appeared.

CHAPTER V.

DOUBLE PLAY.

THE greeting of familiar friends amid new surroundings is a fragment of home at a distance; and thus the call from Clodwig and Bella had for Frau Dournay a home-like charm. Bella embraced her with great warmth, and Clodwig took her hand in both of his.

"Where is Erich?" asked Bella at once, still holding the hand of Aunt Claudine. She seemed to be under the necessity of grasping something.

Frau Dournay, turning uneasy glances from Clodwig to Bella, explained that it had become the rule not to permit such pleasant home events as this friendly call to interrupt the course of instruction. She gave special emphasis to the word *home*.

Sonnenkamp said, with a bow of gratitude to the visitors, that an exception might surely be made to-day; but Clodwig himself begged that it should not.

Bella let fall the hand of Aunt Claudine, and stood with her eyes bent down.

Frau Dournay watched her closely.

Bella looked freshly animated; she was in full dress, and wore a large, light blue, silk cloak, from beneath which, when she reached out her hand, her beautiful round bare arm was displayed.

They walked out into the garden. Sonnenkamp was delighted by the way Frau Dournay explained his art of gardening: however, he soon withdrew to announce the visit to his wife. He would do everything he could, not to have Frau Ceres ill to-day.

Clodwig walked with Aunt Claudine; Bella with the mother. Clodwig and the Aunt were soon engaged in animated conversation. The Aunt, a perfect mistress of the piano, was herself much like a piano, an instrument upon which every one can play, children as well as accomplished performers, and which, when nothing is sought from it, will not render itself of any value.

Bella asked Frau Dournay frequently how all the people appeared to her; but as she received very guarded answers, she herself talked a great deal. Her cheeks glowed. She let the cloak fall back a little; her beautiful shoulders were revealed, full and voluptuous.

"Pity that Clodwig did not know your sister-in-law earlier," she said abruptly.

"He knew her well; and she was, as you know, formerly—unhappily for her—much courted and honored at court. That was undoubtedly before your time."

Bella was silent; the mother threw a brief, searching glance upon her. What ails this lady? Why this restlessness, this flitting from one topic to another?

Erich and Roland came. Bella drew her cloak quickly over her shoulders and held her arms close under it; to Erich she scarcely extended her finger-tips.

Roland was very gay, Erich was quiet and serious; whenever he looked at Bella, he quickly drew his eyes away. She congratulated him on the arrival of his mother, and said:

"I think, if a stranger should meet you on the road, he would see in your look that you still have the happiness of possessing a mother; and what a mother! An indefinable grace leaves a man, when his mother is torn from him."

Bella said this with a tone of deep seriousness, and yet she had at the same time a strange smile on her lips, and she glanced around as if she wanted to gather in all the plaudits her thought deserved.

Sonnenkamp came: he stroked his chin fondly, while he begged the ladies to come to his wife, whom the arrival of such guests had quite recuperated. He proposed that the gentlemen should go to the castle, to view the progress of the works, and examine the localities where the relics of Roman antiquity had been found. Bella interchanged a few jesting speeches with Sonnenkamp, rating him for having deprived them of their dear guests, and then she went with the ladies to the summer-house; the gentlemen proceeded to the fort.

Frau Ceres was soon ready to go with them to the music-room, and Aunt Claudine played for them, without having to be entreated. Bella sat between Erich's mother and Frau Ceres; Miss Perini stood beside Aunt Claudine at the piano.

When the Aunt had finished her first piece, Bella said:

"Fräulein Dournay, do you sometimes accompany your nephew when he sings?"

The Aunt said that she did not.

Erich's mother again threw a quick glance at Bella, who was always thinking of Erich; she did not seem to be able to hide it, or even to wish to hide it. While the Aunt was playing a new piece, Bella said to the mother:

"You must give me something of yourself; give me your sister-in-law to take with me to Wolfsgarten."

"I have no right to dispose of my sister-in-law. But, pardon me, she is not in the least exacting in anything else, but when she is playing, the slightest word spoken disquiets her."

Bella was silent, and the Widow also. But while they were listening to an enlivening piece of Mozart, the thoughts of the ladies flowed in very divergent directions. What Bella thought, can scarcely be defined; her whole being fluctuated to and fro between joy and sadness, renunciation and defiance. But the Widow was confirmed in the reality of an observation she had made, and she already felt herself tainted with the knowledge of it.

When the piece was finished, Bella said:

"Ah! Mozart's is a happy nature; hard as his life was, he was always happy; and he has the power to impart happiness as often as one hears him; even his sorrows and complainings have a certain serenity. Did your husband also love music?"

"Oh yes!" he often said: "Modern humanity gives expression to the imaginative fable-creating power of the human mind in music, while antiquity embodied the same tendency in its myths. Music engenders moods and aspirations that transcend all tangible and visible existence, and transports us waking into dream-land."

They went out on the verandah, where they played with the parrots. Bella told one of the parrots a wonderful story about its cousin at Wolfsgarten, who dwelt in a wonderfully beautiful cage, though he sometimes deserted to the woods. But he was too genteel, and had not learned to get his living in the woods, and so he always had to come back to his golden prison.

Bella's cheeks glowed more and more, and her lips trembled; suddenly it occurred to her that she must bring the visit to a close. She begged of the aunt and mother so earnestly, and with such childish warmth, that she at last received their consent that in a few days the former should make her a visit.

"You shall see," she said again to the Widow, half triumphantly, "Fräulein Dournay is Clodwig's best friend; they are created wholly for one another."

The Widow looked fixedly at her.

Is it then gone so far that this woman wishes to give her husband a substitute for herself?

CHAPTER VI.

A SAD AND MINISTERING MOTHER.

BEFORE they went to the table, the ladies withdrew to make their toilet.

The Widow had unbound her long gray hair, and sat quiet for a long time in her dressing-room, her hands lying folded in her lap. The conviction to which she had been led by unmistakable signs, affected her like a blow on the head. Her heart felt weighed down, and tears pressed to her eyes, though she did not let them escape. Was it for this, then, that a child so nurtured, guarded, inspired with all that is good—that it should end thus? No, not end, but begin in a maze of disorder and desolation, which the eye cannot follow? Is it for this that his mind was stored with all things worth knowing—to use them as a deceptive show; as the mask, the cloak of baseness?

"O my God! my God!" she cried, and covered her face with both hands.

Before her mind's eye arose the vision of the ruin that impended: first, the pure, open, lofty, magnanimous nature of Erich; then she, herself. She could no longer take delight in the look, the words, the appearance of her son; he had wasted them all in deception and lies.

Her eyes then filled with tears, for the thought came to her, what would her dead husband have said to this? How often did he lament, because every one says to himself: "The world is wicked and corrupt to the core; why should I alone shut myself out, and not also give myself up to my pleasures?" And see all the ruin that will follow! This noble-hearted Clodwig, who cherishes a friendship without parallel—and they must see him, greet him, speak to him, and yet wish him dead. Shame! And then he goes away and teaches the boy; teaches him to rule himself, to act generously toward others; and he—yes, it is he! Oh horrible! And this impassioned woman—too proud to devote herself to one of the best of men—what will become of her? And this Sonnenkamp and his wife, and Miss Perini, and the Priest? "See here!" they will all cry out, "See here! Such are your liberals; your men that are always prating of humanity, and of the happiness of working for it; and who, meanwhile, are gratifying their lowest lusts, and eschew no treachery, no lies, no hypocrisy!"

Oh these unhappy women—these women who call themselves unhappy! It's all a lie, what is said in our time about unhappy women. This is the way it is: The young women wish to have men of wealth and standing, and near at hand a paramour of youth and spirit. Why do they never marry a poor man? Because he cannot give them an equipage. And these men whom they obtain as paramours—

"A paramour!" she cried aloud.

She sprang up quickly and pulled at the bell, for she heard a carriage drive up in the courtyard.

She ordered the servant to request her son to come to her at once.

Erich came: he looked much excited. He gazed in astonishment at his mother; he had never seen her thus, with her long hair unbound, and even her face seemed to have grown gray.

"Sit down," she requested.

Erich obeyed.

His mother pressed her hand to her forehead. Ought she to admonish her son directly—openly? What can a mother do, what can parents do, when their child, grown to manhood and independent, wanders from the right way? And if he has already fallen, will he still keep his honor with her? He will—he must lie; it would be a double baseness if he did not shield himself with lies, himself and his—!

"My dear son," she began with a subdued voice, "it seems impossible for me, taken thus suddenly from my solitary, quiet ways, to find myself at home in this restless life. I wonder at your greater power—No, no, not that yet. But what did I wish to say to you? Ah! that's it. The Countess of Wolfsgarten, the wife of our friend"—she gave a quiet, clear emphasis to this word, and made a short pause after it, then went on—"wishes to take Claudine with her to stay."

"That's good! Magnificent!"

"Indeed? And why? Don't you see, then, that I shall be left alone and in a strange house?"

"My dear mother, you are not alone—never. And Aunt Claudine can do a good work at Wolfsgarten; the Countess Bella, notwithstanding all the elegant variety of her life, is still full of disquiet; a nature so genuine, so calm in itself and so quieting in its influence upon others as Aunt Claudine's, will give a contentment and repose to hers, such as nothing else in the world could. I do not deny that you will have to make a sacrifice, but it will be doing a good work."

His mother's eye became calmer; her aspect cleared as if electrically touched, and she said, smiling:

"We each have at last a mission; we are all become educators. May I ask how Countess Bella, the wife of our friend, appears to you?"

It was as if a double-edged sword pierced Erich's heart. He knew what a burden he was on his mother's soul. And perhaps Bella, by a passionate word, has betrayed what nevertheless shall never be; and he stands before his mother a transgressor, a traitor! A short pause followed, and his mother asked again, her manner suddenly changing:

"Why do you not answer me?"

"Mother, I'm still, I think, too immature; I no longer trust so securely to my judgment of men. I have really no knowledge of human nature, even though my dear father used to say, that in psychology lies my chief strength. Perhaps! I can follow closely a mood of the mind back to its antecedents and outward to its results; but real knowledge of men I don't yet possess."

The mother listened to this long introduction, in which Erich was probably trying to collect himself, with a quiet, downward look; but when Erich ceased, she said:

"You will, however, give me your view, if it be an immature one."

"Well, then, I think that in this highly-gifted woman there is a struggle between worldliness and renunciation, between the desire to appear and the longing for reality. It seems to me as if in the development of her life there were something repressed, checked, and as if she were not yet fully ripe for the beautiful task of replenishing, with her own life, the evening of such a noble life as Clodwig's."

"Yes, he is a noble man, and to afflict him were as the profanation of a temple," the mother said with emphasis.

These words were uttered in a severe tone, and she added:

"You have, indeed, hit it well; these Pranckens are a bold, enterprising race. It was believed that Bella would marry her music-teacher; she often played with him: in truth, she did play with him—but that's another thing. Now, however, Bella has met some apparently unimportant experience, which nevertheless has effected a—I don't know what to call it—a revulsion in her nature. In her youth, at an age when she could still pass for young—she was twenty-two or twenty-three—she lived to see her younger sister marry before her; she permitted this with great resignation; but I think, that from time to time a change occurred in her nature which is hard to understand. She became suddenly old, older than she was willing to confess to herself; she had something matronly in her air. That was unreal in her, but—a more bitter thought!—it was also real. Her sister died, leaving no children. The whole chain of events imparted something disordered—strained, to Bella's nature; she really hated this sister, and yet always had the air of being consumed with longing for her. Bella had no mother, or rather she had a mother whose highest triumph it was to hear it said: 'Your daughter is beautiful, but not so beautiful as you were when a girl.' And to be beautiful is the great pride of these Pranckens! Bella is rather a product of that unfortunate class of society, which, when it goes to the theatre, goes only to make sport, playfully mingling its wit with its sneers, and when it attends the church, simply goes to pay their respects to the Almighty;—a class in which a woman is utterly useless, if she be not beautiful, and know not how, by the time she approaches the altar, to intrigue and be pious. Such a creature may say to herself: 'I have in the course of my life covered from eight hundred to a thousand ells of canvas with flowers or some such work for some very superfluous sofa cushions.' Is this a life worth living? Now she herself has no children, no settled, natural duties—"

"And for that very reason," Erich interrupted, "Aunt Claudine would exercise, without her needing to know it, a softening, calming influence; her peaceful nature, which never has to deny itself because it never wills what is foreign to it, would seem specially chosen for the task. As much as I value Countess Bella for herself and as the wife of our friend, we must nevertheless fulfil, before all, our duty to the noble Count Clodwig; it will re-establish and enhance the beauty and purity of his life."

"Very well, Aunt Claudine will go to Wolfsgarten. And now, my dear son, leave me. Yet stay! I must add something, childish as it may seem. When I saw you, to-day, running so lightly through the garden, I thought of your father's joy when he took you on a trip to the mountains, and when you, though only in your eleventh year, were with him in Switzerland; he said, on his return home, that his chief pleasure was to see how safely and well you climbed up and down the mountain-sides, never losing your foothold; and in fact, while your younger brother was always getting wounds and bruises, you never fell once."

It was with a look of double meaning that Erich's mother regarded him, as she drew her hand over his face.

"But we have prattled enough; go now—I must dress for dinner."

She kissed him upon the forehead; he went out.

But outside the door he stood still and folded his hands, and said:

"I bless you, ye Heavenly Powers, that ye yet leave me my mother; she comes to the rescue of us all!"

CHAPTER VII.

THE STATISTICS OF LOVE.

WHEN the guests at the Villa came together again, they found the Doctor accidentally there. Or, was it accident? Did he wish to watch closely the relations of Erich and Bella to each other?

He saluted the Professor's widow with great respect: she was obliged to confess that her husband, who was always very careful to mention the names of his most distant friends, had never, so far as she could remember, spoken the name of Doctor Richard.

"Still I was a friend of his!" exclaimed the Doctor, in a loud voice.

But a little while after he said, in a low tone:

"I need not resort to the common social deceptions in my relations to you. I was, in truth, only casually known to your husband, but I was a pupil of your father-in-law. I allowed myself to be introduced to your son as the friend of your father because that seemed to me the speediest way to be useful to him, for, in his life here and in what it involves, he is exposed to many dangers."

The Widow thanked him sincerely; but she felt a chill at her heart. This man had evidently alluded to Bella.

The Artist, who had painted the portrait of the Wine-count's daughter, was also present. Soon after, the Priest came; and it was regretted that the Major could not also be among them: he had gone off to a St. John's-day festival in the neighborhood. The Major always obeyed the behests of the Masonic fraternity as if they were military orders.

All went very genially at the dinner-table. The Doctor asked the Artist how far he had got with his picture representing the story of Potiphar's wife.

The Artist invited the guests to visit him soon at the atelier, which Herr von Endlich had devoted to his use for the summer months.

"Strange!" cried the Doctor. "She's always called Potiphar's wife, and we never learn what her own name was; she lived on with the name of her husband, and you knights of the brush never let the chance escape you of painting beautiful nudities with more or less discretion. With you the chaste Joseph always cuts a ridiculous figure, and perhaps that's the reason the world affirms that the chaste Joseph is always a ridiculous figure. Æneas and Dido are another such constellation; but Æneas is not considered so ridiculous as the Egyptian Joseph."

It was painful to hear the Doctor go on thus.

The Priest remarked:

"This history, told in the Old Testament, is complementary to the history of the adulteress in the New, and thus supplies another instance of that accordance which, though interrupted for centuries, is at last made good. The Old Testament leaves the discordance standing, the New clears it up."

Clodwig was much pleased with this view; he always retained

something of the enthusiasm of the young student. He was exhilarated, perfectly happy, over any new enlargement and enrichment of his knowledge.

"Reverend Sir, and you, Honored Lady," cried the Doctor, looking from the Priest to the Widow—he was to-day even more given to talk than usual—"you two, with your varied experience in life, can do a friend of mine a great service."

"I?" asked the Priest.

"And I?" asked the Widow.

"Yes, both. Our century has initiated a wholly new examination of the laws of the Universe; certain phenomena—states—sensations, which, it was thought, could not be grasped, are now caught in the net of statistic science and have to take shape according to definite laws. What is there that was deemed more free and inapprehensible, more difficult to follow, than love, than marriage, and yet on this subject statistics give fixed data; an iron law regulates even the number of divorces that occur in a year. My friend goes further; he has illustrated in his own experience that marriages in which the man is much older than the woman, prove, on the average, much happier than those which are contracted in youth, and in what is called the enthusiasm of love. Turn over in mind now, Reverend Sir, and you also, my dear lady, the number of instances which you know, and ask yourselves, whether you do not find this law confirmed."

The Widow remained silent, but the Priest said that religion alone gives consecration to marriage; religion alone gives that humility of heart which is the sure foundation of all beautiful fellowships among men, and of community with God.

In the further course of the conversation, the Priest succeeded in turning it off from the topic which had been so boldly introduced.

Sonnenkamp reported that the Major desired, as soon as the great Gothic hall was completed at the castle, to hold a great Masonic festival in it. He asked Clodwig how the reigning Prince was affected toward Masonry.

Clodwig answered that the Prince formerly belonged to the society, and that he was still its protector, without being a member.

The conversation became general and discursive; they rose from the table in good spirits. The Doctor left.

It was now decided that Aunt Claudine should return with the guests to Wolfsgarten; and, to give her time to make her preparations, they were to remain overnight, for they wanted to take her home with them the very next day.

Bella was very gay and good-humored; she begged Sonnenkamp to let her have one of his parrots; she would have the very wildest, and she promised to tame it.

The evening came on; they must give way to Roland's humor and row with him out on the Rhine. Aunt Claudine joined Bella; Miss Perini retired with Frau Ceres; the Widow remained with Clodwig; and Sonnenkamp excused himself, saying that he had letters to dispatch.

In the boat the gayety and laughter was universal; even Bella laughed and jested with the rest, but she often dipped her hand in the waves and played with her wedding-ring, moving it up and down on her finger, and again and again dipped her hand in the Rhine.

"Do you understand what the Doctor meant?" she once asked Erich.

"If I had been willing to understand it, I should have been obliged to take offence," he replied.

"Now that we are speaking of the Doctor," Bella resumed, "I must tell you of an important fact, which I have forgotten to mention. The Doctor is very good, he is virtue itself, but this rugged virtue once made court to me, and I had to show him how ridiculous he was. It may easily be that the man does not speak well of me. You should know this."

Erich was thoroughly startled. What does this mean? Is it perhaps a feint to neutralize the verdict of the physician? He found no way out.

After awhile Bella asked:

"Can you tell me why I am now so often melancholy?"

"The more highly endowed natures are always melancholy; so Aristotle beautifully says," replied Erich.

Bella held her breath; that was altogether too pedantic an answer.

They were unable to keep up an unbroken conversation; but Bella once more said abruptly to Erich:

"It vexes me—this visit of your mother here."

"What! It vexes you?"

"Yes; it is outrageous that this man with his money should be able so to reverse the true relations of people."

Erich had much to think over in the expression thus incidentally thrown out.

"You have the happiness of being much beloved," said Bella, suddenly.

Erich looked up, alarmed, and glanced at Roland. Bella continued aloud:

"Your mother loves you much."

A little after, she said in a low tone to herself, but Erich heard it:

"No one really loves me, and I know why—no, I don't know why."

Erich looked very hard at her, then grasped an oar, and rolled up high waves.

Meanwhile, his mother, who was seated by Clodwig, was expressing her gratification that Erich had the privilege of intercourse with men so tried and experienced in life. In earlier times it may have been that man's education was completed by the social influence of woman, but now it is consummated only by intercourse with the higher order of men.

Clodwig and the Widow were soon deep in those reciprocal confessions of thought which are the true spiritual greetings of those who have wandered over the same intellectual paths, but far from one another, and under different conditions of life.

The Widow had known Clodwig's first wife well, and spoke of her in heartfelt words; Clodwig looked around as if to make sure that Bella was not near, for in her hearing he had never spoken of his former wife. It was a calumny—the report that he had enjoined upon Bella not to speak of his first wife; Clodwig was not so weak as that, and Bella was not so unfeeling; but he avoided it from tenderness.

The conversation flowed on in soft half-tones; Clodwig and the Widow agreed in the opinion—and they drew it from the same experience in themselves—that it is a happiness in man here below, that he can easily forget everything sad, and only holds fresh in his memory what has brought him pleasure.

"Yes," said Frau Dournay in confirmation, "my husband often said, that through every nature, rich in the forces of life, a Lethe flows, which brings forgetfulness."

The hour which Clodwig and the Professor's widow spent together, was one of those in which the soul gains the deepest knowledge of itself, and the purest sympathy with the universe of thought. They were like two spirits on the farther shore, who calmly and clearly survey the movement of life. There was nothing really painful in their mutual revival of old memories; it was rather a present consciousness of the inexhaustible fulness of existence. Upon this height floated the tones of longing and grief; their own life, and that of those dear to them, lapsed and expanded into the universal being.

But now their mood changed: and Clodwig lamented that earlier in life he had lived too much as a mere looker-on, and, without taking hold and adding his strength to the mass, he had too confidently trusted that the higher thought astir in the world would of itself ripen to its own fulfilment. He declared his joy in the fact that genuine youth is something different; and that Erich, before all others, presented to him an inspiring image of youth, which is at once discreet and bold, temperate, and full of action.

They came unexpectedly back to the statistics of love, but just then Bella entered. She was pale; Clodwig did not mark it. She bade them both go on in their conversation, and sat down quietly by them; but neither the Widow nor Clodwig took up the interrupted theme.

Clodwig spoke of Aunt Claudine; he inquired concerning her tastes, and he was glad that he had a fine telescope with which she could contemplate the stars.

After resting a little, Bella wandered off from them, and went into the park.

CHAPTER VIII.

THE STRUGGLE BETWEEN DUTY AND LOVE.

I MUST speak to you once more this evening, in the park, under the weeping-ash," Erich had said to Bella, as she was stepping from the boat.

"This evening?" she asked.

"Yes."

"And in the park, under the weeping-ash?"

"Yes."

She had of her own accord placed her arm in his, and without a word she permitted him to lead her to the Villa; then she dropped his arm, and went quickly to Clodwig and the Widow. She was not conscious what she wanted there, but she was happy—no, not happy, but quieted—when she saw Clodwig and the Widow so confidential together. "Yes, any one who listens to him, and gives him an animating word in return, is as much to him as I," she thought to herself.

She rose and went into the park. She wandered restlessly about, for she knew that Erich had released himself from Roland, so as to speak to her again. But she could not dream how hard he found it to do; not that Roland did not obey, and had to have a task assigned him every hour, but because Erich was himself disturbed in mind; because, in order that he might for the time being get free from him, he had to impose upon his pupil some great thought, or element of knowledge. The book which he gave him, the passage which he marked out for him to read till he returned, seemed to him profaned, soiled, desecrated, and yet it must be done. It made him heavy at heart, but it should be the last time; he would come forth from this last interview pure and strong, with everything levelled and adjusted.

Thus thinking, he recovered his self-possession and went into the park. He met Bella on the knoll. It was evident she had been weeping bitterly.

As she heard his steps, she withdrew the handkerchief which she had pressed to her eyes.

"You've been crying."

"Yes, for your mother, for myself, for us all! Oh, how often did I hear your mother lamented over, bantered, laughed at, commiserated, because she followed the impulse of her heart and the man of her love. A salary of eight hundred thalers and true love to boot, was for a long time the jest. And she is favored and elevated above us all. She looks with peaceful happiness upon her past, sees her future before her in her son. And what are the rest of them? Puppets, mincing puppets—prattling, piano-playing, dancing, lionizing, medicine-vending puppets! They turn up their noses in contempt over the man there, so rich from the labor of slaves. And our excellent fathers sell their children, and the children sell themselves, for position in society, for horses and carriages, for style and country-seats. The noble rank, this miserable noble rank, is the inherited sin of ancestral pride, ancestral slavery. A peasant-woman, who picks up the heads of corn in the stubble, is happier and freer than the lady who lolls back in her carriage, and, fanning herself cool, is rolled along the road."

"I ask a favor," Erich began, with subdued voice. "Will you give me an hour from your life?"

"An hour?"

"Yes. Will you listen to me?"

"I hear you."

She gazed at him fixedly with those large eyes of hers, while her brows seemed to rise and swell higher and higher; the corners of her mouth were drawn down with angry aversion; her lips parted with a slight feverish panting; there was wanting nothing but the wings on the head, and the coil of serpents knotted under the chin—it was the look of the Medusa.

For a moment Erich was frozen to the soul; then with a strong effort he recovered himself, and proceeded:

"Two questions are now rending my heart. One is, 'Has life, study, the abstraction of thought, deprived me of the power of loving?' The other question is: 'Must a child of humanity, when his destiny has decided what he ought to do, sacrifice his life to its decree?' And these two questions are twined into one, like those knotted snakes' heads under the chin of the Medusa."

"Go on—go on!" gasped Bella.

"Well then; there was a moment when I could have said to the beautiful wife of another, as she sat before me, 'I love you!' and I could have embraced and kissed her, but then," Erich pressed his hand upon his heart, and ground through his teeth, "but then—a moment after, I should have sent a ball through my brain."

Bella let her eyes fall, and Erich went on:

"There was a time when my peace was gone, my pride gone—I had nothing left in the world. You robbed me of my rest, of my thought. It could not go on so. I lost myself, and what did I win? I saw all the desolation this love brought. Was it love, then? No! If I could make light of it as others do, it would indeed be a light matter. But why, then, take this alone with easy indifference, and not everything else besides? Why, then, is not every life devoted to high thoughts, a mere play—all sentiments mere lies of speech?"

With a husky voice, he added:

"But I do not believe that love has a right to override everything; one may perhaps say, that then it is not genuine love. Take courage; look at the world—it knows how to lie so bravely, so respectably, so wisely—the women decked off in their spangles, the men in their wit and wisdom. Look at this abyss, on the brink of which I stand. And then I said to myself, we are placed here in the world to live, and intelligence and culture are given us, that with them we may create life for ourselves—not death. And how could I look still upon an honest man; how could I look upon the sun in heaven; how could I stand forth in the world, frown upon crime, know and name holy things, educate a human soul; how should I take the word mother on my lips and feel in my conscience, that I am one of the worst of men, and that there is not a moment when I, when another than I, need not tremble with fear and anxiety?"

Erich paused; he laid his hand on his forehead, his voice choked, tears rushed to his eyes.

"Speak on," cried Bella; "I hear."

"Well, I shall speak but once to you in this way—only this once; you have the courage to hear the truth. Well, then, that which unites us is not love—must not be love; for love cannot spring from death, fraud, and treachery. Give me your hand—No! I will not take it; for I know that I could not let it fall again. Let me stand here: let me speak to you. Will you hear me? I speak to you as if miles apart—as if from the dead. It must be distance, it must be death, before there is resurrection, before there is life."

"What would you?" Bella cried.

She looked at Erich's hand, as if he were about to draw a weapon from his breast.

He drew a deep breath, and went on.

"It must, nevertheless, be possible that men who still know themselves as they stand, can find their way back from a path of error. My friend, if you understand what happiness is, you are happy, and I am happy; shattered as my heart now is, I know that I shall learn to comprehend my duty and my happiness. I was once so proud, I thought I had penetrated the secret of the world, and had conquered the world. So was it with you, too; but now that we have met, it shall not be to our ruin; we shall awaken to a purer life. I look into the future: there shall come a day when we shall permit ourselves to take each other by the hand and say, or if not say, feel and know, that this was a pure hour, though the struggle was a hard one—an hour in which we rose above ourselves, and because we respected each other, did not debase ourselves, did not throw away our self-respect. This moment is a hard one, it is a crushing one; but that which is now so hard, so crushing, will, in the future, be softening and elevating. We shall preserve each other's purity, that we may not lose our right to life. And that is the duty of life. My friend, a word of my father's comes to my mind: the rational soul, he said, must pursue its duty with the same ardor with which others pursue their passions; so it must be. The stars are coming out above us, and I look up to you as to a star. It shines forth, and remains steadfast in the law of its being and in its purity of light. Ah! I no longer know what I am saying. Let me now bid you farewell. When we meet again—"

"No, do not go!" Bella cried, and seized him by the arm; but quickly, as if she had touched a serpent, she loosened her hold.

She stood two steps from him, drew back her head, and said:

"I thank you."

Erich was about to reply, but—it was better so—he said nothing; he was turning away in silence, when Bella cried:

"One more question! Is it true that you saw Manna Sonnenkamp before you came here?"

"Yes."

"And you love her, and for her sake are here now?"

"No."

"I believe you, and I thank you."

It seemed to be implied in this expression that it was a consolation to her not to have been sacrificed to another love. She looked around her wildly, turned her head quickly to one side and the other, and when she had at last collected herself, said:

"You are right. It is well."

She seemed to be seeking something, which she wanted to give Erich; she did not apparently find it, and an old forgotten thought recurred to her as something harassing, for she cried out suddenly:

"Be warned. Beware of my brother—he can be dangerous."

Erich went away; it was hard for him to return to Roland now, yet he must do it.

He sat quiet for a few minutes near Roland, shading his eyes with his hand; the light pained them, and he dared not look at Roland.

A servant then came and announced that Count Clodwig and the Countess were going away that very evening. Erich and Roland were requested to come down to the courtyard and bid them good-bye.

They went down, and learned that contrary to their original intention, the Wolfsgartens were about to ride off at once: they would send the carriage some other day to bring Fräulein Dournay.

Bella extended her gloved hand to Erich, and said, in a low voice:

"Good-night, Herr Captain."

The carriage drove off.

CHAPTER IX.

SEVERED AND SAVED.

AS they drove home, Bella sat silent in the carriage beside her husband. For a long while neither spoke; at last Count Clodwig remarked:

"My heart is full of joy and happiness; it is a perfect blessing to see a woman of sixty years, whose mind has never harbored a thought which she has cause to repent."

Bella turned around suddenly. What is this? Did he suspect how it had been with her?

That cannot be, or he would not have made the remark. Still, it may be his lofty manner, to try to guide her by pointing out the example of a spotless life.

She was afraid of betraying herself if she gave no answer; and on the other hand, she knew not what to say. With forced composure she said at last:

"This woman is very happy in spite of her poverty; she has a noble, well-educated son."

Now it was Clodwig who turned around, as if some one had pulled him sharply. Could Bella have a suspicion that once the thought had flitted through his mind: 'How would it be if this woman . . . and then Erich were your son.'

He had the advantage of Bella, he need not frame a reply, but in the inmost recesses of his soul he reproached himself for having harbored such a thought, though it had been but for a moment.

Thus the two rode on in silence: they were side by side, but yet each had his own heavy thoughts: they did not exchange another word during the whole ride. It seemed to Bella as if some force must come to lift her up, carry her away into the intangible, into the void. The carriage rattled so curiously, the wheels creaked, and the lady's-maid and the coachman, up there before her eyes, appeared like figures in a fairy-tale, and the shadows in the moonlight, which flitted past, seemed the visions of a dream; the carriage with its occupants was a monster. Anger, shame, pride, humiliation, all together stormed in the heart which had not yet found peace.

She was deeply vexed at herself: she had done with life, still once more this childish, insane emotion had mastered her; for now she called it childish and insane. And had not her self-love been wounded? was it not the first time that she had held out her hand, and it had not been taken?

It occurred to her that Erich had exaggerated his love for her in order to mitigate her shame; aye, her memory made her even find something unnatural, something forced and affected in his tone. Her thoughts returned to Erich. Where is he now? Is he talking to any one? He too must suffer deeply and heavily; he has saved you and himself. Her thoughts spun around as if caught in a whirlwind. Now she felt a scornful triumph. It was only a slight jest, a trial, a bold game! She, Bella the strong, had only attempted to throw a young man on his knees before her, and had he yielded, she would have repelled him with contempt. She can say this—who can contradict her? All her past life bore witness for her, and still before her own self she was ashamed of this lie. But what will come of it now? she again asked. She must be calm; calmly she will meet the man, whom, after all, she only cautioned against an inclination for Manna. That was all! This was the handle by which to take hold of the whole bold venture. But to herself she vowed to root out every passion, every strong emotion from her soul. Yes, she now thanked Fate, which had aroused her with powerful nature's force—her virtue had now been tried by fire.

She removed the veil from her face and looked up at the stars; they should be witnesses that she had overcome all the temptation of an untamed, childish nature, which was unworthy of her. With silent thankfulness she now recalled Erich, as he had said to her: "We have acquired knowledge and culture, so that we may be masters of our own natures."

Still, as they drove up the mountain to Wolfsgarten, a sensation of imprisonment again overcame her, she felt as if her hands were fettered, and she took them from under her cloak. Clodwig imagined she was feeling for his hand; he seized hers and pressed it silently.

Thus they arrived in silence at Wolfsgarten, and when they stood in the brightly illuminated pavilion, Clodwig said:

"We two can well afford to be silent, side by side. The most beautiful of all companionship is that in which each, though bent on his own thoughts, still feels that he is with the other."

Bella nodded; she looked about her with wondering eyes. What is all this? to whom does it all belong? what power has brought her here? where has she been? how would she now be standing here alone by her husband's side, if—

She felt as though she must kneel down before him, take his hand, and beg his forgiveness.

But it is better, so she again consoled herself, not for herself—she fancied herself ready to bear any humiliation—no! for him, if he knows nothing of what is past; it should remain concealed from him. She bent her head. Clodwig kissed her forehead and said:

"Your forehead is hot."

Then they retired.

Bella dismissed her maid, and undressed that night without assistance.

In the mean time, after Clodwig and Bella had left, Erich's mother went with him to the little vine-covered cottage. She led him by the hand, as if he were a little child. She felt his hand tremble, but she did not say a word. When they reached the staircase she said:

"Kiss me, Erich."

Erich felt that his mother wished to find out whether he could still kiss her with pure lips. He kissed her. Mother and son said not another word.

Wiped out, blown away, was all the heaviness from Erich's whirling brain; and the heaviest thought of all—sincerity demands that we say it—the most torturing of all was, still, that for a short time he had repented having been perhaps too puritanical after all, too conscientious; thus the tempter called it. He had repelled a beautiful woman who wanted to embrace him with all the ardor of love. When he surprised himself, on this train of thought, he was deeply unhappy; all pride in his conscientiousness, all the exaltation of purity had left him; he was a sinner without sin itself. He had appeared very high in his own eyes, when he expressed his love for Bella more strongly and represented it as more violent than it really was: now this was avenged; now the scorned and rejected love overcame him with double sinfulness. Long he paced to and fro in the silent night.

There is a wound-fever of the soul, which is not less violent and requires no less forbearance than that of the body. Erich had sacrificed part of his soul to save the rest; he felt this painfully; but as the dew settled on tree and grass and on Erich's face, dew fell upon his soul. The pride of conscious virtue was taken from him, his double repentance had effaced it; he was a child again. And looking back on the little vine-clad cottage he thought:

"As a man I will preserve the child in me!" And then he thought: "You have avoided temptation through the consciousness of your duty; be charitable in judging the rich and the powerful, to whom everything is offered, to whom so much is granted. The consciousness of duty does not restrain them as firmly as him who is in the world to serve others, and who must look to others for services, and who has nothing left when he has lost himself."

The night was far advanced when he returned home, and in his dreams he fancied himself battling with the waters of the Rhine; and he, the confident swimmer, could not subdue the waves. He screamed, but a steam-tug drowned his screams; and from the helm of a vessel, the helms-woman looked down at him mockingly—and suddenly it was not the helms-woman, but a girlish figure with a pair of wings and two shining, flaming eyes.

CHAPTER X.

THE ASSISTANT AND THE WATCHER.

EARLY in the morning a carriage came from Wolfsgarten for Aunt Claudine and the parrot.

For almost thirty years since her marriage with the Professor, the mother had not lived a single day without her husband's sister: now they were to be parted for the first time. It seemed almost inconceivable to both, that one should live apart from the other: still, it had been resolved on, and it had to be.

Sonnenkamp was very attentive: he made the Aunt promise to look upon his house as her home, and to spend only a few days as a guest at Wolfsgarten.

He sent along by the coachman a carefully wrapped basket of grapes and bananas. The cage with the parrot stood on the seat beside the Aunt.

The parrot screamed and scolded as they drove off, and screamed and scolded all the way; he seemed loth to leave Villa Sonnenkamp.

Herr Sonnenkamp proposed a drive to Frau Dournay, to make her forget the separation; the widow rejoined that we must accustom ourselves to the unavoidable by calm consideration, and not by diversion. Roland looked up in surprise; these were Erich's thoughts, his very words.

They passed several very quiet days at the Villa: they scarcely left it, even for the little vine-covered cottage. Bella's visit had disturbed the quiet of the house in a way which still oppressed them all; and they became more and more conscious of this disquiet, because the Aunt was missed by all. Bella had, after all, carried away with her one of the necessities of their life. And perfect silence again pervaded the house.

Erich and Roland were more industrious than ever, for the mother had requested Erich's permission to be present during the lessons, as she had never become acquainted with Erich's method of instruction. Erich knew very well that she meant to incite him to rigorous application, for although she had not said a word about it, she suspected that something must have occurred between Erich and Bella; and she not only wished to bear her son company at all hours, but her presence should encourage him in the conscientious discharge of his duty toward Roland.

So she sat from early morning through the greater part of the day in the room with Roland and Erich. She breathed softly, she even had the strength to deny herself her accustomed needlework; and Erich and Roland derived peculiar incitement from the presence of a third person—a calm philosophic, catholic mind.

At first Roland frequently looked over to the mother, but she shook her head whenever he looked at her; he was to attend wholly to his work and not mind her.

Erich, on the other hand, was at once perfectly free, for during the first hours he had caught himself in the attempt, to so shape his instruction, that his mother should acquire some new information too; then he met her large, expressive glance, which said to him: "That was not my intention."

He returned to his simple method, without any reference to his mother's presence.

Erich's methodical manner of teaching and of concentrating the youth's attention on his studies, made her feel quite happy. She listened with delight, when one day he explained that idleness likes to say: "I am of no consequence—only a single individual." Yes, but a people, all mankind consists only of individuals; a student learns only by hours and days, a fruit ripens by single sunbeams; everything is an individual unit, but the collected units constitute the whole.

Erich was prepared to illustrate the point, and read appropriate passages from Cicero and Xenophon's Memorabilia. He meant Roland to feel that his life was linked to the essential goodness of the life of all ages.

But when his mother was alone with Erich, she said:

"It seems to me, that in explaining everything to your pupil, in your endeavor to give him all knowledge, you cut away from under him the stout prop of fixed principles."

Erich was taken aback; he had hoped that his mother would

express her entire satisfaction: now, she found fault with him; but he felt relieved when she continued pleasantly:

"I must laugh: rightly viewed, my two grounds of objection are but one, objective and subjective. Objectively I consider it dangerous for you to give your pupil whatever he happens to ask for: you follow the zigzag movement of a youthful, roaming mind. And there, by-the-by, lies the danger of private instruction. In this way, it spoils the young mind, which receives what it has felt a desire for, not what is best for it; but the disciplinary power of systematic instruction lies in its forcing the student to receive and proceed consecutively, and not according to his own pleasure. That is discipline for life, since life brings us, not what we would have, but what is proper and necessary for us."

"And what is your second point?" Erich asked, as his mother paused.

"My second point is this. I remember your father's saying, that the first and only correct prop, the basis rather, of all education should be, 'Thou shalt,' and 'Thou shalt not;' plain and simple, without comment, without explanation, without discussion. And now let me ask you: do you not disintegrate his soul? Suppose our Roland should some day be subjected to a conflict, will his philosophy be able to help him? Will he not rather have to fall back upon the ancient, fixed rules, 'Thou shalt,' and 'Thou shalt not?' I call your attention to the subject, Erich, so that you may reflect upon it: others may praise you, it is my duty to warn you. But I will say this much, you have achieved one great result, the youth has a holy reverence for the Spirit of History."

Erich took his mother's hand, and walked with her for a long time, in silence.

Then he explained to her in what way he meant to give Roland, not only knowledge, but a stay for life, so that he might rely upon himself alone.

"My son," rejoined his mother, "you have set yourself too hard a task; you have undertaken to solve a threefold problem at one time: that is impossible. Hear me patiently. You mean, in the first place, to supplement and complete a neglected intellectual education, and direct it into a better channel; you mean, secondly, to endue your pupil with a moral strength, nay more! an enthusiastic moral impulse, without employing the approved levers; and finally, you would make of a youth who is conscious of his wealth, a public-spirited, unselfish, self-sacrificing man. Now pray, why are you laughing? Let me finish, though,—I might add, that you desire to make a boy without a family, sympathetic, a youth without a country, patriotic. Now say, why do you laugh?"

"Pardon me, mother; they call you the Professorin with good reason; you discoursed as if you were sitting in a professor's chair. But allow me to remark that the two-fold or five-fold problem is, in the end, but one. I confess, I have often felt as if I ought to make my work easier; but then I have asked myself whether that was not the prompting of my love of ease. I must try the experiment of trusting a young man to act freely upon his own knowledge."

"Knowledge?" his mother returned. "Knowledge can make a man calm, but not happy, not blessed. Knowledge may be food, which the young soul cannot take. See, my son! meat is good food, but you cannot feed the new-born babe upon meat instead of milk. Do you understand me?"

"Of course; you mean to say that Religion is the milk of the Spirit."

"That's it," said his mother with animation. "Your father used to say: 'No man has ever accomplished anything great, no man has ever done a great deed, who did not believe in God; God is the highest, most living imagination. Until Philosophy shall furnish men a Moral Law which can be cut upon two tables like the Ten Commandments, which can be expressed briefly and unequivocally—until then, Religion must be the first stage, at least, of all Moral Education."

"Mother," replied Erich, gravely, "our faith in God is stronger than theirs who imprison him in a book, a house, a set form of worship."

"My dear," said the mother, "don't let us speak any more about it. Do you hear the butterfly fluttering about in large circles at the window-pane? From its transparency the butterfly supposes the pane to be the air; he imagines he must be able to pass through it, and he will finish by running his head against the glass wall which he takes for air. But enough, I am no match for you. If only your father were living, he could help you."

The conversation took a different turn upon the allusion to his father's death.

CHAPTER XI.

UNEXPECTED SCHOOL INSPECTORS.

IT seemed to Frau Ceres that Frau Dournay did not devote herself sufficiently to her. This excited her jealousy, and to everybody's surprise she declared that she too desired to be present during study-hours—she had far greater need of instruction than all the rest. And now Sonnenkamp came too, and listened to the teaching. But he could never sit unoccupied; whenever he was not smoking, it was his habit to whittle a piece of wood, of which he made all sorts of curious figures; he was peculiarly given to cutting grotesque figures from the roots of vines—only when thus occupied could he listen in silence.

Erich perceived that his course of instruction was interrupted by this motley audience. His mother comprehended his dissatisfaction without his giving it verbal expression: she no longer attended at lessons, and Frau Ceres and Sonnenkamp also stayed away.

While by the conscientious discharge of his duty Erich was enabled to banish all the painful traces of the violent emotion which Bella had stirred in his heart, his mother was full of uneasiness. She had attained an ideal which she had always wished for—daily life and employment in a large garden; and now when she had attained it, it did not afford her full satisfaction.

On one occasion, as she was rambling in the park with her son early in the morning, she said:

"I have made a discovery; I find that I have no talent for being a guest."

Erich did not interrupt her with questions: he knew that she would reach the point, even if it were in a roundabout manner; and the Mother continued:

"I feel that I must be doing something. I cannot always have every thing done for me; and here again we have a point, wherein lies a danger to wealth. The wealthy look upon themselves as guests in the world—they need do nothing themselves, others do everything for them; and, my dear son, I assure you, I can stand it no longer, I must do something. You men can create, work, form, accomplish, and your actions renovate your life; we women can renovate and animate our lives only by loving."

Erich replied to her, that she accomplished enough by her mere existence; but his mother retorted vehemently:

"This is what I can never forgive Schiller; he should never have said the words, they were not worthy of him, 'Common natures pay with what they do; noble ones with what they are.' That sounds like a license for all idlers, with or without the coronet of nobility on their seals."

Erich replied that she might rest contented with her influence on Frau Ceres; but the Mother shook her head, and said nothing. She had indeed hoped for this influence herself, but in Frau Ceres she had met with a nature so enigmatical, so incomprehensible, that she found herself perfectly useless. She would not acknowledge to her son that this house had an oppressive influence on her; that as the family's pride and glory centred in external possessions, so everything here seemed to be moved from without, by strangers—all spontaneous force seemed to be wanting.

Miss Perini always spoke of Frau Ceres as "our dear sufferer." But of what nature was Frau Ceres' complaint?

Frau Dournay had once casually said to Frau Ceres, that she must miss her daughter very much; upon which Frau Ceres started up, her eyes sparkling like those of a serpent about to strike. She sent Miss Perini, who was present, into the garden, and, glancing about furtively, said to the Widow:

"It's not her fault, but mine—only mine. I meant to punish him when I told the child to do so, but I did not intend this."

Frau Dournay begged her to place complete confidence in her, and explain herself fully; but Frau Ceres burst into a laugh, which sounded as if it came from another person.

"No! no! I sha'n't tell it again, and surely not to you."

The dread which had overcome the Widow at her first meeting with Frau Ceres, now revived again; she fancied she now recognized the complaint of the black-eyed woman, who was lazy, or of a lizard-like restlessness by fits and starts; she must be burdened with a thought which she could not entirely reveal, nor yet entirely conceal.

As one continually repeats the same fairy-tale to a child, she often yielded to the importunities of Frau Ceres to tell her of the only thing which seemed to interest her—court-festivities. She might relate the same occurrences to her repeatedly, Frau Ceres always enjoyed them anew. But the Mother laid great stress on the fact that every hour of a princess's life had its allotted duty, and that every station in life demanded its peculiar restraining dignity; she spoke impressively, and often recurred to the thought, that a woman who was born in a republic, as Frau Ceres was, could have no idea of all these things; that the sensation which they produced in her, was most likely what ours would be if we were suddenly carried into another century.

"I understand perfectly whatever you and your son say," remarked Frau Ceres. "All the others, with the exception of the Major, I listen to, to be sure, but I don't know where I am. Would you believe it, I was afraid of you at first."

"Of me? No one was ever afraid of me!"

"I shall tell you some other time. Ah! I'm suffering, I always suffer."

The Mother did not succeed in rousing Frau Ceres from her mode of life, which consisted only of sleeping and waking.

Sonnenkamp always treated the Mother with extreme reverence; it seemed as if he made her an object on which to practise a noble, reserved demeanor. Once, he remarked very modestly that he had observed the law, and had never asked what his wife spoke or desired; he only begged for permission to ask one question: "Had Frau Ceres never spoken of Manna?"

"Of course; but only very briefly."

"And may I not know what she said?"

"I don't know it myself, it remained obscure. But I beg of you, do not tempt me to disloyalty and breach of confidence."

"Breach of confidence?" exclaimed Sonnenkamp, and his lip trembled.

"Ah! it was not the proper word. Your wife confided nothing to me; but I believe—I beg you not to misunderstand me—I imagine that she has a secret fear of Miss Perini, or she is vexed or angry at her. Far be it from me to attempt to injure Miss Perini; I almost regret having said what I did."

"Give yourself no trouble on that point; my wife would gladly dismiss Miss Perini from the house ten times in the course of a single day, and would gladly recall her again as often. I know no one, not even excepting yourself, who is as necessary or as useful to her as Miss Perini."

Frau Dournay longed to leave the house, but her relations to the family had become such, that she could not find a suitable reason for her departure. She had no desire to be made the depositary of secrets, or to solve riddles, and still her mind was incessantly occupied with the daughter of the house. A child, a grown-up girl, who leaves such a house—perhaps such a girl would be an object for her labors: in what way, she could not tell; but it never left her thoughts. She meant to ask the Major about her, Clodwig, Bella; yes she would even offer her services to Prancken himself; but Prancken had not appeared for several weeks. She once made Joseph show her Manna's rooms, and there she felt as if she heard the sweet child calling to her; it seemed to be her duty to give her help and support.

She wrote a letter to the lady Superior, saying that she should call on her within a few days.

CHAPTER XII.

FRAU PETRA.

WHEN Sonnenkamp was alone in the garden, in the hot-houses, in his study, or in the seed-room, there was always a triumphant self-satisfied smile upon his features; indeed he often spoke out loud, for he enjoyed the triumph, of using, according to his own pleasure, persons and relations, which came into his hands. He governed, he bent and directed them, as he did the fruit-trees of his garden.

Frau Ceres' defiance and inertness had at first served to lend to the house and whole establishment a certain aristocratic aspect; for aristocracy appears, at first sight, in the form of self-sufficiency; the aristocrat needs no other human being, he has everything in himself. Whatever comes to him is accepted graciously, but must never assert its claim to the character of a necessity. But the aristocratic aspect had soon become one of mystery which challenged curiosity and scandal.

Sonnenkamp had anticipated it, but he had not expected this disposition to endure so long. The shyness and reserve with which the old inhabitants of the neighborhood refused to be drawn into anything which looked like familiar acquaintance, wounded his pride sorely. It would be difficult ever to overcome their exclusiveness; indeed he must take care not to recognize it; he must be obliging to the most distant; he must not allow them to notice that he is aware of their unwillingness to make his acquaintance.

His acquaintance with Otto von Prancken was the result of their meeting in a stable; it had progressed finely, and promised to procure him, in the future, a firm hold upon the old families. But for all that, Sonnenkamp's house, park, and garden were as yet, on the whole, like tub-plants—foreign and not of the land. But through Erich and his family he took a position in the country, as if it were a matter of course.

Erich had brought about that intimate acquaintance with Clodwig and Bella, which Prancken had not been able to accomplish. The Professor's widow was to do the rest; she must make and receive calls on her own account; her friends would naturally become the guests of the house.

With much circumspection, Sonnenkamp told the Mother how bad it was that his wife was not by nature fitted to call upon the good families of the district, and to cultivate a neighborly feeling. The Mother, on her part, desired to obtain an insight into the life of this country-side, and to thank the people who had shown so much kindness to her son. First, she desired to call at the Doctor's house. Sonnenkamp said that she ought to call upon the Justice's family too. He placed his whole house at her disposal, in case she should want to issue invitations.

It was a fine Sunday in early Autumn, when they prepared to call upon their neighbors.

Frau Ceres had promised to be of the party; but when the time for starting had come, she declared that it was impossible for her to go, and now, for the first time, the Widow noticed a trait of insincerity in her nature: evidently, she had yielded only to escape persuasion; now, unexpectedly, she asserted her own will, and did not even feign sickness.

Miss Perini stayed at home too.

They drove first to Herr von Endlich's, although they had

means of knowing that the family were travelling. They wished to make a blind visit.

Sonnenkamp returned to the Villa, and let Roland, Erich, and the Mother drive to the village; he called after them that they must be careful, and not taste all the wine that would be offered them.

Now, when the Mother was riding along with Erich and Roland, the thought occurred to her that she was not making these calls for herself, but she was unpretending, and was willing to serve her hospitable friend.

On the road, Roland made the carriage stop, for they met the Krischer. Roland presented him to Frau Dournay. She gave him her hand, and said that she would call on him soon.

The Krischer's face brightened, and pointing to Roland, he said:

"Yes, yes; if I had to cut out a grandmother for him, I'd make her just like you."

They laughed, and drove on.

When they came to the town, the bells were ringing in the steeple of the new Protestant church, which looked down cheerfully upon the country from the hill where it stood.

The Mother had the carriage stop, and went to the church with Erich and Roland.

Roland said that this was his first visit to a Protestant church during the service; and though the Mother urged him not to make it to-day, but to accompany her son into the town for awhile, he insisted on going with her.

And so they entered the church, a plain structure and devoid of ornament, just as the congregation had concluded a hymn. The Mother was sorry to hear a sermon severe in sentiment and overstrained in delivery, and she deeply regretted having complied with Roland's wishes.

"When you're old enough," said she, taking his hand as they passed out and caught a refreshing view of the beautiful landscape, "I will make you acquainted with a writer from your native land, from whom you can gain other and higher views of truth."

"Do you mean Benjamin Franklin? I know him."

"No; I mean a preacher who died but a few years ago. He was a man of the highest inspirations. I was so fortunate as to know him personally. He has eaten at our table, and I have shaken him by the hand. He and my husband contracted a speedy and warm friendship."

"You must mean Theodore Parker?" interrupted Erich.

"Certainly; and I always feel it an honor that such a man should have lived with us."

"Why haven't you ever spoken of him?" said Roland, turning to Erich.

"Because I wanted to avoid all interference with the religious creed in which you were born."

Erich said this without any tone of reproach toward his mother; but on hearing him, she started, and repeated that Roland should not make the acquaintance of this man until he was older and his judgment more matured. It happened, however, that whenever anything was shown or mentioned to the boy which for the present was withheld from him, he, accustomed as he was to be denied nothing, took care persistently to urge the point; and if still rebuffed, he would privately look into the matter for himself.

As they came out of church, Erich and Roland were greeted by many people. Erich introduced his mother to the School-director and the Forester, as well as to the wife and sister-in-law of the latter, and they accompanied their friends into the village. The procession was a pleasant one as they thus walked along the highway with new companions; and there is nothing, perhaps, to be compared with that self-satisfied frame of mind in which a crowd of persons of various dispositions are wont to return from church.

"Wasn't the Doctor's wife at church?" asked the Mother.

They said that she never came to church on Sunday morning; she stayed at home to help the country-people, who, on Sundays in particular, came very early to get advice about any complaint they might have. She often prescribed soothing domestic remedies, and left her post only on the Doctor's return. And now, too, Erich for the first time heard that her name was Petra. She held a position in some degree resembling that of Saint Peter, for she made it her duty to examine the people before they could be admitted into the heaven of health.

The three now entered the Doctor's house. The floor and staircase fairly shone with home-like cleanliness, and the walls were covered with well-executed pictures, no one of which seemed to have got there by accident; while upon the tables stood pots with green climbing-plants, sending their creeping tendrils in every direction. In the sitting-room a sewing-table stood beside the window, before which stood a mirror, so placed as to reflect the scene without. Everything was in Sunday trim, and upon the table itself stood a full-blown camelia.

"Yes, Nanny," said a voice in the next room—it was that of the Doctor's wife—"yes, you're forever talking about religion and submission to the Divine will, and yet you seem so impatient and despondent, and are a very hard patient to manage. My husband can give medicine, but love and patience you must find yourself. And you, Anna, you overfeed your child, and then always have to come for help; sense can't be bought at

9.

For, Maud, so tender and true,
As long as my life endures
I feel I shall owe you a debt,
That I never can hope to pay;
And if ever I should forget
That I owe this debt to you
And for your sweet sake to yours;
O then, what then shall I say?—
If ever I *should* forget,
May God make me more wretched
Than ever I have been yet!

10.

So now I have sworn to bury
All this dead body of hate,
I feel so free and so clear
By the loss of that dead weight,
That I should grow light-headed, I fear,
Fantastically merry;
But that her brother comes, like a blight
On my fresh hope, to the Hall to-night.

XX.

1.

STRANGE, that I felt so gay,
Strange, that I tried to-day
To beguile her melancholy;
The Sultan, as we name him,—
She did not wish to blame him—
But he vext her and perplext her
With his worldly talk and folly:
Was it gentle to reprove her
For stealing out of view
From a little lazy lover
Who but claims her as his due?

The Mother took her leave, and Frau Petra did not try to detain her, saying frankly that she had to speak with several persons who were about going home.

Refreshed and cheered, the guests left the house.

They were detained a long time at the Justice's, for his wife and daughter had their toilet to make, and when they at last made their appearance, they were profuse in their apologies for the delay, declaring they had hurried as fast as possible, and they regretted the disordered appearance of everything, though both their dress and the room itself were the picture of neatness.

A messenger was sent for the Justice, who was just then enjoying his Sunday schoppen; and when Frau Dournay was at last seated in the sofa-corner where one could hardly sit comfortably for the piles of embroidered cushions, an agreeable conversation ensued, for very fortunately the Justice's wife had mentioned the name of her father, with whom Erich's mother was acquainted, and the first awkwardness on meeting, gradually gave place to a genial, mutual understanding. Frau Dournay succeeded in engaging Lina in conversation, and drew from her a description of the life in the convent; and she felt very glad that the latter regarded everything in so pleasing a light. Thus encouraged, Lina grew more and more communicative, and talked so much that her mother looked at her in surprise.

The Justice now made his appearance. He had evidently hurried down his schoppen, for of course he could not leave a drop behind. He gave the Professor's widow a warmer and more protracted grasp of the hand than was really necessary; and good-humoredly—any humorous expression on the little man's grave face had such an odd look—assured her of his official protection. He then informed Erich and Roland that the Pole had escaped from the House of Correction, and that reward had been offered for his apprehension, but that the would be glad if he were not retaken.

The wife and daughter of the host brought their hats, and, not perhaps without an eye to enjoying the scenery, accompanied their worthy guest by a circuitous path along the Rhine to the School-director's house. Erich walked with the Justice, who had Roland's arm, and Lina accompanied Frau Dournay.

Lina voluntarily began to speak of Manna, and to tell how from being so merry she had become so sad. She had been so devoted to her father that no one would suppose she could leave him for a day; and Lina now asked Erich's mother to take measures to secure her return.

The Mother carefully avoided making any inquiries, but it seemed to her so strange that this visit which she had made from mere politeness, should have given rise to a new duty. Could she have suspected that Sonnenkamp was only using her to subserve his own purposes, she would have been still more surprised at the various turns a trifling event will take.

The families of the School-director and Forester were not at home, and as the party were driving back, the Doctor's wife stood at her door as they passed and called out for them to stop.

They did so, when the Doctor's wife came up and said that she had forgotten to tell Frau Dournay to be sure to visit Fräulein Milch and the Major to-day. The latter was a very good-natured man but sensitive upon points of etiquette, and never forgave any lack of attention toward Fräulein Milch; and too, that lady, save in some particulars, was a very excellent and worthy person.

In a happy mood, they returned to the Villa.

The first person they met in the courtyard was the Major; he looked rather out of sorts, but his whole face lighted up when the Widow informed him of her intention to pay him and Fräulein Milch a noonday visit, and indeed, take a cup of coffee with them, for unfortunately, she could not drink wine at that hour of the day, as was the custom here.

The Major bowed: he contrived soon to withdraw and send one of the Castellan's children to Fräulein Milch with the joyful tidings.

Erich's mother was in high good spirits, and Erich expressed his delight that she, too, should feel something of the intoxication of enthusiasm with which every one is inspired by life and nature on the Rhine.

"I have been looking into the encyclopædia," said Roland to Erich's mother, in a low tone, as he came to the table. "This is Theodore Parker's birthday: it's the twenty-fourth of August."

The Mother whispered to him not to speak of it to any one but her.

CHAPTER XIII.

SOUR CREAM TURNS SWEET AGAIN.

At no Sunday dinner had the Major ever been as lively as to-day. He even forgot to beckon to Joseph to pour him out another glass of Burgundy.

Frau Ceres smiled embarrassedly as the Widow remarked how many excellent people she had seen to-day, and how, though the river and mountains were such a refreshing sight, a glance into so many noble, sterling homes was still more pleasant.

She added, that though it was true that she knew little of foreign lands, she was sure no country surpassed Germany in real depth of feeling and wide diffusion of culture. Towns and villages which seemed but a name to the traveller as he hastens past, contain within them all that is good and beautiful to adorn humanity.

"No better sermon has been preached to-day within the sound of the church-bell," said the Major to Erich. He then rose. "Here's to the health of Erich's mother—all join me in the toast—long life to her; for, in living, she makes others see life as beautiful and true; and the Creator will bless her for it. Comrades, I mean my—my—long life to Frau Dournay!"

Never before had the Major offered such a long toast, and never had he been happier than to-day. Soon after the repast, he returned home, repeating his toast over and over to himself, as he went, for he was ambitious to be able to repeat to Fräulein Milch his fine speech, word for word. World-wide renown was nothing without her praise; for her opinion was certainly the most to be valued.

When he reached home, and Fräulein Milch complained to him that her sweet cream had soured, and that there was no fresh to be got anywhere in the village, he kept motioning to her not to speak and thus drive his toast out of his mind. He then stood up boldly before her: "This is the speech I made at the table to-day," said he, commencing his recitation. While he was delivering the grand speech, Laadi gazed at her master, and as the Major concluded, barked her appreciation. The Major most assuredly did not mean to lie, but the harangue was certainly finer, or at least longer, as he delivered it before Fräulein Milch, than in its original form.

"I'm so glad," said she, as he finished, "that there were some good people present to hear you." For Fräulein Milch was not on good terms with Herr and Frau Sonnenkamp, and with Miss Perini, least of all.

"Why haven't you got out our beautiful white tablecloth?" asked the Major, looking at the neatly-spread table in the garden.

"Because white is so dazzling in sunlight."

"True: that's all right! Sha'n't I fasten up Laadi? She's so importunate."

"No: leave the dog loose."

The Major seemed quite depressed that he could not do something, too, toward giving a worthy reception to the guests.

After awhile he returned in triumph: he had done a deed which, to him, was a great sacrifice; he had begged the superintendent's cook for a dish of fresh cream. He seldom borrowed or lent, but to-day he must make an exception.

He succeeded in getting it on the table unperceived by Fräulein Milch. He clapped his hand over his mouth that he might not laugh out loud at her look of surprise, on suddenly finding sweet cream on the table. He did still more. He went into the sitting-room and brought his huge, leather-covered, cushioned armchair out into the garden. There it was that Frau Dournay was to be installed; but Fräulein Milch came and showed him, to his dismay, that its appearance would not stand the test of broad daylight; so the two were forced to take it in again.

"Sha'n't we go and meet them?" said the Major, who had drawn out his telescope to its full length. "Just take a look. Wait! I'll arrange it differently. There! I think I see something down the road."

Fräulein Milch asked him to stand very still; and here the Major's face looked as if he were about to weep. "It's hard," said he, laying his hand on Fräulein Milch's shoulder—"it's hard—cruel—sad—very sad—very cruel not to be able to say to Frau Dournay, 'Allow me to present to you my wife.'"

Fräulein Milch hastily turned away; her manner had suddenly become rather stiff.

"What, in the name of Heaven, is the matter?"

The dog barked as if to say, "What does it mean? Why do you look so angry?"

"I'll be quiet now; I'll be quiet! Hush, Laadi!" said the Major, in a pacifying tone, and he was so tired that he was forced to sit down; he tried to light his long pipe, but it went out.

He stood by the garden hedge, drumming on one of the saplings with his fingers, and gazing so vacantly into the distance that his guests stood before him without his seeing them approach.

The meeting between Erich's mother and Fräulein Milch was by no means as cordial as the Major had hoped. Both ladies had a suspicious feeling; and evidently surveyed each other closely. But the Major soon indulged in a secret laugh, for Fräulein Milch did not notice that the sweet cream had been substituted for the sour, but poured it out as if nothing had happened.

"She's much too prudent for that," he soon said, bringing his finger-stump to his forehead. "She'll not call the attention of strangers to it. Oh, she's so clever, she's past finding out."

How much he would have liked to state the fact to the Widow; but he did not intend to speak at all to-day, if he could help it; Fräulein Milch alone should do the talking.

They, however, did not seem to succeed in starting any real conversation, except when the Doctor's wife was mentioned: then Fräulein Milch took occasion to express her respect for that noble woman whose distinction was of the right kind.

"What do you mean by 'distinction of the right kind?'"

"I consider it to consist in the possession of the respect and esteem of every one, whoever he may be."

"Just so, and that may be said in a perhaps greater degree of Frau Dournay," interrupted the Major.

He fancied he saw a somewhat sarcastic expression on Fräulein Milch's countenance, and he did not like it.

Erich's mother asked her hostess if she were a native of the country. She curtly replied in the negative.

The Major at last hit on an expedient. A couple of strange horses must be left in the stable alone together; they may perhaps give each other a few hard knocks but they will finally come to terms. He began to tell Roland and Erich much about the vineyard, which would yield its first wine that season—the virgin wine, as it was called; they must accompany him thither.

And now the two women were alone. As Erich's mother had heard so much good of Fräulein Milch, she at first intended to pay her some compliments, but she found that that was not the best way; so by skilfully turning the conversation she spoke of the singular change which had taken place in her own life, and how much she needed assistance.

This was her cue; for where it was a question of aid and advice, Fräulein Milch was in her element. She stated it as her firm conviction that by keeping one's self-respect intact, the mastery of life is secured. Her mode of expression and considerate manner surprised Erich's mother. She had expected to find a petty, narrow-minded, loquacious housewife, and here was a thoughtful and intelligent mind, which could only have been formed by calm, mature, and great reflection.

"You are more than you seem," she was about to say, but she hastily turned the sentence and again remarked how pleased she was with the bountiful life here, and with the scenery; for one met not only secret nooks, full of refreshing beauty, but also natures, who in their solitude cultivate a fineness of understanding and loftiness of mind.

Fräulein Milch, who, cup in hand, had seated herself a little aside from the table, now drew nearer and gave a penetrative analysis of the characters of Herr and Frau Sonnenkamp.

She made no allusion to Miss Perini; she merely expressed her regret that Herr Sonnenkamp, who was not unkind at heart, had no systematized plan of benevolence. She mentioned this and that case of need—she knew the circumstances of every person for miles around.

"Thank you," Frau Dournay at last said; "thank you for having reminded me of the task which I had quite forgotten, for that is the real cause of my change of residence. Suppose I should plan a scheme of charity on the part of Herr Sonnenkamp, would you lend me your aid?"

Fräulein Milch promised to do so; but she said the best and most proper way would be for Frau Dournay to enlist the interest of the daughter—this would at once remove many difficulties. The girl, who had a serious nature, would thus be restored to her proper position, and Herr Sonnenkamp's boundless wealth being thus intrusted to his daughter, would rest on a secure and firm foundation.

The Professor's widow fixed her beaming eyes upon Fräulein Milch. Awhile ago the Doctor's wife called upon her to bring Manna away from the convent and employ her in labor with and for others, and now this woman repeated the demand.

Frau Dournay then attentively asked still further particulars from the thrifty and sagacious housekeeper in regard to the people of the vicinity; but Fräulein Milch, in a straightforward way, declined giving any opinion in reference to them. She could not judge of them, she said; she saw them, it was true, on Sundays and other holidays going up the mountain, jesting and singing, with their heads decorated with wreaths; but one not in the midst of the merry scene, and who merely looked on from the window or from behind the garden hedge, could form no correct judgment, and sometimes the entire scene of commotion made one feel as when one stops the ears and watches dancing, but hears no music.

Erich's mother again touched upon Manna and, forgetful of the restraint which, with evident difficulty, she had imposed upon herself, Fräulein Milch declared that Manna must have been wounded in some incomprehensible manner, for it was wholly unnatural for her suddenly to fall from pertness into such a state of humility.

"I'll mention to you one little trait in her character and then you'll understand her. A fly was sitting on her hand sucking her blood; she allowed it to suck away quietly and then merely remarked, 'The nasty fly! I gave it a drink and never disturbed it, and it has repaid me by stinging me.' That will show you the nature of the child provided she has not been spoiled in the convent. I can speak the more frankly from the fact that the girl has an aversion to me, an aversion inspired by Miss Perini."

And in a passionate outburst of excitement Fräulein Milch now gave vent to her indignation against Prancken.

She confessed that she disliked him because in a manner ill becoming youthful superciliousness, he made the Major the butt of his witticisms, for he was very pert and overbearing. It was therefore the more remarkable that he should now be playing such a pious *rôle*, which he assumed even before bringing Manna home; there must be some secret machination underlying the matter, a scheme they could not fathom.

And thus pleasantly conversing, the two women learned to know each other. The culture of the Widow was of an easy kind, and hers by birth; she gave much without seeming to do so; that of Fräulein Milch was of a heavy, hard-earned order, every statement she made betraying the labor by which she had gained a deep and independent power of thought; and on observing the ease and fluency with which the Widow expressed herself, Fräulein Milch mentally nodded assent. "Ah yes, to be sure," said she to herself, "this lady has tasted refinement from a bountifully loaded board, but I've had to be my own cook and spread my own table."

From a distance, the Major saw the two women shake hands, and he bestowed upon Laadi the caressing words he would fain have uttered to Fräulein Milch.

"You're a splendid creature, and more sensible than all the rest of the world put together: you're clear as daylight, quiet and solid. What are you looking up at me for, Laadi? I don't mean you."

He returned to the garden, followed by Roland and Erich.

"I think," said the Widow to the Major, as the latter accompanied her a short distance on her way home, "I think that I have now made the acquaintance of not only the two best but also the two happiest people in the neighborhood."

The Major stood a long time watching the retreating forms, and then raising his eyes heavenward he said:

"I thank Thee, Thou architect of all worlds—Thou knowest what I would say by that. Heigh-ho!"

BOOK EIGHTH.

CHAPTER I.

ON GOETHE'S BIRTHDAY.

IT seemed as if from curve to curve the strong-flowing Rhine had become a lake, until, passing the jutting mountains, it continued its course.

In the same manner flowed the story which we have to tell.

Unswervingly, Frau Dournay endeavored to gain the object which appeared to her a necessity; but obstacles presented themselves. First came an exceedingly kind note from Clodwig, inviting Frau Dournay and the whole family of Sonnenkamp to celebrate Goethe's birthday at Wolfsgarten.

The invitation was accepted, but again Frau Ceres and Miss Perini remained at home.

The others drove to Wolfsgarten.

Erich did not express in words, but his eyes betrayed, how he felt himself protected and spiritually upheld in entering his friend's house beside his mother. She appeared as a living witness that he entered with a pure heart and open brow. Nevertheless he could not think of meeting Bella without a feeling of anxiety. Soon the Aunt and Bella met the visitors in the woods. Bella embraced Erich's mother, and again thanked her for making the sacrifice of letting her have dear Claudine. To Erich she gave her hand, saying, with a certain stony look:

"His first thought to-day, young friend, was of you."

She said no more; she did not mention her husband by name.

It began to rain just as they arrived at Wolfsgarten, and the storm continued all day; so they were compelled to remain indoors.

Clodwig was exceedingly gay and happy. It was a day of mirth and pleasure such as can only be celebrated by natures unoppressed by care, and only perhaps on the Rhine.

But the most joyous of all was Roland. He was the uniting and the refreshing element. He looked in every one's face as if to say, "Why don't you enjoy yourself as I do?" He went to and fro, from Frau Dournay to Aunt Claudine, from her to Bella, and then to Clodwig, as if he would tell them all that he was in a truly happy home-circle. He was in such merry spirits that he suddenly exclaimed:

"Oh, when dear sister Manna comes home, she'll see at once

that we've got Uncle and Aunt, and Grandfather and all, just as if they'd grown on trees."

"Where's Prancken?" some one asked.

The reply was that he was staying on the Lower Rhine, with a pious farmer, the so-called Convent-farmer; for there is nothing in our day that is not colored and characterized by the Church.

Prancken was so fortunate as to be in the neighborhood of the convent, as the farmer had obtained a lease of the land on the Island, which he cultivated.

The party assembled in the great saloon, three doors of which led to the covered balcony, which was adorned with flowers and creeping plants, and provided with comfortable seats.

While the company was sitting, quietly conversing, Clodwig suddenly raised his hand as if commanding silence. All understood him, and were still. He had drawn out his watch, and now said:

"At this moment Goethe was born. I beg," he added, with a friendly nod—"I beg Fräulein Dournay and Bella—"

The two understood, seated themselves at the piano, and played, as a duett, Beethoven's Overture to Egmont.

Clodwig leaned back in his chair and listened with closed eyes. Frau Dournay sat beside him. Erich and Roland were on the balcony. Erich held Roland's hands.

When the music ceased, Clodwig said that he had been fortunate enough to know Goethe personally, and he then related many pleasing reminescences.

Frau Dournay regretted that it had not been her privilege to hear the voice of the great genius, and to look into his face; and yet she—when he died—was old enough to know what he was, although she was not able, at that time, to comprehend him fully. She told how, just as they were sitting down to dinner, in her parent's house, a man came in and told them that the news of Goethe's death had just been received. An elderly lady was so overcome, that she could not sit down to dinner. Then for the first time, Frau Dournay continued, she found her husband, who was present, inconsistent in his opinions; for notwithstanding all his veneration for Goethe, he had asserted: that the master had effeminated poetry too much, by placing woman in the centre of the turmoil of life; and he left men in the belief, that poetry and its comprehension was woman's peculiar gift; just as many so-called free-thinkers look upon religion as a mere woman's affair.

Clodwig objected to this conception of Goethe, and said with emphasis that the principal difficulty with modern life, is that it deprecates the so-called worship of Genius. Worship is only possible, indeed, when a theophany—a pure manifestation of the

Infinite is assumed. As soon as limitations are imposed, worship is impossible.

It was hardly noticed that Bella, Claudine, and Sonnenkamp, had left the room; Bella had asked the latter to give her some advice about the new arrangements in her greenhouse.

Thus Clodwig and Frau Dournay were left alone in the room; whilst Erich and Roland remained quietly on the balcony, and heard Clodwig add that, possibly, in the future, Religion would no longer possess any distinct cult, but that all the processes of life would be imbued with the true sanctification of the spirit.

Erich and Roland listened breathlessly, as Clodwig and Frau Dournay told each other of the philosophy and life they had gained from the master; and how that undervalued work of Goethe, "Conversations with Eckermann," whose infinite suggestiveness was discussed in all lights, renewed for them the life and personal intercourse of the old master.

Clodwig mentioned that the youth of the present day had not the old veneration for the master; and Frau Dournay added, that her husband—she always quoting him—had explained that the youth of the day feel themselves, before anything else, members of an organic community; that the real life of the citizen—that active working for the living state, had not been appreciated by Goethe, and it was not his task.

Again the two returned, as in an alternating song, to the enrichment and earnestness of life they had gained from Goethe.

Erich and Roland sat quiet and listened, only once Erich said in a low voice:

"See, Roland, that is glory, that is honor; the highest thing possible to a man is to leave after him such an influence, that his mind still continually reanimates. And people sitting here in after-years, inspire each other by awakening that which has been evolved by one who is done with life."

Roland looked in Erich's great glowing eyes, and Erich could have caught the youth up in his arms when he said:

"Now, for once, I am in the presence of your devotion."

The two in the room spoke on, and now Erich heard his name mentioned, for his mother said: "Erich can read Goethe's poems very well."

Erich at once arose, ready to do it.

Bella, Claudine, and Sonnenkamp were again called, and Erich read to them. But he never did himself as little credit as to-day; for there appeared so many passages which touched upon what his heart and Bella's held in common. Nevertheless, they sat down to dinner cheerfully as if from an hour of devotion.

Clodwig could not cease to bless the good Providence which

had appointed the son of one of the friends there gathered, to stimulate and regulate the life of the son of another.

He continually dwelt on the idea that an all-controlling spirit was constantly providing and preparing one man to weld his energies with those of another.

Quite naturally, he went on to say that Manna ought to leave the convent, as nobody could finish her education as well and worthily as Frau Dournay.

Sonnenkamp and Frau Dournay looked at each other in astonishment: here one openly spoke in their presence what they themselves had secretly thought. Sonnenkamp humbly thanked Clodwig for the warm interest which he showed in his family, and declared that a wish of Clodwig was for him a command: he hoped that Frau Dournay would also accept it as such. She promised to undertake the task, for it was a gratification to make herself useful.

The rain kept on unceasingly. They again assembled in the large room, and now Bella displayed quite unexpected talents for the benefit of the company. She appeared, wrapped in a red velvet cover, which she draped about her like a Grecian robe, and imitated a celebrated Italian actress to the life. She disappeared and came back as a Paris grisette: then she again disappeared and came back as a Tyrolean singer, always fresh, always disguised to perfection.

She created most merriment when, in quick succession, she imitated three beggar-women—a Catholic, a Protestant, and a Jew. And with the same success, she imitated three ways of having toothache, such as a Protestant, a Catholic, and a Jew might show on going to the dentist and having a tooth pulled out. She understood, too, how to imitate her friends and acquaintances, without burlesquing or characterizing them, but always with such exquisite grace and individuality, that one could hardly find words to express their admiration.

Clodwig said softly to Frau Dournay, "You may feel flattered that she plays all this before you, for she would hardly do it before any one with whom she was most nearly connected."

Sonnenkamp added that it was admirable, and a great luxury to possess such talent for yourself alone, and not be obliged to exhibit it before the world.

Erich looked on, it is true, with admiration, but there were in his heart conflicting sentiments. What a rich nature Bella had! It must, indeed, have been hard for her to lock within herself her manifold powers, and to move in the narrow circle of duty. Bella, however, had to-day forced herself to display her talents; she was determined to sweep away every sentiment, every reminiscence that existed between herself and Erich. Erich seemed to see that, but he was silent. Only once Bella addressed him, saying that the Russian Prince, who had gone to Weidman at Mattenheim, wrote frequently, and always remembered him, and that he also spoke very highly of Roland's old tutor, Knopf.

In the way she emphasized the word "tutor," she seemed to wish again to erect a barrier between her and Erich.

Toward evening the rain ceased, and the sun set over the glowing mountains with that inexpressible magnificence of color which can only be produced by the rays beaming through the rainy atmosphere. The party broke up, and all returned home.

The whole day appeared to have been full of dream-pictures. Roland continually expressed his astonishment at the many things the Countess could do. Sonnenkamp gave his hand to Frau Dournay and said:

"If agreeable to you, we will go together to see my daughter to-morrow."

Frau Dournay nodded in assent. Sonnenkamp was exceedingly happy: he really believed in the noble motives of Frau Dournay, and for a moment he felt something of the same nobleness of heart. It is so beautiful, people are so happy who aim at truth, that it well repays them, at least in self-satisfaction.

Soon, however, the consciousness of his triumphing power arose. The world served his plans, and it was his principal pleasure to play with men, and to use them to raise himself by. It came in so very nicely, that Clodwig and Frau Dournay made his secret plan their own; they now had to be grateful that he complied with their wishes, and yet they had to serve him; his principal plan should be carried out by the two, and in this he seemed to find illustrated his own prerogative to be a being of a higher order, disposing of others and gracing them with his friendship.

On the same evening Sonnenkamp ordered the gardener to fill Manna's room next day with her favorite flowers, first among which was the mignonette.

CHAPTER II.

AN ISLAND FIELD IS PLOUGHED.

DEFERENCE, respect, and cheerful readiness to be of service, were manifest in Sonnenkamp's whole manner, as he held out his hand to Frau Dournay when she alighted from the carriage; as he led her to the steamboat, protected her from draughts of air, and chose for her the best points from which to see the scenery; and as he anticipated her needs, and inquired regarding her wishes.

Frau Dournay found, to her annoyance, that she had forgotten a book which she had intended to take with her. She avoided Sonnenkamp's questions as to what book it was; for she could easily presuppose that the writings of the man whom she honored so highly were anything but acceptable to Sonnenkamp. She laughed at herself at the thought that she should have become so absorbed in the world of learning as to even have a book by her on a clear sunny day—and that, too, in an excursion on the Rhine.

Now she must give herself up to the scenery and her reflections.

Sonnenkamp seated himself near her, and his voice was indeed moved when he said that he considered his children very happy—yes! that he almost envied them—that such a woman should enter into the intellectual life of their youth.

The more he spoke the more he became moved. There was a lustre in his eyes, as though a tear had escaped into them. He repeated often that he dare not speak of his youth; that was barren and waste—no kind hand of woman had ever smoothed his brow. A deep agitation was evident, as the strong man, half hiding, half revealing, spoke of his childhood. At last, controlling himself, he came to the main point. Frau Dournay must first of all discover what had caused Manna to turn from him. He bowed, however, immediately, as he added:

"Perhaps they have told her a circumstance which I hold it beneath my dignity to contradict. Should you hear it, my dear Madam, let me assure you, in advance, that it is a lie carved out of the meanest enmity."

Frau Dournay wished to know what this circumstance was; but he said that he could not name it, or he would go mad here on the boat. His appearance, which had smoothed to mildness, suddenly became wild and terrible. Frau Dournay now said that she was about to visit their lady Superior, a friend of her youth; and then she begged that Sonnenkamp would avoid any attempt to force his daughter into a relation with her.

"Children," she said, "must be allowed to find friendship; they cannot inherit it. One must avoid any intrusion upon them, treating them gently and kindly, and waiting till they come of their own accord."

Sonnenkamp found this so judicious, that he promised not to go at once to the island. He would stay at the inn on the other shore till Frau Dournay should send for him.

"You are as kind as you are wise," said he; for in the Widow's caution he saw a wise policy; and, still more, it pleased him thoroughly to be still able to outmanœuvre all stratagems.

While Sonnenkamp and the Mother were going down the Rhine, a rare occurrence took place upon the Convent-island.

Throughout the year there was no horse upon the island, excepting at ploughing season.

Now the wondering pupils pointed out to one another a plough to which a horse was harnessed, and which was turned backward and forward at the point of the island. The plough was guided by a portly peasant in a blue blouse, and with a gray, much-creased hat upon his head. The children stood at a distance, and looked at the plough as though it were a new wonder. They longed to go nearer, and looked toward Manna to see whether she consented. Manna nodded, and they followed the gravel walk along the side of the field. The plougher saluted them by taking off his hat. Manna stood rooted to the spot, as though bewitched. Is not that Herr von Prancken?

He did not speak a word; he ploughed quietly on. As he turned the plough he looked toward her and smiled; it was he!

"That's a handsome peasant," said one of the girls.

"And he looks so stylish," cried another.

"And he has a seal ring on his hand," cried a third. "Who knows whether he's not a nobleman in disguise?"

Manna called to the children to return with her. She went to her cell, from whence one could overlook the field; but she avoided the window. She was flattered that Prancken should have assumed the lowest rank to be near her, and she felt grateful to him for being so modest and considerate as not to speak to her. She reflected whether it was not her duty to speak of the occurrence to the Superior, but she thought that she had no right to expose Herr von Prancken's modest secret; and then there was nothing wrong in it, but much rather it was the noblest expression of deference.

Then she went to the window; she saw him as he quietly finished his work, and he seemed to her, purer, nobler, and more lovable than ever, in this simple occupation. A rosebush stood on her window-sill, a late rose was in bloom. Just then he looked up: she took hold of the flower to break it off and throw it down to him as a sign of recognition, but just as she touched the stem a novice entered and announced that a visitor had arrived, who wished to speak with Manna. The rose remained on the bush.

Manna turned around and realized how confused she was. There is Prancken—there he is guiding the plough. Can it be that he has caused himself to be announced? Or is Countess Bella come? With trembling steps she descended to the reception-room. The lady Superior presented to her an agreeable appearing, well-rounded lady, and said:

"This is my friend, Frau Dournay, the mother of your brother's teacher."

CHAPTER III.

FROM THE WORLD AND OUT OF THE WORLD.

THE first look exchanged between Manna and the Professor's widow was one of surprise; the second, one of calm confidence: each had preconceived an erroneous idea of the other.

Manna remembered Erich's tall form, his resemblance to St. Anthony, and now she saw a small woman of blonde complexion and with gray hair. The Mother, on the other hand, had imagined Roland's sister to be beautiful, and she found her a trim delicate creature, but one who, at first-sight, by no means conveyed an impression of beauty. A mole on her left cheek and another upon her upper lip were especially noticeable: the young girl's complexion was rather dark, and her deep brown eyes shone with a warm and penetrating lustre.

Manna made a formal bow to the Professor's widow, who, rising, gave her her hand with motherly cordiality, saying that it was a pleasure, during this visit with her old friend the lady Superior, to be able to make the acquaintance of the daughter of those who had shown her such hospitality. She laid special emphasis on the fact that she had the pleasure of being intimately acquainted with Manna's mother.

"Is my mother well?" inquired Manna. Her tone of voice, which was low, was pleasant and expressed much feeling.

The Professor's widow told her how her mother was; and she was able to add that the Doctor said that Frau Ceres had never been in such constant good spirits.

"I have a request to make of you," she continued in an animated tone. "Since I have had the pleasure of being a guest in your parents' house, I have strenuously insisted that your brother's course of daily instruction should not suffer the least disturbance or interruption, and so I desire that you too, my dear young lady, should continue your customary regulations. I have the honor to sit with you at table, and after dinner I will be happy if you can devote a quarter of an hour to me."

"If you have any special business with Manna," said the Superior, "I will leave you together."

"I have certainly no special business with her."

Manna gave the Professor's widow her hand and took her leave. She did not know how it had all happened. Why should she have been sent for when there was hardly anything to tell her. To be sent hither and thither by a stranger--for a stranger the lady certainly was—seemed to her unworthy treatment. But as she walked back, during the entire distance, the stranger's cordial, gentle countenance kept rising before her, smiling upon her as if saying, "You are a strange child!"

Manna returned to her cell in a thoughtful frame of mind: she looked out the window and saw Prancken enter a boat with his horse, and now he was landing on the other side.

"Ah, Herr von Prancken!" shouted a voice. The sound came echoing back. What voice was that?

Prancken hastened up the bank and disappeared behind the willows.

Manna longed for the time when she should part from the world and no longer know unrest, for she was now deeply troubled. Here was Prancken. And there was the tutor's mother—what did it all mean? She took up her prayer-book, but in spite of her efforts, her thoughts still lingered on the subject.

The Professor's widow, meanwhile, was seated beside the Superior, while the latter told her what a strange nature Manna's was. She seemed to have really two natures, one docile, pliant, almost without any will of her own; the other perverse, obstinate, and defiant. Her character, too, was strong and grave, it might be a trifle too grave for a girl of seventeen; she often suffered her feelings to get the better of her, and who at her age did not? But she was burdened by some grief which was wholly inexplicable. It was evident that this was caused by her deep feeling in regard to the divisions between her parents, and that she made it, as it were, a personal matter. She inquired particularly of Frau Dournay in reference to the particular characteristics of the parents, but her friend returned only evasive answers.

Both in appearance as well as bearing, the two women were exact opposites.

The form of the Professor's widow was pleasing, and her countenance always expressed observant animation; her hands were plump and full: the Superior was thin, tall, and lank, the expression of her countenance was harsh and grave, as if she had just issued a peremptory command or were upon the point of issuing one; her hands were long and wrinkled. The lives of both had been very trying; her afflictions had given the Professor's widow a really smiling contentment. The Superior, on the other hand, seemed to be constantly arming herself for a firm and inflexible resistance against all opposition.

The first meeting of the two friends after a separation of about thirty years, had been a singular one. The Superior did not hear or pretended not to hear the Professor's widow address her as "thou."

"I never supposed I should see you on earth again," she had abruptly said; and when her friend began to revive old recollections, the Superior replied that her past life was buried; she had destroyed every souvenir that might recall it. She lived only in the future, the only time upon which we have any right to fix our thoughts.

The Superior observed that this strange speech perplexed her old friend, and then remarked with the same composure that she recognized no difference between her relations and acquaintances of past days. All were equally near and equally distant; and no one unable to feel thus ought to devote herself to the sacred calling.

The Professor's widow felt as if she had been shown the door; she, however, had sufficient self-possession to say:

"Yes, you always had an austerity of character which used to frighten me, but which now excites my admiration."

The Superior smiled; but as if vexed to have allowed this polite remark to excite an emotion of complacency, she added:

"I beg, dear Clara, that you will not lead me into vanity: I am at my post, I am on vigilant guard until the Lord of Hosts calls me to himself. I did not use to know—I must say this—that we were living in two different worlds: in mine, no one must rely on his own strength."

The Professor's widow thought that with all her self-denial, the Superior spoke of the power and dignity of the sphere she occupied, with that pride or at least with that feeling of elation which inspires every member of a large and powerful community. In the eyes of her friend, she herself was but a detached, isolated atom floating about no one knew whither.

The two, however, soon found a topic on which they could sympathize—the difficult task of rearing the young.

The Superior was possessed of great experience, while her friend could only fall back on the views and ideas of her deceased husband; and now that she was a learner and listened with gratitude, she too became more gentle, for the Superior felt that she had indeed behaved with too much austerity toward the noble woman; and as in such a state of feeling one is very likely to say things which are really intended to remain unsaid, so it was in this case.

The Superior remarked that at first Manna's situation in the convent had been a trying one; indeed, what had taken place was something unparalleled. The entrance of the young girl seemed to excite a revolt within the walls. Two other Americans, both of good family, were also here, and these would not sit at the same table with the octoroon, for such they considered Manna. They told their fellow-pupils that at home persons of mixed blood were always obliged to occupy railroad cars specially assigned them; and that even in church they were seated apart from the rest of the congregation. And as the majority of the children belonged to the German nobility, they at last united in a unanimous protest against Manna's presence; though of this

Manna knew nothing. Once, when she was asleep, three of the scholars, in the presence of a nun, carefully examined Manna's nails, but found no dark coloring beneath them; and this proving both parents were of pure blood, Manna was endured on sufferance, and by her quickness of comprehension, and her great zeal, she had succeeded in gaining the blue ribbon.

A remark rose to the lips of the Professor's widow, but she repressed it; for it was her wish to preserve a peaceable demeanor, and to avoid any demonstrations of opposition. Her lips quivered; and she wanted to tell her friend that it was her duty to show the children, by word and deed, that God made no distinctions of color, and that this exclusiveness was barbarous and impious.

The Professor's widow repressed the words, and she was forced to keep back much besides; for the Superior now informed her that when the blessing was asked at table, she must have the goodness to clasp her hands.

Her friend's countenance flushed at hearing this.

"My husband," she replied, "is now in the eternal world; and when he stands before the judgment-seat, the Divine Being I know will say to him, 'You have lived according to the convictions of your soul; you have shown yourself faithful, and have done only what you honestly might.' We had no prayer pronounced at our table, but, before we sat down, a moment's silence was preserved, and each one thought over what it meant to renew one's existence from the Source of all life; and our repast was consecrated by good and pure thoughts."

"Very well, very well; I did not mean to wound you," said the Superior. "I was sorry to hear that you had lost your husband, to whom you sacrificed yourself with such beautiful and joyous devotion."

"I was happy with my husband," returned her friend. "Our love was ever new. But we constantly hear that love spoken of which exists between lovers, and between husband and wife; but there is still another kind of love, marvellously new and deep, and this love I think I know. Excuse me for saying that it seems to me as if love has its first real beginning when one possesses a noble son."

"I am glad that you are thus fortunate; but tell me, honestly, have not you yourself found that at least nine out of ten wives are unhappy?"

Her friend was silent, and the Superior continued:

"Your silence is an affirmative answer; and now observe the difference—among a hundred nuns you find hardly one who is unhappy."

Her friend still remained silent; she did not wish to discuss the statement; she was a guest, and was not here to mend or improve matters. The Superior, however, provoked a reply by inquiring:

"Do you know any greater misfortune than that of a young girl who knows herself, and is known by others, to be the heiress of millions? Can it be imagined that she will be sought in marriage simply for her own sake? Her only course is to place herself and her wealth in the keeping of the Eternal. I tell you this—I do not know what your errand may be; though you should have none whatever, you may proclaim what I say. We are not seeking to gain over Manna and the large fortune which will one day be hers: we insist upon her return to the world, and that she shall not return to us save of her own free will. We employ neither force nor intimidation; but then it is our duty to protect those, wherever they may be, who prefer the imperishable to the perishable. And here let us drop the subject: you now understand the whole matter."

The Lady Superior took her leave.

The Professor's widow strolled alone about the island; and it seemed to her a hazardous act, and one of unwarrantable temerity, to seek to tear away, though with loving violence, this child, who was living here in peace, and who was desirous of passing her life among these surroundings.

She was standing on the shore; and, hardly knowing why, she suffered herself to be taken to the mainland, where she was not a little amazed to see, seated beneath the shady linden-trees before the inn, Herr Sonnenkamp and Herr von Prancken, taking their wine.

Prancken was so singularly dressed that she thought she must be mistaken. She was about to turn back; but they called her, and she went to join them in the garden.

Sonnenkamp was in excellent spirits. He congratulated himself on having happened on his friend Prancken; he thought it quite a fine thing for the Baron to turn farmer awhile; and he faintly intimated that he too had once been something of the kind.

"We have no secrets from our friend." Then he said: "Well; does Manna wish to return home with you?"

The Professor's widow replied that not a word had, as yet, been spoken on the subject; and one could hardly wish it. Manna should be allowed to stay the appointed time; and all strenuous interference whatever should be carefully avoided.

Prancken gave a peculiar assent, but Sonnenkamp was vexed that his child should live here as in a herd, while a free and happy existence was prepared for her.

The noon-bell tolled at the convent, and Frau Dournay said that she must return. Sonnenkamp accompanied her to the shore, and whispered to the Mother:

"Don't mind Prancken. We'll give my child freedom in every respect."

Frau Dournay returned to the island: the children were already at table when she entered the dining-hall. Before she sat down, she stood by her chair for a moment, and silently folded her hands. When they had dined and given thanks, the Superior said to Manna, "Now join the friend of your family."

Frau Dournay went with Manna to the little shady grove at the upper end of the island. Cricket went with them, too, and felt herself quite at home with the Mother; indeed, she quietly allowed herself to be seated under a tree with a book until they called for her again.

"But you mustn't take Manna away," cried the child after them from her little bench. Both were startled, for the child, by a natural impulse, seemed to express what the one feared and the other hoped.

CHAPTER IV.

"YOU MUST EXPERIENCE IT IN YOURSELF."

BOTH were silent for some time; at last the Professor's widow said:

"You seem to me called to the higher life by your bitter experience and your knowledge of the dissensions among mankind, at your early age."

"I? Why?" asked Manna, trembling. "What do you know?"

"I know," replied the Widow, "that you have suffered under that dreadful taint which specially mars your great and beautiful country."

"My country? I? Speak plainly."

"It would grieve me to touch a scar; but this very scar is a badge of honor for you, and you yourself are innocent, my child, of being placed amidst this conflict of life."

"I?"

"Yes!"

"How? Tell me everything. What do you know?"

"I mean that it must elevate you, to have been compelled to suffer that humiliation and bitterness yourself; it lends you a higher worth."

"Then tell me plainly at last, what do you know?"

Her tone was quite changed. There was something like a serpent's hiss in the short, angry tone in which Manna uttered this, and her mild eye flashed menacingly.

"Heaven knows, I do not wish to wound you," said the Professorin, "but would rather extend my hand to cherish and tc bless."

She tried to touch Manna's head, who shyly withdrew and exclaimed;

"Tell me outright, I beg of you—who knows it? What do you know?"

"I know nothing, except that on entering the convent you were made to suffer greatly, because two American girls took you for an octoroon, and avoided you."

"Yes, yes, that's it! Now I know why they examined my nails, and Anna Sotway stood by. Ah! well, well! I thank thee, great God, that thou hast let me experience this; that myself, myself, I must submit to the shame of being examined like a slave! Why did they not cut open my veins? I thank thee, my God! But why do you allow them to worship you, while they mock you in your creatures! Then it was not because I wished to be pious and obedient that they received me here, but because I am of pure blood. Shame!"

It seemed an altered being that spoke now, and cried out into the wood:

"Ye trees, why do you each, according to its kind, bud, bloom, and grow with one sun to warm you all, and the birds to sing to you? Woe, woe! where am I?"

"In the right path," said Frau Dournay; and Manna stared at her as if she were a ghost; but the Mother continued: "A pure spirit is renewing itself in you, my child; you have expressed it. When Lessing wrote, 'I do not wish all trees to have the same bark,' he did not foresee that his spirit would be revealed to an unfolding child, in a convent here. His pure spirit is with us now, my child; and I believe Lessing would say to you, 'Forgive them; they will learn that God alone endures, while generations of men are only mutable forms of existence eternally renewed.'"

Manna scarcely seemed to hear her, for she now took hold of Frau Dournay and asked: "Did you not tell me that you had my mother's special confidence?"

"Yes."

"And did she tell you the secret?"

"I do not understand you."

"Speak openly, I know all."

"Your mother did not confide any secret to me."

Manna spasmodically grasped the cross upon her breast, and sat staring long and silently.

The Widow told her, with earnest sincerity, how much she regretted having agitated her so, and that she did not wish to force herself upon her, but would be a loving relative to her.

Still Manna made no answer; at last she turned and kissed the startled woman on the mouth.

"I kiss the lips, which tell me that—the dreadful, and the other. Yes! I was destined to experience it myself, and now I believe that I am consecrated for the sacrifice."

The Mother was at a loss before this enigmatical nature, but at last Manna promised her to be calm: she seated herself on a bench under a pine, leaned against the tree and looked up at the sky.

"Why," she said, as if to herself, "does not a voice come to us out of the air? Oh! I would gladly follow it over hill and dale, through night and death."

Manna wept. The Widow reminded her of her promise to be calm, but Manna declared she could not, for it grieved her to be torn away from here, and go she must, because she could no longer be truthful; she must live untruthfully here, because people had not been true to her.

Now Frau Dournay was shocked to learn, for the first time, that Manna really had not known the circumstance at all, and she trembled at what she had done. She mourned that she could never forgive herself for having so disturbed Manna's young soul. And then Manna turned, and strove to reassure and comfort the unhappy woman who stood before her.

"Believe me! I beseech you," she cried, uplifting her folded hands—"oh, believe me, truth alone gives freedom, and it is terrible that the park, the house, and the splendor are all lies. No, I did not want to say that. Only one thing I beg of you, do not reproach yourself for having told me *this*. When you leave me again, it will do no harm, it will help me. It was intended I should learn that too, and it is well."

Frau Dournay composed herself, and when she praised Manna's love of truth, Manna shook her head and said:

"I do not want to be praised, I do not deserve it. I do not leserve the whole truth, for I myself conceal something."

Frau Dournay felt the trial she had caused the young girl, and succeeded in explaining that the Superior had healed like a physician, without telling the patient the whole, and Manna looked fixedly at the Widow as she continued: "Unfortunately, I too have not been quite open toward you."

"You too?"

"Yes! I have not yet told you that your father came with me. He is waiting for my return on the opposite shore, and hopes you will come home with us."

"My father hides himself from his child and sends a stranger!" said she, speaking to herself. "Come to the Superior with me," she suddenly exclaimed, and taking the Widow by the hand, went with her to the convent.

But now Cricket came and cried: "No! Manna, you must not go, you must not leave me here alone!"

"Come with me," replied Manna, and took the child's hand.

She went to the Superior, and asked permission to go with the Widow to her father, who was expecting her on the other shore.

"Ask him to come here."

"No, I would rather go to him."

Permission was given, but it was not so easy to part fron Cricket, who refused to be comforted until Manna promised hei faithfully to come back.

Manna sat in the boat, and stared into the water. She reached the garden of the inn with Frau Dournay, where Sonnenkamp still sat in the shade of the arbor with Prancken.

"You are going home with us?" cried Sonnenkamp to his daughter, who suffered his embrace, but did not return it.

Prancken, too, was very glad to welcome Manna, and as she gave him her hand he remarked smiling, "My hand has become hard, but my heart remains soft—too soft perhaps."

Manna cast down her eyes. Soon pleasant jests were passed at the manner in which Prancken had settled in the neighborhood. He related humorously how he had adapted himself to his new life; there was a vigorous freshness in his appearance, and a warm, heartfelt tone in all he said. He saw, not without satisfaction, the impression his demeanor made upon Manna. At last, she said that she believed she might speak openly before the strangers, who really were not like strangers; that she had not fully decided, but still felt a strong desire to leave the convent at once, or better still, not to return to it at all from the place where she was, but Frau Dournay or her father might go over and say farewell in her stead.

"May a friend he allowed to say a word?" asked Prancken, as Sonnenkamp loudly expressed his joy.

Manna begged he would speak; and he now explained that as a friend he must see that Manna's actions were judicious and noble. Whatever might have happened, it remained her duty not harshly to break the pure and intimate relations in which she stood to the convent, especially to the Superior; that ingratitude and severity exercised toward others left heaviness and bitterness of soul behind. He therefore thought that as Manna had entered the convent of her own free will and with a pure resolve, she must now leave it in the same way, in kindness and peace. It seemed to him fitting that she should return and remain some time, and then part with quiet consideration from her companions and the pious Sisters. He repeated that he wished nothing more than to see Manna return as soon and as completely as possible to active life, but that it was a friend's duty to save those who were nearest from repentance and self-reproach. It was with more than dignity, it was with a nobleness of demeanor that Prancken suggested all this; and the looks and thoughts of the three who regarded him were strangely at variance. Sonnenkamp was vexed, but admitted to himself that blood imparted something distinguished and controlling. Frau Dournay believed that Prancken intended to win over Manna anew by noble sentiments. Manna herself was overcome.

"You are right," she cried, and took Prancken's hand, which she held for some time. "You have pointed out what is right; I thank you, and will obey you."

Sonnenkamp was beside himself to see his dearest wish again thwarted, but his astonishment increased when the Widow also expressed her assent.

After Manna had begged Prancken to avoid all intercourse with her until she was again under her father's roof, the two ladies, accompanied by Sonnenkamp and Prancken, went to the shore, and were rowed back to the island.

Cricket, who had not ceased crying, was already put to bed, and continued to complain that Manna had gone away. She went to the child and found her still weeping, and the pillow wet with tears. She wiped the child's eyes and soothed her, until she dropped asleep; and as she comforted her and made her kind promises, she herself grew calmer.

CHAPTER V.

NIGHT AND MORNING IN THE CONVENT.

LATE in the evening Manna walked up and down the broad path on the island with the Superior and Frau Dournay, holding each by the hand. It seemed to her as if two great powers were lovingly contending for her, and each in its way seemed worthy of being followed.

The two ladies spoke—the origin of the conversation could hardly be recalled—of fixedness in opinions. Frau Dournay maintained that the chance of salvation consists in the readiness to acknowledge and confess a wrong, an error, or a rash impulse.

The Superior admitted this, but showed how we might always revert to error—to false views on the highest things, unless by fixed and irrefutably revealed teachings, continually proclaimed through an infallible medium, these errors were healed; else we could not determine if we erred or not, and the torment of doubt would never cease.

The Lady Superior had such sure consciousness of the Positive that, brought face to face with it, Frau Dournay had to seek new knowledge and new observation for each incident; and this made her appear undecided and wavering. This sensation was still further heightened by her not feeling herself justified to battle against so firm and so beneficent a faith. A restlessness, such as a spy must experience, who, actuated by the purest patriotism, reconnoitres the enemy's camp, swayed Frau Dournay's manner. She censured herself for having allowed herself to be employed on this mission. But now she was at her post, and must defend her position. She searched for a point where she could be wholly true; and so she informed Manna that her father intended organizing an extensive system of charity, and showed her what a noble vocation it would be for her to assist in this work. The Superior waited for Manna to reply, who said:

"The gifts which my father bestows will not find their way into the proper hands. We can return all that we possess only into the hands of Him who alone can determine where it shall become of use."

There was a hidden meaning in Manna's reply.

Frau Dournay remarked that every poor man is a messenger of mercy, and every needy man presents a claim for sacrifices; that it was not sufficient to give alms, but that we must devote ourselves, personally, to the sufferers. Not the gift which we bestow on the beggar is of importance, but the trouble which we take for his sake. As a gentleman, crossing the streets in Winter, wrapped up in his furs, often willingly gives something to a shivering beggar, his unbuttoning his coat, his looking for the money, is of more value than the gift itself; at least, as far as the giver is concerned."

Manna replied that women could do nothing by themselves in this matter. And the Superior came to her aid by repeating that she decidedly advised Manna against taking the veil, because it was to be feared that her temperament was not suited for it. Turning to Frau Dournay, she said sharply:

"It does not disturb us in the least to have the world reproach us with having aimed at this child's wealth. We do not despise the wealth—we can accomplish great things with it; but it is the child's soul alone which we value. And we care not whether the world believes it or not!"

The Professor's widow was glad when she was alone in the cell in which she was to sleep. She had never passed a night in a cloister. And yet she felt ill at ease; as if she were a traitoress, a spy. Smiling, she said to herself:

"I am really happy to have forgotten Parker's book. It would be fresh treason to have and to read that man's words and thoughts in this house."

She relinquished the idea of influencing Manna; for in the girl's mind processes went on which she could not control, conditions existed which she could not comprehend. This child is a prey to a grief which only the confessional will ever learn, and which, perhaps, can be assuaged only there alone.

Frau Dournay was oppressed with troubled dreams. It seemed to her as if she were transported to Wallenstein's camp, then arrested as a spy, and examined by the Sergeant; and then, suddenly, the Sergeant was changed, and it was Professor Einsiedel, who said to her:

"Do not be afraid! I have influence here, I shall have you released."

And then again she was at Court; and all the noble company laughed at the Sutler-woman—she had acted that part years before, when she was a young, giddy girl. Then she saw her son's eye resting upon her, and she was ashamed to appear before him in this dress.

And so the scenes whirled confusedly through her brain. She felt happy when she awoke, and found that it had all been only a dream.

They rose very early in the cloister; but long before the matin-bell of the church rang, Frau Dournay had arisen and dressed; and then she gazed through the window of the cell upon the landscape, which was more and more fully revealed by the brightening day. The unpleasant recollection of her dreams, like the fog upon the river, was dissipated by the morning sun. She thought of the hundreds of young souls, which still lay sleeping, maturing for a peaceful future. She thought of the nuns, who had renounced life, to whose souls the new day brought nothing of personal interest—only their unvarying duty.

She shuddered at the thought that any one should undertake to disturb such a life.

Whatever irregularities and improprieties may accidentally occur, a holy disposition reigns over these spirits. And now, in the early morning, there came to her again an aphorism of her husband: "You can only oppose an existing, positive religion, with more religion still. In the world, the idea of the Pure i. persecuted, hunted down, obscured. Let no man venture to attack an asylum of that idea, unless it holds a newer and a higher consecration."

The sun had completely overpowered the mists, and shone upon the mountains and the river; the cloister-bell rang; the inmates of the great house were stirring. The Professor's widow went down, and knelt behind a pillar; the Sisters and the children were assembling.

Frau Dournay stayed until the morning service was over; then she went into the dining-hall, and begged Manna and the Superior to allow her to take her leave. They saw her down to the shore.

Frau Dournay exhorted Manna, remaining there, to concentrate her powers, and to live for pure wisdom. She spoke with so much emotion that the Superior held out her hand, while her lips moved, evidently in prayer.

The Widow perceived that her old friend prayed for her. And is there not as good justification for this form as for a fervent but unworded thinking and wishing for one upon whom you would have all happiness showered? With lightened soul she crossed to the other side.

Sonnenkamp was astonished, because, after all, she did not bring Manna; but she declared that, under the circumstances, she would not, on any account, interfere any further. She went back with Sonnenkamp to the Villa. On the boat she developed a complete scheme for the organization of an extended charity; saying that it must be arranged so that Manna might pass from one sanctuary to another.

Sonnenkamp listened in silence and ill-humor; the whole world had conspired against him to make him a pretender to virtue.

Yesterday Prancken had made a similar demand. He had retorted that it was ridiculous that even the nobility should require the appearance of virtue; but Prancken had insisted upon the religious obligation.

Sonnenkamp had shrugged his shoulders because the man kept his mask on even while alone with him; and he did not consent until Prancken added that it would not only justify, but really oblige, the Court to ennoble him. Now Frau Dournay recommended the same thing. The one good point about it was, that she was probably honest in her recommendation.

The return home was not overjoyous; for they came home empty-handed. Indeed, Sonnenkamp felt outraged that he should be called upon for further exertion, while he had not as yet obtained any result.

CHAPTER VI.

THE FORBIDDEN FRUIT IN EDEN.

A STRANGE spirit—it was kept concealed, but was not ghostlike; it was all clearness, but caused much confusion withal—had in the meanwhile appeared at Villa Eden.

On the morning after Frau Dournay's departure, Roland had gone to the vine-covered cottage. Erich had sent him to get a book from the library. Unintentionally, as if driven by an impulse to see how it looked in her absence, he had stepped into Frau Dournay's open room. A book was on the table; it was open, and on the fly-leaf these words were written in English: "To my friend Dournay. Theodore Parker."

Roland was startled. Why, that was the man of whom the Mother had spoken, only a few days before, as of a saint, whom he was not to know until he should have grown considerably older. He took the book, and hid it.

At noon he asked for permission to go to the Krischer's; it was granted. Erich remained at home to finish a letter to Professor Einsiedel. But Roland did not go to the Krischer's; he sat under the high willows by the shore, and read and read. At times he looked off over the stream, and then he read again.

What is all this? Why, here is a soldier—all-inspired, God-fearing soldier—who battles for moral freedom and against slavery. He read of a man, John Brown, who suffered death upon the gallows at Harper's Ferry, for the sake of the abolition of slavery. He read, and saw, and heard, how Parker foretold a great struggle; and the words, "All great charters of humanity are written in blood," fell into the boy's soul like a firebrand. He read on, and further on, until he noticed that it was growing dark. Now, for the first time, he remembered that he had started to go to the Krischer's house. He hastened to the village. On the way he met Erich, who was deeply concerned because Roland had deceived him.

"Where have you been?" asked Erich.

"Here," replied Roland, handing Erich the book.

Roland had partaken of the forbidden fruit of the tree of knowledge; and Erich saw, with wonder, how deep an impression the book had made upon the youth's soul. A new and difficult task devolved upon Erich: Roland must be prevented from communicating his impressions to his father.

"Who is Brown?" asked Roland. "Can you tell me anything about him?"

Erich complied willingly. He told the martyr's story; he dwelt, with emphasis, upon the facts that martyrdom existed in our days as truly as it did in the past: he told his pupil that single-hearted devotion conferred sublimity even upon the man who wears the gay uniform of to-day, upon the military man; parenthetically he tried to show that the costume of any age, and of any caste, can be made to typify the Sublime. But Roland did not enter upon this thought, and Erich undertook, without further delay, the rather difficult work of justifying, or, at least, explaining the position of Sonnenkamp, who had evidently sympathized with the other side.

"Oh yes!" exclaimed Roland, "now I remember when we met the Russian at Clodwig's you said that you could not imagine a white boy and a black boy being friends and playmates. Do you believe in slavery, then?"

Erich endeavored to explain in what sense he had said it; and, while he was speaking, he was glad to see how open the youth's soul was to all impressions, and how it held fast to things which at the time appeared transient and unimportant.

Late into the night Erich sat with Roland, endeavoring to satisfy the lad's sense of justice, and it was almost the severest trial of his life. Roland was to understand that there existed a different mode of looking upon the matter—a mode which sustains slavery as justified and necessary: he was never to let his father know that he accidentally, and through Frau Dournay, had become acquainted with a spirit which must not be invoked in this house.

Erich remembered that his mother had justly advised him to introduce into his teaching only those things which were necessary for other things that were to follow them, and not anything whatever that the youth might happen to desire; now a subject had turned up, in which he need do no more than follow the tracks which the lad's inquiring mind had found of itself. And it ought to have been a cause of rejoicing that he had, of himself, entered upon this path; it was the one that all education should lead up to, and should he, the teacher, now turn his pupil's feet away from that path—should he obscure and destroy the foundation of all morality—the difference between "Thou shalt" and "Thou shalt not"?

"It's like a dream to me!" the boy said. "A great negro held me in his arms. I remember that very distinctly. I remember his woolly hair, which I pulled; he had a smooth face, no beard at all."

"Negroes have no beards," Erich remarked, and the boy continued in a dreamy way:

"I was carried in the arms of negroes—of negroes."

He kept repeating the words in lower and lower tones; then he was silent. Suddenly he passed his hand over his forehead, and asked:

"Do men that are slaves love their own children? Don't you know any song that they sing?"

Erich had not much to say: Roland wanted to know how all the nations of antiquity regarded slavery. Erich was only superficially informed on this question; so he opened his letter to Professor Einsiedel again, and begged him to give him the names of those books in which the state of slavery among the Jews, Greeks, Romans, and the old Germans was fully treated of.

When, at last, Roland was about to go to bed, he got Thomas à Kempis' book and laid it down by the side of Theodore Parker's.

"I wonder," said he, "if the two men stood side by side,

how they would regard each other. I imagine Thomas à Kempis as a very fervent, polished monk, but when I think of Parker, I think of him as if he were a grandson, or a great-grandson, of Benjamin Franklin."

Erich's astonishment increased, as he saw how Roland had penetrated into the mind of each.

Thomas à Kempis tends to make a hermit of a man; leads him to enter more and more into himself, and then to pass off away from the human altogether. Parker, too, first leads man into himself, and then beyond himself—but out, among men.

When, next day, Roland and Erich went to take the letter to Professor Einsiedel to the station, they saw the boat approaching on which Sonnenkamp and Erich's mother were coming up the river; they signalled to them, and went down to the landing.

Roland was surprised to find that Manna had not returned with them; for his father had promised him to bring her home. Sonnenkamp walked ahead with Erich, and inquired of him about the state of his house: he seemed sadly out of humor.

Roland kept the Mother back, to allow the others to precede them some distance, then he asked:

"Has Manna told you, too, that she is an Iphigenia?"

"No! what did she mean by that?"

"I don't know."

Frau Dournay compressed her lips. The truth began to dawn on her: she understood Manna's lamentations, and her thankfulness to God, who had sent this worst of misfortunes upon her. She tried to get at all the circumstances, but Roland interrupted her, telling her that he had read the book which she had forgotten.

The Mother was frightened, but she grew calmer as Roland informed her that Erich had explained the whole matter to him, and that he would guard the secret carefully.

Nevertheless, she was very uneasy. When she re-entered the Villa, she had introduced a spirit which ought not to dwell here. The freedom of her mind was taken from her, for that which she had kept concealed, had burst forth in an influence which she could no longer control, and which at any moment might bring down terror and confusion.

Frau Ceres was again indisposed; Miss Perini was not allowed to leave her for a moment. She begged to be excused from receiving Sonnenkamp and Frau Dournay on their return.

Like a child that is always lighthearted, and lives on from moment to moment, free from thought or trouble, appeared the Major; and every one took pleasure in his steady equanimity. He thought it preferable that Manna should not come now; she should come only when the castle was completed. It would be very fine—the transition from the cloister to the castle. He looked forward with pleasure to the time when they should all be together again; he did not like this eternal travelling and bursting asunder like a bombshell. Why, you could nowhere be better off than here at home; and nowhere could you have more than sky, and water, and mountains, and trees.

The Major was the life of the party which met at supper, and each was lost in his peculiar train of thought. After supper, Frau Dournay accompanied the Major to his house. Far out into the night she sat with Fräulein Milch, who was appointed first-assistant in the charity scheme. She seemed to be cut out for it. She knew all the people, and all about their circumstances; and the first thing she demanded was, that a dozen sewing-machines should be sent into the neighboring villages, and said that she herself would teach the women and the girls how to use them.

Frau Dournay's heart felt stronger, as she returned to the Villa under the light of the stars, escorted by the Major and Fräulein Milch. She was calm, and a saying of Goethe's resounded in her soul, as if it were being sung: "Not by reflection can you learn to know yourself, but by endeavoring to do your duty."

A course of action lay before her, which should elevate her and all about her.

CHAPTER VII.

A NEW GATE IN THE WALL.

FRAU Dournay accompanied the Doctor on his rounds in the country for several days. By this she obtained an insight of her own into the life of the neighborhood.

She now laid before Herr Sonnenkamp the plan which she and Fräulein Milch had sketched. He adopted it with great readiness; and the idea of supplying sewing-machines afforded him special satisfaction. It was not only something American, but it would also give rise to much talk in the world. He himself went to the capital to buy the machines.

Sonnenkamp listened to Frau Dournay with pleasure, as she told him what happiness it had afforded her to be put in the way of doing so much good, formerly through the Princess, and now through Herr Sonnenkamp.

"How is it," he asked, "that the poor, and the people of limited means, hold more firmly together than the rich?"

"I have never considered it," replied Frau Dournay, with an embarrassed smile; "but when I come to think of it, it appears to me that the rich man clings above everything to his possessions, and is forced to think of himself; he can't help it. He cannot occupy himself with the lot of others: his soul, his eye, if I may use the expression, has not the imploring glance of him who sits forlorn by the wayside. But the poor man is always hoping, always waiting; he has nothing but a bundle in his lap, or perhaps only his empty hands; he is dependent on others, and attached to others."

Sonnenkamp was eloquent in commending this kind, indulgent explanation, as he called it, and Frau Dournay was charmed with the courteous bearing and delicacy of the apparently rough and selfish man.

"Perhaps," she continued, and her face flushed, "perhaps we could take an example from the animal world."

"What, for instance?"

She was silent, and only on Sonnenkamp's repeating his question, she said:

"To you I may reveal a half-matured opinion: I was on the point of saying, that ravenous beasts live singly, and wolves go together in herds only when it is necessary to make common cause in order to get their prey; at other times each one lives by himself. Graminivorous animals, on the other hand, always live together in herds; they protect each other by association."

The Professor's widow paused, smiling at her own comparison, and then she continued:

"My wisdom dates from yesterday, and is not of much value. The Krischer told me, that in the Fall the granivorous birds gather together in flocks, but those that feed on insects do not."

Sonnenkamp looked at her encouragingly. To qualify her assertion the Professor's widow resumed:

"For all that, granivorous birds are no more praiseworthy than those that feed on insects; each lives in accordance with the law of its nature."

Sonnenkamp was more and more charmed with Frau Dournay's manner; she decked his board with food which cannot be planted in the garden, nor brought home from the chase.

By degrees the papers eulogistically spread the tidings of Herr Sonnenkamp's successful efforts in promoting the welfare of the people. The Privy-councillor's wife came and wished him joy on his success, adding, that her husband was informed that Herr Sonnenkamp's laudable activity had been favorably noticed at Court.

Now Sonnenkamp's zeal redoubled; he would not allow the public voice to rest; it should speak of him day after day: but Prancken, who had returned from his farming escapade, hinted that it would be preferable to desist for awhile, and then astonish the public anew. He had evidently heard of the favorable impression which Frau Dournay had created at the convent, and of her impressive appeal to Manna; so on Sonnenkamp's now submitting to him his plan of installing Frau Dournay permanently in his house, he approved of it at once.

Presently a path was opened along the shore through blooming meadows, from the Villa to the vine-covered cottage; and one day Sonnenkamp begged Frau Dournay to come with him to the garden, and the whole family had to accompany them.

A new door had been broken into the wall which enclosed the whole park: Sonnenkamp said that Frau Dournay should be the first person to pass through this entrance. He gave the key into her hand and she opened the gate. She went through the gate, along the path; then the whole family, and Prancken, who was with them too, followed her. They went to the vine-covered cottage, and the Widow was astonished to find here her whole household-furniture and her husband's library arranged in perfect order. Aunt Claudine was also present, for Sonnenkamp had persuaded Clodwig to allow her to return.

With a certain pride, Sonnenkamp presented his valet Joseph, who had arranged everything so perfectly as a native son of the University.

Frau Dournay thankfully gave Joseph her hand.

Soon after, the Major made his appearance, and when Frau Dournay asked after Fräulein Milch, he excused her stammeringly; it evidently did not suit him either, that Fräulein Milch remained firm in her resolution never to go into society.

Frau Dournay had not had time to recover from her surprise and touching joy, when Bella and Clodwig too arrived. Arrangements had been made for a cheerful repast in the garden, and Roland gave voice to the universal state of mind by saying:

"Now I've got a permanent grandmother and a permanent aunt safe in the nest."

In the evening Erich received a large parcel of books, with a letter from Professor Einsiedel, and a large sheet covered with memoranda. He had much to say in favor of Erich's project of writing a treatise on the principles and nature of slavery, and thought it a most fertile theme.

Erich locked the books up, for he considered it a blessed thing that Roland thought neither of slavery, nor of free-labor, nor of anything of the kind: he was now aiming at a very different object.

The Privy-councillor's son, the cadet, was now on leave of absence at the villa which his family had just taken possession of, and he exhorted Roland to be very industrious, so that he might be soon fitted to enter the military school. So Roland was intent only on fitting himself for the highest class as speedily as possible; he spoke of it daily with his father and Prancken. But once his father took him aside, and said:

"My child, it is quite right, and it pleases me very much, that you are preparing yourself so earnestly; but you shall enter only when—Observe, I honor you in telling you this. I look upon you as a grown man, who can understand everything—"

He paused and Roland asked:

"When am I to enter?"

"Come nearer, I'll whisper it to you: you shall enter only when you have become noble."

"I noble? And you too?"

"Yes; all of us. And for your sake alone I must attain nobility. You will understand that in time. Does it not make you glad to think that you will be ennobled?"

"Do you know, Father, when I first had respect for nobility?"

Sonnenkamp looked at him inquiringly, and Roland continued:

"At the station, when I saw a delirious drunkard whom every one treated with respect, because he was a Baron. Ah, it's a great thing to be a nobleman!"

Roland now related his encounter on the morning of his flight; and Sonnenkamp was astonished at the wonderful effect everything had on Roland, and to notice how everything lived on within him. Then he said:

"Now give me your hand, and pledge yourself that you will say nothing of this to your Herr Erich, until I see fit to tell him myself. On your word of honor as an officer."

Reluctantly and thoughtfully Roland gave his hand.

His father now proceeded to explain to him how unpleasant it would be if he were to receive his title while in the academy, after having entered as a simple citizen.

Roland inquired why he should not talk about it with Erich.

His father refused to give a reason, and demanded unconditional obedience.

Thus Roland had a twofold secret to guard: one from his father, and one from Erich. It weighed heavily on the youth's mind; and it found curious expression when, one day, he asked Erich:

"Have the negroes a noble class among them in their country?"

"There is no natural institution of nobility," replied Erich. "Individual men are of nobility only if and while others will consider them so."

Erich had believed that Roland's absorbing desire for the military academy had overlaid all former thinking and pondering; and now he perceived that it still lived, and had assumed a curious connection of thought, which he did not know how to explain. But he carefully refrained from deeper investigation.

During his leave of absence, the Privy-councillor's son was generally present at lessons. By agreement with his mother, Sonnenkamp now made the proposal that the young cadet should leave home for a time, to be taught with Roland.

Roland was made perfectly happy by this plan. But Erich opposed it; and on Sonnenkamp's recalling to him that he had formerly thought it desirable to instruct Roland together with a companion, it became a difficult task for Erich to explain to him why this was now impracticable. The course of study on which he had entered with Roland, he said, was entirely determined by the lad's character, entirely personal, so that a companionship and consideration for another's acquirements could now serve only to impede Roland's progress.

By this measure Erich forfeited the good-will not only of Herr Sonnenkamp and the Privy-councillor's wife, but also, for a long while, that of his pupil himself, who was angry and refractory, after the cadet had returned to the capital.

CHAPTER VIII.

MANTRAPS IN THE GARDEN OF THE POETS.

IT was Sonnenkamp's pride that he raised the best wines; but the legend of the jubilant harvest-festival is now no better than a mere fable. Heavy fogs had hung over the valley from early morning, and long before the sun had set they enveloped the entire landscape. The leaves had fallen from the trees, and the hoarfrost glittered on the bare branches, when at last the grapes were gathered and pressed. The Major, to be sure, insisted on firing the customary salute, and he took great pleasure in his two comrades, Erich and Roland, who fired so admirably at his word of command that the threefold shot was but one single report; but this was the beginning and the end of the harvest celebration.

Fires had already been lighted at the Villa, and Sonnenkamp was justified in his pride of having a separate chimney for every stove. It was a real festivity when the Professor's widow had a fire in her sitting-room for the first time. She had invited Erich and Roland, and Fräulein Milch had come of her own accord, and so they all sat together by the open hearth. There was no need of saying how happy they were; they were at home and at peace.

Erich's mother reminded him of how he used to read the great poets to them during the long winter evenings, and asked him to renew what had given them so much pleasure. He promised to do so. He felt under deeper obligations than before, for his refusal to take the Privy-councillor's son into the house had occasioned some disagreeable feeling, which he now would try with all his power to remove.

Sonnenkamp, who owned large hunting-grounds, had had handsome cards printed, and invited the better class of the neighbors to hunting-parties. Invitations also came from the neighbors, and Erich permitted himself and Roland to join in the sport once a week.

Roland was proud of his father's great knowledge of the chase, for Sonnenkamp was looked up to as an authority in such matters by the company, and was listened to with much eagerness when he told of the great times he had had hunting in America. Yes, he had once even taken a flying trip to Algiers, where he had shot a lion, whose skin now lay under his writing-desk. In America he had used it as a robe when he went sleighing; but here, in this country, there were seldom such things as large sleighing-parties.

The pleasantest meals, after the sport was concluded, were always taken at the castle, where a large room had been fitted up for this purpose. Here, indeed, was the Major lord of the castle, and often used to speak of the glorious evenings passed at the Villa, where Erich read the ancient and modern dramas. He had never thought that there was so much beauty in the world, or that one single man could express it all so clearly with his voice.

Erich had read uninterruptedly one evening every week, and the impressions made by his readings were as various as his hearers were different. The Major always sat thoughtfully with folded hands. Frau Ceres lolled on her chair, and occasionally opened her eyes, to show that she was not asleep. Miss Perini brought her work, and occupied herself with it, without being in the slightest degree disturbed. Erich's mother and aunt sat quietly. Sonnenkamp asked them, once for all, to excuse his rudeness; and said good-naturedly, as he turned to Roland:

"Don't you ever get in the habit of having a stick in your hand and whittling."

And so he sat and whittled while Erich read; but ever and anon he would pause, with his knife in one hand and his stick in the other, and look up, but would soon return to his work again.

Roland always took a seat opposite Erich, so as to look full in his face, and often, late at night, would speak to his friend of the wonderful things he had heard.

One evening Erich had been reading Macbeth, and was much pleased when Roland said to him,

"That Lady Macbeth might easily become one of those witches in the opening scene."

Another time, when he had been reading Hamlet, Erich was

not a little surprised when Roland said to him, before going to bed:

"It's curious that Hamlet should say in his soliloquy that no one returns from the other world, when he had seen the ghost of his own father only a little while before, and sees him again soon."

One evening he had been reading Goethe's Iphigenia, and Roland said:

"I never can understand why Manna told me once that she was Iphigenia. If she *were*, I would be Orestes. I, Orestes? I? Why? Do you understand what Manna meant?"

Erich said that he did not.

One evening the Doctor and the Priest were present, and Sonnenkamp asked Erich to read Shakspeare's Othello; Erich looked at Roland. Would it not arouse Roland's perplexity in regard to the negroes, which had fallen to sleep? He did not know how to refuse, nor had he any good pretext at hand for having Roland leave the room.

Erich read. The compass of his voice, and its easy modulations, represented every character at its full value, without at all verging on a theatrical rendering of it. He did not attempt to color strongly, but to produce the idea of sculpture rather than painting—a softened, yet complete, outline of life rather than an imitation of it.

The Doctor nodded to Frau Dournay. Erich's reading seem to afford him great comfort.

The attention of Frau Ceres was now for the first time fully aroused; she did not lean back once during the whole evening, but sat with her face bent forward and a new and unknown expression upon it.

Erich read the whole play at one sitting, and when at the close, in a voice struggling with tears, as of one who *will* not weep, he read Othello's lamentable confession of guilt, great tears ran down the pale and delicate face of Frau Ceres.

The play ended, and Frau Ceres rose abruptly and begged Frau Dournay to accompany her to her room. Miss Perini and the others withdrew with them. The men had risen, but Roland remained on his chair as if spell-bound.

The Major looked at the Doctor and said:

"Isn't this a wonderful man?"

The Doctor nodded.

The Priest sat with folded hands. Sonnenkamp looked at his whittlings and placed them together in a little heap, as if they were splinters of gold, and even stooped to pick up some that had fallen on the floor. As he rose again he asked Erich:

"What do you think of Desdemona's guilt?"

"Guilt and innocence," replied Erich, "are not natural ideas, they are human, social, moral laws. Nature recognizes only the free play of forces, and Shakspeare's plays are a second-nature in this regard: they represent only the free play of the natural forces in man."

"That is it," said the Priest. "Religion is not spoken of in this work; for religion would have tamed these men who act only like the forces of nature, would have made them pliant and subdued them, or, more likely, have rendered them subject to the revealed higher law."

"Fine! very fine!" said Sonnenkamp, whose face was pale, "but allow me to ask the Captain for an answer to my question."

"I can answer your first question," said Erich, "only in the words of our greatest æsthetic writer: 'The poet wished to delineate a lion, and in order to do this, had to represent him rending a lamb!' There's no talk of the lamb's guilt. The lion must act in accordance with his nature. But I think there's something behind even the deep tragic effect of this drama."

"What is it?"

"A girl like Desdemona, motherless and alone, who had been brought up only in the company of men, might easily fall in love with a hero whose affectionate and childish nature, feeling the need of love, would make him fawn at her feet like a tamed lion. Yielding strength, which does not deny its wildness but yet considers itself redeemed from it, forms the source of a love which forgets all things, overcomes difference of race, and obliterates even the black hue of the Moor's skin. When Othello kissed her for the first time, she closed her eyes and he kissed them; this closing of the eyes is not momentary, it lasts for a long time. But this self-deception would result in horror beyond parallel, in raving madness, should Desdemona hold in her arms his child, a being strange and repulsive, inhuman even. She would scream with horror, from her agonized and crushed heart, holding to her breast a child so strange to her! That look which, as Hegel says, is the noblest of all—the first glance which a mother gives her child—would have struck Desdemona with death or madness."

Sonnenkamp, who had been playing nervously with his splinters, swept the whole collection to the floor, and went up to Erich with outstretched hands; his powerful nature was deeply moved, and he cried:

"You're a free man, a free thinker; and your brain isn't befogged with any hocus-pocus. You're the only person who gives me a reasonable explanation of the existence of evil. Yes; the tact of the poet is singularly like prophecy. 'It's against Nature,' said Desdemona's father; and that is the only complete solution of the problem. It's all consistently summed up in this expression, 'It must be so,' like a production of Nature. It is against Nature."

Sonnenkamp had never been heard to speak so before; and Roland, who had been staring abstractedly at the wall, looked up, as if to convince himself that it was his father who was speaking.

Sonnenkamp went on triumphantly, for he noticed the surprise depicted on all their faces:

"Marriage--marriage! The Romans knew what that means. Where marriage is opposed to Nature, there can be no talking about human rights, and equality of rights. These crazy humanitarians are very apes, and have sunk as low as apes in their wisdom. These men who are always building up universal theories and pretences which will never apply to human beasts who are gifted with speech, and are always knaves, and don't understand them at all. Faugh! you noble friend of humanity," cried he, walking up and down the room, "go and give your daughter to a nigger; do it once! Do it! and be in mortal fear every minute that he'll tear your child to pieces. Hug your black relation! Do it, my noble friend of humanity! then come back and preach about the equality of races!"

Sonnenkamp had clenched his fist as if holding an enemy whom he would like to strangle. His eyes blazed; and his mouth writhed and panted like that of a tiger who has sprung on his prey. Suddenly he laid his hand on his breast, as if striving to control himself.

"You and the Poet, Herr Captain, have almost made me drunk," said he, with a forced smile; and repeated his conviction that Erich had hit the mark. A white girl cannot become a negro's wife. That was not a prejudice, but a law of Nature.

"I thank you!" said he, turning to Erich. "You have given me very suggestive thoughts."

Everybody was astonished; and the Doctor said, with a modesty which was not at all usual, "that, from a physiological standpoint, he could only agree with all that had been said; for i was well known that hybrids cannot breed after the third gener ation. But difference of race does not alter the rights of mai any more than his duties, since religion lays the same commands on all."

While speaking the last words, he turned to the Priest, who felt obliged to explain that negroes were capable of having not only family feelings, but also religious convictions and views; and this gave them all the rights of men.

"So?" said Sonnenkamp. "Is that true in fact as well as theory? Why, then, has not the Church commanded the abolition of slavery?"

"Because the Church," added the Priest quietly, "has nothing of the sort to command. The Church has only to do with the immortal soul, and teaches it to prepare for the kingdom of heaven. We can neither order nor define what social position man's body—the veil of his soul—shall occupy. Neither servitude nor freedom is a hindrance to a holy life. Our Lord and Master called the souls of the Jews to the kingdom of heaven, although at that very time they were in bondage to the Romans. Through his apostles he summoned all the peoples, and had not to ask what was their political or social condition. Others may do that. Our kingdom is the kingdom of souls, which are equal, whether they live in white or black bodies, in republics or in tyrannies. We may be glad when their bodies are free, but it is not our duty to enforce that."

"Theodore Parker thought differently," said Roland, rising suddenly.

As if a shot had whistled past his head, Sonnenkamp cried out:

"What? Where did you hear about that man? Who told you about him? What do you mean?"

Roland's whole body trembled as his father seized him by both shoulders and shook him.

"Father!" he cried, with the voice of a man, "I have a free soul, too! I am your son, but my soul is free!"

They were all amazed. It was no longer to be said that Roland's voice was changing.

Sonnenkamp let him go. He breathed so heavily that the motion of his breast was plainly visible. Suddenly he said:

"My son, I am glad; that's fine—that's good! You're a genuine American. That's right! Good!—Glorious!"

Again all were astonished. The fitful and vacillating mood of Sonnenkamp struck them with surprise. But Sonnenkamp continued, mildly:

"I'm glad that you do not let yourself be browbeaten. You're brave—good! Now tell me where you made the acquaintance of Mr. Parker."

Roland told how he had happened to hear it, but said nothing about Frau Dournay's mentioning Parker's name during the visit to the village.

"Why didn't you ever tell me of it?" asked his father.

"I can keep my own counsel," replied Roland. "You once gave me credit for doing so."

"Right, my son; you deserved it."

"It's late; we must go home," said the Major at last, breaking up the company.

Never before, even in the most dangerous positions, as an outpost or in the wildest conflict, had the Major's heart beat so loudly as it had during the reading, and yet it beat louder when the conversation took so dangerous a turn. He continually shook his heavy head, and stretched out his hands as if for aid and defence, and as if saying, "For God's sake, drop all this conversation! It's not good, and can result only in bad!" Then he would look at Sonnenkamp again and shrug his shoulders. "What's the matter with the man? Why should he talk so to us? We don't want to lay a straw in his way, and he ought not to have disturbed us by anything of the sort." Then he meditated that Fräulein Milch was right—he ought to have stayed at home to-day! How comfortable he would have been in the armchair, where Laadi was lying now, and the house had been asleep for two hours, and it will be midnight before he can get home; and good Fräulein Milch was sitting up for him, as she always did. It was a great relief for him to take out his watch and see how late it was.

Frau Dournay came back to the room, and told Roland that his mother wanted to see him, and so Roland went to her.

The men set out for home, and Erich accompanied his mother and the others through the snowy night toward home.

CHAPTER IX.

THE BIRD OF NIGHT IS SHOT.

ERICH walked with the ladies in silence; his mother was the first to speak:

"I am happy," said she, "to find again comfort and support in a saying of your father's: 'Nothing is more useless and enervating than repentance,' was an expression often used by him. The perception of an error committed must be quick and sharp, and then we must return to facts. Notwithstanding all the good I may be able to do, I have deeply repented joining myself to this house so firmly that now any attempt to withdraw from it would be disagreeable. But since we have joined ourselves to it, we must act so as to turn all to the best account."

Erich's aunt, who was not generally given to talking, said how painful it is that people, around whose fate some mystery lies, seem placed under some fearful ban, and see in everything some reference to their secret.

No one spoke for some time. Far up on the crest of the hill they heard the shriek of the horned owl, that foreteller of coming cold, in whose horrid cry, as it rises and falls on the wind, there is not only dolefulness immeasurable, but also a sound of malicious triumph. The three stood still.

"Yes," said Erich, "in spite of all the trouble that Herr Sonnenkamp has taken to rid the neighborhood of owls, he has not succeeded."

Again they walked on silently. In moments of excitement, everything becomes symbolical. The Mother told in a low voice of the incomprehensible agitation of Frau Ceres, and how she had thrown herself on her neck, and sobbed and cried.

"I do not know what to think," added she, "there is some dreadful mystery here which troubles me."

Erich told what had occurred after the ladies had withdrawn, and how Roland had startled him by speaking of Parker. It was evident that Sonnenkamp wished to make the existing condition of slavery agree with some well-founded and just principle.

"Nothing is more natural," replied the Mother; "one who has passed his life surrounded by such conditions, must make some theory of them, and call it a moral principle. I am forced to think of your father again. He has told me a thousand times that men cannot bear to confess even to themselves, that their life and actions are wrong; they must try to make them agree with some principle of justice. But, as I said, we must not distress ourselves: we have a young heart to make noble; this is our part, with its past life and its origin we have nothing to do. The past is history; the present is duty. That is another of your father's maxims, and now good-night."

Erich walked peacefully back to the Villa. The owl had flown down from the hills, and sat screaming on the top of a tree in the park. Erich heard it, and Sonnenkamp heard it as he sat in the ante-room of his wife's chamber. He, the father and husband, was obliged to wait here till his son should come out: he was not permitted to be present while his wife talked with Roland.

At last Roland came out, and his father asked him what his mother had said: he had never done so before, but now felt that he must.

Roland answered that she had said almost nothing—had kissed him and cried, and had then asked him to hold her hand till she went to sleep; she was now sleeping quietly.

"Give me that book of Parker's," said Sonnenkamp.

"I haven't it. Erich's mother took it away from me, and gave me a scolding for reading it in secret; she said I was not old enough."

"Remember me to Herr Erich: you have a better teacher than I thought for," said his father.

Roland went to Erich's room, but he was not there.

The owl hooted again as it sat on the tree in the park. Roland put out the light, opened the window, took the rifle from the wall, and presently a report was heard and the owl fell dead from the tree. Roland ran down and met Erich. He told him he had shot the owl: he then went into the park and brought the bird back with him.

The whole house was alarmed. Frau Ceres awoke, and her first words were:

"Has he murdered himself?"

Sonnenkamp and Roland had to go to her room and show her that they were alive. Roland took the dead owl with him, but his mother would not look at it, and cried because they had robbed her of her sleep.

The father and son left her, and Sonnenkamp praised Roland for shooting the bird so coolly and quickly.

Erich went back to his mother, who must have been awakened by the report, and found her still awake; she, too, had feared that the shot was that of a suicide.

The whole house gradually became quiet again.

Roland's pride in having killed the bird made him forget the occurrences of the evening; he went to bed happy, and soon fell asleep.

A lamp was burning in the castle and another in Sonnenkamp's work-room. Erich stared at them and strange thoughts and pictures passed through his mind—Shakspeare's poem, the men who had listened to it, and, above all, what Roland must have thought; and it seemed fortunate that Roland's delight at having shot the owl had banished all bewilderment and the serious thoughts that would otherwise have troubled him. One deed, one deed alone, had delivered him. Where is it—this great power that unriddles all? It cannot be searched out. There is a great movement in history, and the Divinity manifest in history, which is independent of all will and all endeavor to mould events—this God alone produces the deed. The result, the deed, is not ours; but to be prepared for it, that is our part.

Erich too found rest at last.

Sonnenkamp paced up and down in his great chamber like a prisoner. The lion's skin lay at his feet, and the stuffed head glared at him with awful eyes. He doubled the skin, to cover the head. He thought and thought—what should he do? This Erich is educating his son to be an antagonist to him; and that mother of his, who is always fishing up in spirit some of her husband's bright sayings, and who, as Prancken says, is always calling up the restless ghost of her husband—that dead Professor Hamlet, is—No; she is a noble lady.

But why had he fastened around his neck these beggarly scholars, puffed up with their ideas? He could not shake them off without exciting remark. No: he must use them up, and then throw them away.

He came at last to a satisfactory decision. We must busy ourselves with other things—with amusements; and then straight to our goal. Day after to-morrow will be New-year's.

"On New-year's day we'll all go to the Court city." And with this thought, Sonnenkamp at last went to bed.

CHAPTER X.

THE PLAY OPENS.

THE Krischer knew how to stuff birds, and the first thing in the morning Roland wanted to take the owl to him—the bird was lying by the window, frozen stiff.

All the events of the previous day had vanished before the joy occasioned by his glorious shot.

"Wait!" cried Roland suddenly, as he was spreading the owl's wings—"wait! I just thought of a word I heard in a dream last night. A man who looked very much like Franklin, only he wasn't so fat, said it. I thought I was in a battle, the music and screaming made a fearful noise, and right in the midst of it the man said: 'Reputation—reputation!'—and then all of a sudden thousands of black heads reared themselves,—nothing but black heads, a sea of black heads, and all gnashing their teeth at me; and I woke all in a tremble."

Erich had nothing to reply, and Roland continued:

"To-day is the last day of the year; an entirely new world will commence to-morrow: I don't know why it is, but I long for it."

Erich laid his hand on the boy's forehead—it was at fever-heat.

Roland was called—his mother wanted him; and as he went, Erich's eyes followed him thoughtfully. He went toward the door, for he expected that Sonnenkamp would call him. This man that acted so singularly yesterday, that an explanation would be necessary to-day. What explanation, Erich could not think. As in a vision, he saw Herr Sonnenkamp in his chamber, breathing heavily and trying to master himself. He heard the steps of two persons approaching his chamber, and Roland entered holding his father's hand.

"Mother's gone to sleep again," he said; "but I've some news for you. Erich, we will go together to the Court city and stay there all winter."

"Yes, such is my determination," said Sonnenkamp, after the first salutation. "I hope that your mother will accompany us."

He said quietly: "After the loneliness and solitary life in the country, cheerful society will do us all good. And," he added, watching closely to see what effect his remark would have on Erich, "we will meet your friend Clodwig and his amiable wife in town."

Erich took the look quietly, and answered that he considered himself in duty bound to place himself at the disposal of Herr Sonnenkamp's friends.

"I've thought a good deal about what we were talking of last night," began Sonnenkamp, seating himself beside Erich. "You're a learned man, but a bold one too."

He conducted himself with extreme politeness, almost with delicacy; for it delighted him vastly to have the chance of playing the hypocrite. As long as he could consider the whole world fools, he felt an elevated pleasure which gave him great support. He was in such a good humor, that he said to Erich:

"I hope to convert you now; for you will come to know that one lives best in the world when he acts like a stranger in it, and doesn't trouble himself about the laws of states."

"To a certain extent," answered Erich, "Aristotle agrees with you. He passed most of his life in Athens, where he was not a full citizen, and could live in accordance with his ideas, utterly ignoring and released from what might be called active and passive participation in the government."

"I'm glad to hear that. One's always hearing something new and clever about these old philosophers. Aristotle was a traveller, and went wherever he chose, didn't he? Splendid!"

Sonnenkamp looked very much delighted. These scholars have endless resources; they always know how to find some great historical fact to use as an excuse for whatever is egotistic or ungrateful.

He smiled pleasantly and continued to smile, although Erich said:

"What might be right for so great a philosopher as Aristotle would not be right for everybody; for in that case the world could not exist. Who would ever take parish or state offices?"

Sonnenkamp smiled and smiled. "What geese these German schoolmasters are!" thought he to himself; "they're ready to display their learning an hour before going off on a pleasure-trip." But his face expressed only satisfaction, as he said to Erich:

"I am very grateful. One is always learning from you, you are always ready."

Every word that he said was meant as a dig at Erich; but Erich took it in perfect seriousness, and was very grateful for Sonnenkamp's gratitude. And Sonnenkamp was always delighted with this man, who with all his learning was as unsophisticated as a child.

He requested Erich and Roland to make the necessary preparations for the journey, and a servant having brought word that Frau Ceres was ready to receive him, he left the room.

He entered Frau Ceres' apartment: she turned toward him a wearied, lifeless look, and he expressed his joy that she was again cheering up, and would be able, on the next day, to undertake the journey to the capital. He pictured in alluring colors the splendid life of the capital, to which, fortunately, their acquaintance with the family of the Privy-councillor, Count Wolfsgarten and his wife, and the family of Herr von Endlich would afford stepping-stones.

He added with great assurance:

"Be resolute, and, at the same time, amiable in your manner, my dear Frau Ceres, and you will return to these halls a baroness."

Frau Ceres raised herself up at this, but merely regretted that the dresses ordered in Paris had not yet arrived. Sonnenkamp promised to telegraph at once; and he promised, too, that the Professor's widow should accompany them, and they would place themselves under her guidance.

"You may give me a kiss," said Frau Ceres.

Sonnenkamp did so, and she said:

"I think we shall all be happy yet. Oh, if I could only tell you my dream, but you will never listen to a dream. It's also better that I shouldn't tell it. But it was a bird with great wings, oh ever so large, and I sat on the bird and I was borne up in the air; and I was ashamed because I wasn't dressed, and all the people below looked up at me and cried and hooted and laughed; and then the bird turned about, and there was Frau Dournay, and she said, 'How beautifully dressed you are!' and there I had all my finery on,—my satin dress trimmed with point lace, and—. But I know very well you don't want to listen to my dream."

Sonnenkamp went away in good spirits. The day was a bright one—a fresh, cold, brilliant winter's day; the entire landscape, every rock and every tree, stood out boldly against the blue sky; the Rhine was coated with ice; and a rare stillness hung over the whole country like a suspended breath.

Sonnenkamp was happy; the bright day had driven away all the spectres of the night and one could now awaken to a fresh life. He immediately gave orders at the stable that two carriages should be got ready for the drive to the capital. An hour later, when Sonnenkamp, Roland, and Erich were walking toward the vine-arbor they saw people driving along the road, their horses covered with blankets, already on their way to the capital.

Roland asked to take his pony with him; and it was granted. He wanted to know which dog he might take; only one was permitted, but he could not decide which one to select.

The Widow's large sitting-room now presented much the look of a town fair; on tables and chairs lay large bundles of knit and woven garments for men and women; Fräulein Milch was reading from a large sheet of paper upon which the names of the needy ones were written, with a description of what they were severally to receive, while the Widow and the Aunt compared the carefully arranged bundles with the list. When this was done, Fräulein Milch called in the Krischer with his wife and daughter and the Seven-piper with all his children. They were directed to deliver the various packages to the people whose names were written on them; and this they were very willing to do.

"It's well you're not sending money," said the Krischer; "but there's something lacking yet."

"What is it?"

He was prevented from answering by the entrance of Sonnenkamp and Roland.

Sonnenkamp was pleased with the careful manner in which the money had been expended, and he added a few pleasant words to Fräulein Milch. He had not seen her since the morning Roland ran away.

He asked after the Major, and heard with regret that he had been unwell the past night and had not slept till morning; he was probably still asleep; he had a happy constitution, and always slept off his ailments.

The Widow begged to be excused, if she despatched the things before she devoted herself to her early visitors; she then asked the Krischer what he meant when he said that an important thing was lacking.

"Herr Sonnenkamp, in fact, would be the right man for that," answered the Krischer.

"How?"

"I mean that it's all well and good that people should be well wrapped up and the cold kept out, but good spirits and jollity may still be wanting, and I mean that something should be put in to warm a-body up inside, and it wouldn't be out of the way, if a flask of wine was sent to each one of 'em. The people have their eyes on the hillside vineyards all the year round and work in them, and most of 'em are never able to taste even a drop of wine."

"Good! good!" said Sonnenkamp. "Go to the Butler; tell him to give you a bottle of wine of last year's vintage to add to each package."

Sonnenkamp was in a very extravagant mood to-day; for he placed upon every parcel a piece of money. But he nearly spoiled it all; for he said to the Krischer:

"See what confidence I place in you! I don't doubt you will deliver them all honestly."

All the Krischer's good spirits were clouded over at once; but he checked his anger, and only pressed his lips together.

Roland helped him carry the packages to the cart, which stood before the door. Sonnenkamp was on the point of restraining him from this; but the Widow made a sign to him to permit it. With the last package, Fräulein Milch vanished too.

Sonnenkamp now recounted to the Widow, as they stood in the empty room, the plan of his intended visit to the capital, and invited her to accompany his family.

The Widow declined, courteously but with decision. And Sonnenkamp had much trouble in restraining his ill-humor; for no representations on his part could change her mind. He left the house with a polite manner, but quite out of sorts. Roland promised the Widow to leave Grip to keep watch for them.

The Widow saw that the boy wanted to do something more for her, and was willing to make any sacrifice in her service.

"It will be well with you in life," she said, as she took him by the hand.

Roland felt a thrill of awe pass through his soul. He had received a simple, but the highest blessing.

The Widow had promised to spend the evening at the Villa, where they were going to watch out the old year.

On entering, she passed a great black chest, in the hall. In the reception-room, dresses were spread over all the chairs; and Frau Ceres was as happy as a child. She arranged everything with a dexterity which, at other times, was not observable in her. Soon they betook themselves to the dining-hall, where tea was served.

They all felt that a great crisis was at hand. While at other times conversation flowed along lightly and easily, and no one thought of the lapse of the hour, it now seemed as if it would require a great effort to keep watch till midnight. The Widow felt the suspense, and, so to speak, the shadow of the passing hour. They were, it might be said, no longer present, no longer in company with each other; and the Widow spoke, therefore, more as she felt really prompted, and recounted the story of her introduction into the great world of society.

Frau Ceres was very attentive, and begged her to go on and give further incidents. Suddenly she started up, and asked her husband to leave the room with her for a moment.

Sonnenkamp soon reappeared, and asked Frau Dournay to do his dear little wife a favor.

The Widow declared her readiness to do so. It was now explained that she wanted Frau Dournay to play the Princess, Erich the Marshal of the household, Sonnenkamp the Prince, and the Aunt the Mistress of Ceremonies. The Aunt was averse to the part assigned her, and blushed again and again; but the Widow spoke aside with her, and prevailed upon her to undertake the Princess.

After they had had to wait some time, the folding-doors were thrown open.

Erich stood at the door, with his staff of office in his hand; and as Frau Ceres entered, glittering in pearls and diamonds, he escorted her to his Aunt's throne.

The Princess with gracious condescension lowered the fan she had in her hand, and Frau Ceres made a very courtly obeisance.

"Draw nearer," said the Aunt. "We are much pleased that you have made your home in our country."

"It was my husband's wish," answered Frau Ceres.

"Your excellent husband is very benevolent."

"I thank you," answered Frau Ceres.

"In your place," exclaimed Herr Sonnenkamp, "I would have said: 'Your Highness, it was our duty; and we are fully rewarded since you have deigned to take notice of us.'"

"Please write that out for me, I'll learn it," said Frau Ceres, turning to her husband.

She seemed to have grown younger; her cheeks glowed.

The Widow was very animated, and having said in a low voice to Frau Ceres: "I'm Mistress of Ceremonies," she led her to a seat.

"No, not that way! You must take a little pains with your train, and dispose of it gracefully. So—that's the way; and now open your fan—you're permitted to open it now. It's better to fasten it to the wrist by a slight lacing, as it's very apt to fall."

The play was carried on with a great deal of pleasantry. It struck twelve, and Roland cried:

"Father, hundreds of people are now drinking your health."

Sonnenkamp kissed his son, Frau Ceres kissed the Widow, and then inclined her head and awaited patiently her husband's kiss on her forehead.

Without, the bells rang, and guns boomed.

"Hail to the New Year! Hail to the new life!" cried Erich, seizing the hand of his pupil, who gratefully kissed Erich's hand.

Guns were fired and shouts raised even in the near neighborhood of the Villa, and Sonnenkamp was very angry that the excellent German police suffered such doings; it was nothing but the insolence of low people.

But Erich said:

"It's possible, psychologically considered, to find in this disagreeable firing of guns, an expression of joy. A man of insignificant position, when he cracks off a pistol, has a sort of pleasant surprise at being able to compel the attention of so many people to what he is doing. This is the meaning of this rude custom; it's an effort to give strength and reach to the human voice—you understand—to a man's shouting capacity."

Sonnenkamp laughed, and Erich was gratified to know that he was leading not only his pupil, but the father too, to a kindlier view of human nature.

Sonnenkamp, however, thought: "This walking university, these crammed-up answers ready for every occasion, begin to be tiresome; it is lucky that we shall soon enter a larger circle."

He smiled, and pleasantly bade Erich and Roland good-night.

The Widow and Aunt Claudine, wrapped up in warm furs, and attended by two servants, returned to the vine-clad cottage. Soon all was still, and the New Year was cradled in dreams.

CHAPTER XI.

THE ICE BREAKS.

IN the morning, about the time Erich and Roland were setting out for the vine-clad cottage, a message arrived thither from Fräulein Milch: she invited herself and the Major to become Frau Dournay's guests for the day.

The Widow extolled to Aunt Claudine the delicate tact displayed by the worthy housewife in divining that they would feel lonely to-day.

It snowed without cessation, and the Widow greeted her son and Roland, who passed by in the first carriage, from behind the window-panes. She then bowed to Herr Sonnenkamp and Miss Perini, who returned the salutation from the carriage; Frau Ceres lay back in the corner, copiously enveloped, and did not stir.

Soon after, the Major came, and with him, Fräulein Milch. The Major belonged to the strict military school, and never permitted himself to be diverted by any emotions from an erect bearing; he was to-day only slightly hoarse, and could therefore talk even less than usual. He, however, made his compliments to the Widow and the Aunt no less cordially than formally.

"This year," said he, "we will have lived fifty years together." He pointed to Fräulein Milch, and his hand said: "A better soul than she is, the earth does not bear." But his look said still more, which they could not understand.

The time passed very pleasantly at the table, and Fräulein Milch told what happy reports she had already received concerning the bounteous gifts that had been distributed.

The Major forced himself to master his feeling of illness; he determined to do his duty in conversation with the three ladies. He praised the Widow, because she was not only learned, but could cook such excellent soup.

"Yes, yes," he said, laughingly, "I've actually compelled

Herr Sonnenkamp to have soup served at his table. You see, if I'm obliged to live a single day without soup, it's the same as if I should go with naked feet in my boots—without stockings; the foundation of the stomach is cold."

They all laughed over this comparison, and the Major, stimulated by it, continued:

"You, Frau Dournay, know everything; now tell me why is it that this day, though it's simply a day like yesterday, should be thought to have something peculiar in it, merely because it's called New-year's day? It seems to me as if I had put on fresh linen for the whole year."

Again a general laugh arose, and the Major swallowed his dinner in contentment; he had done his part for the day; he could now leave it all to the others.

After dinner, the Widow would listen to no demur, the Major must take his regular nap; she had a fire made in the library for this purpose, and the Major was not a little proud at being permitted to sleep in the easy-chair.

"Yes," said he, "I can sleep as well as the best professor of them all. But these books, all these books! It's awful that a man should read so many books! I don't know how they can do it."

The Major slept the sleep of the just; he would have had no rest, if he had had a suspicion of what was going on among the women.

Fräulein Milch was sitting at the window by the side of Frau Dournay, and the latter was astonished when she heard the simple-minded housekeeper say how incomprehensible it was that Erich consented to read aloud the thrilling drama of Othello—the Major was quite confused by it; and besides, there were so many things in Sonnenkamp's house which had better be avoided.

"Do you know the play?" asked the Widow.

"Oh yes, yes," answered Fräulein Milch, and her whole face reddened up to the borders of her cap. But the Widow was still more astonished when, after Fräulein Milch remarked, with what art the poet had transported the young bridal pair to the island of Cyprus, where strong wine is made and not always drunk in moderation, she heard her add, what seemed exceedingly strange from her lips, that in such insular loneliness and under a hot sun, wild, burning passions were naturally fermented.

It seemed to the Widow as if she had heard a strange person speak, not the woman whom she had all along known. She, however, gave no sign of what she was thinking, and only asked:

"You think, then, it was improper to read the piece there, because the man used to be a slaveholder?"

"Excuse me, I'd rather not say anything more," replied Fräulein Milch. "I don't like to talk about Herr Sonnenkamp; it pleases me—no, that's not the right word, it satisfies me that he scarcely pays any attention to me, and bears himself toward me as a person of slight importance. I don't take it ill, I'm rather thankful, for I don't find it necessary to pay him any attention in return and to feign friendship toward him."

"No, you shall not escape my question in this way. Can you not tell me what it is you find out of the way?"

"I cannot."

Aunt Claudine, who seemed to observe that Fräulein Milch wanted to communicate something, which she perhaps was not intended to hear, slipped quietly out of the room.

"Now," said the Widow, "we are quite alone. You can tell me everything. Shall I give you an assurance that I can be discreet?"

"Ah, I regret that I have gone so far," Fräulein Milch faltered forth, and pulled at the ribbons of her cap with both hands. "This is the first time in fifty years that I have made a visit or eaten at another's table; I should not have done so; I never have self-restraint enough."

There was a tremulousness in Fräulein Milch's manner, and her brown eyes glowed.

"I thought that you considered me your friend," said the Widow, and held out her hand to her.

"Yes, you are indeed one," cried Fräulein Milch; and she seized her hand in both of hers, and pressed it with ardor. "You don't know how I thank God, that he has granted me this before my death. Ever since I devoted myself to Him, I have given up all people. You are the first one. But, indeed, I think you must know everything; nothing new can be told you."

"I do not know everything. What do you know about Herr Sonnenkamp?"

Fräulein Milch bent her head sorrowfully, and held both her hands before her face, exclaiming:

"Why, then, must I tell it?"

Then she raised her head, and placed her mouth to the ear of the Widow, and whispered something. The Widow drew her head back, and supported herself with both hands upon the sewing-machine which stood before her. No word was spoken. Out of doors, all was still, save the cries of a flock of crows, flying over the frozen Rhine.

"I do not think," said the Widow, at last, "that you would

tell me this on the authority of a mere rumor. Go on, and tell me openly how you know it to be true!"

Fräulein Milch looked around and said:

"I have it from a very trustworthy man, whose nephew sent a child to this country to be educated; he knows the name which Herr Sonnenkamp formerly bore: he knows his whole past history. But, my dear and noble friend, why shouldn't a man, whatever he may have done, assume a new life, a new existence?"

"Of that, another time," interposed the Widow. "Tell me the name of the man who gave you the information."

"Well, here it is. It was Herr Weidmann."

The Widow covered her face with both hands.

"What are you saying of Herr Weidmann?" said the Major, who suddenly entered. "I can tell you, dear Frau Dournay, whoever knows that man, knows one of the best and most honorable men in the world. He's God's masterpiece, with whom God himself is pleased. Day after day, as He looks down from heaven, He must say to Himself, 'The world is not yet wholly bad, for down there I have my Weidmann: there's a man—a genuine man.' In that everything is said, nothing is left out."

The two ladies were relieved by the entrance of the Major. He set out with Fräulein Milch on their way home.

When they had gone a few steps from the door, the Widow called Fräulein Milch back and asked her in a whisper:

"Does the Major know too—?"

"Oh no; he couldn't bear it. Please forgive me for having laid such a burden on you. Believe me, it is not any lighter for me, it's heavier to bear."

The guests departed, and soon after, the postboy brought a letter from the University town. Professor Einsiedel, who for the last twenty years had sent his New-year's congratulations to Frau Dournay, did not wish to fail now. The words that he wrote were cordial and significant; they seemed to come from a different world. She read the postscript a second time, for in it there was a word of greeting to Erich, with the news that the Professor would soon send his essay on slavery, which had been announced and would soon appear; he expressed the hope that Erich would this year complete the work upon which he was engaged.

The Widow looked meditative. What is this then? Erich had never said anything to her of being thus employed. She drew her hand across her forehead as if she would drive away some harassing thought. It suddenly struck her, that she had that very morning remarked sadly to Aunt Claudine, how she no longer could be of any practical use in the world, and yet it was the duty of every one to expend one's self in the service of others. What she did seemed to her as nothing, it was only the gift that signified. She almost involuntarily opened the box in which Sonnenkamp had placed the money intrusted to her. How could she hereafter say to those who receive his bounty, "You do not owe your thanks to me, but to Herr Sonnenkamp?"

She rose hastily, entered the library, and gazed out of the window. It was as if something were actually gnawing within her. Notwithstanding that she struggled hard against it, she found herself absorbed in this new situation, and her clear, intelligent vision seemed for awhile darkened.

Out on the river was heard a rushing and waving, a hissing and crackling, as if a new world was rising up. The ice had broken. Great cakes of ice were floating down the stream, jostling, tilting, grinding, crushing one another, and, massing themselves anew, were floating on. Every cake, large or small, was encircled with a wreath of snow, which was formed from the fine shivers of ice which, as the ice broke up, were ground off and worked up over the edges. The ice-cakes were borne so quickly down, that it was easy to see how swift and strong was the regular flow of the stream.

The sun sank glowing over the Rhine, and the Widow said to herself, half aloud:

"This first day of the year, now fading away, has brought me a terrible experience; it must be borne, and turned to good."

www.ingramcontent.com/pod-product-compliance
Lightning Source LLC
LaVergne TN
LVHW021259110826
845150LV00003B/433

* 9 7 8 1 4 2 5 5 6 0 6 6 9 *